Resounding acclaim for award-winning, *New York Times* bestselling author

DENNIS LEHANE

"Lehane is one of those brave new detective stylists who is not afraid of fooling around with the genre's traditions."
—*Washington Post Book World*

"One of the strongest voices in contemporary detective fiction."
—*Seattle Times*

"For mystery writer extraordinaire Dennis Lehane, elaborate plots and vivid settings serve as mere backdrop for showcasing his greater talent: a prodigious ability to develop unforgettable, emotionally textured characters."
—*Providence Journal-Bulletin*

"One of the best writers of his generation, period."
—*Cleveland Plain Dealer*

"A master of noir."
—*Milwaukee Journal Sentinel*

"One of the very best thriller writers."
—*Denver Rocky Mountain News*

"Dennis Lehane is one of the ten best crime novelists in the United States."
—*Toronto Globe and Mail*

"Lehane is very good indeed."
—*Houston Chronicle*

Books by
Dennis Lehane

CORONADO
SHUTTER ISLAND
MYSTIC RIVER
PRAYERS FOR RAIN
GONE, BABY, GONE
SACRED
DARKNESS, TAKE MY HAND
A DRINK BEFORE THE WAR

A DRINK BEFORE THE WAR

DENNIS LEHANE

DARKNESS, TAKE MY HAND

HARPER

An Imprint of HarperCollins*Publishers*

A Drink Before the War was originally published in paperback by Avon Books in July 1996 and by HarperTorch in December 2000.

Darkness, Take My Hand was originally published in hardcover by William Morrow in July 1996 and in paperback by Avon Books in July 1997 and by HarperTorch in December 2000.

HarperCollins books may be purchased for educational, business, or sales promotional use. For information please write: Special Markets Department, HarperCollins Publishers, 10 East 53rd Street, New York, NY 10022.

FIRST EDITION

ISBN: 978-0-06-117226-7
ISBN-10: 0-06-117226-X

10 RRD 10 9 8 7 6 5 4 3 2

A DRINK BEFORE THE WAR

This novel is dedicated to my parents,

Michael and Ann Lehane, and to

Lawrence Corcoran, S.J.

acknowledgments

During the writing of this novel, the following people provided advice, criticism, encouragement, and enthusiasm, for which I'll always be more grateful than they could possibly know:

John Dempsey, Mal Ellenburg, Ruth Greenstein, Tupi Konstan, Gerard Lehane, Chris Cullen, Courtnay Pelech, Ann Riley, Ann Rittenberg, Claire Wachtel, and Sterling Watson.

*My **earliest memories** involve fire.*

I watched Watts, Detroit, and Atlanta burn on the evening news, I saw oceans of mangroves and palm fronds smolder in napalm as Cronkite spoke of lateral disarmament and a war that had lost its reason.

My father, a fireman, often woke me at night so I could watch the latest news footage of fires he'd fought. I could smell the smoke and soot on him, the clogging odors of gasoline and grease, and they were pleasant smells to me as I sat on his lap in the old armchair. He'd point himself out as he ran past the camera, a hazy shadow backlit by raging reds and shimmering yellows.

As I grew, so did the fires, it seemed, until recently L.A. burned, and the child in me wondered what would happen to the fallout, if the ashes and smoke would drift northeast, settle here in Boston, contaminate the air.

Last summer, it seemed to. Hate came in a maelstrom, and we called it several things—racism, pedophilia, justice, righteousness—but all those words were just ribbons and wrapping paper on a soiled gift that no one wanted to open.

People died last summer. Most of them innocent. Some more guilty than others.

And people killed last summer. None of them innocent. I know. I was one of them. I stared down the slim barrel of a gun, looked into eyes rabid with fear and ha-

1

tred, and saw my reflection. Pulled the trigger to make it go away.

I heard the echoes of my gunshots, smelled the cordite, and in the smoke, I still saw my reflection and knew I always would.

1

The bar at the Ritz-Carlton looks out on the Public Gardens and requires a tie. I've looked out on the Public Gardens from other vantage points before, without a tie, and never felt at a loss, but maybe the Ritz knows something I don't.

My usual taste in clothes runs to jeans and diver's shirts, but this was a job, so it was their time, not mine. Besides, I'd been a little behind on the laundry recently, and my jeans probably would've hopped the subway and met me there before I got a chance to put them on. I picked a dark blue, double-breasted Armani from my closet—one of several I received from a client in lieu of cash—found the appropriate shoes, tie, and shirt, and before you could say, "*GQ*," I was looking good enough to eat.

I appraised myself in the smoked-glass bar window as I crossed Arlington Street. There was a bounce to my step, a bright twinkle in my eyes, and nary a hair out of place. All was right with the world.

A young doorman, with cheeks so smooth he must have skipped puberty altogether, opened the heavy brass door and said, "Welcome to the Ritz-Carlton, sir." He meant it, too—his voice trembling with pride that I'd chosen his quaint little hotel. He held his arm out in front of him with a flourish, showing me the way in case I hadn't figured it out by myself, and before I could thank him, the door had closed behind me and he was hailing the best cab in the world for some other lucky soul.

My shoes clacked with military crispness on the marble floor, and the sharp creases of my pants reflected in the brass ashtrays. I always expect to see George Reeves as Clark Kent in the lobby of the Ritz, maybe Bogey and Raymond Massey sharing a smoke. The Ritz is one of those hotels that is resilient in its staid opulence: the carpeting is deep, rich oriental; the reception and concierge desks are made of a lustrous oak; the foyer is a bustling way station of lounging power brokers toting futures in soft leather attaché cases, Brahmin duchesses in fur coats with impatient airs and daily manicure appointments, and a legion of navy blue-uniformed manservants pulling sturdy brass luggage carts across the thick carpeting with the softest whoosh accompaniment as the wheels find their purchase. No matter what is going on outside, you could stand in this lobby, look at the people, and think there was still a blitz going on in London.

I sidestepped the bellman by the bar and opened the door myself. If he was amused he didn't show it. If he was alive, he didn't show it. I stood on the plush carpet as the heavy door closed softly behind me, and spotted them at a rear table, facing the Gardens. Three men with enough political pull to filibuster us into the twenty-first century.

The youngest, Jim Vurnan, stood and smiled when he saw me. Jim's my local rep; that's his job. He crossed the carpet in three long strides, his Jack Kennedy smile extended just behind his hand. I took the hand. "Hi, Jim."

"Patrick," he said, as if he'd been standing on a tarmac all day waiting for my return from a POW camp. "Patrick," he repeated, "glad you could make it." He touched my shoulder, appraised me as if he hadn't seen me just yesterday. "You look good."

"You asking for a date?"

Jim got a hearty laugh out of that one, a lot heartier than it deserved. He led me to the table. "Patrick Kenzie, Senator Sterling Mulkern and Senator Brian Paulson."

Jim said "Senator" like some men say "Hugh Hefner"—with uncomprehending awe.

Sterling Mulkern was a florid, beefy man, the kind who carried weight like a weapon, not a liability. He had a shock of stiff white hair you could land a DC-10 on and a handshake that stopped just short of inducing paralysis. He'd been state senate majority leader since the end of the Civil War or so, and he had no plans for retirement. He said, "Pat, lad, nice to see you again." He also had an affected Irish brogue that he'd somehow acquired growing up in South Boston.

Brian Paulson was rake thin, with smooth hair the color of tin and a wet, fleshy handshake. He waited until Mulkern sat back down before he did, and I wondered if he'd asked permission before he sweated all over my palm too. His greeting was a nod and a blink, befitting someone who'd stepped out of the shadows only momentarily. They said he had a mind though, honed by years as Mulkern's step-and-fetch-it.

Mulkern raised his eyebrows slightly and looked at Paulson. Paulson raised his and looked at Jim. Jim raised his at me. I waited a heartbeat and raised mine at everyone. "Am I in the club?"

Paulson looked confused. Jim smiled. Slightly. Mulkern said, "How should we start?"

I looked behind me at the bar. "With a drink?"

Mulkern let out a hearty laugh, and Jim and Paulson fell in line. Now I knew where Jim got it. At least they didn't all slap their knees in unison.

"Of course," Mulkern said. "Of course."

He raised his hand, and an impossibly sweet young woman, whose gold name tag identified her as Rachel, appeared by my elbow. "Senator! What can I get you?"

"You could get this young man a drink." It came out somewhere between a bark and a laugh.

Rachel's smile only brightened. She swiveled slightly

and looked down at me. "Of course. What would you like, sir?"

"A beer. Do you have those here?"

She laughed. The pols laughed. I pinched myself and remained serious. God, this was a happy place.

"Yes, sir," she announced. "We have Heineken, Beck's, Molson, Sam Adams, St. Pauli Girl, Corona, Löwenbräu, Dos Equis—"

I cut in before dusk fell. "Molson would be fine."

"Patrick," Jim said, folding his hands and leaning toward me. Time to get serious. "We have a slight . . ."

"Conundrum," Mulkern said. "A slight conundrum on our hands. One we'd like cleared up discreetly and forgotten."

No one spoke for a few moments. I think we were all too impressed by the realization that we knew someone who used "conundrum" in casual conversation.

I shook off my awe first. "What is this conundrum, exactly?"

Mulkern leaned back in his chair, watching me. Rachel appeared and placed a frosted glass in front of me, poured two-thirds of the Molson into it. I could see Mulkern's black eyes holding steady with my own. Rachel said, "Enjoy," and left.

Mulkern's gaze never wavered. Probably took an explosion to make him blink. He said, "I knew your father well, lad. A finer man . . . well, I've never known one. A true hero."

"He always spoke fondly of you, Senator."

Mulkern nodded, that being a matter of course. "Shame, him going early like he did. Seemed fit as Jack LaLane, but"—he tapped his chest with his knuckles—"one never knows with the old ticker."

My father had lost a six-month battle with lung cancer, but if Mulkern wanted to think it was a coronary, who'd complain?

"And now, here's his boy," Mulkern said. "Almost all grown."

"Almost," I said. "Last month, I even shaved."

Jim looked like he'd swallowed a frog. Paulson squinted. Mulkern beamed. "All right, lad. All right. You have a point." He sighed. "I'll tell you, Pat, you get to be my age, and everything but yesterday seems young."

I nodded sagely, completely clueless.

Mulkern stirred his drink, removed the stirrer, and placed it gently on a cocktail napkin. "We understand that when it comes to finding people, no one's better." He spread his hand, palm up, in my direction.

I nodded.

"Ah. No false modesty?"

I shrugged. "It's my job. Might as well be good at it." I sipped the Molson, the bittersweet tang spreading across my tongue. Not for the first time, I wished I still smoked.

"Well, lad, our problem is this: we have a rather important bill coming to floor next week. Our ammunition is heavy, but certain methods and services we employed to garner that ammunition could be . . . misconstrued."

"As?"

Mulkern nodded and smiled as if I'd said, "Atta boy."

"Misconstrued," he repeated.

I decided to play along. "And there is documentation—records of these methods and services?"

"He's quick," he said to Jim and Paulson. "Yes sir. Quick." He looked at me. "Documentation," he said, "exactly, Pat."

I wondered if I should tell him how much I hated being called Pat. Maybe I should start calling him Sterl, see if he minded. I sipped my beer. "Senator, I find people, not things."

"If I may interject," Jim interjected, "the documents are with a person who has recently turned up missing. A—"

"—Formerly trusted employee at the State House," Mulkern said. Mulkern had the "iron hand in the velvet glove" routine down to an art. There was nothing in his manner, his enunciation, his bearing to suggest reproach, but Jim looked like he'd been caught kicking the cat. He took a long pull on his scotch, rattling the ice cubes against the rim. I doubted that he'd interject again.

Mulkern looked at Paulson, and Paulson reached into his attaché case. He pulled a thin sheaf of papers out and handed them to me.

The top page was a photograph, a rather grainy one. A blow-up of a State House personnel ID. It was of a black woman, middle-aged, worn eyes, a tired expression on her face. Her lips were parted slightly, and skewed, as if she were about to voice her impatience with the photographer. I flipped the page and saw a Xerox of her driver's license centered on a white page. Her name was Jenna Angeline. She was forty-one, but looked fifty. She had a class three Massachusetts driver's license, unrestricted. Her eyes were brown, her height—five feet six inches. Her address was 412 Kenneth Street in Dorchester. Her social security number was 042-51-6543.

I looked at the three pols and found my eyes pulled toward the middle, into Mulkern's black stare. "And?" I said.

"Jenna was the cleaning woman for my office. Brian's too." He shrugged. "As jigs go, I had no complaints."

Mulkern was the kind of guy who said, "jigs," when he wasn't sure enough of the company to say, "niggers."

"Until . . . ," I said.

"Until she disappeared nine days ago."

"Unannounced vacation?"

Mulkern looked at me as if I'd just suggested college basketball wasn't fixed. "When she took this 'vacation,' Pat, she also took those documents with her."

"Some light reading for the beach?" I suggested.

Paulson slapped the table in front of me. Hard. Paulson. "This is no joke, Kenzie. Understand?"

I looked at his hand, sleepy eyed.

Mulkern said, "Brian."

Paulson removed the hand to check the whip marks on his back.

I stared at him, still sleepy eyed—dead eyes, Angie calls them—and spoke to Mulkern. "How do you know she took the . . . documents?"

Paulson dropped his eyes from mine, considered his martini. It was still untouched, and he didn't take a drink. Probably waiting for permission.

Mulkern said, "We checked. Believe me. No one else is a logical suspect."

"Why is she?"

"What?"

"A logical suspect?"

Mulkern smiled. A thin one. "Because she disappeared the same day the documents did. Who knows with these people?"

"Mmm," I said.

"Will you find her for us, Pat?"

I looked out the window. Perky the Doorman was hustling someone into a cab. In the Gardens, a middle-aged couple with matching *Cheers* T-shirts snapped picture after picture of the George Washington statue. Sure to wow them back in Boise. A wino on the sidewalk supported himself with one hand on a bottle; the other he held out, steady as a rock, waiting for change. Beautiful women walked by. In droves.

"I'm expensive," I said.

"I know that," Mulkern said. "So why do you still live in the old neighborhood?" He said it like he wanted me to believe his heart still resided there too, as if it meant any more to him now than an alternative route when the expressway got backed up.

I tried to think of a response. Something to do with roots, and knowing where you belong. In the end, I told the truth: "My apartment's rent-controlled."

He seemed to like that.

2

The old neighborhood is the Edward Everett Square section of Dorchester. It's a little less than five miles from the center of Boston proper, which means, on a good day, it takes only half an hour to reach by car.

My office is the bell tower of St. Bartholomew's Church. I've never found out what happened to the bell that used to be there, and the nuns who teach at the parochial school next door won't tell me. The older ones plain don't answer me, and the younger ones seem to find my curiosity amusing. Sister Helen told me once it had been "miracled away." Her words. Sister Joyce, who grew up with me, always says it was "misplaced," and gives me the sort of wicked smile that nuns aren't supposed to be capable of giving. I'm a detective, but nuns could stonewall Sam Spade into an asylum.

The day after I got my investigator's license, the church pastor, Father Drummond, asked me if I'd mind providing some security for the place. Some unfaithfuls were breaking in to steal chalices and candlesticks again, and in Pastor Drummond's words: "This shit better stop." He offered me three meals a day in the rectory, my very first case, and the thanks of God if I set up in the belfry and waited for the next break-in. I told him I didn't come that cheap. I demanded use of the belfry until I found office space of my own. For a priest, he gave in pretty easy. When I saw the state of the room—unused for nine years—I knew why.

Angie and I managed to fit two desks in there. Two

chairs too. When we realized there was no room for a file cabinet, I hauled all the old files back to my place. We splurged on a personal computer, put as much as we could on diskettes, and stowed a few current files in our desks. Impresses the clients almost enough to make them ignore the room. Almost.

Angie was sitting behind her desk when I reached the top step. She was busy investigating the latest Ann Landers column, so I stepped in quietly. She didn't notice me at first—Ann must have been dealing with a real headcase—so I took the opportunity to watch her in a rare moment of repose.

She had her feet propped up on the desk, a pair of black suede Peter Pan boots covering them, the cuffs of her charcoal jeans tucked into the boots. I followed her long legs up to a loose white cotton T-shirt. The rest of her was hidden behind the newspaper except for a partial view of rich, thick hair, the color of rainswept tar, that fell to her olive arms. Behind that newsprint was a slim neck that trembled when she pretended not to be laughing at one of my jokes, an unyielding jaw with a near-microscopic brown beauty mark on the left side, an aristocratic nose that didn't fit her personality at all, and eyes the color of melting caramel. Eyes you'd dive into without a look back.

I didn't get a chance to see them, though. She put the paper down and looked at me through a pair of black Wayfarers. I doubted she'd be taking them off any time soon.

"Hey, Skid," she said, reaching for a cigarette from the pack on her desk.

Angie is the only person who calls me "Skid." Probably because she's the only person who was in my father's car with me the night I wrapped it around a light pole in Lower Mills thirteen years ago.

"Hey, gorgeous," I said and slid into my chair. I don't think I'm the only one who calls her gorgeous, but it's force of habit. Or statement of fact. Take your pick. I nodded at the sunglasses. "Fun time last night?"

She shrugged and looked out the window. "Phil was drinking."

Phil is Angie's husband. Phil is an asshole.

I said as much.

"Yeah, well . . ." She lifted a corner of the curtain, flapped it back and forth in her hand. "What're you gonna do, right?"

"What I did before," I said. "Be only too happy to."

She bent her head so the sunglasses slipped down to the slight bump at the bridge of her nose, revealing a dark discoloration that ran from the corner of her left eye to her temple. "And after you're finished," she said, "he'll come home again, make this look like a love tap." She pushed the sunglasses back up over her eyes. "Tell me I'm wrong." Her voice was bright, but hard like winter sunlight. I hate that voice.

"Have it your way," I said.

"Will do."

Angie and Phil and I grew up together. Angie and I, best friends. Angie and Phil, best lovers. It goes that way sometimes. Not often in my experience, thank God, but sometimes. A few years ago, Angie came to the office with the sunglasses and two eight balls where her eyes should have been. She also had a nice collection of bruises on her arms and neck and an inch-tall bump on the back of her head. My face must have betrayed my intentions, because the first words out of her mouth were, "Patrick, be sensible." Not like it was the first time, and it wasn't. It was the worst time though, so when I found Phil in Jimmy's Pub in Uphams Corner, we had a few sensible drinks, played a sensible game of pool or two, and shortly after I'd broached the subject and he responded with a "Whyn't you fucking mind your own business, Patrick?" I beat him to within an inch of his life with a sensible pool stick.

I felt pretty pleased with myself for a few days there. It's possible, though I don't remember, that I engaged in a few fantasies of Angie and myself in some state of domestic bliss. Then Phil got out of the hospital and Angie didn't come to work for a week. When she did, she moved very precisely and gasped every time she sat down or stood up. He'd left the face alone, but her body was black.

She didn't talk to me for two weeks. A long time, two weeks.

I looked at her now as she stared out the window. Not for the first time, I wondered why a woman like this—a woman who took shit from absolutely nobody, a woman who'd pumped two rounds into a hard case named Bobby Royce when he resisted our kind efforts to return him to his bail bondsman—allowed her husband to treat her like an Everlast bag. Bobby Royce never got up, and I'd often wondered when Phil's time would come. But so far it hadn't.

And I could hear the answer to my question in the soft, tired voice she adopted when she talked about him. She loved him, plain and simple. Some part of him that I certainly can't see anymore must still show itself to her in their private moments, some goodness he possesses that shines like the grail in her eyes. That has to be it, because nothing else about their relationship makes any sense to me or anyone else who knows her.

She opened the window and flicked her cigarette out. City girl to the core. I waited for a summer schooler to scream or a nun to come hauling ass up the staircase, the wrath of God in her eyes, a burning cigarette butt in her hand. Neither happened. Angie turned from the open window, and the cool summer breeze creased the room with the smell of exhaust fumes and freedom and the lilac petals which littered the schoolyard.

"So," she said, leaning back in the chair, "we employed again?"

"We're employed again."

"Ya-hoo," she said. "Nice suit, by the way."

"Makes you want to jump my bones on the spot, doesn't it?"

She shook her head slowly. "Uh, no."

"Don't know where I've been. That it?"

She shook her head again. "I know exactly where you've been, Skid, which is most of the problem."

"Bitch," I said.

"Slut." She stuck her tongue out at me. "What's the case?"

I pulled the information about Jenna Angeline from my inside breast pocket and tossed it on her desk. "Simple find-and-a-phone-call."

She perused the pages. "Why's anyone care if a middle-aged cleaning lady disappears?"

"Seems some documents disappeared with her. State-house documents."

"Pertaining to?"

I shrugged. "You know these politicians. Everything is as secret as Los Alamos until it hits the floor."

"How do they know she took them?"

"Look at the picture."

"Ah," she said, nodding, "she's black."

"Evidence enough to most people."

"Even the resident senate liberal?"

"The resident senate liberal is just another racist from Southie when he ain't residing in the House."

I told her about the meeting, about Mulkern and his lap-dog, Paulson, about the Stepford wife employees at the Ritz.

"And Representative James Vurnan—what was he like in the company of such Masters of State?"

"You ever see that cartoon with the big dog and the little dog, where the little dog keeps panting away, jumping up and down, asking the big dog, 'Where we going, Butch? Where we going, Butch?' "

"Yes."

"Like that," I said.

She chewed on a pencil, then began tapping it against

her front teeth. "So, you gave me the fly-on-the-wall account. What really happened?"

"That's about it."

"You trust them?"

"Hell no."

"So there's more to this than meets the eye, Detective?"

I shrugged. "They're elected officials. The day they tell
the whole truth is the day hookers put out for free."

She smiled. "As always, your analogies are splendid.
You're just a product of good breeding, you are." Her
smile widened as she watched me, the pencil tapping
against her left front tooth, the slightly chipped one. "So,
what's the rest of the story?"

I loosened my tie enough to pull it over my head. "You
got me."

"Some detective," she said.

3

Jenna Angeline, like me, was born and raised in Dorchester. The casual visitor to the city might think this would serve as a nice common denominator between Jenna and myself, a bond—however minimal—forged by location: two people who started out of their separate chutes at identical hash marks. But the casual visitor would be wrong. Jenna Angeline's Dorchester and my Dorchester have about as much in common as Atlanta, Georgia, and Russian Georgia.

The Dorchester I grew up in was working class traditional, the neighborhoods, more often than not, delineated by the Catholic churches they surrounded. The men were foremen, crew chiefs, probation officers, telephone repairmen, or, like my father, firemen. The women were housewives who sometimes had part-time jobs themselves, sometimes even had education degrees from state colleges. We were all Irish, Polish, or close enough to pass. We were all white. And when the federal desegregation of public schools began in 1974, most of the men worked overtime and most of the women went to full time and most of the kids went to private Catholic high schools.

This Dorchester has changed, of course. Divorce—practically unheard of in my parents' generation—is commonplace in mine, and I know a lot fewer of my neighbors than I used to. But we still have access to the union jobs, we usually know a state rep who can get us into civil service. To some extent, we're connected.

Jenna Angeline's Dorchester is poor. The neighborhoods, more often than not, are delineated by the public parks and community centers they surround. The men are dockworkers and hospital orderlies, in some cases postal clerks, a few firemen. The women are the orderlies, the cashiers, the cleaning women, the department store clerks. They are nurses, too, and cops, and civil service clerks, but chances are, if they've reached that kind of pinnacle, they don't live in Dorchester anymore. They've moved to Dedham or Framingham or Brockton.

In my Dorchester, you stay because of community and tradition, because you've built a comfortable, if somewhat poor, existence where little ever changes. A hamlet.

In Jenna Angeline's Dorchester, you stay because you don't have any choice.

Nowhere is it harder to try and explain the differences between these two Dorchesters—White Dorchester and Black Dorchester—than in White Dorchester. This is particularly true in my neighborhood, because we're one of the boundary neighborhoods. The moment you pass through Edward Everett Square heading south, east, or west, you're in Black Dorchester. So, people around here have a lot of trouble accepting the differences as anything other than black and white. A guy I grew up with once put it about as plainly as you'll ever hear it: "Hey, Patrick," he said, "enough of this bullshit. I grew up in Dorchester. I grew up poor. No one ever gave me nothing. My old man left when I was a kid just like a lotta the niggers in the 'Bury. No one *begged* me to learn how to read or get a job or be something. Nobody gave me affirmative action to help me out either, that's for damn sure. And I didn't pick up an Uzi, join a gang, and start doing drive-bys. So spare me this shit. They got no excuse."

People from White Dorchester always call Black Dorchester "the 'Bury." Short for Roxbury, the section of Boston that begins where Black Dorchester ends, where they load dead young black kids into meat wagons on the average of eight a weekend sometimes. Black Dorchester gives up its young on a pretty regular basis too, and those in White Dorchester refuse to call it anything but the 'Bury. Somebody just forgot to change it on the maps.

There's truth to what my friend said, however narrow it is, and the truth scares me. When I drive through my neighborhood, I see poor, but I don't see poverty.

Driving into Jenna's neighborhood, I saw a lot of poverty. I saw a big, ugly scar of a neighborhood with several boarded-up storefronts. I saw one that hadn't been boarded up yet, but was just as closed. The front window was blown out and bullet holes pocked the walls in jagged patterns of lethal acne. The inside was scorched and gutted and the fiberglass sign overhead that once said delicatessen in Vietnamese was shattered. The deli business wasn't what it once was in this neighborhood, but the crack business seemed to be doing just fine.

I turned off Blue Hill Avenue up a rutted hill that looked like it hadn't been paved since the Kennedy administration. The sun was setting, blood red, behind an overgrown yard of rotting weeds at the top of the hill. A group of laconic black kids crossed the street in front of me, taking their time, staring into my car. There were four of them, and one had a broomstick in his hand. He turned his head to look at me and whacked the stick off the street with a harsh snap. One of his buddies, bouncing a tennis ball in front of him, laughed and pointed an admonishing finger at my windshield. They passed over the sidewalk and cut through a rotted brown pathway between two three-deckers. I continued on up the hill, and something primal reassured me that my gun was hanging heavily from the holster on my left shoulder.

My gun is, as Angie would say, "not a fuck-around thing." It's a .44 magnum automatic—an "automag," they call it gleefully in *Soldier of Fortune* and like publications—and I didn't purchase it out of penis envy or Eastwood envy or because I wanted to own the goddamned biggest gun on the block. I bought it for one simple reason: I'm a lousy shot. I need to know that if I ever have to use it, I hit what I'm aiming at and I hit it hard enough to knock it down and keep it there. Shoot some people in the arm with a .32 and they just get angry. Shoot them in the same place with the automag and they ask for a priest.

I've fired it twice. Once when a brain-dead sociopath who was only slightly bigger than Rhode Island wanted me to prove how tough I was. He'd jumped out of his car and was six feet away from me and coming on fast, when I fired a round that went straight through his engine block. He stared at his Cordoba like I'd just shot his dog and almost wept. But the steam pouring out of the torn metal on his hood convinced him that there were things out there that were tougher than the two of us.

The other time was Bobby Royce. He had his hands on Angie's neck at the time, and I blew a chunk out of his leg. Tell you something about Bobby Royce: he got back up. He raised his gun toward me and still had it pointed that way even after Angie's two rounds had picked him up and drilled him against a hydrant and the light had left his eyes. Bobby Royce, going into rigor with his gun pointed at me, flat dead eyes not much different than they'd been when he was breathing.

I was wearing a pearl gray, unstructured linen jacket when I stepped out of my car in front of Jenna's last-known address. It was oversized and concealed the gun entirely. The group of teenagers sitting on the cars in front of Jenna's house was definitely fooled. As I crossed the street toward them, one of them said, "Hey, Five-O, where's your backup?"

The girl beside him giggled. "Under his coat, Jerome."

There were nine of them. Half of them sat on the trunk of a faded blue Chevy Malibu with a bright yellow Denver boot strapped to the front tire because the owner hadn't paid his parking tickets. The rest of them sat on the hood of the car behind the Malibu, a puke green Granada. Two kids slipped off the cars and walked quickly up the street, heads down, hands rubbing their foreheads.

I stopped by the cars. "Jenna around?"

Jerome laughed. He was lean and hard, but held himself loosely in his purple tank top, white shorts, and black Air Jordans. He said, " 'Jenna around?' " in a high-pitched falsetto. "Like he and Jenna old friends." The rest of them laughed. "No, man, Jenna's gone for the day." He looked at me and rubbed his chin. "I'm, like, her service, though. Why don't you leave your message with me?"

The other kids cracked up at "service."

I liked it too, but I was supposed to act like I was in control. I said, "Like have my agent call her agent?"

Jerome looked at me, deadpan. "Yeah, man, like that. Whatever you say."

More laughter. Lots more.

That's me, Patrick Kenzie, got a real way with youth. I walked between the two cars, hard to do when no one moves to the side for you, but I managed. "Thanks for your help, Jerome."

"Hey, man, don't mention it. Just part of the wonderfulness of me."

I started up the front steps of Jenna's three-decker. "I'll put in a good word for you with Jenna when I see her."

"Damn white of you too," Jerome said as I opened the door into the hallway.

Jenna lived on the third floor. I trudged up the steps, smelling the familiar smells of all inner-city three-deckers—chipped, sunbaked wood, old paint, kitty litter, wood and linoleum that had soaked up decades of melting snow and dirt from wet boots, spilled beers and sodas, the ashes of a thousand discarded cigarettes. I was careful not to touch the railing; it looked like it could easily crumble away from the banisters.

I turned into the top hallway and reached Jenna's door, or what was left of it. Something had imploded the wood by the knob, and the knob itself lay in a pile of splinters on the floor. A quick glance at the corridor in front of me revealed a thin stretch of dark green linoleum littered with broken chair legs, a shattered drawer, some shredded clothing, pillow stuffing, pieces of a small transistor radio.

I pulled my gun, inched inside, checking each doorway with my eyes and gun in tandem. The house had that certain stillness that only comes when nothing living remains inside, but I'd been fooled by that stillness before, and I have a rewired jaw to prove it.

It took me ten minutes of laborious, stiff-necked searching to decide the place actually was empty. By this time, my skin was covered in sweat, my back ached, and the muscles in my hands and arms felt about as pliable as Sheetrock.

I let the gun hang loosely from my hand as I went more casually through the apartment, rechecking the rooms, looking at things in more detail. Nothing jumped from the bedroom and danced in front of me with a neon sign overhead that said CLUE!!! Not in the bathroom either. Kitchen and living room were equally uncooperative. All I knew was that someone had been looking for something and delicacy had not been a primary concern. Nothing that was breakable was unbroken, nothing slitable unslit.

I stepped into the corridor and heard a sound to my right. I spun and stared down the fat barrel at Jerome. He crouched, hands in front of his face. "Ho! Ho! Ho, ho, ho, ho! Don't fucking shoot!"

"Jesus," I said, a hard wave of exhausted relief curling over my razor-blade adrenaline.

"God damn!" Jerome straightened up, brushed at his tank top for some reason, smoothed the cuffs of his shorts. "The fuck you carrying that thing for? I ain't seen no elephants 'round here since I don't know when."

I shrugged. "What're you doing up here?"

"Hey, I *live* in this neighborhood, white bread. Seems to me, you the one needs the excuse. And put that fucking thing *away*."

I slid the gun back into my holster. "What happened here, Jerome?"

"You got me," Jerome said, walking inside, looking at the mess like he'd seen it a hundred times before. "Old Jenna ain't been around in over a week. This was done over the weekend." He guessed my next question. "And no, man, no one saw anything."

"I'm not surprised," I said.

"Oh, like people in your neighborhood, they just up and volunteer information to the police all the time too, I bet."

I smiled. "Not on their best days."

"Uh-huh." He looked at the mess again. "This got to be about Roland. Got to be."

"Who's Roland?"

He chuckled at that one, looked at me. "Yeah, right."

"No, I'm serious. Who's Roland?"

He turned and walked out. "Go home, white bread."

I followed him down the stairs. "Who's Roland, Jerome?"

He shook his head the whole way down to the bottom floor. When he reached the porch, where his friends had reassembled on the steps, he jerked his thumb behind him at me as I came through the doorway. "He asking who Roland is."

His friends laughed. I had to be the funniest white man they'd seen in days.

Most of them stood up as I came out on the porch. The girl said, "You want to know who Roland is?"

I walked halfway down the steps. "I want to know who Roland is."

One of the bigger guys stabbed my shoulder with his index finger. "Roland your worst fucking nightmare."

The girl said, "Worse than your wife."

They all laughed and I walked down the steps and cut between the blue Malibu and the green Granada.

"Stay away from Roland," Jerome said. "What kill elephants, don't so much as faze Roland. Cause he ain't human.''

I stopped, turned back, my hand resting on the Malibu. "Then what is he?"

Jerome shrugged, folded his arms across his chest. "He just plain bad. Bad as it gets."

4

Shortly after I got back to the office, we ordered out for some Chinese and went over the day.

Angie had done the paper trail while I followed the physical one. I told her what my trail had brought us, added the names "Jerome" and "Roland" to the first page of our file, entered it into the computer. I also wrote "Break-in" and "Motive?" and underlined the latter.

The Chinese food arrived and we went to work clogging our arteries and forcing our hearts to work double time. Angie told me the results of the paper trail between mouthfuls of pork fried rice and chow mein. The day after Jenna disappeared, Jim Vurnan had gone to the restaurants and shops around Beacon Street and the State House to see if she'd been in recently. He didn't find her, but in a deli on Somerset he got a copy of one of her credit-card receipts from the owner. Jenna had paid for a ham on rye and a Coke with a Visa. Angie had taken the receipt and using the tried-and-true "Hi, I'm (Insert target's name) and I seem to have misplaced my credit card" method, she found that Jenna carried the Visa only, had a spotty credit history (one run-in with a collection agency back in '81), and had last used her card on June 19, the first day she didn't show up to work, at the Bank of Boston on the corner of Clarendon and St. James for a cash advance of two hundred dollars. Angie had then called the Bank of Boston claiming to be a representative of American Express. Mrs. Angeline had applied for a credit card and would they mind verifying her account?

What account?

She got the same response at every bank she tried. Jenna Angeline had no bank account. Which is fine, as far as I'm concerned, but it makes a person harder to find.

I started to ask Angie if she'd missed any banks, but she held up her hand, managed a "Not finished yet," around some spare rib. She wiped her mouth with a napkin and swallowed. Then she downed a gulp of beer and said, " 'Member Billy Hawkins?"

"Of course." Billy would be doing a dime in Walpole Penitentiary if we hadn't found his alibi.

"Well, Billy works for Western Union now, out of one of those Check Cashing Express places." She sat back, pleased.

"Well?"

"Well what?" She was enjoying herself.

I picked up a greasy spare rib and cocked my arm.

She held up her hands. "OK, OK. Billy's going to run a check for us, find out if she's used any of their offices. She can't have survived on two hundred dollars since the nineteenth. Not in this city anyway."

"And when's Billy going to get back to us?"

"He couldn't do anything today. He said his boss would be suspicious if he hung around for too long after the end of his shift, and his shift ended five minutes after I called. He'll have to do it tomorrow. Said he'll call us by noon."

I nodded. Behind Angie the dark sky was streaked with four fingers of scarlet and the slight breeze blew the thinnest wisps of her hair from behind her ear onto her cheekbone. Van Morrison was singing about "crazy love" on the boom box behind me, and we sat in the cramped office, staring at each other in the afterglow of the heavy Chinese food and the humid day and the satisfaction of knowing where our next paycheck was coming from. She smiled, a slightly embarrassed one, but didn't look away, and began tapping that pencil lightly against the chipped tooth again.

I let the stillness settle between us for a good five minutes before I said, "Come home with me."

She shook her head, still smiling, and swiveled the chair slightly.

"Come on. We'll watch a little TV, chat about old times—"

"There's a bed in this story somewhere. I know it."

"Only as a place to sleep. We'll lie down and . . . talk."

She laughed. "Uh-huh. And what about all those lovely young things who tend to camp out on your doorstep and tie up your phone?"

"Who?" I asked innocently.

"Who," she said. "Donna, Beth, Kelly, that chick with the ass, Lauren—"

"That *chick with the ass,* excuse me?"

"You know the one. The Italian girl. The one who goes"—her voice rose about two octaves—" 'Oooooh, Patrick, can we take a bubble bath now? Hee!' That one."

"Gina."

She nodded. "Gi-na. That's the one."

"I'll give them all up for one night with—"

"I know that, Patrick. I hope you don't think that's something to be proud of."

"Well, gee, Mom . . ."

She smiled. "Patrick, the major reason you think you're in love with me is because you've never seen me naked—"

"In—"

"In thirteen years," she said hurriedly, "and we both agreed that was forgotten. Besides, thirteen years is a lifetime to you where a woman is concerned."

"You say it like it's a bad thing."

She rolled her eyes at me. "So," she said, "what's on tomorrow's agenda?"

I shrugged, drank some beer from the can. Summer was definitely here; it tasted like tea. Van had finished singing about "crazy love," and was heading "into the mystic." I said, "I guess we wait for Billy to call, call him at noon if he doesn't."

"Sounds almost like a plan." She drained her beer, made a face at the can. "Any more cold ones?" I reached into my wastebasket, which was doubling as a cooler, tossed a can to her. She cracked it, took a sip. "What do we do when we find Mrs. Angeline?"

"Haven't a clue. Play it by ear."

"You're such a professional at this."

I nodded. "That's why they let me carry a gun."

She saw him before I did. His shadow fell across the floor, crept up the right side of her face. Phil. The Asshole.

I hadn't seen him since I hospitalized him three years ago. He looked better than he had then—lying on the floor holding his ribs, coughing blood onto a sawdust floor—but he still looked like an asshole. He had a hell of a scar beside his left eye, compliments of that sensible pool stick. I'm not sure, but I think I beamed when I noticed.

He wouldn't look at me. He looked at her. "I've been downstairs honking for the last ten minutes, hon'. You didn't hear me?"

"It was pretty noisy outside, and . . ." She pointed at the boom box, but Phil chose not to look at it because that would have meant looking at me.

He said, "Ready to go?"

She nodded and stood. She drained the beer in one long swallow. That didn't seem to make Phil's day. Probably made it worse when she flipped the can airborne in my direction and I tapped it into the wastebasket.

"Two points," she said, coming around the desk. "See you tomorrow, Skid."

"See you," I said, as she took Phil's hand and started walking out the door.

Just before they reached the door, Phil turned, her hand in his, and looked at me. He smiled.

I blew him a kiss.

I heard them work their way down the narrow, winding steps. Van had stopped singing and the quiet that replaced him felt thick and decayed. I sat in Angie's chair, saw them below me. Phil was getting in the car, Angie standing at the passenger door, holding the handle. Her head was down and I got the feeling she was making a conscious effort not to look back up at the window. Phil opened her door from the inside, and a moment after she got in, they pulled out into traffic.

I looked at my boom box, at the cassettes scattered around it. I considered taking Van out and putting in some Dire Straits. Or maybe some Stones. No. Jane's Addiction perhaps. Springsteen? Something really different, then. Ladysmith-Black-Mambazo or The Chieftains. I considered them all. I considered what would best fit my mood. I considered picking up the boom box and hurling it across the room at the exact spot where Phil had turned, Angie's hand in his, and smiled.

But I didn't. It'd pass.

Everything did. Sooner or later.

5

I left the church a few minutes later. Nothing left to keep me. I walked through the empty schoolyard, kicked a can in front of me as I went. I passed through the opening in the short wrought-iron fence that lined the yard and crossed the avenue to my apartment. I live directly across from the church in a blue-and-white three-decker that somehow missed the scourge of aluminum siding that overtook all its neighbors. My landlord is an old Hungarian farmer whose last name I couldn't pronounce with a year of practice. He spends all day fussing about in the yard, and he's said maybe a total of two hundred and fifty words to me in the five years I've lived there. The words are usually the same and there are three of them: "Where's my rent?" He's a mean old bastard, but he's unfriendly.

I let myself into my second-floor apartment and tossed the bills that awaited me on a pile on the coffee table with their relatives. There were no women camped by my door, inside or out, but there were seven messages on my answering machine.

Three were from Gina of the Bubble Bath. Each of her messages was backed by the grunts and moans emanating from the aerobics studio where she worked. Nothing like a little summer sweat to get the wheels of passion turning.

One was from my sister, Erin, long distance from Seattle. "Staying out of trouble, kid?" My sister. I'll have my teeth in a glass and a face like a prune, and she'll still be calling me "kid." Another was from Bubba Rogowski, wondering if I wanted to have a beer, shoot some pool. Bubba sounded drunk, which meant someone would bleed tonight. I nixed the invitation as a matter of course. Someone, I think it was Lauren, called to make nasty promises concerning a pair of rusty scissors and my genitalia. I was trying to recall our last date to decide if my behavior warranted such extreme measures, when Mulkern's voice drifted into the room and I forgot all about Lauren.

"Pat, lad, it's Sterling Mulkern. I assume you're out earning your money, which is grand, but I wonder if you had the time to read today's *Trib?* That dear boy, Colgan, was at my throat again. Ah, the boy would have accused your own father of setting fires just so he could put them out. A real Peck's bad boy, that Richie Colgan. I wonder, Pat, if you might have a word with him, ask him to lighten up a bit on an old man for a time? Just a thought. We've a table for lunch at the Copley, Saturday at one. Don't forget." The recording ended with a dial tone, then the cassette began rewinding.

I stared at the small machine. He wondered if I might have a word with Richie Colgan. Just a thought. Toss in the memory of my father for good measure. The hero fireman. The beloved city councilor. My father.

Everyone knows Richie Colgan and I are friends. It's half the reason people are a little more suspicious of me than used to be the case. We met when we were both majoring in Space Invaders with a Pub Etiquette minor at the Happy Harbor Campus of UMass/Boston. Now Richie's the *Trib*'s top columnist, a vicious bastard if he thinks you're one of the three great evils—an elitist, a bigot, or a hypocrite. Since Sterling Mulkern is an embodiment of all three, Richie orders him for lunch once or twice a week.

Everyone loved Richie Colgan—until they ran his picture over his byline. A good Irish name. A good Irish boy. Going after the corrupt, fat party bosses in city hall and the Statehouse. Then they ran his picture and everyone saw that his skin was blacker than Kurtz's heart, and suddenly he was a "troublemaker." But he sells papers, and his favorite target has always been Sterling Mulkern. Among the monikers he's given the Senator there's "Santa's Evil Twin," "Siphoner Sterling," "Three-Lunch Mulkern," and "Hypo the Hippo." Boston's not a town for the sensitive pol.

And now, Mulkern wanted me to "have a word with him." In for a penny, in for a pound. Next time I saw Mulkern, I decided, I'd give him the "Your money rents, it doesn't buy" speech and tell him to leave my hero father out of it while I was at it.

My father, Edgar Kenzie, had his fifteen minutes of local fame almost twenty years ago. He'd made the front page of both dailies; the photo even hit the wires and ended up on the back pages of the *New York Times* and the *Washington Post*. The photographer damn near won a Pulitzer.

It was a hell of a photograph. My father, swathed in the black and yellow of the BFD, an oxygen tank strapped to his back, climbing *up* a ten story building on a rope of sheets. A woman had come down those sheets a few minutes earlier. Well, halfway down. She'd lost her grip and died on impact. The building was an old nineteenth-century factory that someone had converted into tenements, made of red brick and cheap wood that could have been tissue and gasoline as far as the fire was concerned.

The woman had left her kids inside, telling them, in a moment of panic, to follow her down, instead of the other way around. The kids saw what happened to her and stopped moving, just stood in the black window and looked at their broken doll mother as smoke poured out of the room behind them. The window faced a parking lot and firemen were waiting for a tow truck to get the cars out so they could back a ladder in. My father grabbed an oxygen tank without a word, walked up to the sheets and started climbing. A window on the fifth floor blew out into his chest, and there's another photo, slightly out of focus, of him flapping in the air as shards of glass explode off his heavy black coat. He reached the tenth floor eventually and grabbed the kids—a four-year-old boy, a six-year-old girl—and went back down again. No big deal, he'd say with a shrug.

When he retired five years later, people still remembered him, and I don't think he ever paid for another drink in his life. He ran for city council on Sterling Mulkern's suggestion and lived a good life of graft and large homes until cancer settled into his lungs like smoke in a closet and ate him and the money away.

At home, the Hero was a different story. He made sure his dinner was waiting with a slap. Made sure the homework got done with a slap. Made sure everything went like clockwork with a slap. And if that didn't work, a belt, or a punch or two, or once, an old washboard. Whatever it took to keep Edgar Kenzie's world in order.

I never knew, probably never will, if it was the job that did this to him—if he was just reacting in the only way he knew how to all those blackened bodies he'd found, scorched into final fetal positions in hot closets or under smoking beds—or if he was simply born mean. My sister claims she doesn't remember what he was like before I came along, but she's also claimed, on occasion, that there were never days when he beat us so badly we had to miss school again. My mother followed the Hero to the grave by six months, so I never got to ask her either. But I doubt she would have told me. Irish parents have never been known for speaking ill of their spouses to their children.

I sat back on the couch in my apartment, thinking about the Hero once again, telling myself this was the last time. That ghost was gone. But I was lying and I knew it. The Hero woke me up at night. The Hero hid in waiting—in shadows, in alleys, in the antiseptic hallways of my dreams, in the chamber of my gun. Just as in life, he'd do whatever he damn well pleased.

I stood and walked past the window to the phone. Outside, something sudden moved in the schoolyard across the street. The local punks had shown up to lurk in the shadows, sit in the deep stone window seats and smoke a little reefer, drink a few beers. Why not. When I was a local punk, I'd done the same thing. Me, Phil, Bubba, Angie, Waldo, Hale, everybody.

I dialed Richie's direct line at the *Trib,* hoping to catch him working late as usual. His voice came across the line midway through the first ring. "City desk. Hold." A Muzak version of *The Magnificent Seven* theme syruped its way over the line.

Then I got one of those what's-wrong-with-this-picture answers without ever consciously having asked myself the question. There was no music coming from the schoolyard. No matter how much it announces their position, young punks don't go anywhere without their boom boxes. It's bad form.

I looked past the slit in the curtains down into the schoolyard. No more sudden movement. No movement at all. No glowing cigarette butts or clinking glass bottles. I looked hard at the area where I'd seen it. The school was shaped like an E without the middle dash. The two end dashes jutted out a good six feet farther than the middle section. In those corners, deep shadows formed in the ninety-degree pockets. The movement had come from the pocket on my right.

I kept hoping for a match. In the movies, when someone's following the detective, the idiot always lights a match so the hero can make him. Then I realized how ridiculously cloak-and-dagger this shit was. For all I knew, I'd seen a cat.

I kept watching anyway.

"City desk," Richie said.

"You said that already."

"Meestah Kenzie," Richie said. "How goes it?"

"It goes well," I said. "Hear you pissed off Mulkern again today."

"Reason to go on living," Richie said. "Hippos who masquerade as whales will be harpooned."

I was willing to bet he had that written on a three-by-five card, taped above his desk. "What's the most important bill coming to floor this session?"

"The most important bill—" he repeated, thinking about it. "No question—the street terrorism bill."

In the schoolyard, something moved. "The street terrorism bill?"

"Yeah. It labels all gang members 'street terrorists,' means you can throw them in jail simply because they're gang members. In simplest terms—"

"Use small words so I'll be sure to understand."

"Of course. In simplest terms, gangs would be considered paramilitary groups with interests that are in direct conflict with those of the state. Treat them like an invading army. Anyone caught wearing colors, wearing Raiders baseball caps even, is committing treason. Goes straight to jail, no passing Go."

"Will it pass?"

"Possibly. Good possibility, actually, when you consider how desperate everyone is to get rid of the gangs."

"And?"

"And, it'll get struck down within six months in a courtroom. It's one thing to say, 'We should declare martial law and get these fuckers off the streets, civil rights be damned.' It's another to actually do it, get that much closer to fascism, turn Roxbury and Dorchester into another South Central, helicopters and shit flying overhead day and night. Why the interest?"

I tried to put Mulkern or Paulson or Vurnan with this and it didn't fit. Mulkern, the house liberal, would never publicly stand behind something like this. But Mulkern, the pragmatist, would never take a public stand in favor of the gangs either. He'd simply take a vacation the week the bill came to floor.

"When's it coming to floor?" I asked.

"Next Monday, the third of July."

"There's nothing else coming up you can think of?"

"Not really, no. They got a mandatory seven bill for child molesters will probably sail through."

I knew about that one. Seven years mandatory prison time for anyone convicted of child molestation. No parole possibility. The only problem I had with it was that it wasn't called the mandatory life bill, and that there wasn't a provision that ensured that those convicted would be forced to enter mainstream population, and get back a little of what they gave.

Again Richie said, "Why the interest, Patrick?"

I considered Sterling Mulkern's message: Talk to Richie Colgan. Sell out. For the briefest moment, I considered telling Richie about it. Teach Mulkern to ask me to help him soothe his ruffled feathers. But I knew Richie would have no choice but to put it in his next column, in bold print, and professionally speaking, crossing Mulkern like that would be the same as cutting my wrists in a bathtub.

"Working on a case," I told Richie. "Very hush-hush at the moment."

"Tell me about it sometime," he said.

"Sometime."

"Good enough." Richie doesn't press me and I don't press him. We accept the word no from each other, which is one reason for the friendship. He said, "How's your partner?"

"Still mouthwatering."

"Still not coming across for you?" He chuckled.

"She's married," I said.

"Don't matter. You've had married before. Must drive you nuts, Patrick, a beautiful woman like that around you every day, and nary a single desire to touch your dick in her whole luscious being. Damn, but that's got to hurt." He laughed.

Richie's under the impression that he's a real hoot sometimes.

I said, "Yeah, well, I got to run." Something moved again in the black pocket of the schoolyard. "How about a couple of beers soon?"

"Bring Angie?" I thought I could hear him panting.

"I'll see if she's in the mood."

"Deal. I'll send over a few file reports on those bills."

"*Gracias.*"

He hung up and I sat back and looked through the slit in the curtains. I was familiar with the shadows now, and I could see a large shape sitting within them. Animal, vegetable, or mineral, I couldn't tell, but something was there. I thought about calling Bubba; he was good for times like these when you weren't sure what you were walking into. But he'd called me from a bar. Not a good sign. Even if I could track him down, he'd just want to kill the trouble, not investigate it. Bubba has to be used sparingly, with great care. Like nitro.

I decided to press Harold into service.

Harold is a six-foot stuffed panda bear that I won at the Marshfield Fair a few years back. I tried to give him to Angie at the time; I'd won him for her, after all. But she gave me that look she'd give me if I lit up a cigarette during sex, the withering one. Why she didn't want a six-foot stuffed panda in bright yellow rubber shorts adorning her apartment is beyond me, but since I couldn't find a trash barrel big enough to take him, I welcomed him into my home.

I dragged Harold from the bedroom into the dark kitchen and sat him in the chair by the window. The shade was drawn, and on my way out, I flicked on the light. If someone was watching me from the shadows, Harold should pass as me. Although my ears are smaller.

I crept through the back of the house, took my Ithaca from behind the door, and went down the back stairs. The only thing better than an automag for the total firearms incompetent is an Ithaca .12 gauge shotgun with a pistol grip. If you can't hit your target with that, you're legally blind.

I stepped out into my backyard, wondering if possibly there were two of them. One for the front, one for the back. But that seemed as unlikely as there being one of them in the first place. Paranoia had to be checked.

I hopped a few fences until I got to the avenue, slipped the Ithaca under my blue trench coat. I crossed the intersection and walked past the church on the south side. A road runs behind the church and the school, and I took that north. I passed a few people I knew along the way, gave curt nods, keeping my coat closed with one hand; have gun, will offend the neighbors.

I slipped into the back of the schoolyard, soundless in my Avia high-tops, and pressed close against the wall until I reached the first corner. I was at the edge of the E and he was ten feet away, around another corner, in the shadows. I considered how to approach it. I thought of just walking up on him, fast, but people tend to die that way. I thought of crawling along the ground like they used to on *Rat Patrol,* but I wasn't even positive anyone was there, and if I crawled up on a cat or two kids in a lip lock, I wouldn't be able to show my face for a month.

My decision was made for me.

It wasn't a cat and it wasn't teen lovers. It was a man and he was holding an Uzi. He stepped out from the corner in front of me with the ugly weapon pointed at my sternum, and I forgot how to breathe.

He was standing in darkness and wearing a dark blue baseball cap like they wear in the navy, with gold leafs embroidered on the brim, and gold writing of some sort on the front. I couldn't make out what it said, or maybe I was just too scared to concentrate.

He wore black wraparound sunglasses. Not the best thing to see properly when you wanted to shoot someone in the dark, but with that gun at this range, Ray Charles could put me in the grave.

He wore black clothes over black skin and that's about all I could tell about him.

I started to mention that this neighborhood wasn't known for its courtesy toward its darker neighbors after sunset when something fast and hard hit my mouth, and something else, equally hard, hit my temple, and just before I lost consciousness, I remember thinking: Harold the Panda doesn't fool 'em like he used to.

6

While I slept the sleep of idiots, the Hero came to visit. He was dressed in his uniform, carrying a child under each arm. His face was covered with soot, and smoke rolled off his shoulders. The two children were crying, but the Hero was laughing. He looked at me and laughed. And laughed. The laugh turned into a howl just before brown smoke began pouring from his mouth, and I woke up.

I was on a rug. That much I knew. There was a guy dressed in white kneeling over me. I'd either been committed or he was a paramedic. He had a bag beside him and a stethoscope around his neck. A paramedic. Or a very authentic impersonator. He said, "You gonna be sick?"

I shook my head and threw up on the rug.

Someone started screaming at me in high-pitched gibberish-speak. Then I recognized it. Gaelic. She remembered what country she was in and switched to English with a heavy brogue. It didn't make much difference, but at least I knew where I was now.

The rectory. The screaming banshee was Delia, Pastor Drummond's housekeeper. In a moment, she'd begin hitting me with something. The paramedic said, "Father?" and I could hear the pastor hustling Delia out of the room. The paramedic said, "You finished?" He sounded like he had things to do. A real angel of mercy. I nodded and rolled over onto my back. I sat up. Sort of. I hooked my arms around my knees and sat there, holding on, my head swimming. The walls were doing a psychedelic dance in front of me and my mouth felt like it was full of bloody pennies. I said, "Ouch."

"You got a way with words," the paramedic said. "You also got a mild concussion, some loose teeth, a busted lip, and a hell of a shiner growing by your left eye."

Great. Angie and I would have something to talk about in the morning. The Ray-Ban twins. "That it?"

"That's it," he said, dropping the stethoscope into the bag. "I'd tell you to come down to the hospital with me, but you're from Dorchester, so I figure you're into all that macho bullshit and won't come."

"Mmm," I said. "How'd I get here?"

Pastor Drummond, behind me, said, "I found you." He stepped in front of me, holding my shotgun and the magnum. He placed them gently on the couch across from me.

"Sorry about the rug," I said.

He pointed at the vomit. "Father Gabriel, when he was in his cups, used to do that quite often. If I remember right, that's why we picked that color pattern." He smiled. "Delia's making up a bed for you now."

"Thanks, Father," I said, "but I think if I can walk to the bedroom, I can walk across the street to my own place."

"That mugger might still be out there."

The paramedic picked up his bag from beside me and said, "Have a good one."

"It's been swell for me too," I managed.

The paramedic grimaced and gave us a little wave before letting himself out the side door.

I reached out my hand and Pastor Drummond took it, pulling me up. I said, "I wasn't mugged, Father."

He raised his eyebrows. "Angry husband?"

I looked at him. "Father," I said. "Please. You have to stop getting illicit thrills from my lifestyle. It has to do with a case I'm on. I think." I wasn't even sure. "It was a warning."

He supported me as far as the couch. The room was still

about as stable as quarters on the *Titanic*. He said, "This is some warning."

I nodded. Bad move. The *Titanic* overturned and the room slid sideways. Pastor Drummond's hand pushed me back against the couch. I said, "Yes. Some warning. Did you call the police?"

He looked surprised. "You know, I didn't think of it."

"Good. I don't want to spend all night filling out reports."

"Angela might have, though."

"You called Angie?"

"Of course he called me." She was standing in the doorway. Her hair was a wreck, messy strands hanging over her forehead; it made her look sexier, like she'd just woken up. She was wearing a black leather jacket over a burgundy polo shirt that hung untucked over gray sweatpants and white aerobic sneakers. She had a purse you could hide Peru in, which she dropped on the floor as she crossed to the couch.

She sat beside me. "Don't we look beautiful," she said, her hand under my chin, tilting it upward. "Jesus, Patrick, who'd you run into—an angry husband?"

Father Drummond giggled. A sixty-year-old priest, giggling into his fist. Not my day.

"I think it was a relative of Mike Tyson," I said.

She looked at me. "What, you don't have hands?"

I pushed her hand away. "He had an Uzi, Ange. Probably what he hit me with."

"Sorry," she said. "I'm a little anxious. I didn't mean to snap." She looked at my lips. "This wasn't done with the Uzi. Your temple, maybe. But not the lips. Looks like a speed glove to me, the way it tore the skin."

Angie, the expert on physical abrasions.

She leaned in close, whispered. "You know the guy?"

I whispered back. "No."

"Never saw him before?"

"Nope."

"You're sure?"

"Angie, I wanted this, I would've called the cops."

She leaned back, hands up. "OK. OK." She looked at Drummond. "OK if I take him back to his place, Father?"

"It would make Delia's day," Drummond said.

"Thanks, Father," I said.

He folded his arms. "Some security you are," he said, and winked.

He's a priest, but I could've kicked him.

Angie picked up the guns and then lifted me to my feet with her free hand.

I looked at Father Drummond. "G'night," I managed.

"God bless," he said at the door.

As we went down the steps into the schoolyard, Angie said, "You know why this happened, don't you."

"No, why?"

"You don't go to church anymore."

"Ha," I said.

She got me across the street and up the stairs, the queasiness steadily evaporating as the warmth of her skin and the feel of the blood rushing through her body reawakened my senses.

We sat down in the kitchen. I kicked Harold the Panda out of my chair, and Angie poured us each a glass of orange juice. She sniffed hers before she drank. "What'd you tell the Asshole?" I asked.

"After I told him what happened, he seemed so pleased someone finally kicked your ass, he would've let me fly to Atlantic City with the savings account."

"Glad to know some good came out of this."

She put her hand on mine. "What happened?"

I gave her the rundown from the time she left the office to ten minutes ago.

"Would you recognize him again?"

I shrugged. "Maybe. Maybe not."

She sat back, one leg raised and propped beside her on

the chair, the other tucked under her. She looked at me for a long time. "Patrick," she said.

"Yeah?"

She smiled sadly and shook her head. "You're going to have a hard time getting a date for a while."

7

We were just about to call Billy Hawkins the next day at noon when he walked into the office. Billy, like a lot of people who work in Western Union offices, looks like he just got out of detox. He's extremely skinny and his skin has that slightly yellowish texture of someone who spends all his time indoors in smoke-filled rooms. He accentuates his lack of weight by wearing tight jeans and shirts, and rolls his half-sleeves up to his shoulders as if he has biceps. His black hair looks like he combs it with a clawhammer, and he has one of those drooping Mexican bandit mustaches that nobody, not even your average Mexican bandit, wears anymore. In 1979, the rest of the world went on, but Billy didn't notice.

He plopped himself lazily into the chair in front of my desk and said, "So, like, when you guys going to get a bigger office?"

"The day I find the bell," I said.

Billy squinted. Slowly, he said, "Oh, right. Yeah."

Angie said, "How you doing, Billy?" and actually looked like she cared.

Billy looked at her and blushed. "I'm doing . . . I'm doing all right. All right, Angie."

Angie said, "Good. I'm glad." What a tease.

Billy looked at my face. "What happened to you?"

"Had a fight with a nun," I said.

Billy said, "You look like you had a fight with a truck," and looked at Angie.

Angie gave it a small giggle, and I didn't know who I wanted to pitch out the window more.

"You run that check for us, Billy?"

" 'Course, man. 'Course. You owe me big time on this one too, I'll tell ya."

I raised my eyebrows. "Billy, remember who you're talking to."

Billy thought about it. Thought about the ten years he'd be doing in Walpole, fetching cigarettes for his boyfriend, Rolf the Animal, if we hadn't saved him. His yellow skin whitened considerably, and he said, "Sorry, man. You're right. When you're right, you're right." He reached into the back pocket of his jeans and tossed a somewhat greasy, very wrinkled piece of paper on my desk.

"What am I looking at here, Billy?"

"Jenna Angeline's reference check," he said. "Copped from our Jamaica Plain office. She cashed a check there on Tuesday."

It was greasy, it was wrinkled, but it was gold. Jenna had listed four references, all personal. Under the Job heading, she'd written, "Self-employed," in a small, birdlike scrawl. In the personal references she'd listed four sisters. Three lived in Alabama, in or around Mobile. One lived in Wickham, Massachusetts. Simone Angeline of 1254 Merrimack Avenue.

Billy handed me another piece of paper—a Xerox of the check Jenna had cashed. The check was signed by Simone Angeline. If Billy hadn't been such a slimy-looking dude, I would have kissed him.

After Billy left, I finally got up the nerve to take a look in the mirror. I'd avoided it all last night and this morning. My hair's short enough to make do with a finger comb, so after my shower this morning, that's exactly what I did. I'd skipped shaving too, and if I had a little stubble, I told myself it was hip, very *GQ*.

I crossed the office and entered the tiny cubicle that

someone had once referred to as "the bathroom." It's got
a toilet all right, but even that's in miniature, and I always
feel like an adult locked in a preschool whenever I sit on
it and my knees hit my chin. I shut the door behind me
and raised my head from the munchkin sink and looked in
the mirror.

If I hadn't been me, I wouldn't have recognized my face.
My lips were blown up to twice their size and looked like
they'd French-kissed a weed whacker. My left eye was
fringed by a thick rope of dark brown and the cornea was
streaked with bright red threads of blood. The skin along
my temple had split when Blue Cap hit me with the butt
of the Uzi, and while I slept, the blood had clotted in some
hair. The right side of my forehead where I assume I'd hit
the school wall was raw and scraped. If I wasn't the manly
detective type, I might have wept.

Vanity is a weakness. I know this. It's a shallow de-
pendence on the exterior self, on how one looks instead of
what one is. I know this well. But I have a scar the size
and texture of a jellyfish on my abdomen already, and
you'd be surprised how your sense of self changes when
you can't take your shirt off at the beach. In my more
private moments, I pull up my shirt and look at it, tell
myself it doesn't matter, but every time a woman has felt
it under her palm late at night, propped herself up on a
pillow and asked me about it, I've made my explanation as
quick as possible, closed the doors to my past as soon as
they've opened, and not once, even when Angie's asked,
have I told the truth. Vanity and dishonesty may be vices,
but they're also the first forms of protection I ever knew.

The Hero always gave me a dope slap upside the head
whenever he caught me looking in the mirror. "Men built
those things so women would have something to do," he'd
say. Hero. Philosopher. My father, the Renaissance man.

When I was sixteen, I had deep blue eyes and a nice
smile, and little else to take confidence in, hanging around
the Hero. And if I was still sixteen, staring into the mirror,

working up some nerve, telling myself *tonight* I'd finally do something about the Hero, I'd definitely be at a loss.

But now, damnit, I had a genuine case to solve, a Jenna Angeline to locate, an impatient partner on the other side of the door, a gun in my holster, detective's license in my wallet, and . . . a face that looked like it belonged to a Flannery O'Connor character. Ah, vanity.

When I opened the door, Angie was rifling through her purse, probably looking for a misplaced microwave or an old car. She looked up. "You ready?"

"I'm ready."

She pulled a stun gun from the purse. "What's this guy look like again?"

I said, "Last night he was wearing a blue cap and wraparounds. But I don't know if it's like his regular uniform or anything." I opened the door. "Ange, you won't need the stun gun. If you spot him, lay back. We just want to verify that he's still around."

Angie looked at the stun gun. "It's not for him, it's for me. Case I need something to keep me awake in cow country."

Wickham is sixty miles from Boston, so Angie thinks they don't have telephones yet.

I said, "You can take the girl out of the city . . ."

"But you'll have to shoot her first," she said and headed down the stairs.

She stayed in the church, giving me a minute head start and watching the street through the lower opening of a stained-glass window.

I crossed the street to what I call my "company car." It's a dark green 1979 Volaré. The Vobeast. It looks like shit, sounds like shit, drives like shit, and generally fits in well in most of the places where I have to work. I opened the door, half expecting to hear a rush of feet on the street behind me, followed by the snap of a weapon hitting the back of my skull. That's the thing about being a victim;

you start to think it'll happen to you on a regular basis. Suddenly everything looks suspect and any brightness you may have noticed the day before has dissipated into the shadows. And the shadows are everywhere. It's living with the reality of your own vulnerability, and it sucks.

But nothing happened this time. I didn't see Blue Cap in my rearview as I pulled a U-turn and headed for the expressway. But then, unless he'd really enjoyed last night's encounter, I didn't think I would see him again; I'd just have to assume he was there. I pushed the Vobeast down the avenue, then turned onto the northern on-ramp for I-93 and drove downtown.

Twenty minutes later I was on Storrow Drive, the Charles River running by in copper flashes on my right. A couple of Mass. General nurses lunched on the lawn; a man ran over one of the footbridges with a mammoth chocolate Chow beside him. For a moment, I thought of picking one up for myself. Probably do a hell of a lot better job protecting me than Harold the Panda ever would. But then, I didn't really need an attack dog; I had Bubba. By the boathouse, I saw a group of BU or Emerson students, stuck in the city for the summer, passing around a bottle of wine. Wild kids. Probably had some brie and crackers in their backpacks, too.

I got off at Beacon Street, U-turned again onto the service road, and banged a quick right onto Revere Street, following its cobblestones across Charles Street and up Beacon Hill. No one behind me.

I turned again onto Myrtle Street, the whole street no wider than a piece of dental floss, the tall colonial buildings squeezing in on me. It's impossible to follow someone in Beacon Hill without being spotted. The streets were built before cars, and I presume, before fat or tall people.

Back when Boston was this wonderful mythic world of midget aerobics instructors, Beacon Hill must have seemed roomy. But now, it's cramped and narrow and shares more than a little in common with an old French provincial town—very pleasing to the eye, but functionally a disaster. A truck stopped for a delivery on the Hill can back up traffic for a mile. The streets are apt to be one-way in a northern direction for two or three blocks, then arbitrarily turn one-way to the south. This usually captures the average driver unaware and forces him to turn onto yet another narrow street with much the same problem, and before he knows it, he's back on Cambridge or Charles or Beacon Street, looking up at the Hill, wondering how the hell he ever ended up down here again, but getting the distinct, if irrational, impression that the Hill itself threw him off.

It's a wonderful place to be a snob. The homes are gorgeous red brick. The parking spaces are guarded by the Boston Police. The small cafés and shops are manned by imperious owners who close their doors whenever someone they don't recognize looks as if he may want to enter. And no one can find your address unless you, personally, draw them a map.

I looked in my rearview as I crested the Hill, the gold dome of the State House peeking out through the wrought-iron fence of a roof garden ahead of me. Two blocks behind me, I saw a car driving slowly, the driver's head turning left and right as if looking for an unfamiliar address.

I took a left on Joy Street and coasted the four blocks down to Cambridge Street. As the light turned green and I crossed the intersection, I saw the same car coasting down the hill behind me. At the very top of Joy Street, another car appeared—a station wagon with a broken luggage rack on the roof. I couldn't see the driver, but I knew it was Angie. She'd busted the luggage rack with a hammer one morning, pretending the flimsy metal was Phil.

I turned left on Cambridge Street and drove a few blocks to the Charles Plaza. I pulled into the parking lot, took the ticket at the gate—only three dollars per half hour; what a bargain—and pulled across the lot until I was in front of the Holiday Inn. I walked inside the hotel like I had business there, turned right past the front desk and hopped the elevator to the third floor. I walked down the corridor until I found a window and stared down into the parking lot.

Blue Cap wasn't wearing a blue cap today. He had on a white bicycler's cap, the brim pushed back flat against his forehead. He still wore the wraparounds, though, and a white Nike T-shirt and black sweatpants. He stood just outside of his car—a white Nissan Pulsar with black racing stripes—and leaned on the open door while he decided if he should follow me in or not. I couldn't see his license plate numbers from this angle, and from this height, I could only guess at his age, but I put him at twenty to twenty-five. He was big—six two or so—and he looked like he knew his way around a Nautilus machine.

Out on Cambridge Street, Angie's car idled, double-parked.

I looked back at Blue Cap. No point sticking around. He'd follow me into the hotel or he wouldn't. Either way, it didn't make any difference.

I took the stairs down to the basement, opened a door onto a service driveway that smelled of exhaust fumes, and jumped off the loading dock. I walked past a dumpster that reeked of slowly stewing fruit and worked my way down onto Blossom Street. I took my time, but before you could say slick-as-a-wet-goose, I was back on Cambridge Street.

All over Boston, in places you'd never notice, there are garages. It doesn't compensate for a city as short on parking space as Moscow is on toilet paper, but at least the rental fees are exorbitant. I stepped into one between a hair salon and a florist, strolled along the garage until I came to space number eighteen, and removed the slipcover from my baby.

Every boy needs a toy. Mine is a 1959 Porsche Roadster convertible. It's royal blue, with a wood finish steering wheel and a twin cowl cockpit. True, "cockpit" is a term usually reserved for jets, but when I've taken this thing up to a hundred and forty or so, I've gotten the distinct impression that liftoff's only a few more blurred road signs

away. The interior is a rich white leather. The stick shift
gleams like polished pewter. The horn has a keen horse
emblem on it. I work on it more than I drive it, pampering
it on weekends, polishing it, bringing it new parts. I'm
proud to say I've never gone so far as to give it a name,
but Angie says that's only because I lack the imagination.

It started with the growl of a jungle cat on the first turn
of the key. I took a baseball cap from under the seat, slipped
off my jacket, adjusted my sunglasses, and left the garage.

Angie was still double-parked in front of the Plaza,
which meant Blue Cap was present and accounted for. I
waved and pulled out onto Cambridge, heading toward the
river. She was still behind me when I reached Storrow
Drive, but by the time I got to I-93, I'd left her in the dust,
simply because I could. Or maybe, simply because I'm so
immature. One of the two.

8

The drive to Wickham is not a fun one. You have to switch interchanges every third mile or so, and one wrong turn dumps you in New Hampshire, trying to talk directions with eastern rednecks who don't speak the language. To top it off, there's nothing to look at but the occasional industrial park, or as you get closer to the belt of towns that lie along the Merrimack River, the Merrimack River. Not a pleasant sight. Usually you have to look down a sewer grate to find water as brown and sluggish as the Merrimack's—a casualty of the textile business that built a lot of New Hampshire and Massachusetts. The next thing you see as you drive through this region are the mills themselves, and the sky turns to soot.

I had *Exile on Main St.* pumping through my speakers the whole way so I didn't mind it that much, and by the time I found Merrimack Avenue, the only thing I was worried about was leaving the car unattended.

Wickham is not an upwardly mobile community. It's dingy and gray as only a mill town can be. The streets are the color of a shoe bottom, and the only way to tell the difference between the bars and the homes is to look for the neon signs in the windows. The roads and sidewalks are uneven, the tar cracked and pale. Many of the people, especially the workers as they trudge home from the mills in the dying light, have the look of those who've long ago gotten used to the fact that no one remembers them. It's a place where the people are grateful for the seasons, because at least they confirm that time is actually moving on.

Merrimack Avenue is the main strip. Simone Angeline's address was a good ways past the center of town—the bars, gas stations, mills, and clothing factories were five miles behind me before I reached the twelve hundred block. Angie was back in my rearview mirror by then, and she passed me when I pulled onto a side street and parked the car. I set the Chapman lock and disengaged the radio, taking it with me as I got out. I took one last look back at the car and hoped that we would find Jenna soon. Real soon.

I didn't win my car in a card game or have it bequeathed to me by an overly generous client. I banked my money and waited, banked some more money and waited. Finally I saw it advertised and I went to the bank for a loan. I sat through an excruciating interview with a condescending loan officer who reminded me of every bitter, high-school geek who sees his adult life as a mission to avenge adolescence by being a total prick to anyone he assumes would have treated him badly in homeroom. Luckily, my practice grew and my fees rose and I soon had that monkey off my back. But I still pay the price of being constantly anxious about the only material possession I've ever given a damn about.

I slid into the passenger seat of Angie's car and she took my hand. "Don't wowwy, baby, nothing will happen to your pride and joy. I promise."

She's funny enough to shoot sometimes.

I said, "Well, least in this neighborhood, nobody will be suspicious of *this* thing."

She said, "Oh, good one. You ever think of going into stand-up?"

It went like that. We sat in the car and passed around a can of Pepsi and waited for our meal ticket to make a guest appearance.

By six o'clock we were cramped and sick of each other and even sicker of looking at 1254 Merrimack Avenue. It was a faded A-frame that might have been pink once. A

Puerto Rican family had entered it an hour ago, and we'd watched a light go on in the second-floor apartment a minute or so later. Short of our second can of Pepsi exploding all over the dashboard when I opened it, that was the closest we'd come to excitement in four hours.

I was looking through the tape collection on Angie's floor, trying to find a group I'd heard of, when she said, "Heads up."

A black woman—rope thin, with a stiff, almost regal bearing—was stepping from an '81 Honda Civic, her right arm around a bag of groceries, resting them on her hip. She looked like the picture of Jenna, but younger by a good seven or eight years. She also seemed to have too much energy for the tired woman in the photograph. She slammed the car door with her free hip, a hard, swift move that would have left Gretzky on the ice with a wet ass. She marched to the front door of the house, slid her key into the lock, and disappeared inside. A few minutes later, she appeared in silhouette by the window, a telephone receiver to her ear.

Angie said, "How do you want to play it?"

"Wait," I said.

She shifted in her seat. "I was afraid you were going to say that." She held her chin with her fingers, moved it around in a semicircle for a moment. "You don't think Jenna's in there?"

"No. Since she disappeared, she's played it relatively careful. She has to know her apartment's been trashed. And the beating the guy in the schoolyard gave me tells me she's probably into more than the petty theft we're after her for. With people like that after her—maybe this Roland guy too—I don't think she's going to set herself up in her sister's place."

Angie half shrugged, half nodded in that way she has, and lit a cigarette. She hung her arm out the window and the gray smoke pooled by the rearview mirror, then separated into equal strands and floated out the windows. She said, "If we're smart enough to figure out where she is, wouldn't someone else be? We can't be the only ones who know about the sister."

I thought about it. It made sense. If whoever "they" were had put a tail on me in the hopes of following me to Jenna, then they must have put a tail on Simone. "Shit."

"Now, what do you want to do?"

"Wait," I repeated, and she groaned. I said, "We follow Simone when she goes somewhere—"

"*If* she goes somewhere."

"Positive energy, please. When she goes somewhere, we follow, but we hang back first, see if we have company."

"And if our company is already on to us? If they're watching us right now as we speak, thinking the same thing? What then?"

I resisted the urge to turn around and look for other cars with two immobile occupants, staring in our direction. "We deal with it," I said.

She frowned. "You always say that when you don't have a clue."

"Do not," I said.

At seven-fifteen, things started happening.

Simone, wearing a navy blue sweatshirt over a white T-shirt, faded jeans, and generic sneakers the color of an oyster, walked out of the house with determination and opened her car the same way. I wondered if she did everything the same way—with that set look on her face, that the-hell-with-you-if-you-can't-keep-up air about her. Could people *sleep* that way?

She went straight up Merrimack, so we gave her a few blocks, waiting to see if we were the only interested party. It seemed to be the case, and if not, I wasn't about to lose my only lead. We pulled out, and with one last look at my thirty-seven thousand dollars worth of automobile—insurance company estimate, mind you—we tailed her through Wickham. She went straight through the center of town and hopped on I-495. I was tired of being in the car and hoped like hell she didn't have Jenna stowed away in Canada. Thankfully, that didn't seem to be the case, because she got off the expressway a few miles later, turning off into Lansington.

If possible, Lansington is uglier than Wickham, but in imperceptible ways. In most respects, they're identical. Lansington just feels dingier.

We were waiting at a traffic light near the center of town, but when the light turned green, Simone didn't move. I felt two cold spades press together around my heart and Angie said, "Shit. Think she's on to us?"

I said, "Use the horn."

She did and Simone's hand went up in apology as she realized the light had changed. It was the first undetermined thing she'd done since I'd seen her, and it felt like a jump start: we were close.

All around us were squat two-story clapboard buildings, circa the late 1800s. Trees were sparse and gnarled in hideous ways where we saw them. The traffic lights were old, still round, no Walk/Don't Walk signals or neon pictures for those who couldn't understand the Walk/Don't Walk parts. The lights made clicking sounds when they changed, and as we drifted along the two-lane road, I felt that we could just as easily have been in rural Georgia or West Virginia.

Ahead of us, Simone's left blinker went on, and a fraction of a second later, she pulled off the road into a small dirt parking lot filled with pickup trucks, a Winnebago, a couple of dusty American sports cars, and those wretched testaments to Detroit's bad taste—El Caminos. Two of them. A car that couldn't decide whether it wanted to be a truck; a truck that couldn't decide whether it wanted to be a car—obscene, hybrid results.

Angie kept going and a half mile down the road, we U-turned and went back. The parking lot belonged to a bar. Just like Wickham, you wouldn't have known what it was without the small neon Miller High Life signs in the windows. It was a low two-story building, a little deeper than most of the houses, stretching back an extra ten yards or so. From inside I could hear glasses clinking, a smattering of laughter, the babble of voices, and a Bon Jovi song coming off the jukebox. I amended that last thought; maybe it was just a stereo tuned to a radio station and no one inside had actually paid money to listen to Bon Jovi. Then I looked at the pickups and the bar again, and I wasn't hopeful.

Angie said, "We going to wait here too?"

"Nope. Going in."

"Goody." She looked at the building. "Thank God I'm licensed to carry a firearm." She checked the load in her .38.

"Damn straight," I said, climbing out of the car. "First thing you do when we get inside, shoot the stereo."

Simone was nowhere in sight when we entered. This was pretty easy to ascertain, because the moment we stepped through the door, everyone stopped moving.

I was wearing jeans, a denim shirt, and a baseball cap. My face looked like I'd had a disagreement with a pit bull, and the jacket that covered my gun was a raggy, faded army thing. I fit right in.

Angie was wearing a dark blue football jacket with white leather sleeves over a loose white cotton shirt that hung untucked over a pair of black leggings.

Guess which one of us they were looking at.

I looked at Angie. New Bedford isn't terribly far from here. Big Dan's Bar is in New Bedford. That's where a bunch of guys threw a girl down on a pool table and had their version of fun at her expense while the rest of the bar cheered them on. I looked at the patrons of this bar—a Heinz 57 mix of eastern rednecks, white trash, mill workers only recently immigrated from the Third World, Portuguese, a couple of black guys—all poor and hostile and gearing up to let off some steam. Probably came here because Big Dan's was closed. I looked at Angie again. I wasn't worried about her; I was considering what would happen to my business if my partner shot the dicks off a barful of people in Lansington. I wasn't sure, but I didn't think we'd be able to keep that office in the church.

The barroom was larger than it looked from the outside. To my left, just before the bar itself, was a narrow staircase of unfinished wood. The bar ran halfway down the floor on the left side. Across from it were a few tables for two against a dark plywood wall. Past the bar, the place opened up and I could see pinball and video machines on the left and the corner of a pool table on the right. A pool table. Terrific.

The place was medium to crowded. Just about everyone wore a baseball cap, even those who I assume were women. A few people had mixed drinks, but for the most part, this was Budweiser country.

We walked up to the bar and folks went back to what they were doing, or pretending to.

The bartender was a young guy, good-looking and bleached blond, but a townie if he was working this place. He gave me a slight smile. Then he gave one to Angie that, in comparison, looked as if his lips exploded. "Hi. What can I get you?" He leaned on the bar and looked into her eyes.

Angie said, "Two Buds."

"My pleasure," Blondie said.

"I'll bet," she said and smiled.

She does this all the time. Flirts her ass off with everyone but me. If I wasn't such a rock of self-confidence, it would annoy me.

My luck was good tonight, though. I felt it the moment the Bon Jovi song ended. While Blondie went for the beers, I looked at the stairs. In what passes for a moment of stillness in a bar, I could hear people moving around overhead.

When Blondie placed both beers in front of Angie, I said, "Is there a back door to this place?"

He turned his head slowly in my direction, looking at me as if I'd just bumped his knee stepping onto the bus. "Yeah," he said with extreme slowness and nodded in the direction of the pool table. Through the smoke that hung over the back I saw the door. He was looking at Angie again, but out of the corner of his mouth, he said, "Why, you planning on sticking the place up?"

"No," I said. I flipped through all the cards in my wallet until I found the right one. "I'm planning on citing you for building code violations. Lots of them, asshole." I flipped the card on the bar. It said, "Lewis Prine, State Building Inspector." Lewis made the mistake of leaving me unattended in his office once.

Blondie stopped looking at Angie, though I could see it hurt. He stepped back a bit and looked at the card. "Don't you guys have badges or something?"

I had one of those too. Good thing about badges, most of them look pretty much the same to the untrained eye, so I don't have to carry fifty of them around with me. I flipped it at him, then put it back in my pocket. "All you got's that one back door?" I said.

"Yeah," he said. Nervous. "Why?"

"Why? *Why?* Where's the owner?"

"Huh?"

"The owner. The owner."

"Bob? He's gone home for the night."

My luck was still holding. I said, "Son, how many floors you got here?"

He looked at me as if I'd just asked what the atmospheric density of Pluto was. "Floors? Uh, two. We got two. Rooming house's upstairs."

"Two," I repeated with an air of moral revulsion. "Two floors and the only exits are on the first."

"Yeah," he said.

" 'Yeah'? How people on the second floor supposed to get out if there's a fire?"

"A window?" he suggested.

"A window." I shook my head. "How about I take you up there right now, see how well you land jumping out a fucking window? A window. Jesus."

Angie crossed her legs, sipping her beer, enjoying this.

Blondie said, "Well . . ."

I said, "Well *what?*" I gave Angie the get-ready look. She raised her eyebrows and downed her beer happily. "Boy," I said, "you're gonna learn some shit tonight," and I crossed the floor to the plywood wall and pulled the fire alarm.

No one in the barroom ran for an exit. No one really moved at all. They just turned their heads and looked at me. They seemed a bit pissed off.

But on the second floor, no one could tell if there was a fire or not. Bars always smell like smoke.

A rather large woman with a rather small sheet over her nude body and a skinny guy with a lot less coverage came down first. They barely glanced at the bar before they hopped out the door like rabbits during hunting season.

Two kids were next. Sixteen or so, both with a little acne. Probably registered as Mr. and Mrs. Smith. They flattened against the wall as soon as they cleared the last step, staring at all of us, chests heaving.

Then suddenly, Simone was there, looking very put out, looking to find someone responsible, her eyes working their way from Blondie, around the crowd of hicks, and finally settling on *moi*. I glanced at her but passed by, my eyes slowing and holding at a point just over her shoulder.

On Jenna Angeline.

Angie left my shoulder and disappeared around the corner, on the other side of the plywood wall. I waited, my eyes fixed on Jenna Angeline, hers finally meeting mine. They were eyes that screamed resignation. Old, old eyes. Brown and numb and too beaten to show fear. Or joy. Or life. Something passed through them, briefly, and I knew that she recognized me. Not who I was. What I represented. I was just another form of cop or collection agent or land-

lord or boss. I was authority, and I was coming to decide
something about her life whether she liked it or not. She
recognized me all right.

Angie had found the main cables and the clarion blast
bleated away to nothing in one wheezing second.

I was the center of attention now, and I knew I was about
to face resistance, at the very least from the Angeline sisters. Everyone except them, the bartender, and a big, going-
to-fat, ex-football player type to my right faded slightly
behind a haze of gauze. The football player was leaning
forward on his toes and Blondie had his hand under the
bar. Neither of the Angeline sisters looked like they had
any intention of moving without help from a crane.

My voice seemed loud and hoarse when I said, "Jenna,
I need to talk to you."

Simone grabbed her sister's arm and said, "Come on,
Jenna, let's go," and started leading her toward the door.

I shook my head and stepped in front of the door, my
hand already in my jacket as the football player made his
move. Another hero. Probably a member of the auxiliary
fire department. His right hand was heading toward my
shoulder and his mouth was open, a gruff voice saying,
"Hey, asshole, leave the women alone." Before he reached
my shoulder, my hand cleared my jacket and whacked his
arm away and brushed my gun against his lips.

I said, "Excuse me?" and dug the muzzle of the gun
hard against his upper lip.

He looked at the gun. He didn't say anything.

I didn't move my head, just kept my eyes on the barroom, looked everyone in the eye who'd meet mine. I felt
Angie beside me, her gun steady, her breathing shallow.
She said, "Jenna, Simone, I want you to get in your car
and drive to the house in Wickham. We'll be right behind
you and if you try to take off, believe me, our car's a lot
faster than yours and we'll end up talking in a ditch
somewhere."

I looked at Simone. "If I wanted to hurt you, you'd be dead now."

Simone gave off some sort of body language that only a sister would recognize, because Jenna put a hand on her arm. "We do what they say, Simone."

Angie opened the door behind me. Jenna and Simone passed by and walked out. I looked at Football Player, then pushed his face back with the gun. I felt the weight of it in my arm, the muscles beginning to ache, my hand stiffening and sweat popping out of the glands all over my body.

Football Player met my eyes and I could see he was thinking about being a hero again.

I waited. I leveled the gun and said, "Come on."

Angie said, "Not here. Let's go." She took my elbow, and we backed out of the bar into the night.

9

"Sit down, Simone. Please." Everything Jenna said came out as a weary plea.

We'd been back at the house for ten minutes and had spent all our time dealing with Simone's ego. So far, she'd tried to push past me twice, and now she was walking toward the phone.

"Man don't come into my house, tell me how to act," she told Jenna, then looked at Angie. "And the man ain't going to shoot me with the neighbors awake upstairs." She'd started to believe that by the time she reached the phone.

I said, "Simone, who're you going to call? The police? Fine."

Jenna said, "Put the phone down, Simone. Please."

Angie looked bored and antsy. Patience is not one of her prime virtues. She walked over and pulled the phone cord out of the wall.

I closed my eyes, then opened them. "Jenna, I'm a private investigator, and before any of us decides to do anything else, I have to talk to you."

Simone looked at the phone, then at Angie and me, finally at her sister. She said, "Your bed, girl, lie in it," and sat down on the couch.

Angie sat beside her. "You have a very nice place here."

This was true. It was small, and the outside was nothing to look at, and it wasn't like there was a baby grand by the window, but Simone definitely had an eye. The floor had

67

been stripped, the blonde wood underneath polished to a high gloss. The couch where Simone and Angie sat was a light cream color with an oversize throw pillow that Angie was itching to hug to her chest. Jenna sat in a mahogany shell chair to the right of the couch and I leaned on its twin across from her. Four feet from the windows the floor rose eight inches and a small alcove had been created around the two windows facing the street, cushions on the window seats, a small wooden magazine rack, a hanging plant overhead, and the wooden telephone desk. A bookcase ran the length of the half wall behind Jenna and I saw poetry by Nikki Giovanni, Maya Angelou, Alice Walker, and Amiri Baraka, plus novels by Baldwin and Wright as well as Gabriel García Márquez, Toni Morrison, Pete Dexter, Walker Percy, and Charles Johnson.

I looked at Simone. "Where'd you go to school?"

She said, "Tuskegee," a little surprised.

"Good school." A friend of mine played ball there for a year before he found out he wasn't good enough. I said, "Nice book collection."

"You just surprised the nigger knows how to read."

I sighed. "Right. That's it, Simone." I said to Jenna, "Why'd you quit your job?"

Jenna said, "People quit their jobs every day."

"This is true," I said, "but why'd you quit yours?"

She said, "I didn't want to work for them no more. Plain and simple."

"And when you raided their files, how plain and simple was that?"

Jenna looked confused. So did Simone. It's possible they actually were, but then, if she had stolen the files, looking completely aware of what I was talking about probably wasn't the best idea. Simone said, "What the hell are you talking about?"

Jenna was watching me steadily, her hands kneading the fabric of her skirt. She was considering something and, for a moment, the intelligence that entered her eyes swamped all that weariness like a wave over a rowboat. Then it was gone again and the eyes dulled. She said, "Simone, I'd like to talk to this man alone for a few minutes."

Simone didn't like it, but after a minute or so, she and Angie went into the kitchen. Simone's voice was loud and unhappy, but Angie has a way with loud and unhappy. You don't live in a marriage of arbitrary rages, unfounded jealousies, and sudden accusations without growing adept at dealing with another's hostility in a small room. When dealing with whiners or ragers of any sort—those who always see themselves as victims of life's vast conspiracy to ruin their day or are unreasonable or choking on some predictable, paltry anger—Angie's gaze grows flat and level, her head and body become as still as a statue, and the whiner or the rager vents until that gaze forces them to sputter, to weaken, to exhaust themselves. You either wither under the calm logic of it, blanch in the face of its daunting maturity, or you lash out against it, like Phil, and negate yourself. I know; I've been the focus of that gaze a time or two myself.

In the living room, Jenna's eyes were fastened firmly on the floor and if she kneaded that skirt any harder the thread would begin pooling at her feet. She said, "Whyn't you tell me why you've come up here for me."

I thought about it. I've been wrong about people before. Several times. I go on the presumption that everyone's full of shit until proven otherwise, and this usually serves me in good stead. But every now and then, I think a person has proven himself otherwise, only to discover the shit later, usually in painful ways. Jenna didn't strike me as a liar. She didn't look like she knew how, but often it's people just like that who wouldn't know the truth if it was wearing an ID card on its lapel.

I said, "You have certain documents. I was hired to retrieve them." I spread my hands, palms up. "Simple as that."

"Documents?" she said, spitting it. "Documents. Damn." She stood and began pacing and suddenly she looked a lot stronger than her sister, a lot more determined. She had no trouble meeting my eyes now. Hers were red and hard, and I realized, once again, that people aren't born weary and beaten, they get that way.

She said, "Let me tell *you,* Mr. Kenzie"—and pointed a stiff finger at me—"that's one hell of a funny word. 'Documents.'" Her head was down again and she was pacing in a tight circle with borders only she could see. "Documents," she said again. "Well, OK, call them what you will. Yes, sir. Call them what you will."

"What would you call them, Mrs. Angeline?"

"I ain't no missus."

"OK. What would you call them, Ms. Angeline?"

She looked at me, her whole body beginning to quiver with rage. The red of her eyes had darkened and her chin was pointed out straight and unyielding. She said, "All my life, nobody ever need me. Know what I mean?"

I shrugged.

"Need," she said. "Nobody ever need me. People *want* me, sure. For a few hours or so, a week maybe, they say, 'Jenna clean room one-oh-five,' or 'Jenna, run down the store for me,' or real sweet they say, 'Jenna, honey, come on over here and lie down a spell.' But then, when they done, I'm just a piece of furniture again. Don't care if I'm around; don't care if I ain't. People can always find someone to clean for 'em, or run to the store for 'em, or lie down with 'em."

She walked back to her chair and rummaged through her purse until she found a pack of cigarettes. "Hadn't smoked in ten years—until a few days ago." She lit one, blew the smoke out in a rush that clouded the small room. "Ain't no documents, Mr. Kenzie. You understand? Ain't no documents."

"Then what—"

"There are things. There *are* things." She nodded to herself, stabbed her cigarette downward into the air, kept pacing.

I leaned forward in my chair a bit, my head following her like I was at Wimbledon. I said, "What things, Ms. Angeline?"

"You know, Mr. Kenzie," she said, as if she hadn't heard me, "all of a sudden, everyone looking for me, hiring people like yourself, hiring worse people probably, trying to find Jenna, to talk to Jenna, to get what Jenna got. All of a sudden, everyone *need* Jenna." She crossed the floor quickly to me, her cigarette poised over me like a butcher knife, her jaw clenched. She said, "Nobody getting what I got, Mr. Kenzie. You hear me? No one. 'Cept who I decide to give it to. I make the decision. I get what I want. I do a little using myself. Send someone to the store for *me*, maybe. See people work for *me* for a change. See them fade into furniture when I don't have no use for them anymore." She stabbed the glowing cigarette in toward my eye. "*I decide*. Jenna Angeline." She leaned back a bit, took a drag on the cigarette. "And what I got ain't for sale."

"Then what's it for?"

"Justice," she said through a stream of smoke. "And lots of it. People going to be in pain, Mr. Kenzie."

I looked at her hand, shaking so badly the cigarette quivered up and down like a recently abandoned diving board. I heard the anguish in her voice—a torn, slightly hollow sound—and saw its ravages on her face. She was a wreck of a person, Jenna Angeline. A heart beating fast in a shell of a body. She was scared and tired and angry and howling at the world, but unlike most people in the same situation, she was dangerous because she had something that, at least as far as she was concerned, would give her something back in this world. But the world usually doesn't work that way, and people like Jenna are time bombs; they might take a few people down with them, but they'll go up in the inferno too.

I didn't want anything bad to happen to Jenna, but I was even more certain that I wasn't going to get hit with any shrapnel if she self-destructed. I said, "Jenna, here's my problem: we call this sort of case a 'find-and-a-phone-call' because that's pretty much all I'm paid to do—find you and call the client and then go on my merry way. Once I make the phone call, I'm out of it. The client usually brings in the law or deals with it personally or whatever. But I don't stick around to find out. I'm—"

"A dog," she said. "You run around with your nose on the ground, sniffing through bushes and piles of warm shit until you find the fox. Then you step back and let the hunters shoot it dead." She stabbed out her cigarette.

It wasn't the analogy I would have chosen, but it wasn't entirely false no matter what I wanted to think. Jenna sat back down and looked at me and I held her dark eyes. They had the odd mixture of terror and resilient bravery of a cat backed into a corner; the look of someone who isn't sure she's up to the task, but has decided there's no other way out but straight ahead. It's the look of the crumbling soul trying to pull it all together for one last worthwhile breath. It's not a look I've ever seen in the eyes of people like Sterling Mulkern or Jim Vurnan or Brian Paulson. I never saw it on the Hero's face or a president's or a captain of industry's. But I've seen it in the faces of most everyone else.

"Jenna, you tell me what you think I should do."

"Who hired you?"

I shook my head.

"Well, it was either Senator Mulkern or Socia, and Socia'd just have you shoot me where I sit, so it got to be Senator Mulkern."

Socia? "Is Socia any relation to Roland?" I asked.

I could have broadsided her with a wrecking ball and had less impact. She closed her eyes for a moment and rocked in place. "What you know about Roland?"

"I know he's bad news."

"You stay away from Roland," she said. "You hear? Away from him."

"That's what people keep telling me."

"Well," she said, "you listen."

"Who's Roland?" I asked.

She shook her head.

"OK. Who's Socia?"

Another head shake.

"I can't help you, Jenna, if—"

"Ain't asking for your help," she said.

"Fine," I said. I stood up and walked over to the phone. I reconnected it, began to dial.

She said, "What're you doing?"

I said, "Calling my client. You can talk to him. My job's done."

She said, "Wait."

I shook my head. "Sterling Mulkern, please."

An electronic voice was telling me the time when Jenna pulled the phone cord out of the wall again. I turned and looked at her.

She said, "You got to trust me."

"No, I don't. I can leave you here and walk down to the nearest phone booth and make my call there."

"But what if—?"

"What if what?" I said. "Lady, I got better things to do than fuck around with you. You got a card to play? Play it."

She said, "What sort of documents you supposed to be looking for?"

No point in lying. I said, "They pertain to an upcoming bill."

"Oh, they do?" she said. "Well, Mr. Kenzie, someone been lying to you. What I got don't have nothing to do with bills and politics or the State House."

Everything has to do with politics in this town, but I let it go. "What do they pertain—No, fuck it. What do you got, Ms. Angeline?"

"I got some things in a safety-deposit box in Boston. Now, you want to find out what those things are, you come with me tomorrow when the banks open, and we'll see what you're made of.''

"Why should I?" I said. "Why shouldn't I call my client right now?"

She said, "I think I know people pretty well, Mr. Kenzie. Ain't much of a talent for a poor black woman to have, but it's the only one I got. And you, well, maybe you don't mind being someone's dog every now and again, but you sure ain't nobody's bag boy.''

10

Angie said, "**Are** you out of your fucking mind?" It came out in a harsh whisper. We were sitting in the alcove, looking out at the street. Jenna and Simone were in the kitchen, probably having a similar conversation.

I said, "You don't like it?"

"No," she said, "I don't like it."

"Twelve hours more or less won't make much difference."

"Bullshit. Patrick, this is retarded. We were hired to find her and call Mulkern. OK. We found her. Now, we should be making the call and going home."

"I don't think so."

"*You* don't think so?" she hissed. "How nice. Except you're not the only component in this equation. This is a partnership."

"I know it's—"

"Do you? I have a license too. Remember? You may have started the agency, but I've put my time in now too. I get shot at and beat up and sit on forty-eight-hour stakeouts too. I'm the one who had to sweat out the DA's decision whether to indict on Bobby Royce. I have a say, here. Fifty percent of one."

"And you say?"

"I say this is bullshit. I say we do what we were hired to do and go home."

"And I say . . ." I checked myself. "And I *ask* that you trust me on this and give me till morning. Hell, Ange, we'd end up sitting on her till then anyway. Mulkern's not going to get out of bed and drive up to Wickham at this time of night anyway.''

She considered that. Her olive skin was darkened to the shade of coffee in the ill-lit alcove and her full lips were pursed tightly. She said, ''Maybe. Maybe.''

''Then what's the problem?'' I said and started to get up.

She grabbed my wrist. ''Not so fast, boy.''

''What?''

''Your logic is good, Skid; it's your motives I have a problem with.''

''What motives?''

''You tell me.''

I sat back down, sighed. I looked at her, gave it my best ''Who me?'' look. ''I don't see that it hurts to learn everything we can while we have the chance. That's my only motive.''

She shook her head slowly, watching me steadily and with some sadness. She ran a hand through her hair, let the loose bangs fall back down on her forehead. ''She's not a cat somebody left out in the rain, Patrick. She's a grown woman who committed a crime.''

''I'm not so sure,'' I said.

''Either way it's irrelevant. We're not social workers.''

''What's your point, Ange?'' I said, suddenly tired.

''You're not being honest with yourself. Or me.'' She stood up. ''We'll play it your way if you want. I can't say it'll make all that much difference. But, remember something.''

''What?''

''When Jim Vurnan asked us if we'd take the job, I was willing to refuse it. You're the one who said working for Mulkern and his kind wouldn't be a problem.''

I held out my hands. ''And my position hasn't changed.''

''I hope it hasn't, Patrick, because we're not so goddamn successful that we can afford to botch a job like this.''

She walked out of the alcove, into the kitchen.

I looked at my reflection in the glass. It didn't seem too pleased with me either.

I pulled my car in front of the house where I could keep an eye on it from the alcove. Nothing was stolen or broken or keyed and I thanked the great auto god in the sky.

Angie came back out of the kitchen and called Phil to tell him she'd be staying overnight and it turned into an ordeal, his voice plainly audible through the receiver as he ranted on about *his* fucking needs, damnit. Angie got a blank, faraway look on her face, and she held the receiver in her lap and closed her eyes for a moment. She turned her head and opened her eyes. "You need me?"

I shook my head. "I'll see you at the office tomorrow around ten or so."

She spoke back into the phone in a voice so soft and placating that it made me nauseous, and shortly after she hung up, she was gone.

I'd checked to see that it was the only phone and bolted the back door so no one could open it without making noise. I sat in the window seat and listened to the house. Through the bedroom wall, I could hear Jenna still trying to explain our deal to Simone.

Earlier, Simone had made some squawking noises about kidnapping and federal offenses, quoting me a whole shitload of legal references that she learned from *L.A. Law.* She was on something of a tear, babbling at the top of her voice about "enforced incarceration" or some such nonsense, when I assured her that the alternative to my handling of the situation would be a swift legal execution of her sister's affairs by Sterling Mulkern and company. She shut up.

The voices in the bedroom died out and a few minutes later I heard the door open and Jenna's reflection rose up over my shoulder in the window. She was wearing an over-size T-shirt over a pair of old, gray sweatpants, and her face was scrubbed clean of makeup. She held two cans of beer in her hand and when I turned, she put one in my hand. She said, "My sister made me promise to replace these."

"I'll bet."

She smiled and sat on the window seat across from mine. "She told me to tell you to stay out of her fridge. She don't want you touching her food."

"Understandable," I said and cracked the beer. "Maybe I'll go in after you guys fall asleep, move things around just to piss her off."

She took a sip of the beer. "She's a good girl, Simone. Just really angry."

"At?"

"Who you got? The world in general, I s'pose. The white man in particular."

"I don't suppose I'm doing much to change her impression."

"No, you're not."

She seemed almost serene, sitting there in the window, head resting against the pane, beer in her lap. Without any makeup, she looked younger somehow, less exhausted. Once, she might have even been pretty, someone men commented on as she walked down the street. I tried to picture her that way—a young Jenna Angeline with a glow of confidence flushing her face because she was young and under the illusion that her youth and her beauty gave her options—but I couldn't. Time had laid too heavy a hand on her.

She said, "Your partner, she didn't seem all that pleased, either."

"She wasn't. It was all up to her, we'd have made the phone call and gone home by now."

She nodded and took another sip of the beer. She shook her head slightly. "Simone," she said, "sometimes I don't understand that girl."

"What's to understand?" I said.

"All that hate," she said. "You know?"

"There's a lot to hate out there," I said.

"I know," she said. "Believe me, I know. Seems there's so much, you got to kind of pick and choose. Earn what you hate, I guess. Simone, now, she just hate everything. And sometimes . . ."

"What?"

"Sometimes, I think she hate cause she don't know what else to do with herself. I mean, me, I got good reason to hate what I hate, believe me. But her, I'm not so sure she's . . ."

"Earned it?"

She nodded. "Exactly."

I thought about that. I couldn't see much to argue with. I've learned more about the capacity to hate than anything else since I started doing this work.

She drank some more beer. "Seems to me, the world going to give you plenty to be angry about, either way. Getting a chip on your shoulder before you've even seen how bad it can be, what the world can do to you when it really sets its mind to it . . . seems to me, that's just foolish thinking."

"Damn straight," I said and held up my can. She smiled, a small one, and glanced her can off mine, and I realized what part of me had known since I'd first seen her photograph: I liked her.

She finished her beer a minute or so later and went to bed with a small wave behind her as she entered the bedroom.

The night passed slowly and I shifted in my seat a lot, paced a bit back and forth, stared at my car. Angie was home now, taking another few steps in that grotesque dance of pain she called a marriage. A harsh word, a slap or two, a few screamed accusations, and on to bed until the next day. Love. I wondered again why she was with him, what possessed a person of her quality and judgment to put up with such shit, but before I slipped completely into the realms of the self-righteous, my palm rested on my abdomen, on the patch of scar tissue, which always reminded me of the price of love in its least idealized form.

Thank you, father.

Sitting in the quiet of the dark living room, I also remembered my own marriage, which had lasted about a minute and a half. Angie and Phil at least had a sense of dedication to the love between them, however twisted that love might be, which Renee and I never had. The only thing our marriage had taught me about love was that it ends. And looking out at the empty street from Simone Angeline's window seat, it occurred to me that one of the reasons I'm successful at the work I do is that come three o'clock in the morning, when most of the world is asleep, I'm still up doing my job because I don't have any place better to be.

I played some solitaire and told my stomach it wasn't hungry. I considered raiding Simone's fridge but figured she might have booby-trapped it; I'd grab the mustard and trip a wire, take an arrow in the head.

Dawn came in a faded line of pale gold that pushed up the black cover of night, then an alarm clock went off in the next room, and soon I heard the shower running. I stretched until I heard the satisfactory crack of bones and muscles, then did my morning regimen of fifty sit-ups and fifty push-ups. By the time I'd finished, the second turn in the shower had been taken, and the two sisters were standing by the door, ready to go.

Simone said, "You take anything from my fridge?"

"No," I said, "but I think I may have mistaken it for the toilet last night. I was really tired. Do you keep vegetables in the toilet?"

She brushed past me into the kitchen. Jenna looked at me and shook her head. She said, "Bet you were real popular in the second grade."

"Good humor has no age limit," I said, and she rolled her eyes.

Simone had a job, and I'd debated all night whether I should let her go to it. In the end I figured Simone hadn't shown any homicidal tendencies toward her sister that I'd noticed, so I was pretty sure she'd keep her mouth shut.

As we stood on the porch watching her drive off, I said, "Does this Socia guy know about Simone?"

Jenna was working her way into a light cardigan even though the temperature was already on a steady cruise toward the seventies at eight in the morning. She said, "He met her. Long time ago. In Alabama."

"How long since she moved up north?"

She shrugged. "Two months."

"And Socia definitely doesn't know she's here?"

She looked at me like I was drugged. "We both be dead now, Socia knew that."

We walked to my car and Jenna looked at it as I opened the door. "Never grew up totally, did you, Kenzie?"

And I'd once thought the car would impress people.

The drive back was as boring as the one up. I had Pearl Jam's *Ten* playing, and if Jenna minded, she didn't say anything. She didn't talk much, period, just stared out at the road and kneaded the bottom of her cardigan with her thin fingers when they weren't occupied with a cigarette.

As we neared the city, the Hancock and Prudential buildings rising up in pale blue to greet us, she said, "Kenzie."

"Yeah."

"You ever feel needed?"

I thought about it. "Sometimes," I said.

"Who by?"

"My partner. Angie."

"You need her?"

I nodded. "Sometimes, yeah. Hell, yeah."

She looked out the window. "You best hold on to her then."

*   *   *

Rush hour was in full swing by the time we got off 93 near Haymarket, and it took us close to half an hour to move the mile up onto Tremont Street.

Jenna's safety-deposit box was in the Bank of Boston on Tremont, across from the Boston Common at the Park Street corner. The Common runs back in a mall of cement here, past two squat buildings that serve as the Park Street T-station entrances, past a gaggle of vendors and street musicians and newspaper hawkers and winos. Crowds of businessmen and women and politicians walk briskly up the walkways where the Common turns green again and rises in a slope to the steep steps that climb to Beacon Street, the State House towering overhead, its gold dome looking down on the minions.

It's impossible to park on Tremont or even idle there for more than thirty seconds. A platoon of meter maids, imported from the female Hitler Youth shortly after the fall of Berlin, roam the street, at least two to a block, pit bull faces on top of fire hydrant bodies, just waiting for someone stupid enough to stall traffic on their street. Say, "Have a nice day," to one of them and she'll have your car towed for being a smart-ass. I turned onto Hamilton Place, behind the Orpheum Theater, and parked in a loading zone. We walked the two blocks to the bank. I started to walk in with her, but she stopped me. "An old black lady going into a bank with a big young white boy. What they going to think?"

"I'm your gigolo?"

She shook her head. "They going to think you're the law, escorting the nigger who got caught doing something. Again."

I nodded. "All right."

She said, "I didn't go through all this just so I could run on you now, Kenzie. I could have climbed out a window last night, that was the case. So, whyn't you wait across the street?"

Sometimes you got to trust people.

She went in alone, and I crossed Tremont and stood near Park Street Station, in the middle of the mall, the shadow of Park Street Church's white spire falling on my face.

She wasn't in there long.

She came out, saw me, and waved. She waited for a break in the traffic then came across the street. Her stride was full, her purse held tightly in her hand as she came across the mall. Her eyes had brightened, brown marble with flames glowing in the center, and she looked much younger than the picture I'd been given.

She came up close to me and said, "What I got here is a little part of it."

I said, "Jenna—"

"No, no," she said. "It's something, believe me. You'll see." She glanced up at the State House, then looked back at me. "You prove you're ready to help me on this, show what side you're on, and I give you the rest. I give you . . ." Her eyes lost their fire and filled; her voice stuck like a worn clutch. "I give you . . . the rest," she managed. I hadn't known her for more than twelve hours, but I had the feeling that whatever "the rest" was, it was bad. Tearing her apart from the inside out.

She smiled then, a nice soft one, and touched her hand to my face. She said, "I think we're going to turn out all right, Kenzie. Maybe the two of us get some justice while we're at it." The word "justice" came off her tongue as if she were trying to taste it.

I said, "We'll see, Jenna."

She reached into her purse and handed me a manila envelope. I opened it and extracted an eight-by-eleven black-and-white photograph. It was slightly grainy, as if it had been transferred from another type of film, but it was clear. There were two men in the photograph, standing by a cheap chest and mirror, drinks in their hands. One of them was black, the other, white. The black guy I didn't know. The white guy was wearing a pair of boxer shorts and black socks. His hair was brown, the gray that would consume it in a tin sheath, still a few years off. He was smiling tiredly, and the picture seemed old enough that possibly he'd only been Congressman Paulson at that point.

I said, "Who's the black guy?"

She looked at me and I could tell she was sizing me up. The wet ass hour, as it were, deciding if she could trust me. I felt like we were in a pocket—the crowds of people hurrying past us, not really there but existing on a matte screen behind us, like in an old movie.

Jenna said, "What're you in this for?"

I was considering my answer when something familiar moved out of the screen to our right, heading for our pocket, and I recognized it as if I was underwater—a blue baseball cap with yellow stitching.

I said, "Get down," and had my hand on Jenna's shoulder when Blue Cap set himself into his stance and a hammering metallic chatter drilled the morning air. The first burst of bullets slammed through the front of Jenna's chest as if it wasn't there, and I ducked as they blew past my head, still trying to pull her down as her chest jerked forward at all sorts of angles. Blue Cap had his finger pulled back on the trigger and the gun at full auto, the metal stitching slicing from Jenna's body to the cement, coming around in an arc for me. The crowd in the mall had turned into a stampede, and as I cleared my gun from its holster, someone trampled my ankle. Jenna's body crashed down on top of mine, and cement chips shot off the ground into my face. He was firing more methodically now, trying to get around Jenna's body to hit mine. In a moment, he'd just begin firing into her body again, and the bullets would pass through it as if it were paper and punch their way into mine.

Through the blood in my eyes, I could see him raising the Uzi up over his head, then bending it in at an angle, the muzzle a white flame. The line of bullets jackhammered toward my forehead and stopped suddenly in a white cloud of cement dust. The slim clip dropped from the gun toward the pavement and he had another one slammed home before it hit the ground. He pulled back on the bolt and I leaned out from under Jenna's body and fired.

The magnum went off with a harsh *whoomp* and he flipped into the air sideways as if he'd been broadsided by a truck. He came back down onto the pavement and bounced, the gun skittering out of his hand. I rolled Jenna off me, wiped her blood from my eyes, and watched him try to crawl to his Uzi. It was eight feet away and he was having a hard time covering the distance because his left ankle was almost completely obliterated.

I walked over and kicked him in the face. Hard. He groaned and I kicked him again, and he went out.

I crossed back to Jenna and sat on the cement in a growing puddle of her blood. I lifted her off the pavement and held her in my arms. Her chest was gone and so was she. No last words, just death, splayed out like a broken doll at the edge of the Boston Common at the beginning of a new day. Her legs were askew, and the curious vultures were coming back for a second look now that the shooting was over.

I pulled her legs together and tucked them under her. I looked at her face. It told me nothing. Another death. The more I see, the less I know.

No one needed Jenna Angeline anymore.

11

Like the Hero, I made the front page of both newspapers. Some rookie photographer was in the crowd when the shooting started, and once he'd cleaned the mess out of his underpants, he came back.

I'd walked back to Blue Cap by this time and picked up his Uzi by the sling. I slid it over my shoulder and squatted down beside him, my head down, magnum in my hand. That's when the photographer took his shots. I never noticed him. One shot showed me squatting by Blue Cap, a strip of green and the State House beyond us. In the extreme right foreground, almost out of focus, was Jenna's corpse. You could barely notice her.

The *Trib* carried it in the bottom left corner of page one, but the *News* plastered it completely over the front page with a hysterical black headline across the Statehouse— HERO P.I. IN MORNING GUNFIGHT!!! How they could print "hero" with Jenna's corpse lying in plain view was just beyond me. I guess LOSER P.I. IN MORNING GUN- FIGHT didn't have the same ring.

The police showed up around that time and hustled the photographer behind a hastily set up sawhorse. They took my gun and the Uzi and gave me a cup of coffee and we went over it. And over it.

An hour later I was at headquarters on Berkeley Street and they were deciding whether to book me or not. They read me my rights in English and Spanish while they figured out what to do.

I know quite a few cops, but none I recognized seemed to be taking part in this investigation. The two guys who had been assigned to me looked like Simon and Garfunkel on a bad day. Simon's name was Detective Geilston, and he was short, neatly dressed in dark burgundy pleated trousers, a light blue oxford with a roll in the collar and cream crisscross stripes. He wore a burgundy tie with a subtle blue diamond pattern. He looked like he had a wife and kids and CD accounts. He was Good Cop.

Bad Cop was Garfunkel, or Detective Ferry as they called him around the station. He was tall and lanky and wore a drab brown two-piece suit that was too short in the arms and legs. Underneath he wore a wrinkled white shirt and a dark brown knit tie. Mr. Fashion. His hair was strawberry blond, but a wide bare patch ran up the middle now and the bushy remains shot out from the sides of his head like a cleaved afro.

They'd both been friendly enough at the crime scene—giving me cups of coffee and telling me to take my time, take it slow, relax—but Ferry started getting more and more pissed off the more I kept answering his questions with, "I don't know." He got downright nasty when I refused to tell him who had hired me or exactly what I was doing with the deceased. Since I hadn't been booked yet, the photograph was folded and tucked into the ankle of one of my high-tops. I had a feeling what would happen if I gave it up—a formal inquiry, maybe a few nasty details about Senator Paulson's lifestyle, maybe nothing at all. But definitely no arrests, no justice, no public acknowledgment of a dead cleaning lady who'd only wanted to be needed.

If you're a private detective, it helps to be nice to cops. They help you out from time to time and vice versa and that's how you build contacts and keep business thriving. But I don't tolerate animosity very well, especially when my clothes are saturated with someone else's blood and I haven't eaten or slept in twenty-four hours. Ferry was standing with one foot on the chair beside me in the interrogation room, telling me what was going to happen to my license if I didn't start "playing ball."

I said, " 'Playing ball'? What, do you guys have a police cliché manual or something? Which one of you says, 'Book him, Danno'?"

For the thirtieth time that morning Ferry sighed deeply through his nostrils and said, "What were you doing with Jenna Angeline?"

For the fiftieth time that morning, I said, "No comment," and turned my head as Cheswick Hartman walked through the door.

Cheswick is everything you could want in an attorney. He's staggeringly handsome, with rich chestnut hair combed straight back off his forehead. He wears eighteen-hundred-dollar custom-made suits from Louis and he rarely wears the same one twice. His voice is deep and smooth like twelve-year-old malt and he has this annoyed look that he gets just before he buries an opponent with a barrage of Latin phrases and flawless elocution. Plus, he has a really nifty name.

Under normal circumstances, I'd have to have won the lottery to afford Cheswick's retainer, but a few years ago, just when he was being considered for partnership in his firm, his sister, Elise—a sophomore at Yale—developed a cocaine problem. Cheswick controlled her trust fund, and by the time Elise's addiction had blossomed into an eight-ball-a-day habit, she'd depleted her yearly allowance and still owed several thousand more to some men in Connecticut. Rather than tell Cheswick and risk his disappointment, she made an arrangement with the men in Connecticut, and some pictures were taken.

One day Cheswick got a phone call. The caller described the photos and promised they'd be on the desk of the firm's senior partner by the following Monday if Cheswick didn't come up with a high five-figure sum by the end of the week. Cheswick was livid. It wasn't the money that bothered him—his family fortune was huge—it was the advantage they'd taken of both his sister's problem and his love for her. So concerned was he for his sister that not once during our first meeting did I get the feeling it was the jeopardy to his job that angered him, and I admired that.

Cheswick got my name from a guy he knew in legal aid, and gave me the money to deliver with the express demand that I bring back all photos and negatives, and an absolute assurance that this would stop here and now. Elise's debt, I was to tell these men, was paid in full.

For reasons I can't even remember anymore, I brought Bubba along for the ride when I went down to Connecticut. After finding out that the blackmailers were a rogue group with no connections, no real muscle, and absolutely no juice with any politicians, we met two of them in a Hartford high-rise. Bubba held one guy by his ankles out a twelfth floor window while I negotiated with the guy's partner. By the time Bubba's victim had voided himself, his partner had decided that yes, one dollar was a very fair settlement price. I paid him in pennies.

Cheswick has been returning the favor to me by representing me gratis ever since.

He raised his eyebrows at the blood on my clothes. Very quietly he said, "I'd like a moment alone with my client, please."

Ferry crossed his arms and leaned in toward me. "So fucking what," he said.

Cheswick yanked the seat out from under Ferry's foot. "So fucking get out of the room now, *Detective,* or I'll slap this department with enough false arrest, harassment, and unlawful detainment citations to keep you in court until long after you've reached your twenty." He looked at me. "Have you been Mirandized?"

"Yes."

"Of course he's been fucking Mirandized," Ferry said.

"You're still here?" Cheswick said, reaching into his briefcase.

Geilston said, "Come on, partner."

Ferry said, "Hell no. Just because—"

Cheswick was looking at the both of them flatly, and Geilston had his hand on Ferry's arm. He said, "We don't mess with this, Ferry."

Cheswick said, "Listen to your partner, Detective."

Ferry said, "We'll meet again." Professor Moriarty to Sherlock Holmes.

Cheswick said, "At your inquest, no doubt. Start saving now, Detective. I'm expensive."

Geilston gave one last tug on Ferry's arm and they left the room.

I said, "What's up?" expecting he had something private to tell me.

"Oh, nothing," he said. "I just do that to show them who's boss. It gives me a woody."

"Swell."

He looked at my face, at the blood. "You're not having a good day, are you?"

I shook my head slowly.

His voice lost its levity. "Are you all right? Really? I've heard snippets of what happened, but not much."

"I just want to go home, Cheswick. I'm tired and I got blood all over me, and I'm hungry, and I'm not in the best of moods."

He patted my arm. "Well, I have good news from the DA then. From everything he's heard, they have nothing to charge you with. You are to consider yourself released pending further investigation, don't take any sudden trips, blah, blah, blah."

"My gun?"

"They keep that, I'm afraid. Ballistic tests, etcetera."

I nodded. "Figures. Can we leave now?"

"We're gone," he said.

He took me out the back entrance to avoid the press, and that's when he told me about the photographer. "I confirmed it with the captain. The man definitely took pictures of you. He strings for both papers in town."

I said, "I saw them hustling him out of there, but it didn't register."

We walked through the parking lot toward his car. His hand was on my back, as if he were ready to run interference for me or simply to hold me up. I wasn't sure which. He said, "Are you OK, Patrick? You may want to stop at Mass. General, have yourself checked out."

"I'm fine. What about the photographer?"

"You'll be on the front page of the *News* late edition, which should be coming out any minute now. I hear the *Trib* picked it up too. The papers love this sort of thing. Hero detective, a morning—"

"I'm no hero," I said. "That's my father."

We drove through the city in Cheswick's Lexus. It seemed strange, everyone going about their business. I'd half expected time to have stopped, everyone frozen in place, holding their breath, awaiting further news. But people ate lunch, made phone calls, canceled dentist appointments, got their hair cut, made dinner plans, worked their jobs.

Cheswick and I argued about my ability to drive in my present state, but in the end he dropped me back at Hamilton Place and told me to call him day or night on his private line if I required his services. He drove up Tremont, and I stood outside my car, ignored the ticket on the windshield, and looked at the Common.

In the four hours since it had happened, everything had gone back to normal. The barricades had been taken away, all the questions asked, all the witnesses' names written down. Blue Cap had been lifted into an ambulance and driven off. They'd rolled Jenna into a body bag and zipped it up, carted her off to the morgue.

Then someone had come along and hosed the blood off the cement until everything was clean again.

I took one last look and drove home.

12

When I got home, I called Angie across the street. "You heard?"

"Yes." Her voice was small and quiet. "I called Cheswick Hartman. Did he—?"

"Yeah. Thanks. Look, I'm going to take a shower, get into some clean clothes, eat a sandwich. Then I'll be over. Any calls?"

"A ton," she said. "But they'll keep. Patrick, are you OK?"

"No," I said, "but I'm working on it. I'll see you in an hour."

The shower was hot and I kept turning it hotter, the jet blast pounding into the top of my head, water pellets drumming against my skull. No matter how lapsed, I'm still sort of Catholic, and my reactions to pain and guilt are all tied up with words like "scalding" and "purge" and "white-hot." In some theological equation of my own making, heat=salvation.

I stepped out after twenty minutes or so and dried slowly, my nostrils still thick with the clogging scent of blood and the bitter aroma of cordite. Somewhere in all the shower steam, I told myself, was the answer, the relief, the purchase necessary to turn the next corner and get past all this. But the steam cleared, and nothing remained but me and my bathroom and the smell of something burning.

I wrapped the towel around my waist and entered the kitchen and saw Angie blackening a steak on my stove.

Angie cooks about once every leap year and never with any
success. If it was up to her, she'd trade in her kitchen for
a take-out counter.

I instinctively hitched the towel up over my scar and
came up behind her and reached around her waist to shut
off the burner. She turned in my arms, her chest against
mine, and I guess it's the consummate declaration of my
state of mind that I stepped around her and checked the
rest of the oven for damage.

She said, "What'd I do wrong?"

"I think your first mistake was turning on the stove."

She slapped the back of my head. "See the next time I
cook for *you.*"

"And they say Christmas comes only once a year." I
turned from the stove and saw her watching me the way
you watch a baby walking on the edge of a swimming pool.
I said, "Thank you for the gesture. Really."

She shrugged, continued staring at me, those caramel
eyes warm and slightly damp. "You need a hug, Patrick?"

I said, "God, yes."

She felt like everything good. She felt like the first warm
gust of spring and Saturday afternoons when you're ten
years old and early summer evenings on the beach when
the sand is cool and the waves are colored scotch. Her grip
was fierce, her body full and soft, and her heart beat rapidly
against my bare chest. I could smell her shampoo and feel
the downy nape of her neck against my chin.

I stepped back first. I said, "Well . . ."

She laughed. "Well . . ." She said, "You're all wet,
Skid. My shirt's soaked now." She took a step back.

"Happens sometimes when you take a shower."

She took another step back, looked down at the floor.
"Yeah, well . . . ," she said again, "you have a pile of
messages over there. And . . ." She stepped past me, picked
up the steak, and carried it toward the garbage. "And . . .
and I still can't cook, obviously."

I said, "Angie."

She kept her back to me. "You almost died this morning."

"Ange—"

"And I'm very sorry about Jenna, but you almost died."

"Yes."

"I wouldn't have . . ." Her voice cracked and I could hear her inhale until she got it under control. "And I wouldn't have handled it very fucking well, Patrick. I don't like thinking about it, and it's got me a little . . . off, right now."

I heard Jenna's voice in my head when I told her Angie needed me. "You best hold on to her then." I took a few steps across the floor and put my hands on her arms.

She tilted her head back so that it nestled under my chin.

The air seemed impossibly still in the kitchen and I don't think either of us took a breath. We stood there, our eyes closed, waiting for the fear to go away.

It didn't.

Angie's head left my chin and she said, "Let's get past this. Do some work. We're still employed, right?"

I let go of her arms and said, "Yeah, we're still employed. Let me change and we'll get to work."

I came back out a few minutes later in an oversize red sweatshirt and a pair of jeans.

Angie turned from the kitchen counter, a plate in her hand, a sandwich on it. "I think I'm safe around deli meat."

"Didn't try to cook it or anything, did you?"

She gave me that look.

I got the point and took the sandwich. She sat across the table from me as I ate. Ham and cheese. A little heavy on the mustard, but otherwise fine. I said, "Who called?"

"Sterling Mulkern's office. Three times. Jim Vurnan's office. Richie Colgan. Twice. Twelve or thirteen reporters. Also, Bubba called."

"What'd he have to say?"

"You really want to know?"

Usually one doesn't with Bubba, but I was feeling loose. I nodded.

"He said to call him next time you go 'a coon hunting.' "

That Bubba. Hitler might have won the war with Bubba at his side. I said, "Anyone else?"

"No. But Mulkern's office sounded pretty pissed off by the third call."

I nodded and chewed.

Angie said, "You going to tell me what we're into here, or you just going to sit there and do your village idiot impersonation?"

I shrugged, chewed some more, and she took the sandwich away from me. "I believe I've been chastised," I said.

"You'll be a lot worse than that, you don't start talking."

"Ooooh. Tough girl. Scold me some more," I panted.

She looked at me.

"All right," I said. "But we're going to need liquor for this."

I made us two scotches neat. Angie took one sip of hers and poured it down the sink without a word. She grabbed a beer from the fridge, sat back down, and raised an eyebrow.

I said, "We may be in over our heads on this one. Way over our heads."

"So I gathered. Why?"

"Jenna didn't have any documents that I saw. That was bullshit."

"Which you half-figured."

"True," I said, "but I didn't think it would be too far off the mark. I don't know what I thought she had, but I didn't think it was this." I handed her the photo of Paulson in his skivvies.

She raised her eyebrows. "OK," she said slowly, "but still, so what? This picture's, like, six or eight years old, and all it shows is Paulson, half-dressed. However unappetizing, it's not news. Not worth killing over."

"Maybe," I said. "Look at the guy with Paulson, though. He doesn't look like he runs in the same circles exactly."

She looked at the guy. He was slim, wearing a blue crewneck shirt over a pair of white trousers. He wore a lot of gold—on his wrists, his neck—and his hair looked simultaneously matted and flyaway. His eyes were all sullen reproach, those of the terminally angry. He looked to be about thirty-five.

"No, he doesn't," she said. "We know him?"

I shook my head. "He could be Socia. He could be Roland. He could be neither. But he definitely doesn't look like a state rep."

"He looks like a pimp."

"That too." I pointed to the cheap chest and mirror in the photo. Reflected in the mirror was a bed, unmade. Beyond that, the corner of a door. On the door were two square pieces of paper. I couldn't make out what they said, but one looked like the rules and regulations of a motel, and the smaller one below it looked like a check-in, check-out time reminder. A Do-Not-Disturb sign hung from the doorknob. "And this looks like . . ."

"A motel," she said.

"Ver-ry good," I said. "You should be a detective."

"You should stop impersonating one," she said and flipped the photo back on the table. "So, what's all this mean, Sherlock?"

"You tell me, Spanky."

She lit a cigarette and sipped her beer and thought about it. "These photos might be the tip of the iceberg. Maybe there're more of them, and they're a lot worse. Someone, either Socia or Roland or—dare I say it?—someone in the political machine had Jenna eliminated because they knew she'd blow the whistle on whatever it is. That what you're thinking?"

"That's what I'm thinking."

"Well," she said, "either they're really dumb, or you are."

"Why's that?"

"Jenna had the pictures in her safety-deposit box, correct?"

I nodded.

"And when someone is murdered, standard police procedure is to get a court warrant and open every can of worms the victim had in her pantry. Of which, the safety-deposit box is definitely one. I assume they've already figured the bank was the last place before she . . ."

"Died," I said.

"Yes. So, they're probably on their way down to open it as we speak. And anyone with half a brain could have foreseen that."

"Maybe they figured she'd taken everything out of there and given it to me."

"Maybe," she said. "But that's leaving an awful lot to chance. Don't you think? Unless, somehow, they were positive that she wasn't going to leave anything behind in there."

"How would they know?"

She shrugged. "You're a detective. Detect."

"I'm trying."

"Something else," she said, putting her beer down, sitting up.

"Pray tell."

"How'd they know you were going to be there this morning?"

I hadn't given it much thought. "Blue Cap," I said.

She shook her head. "We lost Blue Cap yesterday. I mean, I don't know about you, but I don't think he was hanging around on the interstate this morning, waiting to spot you driving by in a car he doesn't even know you own. *Then* he tailed you to the Common? Uh-uh. I don't buy it.''

''Only two people knew where Jenna and I were going this morning.''

''Damn right,'' she said. ''And I'm one of them.''

13

Simone Angeline's eyes were ringed with red on the other side of the chain, and fresh tears welled in her sockets. Her hair was matted to one side of her face and she looked like she'd skipped a few decades and turned seventy when no one was looking. Her teeth gritted when she saw us. "You get the fuck off my porch."

I said, "OK," and kicked the door in.

Angie came in behind me as Simone made a scramble for the small telephone desk in the alcove. She wasn't going for the phone. She was going for the drawer underneath, and as she opened it, I put my hand behind the desk and brought the whole thing toppling down on top of her. The contents of the drawer—a small red phone book, some pens, and a .22 target pistol—bounced off her head on their way to the floor. I kicked the gun under the bookcase and grabbed Simone by the front of her shirt and dragged her over to the couch.

Angie closed the door behind her.

Simone spat in my face. "You killed my sister."

I slammed her back against the couch and wiped the spittle off my chin. Very slowly I said, "I failed to protect your sister. There's a difference. Someone else pulled the trigger, and you put the gun in his hand. Didn't you?"

She bucked against my hand and clawed at my face. "No! You killed her."

I pushed her back again and knelt on her hands. I whispered in her ear, "The bullets came through Jenna's chest like it wasn't there, Simone. Like it wasn't fucking there. She had so much blood coming out of her body that just the small percentage that got on me was enough to make the cops think I'd been shot. She died screaming in the middle of the morning with her legs spread out in front of her while a crowd of people watched, and the motherfucker who pulled the trigger used a whole clip on her and didn't so much as blink.''

She was trying to head-butt me now, rocking forward on the couch as much as she could manage with my 180 pounds on top of her. "You goddamned bastard."

"That's right," I said, my mouth still a half inch from her ear. "That's right. I'm a bastard, Simone. I held your sister in my lap while she died and there wasn't a damn thing I could do about it, and I earned the right to be a bastard. But, you, you don't have any excuse. You picked her execution spot and stayed out here, sixty miles away, while she screamed her final breath. You told them where she was going and you let them kill her. Didn't you, Simone?"

She blinked.

I screamed, "Didn't you?"

Her eyes rolled back in her head for a moment and then her head dropped, the sobs tearing out of her as if someone was reaching in there and pulling them out. I stepped back because there was nothing left of her now. The sobs grew louder, gasping wracks from her heaving chest. She balled into a fetal position and banged her fists against the arm of the couch, and every time the sobs seemed to have subsided they picked up again, only louder, as if each breath pierced her like something heavy and sharp.

Angie touched my elbow, but I shrugged it off. Patrick Kenzie, great detective, able to terrorize a near-catatonic woman into hysterics. What a guy. For an encore, maybe I'd go back home and mug a nun.

Simone turned on her side, her eyes closed, speaking with half her mouth still buried in the couch. "You were working for *them*. I told Jenna she was a fool, trusting you and those fat white politicians. Ain't one of them ever gave a damn for a nigger, ain't one of them ever will. I figured as . . . as soon as you got what you wanted from her, you'd . . ."

"Kill her," I said.

Her head stretched out onto the arm and gagging sounds emanated from her throat. After a few minutes, she said, "I called him, because I figured no man could . . ."

"Who'd you call?" Angie said. "Socia? Was it Socia?"

She shook her head a few times, then nodded. "He . . . he said he'd take care of it, talk some sense into her fool head. That's all. I figured no man could do . . . that to his wife."

His wife?

She looked at me. "She never could have won. Not against all them. Not her. She . . . couldn't."

I sat on the floor beside the couch and held up the photograph. "Is this Socia?"

She looked at it long enough to nod, then buried her head back in the couch.

Angie said, "Simone, where's the rest of it? Is it in the safety-deposit box?"

Simone shook her head.

"Then where is it?" I said.

"She wouldn't tell me. She just said, 'In a safe place.' She said she put just the one picture in the safety-deposit box to throw them off the scent, case they ever follow her there."

I said, "What else is there, Simone? Do you know?"

She said, "Jenna said they were 'bad things.' That's all she'd say. She'd get all tight lipped and antsy if I asked her about it. Whatever it was, it shook her up every time she talked about it." She raised her head and looked past my shoulder as if someone stood behind me. She said, "Jenna?" and began sobbing again.

She was trembling violently and I didn't think she had

much left in her. I'd done my damage, and she'd do the rest to herself in the days and years ahead. So, I let my anger go, let it flush out of my heart and body until all I saw before me was a trembling heap of humanity on a sofa. I reached out and touched her shoulder.

She screamed. "Don't you fucking touch me!"

I pulled the hand back.

"Get the hell off my floor and the hell out of my house, white man, and take your whore with you."

Angie took a step toward her on the word "whore," then stopped and closed her eyes for a second, then opened them. She looked at me and nodded.

There wasn't anything else to say, so we left.

14

We were halfway back to Boston, avoiding any conversation about Simone Angeline or the scene in her apartment, when Angie sat up suddenly in her seat and said, "Aargghh," or a reasonable facsimile. She stabbed her index finger into the eject button of my cassette player hard enough to send *Exile on Main St.* past me like a missile. It bounced off the back of the seat and fell to the floor. Right in the middle of "Shine a Light," too. Sacrilege.

I said, "Pick it up."

She did and flipped it onto the seat beside my hip. She said, "Don't you have any New Music?" New Music, I guess, is all those bands Angie listens to. They have names like Depeche Mode and The Smiths and they all sound the same to me—like a bunch of skinny white British nerds on Thorazine. The Stones, when they started, were a bunch of skinny white British nerds too, but they never sounded like they were on Thorazine. Even if they were.

Angie was looking through my cassette case. I said, "Try the Lou Reed. More your style."

After putting in *New York,* listening for five minutes, she said, "This is all right. What, you buy it by mistake?"

Just outside the city limits, I pulled into a Store 24 and Angie went in for cigarettes. She came out with two late editions of the *News* and handed me a copy.

That's how I confirmed that I'd become the second generation of Kenzie to achieve a sort of immortality in newsprint. I'd always be there, frozen in time and black-and-white on June 30, for anyone who wished to access the file on a microfiche. And that moment, that most personal of moments—squatting by Blue Cap with Jenna's corpse behind me, my ears ringing and my brain trying to re-anchor in my skull—none of it was completely mine anymore. It had been spat out for the breakfast consumption of hundreds of thousands of people who didn't know me from Adam. Possibly the most intensely personal moment of my life and it would be rehashed and second-guessed by everyone from a barfly in Southie to two stockbrokers riding the elevator in some skyscraper downtown. The Global Village Principle at work, and I didn't like it one bit.

But I did finally learn Blue Cap's name. Curtis Moore. He was listed in critical condition at Boston City and doctors were said to be working frantically to save his foot. He was eighteen years old and a reputed member of the Raven Saints, a gang that ran out of the Raven Boulevard Projects in Roxbury and favored New Orleans Saints baseball caps and team memorabilia. His mother was pictured on page three, holding a framed photograph of him when he was ten years old. She was quoted as saying, "Curtis never ran with no gang. Never did nothing wrong." She demanded an investigation, said the whole thing was "racially motivated." She managed to compare it to the Charles Stuart case, of course, in which the DA and just about everyone else had believed Charles Stuart's story that a black guy had killed his wife. They'd arrested a black guy, and possibly would have sent him up if the insurance policy Stuart had taken out on his wife hadn't finally raised a few eyebrows. And when Chuck Stuart took a 9.5 swan dive off the Mystic River bridge, it pretty much confirmed what a lot of people had already thought was obvious in the first place. Shooting Curtis Moore had about as much in common with the Stuart case as Howard Beach has in common with Miami Beach, but there wasn't much I could do about it standing outside a Store 24.

Angie snorted loudly and I knew she was reading the

same article. I said, "Lemme guess—the 'racially motivated' line."

She nodded. "The nerve of you, shoving that Uzi into
that poor boy's hand and forcing him to pull the trigger."

"I don't know what comes over me sometimes."

"You should have tried to talk with him, Patrick. Told
him you understood the life of deprivation that put that gun
in his hand."

"I'm such a prick that way." I tossed the paper in the
backseat and got behind the wheel and headed into the city.
Angie kept looking at the paper in the dim light and
breathing heavily through her nostrils. Eventually, she
bunched it in her hand and threw it on the floor.

She said, "How can they look at themselves in the mirror?"

"Who?"

"People who say such . . . shit. 'Racially motivated.'
Please. 'Curtis never ran with no gang.' " She looked down
at the paper and spoke to the picture of Curtis's mother.
"Well he wasn't out till three A.M. every night with the
fucking Boy Scouts, lady."

I patted her shoulder. "Calm down."

"It's bullshit," she said.

"It's a mother," I said. "Say anything in the world to
protect her child. Can't blame her."

"Oh, no?" she said. "Then, why bring race into it if all
she wants to do is protect her child? What's next—Al
Sharpton going to come to town, hold a vigil for Curtis's
foot? Pin Jenna's death on the white man too?"

She was sounding off. Reactionary white rage. I hear
more of it lately. A lot more of it. I've said similar things
on occasion myself. You hear it most among the poor and
working class. You hear it when brain-dead sociologists
call incidents like the wilding attack in Central Park a result
of "uncontrollable" impulses, and defend the actions of a
group of animals with the argument that they were only
reacting to years of white oppression. And if you point out
that those nice, well-bred animals—who happen to be

black—probably would have controlled those actions just fine if they'd thought that female jogger was protected by an army of her own, you're labeled a racist. You hear it when the media makes a point out of race. You hear it when a bunch of possibly well-intentioned whites get together to sort it all out and end up saying, "I'm no racist *but*..." You hear it when judges who forcibly desegregate public schools with bussing put their own children in private schools, or when, recently, a circuit court judge said he'd never seen evidence to suggest that street gangs were any more dangerous than labor unions.

You hear it most when politicians who live in places like Hyannis Port and Beacon Hill and Wellesley make decisions that affect people who live in Dorchester and Roxbury and Jamaica Plain, and then step back and say there isn't a war going on.

There is a war going on. It's happening in playgrounds, not health clubs. It's fought on cement, not lawns. It's fought with pipes and bottles, and lately, automatic weapons. And as long as it doesn't push through the heavy oak doors where they fight with prep school educations and filibusters and two-martini lunches, it will never actually exist.

South Central L.A. could burn for a decade, and most people wouldn't smell the smoke unless the flames reached Rodeo Drive.

I wanted to sort this out. Now. To wade through it all, in the car with Angie, until our places in this war were clearly defined, until we knew exactly where we stood on every issue, until we could look into our hearts and be satisfied with what we saw there. But I feel this way a lot, and everything always ends up in circles, coming back to me with nothing solved.

I said, "What're you going to do, right?" and pulled to the curb in front of her house.

She looked at the front page of the paper, at Jenna's body. She said, "I can tell Phil we're working late."

"I'm fine," I said.

"No, you're not."

I half laughed. "No, I'm not. But you can't come into my dreams with me, protect me there. So, otherwise, I can handle it."

She was out of the car now, and she leaned back in and kissed my cheek. "Be well, Skid."

I watched her climb the stairs to her porch, fumble with her keys, then open the door. Before she got inside, a light went on in the living room and the curtain parted slightly. I waved at Phil, and the curtain fluttered closed again.

Angie entered her home and shut off the light in the hallway and I drove off.

The light was on in the belfry. I pulled to the curb in front of the church and walked around to the side door, acutely aware of the fact that my gun was sitting in the police-station evidence room. There was a note on the floor as I entered: "Don't shoot. Two black men in one day will give you a bad rep."

Richie.

He was sitting behind my desk when I entered. He had his feet up and a Peter Gabriel tape going on my boom box, a bottle of Glenlivet on the desk and a glass in his hand. I said, "Is that my bottle?"

He looked at it. "I believe so, son."

"Well, help yourself," I said.

"Thank you," he said and poured another shot into his glass. "You need ice."

I found a glass in my drawer, made a double. I held up the paper. "Seen it?"

"I don't read that rag," he said. Then, "Yeah, I saw it."

Richie is not one of those Hollywood blacks with skin like coffee regular and Billy Dee Williams eyes. He's black, black as an oil slick, and he's not what one would call handsome. He's overweight, always has a five o'clock shadow, and his wife buys his clothes. A lot of times, his ensemble looks like she's experimenting again. Tonight he was wearing beige cotton trousers, a light blue shirt, and a pastel tie that looked like a poppy field had exploded on it and someone had doused the flame with rum punch. I said, "Sherilynn went shopping again?"

He looked at the tie and sighed. "Sherilynn went shopping again."

I said. "Where? Miami?"

He lifted the tie for closer inspection. "You'd think so, wouldn't you?" He sipped his scotch. "Where's your partner?"

"With her husband."

He nodded, and simultaneously, we said, "The Asshole."

"When's she going to pump a round into that boy?" he asked.

"I've got my fingers crossed."

"Well, you call me when she does. I got a bottle of Moët sitting at home for the occasion."

"To that day." I held up my glass. He met it. "Cheers." I said, "Tell me about Curtis Moore."

"Gimpy?" he said. "That's what we're calling ol' Curtis these days. Brings a tear to your eye, doesn't it?" He stretched back in the chair.

"Tragic," I said.

"It's too bad," he said. "Don't take it too lightly, though. Curtis's friends might come looking for you and they are particularly heinous motherfuckers."

"How big are the Raven Saints?"

"Not big by L.A. standards," he said, "but this ain't L.A. I'd say they got seventy-five hardcore and another sixty or so peripheral."

"So what you're saying is I got a hundred thirty-five black guys to be wary of."

He put his glass down on the desk. "Don't turn this into a 'black thing,' Kenzie."

"My friends call me Patrick."

"I'm not your friend when I hear shit like that come out of your mouth."

I was angry and damned tired, and I wanted someone to blame. My emotions were running hard along open nerve endings that stopped just short of breaking my skin, and I was feeling stubborn. I said, "Tell me about a white gang that runs around with Uzis and I'll be afraid of white people too, Richie. But until then—"

Richie banged his fist down on the desk. "The fuck you call the Mafia? Huh?" He stood up and the veins in his neck were thick, poking out as hard as I figured mine were. "The Westies in New York," he said, "those nice boys, Irish like yourself, who specialized in murder and torture and cowboy bullshit. What color were they? You going to sit there and tell me the brothers invented murder too? You going to try and pass that shit off on me, Kenzie?"

Our voices were loud in the tiny room, hoarse, slipping under the cheap walls and reverberating. I tried to talk calmly, but my voice didn't come out that way; it sounded harsh and slightly alien. I said, "Richie, one kid gets hit by a car because a bunch of retard Hitler Youth chase him into the road in Howard Beach—"

"Don't you *even* bring up Howard Beach."

"—and it gets treated like a national tragedy. Which it is. But," I said, "a white kid in Fenway gets stabbed *eighteen* times by black kids, and no one says a goddamn thing. 'Racial' never comes into it. It's off the front page the next day, and it's filed as homicide. *No* racial incident. You tell me, Richie, what the fuck is that?"

He was staring at me, holding his hand a foot in front of him, then moving it to his head where it massaged his neck, then down onto the desk, where he looked at it, not sure what to do with it. He started to speak a couple of times. Stopped. Eventually, he said quietly, but almost in a hiss, "Those three black kids killed the white boy, you think they'll do hard time?"

He had me there.

"Huh?" he said. "Come on. Tell the truth."

I said, "Of course. Unless they get a good lawyer, get—"

"No. No lawyers. No technicality bullshit. If they go to trial and it reaches jury, will they be convicted? Will they end up doing twenty to life, maybe worse?"

"Yeah," I said. "Yeah, they will."

"And if some white guys killed a black guy and it wasn't, let's pretend, called a racial incident, if it wasn't considered a tragedy, what then?"

I nodded.

"What then?"

"There's a better chance they'd get off."

"Damn right," he said and dropped back into the chair.

"But, Richie," I said, "that sort of logic is beyond the average guy on the street, and you know it. Joe from Southie sees a black death turned into a racial incident, then sees an identical white death called a homicide, and he says, 'Hey that ain't right. That's hypocritical. That's a double standard.' He hears about Tawana Brawley, and loses his job to affirmative action, and he gets pissed off." I looked at him. "Can you blame him?"

He ran his hand through his hair and sighed. "Aww, shit, Patrick. I don't know." He sat up. "No, OK? I can't blame the guy. But what's the alternative?"

I poured myself another shot. "It ain't Louis Farrakhan."

"And it ain't David Duke," he shot back. "I mean, what—we're supposed to do away with affirmative action quotas, minority grants, racial incident cases?"

I pointed the bottle at him and he leaned forward with his glass. "No," I said, pouring his drink, "but . . ." I leaned back. "Damnit, I don't know."

He half smiled and leaned back in the chair again, looking out the window. The Peter Gabriel tape had ended and from the street came the sound of the occasional car scooping up air as it hummed past on the asphalt. The breeze coming through the screen had cooled and as it drifted into the room, I felt the weight of the atmosphere dissipating. Somewhat anyway.

"Know what the American way is?" Richie asked, still looking out the window, his elbow up, drink poised halfway to his mouth.

I could feel the anger in the room beginning to fuse with the slow rush of scotch in my blood, dissolving in the liquor's undertow. I said, "No, Rich. What's the American way?"

"Finding someone to blame," he said and took a drink. "It's true. You out working a construction job and you drop a hammer on your foot? Hell, sue the company. That's a ten-thousand-dollar foot. You're white and you can't get a job? Blame affirmative action. Can't get one and you're black? Blame the white man. Or the Koreans. Hell, blame the Japanese; everyone else does. Fucking whole country's filled with nasty, unhappy, confused, pissed-off people, and not one of them with the brain power to honestly *deal* with their situation. They talk about simpler times—before there was AIDS and crack and gangs and mass communications and satellites and airplanes and global warming—like it's something they could possibly get back to. And they can't figure out why they're so fucked up, so they find someone to blame. Niggers, Jews, whites, Chinks, Arabs, Russians, pro-choicers, pro-lifers—who do you got?"

I didn't say anything. Hard to argue with the truth.

He slammed his feet down on the floor and stood up, began pacing. His steps were a little uncertain, as if he expected resistance after each one. "White man blames people like me because they say quotas got me where I am. Half of 'em can't so much as read, but they think they deserve my job. Fucking pols sit in their leather chairs with their windows looking out on the Charles and make sure their stupid-fuck white constituents think the reason they're angry is because I'm stealing food from their children's mouths. Black men—brothers—they say I ain't black anymore because I live on an all-white street in a pretty much all-white neighborhood. Say I'm sneaking into the middle class. Sneaking. Like, because I'm black, I should go live in some shithole on Humboldt Avenue, with people who cash their welfare checks for crack money. Sneaking,'' he repeated. ''Shit. Heteros hate homos, now homos are ready to 'bash back,' whatever the fuck that means. Lesbians hate men, men hate women, blacks hate whites, whites hate blacks, and . . . everyone is looking for someone to blame. I mean, hell, why bother looking in the mirror at your own damn self when there's so many other people out there who you *know* you're better than.'' He looked at me. ''You know what I'm saying, or is it the booze talking?''

I shrugged. ''Everyone needs someone to hate for some reason.''

''Everyone's too damn stupid,'' he said.

I nodded. ''And too damn angry.''

He sat down again. ''Goddamn.''

I said, ''So where's that leave us, Rich?''

He held up his glass. ''Crying into our scotch at the end of another day.''

The room was still for a while. We each poured another drink in silence, sipped them a bit more slowly. After five minutes of this, Richie said, ''How do you feel about what happened today? Are you OK?''

Everyone kept asking me that. I said, ''I'm all right.''

''Yeah?''

''Yeah,'' I said. ''I think.'' I looked at him, and for some reason I wished he'd met her. I said, ''Jenna was decent. A good person. All she wanted was, once in her life, not to be pushed under the rug.''

He looked at me and leaned forward, his glass extended. ''You're going to make people pay for her, aren't you, Patrick?''

I leaned forward and met his glass with mine. I nodded. ''In spades,'' I said, then held up my hand. ''No offense.''

15

Richie left a little after midnight, and I carried the bottle across the street to my apartment. I ignored the blinking red light on my answering machine and flicked on the TV. I dropped into the leather La-Z-Boy, drank from the bottle, watched *Letterman,* and tried not to see Jenna's death dance every time my eyelids reached half-mast. I don't usually indulge in hard liquor to excess, but I was putting one hell of a dent in the Glenlivet. I wanted to pass out, no dreams.

Richie had said Socia sounded familiar, but he couldn't quite place him. I assessed what I knew. Curtis Moore was a member of the Raven Saints. He had killed Jenna, most likely at someone else's behest, that someone probably being Socia. Socia was Jenna's husband, or had been. Socia was friendly enough with Senator Brian Paulson to have had snapshots taken with him. Paulson had slapped the table in front of me at our first meeting. "This is no joke," he'd said. No joke. Jenna was dead. Well over a hundred · urban warriors who weren't afraid to die had a bone to pick with me. No joke. I was scheduled to meet Mulkern and crew for lunch tomorrow. I was drunk. Maybe it was me, but Letterman seemed to be getting stale. Jenna was dead. Curtis Moore was missing a foot. I was drunk. A ghost in a fireman's uniform was looming up in the shadows behind the TV. The TV was getting harder to focus on. Probably the vertical hold. The bottle was empty.

*   *   *

The Hero swung his fire ax into my head and I sat bolt upright in the chair. The TV screen was snowing. I trained a blurry eye on my watch: 4:15 A.M. Molten fire surged under my sternum. All the nerves in my skull were freshly exposed by the ax, and I stood up and just made the bathroom before I yakked up the Glenlivet. I flushed the toilet and lay on the cool tile, the room smelling of scotch and fear and death. This was the second time in three nights I'd thrown up. Maybe I was getting bulimia.

I made it to my feet again and brushed my teeth for half an hour or so. I stepped into the shower, turned it on. I stepped back out, removed my clothes, and got back in. By the time I finished, it was almost dawn. Three Tylenol, and I fell on top of my bed, hoping that whatever I had up-chucked contained all those things that made me afraid to sleep.

I dozed on and off for the next three hours, and, thankfully, no one came to visit. Not Jenna, not the Hero, not Curtis Moore's foot.

Sometimes, you get a break.

"I hate this," Angie said. "I . . . hate . . . it."

"You look like shit too," I offered.

She gave me that look and went back to fiddling violently with the hem of her skirt in the back of the taxi.

Angie wears skirts about as often as she cooks, but I'm never disappointed. And for all her bitching, I don't think it's as painful for her as she pretends. Too much thought had gone into what she was wearing for the result to be anything less than "Wow." She wore a dark cranberry silk-crepe wraparound blouse and a black suede skirt. Her long hair was brushed back off her forehead, pinned back over her left ear, but tumbling loosely along the right side of her face, cowling in slightly around her eye. When she raised her eyes from under her long lashes and looked at me, it hurt. The skirt was damn near painted on and she kept tugging at the hem to get comfortable, squirming in the backseat of the cab. The sight, all in all, wasn't hard to take.

I was wearing a gray herringbone double-breasted with a subtle black crisscross pattern. The jacket was tight where it hugged my hips for that cosmopolitan look, but fashion designers are usually kinder to men, and all I had to do was unbutton it.

I said, "You look fine."

"I know I look fine," she said, scowling. "I'd like to find whoever designed this skirt, because I *know* it was a man, and shove him into it. Turn his ass soprano real quick."

The cab dropped us on the corner, across from Trinity Church.

The doorman opened the door with a "Welcome to the Copley Plaza Hotel," and we went in. The Copley is somewhat similar to the Ritz: they were both standing long before I was born; they'll still be here long after I'm gone. And if the employees at the Copley don't seem as plucky as those at the Ritz, it's probably because they have less to be plucky about. The Copley's still trying to bounce back from its status as the city's most forgotten hotel. Its latest multimillion-dollar refurbishment will have to go a long way to erase its once dark corridors and staid-to-the-point-of-death atmosphere from people's minds. They started with the bar, though, and they've done a good job. Instead of George Reeves and Bogey, I always expect to see Burt Lancaster as J. J. Hunsecker holding court at a table, a preening Tony Curtis at his foot. I mentioned this to Angie as we entered.

She said, "Burt Lancaster as who?"

I said, *"Sweet Smell of Success."*

She said, "What?"

I said, "Heathen."

Jim Vurnan didn't rise to meet me this time. He and Sterling Mulkern sat together in oaken shadows, their view protected from the trivialities of the outside world by dark brown slats. Pieces of the Westin Hotel peeked in through the window slats, but unless you were looking for it, you wouldn't notice. Which is just as well I suppose—the only hotel uglier than the Westin in this city is the Lafayette and the only hotel uglier than the Lafayette hasn't been built yet. They noticed us about the time we reached their booth. Jim started to get up, but I held up my hand and he slid over to make room for me. If only they made dogs and spouses as accommodating and loyal as they made state reps.

I said, "Jim, you know Angie. Senator Mulkern, this is my partner, Angela Gennaro."

Angie held out a hand. "Pleased to meet you, Senator."

Mulkern took the hand, kissed the knuckles, and slid along his seat, leading the hand with him. "The pleasure is completely mine, Ms. Gennaro." That smoothie. Angie sat down beside him, and he let go of her hand. He looked at me with a raised eyebrow. "Partner?" He chuckled.

Jim chuckled too.

I thought it rated a slight smile. I sat beside Jim. "Where's Senator Paulson?" I asked.

Mulkern was smiling at Angie. He said, "Couldn't get him away from his desk this afternoon, I'm afraid."

I said, "On Saturday?"

Mulkern took a sip of his drink. "So, tell me," he said to Angie, "where is it that Pat's been hiding you?"

Angie gave him a brilliant smile, all teeth. "In a drawer."

"Is that a fact?" Mulkern said. He drank some more. "Oh, I like her, Pat. I do."

"People usually do, Senator."

Our waiter came, took our drink orders, crept away silently on the deep carpet. Mulkern had said lunch, but all I saw on the table were glasses. Maybe they'd discovered a way to liquefy the menu.

Jim touched my shoulder. "You had quite a day yesterday."

Sterling Mulkern held up the morning *Trib.* "A hero like your father now, lad." He tapped the paper. "You've seen it?"

"I only read 'Calvin and Hobbes,' " I said.

He said, "Yes, well . . . wonderful press, really. Great for business."

"But not for Jenna Angeline."

Mulkern shrugged. "Those who live by the sword . . ."

"She was a cleaning woman," I said. "Closest she ever came to a sword was a letter opener, Senator."

He gave me the same shrug and I saw that his mind wasn't for the changing. People like Mulkern are used to creating the facts on their own, then letting the rest of us in.

"Patrick and I were wondering," Angie said, "if the death of Ms. Angeline means our work for you is done."

"Hardly, my dear," he said. "Hardly. I hired Pat, and you as well, to find certain documents. Unless you've brought those to the table with you, you're still working for me."

Angie smiled. "Patrick and I work for ourselves, Senator."

Jim looked at me, then down at his drink. Mulkern's face stopped moving for a moment, then he raised his eyebrows, amused. He said, "Well, exactly why did I sign that check made out to your agency?"

Angie never missed a beat. "Service charges for the loan of our expertise, Senator." She looked up as the waiter approached. "Ah, the drinks. Thank you."

I could have kissed her.

Mulkern said, "Is that the way you see it, Pat?"

"Pretty much," I said and sipped my beer.

"And, Pat," Mulkern said, leaning back, gearing up for something, "does she usually do all the talking when you're together? And all other duties, I'm assuming?"

Angie said, "She doesn't appreciate being spoken of in the third person when *she's* in the room, Senator."

I said, "How many drinks you had, Senator?"

Jim said, "Please," and held up his hand.

If this had been a saloon in the Old West, the place would have cleared about now, the loud rustling of fifty chairs pushing back from tables, wood scraping against wood. But it was a posh bar in Boston in the middle of a Saturday afternoon, and Mulkern didn't look like he'd wear a six-gun real well. Too much belly. But then, in Boston, a gun never was much of a match for a signature in the proper place, or a well-chosen slur dropped at precisely the right moment.

Mulkern's black eyes were staring at me from under heavy lids, the look of a snake whose lair has been invaded, the look of a violent drunk itching for a fight. He said, "Patrick Kenzie," and leaned across the table toward me. The bourbon on his breath could have ignited a gas station. "Patrick Kenzie," he repeated, "now you listen to me. There is absolutely no way I will be spoken to in this manner by the *son* of one of my *lackeys*. Your father, dear boy, was a dog who jumped when I told him to. And you have no other hope in this town but to carry on in his footsteps. Because"—he leaned in farther and suddenly grasped my wrist on the table, hard—"if you show disrespect to me, boyo, your business will be lonelier than an AA meeting on St. Patrick's Day. One word from me, and you'll be ruined. And as for your girlfriend here, well, she'll have a lot more to worry about than a few pops in the eye from her deadbeat husband."

Angie looked fit to decapitate him, but I put my free hand on her knee.

I took it back and reached into my breast pocket to remove the Xerox I'd made of the photograph. I held it in my hand, away from either Mulkern or Vurnan, and smiled slightly, coldly, I imagine, my eyes never leaving Mulkern's. I leaned back a little, away from his toxic halitosis, and said, "Senator, my father was one of your lackeys. No argument. But, dead or alive, he can piss up a rope as far as I'm concerned. I hated the bastard, so don't waste your distilled breath on appeals to my sentimentality. Angie is family. Not him. Not you." I flicked my wrist and my hand came free of his. Before he could pull his back, I closed mine around it and yanked. "And Senator," I said, "if you ever threaten my livelihood again"—I flipped the photocopy on the table in front of him—"I'll blow a fucking hole in your life."

If he noticed the photocopy, he didn't show it. His eyes never left mine, just grew smaller, pinpoints of focused hatred.

I looked at Angie and let go of Mulkern's hand. "I'm done," I said and stood up. I patted Jim's shoulder. "Always a pleasure, Jim."

Angie said, "Bye, Jim."

We walked away from the table.

If we made it to the door, I'd be on welfare come autumn. If we made it to the door, the picture meant nothing more than guilt by association and they had nothing to hide. I'd have to move to Montana or Kansas or Iowa or one of those places where I imagine it's so boring no one would want to wield political influence. If we made it to the door, we were done in this city.

"Pat, lad."

We were eight or nine feet from the door; my faith in human nature was restored.

Angie squeezed my hand and we turned around like we had better things to do.

Jim said, "Please, come back and sit down."

We approached the table.

Mulkern held out his hand. "I'm a tad peckish this early in the day. People seem to misunderstand my sense of humor."

I took the hand. "Ain't that always the way."

He held it out to Angie. "Ms. Gennaro, please accept the apologies of an ornery old man."

"It's already forgotten, Senator."

"Please," he said, "call me Sterling." He smiled warmly and patted her hand. Everything about him screamed sincerity.

If I hadn't upchucked the night before, I think we all would have been in danger.

Jim tapped the photocopy and looked at me. "Where did you get this?"

"Jenna Angeline."

"It's a copy," he said.

"Yes, it is, Jim."

"The original?" Mulkern said.

"I have it."

"Pat," Mulkern said, his smile keeping his voice in check, "we hired you for the purpose of retrieving documents, not their photocopies."

"I keep the original of this one until I find the rest of them."

"Why?" Jim asked.

I pointed at the front page of the newspaper. "Things have gotten messy. I don't like messy. Ange, do you like messy?"

Angie said, "I don't like messy."

I looked at Vurnan and Mulkern. "We don't like messy. Keeping the original is our way of stepping around the mess until we're sure what it is."

"Can we help you, Pat, lad?"

"Sure. Tell me about Paulson and Socia."

"A foolish indiscretion on Brian's part," Mulkern said.

"How foolish?" Angie asked.

"For the average man," Mulkern said, "not very. But for one in the public eye, extremely foolish." He nodded at Jim.

Jim folded his hands together on the table. "Senator Paulson engaged in a night of . . . illicit pleasure with one of Mr. Socia's prostitutes six years ago. I can hardly make light of it under the circumstances, but in the grand scheme of things, it amounts to little more than an evening of wine and women.''

"None of these women being Mrs. Paulson," Angie said.

Mulkern shook his head. "That's irrelevant. She's a politician's wife; she understands what's expected of her at a time like this. No, the problem would arise if any documentation of this affair ever surfaced in the public eye. Brian is presently a very strong, silent voice advocating the street terrorism bill. Any association with people of . . . Mr. Socia's type could be very damaging.''

I wanted to ask how anyone could be a "strong, silent voice," but I figured it might reveal my lack of political savvy. I said, "What's Socia's first name?''

Jim said, "Marion," and Mulkern glanced at him.

"Marion," I repeated. "And how did Jenna come into play in this? How did she get ahold of these pictures?''

Jim looked at Mulkern before answering. The telepathic pols. He said, "The best we can figure it, Socia sent the photographs as an extortion attempt of some sort. Brian got very drunk that night, as you might imagine. He passed out in his chair with the photos on his desk. Then Jenna came to clean, and we assume . . .''

Angie said, "Wait a sec'. You're saying Jenna got so morally repulsed by photographs of Paulson with a hooker that she took them? Knowing her life wouldn't be worth a dollar if she did?'' She sounded like she believed it less than I did.

Jim shrugged.

Mulkern said, "Who can tell with these people?''

I said, "So, why would Socia have her killed? Doesn't seem to me that he had all that much to lose by pictures of Paulson and some hooker going public.''

Before he spoke, I knew Mulkern's answer, and I wondered why I even bothered asking in the first place.

"Who can tell with these people?" he said again.

16

The rest of the day was a wash.

We returned to the office and I flirted with Angie and she told me to get a life and the phone didn't ring and nobody just happened by our belfry. We ordered a pizza and drank a few beers and I kept thinking about how she'd looked in the back of the taxi, squirming in that skirt. She looked at me a couple of times, guessed what I was thinking, and called me a perv. One of those times I was actually having a purely innocent thought about my long-distance phone service, but there've been so many other times it sort of made up for it.

Angie's always had this thing about the window behind her desk. She spends half her time staring out it, chewing on her lower lip or tapping a pencil against her teeth, off in her own world. But today it was as if there was a movie out there only she could see. A lot of her responses to my comments began with a "Huh?" and I got the feeling she wasn't even in the same hemisphere. I figured it had to do with the Asshole, so I let her be.

My gun was still down at police headquarters, and I had no intention of going about town holding only my dick and an optimistic attitude with the Raven Saints looking for me. I needed one that was completely virgin, because the Commonwealth has very definite laws about unregistered handguns. Angie would need one too in case we got into something together, so I tracked down Bubba Rogowski and ordered two traceless pieces from him. He said no problem, I'd have them by five. Just like ordering the pizza.

I called Devin Amronklin next. Devin's assigned to the mayor's new Anti-Gang Task Force. He's short and powerful and people who try to cause him harm only make him angry. He has scars long enough to qualify as mile markers, but he's a pretty swell guy to have around if you're not at a cocktail party in Beacon Hill.

He said, "Love to talk, but I got shit to do. Meet me at the funeral tomorrow. You earned some points for Curtis the Gimp, no matter what that asshole Ferry told you."

I hung up and felt a slight swell of warmth in my chest, like hard liquor on a cold night before the bitter kicks in. With Bubba and Devin around, I felt safer than a condom at a eunuchs' convention. But then I realized, as I always do, that when someone wants to kill you, really kill you, nothing but caprice will save you. Not God, not an army, certainly not yourself. I had to hope my enemies were stupid, untimely, or had extremely short attention spans when it came to vengeance. Those would be the only things keeping me from the grave.

I looked over at Angie. "What's up, gorgeous?"

She said, "Huh?"

"I said, 'What's up, gorgeous.' "

The pencil went tap-tap-tap. She crossed her ankles on the windowsill, swiveled the chair partway in my direction. She said, "Hey."

I said, "What?"

"Don't do that anymore. OK?"

"Do what?"

She turned her head, met my eyes. "The gorgeous stuff. Don't do that anymore. Not now."

I said, "Well gee, Mom . . ."

She swiveled the chair all the way around to face me, her legs coming off the windowsill. "And don't do that shit either. That 'Well gee, Mom . . . ' like you're being innocent. You're not being innocent." She looked out the window for a moment, then back at me. "You can be some kind of asshole sometimes, Patrick. You know that?''

I put my beer down on the corner of the desk. ''Where is this coming from?''

''It's just coming,'' she said. ''OK? It's not easy . . . It's not . . . I come here every day from my fucking . . . home, and I just want . . . Jesus. And I, I have to deal with you calling me 'gorgeous' and hitting on me like it's a god-damned reflex action and looking at me the way you do and I . . . just . . . want it to stop.'' She rubbed her face harshly with her hands and ran them back through her hair, groaning.

I said, ''Ange—''

''Don't Ange me, Patrick. Don't.'' She kicked a lower drawer of her desk. ''You know, between men like Sterling Mulkern the fat fuck, and Phil, and *you*, I just don't know.''

It felt like there was a poodle lodged in my throat, but I managed to say, ''Don't know what?''

''Anything!'' She dropped her face into her hands, then looked up again. ''I just don't know anymore.'' She stood up hard enough to spin her chair a full revolution and walked toward the door. ''And I'm sick of being asked the fucking questions.'' She walked out.

The sound of her heels echoed off the steps like bullets, cracking upward and through the doorway. I felt a heavy ache behind my eyes, the steel spikes of a grate that had its back to a dam.

The sound of her heels stopped. I looked out the window, but she wasn't outside. The scraped beige paint of her car roof shone dully under the streetlight.

I took the stairs three at a time in the dark, the steep narrow space curving and dropping in a black rush before me. She was standing a few feet past the bottom step, lean-ing against a confessional. A lit cigarette stood straight out between her lips and she was placing the lighter back in her purse when I rounded the bend.

I stopped dead and waited.

She said, ''Well?''

I said, "Well what?"

"This conversation sounds like it's going to be a winner."

I said, "Please, Angie, give me a break here. This sort of is coming out of the clear blue sky to me." I caught my breath as she watched me with opaque eyes, the kind that told me a challenge had been issued and I'd better figure out what it was, quick. I said, "I know what's wrong—about Mulkern, Phil, me. You got a lot of asshole men in—"

"Boys," she said.

"OK," I said. "A lot of asshole boys in your life right now. But, Ange, what's *wrong?*"

She shrugged and flicked an ash on the marble floor. "Probably burn in hell for that."

I waited.

"Everything's wrong, Patrick. Everything. When I thought about you almost dying yesterday, it made me think of a lot of other things too. And, I mean, Jesus Christ—this is my life? Phil? Dorchester?"—she swept her hand around the church—"This? I come to work, I fend you off, you have your fun, I go home, get slapped around once or twice a month, make love to the bastard sometimes the same night, and . . . that's all? That's who I am?"

"Nobody says it has to be."

"Oh, right, Patrick. I'll become a brain surgeon."

"I can—"

"No." She dropped her cigarette on the marble, ground it out. "It's a game to you. It's—'I wonder how *she* is in bed?' And then, once you know, you move on." She shook her head. "This is my life. No game."

I nodded.

She smiled, a rueful one, and in the little bit of light that shone through the green stained glass to my right I could see that her eyes were wet. She said, "Remember what it used to be like?"

I nodded again. She was talking about before. Before,

when there weren't any limits. Before, when this place was a slightly drab, slightly bluesy romantic locale, and not a simple reality.

She said, "Who would've thought, right? Kinda funny, huh?"

"No," I said.

17

Bubba never made it to my office that night. Typical.

He came to my apartment the next morning while I was deciding what to wear to Jenna's funeral. He sat on my bed as I worked on my tie and said, "You look like a fag with that tie."

I said, "Didn't you know?" and blew him a kiss.

Bubba moved a foot down the bed. "Don't even fucking kid about that, Kenzie."

I considered pushing it, seeing how antsy I could make him. But pushing Bubba is a good way to find out real quick how well you fly, so I went back to working on my tie.

Bubba is an absolute anachronism in these times—he hates everything and everybody except Angie and myself, but unlike most people of similar inclination, he doesn't waste any time thinking about it. He doesn't write letters to the editor or hate mail to the president, he doesn't form groups or stage marches or consider his hate as anything other than a completely natural aspect of his world, like breathing or the shot glass. Bubba has all the self-awareness of a carburetor and takes even less notice of anyone else—unless they get in his way. He's six feet four inches, 235 pounds of raw adrenaline and disassociated anger. And he'd shoot anyone who blinked at me the wrong way.

I prefer not to consider this loyalty too closely, which is fine with Bubba. As for Angie, well, Bubba once promised to sever each of Phil's limbs and put them back on again—

backward—before we talked him out of it. We promised him, swore to God in fact, that we'd take care of it some day and call him before we did. He relented. He called us losers and shitheads and every other expletive you can think of, but at least we didn't have a Murder One Conspiracy hanging over our heads.

The world according to Bubba is simple—if it aggravates you, stop it. By whatever means necessary.

He reached into his denim trench coat and tossed two guns onto my bed. "Sorry I was late."

"No problem," I said.

He said, "I got some missiles you could use."

I considered the knot in my tie, kept my breathing regular. "Missiles?" I said.

"Sure," he said. "Got a couple of stingers would fix those homeboys just right."

Very slowly I said, "But, Bubba, wouldn't they take out, like, half a neighborhood while they were at it?"

He thought about that for a second. "What's your point?" he said. He stuck his hands behind his head and leaned back on the bed. "So, you interested or what?"

"Maybe later," I said.

He nodded. "Cool." He reached into his jacket again and I waited for him to pull out an antitank gun or some claymores. He tossed four grenades on my bed. "In case," he said.

"Yeah," I said like I understood, "those could probably come in handy."

"Fucking A right," he said. He stood up. "You're good for the cost of the guns, right?"

I eyed him in the mirror and nodded. "I can pay you later this afternoon if you really need it."

"Nah. I know where you live." He smiled. Bubba's smile has been known to induce month-long periods of insomnia. He said, "You call me, day or night, you need anything." He stopped at the bedroom door. "A beer soon?"

"Oh," I said, "absolutely."

"Righteous." He waved and left.

I felt like I always felt after Bubba left—like something hadn't exploded.

I finished with the tie and crossed to the bed. In between the grenades were two guns—a .38 Smith and a nickle-plated Browning Hi-Power nine millimeter. I put on my suit jacket, slipped the Browning into my holster. I put the .38 in the pocket of the jacket and appraised myself in the mirror. The swelling on my face had gone down and my lips were semihealed. The tissue around my eye had yellowed and the scrapes on my face were starting to fade to pink. I was still no dream date, but I wasn't in the running for the Elephant Man contest, either. I could go out in public without fear of pointed fingers and muffled giggles. And if not, I was packing serious heat; anyone giggled, I'd shoot him.

I looked at the grenades. Didn't have a clue what to do with them. I had the feeling that if I left the house, they'd roll off the bed, take out the entire building. I picked them up, gingerly, and put them in the fridge. Anyone broke in to steal my beer, they'd know I meant business.

Angie was sitting on her steps when I pulled up. She wore a white blouse and a pair of black pants that tapered at her ankles. *She* was looking like a dream date, but I didn't mention it.

She got in the car and we drove for quite a while without a word. I'd purposely put a Screaming Jay Hawkins tape in the player, but she didn't so much as flinch. Angie likes Screaming Jay about as much as she likes being called a chick. She smoked a cigarette and stared out at the land-scape of Dorchester as if she'd just emigrated here.

The tape ended as we entered Mattapan, and I said, "That Screaming Jay, he's good enough to play twice. Heck, I might just rip out the eject button, play him for eternity."

She chewed a hangnail.

I ejected Screaming Jay and replaced him with U2. The tape usually rocks Angie in her seat, but today it might as well have been Steve and Edie; she sat there like she'd had lithium with her morning coffee.

We were on the Jamaica Plain Parkway and the Dublin boys were into "Sunday Bloody Sunday," when Angie said, "I'm working some things out. Give me time."

"I can deal with that."

She turned on the seat, tucking her hair behind her ear in the wind. "Just lay off the 'gorgeous' stuff for a little while, the invitations to your shower, things like that."

"Old habits die hard," I said.

"I'm not a habit," she said.

I nodded. "Touché. You want to take some time off maybe?"

"No way." She tucked her left leg under her right. "I love the job. I just need to work through things and I need your support, Patrick, not your flirtations."

I held out my right hand. "You got it." I almost tacked a "gorgeous" to the end of that, but thankfully, I didn't. Mama Kenzie may have raised a fool, but she didn't raise no suicide.

She took my hand, shook it. "Bubba catch up with you?"

"Uh-huh. He brought you a present." I reached into my pocket, handed her the .38.

She hefted it. "He's so sentimental sometimes."

"He offered us the use of a couple of stingers, in case there's a country we want to overthrow anytime soon."

"I hear the beaches in Costa Rica are nice."

"Costa Rica it is then. You speak Spanish?"

"I thought you did."

"I *failed* it," I said. "Twice. Not the same thing."

"You speak Latin."

"OK, we'll overthrow Ancient Rome."

The cemetery was coming up on our left and Angie said, "Jesus Christ."

I looked as I made the turn onto the main road. We'd expected the sort of funeral cleaning ladies usually get—one rung higher than a pauper's—but there were cars everywhere. A bunch of beat-up street sleds, a black BMW, a silver Mercedes, a Maserati, a couple of RX-7s, then a full squadron of police cruisers, the patrolmen standing out of their units watching the grave site.

Angie said, "You sure this is the right place?"

I shrugged and pulled over onto the lawn, completely confused. We left the Porsche and crossed the lawn, pausing a couple of times when Angie's heel caught the soft soil.

The minister's baritone was calling upon the Lord our God to welcome his child, Jenna Angeline, into the Kingdom of Heaven with the love of a father for a true daughter of the spirit. His head was down as he spoke, peering at the coffin that sat on brass runners over the deep black rectangle. He was the only one looking at it, though. Everyone else was too busy looking at each other.

The group on the southern side of the coffin was headed by Marion Socia. He was taller than he'd appeared in the photograph, his hair shorter, tight curls hugging an oversize head. He was thinner, too, the thin of adrenaline burn. His slim hands twitched constantly by his sides, as if grasping for the trigger of a gun. He was wearing a simple black suit with white shirt and black tie, but it was expensive material—silk, I guessed.

The boys behind him were dressed exactly the same, their suits of varying quality, deteriorating steadily the farther back they stood from Socia and the grave. There were at least forty of them, the whole group in a taut, structured formation behind its leader. A conspicuous air of Spartan devotion. None of them, except Socia, looked much over seventeen, and some didn't look old enough to have had an erection yet. They all stared beyond the grave in the same direction as Socia, their eyes devoid of youth or movement or emotion, flat and clear and focused.

The object of their attention was on the other side of the grave, directly across from Socia. A black kid, as tall as Socia, but more solid, his body the healthy hard that a male achieves only before the age of twenty-five. He wore a black trench coat over a midnight blue shirt, buttoned at the top, no tie. His pants were pleated charcoal with light blue specks woven into the fabric. He had a single gold earring hanging from his left ear and his hair was cut in a sloping high-top fade, the sides of his head cropped extremely close, matching stripes cut into what little hair remained there. The back of his head was shorn just as close and something had been carved there too. From my vantage point, I couldn't be positive, but it looked like the shape of Africa. He held a black umbrella in his hand, pointed at the ground, even though the sky was about as cloudy as freshly blown glass. Behind him was another army: thirty of them, all young, all dressed semiformal, but not a tie among them.

The first white person we noticed was Devin Amronklin. He was standing a good fifteen yards behind the second group, chatting with three other detectives, all four of them flashing their eyes back and forth between the two gangs and the cops on the road.

Beyond all of this, facing the foot of the coffin, I noticed a few older women, two men dressed in the clothes of State House sanitary personnel, and Simone. Simone was staring at us when we noticed her and she held the look for a solid minute before looking off at the firm elms that surrounded the cemetery. Nothing about her look suggested she'd come past me on the way out, invite me over for tea and a healing racial debate.

Angie took my hand and we walked over to Devin. He gave us each a curt nod, but didn't say anything.

The minister finished his eulogy and hung his head one last time. No one else followed suit. There was something alien about the stillness, something dangerously false and ponderous. A pigeon, gray and fat, swooped over the silence, small wings flapping fast. Then the crisp morning air cracked open with the mechanical whir of the coffin descending into the black rectangle.

The two groups moved as one, fading forward ever so slightly like slim trees in the first gust of a storm. Devin put his hand on his hip, a quarter inch from his gun, and the other three cops did the same. The air in the cemetery seemed to suck into itself and disappear in its own vortex. A current of electricity streamed into its place, and my teeth felt like they were gritted into tin foil. A gear ground somewhere in the dark hole, but the coffin continued on down. In those few moments of some of the most severe quiet I've ever felt, I think if someone had sneezed they'd have spent the rest of the day shoveling bodies off the lawn.

Then the kid in the trench coat took one step closer to the grave. Socia was a millisecond behind him, taking two steps to compensate. Trench Coat took the challenge and they reached the edge of the grave simultaneously, their bearings interchangeable, heads straight and immobile.

Devin said, "Calm. Everyone. Calm," in a whisper.

Trench Coat bent, a stiff squat, and picked up a white lily from a small pile by his feet. Socia did the same. They looked at each other as they extended their arms over the grave. The white lilies never quivered. They held their arms straight out, neither dropping his lily. A test whose limit only they knew. I didn't see which of them opened his hand first but suddenly the lilies fell toward the grave in nearly weightless surrender.

Each took two steps back from the grave.

Now it was the gangs' turn. They mimicked what Socia or Trench Coat had done, depending on their affiliation. By the time the line had dwindled to the lowest level members of each group, though, they were picking up the lilies and dropping them into the blackness in record time, barely taking a few precious moments to stare into each other's eyes and show how unafraid they were. I heard the cops behind me begin breathing again.

Socia had moved to the foot of the grave, hands folded together, staring at nothing. Trench Coat stood near the head, hand on his umbrella, eyes on Socia.

I said to Devin, "OK to talk now?"

He shrugged. "Sure."

Angie said, "The hell's going on here, Devin?"

Devin smiled. His face was only slightly colder to look at than the black hole everyone was dropping lilies into. "What's going on," he said, "is the beginning of the biggest bloodfest this city's ever seen. It'll make the Coconut Grove fire seem like a trip to EPCOT."

A block of ice the size of a baseball nestled against the base of my spine and chilled sweat slid past my ear. I turned my head and my eyes passed over the grave and locked with Socia's. He was completely still, his eyes looking directly at me as if I weren't there. I said, "He doesn't seem too friendly."

Devin said, "You amputated the foot of his favorite lieutenant. I'd say he's downright livid."

"Enough to kill me?" It wasn't easy, but I continued to meet that sullen gaze that told me I'd already ceased to exist.

"Oh, without a doubt," Devin said.

That's Devin for you. All heart.

"What's my move?" I asked.

"A plane ticket to Tangiers would be my suggestion. He'll still get to you but at least you could say you'd seen the world." He scuffed the thick, stubby grass in front of him. "Word on the street, though, is he wants to talk with you first. Seems to think you got something he needs." He raised his foot, used his hand to brush the grass off his shoe. "Now, what could that be, Patrick?"

I shrugged. Those eyes never left me. I've seen frozen ponds with more empathy. I said, "The man's deluded."

"No argument there. Hell of a good shot though. I hear

he likes to pull the trigger a lot, hit his victims in superficial places. You know, take his time. Give them the head shot about a half hour after they start begging for it. A real humanitarian, our Socia." He crossed his hands in front of him, cracked the knuckles. "So, why does he think you have something he needs, Patrick?"

Angie squeezed my hand and slipped her other hand under my arm. It felt warm and slightly bittersweet. She said, "Who's the guy with the umbrella?"

Devin said, "I thought you two were detectives."

Trench Coat had turned now, too. He was following Socia's gaze, his eyes landing on me as well. I felt like a minnow in a shark tank.

Angie said, "No, Devin, we're still studying. So, tell us—who's the guy with the umbrella?"

He cracked his knuckles again, sighed with the ease of a man drinking a beer in a hammock. "That's Jenna's son."

I said, "Jenna's son."

"Did I stutter? Jenna's son. He runs the Angel Avengers."

Angel Avenue runs through the heart of Black Dorchester. It's not a place where you stop at red lights. Even in broad daylight.

"He got a hard-on for me, too?"

"Not as far as I know," he said.

Angie said, "Is Socia his father?"

Devin looked at the two of them, then the two of us. He nodded. "But I think it was the mother who named him Roland."

18

"One angry child, our Roland," Devin was saying.

I sipped some coffee. "He didn't look much like a child to me," I said.

Devin swallowed a hunk of doughnut, reached for his coffee. "He's sixteen years old."

Angie said, "Sixteen?"

"Just *turned* sixteen," Devin said, "last month."

I thought of what I'd seen of him—a tall, muscular body, the bearing of a young general, standing on the small knoll above his mother's grave, umbrella in hand. He looked like he already knew his place in this world—at the forefront, with his minions behind him.

When I was sixteen, I barely knew my place in the school lunch line. I said, "How's a sixteen-year-old boy run a network like the Avengers?"

"With a big gun," Devin said. He looked at me, shrugged. "He's a pretty smart boy, Roland is. He's got balls the size of truck radials, too. A good thing to have if you want to run a gang."

"And Socia?" Angie asked.

"Well, I'll tell you something about Roland and his daddy, Marion. They say the only natural force in this city that's possibly more dangerous than Roland is his daddy. And believe me, I've sat in a cold interrogation room with Marion for seven hours: the man has a cavity where his heart should be."

"And he and Roland are about to go head to head?"

141

"Seems to be the case," Devin said. "They ain't Ward and the Beav', that's for sure. Take my word, Roland's not walking around breathing because of any help from his old man. Socia was born without paternal instincts. The Avengers used to be a sort of brother gang to the Saints. But Roland changed all that about three months ago, broke away from his old man's organization. Socia's tried to hit Roland at least four times that we know of, but the kid doesn't die. A lot of bodies been showing up in Mattapan and the 'Bury the last few months, but none of them has been Roland."

Angie said, "But sooner or later . . ."

Devin nodded. "Something's got to give. Roland hates his old man something fierce. No one knows why exactly. Although now, with Jenna dead, he pretty much has all the motivation he needs, doesn't he?"

"He was close to her?" I asked.

Devin shrugged, his large palms up in front of him. "I don't know. She visited him a lot when he was in juvie lockup at Wildwood, and some say he'd drop by her place every now and then, leave her some cash. But it's really hard to say—Roland's got about as much love in him as his father."

"Great," I said. "Two machines without emotion."

"Oh, they got plenty of emotion," Devin said. "It's just all hate." He caught the waitress's eye. "More coffee."

We were sitting in the Dunkin' Donuts on Morton Street. Outside the window a few guys passed around a bottle in a brown paper bag, drinking Sunday into Monday. Across the street, four punks prowled, eyes roving, every now and then one of them banging his fist off the top of another's— jacked up on hate and pain and ready to ignite as soon as they found a spark. Down the block, a young girl pushing a carriage veered it off the curb and began crossing to the other side of the street, head down, hoping they wouldn't notice her.

Devin said, "You know, it's too bad about Jenna. Don't

seem right, a woman like that being stuck with two stone killers like Socia and Roland. Shit, the worst thing the woman ever did was rack up a lot of parking tickets. And who the hell doesn't in this city." He dipped his second doughnut into his third cup of coffee, his voice as inflectionless as a single piano key struck over and over again. "Too bad." He looked at us. "Opened her safe-deposit box last night."

Very slowly I said, "And?"

"Nothing," he said, watching me. "A government bond, some jewelry wasn't worth the rental fee on the box."

A muffled explosion went off outside, and the inside of the doughnut shop rattled. I looked toward the window and saw the group of punks. One of them was staring in, the veins in his neck prominent, his face a war mask. He met our eyes and his hand shot out again into the window. A couple of people flinched but the window didn't break. His friends laughed but he didn't. His eyes were red, blazing with rage. He hit the window one more time, got a few more flinches, and then his friends pulled him away. He was laughing by the time he reached the corner. Nice world.

I said, "No one knows why Roland has this beef with Socia?"

"Could be anything. You weren't particularly fond of your old man, were you, Kenzie?"

I shook my head.

He pointed at Angie. "You?"

"My father and I got along all right," she said. "When he was home. My mother and I were another story."

"I hated my old man," Devin said. "Turned every waking hour in my house into the Friday night fights. Took so much shit from him growing up, I swore I'd never take it from anyone else for the rest of my life, even if that meant dying young. Maybe Roland's like that. His juvie sheet is one long list of authority problems, going back to the fifth grade when he split open the substitute teacher's head. Bit off some of his ear too."

Fifth grade. Jesus.

Devin said, "Fucked up his share of social workers too, not to mention another teacher. Kicked a cop's head through the windshield of his cruiser when he was taking him to juvie once. Broke the nose of an emergency-room doctor, this while he had a bullet lodged near his spine. Come to think of it—everyone Roland's jammed on has been male. He doesn't respond well to female authority, either, but he doesn't get violent, he just walks away."

"What about Socia?"

"What about him?"

"What's his deal?" I said. "I mean, I know he runs the Saints, but besides that."

"Marion is a true opportunist. Up till about ten years ago, he was just a small-time pimp. A very vicious small-time pimp, but he didn't give the computer an overload when you keyed his name into it."

"And then?"

"Then came crack. Socia knew what it would mean, long before it made the cover of *Newsweek*. He killed the mule of one of the Jamaican syndicates, took over the man's action. We all figured he had about a week to live after that, but he flew to Kingston, showed the Boss the size of his balls, dared him to retaliate." Devin shrugged. "Next thing you know, the man to see for crack in this town was Marion Socia. This was back in the early days, but even now, with all the competition, he's still the top man. He's got an army of kids willing to die for him, no questions asked, and he's got a network that's so detailed, you could bust one of his upper-echelon suppliers and still be four or five buffer people removed from Socia himself."

We sat silent for a while, drinking our coffee.

Angie said, "How's Roland ever hope to beat Socia?"

Devin shrugged. "You got me. I got a hundred bucks on Socia in the pool, myself."

"The pool?" I said.

He nodded. "Of course. The departmental pool, see who

wins the gang war. They don't pay me enough to do this job, so I got to take my perks where I find them. Odds on Roland are about sixty to one."

Angie said, "They looked pretty even at the funeral."

"Looks can be deceiving. Roland's tough, he's smart, and he's got a pretty good posse working for him up on Angel Avenue. But he's not his father, not yet. Marion is ruthless and he's got nine lives. There ain't a member of the Saints who isn't convinced he's Satan. You fuck up even slightly in Socia's organization and you die. No outs. No compromises. The Saints think they're in a holy war."

"And the Avengers?"

"Oh, they're dedicated. Don't doubt that. But, push come to shove, enough of them die, they'll back down. Roland's going to lose. Bank on it. Couple years from now, it might be a different story, but he's too green right now." He looked down at his cold coffee and grimaced. "What time is it?"

Angie looked at her watch. "Eleven."

"Hell, it's noon somewhere," he said. "I need alcohol." He stood up, dropped some coins on the table. "Come on, kids."

I stood. "Where?"

"There's a bar around the corner. Lemme buy you a drink before the war."

The bar was small, cramped, and the black rubber tile on the floor smelled of stale beer and wet soot and sweat. It was one of those paradoxes that are common in this city—a white Irish bar in a black neighborhood. The men who drank here had been drinking here for decades. They walled themselves up inside with their dollar drafts and their pickled eggs and their frozen attitudes and pretended the world outside hadn't changed. They were construction workers who'd been working within the same five-mile radius since they got their union cards because something's always being built in Boston; they were foremen from the docks, from the General Electric plant, from Sears and Roebuck. They chased cut-rate whiskey with impossibly cold beer at eleven o'clock in the morning and watched a videotape of the Notre Dame–Colorado Orange Bowl from last New Year's.

When we entered, they glanced at us long enough to assess our color, then resumed their argument. One of them was up on his knees atop the bar, pointing at the screen, counting some of the players. He said, "There, they got eight on the defense alone. Fucking eight. You tell me again about Notre Dame."

The bartender was an old-timer with slightly fewer scars on his face than Devin. He had the bored, opaque face of someone who's definitely heard it all and made up his mind about most of it years ago. He raised a tired eyebrow at Devin. "Hey, Sarge, what can I get you?"

"Bullshit, bullshit, bullshit, bullshit," someone by the TV said. "Count 'em again."

"Fuck you—count 'em again. *You* count 'em."

Devin said, "What's the thrust of the intellectual discourse at the other end of the bar?"

The bartender wiped the bar in front of us as we sat down. "Roy—the guy on the bar—he claims Notre Dame's the better team because they got less niggers. They're counting to decide."

"Hey, Roy," someone yelled, "the fucking quarterback's a nigger. How white can the Fighting Irish be?"

Angie said, "If I wasn't used to this, I'd be embarrassed."

Devin said, "We could shoot 'em all, maybe get a medal for it."

I said, "Why waste the bullets?"

The bartender was waiting. Devin said, "Oh, sorry, Tommy. Three drafts and a shot."

Someone less familiar with him might have assumed he'd ordered for the three of us. I wasn't fooled. "A draft," I said.

Angie said, "Me too."

Devin hammered a box of unopened cigarettes against his wrist, then removed the wrapping. He took one, offered the pack. Angie took another. I resisted. With pain, as always.

At the other end of the bar, Roy—his pale, hairy belly spilling out of a sweaty blue softball shirt—was banging his finger off the TV faster than tapped Morse code on a sinking ship. "One nigger, two, three, four, five . . . six, another makes seven, eight, nine. Nine and that's just the offense. Buffaloes my ass. Colorado Spearchuckers."

Someone laughed. Someone always does.

I said, "How do these fucks stay alive in this neighborhood?"

Devin considered the jar of pickled eggs. "I have a theory about that." Tommy set the three beers in front of him, placed the shot beside them, went back for ours. The shot disappeared down Devin's throat before I saw him pick it up. He wrapped a hand around one of the frosted mugs, downed half a pint before he spoke again. "Cold," he said. "My theory is this—people like that, you got two choices: you either kill 'em or you let 'em be, because you'll never change their minds. I figure the folks in this neighborhood are just too tired to kill 'em." He polished off the rest of his first beer. He still had half a cigarette and two of his drinks were gone.

I always feel like a Chevette with a bad tire chasing a Porsche when I try to keep up with Devin at a bar.

Tommy placed two beers in front of Angie and me, poured another shot into Devin's shot glass.

Angie said, "My father used to come to this bar."

Devin inhaled the second shot sometime while I blinked. "Why'd he stop?"

"He died."

Devin nodded. "That'd do it, sure." He started on his second pint. "Your old man, Kenzie, the hero fireman, he come to places like this?"

I shook my head. "He drank at Vaughn's on Dot Avenue. Only place he went. Used to say, 'A man who ain't faithful to his bar ain't much better than a woman.' "

"A real prince, his father," Angie said.

"Never met the man," Devin said. "Saw that picture though. Two kids from a burning tenth floor." He whistled and drank the rest of his second pint. "Tell you what, Kenzie—you got half the balls your old man had, you might live through this."

A burst of laughter blew across from the other side of the bar. Roy was pointing at the screen, saying, "Nigger, nigger, nigger, nigger, nigger, nigger, nigger," doing a little drunken dance on his knees. Soon, they'd start telling AIDS jokes, really bust a gut.

I thought about what Devin said. "Your concern is touching," I told him.

He grimaced, his eyebrows furrowed, the third pint washing down his throat. He put it down, wiped his mouth with a cocktail napkin. He said, "Tommy," and waved his arm like a third-base coach sending the runner home. Tommy came down with two more pints and poured him another shot. Devin held up his hand, downed the shot, and Tommy poured another one. Devin nodded, and he left.

Devin turned on the stool, looked at me. "Concern?" he said. He chuckled, a graveyard chuckle. "Tell you what concern changes—nothing. I'm concerned that this city's going to rip itself apart this summer. Won't stop it from happening. I'm concerned too many kids are dying too young over sneakers and hats and five bucks worth of Grade Z cocaine. Guess what though? They're still dying. I'm concerned that shitheads like that"—he jerked a thumb down the bar—"are actually allowed to reproduce and raise new shitheads just as stupid as they are, but it doesn't stop them from mating like rabbits." He threw back the shot, and I had the feeling I'd be driving him home. He was favoring the right elbow on the bar over the left, taking deeper drags on his cigarette. "I'm forty-three years old," he said and Angie sighed quietly. "I'm forty-three," he repeated, "and I got a gun and a badge and I go into gang zones every night and pretend I'm actually doing something, and my *concern* doesn't change the fact that I'm not. I slam sledgehammers into doors in projects that smell of things you couldn't even begin to identify. I go through doors and people shoot at me and children cry and mothers scream and someone gets busted or someone gets killed. And then, then I go home to my shitty little apartment and eat microwave food and sleep until I have to get up and do it again. This," he said, "is my life."

I raised my eyebrows at Angie and she smiled softly, both of us remembering her voice in the chapel the night before. "This is my life?" Lot of people taking stock of their lives these days. Judging by Devin and Angie, I wasn't sure how bright that was.

Somebody down the end of the bar said, "Look at that fucking nigger run, though."

Roy said, "Of course he can run, moron. Been hightailing it from the po-lice since he was two. Probably thinks that's a stolen radio under his arm, 'stead of a football."

Lots of laughter from the group. Wits, one and all.

Devin was watching them now, hollow eyes staring from behind the stream of smoke that flowed from his cigarette. He took a drag from it, the fat forgotten ash tipping forward and dropping to the bar. He didn't seem to notice, even though half of it hit his arm. He downed the rest of his pint and stared at the group and I had the feeling there was going to be some property damage.

He stubbed out his cigarette halfway and stood up. I reached out my hand, stopping three inches from his chest. "Devin."

He pushed it away like it was a subway turnstile and walked down the bar.

Angie turned on her seat, followed him with her eyes. "Eventful morning."

Devin had reached the other end of the bar. One by one,

the men sensed him and turned around. He stood with his legs spread slightly, planted on the rubber tile, his arms hanging loosely by his sides. His hands made small circular motions.

Tommy said, "C'mon, Sarge. Not my place."

Devin said, "C'mere, Roy," very quietly.

Roy climbed off the bar. "Me?"

Devin nodded.

Roy stepped through his friends, pulling the shirt down over his belly. The second he let go of it, it rolled back up like a disobedient shade. Roy said, "Yeah?"

Devin's hand was back down by his side before most of us realized he'd used it. Roy's head snapped back and his legs buckled and he was quite suddenly on the floor with a shattered nose and blood jetting above his face in a small fountain.

Devin looked down at him, kicked his foot lightly. "Roy," he said. He kicked the foot again, a little harder. "Roy, I'm talking to you."

Roy moaned something and tried to raise his head, his hands filling with blood.

Devin said, "A nigger friend of mine asked me to give you that. He said you'd understand."

He walked back down the bar and took his seat again. He made another pint disappear and lit another cigarette. "So, whatta you think?" he said. "Is Roy concerned now?"

19

We left the bar about an hour later. Roy's friends had already taken him out, presumably to the emergency room at City. They gave Angie and me their hard-guy stares as they dragged Roy past, but they avoided Devin's flat gaze as if he were the Antichrist.

Devin tossed an extra twenty on the bar for Tommy's lost business. Tommy said, "You're a real pisser, Sarge. You gonna come in, put money down for every other fucking day they don't come back?"

Devin grumbled, "Yeah, yeah, yeah," and did a drunken shuffle toward the door.

Angie and I caught up with him on the street. I said, "Let me give you a ride home, Dev."

Devin shuffled his way into the Dunkin' Donuts parking lot. He said, "Thanks anyway, Kenzie, but I got to stay in practice."

I said, "For what?"

"Case I ever drink and drive again. I'll want to remember how I managed this time." He turned, walking backward, and I waited for him to tip.

He reached his rusted Camaro, got his keys out of his pocket.

I said, "Devin," and stepped toward him, reaching for the keys.

His hand closed around my shirt, the knuckles pressing into my Adam's apple, and he walked me back a few feet, his eyes swimming with ghosts. He said, "Kenzie, Kenzie," and pushed me back against a car. He tapped my cheek lightly with his other hand. He's got big hands, Devin. Like steaks with fingers. "Kenzie," he said again and his eyes grew hard. He shook his head from side to side slowly. "I'll drive. OK?" He let go of my collar and brushed at the wrinkles he'd left behind in my shirt. He gave me a smile that had no soul. "You're all right," he said. He turned back to his car and nodded at Angie. "Take care of yourself, Stone Fox." He opened the door and climbed in the car. It took two turns of the ignition for the engine to turn over, then the exhaust pipe banged off the small exit ramp and the car dropped into the street. He weaved into traffic, cut off a Volvo, and turned a corner.

I raised my eyebrows and whistled softly. Angie shrugged.

We drove downtown and got the Vobeast out of the parking lot for a little less than it would have cost me to put a kid through med school. Angie drove it, following me to the garage where I returned the Porsche to its happy home and climbed in with her. She slid across the seat and I chugged the rolling scrap metal onto Cambridge.

We drove through downtown, past where Cambridge becomes Tremont, past the place where Jenna went down like a rag doll in the morning sunlight, past the remains of the old Combat Zone, dying a slow but sure death at the hands of development and the X-rated video boom. Why jack off in a scuzzy movie theater when you can jack off in the comfort of your own scuzzy home?

We drove through South Boston—Southie to everyone who isn't a tourist or a newscaster—past strings of drab three-deckers, packed like a line of Port-o'-Potties at a rock concert. Southie amazes me. A good percentage of it is poor, overcrowded, relentlessly unkempt. The D Street housing projects are as bad as anything you'll find in the Bronx—dirty, poorly lit, teeming with angry, crew-cut punks who roam its streets with bloodlust and baseball bats. During a St. Patrick's Day parade a few years ago, a very

Irish kid with a shamrock on his T-shirt wandered in there. He ran into a pack of other Irish kids who also had shamrocks on their T-shirts. Only difference between his T-shirt and theirs was that his said "Dorchester" in green over the shamrock and theirs said "Southie." The D Street kids solved the difference by tossing the kid off a roof.

We were driving up Broadway, past the babies in curlers pushing babies in carriages, past the double- and triple-parked cars and the "Niggers Stay Out" spray-painted on a store grate. Broken glass glittered from the darkness of filthy curbs and trash blew from under cars into the street. I thought of how I could step from this car and poll twenty people here, ask them why they hated "the niggers" so bad, and maybe half would probably tell me, " 'Cause they got no fucking pride in their communities, man." So what if Broadway in Southie was identical to Dudley in Roxbury, if slightly lighter?

We crossed into Dorchester, rode up around Columbia Park and down into the neighborhood. I pulled in front of the church and we could hear the phone ringing as we climbed the stairs. Busy day. I caught it on the tenth ring. "Kenzie-Gennaro," I said.

Angie dropped into her seat as the voice on the other end said, "Hold on. Someone here want to talk with you."

I took the receiver with me as I went around the desk and sat down. Angie gave me a "Who is it?" look and I shrugged.

A voice came on the line. "Mr. Kenzie?"

"Last time I checked."

"This Patrick Kenzie?" The voice had an edge to it, someone not used to dealing with smart-asses.

"Depends," I said. "Who's this?"

"You're Kenzie," the voice said. "How's the breathing?"

I inhaled audibly, sucking it way back and expelling it in a long rush. I said, "Much better since I quit smoking, thanks."

"Uh-huh," the voice said, slow like freshly sapped maple. "Well, don't get too used to it. Might be all that more depressing when you can't do it no more." The maple voice was thick but light, a hint of lazy Southern afternoons hidden behind years of Northern living.

I said, "You always talk this way, Socia, or you just in a particularly elliptical mood today?"

Angie sat up and leaned forward.

Socia said, "Only reason you're still walking, Kenzie, is because we got things to talk about. Hell, I might just send someone over anyway, have them take a hammer to your spine. All I need's your mouth as it is."

I sat up and scratched an itch near the small of my back. I said, "Send them by, Socia. I'll do some more amputations. Pretty soon you'll have an army of cripples. The Raven Gimps."

"Easy to talk that way, sitting nice and safe in your office."

"Yeah, well look, *Marion,* I got a business to run."

"You sitting down?" he said.

"Sure am."

"In that chair by the boom box?"

Everything went cold inside of me, a flush of chipped ice spilling through my arteries.

Socia said, "You sitting in that chair, I wouldn't get up anytime soon, less you want to see your ass blow past your head on its way out the window." He chuckled. "Was nice knowing you, Kenzie."

He hung up and I looked at Angie and said, "Don't move," even though her moving wasn't the problem.

"What?" She stood up.

The room didn't explode, but I damn near fainted. At least we knew he didn't put a bomb under her chair too, just for fun. I said, "Socia said there's a bomb under my chair."

She froze, a wax statue in mid-stride. The word "bomb"

will do that to people. She took a deep breath. "Call the bomb squad?"

I tried not to breathe. The possibility existed, I told myself, that the weight of the oxygen going into my lungs could put pressure on my lower extremities and detonate the bomb. It also occurred to me how ludicrous that was since the bomb was obviously triggered by a release of pressure, not a gain. So now, I couldn't exhale. Either way I wasn't breathing.

I said, "Yeah, call the bomb squad." It sounded funny, talking while I held my breath, like Donald Duck with a cold. Then I closed my eyes and said, "Wait. Look under the chair first."

It was an old wooden chair, a teacher's chair.

Angie put the phone down. She knelt by the chair. It took a few moments for her to do that. No one wants their eyes an inch from an explosive. She bent her head under the chair and I heard her exhale loudly. She said, "I don't see anything."

I started to breathe again, then stopped. Possibly it was in the wood itself. I said, "Look like someone might have tampered with the wood?"

She said, "What? I can't understand you."

I took a chance and let out my breath and repeated the question.

She was down there for six or seven hours, or so it seemed, before she said, "No." She slid back out from under the chair and sat back on the floor. "There's no bomb under the chair, Patrick."

"Great." I smiled.

"So?"

"So, what?"

"Are you going to stand up?"

I thought of my ass flying over my head. "There's a rush?"

"No rush," she said. "Why don't you stand up?"

"Maybe I like it here."

"Stand up," she said and stood herself. She held her arms out to me.

"I'm working up to it."

"Stand," she said. "Come to me, baby."

I did. I put my arms on the chair and did it. Except, somehow, I was still sitting. My brain had moved, but my body was of another opinion. How professional were Socia's people? Could they fit a bomb seamlessly into a wooden chair? Of course not. I've heard of people dying in a lot of ways, but getting blown up by a completely undetectable bomb in a thin wooden chair isn't one of them. Course, maybe I was being honored by being the first.

"Skid?"

"Yeah?"

"Anytime you're ready."

"OK. Well, see I—"

Her hands grabbed mine and she yanked me up out of the chair. I fell against her and we banged into the desk and didn't blow up. She laughed, an explosion in itself, and I realized she hadn't been entirely sure herself. But she'd pulled me out anyway. She said, "Oh, Jesus!"

I started to laugh too, the laugh of someone who hasn't slept in a week, a laugh along a razor blade. I held on to her, my hands tight around her waist, her breasts rising and falling against my chest. We were both drenched in sweat, but her eyes were pulsing, the dark pupils large and drunk with the taste of a moment that wasn't our last on earth.

I kissed her then and she returned it. For a moment, everything was heightened—the sound of a car horn four stories below, the smell of fresh summer air mingling with spring's dust in the window screen, the salty whiff of fresh perspiration at our hairlines, the slight pain from my still swollen lips, the taste of her lips and tongue still slightly cool from the pale ale we'd drunk an hour before.

Then the phone rang.

She pulled back, her hands on my chest, and slid away from me along the desk. She was smiling, but it was one of disbelief and her eyes were already taking on a spectre of regret and fear. God only knows what mine looked like.

I answered the phone with a hoarse, "Hello."

"You still sitting down?"

"No," I said. "I'm looking out the window for my ass."

"Uh-huh. Well, just remember, Kenzie—anyone can get to anyone, and *anyone* can get to you."

"What can I do for you, Marion?"

"You gone come see me, have a chat with me."

"I am, am I?"

"Bet your ass." He chuckled softly.

"Well, Marion, I'll tell you, I'm booked solid till October. Why don't you try back around Halloween?"

All he said was, "Two-oh-five Howe Street." It was all he had to say. It was Angie's address.

I said, "Where and when?"

He gave it another soft chuckle. He'd read me perfectly and he knew it and knew I knew it too. "We'll meet someplace crowded so you have the illusion of safety."

"Damn white of you."

"Downtown Crossing," he said. "Two hours. In front of Barnes and Noble. And you come alone, or I might just have to pay a visit to that address I mentioned."

"Downtown Crossing," I repeated.

"In two hours."

"So I'll feel safe."

He chuckled again. I figured it was a habit of his. "Yeah," he said, "so you'll feel safe." He hung up.

I did the same and looked at Angie. The room was still overcrowded with the memory of our lips touching, of my hand in her hair and her breasts swelling against my chest.

She was in her seat, looking out the window. She didn't turn her head. She said, "I won't say it wasn't nice, because it was. And I won't try and blame it on you, because I was just as guilty. But I will say, it won't happen again."

Hard to find a loophole in that.

20

I took the subway to Downtown Crossing, climbed up some steps that hadn't been hosed down since the Nixon years, and stepped onto Washington Street. Downtown Crossing is the old shopping district, before there were malls and shopping plazas, back when stores were stores and not boutiques. It was refurbished in the late seventies and early eighties like most of the city, and after they opened a few boutiques, business came back. Mostly younger business—kids who were bored with the malls, or too cool or too urban to be caught dead in the suburbs.

Washington Street is blocked off to auto traffic for three blocks where most of the shops are, so the sidewalks and streets teem with people—people going to shop, people returning from shopping, and most of all, people hanging out. The sidewalk in front of Filene's was lined with merchant carts and packed with teenage girls and boys, black and white, leaning against display windows, goofing on adult passersby; a few couples French-kissed with the desperation of those who don't share a bed yet. Across the street, in front of The Corner—a minimall with shops like The Limited and Urban Outfitters, plus a large food court where three or four brawls break out a day—a pack of black kids manned a radio. Chuck D and Public Enemy pounded "Fear of a Black Planet" from speakers the size of car tires, and the kids settled back and watched people walk around them. I looked at all the black faces in the massive crowd and tried to guess which ones were Socia's crew, but I couldn't tell. A lot of the black kids were part of the coming-from-shopping or going-to-shop crowd, but just as many were packed together in gangs, and some had that lazy, lethal look of street predators. There were plenty of white kids strewn throughout the crowd who looked similar, but worrying about them wasn't a concern now. I didn't know much about Socia, but I doubted he was an equal opportunity employer.

I saw immediately why Socia had picked this location. A person could be dead ten minutes, lying facedown on the street, before someone paused to wonder what he was stepping on. Crowds are only slightly safer meeting places than abandoned warehouses, and in abandoned warehouses, you sometimes have room to move.

I looked across the street, past The Corner, my eyes bouncing along the heads in the crowd like sheet music, slowing as they reached Barnes and Noble. The crowd thinned somewhat here, a few less teenagers. Guess bookstores aren't ideal places to pick up babes. I was ten minutes early and I figured Socia and his crew had gotten here twenty minutes before me. I didn't see him, but then I didn't expect to. I had the feeling he would suddenly appear an inch away from me, a gun between my shoulder blades.

It didn't come between my shoulder blades. It came between my left hip and the bottom of my rib cage. It was a big .45 and seemed even bigger because of the nasty-looking silencer on the end. Socia wasn't the one holding it either. It was a kid, sixteen or seventeen, but hard to tell with the black leather watch cap pulled down low over a pair of red Vuarnets. He had a lollipop in his mouth that he shifted from one side of his tongue to the other. He was smiling around it, like he'd just lost his virginity, and he said, "Bet you feel seriously fucking retarded about now, don't you?"

I said, "Compared to what?"

Angie stepped out of the crowd with her gun against

Lollipop's crotch. She was wearing a cream-colored fedora on her head, and her long black hair was tied in a bun under it. She wore sunglasses that were bigger than Lollipop's and ran the gun muzzle over Lollipop's balls. She said, "Hi."

Lollipop's smile faded, so I replaced it with my own. "Having fun yet?"

The crowd all around us kept moving at their escalator pace, oblivious. Urban myopia. Angie said, "So what's our next move?"

Socia said, "That depends."

He was standing behind Angie and by the way her body tensed, I knew there was another gun back there with him too. I said, "This is getting ridiculous."

Four of us stood in a crowd of thousands, all interconnected like blood cells by fat squat pieces of metal. Someone in the crowd jostled my shoulder, and I hoped like hell no one had a hair trigger.

Socia was watching me, a benign expression on his worn face. He said, "Somebody start shooting, I'll be the one walks away. How 'bout that?"

He almost had a point—he'd shoot Angie, Angie would shoot Lollipop, and Lollipop would definitely shoot me. Almost.

I said, "Well, Marion, seeing how this is already about as crowded as a Japanese camera convention, I don't figure one more body'll hurt. Look at Barnes and Noble."

He turned his head slowly, looked across the street, didn't see anything that alarmed him. "So?"

"The roof, Marion. Look at the roof."

All he could see was a target scope and the muzzle of Bubba's rifle. Big target scope, though. The only way to miss with a scope that big would be in the event of an instant solar eclipse. Even then, you'd have to be lucky.

I said, "We're all in this together, Marion. If I nod, you go first."

Socia said, "I'll take your girlfriend with me. Believe it."

I shrugged. "She ain't my girlfriend."

Socia said, "Like you don't care, Kenzie. Try that shit on someone who—"

I said, "Look, Marion, you're probably not used to this, but what you got here is a no-win situation and not much time to think about it." I looked at Lollipop. I couldn't see his eyes, but drops of sweat were doing relay races down his forehead. Not easy holding a gun steady all this time. I looked back at Socia. "The guy on the roof, he might just get ideas of his own real soon. Figure he can pull the trigger fast, twice"—I glanced at Lollipop—"and take the two of you out before you get a shot off. He might decide to do that on his own, before I nod. Before I do anything. He's been known to . . . act on his own inner voice before. He's not real stable. You listening, Marion?"

Socia was in his Place—wherever it is people like him go to hide their fear and emotion. He looked around slowly, up and down Washington Street, but never once at the roof. He took his time about it, then looked back at me. "What's my guarantee I put my gun back in my pocket?"

"Nothing," I said. "You want guarantees, go to Sears. I can guarantee you'll be dead if you don't." I looked at Lollipop. "Hell, I'm fixing to use this kid's gun on him as it is."

Lollipop said, "Sure you are, man," but his voice sounded hoarse, an untaken breath sitting atop his esophagus.

Socia looked up and down the street again, then shrugged. His hand came out from behind Angie's back. He held the gun where I could see it—a Bren nine millimeter—then stepped from behind Angie and put it inside his jacket. He said, "Lollipop, put it away."

The kid's name was actually "Lollipop." Patrick Kenzie, Psychic Detective. Lollipop's lip was curled upward toward his nose and his breathing was hard, showing me how tough he was, the gun still in my side, but the hammer down. Stupid. He looked ready to prove his manhood, not because he wasn't terrified, but because he was. Usually the way it works. But he was too busy watching my face, proving how much of a man he was. I pivoted slightly with my hip, no big movement, and the gun was suddenly pointed at air. I took the gun hand in mine, snapped my forehead off the bridge of his nose, cracking the Vuarnets in half, and shoved the gun into his stomach with his own hand. I pulled back the hammer. "You want to die?"

Socia said, "Kenzie, let the boy go."

Lollipop said, "I die if I have to," and bucked against my hand, a line of blood running thickly down his nose. He didn't look pleased at the prospect, but he didn't look unwilling.

I said, "Good. Because next time you pull a gun on me, Lollipop, that's exactly what'll happen." I eased the hammer back down and flicked the safety forward, then ripped the gun from his sweaty hand and put it in my pocket. I raised my hand and Bubba's rifle disappeared.

Lollipop was breathing hard and his eyes never left mine. I'd taken a lot more than his gun. I'd taken his pride, the only commodity worth a damn in his world, and he'd definitely kill me if there was a next time. I was getting real popular these days.

Socia said, "Lollipop, disappear. Tell everyone else to pull back too. I catch up with you later."

Lollipop gave me one last look and entered the stream of people heading down the street toward Jordan Marsh. He wasn't going anywhere. I knew that much. He and the rest of them, whoever and wherever they were, would stay in the crowd, keeping watch on their king. Socia was way too smart to leave himself unprotected. He said, "Come on, let's go sit—"

I said, "Let's sit down right over there."

He said, "I got a better place in mind."

Angie tilted her head in the direction of Barnes and Noble. "You don't have any choice, Socia."

We walked past Filene's and sat on a stone bench in the
small cement plaza next door. The scope appeared on the
roof again, tilted in our direction. Socia saw it too.

I said, "So, Marion, tell me why I shouldn't do you right
here, right now."

He smiled. "Shit. You already in enough trouble with
my people as it is. I'm like a god to these boys. You want
to fuck with that, be the target of a holy war, go on ahead."

I hate when people are right.

I said, "OK. Why don't you tell me why you're allowing
me to live?"

"I'm swell that way sometimes."

"Marion."

"No matter what, though," he said, "I might just kill
you for calling me 'Marion' all the time." He sat back on
the bench, one leg up there with him, his hands clasped
around the knee. A man out for some fresh air.

Angie said, "Well, what do you want from us, Socia?"

"Hell, little girl, you ain't even a part of this. We might
let you go on about your life after this is done." He pointed
a finger at me. "Him, though, he stick his nose in where
it don't belong, shoot one of my best men, fuck with all
this shit that ain't his to fuck with."

Angie said, "A common complaint among the married
men in our neighborhood." That Angie, what a hoot.

Socia said, "Joke all you want." He looked at me. "But
you know this ain't a joke, don't you? This is the end of
your life, Kenzie, and it's happening."

I wanted to say something funny, but nothing came to
mind. Nothing came even close. It was definitely happening.

Socia smiled. "Uh-huh. You know it. Only reason you're
alive right now is because Jenna gave you something, and
she told you something else. Now, where's it at?"

I said, "In a safe place."

"In a safe place," he repeated, rolling it off his tongue, slightly nasal inflection. His imitation of Whitespeak. "Yeah, well, whyn't you tell me where this safe place is," he said.

"Don't know it," I said. "Jenna never told me."

"Bullshit," he said and leaned toward me.

"I'm not busting my ass to convince you here, Marion. I'm just telling you so that when you toss my office and apartment and don't find anything, you won't be too surprised."

"Maybe I get some friends, we toss you."

"Your prerogative," I said. "But you and your friends better be real good."

"Why? You think you're real good, Kenzie?"

I nodded. "At this, yeah, I'm real good. And so's Angie, maybe better. And that guy on the roof, he's better than both of us."

"And he's not too fond of black people," Angie said.

"So, you two real proud of yourselves? Got yourselves a three-man KKK to keep the black man from your door?"

I said, "Oh, please, Socia, this ain't color. You're a fucking criminal. You're a douche bag who uses kids to do his dirty work. Black or white, that wouldn't change. And if you try and stop me on this, chances are you'll succeed and I'll die. But you won't stop him." Socia looked up at the roof. "He'll come at you and your whole gang and take you all out and probably half the 'Bury with you. He has about as much conscience as you and even less of a sense of public relations."

Socia laughed. "You trying to scare me?"

I shook my head. "You don't scare, Marion. People like you never do. But you do die. And if I die, so do you. Simple fact."

He sat back on the bench again. Crowds passed us in a steady stream and Bubba's target scope never moved. Socia tilted his head forward again. "All right, Kenzie. We'll give you this round. But, either way, don't matter what, you'll pay up for Curtis.''

I shrugged, a heavy weight behind my eyes.

''You got twenty-four hours to find what we're both looking for. If I find it before you, or you find it and don't get it right over to me, your life won't be worth piss.''

''Neither will yours.''

He stood up. ''Lotta people tried to kill me over the years, white boy. No one figured a way to do it right yet. Either way, that's the workings of the world.''

He walked off into the crowd, the big scope on the roof following him every inch of the way.

21

Bubba met us at the parking garage on Bromfield Street where Angie had parked the Vobeast. He was standing out front as we came up the street, chewing a wad of gum the size of a chicken, blowing bubbles big enough to drive passersby to the curb. He said, "Hey," as we approached, then started on a fresh bubble. A verbal treasure trove, our Bubba.

"Hey," Angie said in a deep baritone that matched his own. She slid her arm around his waist and squeezed. "My God, Bubba, is that a Russian assault rifle under your coat or are you just happy to see me?"

Bubba blushed and his chubby face bloomed for a moment like a cherubic schoolboy. A schoolboy who would put nitro in the toilets, but just the same. He said, "Get her off me, Kenzie."

Angie raised her head and chewed on his earlobe. "Bubba, you're all the man I need."

He giggled. This psychopathic behemoth with a bad attitude and he giggled and pushed her away gently. He looked sort of like the Cowardly Lion when he did it, and I waited for him to say, "Aww g'won." Instead he said, "Cut it out, you tramp," and then checked to see if she was offended.

She caught the look of mortification on his face and it was her turn to giggle, hand over her mouth.

That Bubba. Such a lovable sociopath.

We headed up the garage ramp and I said, "Bubba, you

)

going to be able to stick around for a while, keep a watch on us mere mortals?''

''Course I am, man. I'm there. The whole ride.'' He reached out and punched my arm playfully. All the feeling drained out of it and it would be a good ten minutes, maybe more, before it came back. Still, it was better than an angry Bubba punch. I'd taken one of those a few years ago—the only time I was ever stupid enough to argue with him—and after I came to, it took a week for my head to stop echoing.

We reached the car and climbed in. As we were leaving the garage, Bubba said, ''So, we gonna blow these homeboys back to Africa or what?''

Angie said, ''Now, Bubba . . .''

I knew better than to try and enlighten Bubba on racial matters. I said, ''I don't think it'll be necessary.''

He said, ''Shit,'' and sat back.

Poor Bubba. All dressed up and no one to shoot.

We dropped Bubba off at the playground near his home. He walked up the cement steps and trudged past the jungle gym, kicked a beer bottle out of his way, his shoulders hunched up to his ears. He kicked another bottle and it spun off a picnic table and shattered against the fence. Some of the punks hanging out by the picnic table looked away. No one wanted to catch his eye by mistake. He didn't notice them though. He just kept walking to the fence at the back of the playground, found the jagged hole there and pushed through it. He walked through some weeds and disappeared around the corner of the abandoned factory where he lives.

He has a bare mattress tossed down in the middle of the third floor, a couple of cartons of Jack Daniels, and a stereo that plays nothing but his collection of Aerosmith recordings. The second floor is where he keeps his arsenal and two pit bulls named Belker and Sergeant Esterhaus. A rottweiler named Steve prowls the front yard. If all this *and* Bubba isn't enough to deter trespassers or government of-

ficials, almost every other floorboard in the place is booby-
trapped. Only Bubba knows the right ones to step on. Some
walking suicide once tried to get to Bubba's stash by forcing him to lead him there at gunpoint. Every other month
or so, for about a year after that, pieces of the guy were
popping up all over the city.

Angie said, "If Bubba could have been born in another
time, like say the Bronze Age, he would have been all set."

I looked at the lonely hole in the fence. "Least he would
have had someone who shares his sensibilities."

We drove back to the office, and inside, began kicking
around Jenna's possible hiding places.

"The room above the bar?"

I shook my head. "If she had, she'd have never left them
behind when we came and got her. Place didn't look very
burglar proof to me."

She nodded. "OK. Where else?"

"Not the safety-deposit box. Devin wouldn't lie about
that. Simone's?"

She shook her head. "You're the first person she showed
anything to, right?"

"I think we're working under that assumption, yeah."

"So, that means you're the first person she trusted. She
probably figured Simone's view of Socia was too naive.
And she was right, I'd say."

I said, "If they were in her apartment in Mattapan,
someone would have them by now and there'd be no reason
for any of this."

"So, what's that leave?"

We spent a good ten minutes not coming up with an
answer to that one.

"Shit!" Angie said at the end of those ten minutes.

"Apt," I said. "Not too helpful though."

She lit a cigarette, placed her feet up on the desk, and
stared at the ceiling. More Sam Spade than I'd ever be. She
said, "What do we know about Jenna?"

"She's dead."

She nodded. Softly she said, "Besides that."

"We know she was married to Socia. Common-law or legal, I don't know, but married."

"And had his child. Roland."

"And has three sisters from Alabama."

She sat up in her chair, her feet banging off the floor. "Alabama," she said. "She sent it down to Alabama."

I thought about it. How well did Jenna know these sisters anymore? How much could she trust them? Hell, how much could she trust the mail? This was her chance to be needed, to get a little "justice." To do a little of what people had been doing to her all her life. Would she risk that by putting the major proponent of her vengeance in transit?

"I don't think so," I said.

Angie said, "Why not?" She said it sharply. Her idea—she wasn't going to just let go of it.

I explained my reasoning.

"Maybe," she said, her voice slightly deflated. "Let's keep it on the burner though."

"Agreed." It wasn't a bad idea, and if it came to it, we'd follow it down, but it didn't quite *fit*.

It goes like this a lot. We sit around the office and bounce ideas off each other and wait for divine intervention. When that doesn't come, we chase down each possibility, and usually—not always, but usually—we end up tripping over something that should have been obvious from the beginning.

I said, "We know she had trouble with creditors a few years back."

Angie said, "Yeah. So?"

"I'm brainstorming here. I never promised pearls of wisdom."

She frowned. "She has no record, right?"

"Except for a bunch of parking tickets."

Angie flicked her cigarette out the window.

I started thinking about the beers in my apartment. Heard them calling me, asking for company.

Angie said, "Well, if she had all those parking tickets . . ."

We looked at each other and said it together: "Where's
the car?"

22

We called George Higby at the Registry of Motor Vehicles. It took us fifteen tries to get past the busy signal, and then, once we did, a recorded voice told us that all the lines were busy. Our call would be taken in the order it was received and please stay on the line. I hadn't been planning on doing much till the end of the month anyway, so I cradled the phone against my neck and waited.

The silence ended after about fifteen minutes and the phone rang on the other end—once, twice, three times; four, five, six. A voice said, "Registry of Motor Vehicles."

I said, "George Higby, Vehicle Registration, please."

The voice hadn't heard me. It said, "You have reached the Registry of Motor Vehicles. Our business hours are nine to five P.M., Monday through Friday. If you need further assistance and have a Touch-Tone phone, please press 'one' now." A sonic beep went off in my ear about the same time I realized it was Sunday. If I pressed "one," I'd get another computer that would gladly connect me to another computer and by the time I got pissed off enough to throw my phone through the window, all the Registry computers would be having a good old yuck for themselves.

I just fucking love modern technology.

I hung up and said, "It's Sunday."

Angie looked at me. "Yes, it is. Tell me the date and you'll be my idol."

"Do we have George's home number around here?"

"Possibly. Would you like me to find out?"

"That'd be peachy."

She wheeled her chair over to the PC and entered her password. She waited a moment and her fingers began singing over the keys so fast the computer had a hard time keeping up. Served it right. Probably hung out with the Registry computers on its off days.

Angie said, "Got it."

"Give it to me, baby."

She didn't, but she gave me the number.

George Higby is one of those hapless souls who goes through life expecting the rest of the world to be as nice as he is. Since he gets out of bed each morning with the desire to make the world a better place, a slightly easier place to get along in—he doesn't understand that there are actually people who get up with the desire to make the rest of the world suffer. Even after his daughter eloped with a guitar player twice her age who left her strung out in a Reno motel room; even after she then ran into some especially nasty people and ended up working her sixteen-year-old body on the back streets of Vegas; even after Angie and I flew out there and took her away from these nasty people with the assistance of the Nevada State Police; even after this sweet apple of his eye blamed the mess she'd made completely on him; even after all this—George still meets the world with the nervous smile of someone who only knows how to be open and decent and prays that, maybe just once, the world might reward him. George is the sort of raw material out of which most organized religions create their foundations.

He answered the phone on the first ring. He always does. He said, "This is George Higby," and I half expected him to follow it with, "Want to be friends?"

"Hi, George, it's Patrick Kenzie."

"Patrick!" George said, and I have to admit that the enthusiasm in his voice made me happy to be me all of a sudden. I felt as if I'd been put on this earth for one reason:

to call George on July 2 and make his day. He said, "How are you?"

"I'm great, George. How about yourself?"

"Very good, Patrick. Very good. I can't complain."

George was the kind who never could.

I said, "George, I'm afraid this isn't a strictly social call," and realized with more than a small measure of guilt that I'd never made a "strictly social call" to George and probably never would.

"Well, no problem, Patrick," he said, his voice dropping an octave for a moment. "You're a busy man. What can I do for you?"

"How's Cindy?" I asked.

"You know kids today," he said. "At this point in her life, her father is hardly the most important thing to her. That will change, of course."

"Of course," I said.

"Got to let them grow up."

"Sure," I said.

"And then they come back to you."

"They do," I said. Sure they do.

"But enough about me," he said. "I saw you in the papers the other day. Are you all right?"

"Fine, George. The media blew it all out of proportion."

"They'll do that sometimes," he said. "But then, where would we be without them?"

I said, "The reason I called, George, I need a license number and I can't wait until tomorrow."

"You can't get it through the police?"

"No. I need to play this one out by myself for a little while longer before I take it to them."

"OK, Patrick," he said, thinking about it. "OK," he repeated, brightening a bit. "Yeah, we can do that. You'll have to give me ten minutes or so to access the computer down there. Is that all right? Can you wait that long?"

"You're doing me the favor, George. Take all the time

you need." I gave him Jenna's name, driver's license number, and address.

"OK. Fifteen minutes at most. I'll call you back."

"You have my number?"

"Of course," he said, as if we all keep the phone numbers of people we met twice two years ago.

"Thanks, George," I said and hung up before he could say, "No, thank *you.*"

We waited. Angie shot a Nerf ball through the hoop above the boom box, and I tossed it back to her each time. She's got a nice arc, but she doesn't use the backboard enough. She leaned back in the chair and sent one up in a high arc. Before the foam ball swished through the hoop she said, "We going to call Devin in on this one?"

I tossed the ball back to her. "Nope."

"Why not, exactly?" She put another one up and missed.

"Because we're not. Use the backboard a little more."

She tossed the ball up above her, bouncing it off the ceiling. "It's not standard procedure," she said in singsong.

"Standard procedure? What, we're the army now?"

"No," she said, the Nerf bouncing off her fingers, down her leg, and across the floor. She turned in her chair. "We're detectives who have a pretty good relationship with the police, and I'm wondering why we're risking that by not letting them in on evidence in a Murder One investigation."

"What evidence?" I leaned out of my chair and scooped up the ball.

"The picture of Socia and Paulson."

"Doesn't prove anything."

"That's for them to decide. Either way, it was the last thing the murder victim gave you before she was killed. That definitely makes it something they'd be interested in."

"So?"

"So, this should be a dual investigation is 'so.' We should be telling them we're going to look at Jenna's car. We should be asking them for the plate number, not having poor George break into the Registry computers.''

"And if they were to come across the evidence our clients hired us to find before we do?''

"Then, once they're finished with it, they hand it over to us.''

"Just like that?''

"Just like that.''

"And if it's incriminating? If it's against our clients' best interests to have the police see it, what then? How good is our business then? If Mulkern wanted to get the police to look for those 'documents' he would have. Instead, he hired us. We're not *law enforcement*, Ange, we're private investigators.''

"No shit, Sherlock. But—''

"But what? Where the hell's this coming from? You're talking like a novice.''

"I'm no fucking novice, Skid. I just think you should level with your partner about your motives.''

"My motives. And what are my motives, Ange?''

"You don't want the police to get their hands on this, not because you're afraid of what they'll do with it. You're afraid of what they won't do. You're afraid it might just be so bad, as bad as Jenna said, and someone in the State House will make a phone call and the evidence will disappear.''

I kneaded the foam ball in my hand. "You're suggesting my motives are contrary to the interests of our clients?''

"You're damn right I am. If these 'documents' are as bad as Jenna said, if they incriminate Paulson or Mulkern, what're you going to do then? Huh?''

"We'll have to see.''

"Bullshit we'll have to see. Bullshit. This job should have been over half an hour after we found Jenna in Wickham. But you wanted to play things out, be a goddamn social worker. We're private investigators. Remember? Not moralists. Our job is to turn over what we're hired to find to the people who hired us to find it. And if they cover it up, if they buy off the police, fine. Because we're out of it. We do our job and we get paid. And if—"

"Wait a minute—"

"—you don't do this, if you turn this into some sort of personal crusade to get back at your father through Mulkern, we can kiss this business and this partnership goodbye."

I sat forward, my face two feet from hers. I said, "My father? My fucking father? Where's he come into this?"

"He's been in this. He's Mulkern, he's Paulson, he's every politician you ever met who shakes your hand with one hand and stabs you in the back with the other. He's—"

"Don't you talk about my father, Angie."

"He's dead," she yelled. "Dead. And I'm real sorry to inform you but lung cancer took care of him before you got the chance to do it yourself."

I moved closer. "You my analyst now, Ange?" My face felt warm and the blood rippled through my forearms, tingling my fingers.

"No, I'm not your fucking analyst, Patrick, and why don't you back the fuck up?"

I didn't move. The trip switch on my temper had been kicked over and I stared into her eyes. They were zipping from side to side with bolts of anger. I said, "No, Ange, you back the fuck up, and take your pop psychology degree and your sentiments about my father with you. And maybe I won't try and analyze your relationship with that Husband of the Year who treats you so well."

The phone rang.

Neither of us moved. Neither of us looked at it. Neither of us softened or backed up.

Two more rings.

"Patrick."

"What?"

Another ring.

"That's probably George."

I felt my jaw unclench a bit, and I turned and picked up the phone. "Patrick Kenzie."

"Hi, Patrick. It's George."

"Georgie," I said, working some false excitement through my vocal cords.

"Do you have a pencil?"

"Detectives always have pencils, George."

"Ha. Of course. Jenna Angeline's car is a nineteen seventy-nine Chevy Malibu. Light blue. License number DRW-four seven nine. There's a boot order in effect on it as of June third."

I felt the rush building from the pit of my stomach, the blood pounding into my heart from open valves. "A boot order?"

"Yes," George said. "The Denver boot. Ms. Angeline didn't like paying her parking tickets it seems."

The Denver boot. The yellow, immovable tire lock. The blue Malibu Jerome's friends had been sitting on when I went to Jenna's place. Parked in front of the house. Not going anywhere anytime soon.

I said, "George, you are the greatest. Swear to God."

"I helped?"

"Damn right you helped."

"Hey, how about having a beer together sometime soon?"

I looked at Angie. She was peering at something on her lap, her hair covering her face, but the anger hung in the room like exhaust fumes. I said, "I'd really like that, George. Give me a call at the end of next week? I should have wrapped this up by then." Or died trying.

"You got it," he said. "You got it."

"Take care, George."

I hung up and looked at my partner. She was doing the pencil against her tooth thing again, looking at me, her eyes flat and impersonal. Her voice was pretty much the same. "I was out of line."

"Maybe not. Maybe I'm just not ready to probe that part of my psyche yet."

"Maybe you'll never be."

"Maybe," I said. "What about you?"

"And the Asshole, as you so kindly refer to him?"

"That guy, yeah."

"Things are coming," she said. "They're coming."

"What do you want to do about the case?"

She shrugged. "You know what I want to do. But, then, I'm not the one who had to watch Jenna die, so I'll let you call it. Just remember, you owe me one."

I nodded. I held out my hand. "Pals?"

She grimaced and reached across and slapped my palm. "When weren't we?"

"About five minutes ago." I laughed.

She chuckled. "Oh, yeah."

We parked at the top of the hill, looking down on Jenna's three-decker and the blue Malibu parked out front. The yellow boot was apparent even in the fading light. Bostonians get parking tickets and traffic citations with a consistency most pro sports teams would envy. They also tend to wait until their driver's licenses are about to be renewed before paying attention to them. City officials realized this after a while, took a look at their dwindling coffers, wondered where the graft necessary to put their children through college and their asses on the Vineyard was going to come from, and brought in the Denver boot. It comes, obviously, from Denver, and it clamps around your tire, and that car ain't going anywhere until all those parking fines are paid in full. Tampering with one is a serious offense, punishable by prison and/or a stiff fine. This doesn't deter anyone half as much as the fact that the damn things are almost as hard to remove as an old chastity belt. A friend of mine did it once, with a ballpeen hammer, a chisel, and a whack in just the right place. But the boot must have been defective, because he could never repeat the feat. Depressed the hell out of him too; he could have been set for life—boot destroyer for hire. Making more money than Michael Jackson.

If Jenna had hidden something in that car, it would make a perverse bit of sense. Sure, a car sitting untended in Boston for more than four or five minutes usually loses its stereo and speakers, and more often than not, the rest of it as well. But the chopping block market for fifteen-year-old Chevies ain't what it used to be, and no self-respecting car thief is going to waste precious time screwing around with the boot. So, unless she hid it in her stereo, there was a good chance it was still there. If she'd hidden anything there in the first place. Big if.

We sat and watched the car, waiting for darkness to fall. The sun had set but the sky still held its warmth, a canvas of beige streaked with wisps of orange. Somewhere behind or in front of us—in a tree, on a roof, in a bush, at one with the natural urban world—Bubba lurked in wait, his eyes as constant and emotionless as T. J. Eckleburg's.

We had no music going, because the Vobeast has no radio, and it was damn near killing me. God only knows how people kept their sanity before rock and roll. I considered what Angie had said about my motives, about my father, about taking my anger out on Mulkern and his cronies, anger at a world that had settled the score with my father before I had a chance to. If she was wrong, we'd find out when we finally got our hands on the evidence and I turned it over for another signed check, including the bonus. If she was right, we'd find out about that too. Either way, I didn't like thinking about it.

There was, come to think about it, way too much happening lately that required pauses for introspection. I've never made any bones about it—I love investigating things, as long as I'm not one of them. But suddenly, there were all these hot-blooded confrontations with people in my life—Richie, Mulkern, Angie. All of a sudden I was being asked to reevaluate myself in terms of racism, politics, and the Hero. My three least favorite subjects. Much more introspection and I'd end up growing a long white beard, maybe wearing a white smock, sipping a glass of hemlock while I read *The Crito*. Maybe I'd move to Tibet, climb a mountain with the Dalai Lama or head to Paris and wear nothing but black, grow myself a keen goatee and talk about jazz all the time.

Or maybe I'd do what I always do—hang out and see what develops. Fatalist to the core.

Angie said, "What do you think?"

The sky was turning to ink, and there wasn't a working streetlight for miles. I said, "Time for a little B and E."

There was no one on the stoops as we came down the hill, but that wouldn't last much longer on a humid Sunday night. This wasn't the type of neighborhood where people took off to the Cape for the Fourth of July. We had to get in, find whatever it was we were looking for, and get out. People who don't have much usually protect what they've got in lethal ways. Whether the trigger's pulled by a Bobby Royce or a little old lady, the damage can often be damn similar.

Angie pulled the slim jim from her jacket as we approached the car, and before you could say "grand theft auto," she'd slid it down beside the window and popped the lock. I had no idea what sort of house Jenna had kept— the only time I'd seen it someone had gone through it like a storm front—but she kept a pristine car. Angie took the backseat, reaching down under the seat and behind it, pulling up the mats, looking for telltale tears in the carpet.

I did pretty much the same in the front seat. I pulled open the ashtray, found it brimming with Marlboro butts, closed it. I took what looked like warranties and repair records and an owner's manual from the glove compartment, but I stuffed it all in the plastic bag I'd brought anyway. Easier to check through it all when we got out of here. I reached under the dashboard, ran my hand around, didn't find anything taped there. I checked the door panels for rips or cuts in the seams. Nada. I took a screwdriver to the running panel on the passenger side; maybe Jenna'd seen *The French Connection.* I opened it: Maybe she hadn't.

Angie was doing the same to the panel on the driver's side. When she removed it, she didn't shout "Eureka," so I figured she hadn't found any more than I had. We were steadily getting nowhere when someone said, "Ain't they pretty?"

I sat up in the seat, my hand on my gun, and saw the girl who'd been sitting on the steps the last time I'd been here. Jerome was standing beside her and they were holding hands. Jerome said, "You meet Roland yet?"

I sat up in the seat. "Haven't had the pleasure."

Jerome looked at Angie, kept looking, not wide-eyed, just interested. He said, "The fuck you doing in his mother's car, man?"

"Working."

His girlfriend lit a cigarette. She took a drag, blew the smoke in my direction. A thick ring of red lipstick looped around the white filter. She said, "He's the man was there when Jenna got herself killed by Curtis."

Jerome said, "I know that, Sheila. Damn." He looked at me. "You're a detective, right?"

I looked at Sheila's cigarette again. Something about it annoyed me, but I couldn't figure out what yet. I said, "Yeah, Jerome. Got a badge and everything."

Jerome said, "Beats working for a living."

Sheila took another hit off her cigarette, placed another red ring slightly above the first.

Angie sat up in the seat and lit one too. Carcinogen city.

I looked at Sheila, then at Angie. I said, "Ange."

"Yeah?"

"Did Jenna wear lipstick?"

Jerome was watching us with a cocked eyebrow, his arms folded across his chest. Angie thought about it. She took a few more drags off her cigarette, blew the smoke out in slow streams. She said, "Yeah. Come to think of it. It was subtle, a light pink, but yeah."

I flipped open the car ashtray. "What kind of cigarettes she smoke, you remember?"

"Lights, I think. Or Vantage, maybe. Definitely something with a white filter."

"But she'd just started again," I said, remembering Jenna's claim that she hadn't smoked in ten years until the events of the past few weeks caused her to start back up.

The cigarettes in the ashtray had cork filters and no lipstick rings on them. I yanked the ashtray out, swung my legs out of the car. "Step back for a sec' please, Jerome."

"Yassuh, bawse, whatever you say."

"I said 'please,' Jerome."

Jerome and Sheila took two steps back. I dumped the ashtray on the sidewalk. Jerome said, "Hey, man, some of us got to live here."

Metal gleamed up through the pile of ash. I reached down, scattered the ash, and picked up a key. I said, "We got what we came for."

Angie said, "Neato," and got out of the car.

Jerome said, "Congratulations. Now, pick that shit back up, man."

I held the ashtray by the curb and brushed everything back into it. I put it on the seat and got out of the car. I said, "You're all right, Jerome."

Jerome said, "Thanks. Just knowing I please white folks like yourself makes me a complete man."

I smiled and we walked back up the hill.

It was a locker key, number 506. Could have belonged to a locker at Logan Airport or the Greyhound Station in Park Square or the Amtrak Terminal at South Station. Or any number of bus depots in Springfield or Lowell or New Hampshire or Connecticut or Maine or God knew where else.

Angie said, "So, what do you want to do? Check them all?"

"Don't have much choice."

"That's a lot of places."

"Look on the bright side."

"Which is?"

"Think of all the overtime we can pay ourselves."

She hit me, but not as hard as I thought she would.

23

We decided we'd start in the morning. There were a lot of lockers in the state and we'd need all the energy we had; right now, we were running on fumes. Angie went home and Bubba followed. I slept in the office because it was harder to approach than my apartment; footsteps in the empty church would echo like cannon shots.

While I slept, a knot the size of a seashell worked its way into my neck, and my legs cramped up where they bent on the cot against the wall.

And sometime while I slept, war broke out.

Curtis Moore was the first to fall in the line of duty. Shortly after midnight a fire broke out at the nurse's desk in the prison hospital ward. The two cops on duty by Curtis's bed got up to take a look. It wasn't much of a fire—a rag doused in rubbing alcohol tossed in a trash can, a match thrown in for combustion. The two cops and the nurse found a fire extinguisher, doused it, and then it didn't take the cops too long to figure out a possible motive behind it. By the time they burst back in the room, Curtis had a hole the size of a hand in his throat and the initials J. A. carved into his forehead.

Three members of the Raven Saints met their blaze of glory next. Coming back from a late game at Fenway Park and a little subway wilding for a nightcap, they stepped out of Ruggles Station and had a one-sided conversation with an AK-47 pointed from a car. One of them, a sixteen-year-old named Gerard Mullins, took a burst to his upper thighs and abdomen, but didn't die. He played possum in the shadows until the car drove away, and then he started crawling toward Columbus Avenue. He was halfway between the subway station and the corner when they came back and stitched a line from just below his ear to just above his ankle.

Socia was stepping out of a bar on South Huntington, two soldiers a few feet behind him, when James Tyrone, a fifteen-year-old member of the Angel Avengers, stepped from behind a van with a .45 aimed at Socia's nose. He pulled the trigger and the gun jammed, and by the time Socia's bodyguards stopped firing, he was in the middle of South Huntington turning the yellow divider line a dark red.

Three Avengers went down in Franklin Park next. Then, two more Saints caught it while sitting on a stoop in Intervale. Another cycle of retaliation followed that one, and by the time the sun came up, the worst night in Boston gang history leveled out at twenty-six wounded, twelve dead.

My phone started ringing at eight. I grabbed it somewhere around the fourth ring. I said, "What?"

Devin said, "You heard?"

I said, "No," and tried to go back to bed.

"Boston's favorite father-and-son team just went to war."

My head dropped off the side of the cot. "Oh, no."

"Oh, yes." He gave me the rundown.

"Twelve dead?" I said. "Jesus." Maybe par for the course in New York, but here it was astronomical.

"Twelve at the moment," he said. "Probably five or six on the critical list who won't make Independence Day. It's a wonderful life, isn't it?"

"Why're you calling me at eight in the morning with this, Dev?"

"Because I want you down here in an hour."

"Me? Why?"

"Because you were the last person to talk to Jenna Angeline, and someone just happened to drill her initials onto Curtis Moore's head. Because you met with Socia yesterday and didn't tell me. Because word around town is you got something both Socia and Roland are willing to kill for, and I'm tired of waiting for you to tell me what that is out of the goodness of your heart. You, Kenzie, because lying is second nature to you, but it's harder to do in an interrogation room. So, get your ass down here and bring your partner with you."

"I think I'll bring Cheswick Hartman with me too."

"Go right ahead, Patrick. And that'll please me so much, I'll press obstruction charges against you and toss you in jail for a night. By the time Cheswick gets you out, all the fuckers we arrested last night from the Saints and Avengers ought to know your ass real intimately."

"I'll be there in an hour," I said.

"Fifty minutes," he said. "The clock started ticking when you picked up the phone." He hung up.

I called Angie, told her I'd be ready in twenty minutes. I didn't call Cheswick.

I called Richie at home but he was already at work. I tried him there.

"How much you know?" he asked.

"Nothing more than you guys."

"Bullshit. Your name keeps coming up in this one, Patrick. And weird shit's going down at the State House."

I was working my way into a shirt, but I stopped, my right arm sticking out, frozen, like it was in a cast. I said, "What weird shit?"

"The street terrorism bill."

"What about it?"

"It was supposed to go to floor today. Early. So everyone could beat the traffic up to the Cape for the Fourth."

"And?"

"And no one is there. The State House is empty. Twelve kids died last night in gang violence and the next morning, when a bill that's allegedly going to start curbing all that shit is supposed to go to floor, suddenly no one's interested anymore.''

"I got to go," I said.

I could have airmailed the phone to Rhode Island and still heard his voice. "What the fuck do you know?''

"Nada. Got to run.''

"No more favors, Patrick. No more.''

"Love it when you scold me." I hung up.

I was waiting in front of the church when Angie pulled up in that brown thing she calls a car. On weekends and holidays, Phil has no need for it; he stocks up on Budweiser and settles into the Barcalounger and watches whatever's on TV. Who needs a car when Gilligan still hasn't gotten off the island? Angie drives it whenever she can so she can listen to *her* tapes; she also claims I'm a lousy driver behind the wheel of the Vobeast because I don't care what happens to it. This isn't entirely true; I would care if something happened to it and I'd like some money from the insurance company if it ever did.

The ride from Angie's to Berkeley Street took less than ten minutes. The city was empty. Those who had gone to the Cape had left Thursday or Friday. Those who were going to the Esplanade for tomorrow's concert and fireworks hadn't started camping out yet. Everyone had taken the day off. During the ride, we saw something few Bostonians ever see—empty parking spaces. I kept asking her to stop at each one and back in and out again, just to see what it felt like.

Upper Berkeley, by Police Headquarters, was different. The block was cordoned off with sawhorses. A beefy patrolman waved us around the block. We could see vans with satellite dishes on top, cables running like overweight pythons across the street, white TV trucks parked on the sidewalk, and the black Crown Victorias of the upper police brass parked three-deep by the curb.

We swung over to St. James and parked easily enough, then walked back to the rear door of the building. A young black cop stood in front of the door, hands crossed behind his back, legs spread in military stance. He glanced at us. "Press goes through the front door."

"We're not press." We identified ourselves. "We have an appointment with Detective Amronklin."

The cop nodded. "Go up these stairs. Fifth floor, take a right. You'll see him."

We did. He was sitting on a table at the end of a long corridor with his partner, Oscar Lee. Oscar is big and black and just as mean as Devin. He talks a little less but drinks just as much. They've been partners so long they even got their respective divorces on the same day. Each has taken a bullet for the other, and penetrating just the surface of their relationship would be as easy as digging through cinder block with a plastic spoon. They noticed us at the same time, looked up, and held their tired eyes on us as we walked down the corridor toward them. They both looked like shit, tired and cranky, ready to stomp on anyone who didn't give them what they wanted. They both had splotches of blood on their shirts and coffee cups in their hands.

We entered the office and I said, "Hey."

They nodded. If they became more similar they'd be joined at the hip.

Oscar said, "Have a seat, folks."

There was a scarred card table in the middle of the room with a telephone and a tape recorder on it. We took seats on the side closest to the wall, and Devin sat down on my right, beside the phone, while Oscar sat to Angie's left, beside the tape recorder. Devin lit a cigarette and Oscar turned on the tape recorder. A voice said: "Recording copied August the sixth, nineteen ninety-three. Listed under bar code number 5756798. Evidence room, Boston police headquarters, precinct nine, 154 Berkeley Street."

Devin said, "Turn it up a bit."

Oscar did, and there were fifteen or twenty seconds of dead air, then the sound of a low rumble and lots of metal on metal sounds, as if a dinner party of ten were all rubbing their knives and forks together. Water dripped somewhere in there too. A voice said, "Cut him again."

Devin looked at me.

The voice sounded like Socia's.

Another voice: "Where?"

Socia: "Fuck do I care? Be inventive. That knee looks sensitive."

There was a moment when the only sound was the dripping water, then someone screamed, long and loud and shrill.

Socia laughed. "I'm doing one of your eyes next, so why don't you tell me, get it over with."

The other voice: "Get it over with. He ain't fucking with you, Anton."

"I ain't fucking with you, Anton. You know that."

A low, wheezing sound. Weeping.

Socia: "Too many tears coming out of that eye. Take it out."

I sat up in my chair.

The other voice said, "What?"

Socia: "I stutter? Take it out."

There was a soft, unpleasant sound, the sound a shoe makes when it steps into slush.

And then the scream. Impossibly high-pitched, a mixture of excruciating pain and horrified disbelief.

Socia: "It's on the floor in front of you, Anton. Give me the name, fuck. Who turned you?"

The screaming hadn't subsided yet. It rang clear and hard and steady.

"Who turned you? Stop screaming." A harsh flesh-on-flesh sound. The screaming blew up to a louder pitch.

"Who fucking turned you?"

The screaming was defiant now, an angry howl.

"Who fu— Fuck it. Rip out the other one. No, not with that. Get a fucking spoon, man."

There was a sound of soft footsteps, squeaking a bit as they walked away from wherever the microphone was.

The screaming turned into a whimper.

Socia, in a soft whisper: "Who turned you, Anton? It'll be over quick, soon as you tell me."

The whimper screeched something unintelligible.

Socia said, "I promise. It'll all be over, soon as you tell me. You'll die quick and painless."

A torn sob, ragged breathing, gasping for air, a steady weeping that lasted for over a minute.

"Come on now. Tell me."

From the sob came: "Na. Na I—"

"Hand me that fucking spoon."

"Devin. The cop! Devin!" It sounded like the words had been pushed out of the body through a torn hole.

Devin reached over and shut off the tape recorder. I realized I was sitting rigid in my chair, half out of it, my spine bowed. I looked at Angie. Her skin was white, her fists tight against the arms of the chair.

Oscar looked bored, staring up at the ceiling. He said, "Anton Meriweather. Sixteen years old. Devin and me turned him in December and he informed on Socia. He was a soldier with the Saints. Oh yeah, he's dead."

I said, "You have this tape. Why's Socia still walking around?"

Devin said, "You ever see a jury try to make a decision on a voice ID? You ever seen how many people a defense attorney will find who sound just like the guy on that tape? Did you hear anyone call Socia by name on that tape?"

I shook my head.

"I just want you to know who you're dealing with here, kids. After Anton gave my name up, they worked on him for another ninety minutes. Ninety minutes. Long time to be alive with your eye ripped out. When we found him, three days later, I didn't recognize him. Neither did his mother. We had to do a dental just to be sure it was Anton.''

Angie cleared her throat. "How'd you get that recording?''

Oscar said, "Anton was wearing it. Between his legs. He knew he had the whole thing on tape, all he had to do was say Socia's name, and his brain froze up and he forgot. Pain'll do that.'' He looked at Devin, then back at me. "Mr. Kenzie, I ain't going to try and turn this into good cop/bad cop, but Devin's a friend of yours, and I'm not. I liked Anton a whole hell of a lot though. So I want to know what you know about the shit going on and I want to know now. You figure a way to do that without compromising your clients, that's OK with me. But if you can't figure a way, you're going to tell me anyway. 'Cause we're tired of picking bodies up off the street.''

I believed him. "Ask the questions.''

Devin said, "What'd you and Socia talk about yesterday?''

"He thinks I have incriminating evidence on him, things Jenna Angeline gave me. He wants to trade me my life for the evidence. I told him if I died, so did he.''

"Compliments of Bubba Rogowski,'' Oscar said.

I raised my eyebrows slightly, then nodded.

Devin said, "What kind of evidence do you have against Socia?''

"Nothing—''

"Bullshit,'' Oscar said.

"True shit. I don't have anything that could get Socia convicted of so much as jaywalking.''

Angie said, "Jenna Angeline promised us there were things that *she* had access to, but she died before she could tell us what or where they were.''

"Word on the street is Jenna gave you something right before Curtis Moore popped her,'' Oscar said.

I looked at Angie and she nodded. I reached into my

pocket, pulled out another Xerox of the photo. I passed it to Devin. "That's what she gave me."

Devin looked at it, looked hard at Paulson, flipped it to Oscar. "Where's the rest of it?"

"That's all there is."

Oscar looked at it, looked at Devin. He nodded, looked at me. "You're fucking with the wrong people," he said. "We will throw your tight ass in jail."

"That's all I got."

He slammed a bear's hand down on the table. "Where's the original? Where are the others?"

"I don't know where the others are, and I have the original," I said. "And I'm not giving it up. Throw me in jail. Toss me in a cell with a couple of Saints. Whatever. I don't care. Because I got a lot better chance staying alive in that hole with that picture hidden somewhere than I do out on the street without it."

"You don't think we can protect you?" Devin said.

"No, guys, I don't think you can protect me. I don't have anything on Socia, but he thinks I do. As long as he thinks that, I breathe. Soon as he realizes I'm bluffing, he plays catch-up for Curtis Moore and I end up like Anton." I thought of Anton and felt nauseous.

Oscar said, "Socia's got too much on his slate right now to worry about you."

"That's supposed to make me feel better? What, I got a week or so of happiness before he cleans his slate and remembers me? No way. You want to hear what I think about this, or you want to keep chasing your tails around this point?"

They looked at each other, communicating the way only guys like them can. Devin said, "All right. Tell us what you think's going on."

"Between Socia and Roland—I don't have a clue. Honestly." I picked the photocopy off the table, held it up so they could see it. I said, "But I do know the street terrorism bill was supposed to go before the state senate this morning.''

"So?"

"So it didn't. Today of all days, and they're all acting like suddenly the problem's disappeared.''

Devin looked at the photocopy, raised an eyebrow. He picked up the phone in front of him, punched a few numbers, waited. "Patch me through to Commander Willis, State House Police." He drummed his fingers on the table, looked at the photocopy. He reached out, took it out of my hands, placed it in front of him, looked at it some more. The rest of us had nothing better to do, so we watched him. "John? This is Devin Amronklin. . . . Yeah, I got my hands full. . . . Huh? . . . Yeah, I think there'll be more. Plenty more. . . . Look, John . . . I need to ask you something. Any pols come in today?" He listened. "Well, the Guv, of course. What else is he going to do? And . . . yeah, yeah. But what about that bill they were sup— Uh-huh . . . And who was that? . . . Sure, take your time." He let the phone drop to his neck and drummed his fingers some more. He brought it up to his ear. "Yeah, I'm here. . . . OK, John. Thanks a lot. . . . No, nothing, really. Just curious. Thanks again." He looked at the three of us. "On Friday, someone moved that they all enjoy the long weekend like everyone else.''

"Who was that someone?" Angie asked.

Devin tapped the photocopy. "A Senator Brian Paulson," he said. "Mean anything to you?"

I stared back at him.

"No cameras or tape recorders in the walls," he said.

I glanced at the photocopy. "I can't reveal the names of my clients.''

Devin nodded. Oscar smiled. They liked that. I'd just told them exactly what they wanted to know. Devin said, "This is big, isn't it?"

I shrugged. Another confirmation.

Devin looked at Oscar. "You got anything else?"

Oscar shook his head. His eyes were bright.

Devin said, "Let's walk them down. Sound good to you, Detective Lee?"

When we stepped out the back door, Oscar told the young cop to go get a cup of coffee. He shook Angie's hand, then mine. He said, "Depending how far this goes, we could lose our badges on this one."

I said, "I know."

Devin looked around the back of the building. "Bucking city hall's one thing, the State House is something else entirely."

I nodded.

Oscar said, "Vine," and looked at Devin.

Devin sighed. "No shit."

Angie said, "Vine?"

Oscar said, "Chris Vine. Vice cop a few years back. Swore he had evidence on a senator, hinted about it going higher than that."

I said, "What happened?"

Devin said, "Someone found two kilos of heroin in his locker."

"Box of hypodermics too," Oscar said.

Devin nodded. "Couple weeks later, Vine ate his gun."

Oscar gave Devin another look. There was something alien in both their eyes. It might have been fear. Oscar said, "You be careful, the both of you. We'll contact you."

"Agreed."

Devin said, "If you're still tight with Richie Colgan, I'd say now might be a good time to use him."

"Not quite yet."

Oscar and Devin looked at each other again, let out big bursts of breath. Oscar looked up at the sky. "Going to be a serious shitstorm any day now."

Angie said, "And the four of us without umbrellas."

We all got a chuckle out of that. A short one though. Laughter at a wake.

24

We took Boylston down to Arlington and came back around the block to the Greyhound Station. We waded through a listless sea of hookers, pimps, grifters, and assorted terminal cases before we found the dark green metal checkerboard of lockers. Number 506 was at the top of its row and I had to reach up a bit to try the key.

It didn't fit. One down.

We tried a couple of smaller places. Nothing.

We drove out to the airport. Logan Airport has five terminals, lettered A through E. A had no 506. B terminal had no lockers. C had no 506 in Arrivals. We walked down to Departures. Like the rest of the city, it was a ghost town, the waxed floor still slick and unscuffed, reflecting the bright fluorescents overhead. We found 506, took a deep breath, let it out when the key didn't fit.

Same thing in D and E.

We tried some places in East Boston, Chelsea, Revere—nada.

We stopped at a sandwich shop in Everett and took a seat by the window. The morning had died and the sky had hardened to a damp newspaper gray. It didn't seem particularly cloudy, just resolutely sunless. A red Mustang pulled in across the street and the driver looked in the record store in front of him, probably waiting on a friend.

Angie said, "You think he's the only one?"

I shook my head, swallowed a bite of roast beef. "He's the point man."

We both looked across at him. He was parked a good forty yards back, a thin black head shaven till it gleamed. No sunglasses this time. Probably didn't want anything obstructing his vision when he took a shot at me.

"Where do you think Bubba is?" I said.

"If we could see him, he wouldn't be doing his job."

I nodded. "Still, be nice if he fired a flare every now and then, if only for my peace of mind."

"He *is* your peace of mind, Skid."

Hard to argue with the truth.

We led the Mustang back with us through Somerville and up onto 93, heading into the city. We got off at South Station and parked on Summer Street. The Mustang cruised past, following the traffic past the post office. He turned right, and we got out and walked up to the main entrance.

South Station used to look like a great location for a gangster movie. It's huge, with enormous cathedral ceilings and parquet marble floors that seem to run on into infinity. Used to be all this space was interrupted only by a wooden newsstand, a shoeshine booth, and a few dark mahogany circular benches, expansive and double-tiered like human water fountains. It was the perfect place to wear powder-blue wool suits and matching fedoras, sit and watch people from behind a newspaper. Then came hard times, forgotten times, and the marble grew brown and scuffed, the newsstand needed a paint job or a wrecking ball, and the shoeshine stand disappeared entirely. Then, a few years ago, refurbishment. Now there's a hot dog/pizza place with a yellow neon sign, an Au Bon Pain with Cinzano umbrellas over black wrought-iron tables, and a new newsstand that looks like a cross between a fern bar and a bookstore. The whole place looks smaller, the moody dark hues that pooled in shadows around shafts of faded sunlight have been replaced with glaring bright lights and an ambience of faked happiness. Spend all the money you want on ambience, it still won't change the fact that a train station is a place where people wait, usually without much glee, for a train to come take them away.

The lockers are in the back near the rest rooms. As we headed toward them, an old guy with stiff white hair and a PA system for vocal cords announced: "The Ambassador bound for Providence, Hartford, New Haven, and New York City, now boarding on track thirty-two." If the little dink had had a megaphone I would have lost an ear.

We walked down a dark corridor and stepped into yesterday. No glaring fluorescents, no ferns, just marble and dim yellow lamps that were one step removed from candles. We searched the rows of lockers in the semidarkness, trying to make out the faded, stenciled brass numbers, until Angie said, "Here."

I patted my pockets. "You got the key, right?"

She looked at me. "Patrick."

"Where's the last place we used it?"

"Patrick," she said again, only this time her teeth were gritted.

I held it up. "God, you can't take a joke anymore."

She snatched the key from my hand, slipped it into the lock, and turned it.

I think she was more surprised than I was.

The bag inside was blue plastic. The word "Gap" was stenciled in white letters across the middle. Angie handed it to me. Light. We looked back in, felt around. Nothing more. Angie let the door clang behind us and I carried the bag in my left hand as we walked back down the corridor. A veritable spring to our steps. Payday.

Or Payback Day, depending on your perspective.

The bald kid who'd been driving the Mustang was coming across the terminal toward us fast. He saw us, surprised, and started to turn away. Then he noticed the bag. Real bright fucking move on my part, not putting it under my coat. Baldie raised his right hand over his head and his left dug under his warm-up jacket.

Two kids disengaged themselves from the corner of the

Au Bon Pain counter, and another one—a guy, older than the three of them—sauntered toward us from the left, near the entrance.

Baldie had his gun clear now, holding it down by his leg, walking casually, his eyes never leaving us. The terminal was packed, the oblivious crowd between us and Baldie scooping up their coffee cups and newspapers and luggage and heading out toward the track. Baldie was starting to smile, the crowd and twenty yards all that remained between us. My gun was in my hand now, the bag in front of it. Angie had her hand stuffed in her pocket, both of us taking tender steps forward as the crowd streamed past us, jostling us every now and then. Baldie was moving just as slowly, but with confidence, as if all his movements had been choreographed. His smile was huge, an adrenaline junkie's smile, sucking its fuel from the tension. Fifteen yards between us now, and Baldie starting to rock forward just a bit as he walked, getting high off it.

Then Bubba stepped out of the crowd and blew off the back of his head with a shotgun.

The kid vaulted up in the air, arms spread wide, chest out in a swan dive, and hit the ground on his face. The crowd erupted, scattering across the marble, crashing into one another, no real sense of direction except to get as far away from the corpse as possible, like pigeons without wings, tripping and sliding, trying to scramble back up off the marble before they got trampled. The guy on our left aimed an Uzi, one-handed, straight across the terminal at us and we dropped to our knees as it let loose, the ricochets chucking out pieces of the wall behind us. Bubba's shotgun went off again, and the guy jerked up in the air like he'd just pulled the rip cord on a parachute. He flew back through a window but only half the glass shattered. He hung there, half in, half out, in a glass web.

I took aim at the other two kids as Bubba jacked the shells out of the shotgun and slammed two more home. I squeezed off three shots and the kids dove into a fray of black iron tables. It was impossible to get a clear shot with the crowd in the way, so Angie and I fired at the tables, the bullets popping off the black iron legs. One of the kids rolled onto his back as Bubba turned in his direction. He fired a .357 and the round hit Bubba high in the chest. The shotgun shattered the glass six feet above their heads, and Bubba went down.

A police unit came off Atlantic, bounced straight up onto the curb, and stopped just short of the glass doors. What remained of the crowd seemed to have all come to its senses at once; everyone lay flat on their bellies on the marble, hands protecting heads, luggage providing extra cover like leather retaining walls. The two kids stumbled over the tables and headed toward the tracks, firing in at us from the other side of the windows.

I started toward the middle of the terminal, toward Bubba, but a second police unit jumped the curb, skidding to a stop. The first two cops were already inside, pumping rounds at the two kids near the tracks. Angie grabbed my arm and we ran toward the corridor. The window to my left shattered, dropping out of the pane in a white cascade. The cops were coming closer, firing with accuracy now as the two kids stumbled into each other, trying to get a clear shot at us. Just before we made the corridor, one of them suddenly spun around like a top and sat down. He looked confused, glass falling around him like snow.

Angie kicked the alarm bar on the back door and the siren blast filled the terminal, bleating its call onto the street as we ran behind a row of trucks toward the corner. We cut out into traffic and went around the block, charging back up to Atlantic. We stopped on the corner, took a couple of deep breaths, held them as two more cruisers blew past us. We waited for the light, sweat pouring off our faces. When it turned red, we trotted across Atlantic, through the red dragon's arch and down into Chinatown. We walked up Beach Street, past some men icing down their fish, past a woman tossing a barrel of fetid water off the back of a tiny loading dock, past an old Vietnamese couple, still dressed in the garb they'd worn during the French occupation. A small guy in a white shirt argued with a beefy Italian truck driver. The truck driver kept saying, "We go through this every day. Speak fucking English, goddamnit," and the small guy said, "No speak English. You charge too fucky much, goddamnit." As we passed, the truck driver said, "Now 'too fucky much' that I can understand." The small guy looked fit to shoot him.

We caught a cab at the corner of Beach and Harrison, told the Iranian driver where we wanted to go. He looked at us in the rearview. "Tough day?"

No matter where you are, "tough day" and "too fucky much" seem to be part of the universal language. I looked at him and nodded. "Tough day," I said.

He shrugged. "Me too," he said and pulled onto the expressway.

Angie leaned her head against my shoulder. "What about Bubba?" Her voice was hoarse and thick.

"I don't know," I said and looked at the Gap bag in my lap.

She took my hand and I held on tight.

25

I **sat in** the front pew of St. Bart's and watched Angie light a candle for Bubba. She stood over it for a moment, her hand cupped around it until the yellow flame grew fat with oxygen. Then she knelt and bowed her head.

I started to bow mine, then stopped halfway, caught in the middle as always.

I believe in God. Maybe not the Catholic God or even the Christian one because I have a hard time seeing any God as elitist. I also have a hard time believing that anything that created rain forests and oceans and an infinite universe would, in the same process, create something as unnatural as humanity in its own image. I believe in God, but not as a he or a she or an it, but as something that defies my ability to conceptualize within the rather paltry frames of reference I have on hand.

I stopped praying—or bowing, for that matter—a long time ago, around the time my prayers became whispered chants pleading for the Hero's demise and the courage necessary to have a hand in it. I never did get the courage, and the demise happened slowly, witnessed by my impotent stew of leftover emotions. Afterward, the world went on and any contract between God and myself had severed, interred in the hole with my father.

Angie stood up, blessed herself, and walked down off the carpeted altar to the pew. She stood there, looking down at the Gap bag beside me, and waited.

Bubba was dead, dying, or severely wounded because of

this innocuous-looking bag. Jenna was dead too. So were
Curtis Moore and two or three guys in the Amtrak station
and twelve anonymous street kids who'd probably felt dead
for a long time. By the time this was all over, Socia or I
would join those statistics too. Maybe both of us. Maybe
Angie. Maybe Roland.

A lot of pain in such a simple plastic bag.

"They'll get here soon," Angie said. "Open it."

"They" were the police. It wouldn't take Devin and Oscar long to identify the Unidentified White Male and the
Unidentified White Female who shot it out at the train station with gang members, aided by a known gunrunner
named Bubba Rogowski.

I loosened the string at the top of the bag, reached in,
and my hand closed around a file folder, maybe a quarter-
inch thick. I pulled it out and opened it. More photographs.

I stood and laid them out on the pew. There were twenty-
one in all, their surfaces splintered by the triangles of
shadow and light cast by the stained-glass windows. Not
one of them contained anything I'd want to look at; all of
them contained things I had to.

They were from the same camera and location that produced the photograph Jenna had given me. Paulson was in
most of these, Socia in a few. The same scuzzy motel room,
the same grainy texture to the film, the same high camera
angle, leading me to assume they were stills from a videotape, the camera probably positioned eight or ten feet up,
possibly behind a double mirror.

In most of the photos, Paulson had removed his underwear but retained his black socks. He seemed to be enjoying himself on the small twin bed with torn, stained sheets.

The same couldn't be said for the other person on the
bed. The object of Paulson's affection—if you could call
it that—was a child. A young, extremely skinny black boy
who couldn't have been any older than ten or eleven. He
wasn't wearing any socks. He wasn't wearing anything at
all. He didn't seem to be having as much fun as Paulson.

He did seem to be in a lot of pain.

Sixteen of the twenty-one photographs captured the sex act itself. In some of these, Socia appeared, leaning into the frame to give Paulson what appeared to be directions. In one, Socia's hand gripped the back of the child's head, yanking it back toward Paulson's chest, like a rider reining in a horse. Paulson didn't seem to mind or even notice, his eyes glazed, his lips pursed in pleasure.

The child seemed to mind.

Of the five remaining photographs, four were of Paulson and Socia as they drank dark liquid from bathroom glasses, chatting it up, leaning against the dresser, having a swell old time. In one of those, the boy's slim leg was apparent, just out of focus, tangled in the filthy bedsheets.

Angie said, "Oh, my God," in a cracked, high-pitched voice that sounded like it came from someone else. The knuckles of her right hand were in her mouth, and her whitening skin rippled. Tears welled in her sockets. The warm, stilted air in the church closed in on me for a moment, a weight against my chest that left me slightly light-headed. I looked down at the photographs again, and nausea eddied against the walls of my stomach.

I forced myself to look down at the photos, to hold my eyes there, and soon, my eyes were drawn to the twenty-first the way they would drift toward and fasten onto a single flame in the corner of a dark screen. This was the photograph, I knew, that had already burned its way into my dreams and my shadows, into that part of my mind that I have no control over. Its image would reappear in all its wanton cruelty for the rest of my life, particularly when I was least prepared for it. It was not taken during the act, but afterward. The boy sat on the bed, uncovered and oblivious, his eyes taking on the ghostly image of what he'd already ceased being. In those eyes was the shriveled cast of dead hope and a closed door. They were the eyes of a brain and a soul that had collapsed under the weight of sensory overload. The eyes of the walking dead, their owner oblivious to his loss, his nakedness.

I shuffled the photographs back into a pile and closed the file. Numbness was already settling in, clotting the flow of horror and bewilderment. I looked at Angie, saw the same process taking place in her. The shakes had stopped and she stood very still. It wasn't a sweet feeling, possibly it was harmful in the long run, but at the moment, it was absolutely necessary.

Angie looked up, her eyes red but dry. She pointed at the file. "No matter what, we take them down."

I nodded. "Going to have to take it to them."

She shrugged and leaned back against the baptismal font. "Oh well."

I took one photo from the folder—one that showed the act—the boy, Socia, and Paulson's body but not his head. Socia was Devin's, maybe, but Paulson was mine. I took the rest of the folder to one of the rear confessionals, stepped through the heavy burgundy partition, and bent by the floor. I used my penknife on a square of marble that's been loose since I was an altar boy. I lifted it out and placed the folder down in the two-foot hole. Angie was behind me now, and I held out my hand. She placed her .38 in it and I added the nine millimeter, then closed the hole back up again. The square fit neatly, without any noticeable gaps, and I realized then that I'd co-opted one of the great Catholic traditions: concealment.

I stepped back out of the confessional and we walked down the center aisle. At the door, Angie dipped her fingers into the holy water and blessed herself. I thought about it, figuring I'd need all the help I could get on this one, but there's one thing I hate more than a hypocrite: a pious one. We pushed open the heavy oak doors and stepped into the late afternoon sunlight.

Devin and Oscar were parked out front, leaning over the hood of Devin's Camaro, a spread of McDonald's food in front of them. They didn't so much as look up at us before

Devin said, around a mouthful of Big Mac, "You have the
right to remain silent. Anything you say can and will be
used against you in a court of law. Hand me those fries,
partner. You have a right to an attorney. . . ."

It was well into the next morning before they finished
with us.

Devin and Oscar were obviously taking a lot of heat.
Gangland shootouts in Roxbury or Mattapan are one thing,
but when it rises from the ghettos and rears its ugly head
in the heart of the city, when Joe and Suzy Citizen have to
stumble over their Louis Vuitton luggage to duck out of
the way of gunfire, then there's a problem. We were cuffed.
We were booked. Devin took the photo from me without a
word before we got to the station, and they took everything
else shortly after.

I stood in a lineup with four cops who didn't look remotely like me, and stared into a white light. Beyond it, I
heard a cop saying, "Take your time. Look closely," followed by a woman's voice: "I didn't really get a good
look. I only saw the big black guy."

Lucky me. If there's gunfire, people usually see the black
guy.

Angie and I met up again later when they sat us down
on a bench beside a mangy wino named Terrance. Terrance
smelled like a banana stew, but he didn't seem to mind. He
gladly explained to me, while brushing his teeth with his
index finger, why the world was so out of control. Uranus.
The good green folks who inhabit this planet don't have
the technology to build modern cities; Terrance told us they
can build farmhouses that would make your mouth water,
but skyscrapers are beyond them. "But they want 'em bad,
you see?" Now that we'd built all those skyscrapers, the
Urani were ready to take over. They pissed through the
rain, filling our water supply with a violence-inducing drug.
Within ten years, Terrance confided in us, we'd have all

killed each other off and the cities would be theirs. A big
green party in the Sears Tower.

I asked Terrance where he'd be then, and Angie elbowed
me in the ribs for encouraging him.

Terrance stopped brushing his teeth for a moment and
looked at me. "Back on Uranus, of course." He leaned in
close and I almost passed out from the smell. "I'm one of
them."

I said, "Of course you are."

They came and got Terrance a few minutes later, took
him off to his spaceship or a secret meeting with the government. They left us where we were. Devin and Oscar
walked by a few times without glancing our way. A lot of
other cops did the same, not to mention some hookers, an
army of bail bondsmen, a bunch of PDs with awkward
briefcases and the lean faces of those who don't have time
to eat. As darkness fell, then deepened, a lot of hard-
looking guys, built like Devin—powerful and low to the
ground—headed toward the elevators, bulky Teflon vests
under dark blue windbreakers, M-16s in their hands. The
Anti-Gang Task Force. They held the elevators until Devin
and Oscar joined them, then they all went down in two
cars.

They never offered us a phone call. They'd do that just
before or within the first few minutes of our interrogation.
Someone would say, "What, nobody told you you could
make a phone call? Jeeze. All our lines must have been
busy."

A kid in patrolman's blues brought us some lukewarm
coffee from a machine. The old cop who'd taken our prints
stood across from us behind a desk. He stamped a stack of
papers, answered the phone a lot, and if he remembered us
at all, he was doing a good job of hiding it. At one point,
when I stood up to stretch, he half-glanced my way and out
of the corner of my eye I saw a cop appear in the hallway
on my left. I got a drink from the water fountain—not an

easy thing to manage with your hands cuffed—and sat back down.

Angie said, "They won't tell us about Bubba will they?"

I shook my head. "If we ask about him, it puts us at the crime scene. If they tell us before we ask, they lose everything, gain nothing."

"Pretty much what I figured."

She slept for a while, her head on my shoulder, her knees close to her chest. The weight of her body probably would have cramped a muscle after a while if there'd been any left to cramp; after nine or ten hours on this bench, a simple stretching exercise would have been orgasmic.

They'd taken my watch, but the darkest blue of night had already begun to give way to the first false light of early morning by the time Devin and Oscar returned. I guessed it was around five. Devin said, "Follow us, Kenzie," as he passed.

We peeled ourselves off the bench and staggered down the hallway after them. My legs refused to straighten completely and my lower back felt like I'd swallowed a hammer. They led us into the same interrogation room where'd we'd met about twenty hours before, let the door swing back into my face as I approached. I pushed it open with my cuffed hands and we did our Quasimodo imitations through the doorway.

I said, "You ever hear of the ACLU?"

Devin tossed a walkie-talkie down on the table in front of him. He followed with a huge ring of keys, then sat back in a chair and watched us. His eyes were ragged and red, but darkly vibrant, an amphetamine vibrancy. Oscar's looked the same. They'd probably been up forty-eight hours straight. Someday, when all this was over and they were both spending Sundays in their La-Z-Boys watching football games, their hearts would finally play catch up, do what no bullet had ever managed. Knowing them, they'd probably go the same day too.

I held out my hands. "You going to take these things off?"

Devin looked at my wrists, then at my face. He shook his head.

Angie sat down. "You're an asshole."

"I am," Devin said.

I took a seat.

Oscar said, "Case you two are interested, they upped the ante in the war tonight. Someone fired a grenade through the window of a Saints' crack house. Took out damn near everyone inside, including two babies, couldn't have been more than nine months, the oldest. We're not positive yet, but we think two of the dead might have been white college kids, there on a buy. Probably the best thing could have happened. Maybe somebody'll care now."

I said, "What'd you do with that photograph?"

"Filed it," Devin said. "Socia's already wanted for questioning on seven deaths in the last two nights. If he ever comes to ground, that photo will be one more thing to nail him with. The white guy in the photo, the one on top of the little kid—somebody tells me who he is, maybe we can do something about it."

"Maybe if I was allowed back out on the street, I could do something in ways you couldn't."

Devin said, "Like shoot up another train station?"

Oscar said, "You wouldn't last five minutes on the street anymore, Kenzie."

Angie said, "Why's that?"

"Because Socia knows you have incriminating evidence on him. Hard evidence. Because your main protection, Patrick, ain't in the game anymore and everyone knows it. Because your life ain't worth a nickel bag as long as Socia's still walking around."

"So what's the charge?" I asked.

"Charge?"

"What're you charging us with, Devin?"

Oscar said, "Charging?" Couple of parrots, these two.

"Devin."

"Mr. Kenzie, I have nothing to hold you on. My partner and I *were* under the impression that you might have been involved in some nasty business down at South Station early yesterday afternoon. But, since no witnesses can place you there, what can I say? We fucked up. And we're too sorry about it, believe me."

Angie said, "Take the cuffs off."

"Would that we could find the key," Devin said.

"Take the fucking cuffs off, Devin," she said again.

"Oscar?"

Oscar pulled out all his pockets.

"Oscar doesn't have them either. We'll have to call around."

Oscar stood up. "Maybe I take a look around, see if I can scare them up."

He left and we sat there, Devin watching us. We watched him back. He said, "Think about protective custody."

I shook my head.

"Patrick," he said in a tone my mother used to use, "it's a rolling battleground out there. You won't make it until sunrise. Angie, neither will you if you're with him."

She tilted her chair back, turned her beautiful, weary face toward me. She said, " 'Nobody hands me my guns and says run. Nobody.' " Just like James Coburn in *The Magnificent Seven.* Her full mouth burst wide, the smile that blew into my chest was devastating. At that moment, I think I knew what love was.

We looked at Devin.

He sighed. "I saw the movie too. Coburn died in the end."

"There's always reruns," I said.

"Not out there, there isn't."

Oscar came back through the door. He said, "Well, lookee here," and held up a small key ring.

"Where'd you find 'em?" Devin asked.

Oscar tossed them onto the table in front of me. "Right

where I left them. Funny how that works sometimes, huh.''

Devin pointed at us. ''They think they're cowboys.''

Oscar pulled back his chair and settled heavily into it. ''Then we'll bury them with their boots on.''

26

We couldn't go home. Devin was right. I had no more cards to play, and Socia had nothing to gain as long as I continued breathing.

We sat around for another two hours while they finished up some paperwork and then they took us out a side door and drove us a few blocks away to the Lenox Hotel.

As we got out of the car, Oscar looked over at Devin. "Have a heart. Tell 'em."

We stood on the curb, waited.

Devin said, "Rogowski's got a broken collarbone and he lost a shitload of blood, but he's stable."

Angie sagged against me for a moment.

Devin said, "Been swell knowing you," and drove off.

The folks at the Lenox didn't seem too pleased we'd chosen their hotel at eight in the morning, sans luggage. Our clothes, appropriately, looked as if we'd sat on a bench all night, and my hair was still speckled with chips of marble from the shoot-out at South Station. I gave them my Visa Gold Card and they asked for more ID. While the concierge copied the numbers of my driver's license onto a pad of paper, the reservations clerk called in my Visa number for authorization. Some people you can never please.

After they ascertained that I was who I said I was and that we probably wouldn't make off with much more than a bath towel and some sheets, they gave us a room key. I signed my name and looked up at the reservations clerk.

"Is the TV in our room bolted to the wall or could it just roll on out of there?"

She gave me a very tight smile but didn't answer.

The room was on the ninth floor, overlooking Boylston Street. Not a bad view. Directly below us wasn't much—a Store 24, a Dunkin' Donuts—but beyond, a nice stretch of brownstones, some with mint-green roof gardens, and beyond them, the dark, rolling Charles striped against a pale, gray sky.

The sun was rising steadily. I was dead tired, but more than sleep, I needed a shower. Too bad Angie's quicker than I am. I sat in a chair and flicked on the TV. Bolted to the wall, of course. The early news was running a commentary about yesterday's gang violence in South Station. The commentator, broad-shouldered with bangs that looked as if they'd been sharpened to points with a razor, was damn near quivering with righteous anger. Gang violence, he said, had finally reached our front doors and something had to be done about it, no matter what.

It's always when it reaches our "front doors" that we finally consider it a problem. When it's confined to our backyards for decades, no one even notices it.

I turned off the TV, switched places with Angie when she came out of the bathroom.

By the time I'd finished, she was asleep, lying on her stomach, one hand still on the phone where she'd hung it up, the other still closed around the top of the towel. Beads of water glistened on her bare back above the towel line, her slim shoulder blades rising and falling with each breath. I dried off and went to the bed. I pulled the covers out from under her and she groaned softly, raising her left leg closer to her chest. I placed the sheet over her and shut off the light.

I lay down on the right side of the bed, a few feet away from her on top of the sheet, and prayed she didn't roll over in her sleep. If her body touched mine, I was afraid I'd dissolve into it. And probably not mind.

That being the major problem, right there, I turned onto my side, facing the wall, and waited for sleep.

Some time, shortly before I woke up, I saw the boy in the photos. The Hero was carrying him down a dank hallway, both of them enshrouded in shower steam. Water dripped steadily from the ceiling. I yelled something to the boy, because I knew him. I knew him in that dank hallway as his legs kicked out from under my father's arm. He seemed small in my father's arm, smaller still because he was naked. I called to him and my father turned back toward me; Sterling Mulkern's face was under the dark fireman's helmet. He said, "If you had half the balls your old man had . . ." in Devin's voice. The boy turned too, the face craning around my father's elbow bored and disinterested, even as his bare legs flailed. His eyes were empty, like a doll's, and I felt my legs buckle when I realized nothing would ever shock or scare him again.

I woke up to Angie kneeling over me, her hands on my shoulders. She said, "It's OK, it's OK," in a soft whisper.

I was very aware of her bare legs against mine as I said, "What?"

"It's OK," she said. "Just a dream."

The room was pitch dark but light exploded behind the heavy curtains. I said, "What time is it?"

She stood up, still wearing the towel, and walked to the window. "Eight o'clock," she said. "P.M." She opened the curtain. "On the Fourth of July."

The sky was a canvas of explosive colors. Whites, reds, blues, even some orange and yellow. A clap of thunder rocked the room and a starburst of blue and white ignited the sky. A shooting star of red rocketed through the middle and set off a smaller starburst that bled all over the blue and white. The whole display hit its peak then collapsed at once, the colors arcing downward and sputtering out in a cascade of dying embers. Angie opened the windows and the Boston Pops boomed Beethoven's Fifth as if they had a wall of speakers wrapped around the Hub.

I said, "We slept fourteen hours?"

She nodded. "Shoot-outs and interrogations will do that to you, I guess."

"I guess so."

She came back to the bed, sat on the corner. "Boy, Skid, when you have a nightmare, you have a *nightmare*."

I rubbed my face. "Sorry I woke you."

"Had to get up some time. Speaking of which, do we have a plan of any sort?"

"We have to find Paulson and Socia."

"That's an objective, not a plan."

"We need our guns."

"Definitely."

"Probably not going to be easy getting to them with Socia's people all over the place."

"We're the inventive type."

We took a cab back to the neighborhood, gave the driver an address about a half-mile past the church. I didn't see anyone lurking in the shadows as we passed, but you're not supposed to: that's why there are shadows; that's why they lurk. Some kids—ten or twelve years old at most—were shooting bottle rockets at the passing cars, tossing packs of firecrackers out into the middle of the avenue. The car directly behind us took a direct hit to its windshield and screeched to a halt. The guy jumped out running, but the kids were gone before he'd even reached the curb, hopping fences like hurdlers, disappearing into their own backyard jungle.

Angie and I paid the cabbie and walked through the backyard of the public grammar school—the "project" school we called it when we were kids, because only the kids from the housing projects went there. In the back of the schoolyard, hanging in a loose pack around the fire escape, twenty or so of the older neighborhood kids pounded back some beers, a boom box tuned to WBCN, a few passing around a joint. When they saw us, one of them turned the boom box up louder. J. Geils Band's "Whammer Jammer." Fine with me. They had already decided we weren't cops and now they were deliberating how bad they were going to scare us for being stupid enough to walk through their hangout.

Then a few of them recognized us as we passed under a streetlight and seemed pretty depressed—can't scare people who know your parents. I recognized their leader, Colin, right off. Bobby Shefton's kid; good-looking, even if he was as obviously Irish as a potato famine—tall, well-built, a short-cropped head of dirty blond hair around a chiseled face. He was wearing a white and green BNBL tank top and a pair of pleated walking shorts. He said, " 'S up, Mr. Kenzie?"

They nodded to Angie. No one wants to get too well acquainted with a woman whose husband's jealous streak is legend.

I said, "Colin, how'd you guys like to make fifty bucks before the liquor store closes?"

His eyes lit up for a moment before he remembered how cool he was. He said, "You go in and buy the shit for us?"

"Of course."

They kicked the idea around for a second and a half or so. "You got it. What do you need?"

I said, "It involves screwing with people who might be packing."

Colin shrugged. "Niggers ain't the only ones with guns anymore, Mr. Kenzie." He pulled his own from under his tank top. A couple of other kids did too. "Since they tried to take over the Ryan playground a couple months back, we stocked up a bit." For a moment I thought back to my days on this fire escape—the good old days of tire irons and baseball bats. When a switchblade was rare. But the ante kept getting upped, and obviously, everyone was willing to meet it.

My plan had been to get them to pack around us as we walked back up to the church. With hats, in the darkness, we could probably pass as kids, and by the time Socia's people figured it out, we'd be in the church with our guns. It had never been much of a plan. And I realized now that I'd missed the obvious because of my own racism. If the black kids had guns, only went to figure, the white kids would have them too.

I said, "Tell you what. I changed my mind. I'll give you a hundred bucks *and* the booze for three things."

Colin said, "Name 'em."

"Let us rent two of your guns." I tossed him my car keys. "And go boost my car from in front of my house."

"That's two things."

"Three," I said. "Two guns and one car. What're they teaching you kids these days?"

One of the kids laughed. "Helps if you go to school."

Colin said, "You just want to rent the guns? You'll definitely bring them back?"

"Probably. If not, we'll kick in enough to buy you two more."

Colin stood, handed me his gun, butt first. A .357, scratched along the barrel, but well oiled. He slapped a buddy's shoulder and the buddy handed his gun to Angie. A .38. Her favorite. He looked at his buddy. "Let's go get Mr. Kenzie's car."

While they were gone, we walked across the street to the liquor store and filled their order—five cases of Bud, two liters of vodka, some OJ, some gin. We carried it back across the street and had just given it to the kids when the Vobeast came hurtling down the avenue and smoked rubber the last quarter block to the curb. Colin and his pal were out of it before it stopped rolling. "Get going, Mr. Kenzie. They're coming."

We scrambled into the car and pulled off the curb as the headlights loomed large and malevolent in back of us. There were two sets of headlights and they were right behind us, three silhouettes in each car. They started firing half a block past the school, the bullets ripping into the Vobeast. I cut across the wrong lane of traffic and jumped the divider strip as we entered Edward Everett Square. I banged a right past a tavern, punched the pedal as we lit down the small, densely packed street, the cars fat on both sides. In my rearview, I saw the first car spin around the corner and straighten out cleanly. The second car, though, didn't make the turn. It bounced off a Dodge and the front axle snapped in two. Its fender plowed into asphalt and it flipped up onto its grill.

The first car was still firing away, and Angie and I kept ducking our heads, not sure which explosions came from a gun muzzle and which came from the barrage of fireworks in the sky overhead. Straight out, like this, there was no way we'd last. A Yugo could outrun the Vobeast, and the streets were growing tighter and tighter with less cover and more parked cars.

We crossed over into Roxbury and my back window imploded. I took enough shards of glass in my neck to think I'd been shot for a moment, and Angie had a cut on her forehead that was bleeding a thick river down her left cheekbone. I said, "You OK?"

She nodded, scared but pissed off too. She said, "Goddamn them," and swiveled on the seat, pointing the .38 at the space where the window used to be. My ear exploded as she squeezed off two shots, her arm steady.

Angie's one hell of a shot. The windshield of the car splattered into two big spiderwebs. The driver spun the wheel and they rammed a white panel truck, bounced back into the street sideways.

I didn't stop to check their condition. The Vobeast careened onto a badly paved stretch of road that rocked our heads off the ceiling. I spun the wheel to the right and turned onto a street that was only marginally better. Someone screamed something at us as we went past, and a bottle shattered against the trunk.

The left side of the street was one big abandoned lot, scorched overgrown weeds pouring up out of piles of gravel, crumbled cinder block and brick. To our right, houses that should have been condemned a half-century ago sagged toward the earth, carrying the weight of poverty and neglect with them until the day they'd spill into one another like dominoes. Then the right side of the street would look identical to the left. The porches were crowded and no one seemed too pleased with the whiteys in the rolling piece of shit tearing down their street. A few more bottles hit the car, a cherry bomb blew up in front of us.

I reached the end of the street, and just as I saw the other car appear a block back, I took a left. The street I turned onto was even worse, a bleak, forgotten path through brown weeds and the skeletal remains of abandoned tenements. A few kids stood by a burning trash can tossing firecrackers inside, and behind them two winos tackled one another for the rights to that last sip of T-bird. Beyond them, the condemned tenements rose in crumbling brick, the black windows empty of glass, singed in places by some forgotten fire.

Angie said, "Oh, Christ, Patrick."

The street dead-ended, no outlet, twenty yards away. A heavy cement divider and years of weeds and rubble stood in our way. I looked behind me as I began to apply the brakes, and saw the car turning the corner toward us. The kids were walking away from the barrel, smelling the battle and getting out of the line of fire. I stood on the brakes and the Vobeast gave me a belligerent "fuck you" in reply. Metal clacked against metal, and I might as well have been in a Flintstone car. It seemed to almost pick up a last burst of speed just before we hit the divider.

My head popped off the dashboard and a rush of metal taste fragmented within my mouth as the impact shook me. Angie had been a little more prepared. She snapped forward, but her seatbelt held her in place.

We barely looked at one another before we jumped out

of the car. I scrambled across the hood as the brakes behind
us squealed on the torn cement. Angie was sprinting like
an Olympian across the lot of weeds and cinder block and
broken glass, her chest out, her head thrown back. She was
a good ten yards ahead of me by the time I got going. They
fired from the car, the bullets chunking into the ground
beside me, what remained of natural soil spitting up between the garbage.

Angie had reached the first tenement. She was looking
at me, waving me to go faster, her gun pointed in my general direction, craning her head for a clear shot. I didn't
like the look in her eyes at all. Then I noticed the shafts of
light jerking up and down in front of me, shining off the
tenement, jagged where my body blocked them. They'd
driven in after us. Exactly what I'd been afraid of.
Somewhere in all these weeds and gravel, roads had existed
before this area was condemned. And they'd found one.

A burst of gunfire stitched a pile of torn brick as I
jumped over it and reached the first tenement. Angie turned
as I came through the doorway and we ran inside, ran without thinking, without looking, because we were running
into a building that had no back wall. It had crumbled some
time ago, and we were just as out in the open as we'd been
before.

The car came across the middle of the building, rocketing
over an old metal door ahead of us. I took aim because
there was nothing to hide behind. The front passenger and
the guy in the backseat were sticking black weapons out
the windows. I got off two shots that punched the front
door before they let loose, tongues of fire bursting from
their muzzles. Angie dove to her left, landing behind an
overturned bathtub. I went up in the air, nothing to cover
me, and I was halfway down when a bullet burned across
my left bicep and snapped me around in midair. I hit the
ground and fired again, but the car had gone out the other
side and was circling for another pass.

Angie said, ''Come on.''

I got up and saw what she was running for. Twenty yards ahead of us were two more tenement towers, intact it seemed, and packed close together. Between them was a dark blue alley. A hazy yellow streetlight shone at the end of it, and it was much too thin for a car to work its way into. Silhouettes of misshapen hulks of metal stood out in dark shadows between the two towers.

I ran across the open lot, hearing the engine coming off to my left, blood pouring down my arm like warm soup. I'd been shot. Shot. I saw their faces again as they fired, and I heard a voice that I soon realized was mine saying the same thing, over and over again: "Fucking niggers, fucking niggers."

We reached the alley. I looked behind me. The car was stalled by something in the gravel, but the way they were rocking it from the inside, I didn't think they'd stay that way long. I said, "Keep going."

Angie said, "Why? We can pick them off as they come in."

"How many bullets you got left?"

"I don't know."

"Exactly," I said. "We could run out trying to pick them off." I worked my way over an upturned dumpster. "Trust me."

Once we made it to the end of the alley, I looked back and saw the headlights arcing to the left, moving again, coming around to meet us. The road at the end of the alley was a faded yellow cobblestone. We stepped out onto it, hearing the big engine roaring closer. The yellow streetlight we'd seen was the only one for two blocks. Angie checked her gun. "I have four bullets."

I had three. She was the better shot. I said, "The street-light."

She fired once and stepped back as the glass fell in a small shower to the street. I jogged across the street into a mass of brown weeds. Angie climbed down behind a torched car directly across from me. Her eyes peered over the blackened hood, looking at me, both of our heads nodding forward, the adrenaline rippling through us like fission.

The car fishtailed around the corner, hurtling over the torn cobblestone toward us, the driver craning his head out the window, looking for us. The car began to slow as it got closer, trying to figure out where we could have gone. The shotgun passenger turned his head to his right, looked at the scorched car, didn't see anything. He turned back, and started to say something to the driver.

Angie stood up, took aim over the blackened hood, and fired two shots into his face. His head snapped to the side, bounced off his shoulder, and the driver looked at him for one moment. When he looked back, I was running up to the window, gun extended. He said, "Wait!" through the open window and his eyes loomed large and white just before I pulled the trigger and blew them out through the back of his head.

The car went left, hit an old shopping cart on its way to the curb, bouncing up and over it before ramming a wooden telephone pole and cracking the wood at a point about six feet off the ground. The guy in the backseat shattered the window with his head. The telephone pole wavered in the fragrant summer breeze for a moment, then dropped forward and crushed the driver's side of the car.

We approached slowly, guns pointed at the hole in the back window. We were about three feet away, side by side, when the door creaked open, the lower corner hitting the sidewalk. I took a deep breath and waited for a head to show. It did, followed by a body that dropped to the pavement, covered in glass and blood.

He was alive. His left arm was twisted out behind him at an impossible angle and a large flap of skin was missing from his forehead, but he was trying to crawl anyway. He got two or three feet before he collapsed, rolling over onto his back, breathing hard.

Roland.

He spit some blood onto the sidewalk and opened one eye to look at me. The other eye was already beginning to swell under the mask of blood. He said, "I'll kill you."

I shook my head.

He managed to sit up a bit, resting on his good arm. He said, "I'll kill you. The bitch too."

Angie kicked him in the ribs.

All the pain he was in and he rolled his head at her and smiled. " 'Scuse me."

I said, "Roland, you got this all backward. We're not your problem. Socia's your problem."

"Socia dead," he said, and I could tell a few of his teeth were broken. "He just don't know it yet. Most of the Saints coming over with me. I get Socia any day now. He lost the war. Just a matter of picking his coffin."

He managed to open both eyes then, for just a moment, and I knew why he wanted me dead.

He was the kid in the photographs.

"You're the—"

He howled at me, a stream of blood jetting from his mouth, trying to lunge for me when he couldn't even get off the ground. He kicked at me and banged his fist off the ground, probably driving shards of glass all that much farther into the skin and bone. His howl grew louder. "I fucking kill you," he screamed. "I fucking kill you."

Angie looked at me. "We let him live, we're both dead."

I considered it. One shot is all it would take. Out here on the cusp of the urban wasteland with no one around to question. One shot and no more Roland to worry about. Once we settled with Socia, back to our regular life. I looked down at Roland as he arched his back and jerked up, trying to stand, like a bloody fish on newspaper. His sheer effort scared the shit out of me. Roland didn't seem to know pain or fear any longer, just *drive*. I looked at him steadily, considering it, and somewhere in that raging, hulking mass of hatred, I saw the naked child with the dying eyes. I said, "He's already dead."

Angie stood over him, gun pointed down, hammer pulled back. Roland watched her and she stared back at him flatly. But she couldn't do it either, and she knew no amount of standing there would change that. She shrugged and said, "Have a nice day," and we walked toward the Melnea Cass Boulevard, four blocks west, shining like civilization itself.

27

We flagged down a bus and climbed on. Everyone on it was black and when they saw us—bloody, torn clothes—most of them found some sort of excuse to move to the back. The bus driver closed the door with a soft *whoosh* and pulled off down the highway.

We took seats near the front, and I looked at the people on the bus. Most of them were older; two looked like students, one young couple held a small child between them. They were looking at us with fear and disgust and some hatred. I had an idea what it must be like to be a couple of young black guys in street clothes boarding a subway car in Southie or White Dorchester. Not a nice feeling.

I sat back and looked out the window at the fireworks in the black sky. They were smaller now, less colorful. I heard an echo of my voice as a carload of murderers chased me across an open lot firing bullets at my body, and my hatred and fear distilled into color. "Fucking niggers," I'd said, over and over. I closed my eyes, and in the darkness, they still took note of the light bursting above me in the sky.

Independence Day.

The bus dropped us at the corner of Mass. Ave. and Columbia. I walked Angie back to her house and when we reached it, she touched my shoulder. "You going to get that looked at?"

For all the pain, when I looked at it on the bus, I realized it had only grazed me, cutting the skin like the slash of a good knife—hardly lethal. It needed cleaning and it hurt like hell, but it wasn't worth a cosmetic job in an over-crowded emergency room at the moment. "Tomorrow," I said.

Her living-room curtain parted slightly: Phil, thinking he was the detective. I said, "You better go in."

The prospect didn't seem to appeal to her all that much. She said, "Yeah, I guess I better."

I looked at the blood on her face, the cut on her forehead. "Better clean that up too," I said. "You're looking like an extra in *Dawn of the Dead*."

"You always know the right thing to say," she said and started toward the house. She saw the parted curtain and turned back toward me, a frown on her face. She looked at me for almost a full minute, her eyes large and a little sad. "He used to be a nice guy. Remember?"

I nodded, because I did. Phil had been a great guy once. Before bills came and jobs went and the future became a vicious joke of a word, something to describe what he'd never have. Phil hadn't always been the Asshole. He'd grown into it.

"Good night," I said.

She crossed the porch and went inside.

I walked up onto the avenue, headed toward the church. I stopped in the liquor store and bought myself a six-pack. The guy behind the counter looked at me like he figured I'd die soon; a little over an hour ago—one that seemed like a lifetime now—I'd bought enough liquor to start my own company, and now I was back for more. "You know how it is," I said. "Fourth of July."

The guy looked at me, at my bloody arm and dirty face. "Yeah," he said, "tell that to your liver."

I drank a beer as I walked up the avenue, thinking about Roland and Socia, Angie and Phil, the Hero and me. Dances of pain. Relationships from hell. I'd been a punch-ing bag for my father for eighteen years, and I'd never hit back. I kept believing, kept telling myself, It'll change; he'll get better. It's hard to close the door on optimistic expectations when you love someone.

Angie and Phil were the same way. She'd known him when he was the best-looking guy in the neighborhood, a charmer and natural leader who told the funniest jokes, the warmest stories. He was everyone's idol. A great guy. She still saw that, prayed for it, hoped against hope—no matter how cynically she viewed the rest of the world—that people change for the better sometimes. Phil had to be one of those people, or what gave anything purpose?

And then there was Roland—taking all that hate and ugliness and depravity that had been shoved into him since childhood at every turn, and spinning around and spewing it back at the world. Waging war against his father and telling himself that once it was done, he'd be at peace. But he wouldn't. It never works that way. Once that ugliness has been forced into you, it becomes part of your blood, dilutes it, races through your heart and back out again, staining everything as it goes. The ugliness never goes away, never comes out, no matter what you do. Anyone who thinks otherwise is naive. All you can hope to do is control it, to force it all into one tight ball in one tight place and keep it there, a constant weight.

I reached the belfry—still less risky than my apartment—and went inside. I sat at my desk, drank my beer. The sky was empty now, the celebration ended. The Fourth would be the fifth soon and the migration back from the Cape and the Vineyard had probably already begun. The day after a holiday is like the day after your birthday—everything seems old, like tarnished copper.

I placed my feet up on the desk and leaned back in the chair. My arm still burned and I straightened it out in front of me and poured half a beer on it. Homemade anesthesia. The cut was wide but shallow. In a few months the scar tissue would pale from a dull red to a duller white. It would barely be noticeable.

I raised my shirt, looked at the jellyfish on my abdomen,

the scar that would never fade, never be mistaken for anything innocuous, for anything but what it was: a mark of violence and depraved indifference, a cattle brand. The Hero's legacy, his stamp on this world, his attempt at immortality. As long as I was alive, carrying this jellyfish on my stomach, then so was he.

When I was growing up, my father's fear of flame burgeoned in direct proportion to his success in fighting it. By the time he reached the rank of lieutenant, he'd turned our apartment into a battle zone against fire. Our refrigerator contained not one, but three boxes of baking soda. Two more in the cupboard below the sink, one above the oven. There were no electric blankets in my father's home, no faulty appliances. The toaster was serviced twice a year. Every clock was mechanical. Electrical cords were checked twice a month for cracks in the rubber; sockets were investigated every six weeks. By the time I was ten, my father pulled all plugs from the sockets nightly to minimize any stray currents of malevolent electricity.

When I was eleven, I found my father sitting at the kitchen table late one night, staring at a candle he'd placed before him. He was holding his hand over the flame, patting it occasionally, his dark eyes fixed on the ropes of blue and yellow as if they could tell him something. When he saw me, his eyes widened, his face flushed, and he said, "It can be contained. It can," and I was stunned to hear the thinnest chords of uncertainty in the deep timbre of his voice.

Because my father's shift began at three in the afternoon and my mother worked nights as a cashier at Stop and Shop, my sister, Erin, and I were latchkey kids long before the term became fashionable. One night, we tried to cook blackened redfish, something we'd had during a trip to Cape Cod the previous summer.

We poured every spice we could find into the skillet, and within minutes, the kitchen had filled with smoke. I opened the windows while my sister unlatched the front and back doors. By the time we remembered what caused the smoke in the first place, the pan had caught fire.

I reached the oven just as the first fat parachute of blue flame floated into a white curtain. I remembered the fear in my father's voice. "It can be contained." Erin picked the pan up off the burner and brown grease splattered her arm. She dropped the pan, and the contents spread across the top of the oven like napalm.

I thought of my father's reaction when he discovered we'd allowed *it* into his home, the embarrassment he'd feel, the rage that his embarrassment would turn into, thickening the blood in his hands until they turned to fists and came looking for me.

I panicked.

With six cartons of baking soda in reach, I grabbed the first liquid I saw off the top of the fridge and poured a half-pint of eighty proof vodka into the middle of a grease fire.

A tenth of a second after, I realized what was going to happen and I tackled my sister just before the top half of the room exploded. We lay on the floor and watched in awe as the wallpaper above the oven stripped away from the wall, as a cloud of blue, yellow, black, and red mushroomed across the ceiling, as a hundred fireflies erupted into the side of the fridge.

My sister rolled away and grabbed the fire extinguisher from the hall. I got one from the pantry, and as if the last five minutes hadn't happened, as if we were truly the children of an illustrious firefighter, we stood in the center of the kitchen and doused the oven, the wall, the ceiling, the fridge, and the curtain. Within a minute, black-and-white foam covered our bodies like birdshit.

Once our adrenal glands had closed their floodgates and our shakes had stopped, we sat down in the center of our ruined kitchen, and stared at the front door where my father entered every night at eleven-thirty. We stared at it until we both wept, kept staring long after we'd run out of tears.

By the time my mother returned from work, we'd fanned

all the smoke out of the apartment, wiped all scorch marks off the fridge and oven, and thrown away the charred strips of wallpaper and what remained of the curtain. My mother looked at the black cloud burned into her ceiling, at the scorched wall, and sat down at the kitchen table and stared blankly at something in the pantry for a full five minutes.

Erin said, "Mum?"

My mother blinked. She looked at my sister, then at me, then at the vodka bottle on the counter. She tilted her head toward it and looked at us. "Which of you . . . ?"

I couldn't speak, pointed a finger at my chest.

My mother walked into the pantry. For a small, thin woman, she moved as if she were overweight, with slow lumbering steps. She returned with the iron and ironing board, placed them in the center of the kitchen. In times of crisis, my mother always clung to routine, and it was time to iron my father's uniforms. She opened the window and began pulling them from the clothesline. With her back to us, she said, "Go to your rooms. I'll see if I can talk to your father."

I sat on the corner of my bed, hands in my lap, facing the door. I left the lights off, closed my eyes in the darkness, my hands clasped tight.

When my father came home, his usual thumping about the kitchen—tossing his lunch box on the table, rattling ice cubes in a glass, falling heavily into a chair before pouring his drink—was mute. The silence in the apartment that night was longer and thicker and more pregnant with dread than I have ever experienced since.

My mother said, "A mistake, that's all."

"A mistake," my father said.

"Edgar," my mother said.

"A mistake," my father said again.

"He's eleven. He panicked."

"Uh-huh," my father said.

Everything else that happened seemed to unfold in that weird compression of time that people experience just be-

fore they get in a car wreck or fall down a flight of stairs—
everything speeds up and everything slows down. A lifetime passes, in all its minute detail, in the space of a second.

My mother screamed, "No!" and I heard the ironing
board topple to the kitchen linoleum, and my father's footsteps hammered the floorboards toward my room. I tried to
keep my eyes closed, but when he kicked the door in, a
splinter grazed my cheekbone, and the first thing I saw was
the iron in my father's hand, the electrical cord and plug
missing. His knee hit my shoulder and knocked me back
on the bed and he said, "You're so desperate to find out
what it feels like, boy?"

I looked in his eyes because I didn't want to look at the
iron, and what I saw in those dark pupils was an unnerving
mixture of anger and fear and hatred and savagery and yes,
love, some bastardized version of that too.

And that's what I fixated on, clung to, prayed to, as my
father ripped my shirt up to my sternum and pressed the
iron against my stomach.

Angie once said, "Maybe that's what love is—counting
the bandages until someone says, 'Enough.' "

Maybe so.

Sitting at my desk, I closed my eyes, knowing I'd never
sleep with the adrenaline doing its stock-car derby in my
blood, and when I woke up an hour later, my phone was
ringing.

I managed to say, "Patr—" before Angie's voice tum-
bled over the line. "Patrick, come over here. Please."

I reached for my gun. "What's the matter?"

"I think I just got divorced."

28

When I got there, there was a squad car double-parked in front of the house. Directly behind it was Devin's Camaro. He was standing on the porch with Oscar, talking to another cop, a kid. Too many cops were starting to look like kids to me, I thought, as I climbed the steps.

They were standing over a huddled lump of flesh by the railing, the young cop giving it smelling salts. It was Phil, and my first thought was, Jesus Christ, she killed him.

Devin looked at me and raised his eyebrows, a smile the size of Kansas on his face. He said, "We answered the call because we asked that anything at her or your address be rerouted to us." He looked down at Phil, at the contusions that covered his face like lesions. He looked back at me. "Oh happy day, huh?"

She was wearing a white shirt over a pair of faded cobalt shorts. There was a red bubble on her lower lip and mascara ran down her face. Her hair was in her eyes as she stepped gingerly out onto the porch in bare feet. She saw me then and came toward me in a rush. I held her and her teeth dug into my shoulder. She was crying softly.

I said, "What did you do?" trying to keep the happy surprise out of my voice, but probably not succeeding.

She shook her head and held on tightly.

Devin was leaning against Oscar, the two of them happier than I'd seen them since they both stopped paying alimony on the same day. Devin said, "Wanna know what she did?"

Oscar said, "Make him beg."

Devin reached into his pocket, giggling. He held a Taser gun up in front of my face. "This is what she did."

"Twice," Oscar said.

"Twice!" Devin repeated gleefully. "Damn lucky he didn't have a friggin' coronary."

"Then," Oscar said, "she laid a beating on him."

"Went nuts!" Devin said. "Nuts! Booted him in the head, the ribs, punched the fuck out of him. I mean, look at him!"

I'd never seen Devin so thrilled.

I looked. Phil was coming to now, but once he felt all that pain, I'm quite sure he would've preferred sleep. Both eyes were almost completely swollen. His lips were black. He had dark bruises over seventy-five percent of his face at least. If what Curtis Moore had done to me had made me look like I'd been in a car accident, Phil looked like he'd been in a plane crash.

The first thing he said when he came to was, "You're arresting her, right?"

Devin said, "Of course, sir. Of course."

Angie stepped out of my arms, looked at him.

Oscar said, "You're pressing charges, sir?"

Phil used the railing to get to his feet. He held onto it like it might just up and run away any second. He started to say something, then leaned over the railing and threw up into the yard.

"Pretty," Devin said.

Oscar walked over to Phil, put a hand on his back as he retched some more. Oscar talked to him in a low soft voice, as if there was nothing out of the ordinary going on, as if he was used to carrying on conversations with people who vomited all over their lawns. "See, sir, the reason I ask if you're going to press charges is 'cause some people don't like to do that in this sort of situation."

Phil spit a few times into the yard, wiped his mouth with

his shirt. Always the gentleman. He said, "What do you mean—'this sort of situation'?"

"Well," Oscar said, "this sort of situation."

Devin said, "Sort of situation where a tough guy like yourself gets his ass handed to him by a woman couldn't weigh more than a hundred fifteen pounds soaking wet. Sort of situation that can become real popular conversation in neighborhood bars. You know," he said, "sort of situation that makes a guy look like a serious pussy."

I coughed into my hand.

Oscar said, "Won't be so bad, sir. You just go on into court, tell the judge your wife likes to beat you up every now and then, keep you in line. That sort of thing. Ain't like the judge'll check to see if you're wearing a dress or anything." He patted him on the back again. Not hard enough to send him down the block, but close. He said, "You feeling better now?"

Phil turned his head, looked at Angie. "Cunt," he said.

No one held her back because no one wanted to. She came across the porch in two strides as Oscar stepped out of the way and Phil barely got an arm up before she clocked him in the temple. Then Oscar stepped forward again, pulled her back. She said, "Phillip, I'll kill you if you *ever* come near me again."

Phil put a hand to his temple and looked on the verge of tears. He said, "You guys saw that."

Oscar said, "Saw what?"

Devin said, "I'd take the lady at her word, Phillip. She has a gun and a permit to use it from what I understand. It's a miracle you're still breathing as it is."

Oscar let Angie go and she walked back to Devin and me. I thought I saw smoke coming out of her ears for a moment. Oscar said, "You going to press charges or not, Phillip?"

Phil took a moment to consider it. Thought about the bars he'd be unable to show his face in. Every one in this neighborhood for sure. Thought of the whistles and homosexual jokes that would follow him to the grave, the bras and panties that would show up in his mailbox on a regular basis. He said, "No, I'm not pressing charges."

Oscar tapped his cheek with his hand. "That's real manly of you, Phillip."

The young cop came out of the house carrying Angie's suitcase and set it in front of her.

"Thank you," she said.

We heard a sound like a cat lapping at wet food, and when we looked over, we saw that Phil was weeping into his hands.

Angie gave him a glare of such withering and final scorn that the temperature on the porch must have dropped by ten degrees. She picked up her suitcase and walked to Devin's car.

Oscar slapped Phil's hip and Phil's face came out of his hands. He looked up into Oscar's huge face and Oscar said, "Anything happens to her while me and him"—he pointed at Devin—"are alive, I mean anything, like she gets hit by some lightning or her plane crashes or she breaks a nail, *anything*—and we're going to come play with you, Phillip. Know what I mean?"

Phil nodded and then the convulsions returned and he began sobbing again. He hit his fist against the railing and got them under control and his eyes fell on mine.

I said, "Bubba really misses you, Phil."

He began to shake.

I turned and as I walked down the steps, Devin said, "Hey, Phil, is payback a bitch, or what?"

Phil turned around and got sick again. We walked down to Devin's car and I sat in the backseat with Angie. Camaros have just enough legroom in their backseats to make a dwarf comfortable, but tonight I wasn't complaining. Devin pulled down the street, looked in his rearview at Angie a few times. "No accounting for taste, is there?"

Oscar looked back at Angie. "Boggles the mind. Absolutely boggles the mind."

29

Devin said, "Socia's definitely lost the war. He's been underground for two days, and half his guys have gone over to the Avengers. No one counted on Roland being such a tactician." He looked back at us. "Marion won't last the week. Lucky for you, huh?"

"Yeah," I said, thinking, that still leaves Roland.

"Not for me," he said. "I lost a hundred bucks in the fucking pool."

Oscar said, "Should have bet on Roland."

"Now you tell me."

They dropped us off at my apartment. Oscar said, "We'll have a unit roll the block every fifteen minutes. You'll be fine."

We said good night, walked up to the apartment. There were eight messages on my answering machine but I ignored it. I said, "Coffee or beer?"

"Coffee," Angie said.

I put some in the filter, turned on the Mr. Coffee. I took a beer from the fridge, came back into the living room. She was curled in the corner of the couch, looking smaller than I'd ever seen her. I sat across from her in an armchair and waited. She placed an ashtray on her thigh, lit a cigarette, her hand trembling. She said, "Hell of a Fourth, huh?"

"Hell of a Fourth," I agreed.

She said, "I came home and I was not in good shape."

"I know."

"I mean, I just killed someone for God's sake." Her

hand trembled so badly the ash dropped off the cigarette onto the couch. She brushed it into the tray. "So, I came in and there he is, bitching at me about the car still being parked down at South Station, about me not coming home last night, asking me—no, telling me—that I was fucking you. And I think to myself, I just got in the door, damn lucky to be alive, blood all over my face, and he can't think of anything more original to say than 'You're fucking Pat Kenzie'? Christ." She ran a hand up her forehead, pulled the hair back off her face, held it there. "So, I said, 'Get a life, Phillip,' or something to that effect and I start walking by him and he goes, 'Only thing you'll be able to fuck once I get finished with you, babe, is yourself.' " She took a drag on the cigarette. "Nice, huh? So, he grabs my arm and I get my free hand in my purse and I shoot him with the stun gun. He hits the floor, then he half gets up and I kick him. He's off balance, goes tumbling back out the door onto the porch. And I hit him with the stun gun again. And I'm staring down at him, and it all went away. I mean everything—every feeling I ever had for him just sort of flushed out of my system and all I saw was this piece of shit who had *abused* me for twelve years, and I . . . went a little hoopy."

I doubted that part about the feelings. They'd come back. They always did, usually when you were least prepared for them. I knew she'd probably never love him again, but the emotion would never leave, the reds, the blues, the blacks of all the different things she had felt during that marriage, they'd reverberate time and again. You could leave a bedroom, but the bed stayed with you. I didn't tell her this, though; she'd learn it soon enough on her own.

I said, "Judging by what I saw, you went a lot hoopy."

She smiled slightly, let her hair fall back in front of her eyes. "Yeah. I suppose so. Long time coming though."

"No argument," I said.

"Pat?" She's the only person who can call me that without setting my teeth on edge. On those rare times she does, it sounds OK, it feels kinda warm.

"Yeah?"

"When I was looking down at him, afterward, I kept thinking about the two of us in that alley with the car heading around the block toward us. And I was terrified then, don't get me wrong, but I wasn't half as terrified as I could have been, because I was with you. And we always seem to make it through things if we're together. I don't doubt things as much when I'm with you. You know?"

"I know exactly," I said.

She smiled. Her bangs covered her eyes and she kept her head down for a moment. She started to say something.

Then the phone rang. I damn near shot it.

I got up, grabbed it. "Hello."

"Kenzie, it's Socia."

"Congratulations," I said.

"Kenzie, you have to meet me."

"No, I don't."

"Jesus, Kenzie, I'm a dead man you don't help me."

"Listen to what you just said, Marion, and think."

Angie looked up and I nodded. The softness in her face receded like surf from a reef.

"All right, Kenzie, I know what you're thinking, sitting there all safe, saying, 'Socia done now.' But I ain't done. Not yet. And I have to, I'll come looking for you and make sure I take you with me on the way to the grave. You got what I need to stay alive and you gone give it to me."

I thought about it. "Try and take me out, Socia."

"I'm a half mile from your house."

That stopped me, but I said, "Come on over. We'll have a beer together before I shoot you."

"Kenzie," he said, suddenly sounding weary, "I can get to you and I can get to your partner, that one you look at like she hold all the mysteries to life. You ain't got that psycho with the hardware to protect you no more. Don't make me come for you."

Anyone can get to anyone. If Socia made it his sole objective to make sure my funeral preceded his by a few days or a few hours, he could do it. I said, "What do you want?"

"The fucking pictures, man. Save both our lives. I'll tell Roland if he kill me or you, those pictures definitely see the light. That's exactly what he don't want, people saying Roland take it up the bunghole."

What a prince. Father of the Year.

I said, "Where and when?"

"Know the expressway on-ramp, beside Columbia Station?"

It was two blocks away. "Yeah."

"Half an hour. Underneath."

"And this'll get you both off my back?"

"Fucking right. Keep me and you breathing for some time."

"Half an hour."

We got the photographs and guns from the confessional. We Xeroxed the photos on the machine Pastor Drummond uses for his Bingo sheets in the basement, put the originals back in their place, and went back to my apartment.

Angie drank a tall cup of black coffee and I checked our weapons supply. We had the .357 with two bullets left, the .38 Colin had given us and the .38 Bubba had acquired for us, the nine millimeter, and the .45 I'd taken off Lollipop, silencer attached. We also had four grenades in the fridge, and the Ithaca twelve-gauge.

I put on my trench coat and Angie put on her leather jacket and we took everything but the grenades. Can't be too safe with people like Socia. I said, "Hell of a Fourth," and we left the apartment.

Part of I-93 stretches over the neighborhood. Underneath it, the city leaves three deposits—sand, salt, and gravel—for emergencies. These three cones rise up twenty feet, the bases about fifteen feet wide. It was summer, so they weren't in all that much use. In Boston though, you have to be prepared. Sometimes Mother Nature plays a joke or two on us, drops a snowstorm on us in early October just to show what a card she is.

You can enter the area from the avenue or from the back entrance of the Columbia/JFK subway station or from Mosley Street if you don't mind climbing over some shrubs and walking down an incline.

We climbed some shrubs and walked down the incline, kicking clouds of brown dirt in front of us until we reached bottom. We stepped around a green support beam and came out between the three cones.

Socia was standing in the middle, where the bottoms converged into a ragged triangle. A small kid stood beside him. Unformed cheekbones and baby fat betrayed his age, even if he thought the wraparounds and the hat on his head made him look old enough to buy a pint of scotch. If he was any older than fourteen, he aged well.

Socia's hands hung empty by his sides, but the kid's were dug into the pockets of a team jacket, and he flapped them back and forth against knobby hips. I said, "Take your hands out of your pockets."

The kid looked at Socia, and I pointed the .45 at him. "Which word didn't you understand?"

Socia nodded. "Take 'em out, Eugene."

Eugene's hands came out of the jacket slowly, the left empty, the right holding a .38 that looked twice as big as his hand. He tossed it into the salt pile without my asking, then started to place his hands back in his pockets. He changed his mind and held them out in front of him as if he'd never noticed them before. He folded them across his chest eventually and shifted his feet. He didn't seem to know exactly what to do with his head either. In quick, rodent's motions, he looked at me, then at Angie, over at Socia, back at the place where he'd tossed the gun, then up at the dark green underside of the expressway.

All the salt and exhaust fumes and cheap wine aromas

down here, and the stench of the kid's fear hung in the air like a fat cloud.

Angie looked at me and I nodded. She disappeared around the cone on our left while I watched Socia and Eugene. We knew no one was hanging around on the expressway above, because we'd checked as we came down Mosley. No one was on the roof of the subway station; we'd scoped it out coming down the hill.

Socia said, "Just me and Eugene. No one else."

I didn't see much reason to doubt him. Three days had aged Socia faster than four years in the White House had aged Carter. His hair was mangy. His clothes hung on him like they'd hang on a wire hanger, and there were beige food stains on the fine linen. His eyes were pink, a crack head's eyes, all burning adrenaline and shadow seeking. His thin wrists trembled and his skin had the pallor of a mortician's handiwork. He was on borrowed time, and even he knew he was way past due.

Looking at him, for a twentieth of a second or so, I felt something akin to pity. Then I remembered the photos in my jacket, the skinny boy he'd killed, a hardened robot rising up from the ashes who looked like the boy, talked like the boy, but had left his soul back in a motel room with stained sheets. I heard the tape of him popping Anton's eye from the socket. I saw his wife going down in a hail of bullets on a soft summer morning, eyes glazed with eternal resignation. I thought of his army of Eugenes, who closed their glass eyes and hurtled forward to die for him, inhaled his "product," and exhaled their souls. I looked at Marion Socia and it wasn't a "black thing" or a "white thing," it was a human thing. Just knowing he existed made me hate the nature of the world.

He nodded toward Eugene. "Like my bodyguard, Kenzie? Am I scraping the bottom of the barrel, or what?"

I looked at the boy, could only imagine what those words did to the eyes behind those glasses.

I said, "Socia, you're a fucking pig."

"Yeah, yeah, yeah." He reached into his pocket and I placed the .45 against his throat.

He looked down at the silencer nestled against his Adam's apple. "Think I'm foolish?" He pulled a small pipe from his pocket. "Just grabbing some lightning." I took a step back as he extracted a thick rock from his other pocket and placed it in the pipe. He lit it and sucked back hard, closing his eyes. In a frog's voice he said, "You bring what I need?" He opened the lids again and the whites of his eyes fluttered like a bad TV.

Angie came up beside me, and we stared at him.

He chucked the smoke from his lungs in a blast and smiled. He handed the pipe to Eugene. "Aaah. What you two looking at? Little repressed white children appalled by the big black demon?" He chuckled.

"Don't flatter yourself, Socia," Angie said. "You're no demon. You're a garden snake. Hell, you aren't even black."

"Then what am I, missy thing?"

"An aberration," she said and flicked her cigarette off his chest.

He shrugged, brushed at the ash on his jacket.

Eugene was sucking the small pipe as if it were a reed poking above a waterline. He handed it back to Socia and tilted his head back.

Socia reached out and slapped my shoulder. "Hey, boy, give me what I come for. Save us both from that crazy dog."

" 'That crazy dog'? Socia, you created him. You stripped him bare and left him with nothing but hate by the time he was ten."

Eugene shifted on his feet, looked at Socia.

Socia snorted, toked from the pipe. The smoke flowed slowly out of the corners of his mouth. "What do you know about anything, white boy? Huh? Seven years back, that bitch took my boy away from me, tried to teach him all about Jesus and how to behave for the white man, like he had a chance in the first place. Little nigger boy from the ghetto. She try and slap a restraining order on me. On me. Keep me away from my own child so she could fill his head with a lot a shit about the American Dream. Shit. American Dream to a nigger is like a centerfold hanging in a prison cell. Black man in this world ain't nothing unless he can sing or dance, throw a football, make you whiteys happy.'' He took another hit off the pipe. ''Only time you like looking at a nigger is when you in the audience. And Jenna, bitch tries to pass all that Tom bullshit onto my boy, tell him God will provide. Fuck that. Man does what he does in this world and that's it. Ain't no accountant up above taking notes, no matter what the preachers say.'' He tapped the pipe hard against his leg, dumping the ash and resin, his face flushed. ''Come on now, Kenzie, give me that shit and Roland leave you alone. Me too.''

I doubted that. Socia would leave me alone until he was secure again, if that ever happened. Then he'd start worrying about all the people who had something on him, who'd seen him beg. And he'd wipe us all out to preserve his illusion of himself.

I looked at him, still scrambling to decide if I had any options other than the one he offered. He stared back. Eugene took a step away from him, a small one, and his right hand scratched his back.

''Come on. Give it here.''

I didn't have much choice. Roland would definitely get to me if I didn't. I reached into my pocket with my free hand and extracted the manila envelope.

Socia leaned forward slightly. Eugene's right hand was still scratching at his back and his left foot tapped up and down on the cement. I handed the envelope to Socia, and Eugene's foot picked up speed.

Socia opened the clasp and stepped back under the streetlight to survey his handiwork. ''Copies,'' he said.

''Very good. I keep the originals.''

He looked at me, saw it wasn't negotiable, and shrugged.

He looked at them one by one, taking his time, as if they were old postcards. A couple of times, he chuckled softly.

I said, "Socia, there's something I don't get."

He smiled, a ghostly one. "Lot you don't get, white boy."

"Well, at this particular moment in time, then."

"What is it?"

"Did you transfer the original photos from videocassette?"

He shook his head. "Eight millimeter home movie camera."

"So, if you have the original film, why are all these people dying?"

He smiled. "Don't have the original." He shrugged. "First house Roland's boys hit was a place I keep on Warren. Firebombed it, hoping I was in it. I wasn't."

"But the film is?"

He nodded, then looked back down at the Xeroxed photos.

Eugene was leaning forward, craning his head to get a look over Socia's shoulder. His right hand was buried behind his back now and his left scratched furiously along his hip. His small body rippled, and I could hear a hum coming from his mouth, a low buzzing sound I doubt he knew he was making. Whatever it was that he was getting ready to do, it was coming soon.

I took a step forward, my breathing shallow.

Socia said, "Well, how about all this? Boy could have been a movie star. Eh, Eugene?"

Eugene made his move. He bounced forward, a stumble almost, and his hand cleared his back with a pistol in it. He jerked his arm up but it glanced off Socia's elbow. Socia was turning away as I stepped forward, pivoting as I grasped Eugene's wrist, turning my back in toward his chest. Socia's ankle turned against the pavement. He tipped toward the ground and the gun boomed twice in the still humid air. I snapped my elbow back into Eugene's face and heard bone crack.

Socia bounced off the pavement and rolled into the salt cone, the photocopies exploding in a flurry. Eugene dropped the gun. I let go of his slick wrist and he fell straight back to the pavement, a soft pop as his head hit cement.

I picked up the gun and looked at Angie. She stood in a target shooter's stance, her arm steady as it swung the .38 back and forth between Socia and Eugene.

Eugene sat up, hands on his legs, blood flowing from a broken nose.

Socia lay against the salt pile, his body slack in the dark shadow of the expressway. I waited, but he didn't move.

Angie stepped over to him and looked down. She reached out for his wrist and he rolled over on his back. He looked at us and laughed, a rich, explosive bellow. We watched as he tried to get control of it, but it was beyond him. He tried to sit up straight against the cone, but the movement loosened the salt above him and it cascaded down inside his shirt. This made him laugh even harder. He slid back down into the salt like a drunk on a waterbed, slapping it with his hand, the laughter rippling into the atmosphere and momentarily overpowering the din of cars passing overhead.

Eventually he sat forward, holding his stomach. "Hoo boy. Ain't there no one to trust in this world no more?" He giggled and looked at the boy. "Hey, Eugene, how much Roland pay you to Judas me?"

Eugene didn't seem to hear him. The color of his skin had taken on the unhealthy hue of someone fighting back nausea. He took deep breaths and held a hand to his heart. He seemed oblivious to the broken nose, but his eyes were wide with the enormity of what he'd just attempted and what it had gotten him. Unfathomable terror swam in his irises, and I could tell his brain was scrambling to get past it, searching his soul for the courage necessary to achieve resignation.

Socia stood and brushed some salt from his suit. He shook his head slowly, then bent to pick up the scattered photocopies. "My, my. Ain't going to be a hole deep enough or a country wide enough to hide your ass in, child. Roland or no Roland, you dead."

Eugene looked at his shattered sunglasses lying on the ground beside him and threw up on his lap.

Socia said, "Do that all you want. Won't help you none."

The back of my neck and the lower half of my ears felt sickly warm, the blood boiling in a whirlpool just below the skin. Above us, the metal expressway extension rattled as a convoy of semis roared over in a screaming cacophony.

I looked down at the boy and I felt tired—horrendously tired—of all the death and petty hate and ignorance and complete and utter carelessness that had assaulted me in a maelstrom this last week. I was tired of all the brick-wall debating—the black versus white, the rich versus poor, the mean versus innocent. Tired of spite and senselessness and Marion Socia and his offhand cruelty. Too tired to care about moral implications or politics or anything except the glass eyes of this boy on the ground who didn't seem to know how to cry anymore. I was exhausted by the Socias and the Paulsons, the Rolands and the Mulkerns of this world, the ghosts of all their victims whispering a growling wind of pleas into my ear to make someone accountable. To end it.

Socia was searching the shadows between the cones. "Kenzie, how many of these pictures were there?"

I pulled back the hammer on the .45 as the truck tires overhead slapped the heavy metal with relentless fury, roaring onward to a destination that could have been a thousand miles away or right next door.

I looked at the nose I'd broken. When did he forget how to cry?

"Kenzie. How many fucking pictures you give me?"

Angie was staring at me, and I knew the sounds that howled from above raged in her head too.

Socia scooped up another photocopy. "Fuck, man, this better be all of it."

The last of the trucks rattled past, but the wail continued, pounding at a fever pitch against my eardrums.

Eugene groaned and touched his nose.

Angie looked over at Socia as he searched the ground in a crablike walk. She looked back at me and nodded.

Socia straightened and stepped under the light, holding the photocopies in his hand.

I said, "How many more will it take, Socia?"

He said, "What?" shuffling the edges of the photocopies into a neat stack.

"How many more people are you going to chew up before it's finally enough? Before even *you* get sick of it?"

Angie said, "Do it, Patrick. Now."

Socia glanced at her, then over to me, his eyes a blank. I don't think he understood the concept of my question. He stared at me, waiting for me to elaborate. After a minute or so, he held up the photocopies. His thumb rose up the front one, pressing between Roland's bare thighs. He said, "Kenzie, is this all of it or not?"

"Yeah, Socia," I said, "this is all of it." I raised the gun and shot him in the chest.

He dropped the photocopies and raised a hand to the hole, stumbling back but staying on his feet. He looked at the hole, at the blood on his hand. He seemed surprised, and for a brief moment, terribly afraid. "The fuck you do that for?" He coughed.

I pulled back on the hammer again.

He stared at me, and the fear left his eyes. The irises peppered over with a cold satisfaction, a dark knowledge. He smiled.

I shot him in the head and Angie's gun went off at the same time. The bullets hammered him back into the salt

· pile, and he rolled onto his back and slid to the cement.

Angie's body was shaking a bit, but her voice was steady. "Guess Devin was right."

I looked down at Socia. "How's that?"

"Some people, you either kill them or leave them be, because you'll never change their minds."

I bent down and began picking up the photocopies.

Angie knelt by Eugene and cleaned his nose and face with a handkerchief. He didn't seem surprised or elated or disturbed by what had happened. His eyes were glazed, somewhat off-center. Angie said, "Can you walk?"

"Yes." He stood up unsteadily, closed his eyes for a few seconds, then exhaled slowly.

I found the photocopy I was looking for, wiped it off with some gravel, and placed it in Socia's jacket. Eugene stood firmly now. I looked at him. "Go home," I said.

He nodded and walked off without a word. He climbed the incline and disappeared on the other side of the shrubs.

Angie and I took the same route a minute later, and as we walked toward my apartment, I slipped my arm around her waist and tried not to think about it.

30

His last week alive, my father's six-foot two-inch frame weighed 112 pounds.

In his hospital room at three in the morning, I listened to his chest rattle like shards of broken glass boiling in a pot. His exhalations sounded as if they were forcing their way out through layers of gauze. Dried spittle whitened the corners of his mouth.

When he opened his eyes, the green irises seemed to swim, anchorless amid the white. He turned his head in my direction. "Patrick."

I leaned in toward the bed, the child in me still cautious, still watching his hands, ready to bolt if they moved too suddenly.

He smiled. "Your mother loves me."

I nodded.

"That's something to—" He coughed and the force of it bowed his chest, brought his head off the pillow. He grimaced, swallowed. "That's something to take with me. Over there," he said and rolled his eyes back into his head as if they could catch a glimpse of where he was going.

I said, "That's nice, Edgar."

His feeble hand slapped my arm. "You still hate me, do you?"

I looked in those unhinged irises and nodded.

"What about all that shit the nuns taught you? What about forgiveness?" He raised a tired, amused eyebrow.

"You used it all up, Edgar. A long time ago."

The feeble hand reached out again, grazed my abdomen. "Still mad about that little scar?"

I stared at him, giving him nothing, telling him there was nothing left to take anymore, even if he were strong enough.

He waved the hand in a dismissive gesture. "Fuck ya, then." He closed his eyes. "What'd you come for?"

I sat back, looked at the wasted body, waiting for it to stop having an effect on me, for that poisonous sludge of love and hate to quit sluicing through my body. "To watch you die," I said.

He smiled, eyes still closed. "Ah," he said, "a vulture. So you are your father's son, after all."

He slept for a while after that, and I watched him, listening to the broken glass rattling through his chest. I knew then that whatever explanation I'd been waiting for my whole life was sealed in that wasted frame, in that rotted brain, and it was never coming out. It was going to ride with my father on his black journey to that place he saw when he rolled his eyes back into his skull. All that dark knowledge was his alone, and he was taking it with him so he'd have something to chuckle about during the trip.

At five-thirty, my father opened his eyes and pointed at me. He said, "Something's burning. Something's burning." His eyes widened and his mouth opened as if he were about to howl.

And he died.

And I watched him, still waiting.

31

It was one-thirty in the morning on the fifth of July when we met Sterling Mulkern and Jim Vurnan at the Hyatt Regency bar in Cambridge. The bar is one of those revolving lounges, and as we flowed around in a slow circle, the city glittered and the red stone footbridges on the Charles seemed old and good and even the ivy-covered brick of Harvard didn't annoy me.

Mulkern was wearing a gray suit over a white shirt, no tie. Jim was wearing an angora crew-neck sweater and tan cotton pants. Neither of them looked pleased.

Angie and I wore the usual and neither of us cared.

Mulkern said, "I hope you have a good reason for calling us out at this hour, lad."

I said, "Of course. If you wouldn't mind, please tell me what our deal was."

Mulkern said, "Come now. What's this?"

I said, "Repeat the terms of the contract we made."

Mulkern looked at Jim and shrugged. Jim said, "Patrick, you know damn well we agreed to your daily fee plus expenses."

"Plus?"

"Plus a seven thousand dollar bonus if you produced the documents that Jenna Angeline stole." Jim was irritable; maybe his blond Vassar wife with the Dorothy Hamill do was making him sleep on the couch again. Or maybe I'd interrupted their bimonthly tryst.

I said, "You advanced me two thousand dollars. I've

worked on this for seven days. Actually, if I wanted to be technical, this is the morning of the eighth, but I'll give you a break. Here's the bill." I handed it to Mulkern.

He barely glanced at it. "Ludicrously exorbitant, but we hired you because you allegedly justify your fees."

I sat back. "Who put Curtis Moore on to me? You or Paulson?"

Jim said, "What in the hell are you talking about? Curtis Moore worked for Socia."

"But he managed to begin tailing me about five minutes after our first meeting." I looked at Mulkern. "How convenient."

Mulkern's eyes showed nothing, a man who could withstand a thousand suppositions, no matter how logical, as long as there was no proof to back them up. And if there was proof, he could just say, "I don't recall."

I sipped my beer. "How well did you know my father?"

"I knew your father well, lad, now get on with it." He looked at his watch.

"You knew he beat his wife, abused his children."

Mulkern shrugged. "Not my concern."

"Patrick," Jim said, "your personal life is irrelevant here."

"Somebody has to have a concern here," I said. I looked at Mulkern. "If you knew about my father, Senator, as a public servant, why didn't you do something about it?"

"I just told you, lad—not my concern."

"What is your *concern,* Senator?"

"The documents, Pat."

"What is your concern, Senator?" I asked again.

"The Commonwealth of course." He chuckled. "I'd love to sit here and explain the utilitarian concept to you, Pat, but I haven't the time. A few cuffs on the side of the head from your old man is not a call for action, boy."

A few cuffs. Two hospital stays in the first twelve years of my life.

I said, "Did you know about Paulson? I mean, every-thing?"

"Come now, boy. Complete your contract and let's go about our separate ways." His upper lip was slick with perspiration.

"How much did you know? Did you know he was fuck-ing little boys?"

"There's no need for that sort of language here," Mul-kern said and smiled, looking around the room.

Angie said, "Tell us what sort of language fits your sense of propriety and we'll see if it applies to child molestation and prostitution and extortion and murder."

"What're you talking about now?" Mulkern said. "Crazy talk is what I'm hearing. Crazy talk. Give me the documents, Pat."

"Senator?"

"Yes, Pat?"

"Don't call me 'Pat.' It's something you do to a dog, not something you call a person."

Mulkern sat back and rolled his eyes. I obviously had no grip on this edge of the planet. He said, "Lad, you—"

"How much did you know, Senator? How much? Your aide-de-camp is doing little kids and people end up dying all over the place because he and Socia took a couple of home movies for themselves and things got out of hand. Didn't they? What'd Socia blackmail Paulson so he'd change the nature of his pressure on the street terrorism bill? And Paulson, what'd he have a few too many drinks mourning his lost innocence, and Jenna found them? Found photos of her son being molested by the man she worked for? Maybe even voted for? How much did you know, Sen-ator?"

He stared at me.

"And I was the magnet," I said. "Wasn't I?" I looked at Jim and he stared back, blank-faced. "I was supposed to lead Socia and Paulson to Jenna, help them clean up the mess. Is that it, Senator?"

He met my anger and indignation, and he smiled. He knew I had nothing on him, just questions and suppositions. He knew that's all anyone ever had, and his eyes hardened in victory. The more I asked, the less I'd get. The way of things.

He said, "Give me the documents, Pat."

I said, "Let me see the check, Sterl."

He held out his hand and Jim put a check in it. Jim was looking at me as if we'd been playing the same game together for years, yet only now was he realizing that I had no grasp of the rules. He shook his head slowly, a den mother's motion. Jim would've made some fine convent a good nun.

Mulkern filled in the "pay to the order of" part of the check but left the amount blank. He said, "The documents, Pat."

I reached down to the seat and handed him the manila envelope. He opened it, took the photos out, held them on his lap. He said, "No copies this time? I'm proud of you, Pat."

I said, "Sign the check, Senator."

He leafed through the rest of the photos, smiled sadly at one, put them back in the envelope. He picked up the pen again, tapped it against the tabletop lightly. He said, "Pat, I think you need an attitude adjustment. Yes. So I'm going to cut your bonus in half. How about that?"

"I made copies."

"Copies don't mean a thing in court."

"They can make a hell of a stink though."

He looked at me, sized me up in a second, and shook his head. He bent toward the check.

I said, "Call Paulson. Ask him which one's missing."

The pen stopped. He said, "Missing?"

Jim said, "Missing?"

Angie said, "Missing?" just to be a smart-ass.

I nodded. "Missing. Paulson can tell you there were twenty-two in all. You got twenty-one in that envelope."

"And where would it be?" Mulkern asked.

"Sign the check and find out, dickhead."

I don't think Mulkern had ever been called a "dickhead" in his life. He didn't seem too fond of it either, but maybe it would grow on him. He said, "Give it to me."

I said, "Sign that check, no 'attitude adjustments,' and I'll tell you where it is."

Jim said, "Don't sign it, Senator."

Mulkern said, "Shut up, Jim."

I said, "Yeah, shut up, Jim. Go fetch the senator a bone or something."

Mulkern stared at me. It seemed to be his main method of intimidation and it was lost on someone who'd just spent the past few days getting shot at. It took him a few minutes, but I think he got it. He said, "Whatever happens, I'll ruin you." He signed the check with the proper amount and handed it over.

"Shucks," I said.

"Hand over the photograph."

"I told you I'd tell you where it was, Senator. I never said I'd hand it over to you."

Mulkern closed his eyes for a moment and breathed heavily through his nostrils. "Fine. Where is it?"

"Right over there," Angie said and pointed across the bar.

Richie Colgan stuck his head out from behind a fern. He waved to us, then looked at Mulkern and smiled. A big smile. The corners of his mouth damn near reached his eyelids.

Mulkern said, "No."

Angie said, "Yes," and patted his arm.

I said, "Look on the bright side, Sterl—you didn't have to write Richie a check. He fucked you over for free." We stood up from the table.

Mulkern said, "You're done in this town. You won't even be able to get welfare."

I said, "No kidding? Hell then, I might as well just go

over to Richie and tell him you gave me this check for my help in covering up your involvement in this whole affair.''

Mulkern said, ''And what would you have then?''

''I'd have you in the same position you're ready to put me in. And hell if it wouldn't make my day.'' I reached down, picked up my beer, finished it. ''Still want to wreck my name, Sterl?''

Mulkern held the envelope in his hand. He said, ''Brian Paulson's a good man. A good politician. And these photos are almost seven years old. Why bring this to the surface now? It's old news.''

I smiled and quoted him: '' 'Everything but yesterday seems young,' Senator.'' I nudged Jim with my elbow. ''Ain't that always the way?''

32

We tried to have a conversation with Richie in the parking lot but it was like trying to talk to someone as he passed by on a jet. He was rocking forward on his feet and he kept interrupting to say, "Hold that thought, would you?" Then he'd whisper something into his handheld tape recorder. Probably wrote most of his column standing in the parking lot of the Hyatt Regency.

We said our good-nights and he bounced on the balls of his feet all the way to his car. We might have killed Socia, but Richie was going to bury Paulson.

We took a cab home; the still streets were littered with the residue of fireworks; the wind carried a bitter tang of gunpowder. The rush of burying Mulkern's whipping boy in front of him was already beginning to dissipate, leaking out of the cab onto those desolate streets, drifting off somewhere into the shadows that swept over us between the streetlights.

When we reached my place, Angie went straight to the fridge, took a bottle of zinfandel from the door. She took a glass too, though after watching her drink it, there didn't seem much point; the only way she could have gone through it any faster would have been intravenously. I took a couple of beers and we sat in the living room with the windows open, listening to the breeze blow a beer can down the avenue, tipping it against the asphalt, rolling it steadily toward the corner.

I knew that in a week or so, I'd look back on this with

pleasure, savor the look on Mulkern's face as he realized he'd just paid me a large sum of money to blow a hole in his life. Somehow I'd managed to pull off the rarest of feats—I'd made someone in the State House accountable. In a week or so, that would feel good. Not now though. Now we were facing something else entirely, the air heavy with the impending weight of our own consciences.

Angie was halfway through the bottle when she said, "What's going on?"

She stood up, the wine bottle hanging loosely between her index and middle fingers, tapping against her thigh.

I got up, not sure I was ready to face this yet. I got two more beers, came back. I said, "We killed someone." It sounded simple.

"In cold blood."

"In cold blood." I opened one beer, placed the other on the floor beside the chair.

She drained her glass, poured some more. "He wasn't dangerous to us."

"Not at that moment, no."

"But we killed him anyway."

"We killed him anyway," I said. It was numbing and repetitious, this conversation, but I had the feeling we were each trying to say exactly what we'd done, no bullshit, no lies to come back and haunt us later.

"Why?" she asked.

"Because he repulsed us. Morally." I drank some beer. It could have been water for all I tasted it.

"A lot of people morally repulse us," she said. "We going to kill them too?"

"I don't think so."

"Why not?"

"Not enough bullets."

She said, "I don't want to joke about this. Not now."

She was right. I said, "Sorry."

She said, "In the exact same situation, we'd do it again."

I thought of Socia holding up the photograph, running

his finger between his son's legs. I said, "Yes, we would."

"He was a predator," she said.

I nodded.

"He allowed his child to be molested for money, so we killed him." She drank some more wine, not quite inhaling it anymore. She was standing in the middle of the floor, pivoting slowly on her left foot every now and then, the bottle swinging like a pendulum between her fingers.

I said, "That's about the size of it."

She said, "Paulson did similar things. He molested that child, probably hundreds of others. We knew that. We didn't kill him."

I said, "Killing Socia was an impulse. We didn't know we were going to do it when we met him."

She laughed, a short harsh sound. "We didn't, huh? Why'd we take a silencer with us?"

I let the question fall between us, tried not to answer it. Eventually I said, "Maybe we did go there knowing we'd kill him given half an excuse. He deserved it."

"So did Paulson. He's alive."

"We'd go to jail if we killed Paulson. Nobody cared about Socia. They'll chalk it up to the gang war, be happy he's gone."

"How convenient for us."

I stood up, came across to her. I put my hands on her shoulders, stopped her lazy pivot. I said, "We killed Socia on impulse." If I said it enough, maybe it'd become true. "We couldn't get to Paulson. He's too well insulated. But we took care of him."

"In very civilized fashion." She said "civilized" the way some people say "taxes."

"Yes," I said.

"So we took care of Socia according to the laws of the jungle, and we dispatched Paulson in accordance with the laws of civilization."

"Exactly."

She looked into my eyes and hers were swimming with

alcohol and exhaustion and ghosts. She said, "Civilization seems to be something we choose when it fits our purpose."

Not much I could argue with there. A black pimp was dead and a white child molester was preparing a press release over a bottle of Chivas somewhere, each one as guilty as the other.

People like Paulson would always be able to hide behind power. They might face disgrace, they might even do six months in a federal country club and face public castigation, but they'd breathe. Paulson might actually come out of this OK. A few years back, a congressman who'd admitted to having sex with a fifteen-year-old boy was reelected. I guess, to some people, even statutory rape is relative.

And people like Socia could slip through for a while, maybe a long while. They'd kill and maim and make the lives of everyone around them ugly and bleak, but sooner or later, they usually ended up like Socia himself—brain leaking out under an expressway. They ended up on page thirteen of the Metro section and the cops shrugged and didn't work too hard to find their killers.

One disgraced, one dead. One breathing, one dead. One white, one dead.

I ran my hands through my hair, felt the grit and oil from the last day, smelled the trash and waste on my fingers. At that moment, I truly hated the world and everything in it.

L.A. burns, and so many other cities smolder, waiting for the hose that will flood gasoline over the coals, and we listen to politicians who fuel our hate and our narrow views and tell us it's simply a matter of getting back to basics while they sit in their beachfront properties and listen to the surf so they won't have to hear the screams of the drowning.

They tell us it's about race, and we believe them. And they call it a "democracy," and we nod our heads, so pleased with ourselves. We blame the Socias, we occasionally sneer at the Paulsons, but we always vote for the Sterling Mulkerns. And in occasional moments of quasi-lucidity, we wonder why the Mulkerns of this world don't respect us.

They don't respect us because we are their molested children. They fuck us morning, noon, and night, but as long as they tuck us in with a kiss, as long as they whisper into our ears, "Daddy loves you, Daddy will take care of you," we close our eyes and go to sleep, trading our bodies, our souls, for the comforting veneers of "civilization" and "security," the false idols of our twentieth-century wet dream.

And it's our reliance on that dream that the Mulkerns, the Paulsons, the Socias, the Phils, the Heroes of this world depend upon. That's their dark knowledge. That's how they win.

I gave Angie a weak smile. "I'm tired," I said.

"Me too." She gave me her own weak smile. "Exhausted." She walked to the couch, spread the sheet I'd left across it. She said, "We'll figure it out someday. Right?"

"Yeah. Someday," I said, walking toward my bedroom. "Sure."

33

The photograph we'd given Richie showed Senator Paulson in all his glory. It showed very specifically what he got his sense of glory from. Roland's body took up a third of the frame and you got a good sense of his age, of the youth in the body under Paulson. No doubt about his sex. But unlike most of the other photographs, you couldn't see Roland's face, just his small ears and head. Socia was standing in the bedroom, watching with a bored expression on his face, smoking a cigarette.

The *Trib* ran the photo with appropriate softening and black bars over the places you'd imagine. Beside the photograph was another—one of Socia lying on his back in the gravel, his body looking like an inflatable doll someone had forgotten to inflate. His head was thrown back, the small pipe still in his hand. Over the photo it said: MAN IN PAULSON PIC KILLED GANGLAND-STYLE.

In addition to his column, Richie's byline ran over the Socia murder story too. He said the police had no suspects as of yet, that any fingerprints could have been obscured if the killer had had the sense to rub his hands in the gravel before he touched anything. The killer had. He mentioned that the Xerox of the Paulson photo had been discovered in Socia's bloody linen jacket. He mentioned Socia's common-law marriage to Jenna Angeline, the same Jenna Angeline who'd been a cleaning woman for, among others, Senators Paulson and Mulkern. They reran her death photograph too, the State House looming up behind her.

It was the biggest local scandal since the DA bungled the Charles Stuart case. Maybe bigger. We'd have to wait until it all came out in the wash.

One thing that wouldn't come out in the wash was Roland. I doubt Paulson knew the identity of the child he'd been with that day; over the ensuing years, I'm sure there were so many more. And if he did know, I doubted he'd be shouting it from the rooftops. Socia wasn't up to much public speaking these days, and Angie and I were unequivocally not involved.

Richie was one hell of a reporter. He tied Paulson to Socia and Socia to Jenna by the third paragraph, then noted that Paulson had gone on record in Friday's legislative session motioning for an extra day off, the precise day the street terrorism bill was scheduled to come to the floor. Richie never insinuated, he never accused. He just laid fact after fact down on everyone's breakfast table and let them draw their own conclusions.

I had my doubts about how many of them would get it, but I figured enough would figure it out.

Paulson was reportedly on vacation at the family home in Marblehead, but by the time I caught the morning news on TV, there were Devin and Oscar in front of the cameras in Marblehead. Oscar said, "Senator Paulson has one hour to turn himself in to the Marblehead Police Department or we're going in after him."

Devin didn't say anything. He stood beside his partner, beaming, a cigar the size of a Boeing in his mouth.

The reporter said to Oscar, "Sergeant Lee, your partner looks rather pleased about this."

Oscar said, "He's so happy he don't know whether to shit or—" and they cut to a commercial.

I flipped around, saw Sterling Mulkern on Channel Seven. he was coming up the State House steps, an army of people trotting beside him, Jim Vurnan trying to keep pace a few steps back. He sliced through the mass of microphones like an oar through a dead sea, a chant of "No comment," coming from his lips all the way through the front doors. I was kind of hoping he'd keep things lively, throw in a few "I don't recalls" to break up the monotony, but I guess pleasing me wasn't at the top of his "to do" list this morning.

Angie had been awake for a few minutes by this time, her face propped up on the arm of the couch where she'd slept, her eyes puffed with sleep, but alert. She said, "Sometimes, Skid, this job ain't half bad."

I was sitting on the floor at the foot of the couch. I looked at her. "Does your hair always stand on end first thing in the morning?"

Not a smart thing to say when you're sitting near someone's foot. The next thing I said was, "Ouch."

She got up, tossed the sheet over my head, and said, "Coffee?"

"I'd love some." I pulled the sheet off my face.

"Make enough for the both of us then, would you?" She stumbled into the bathroom and turned the shower on.

On Channel Five, the two anchors were in early, promising to stay with me until all the facts were in. I wanted to tell them they'd be having pizzas delivered to the station for the next ten years if that's what they were waiting for, but I let it slide. They'd figure it out.

Ken Mitchum, on Channel Seven, said it was possibly the biggest scandal since the Curly years.

Channel Six was doing the Charles Stuart comparison by the time I caught up with them, paralleling the racial overtones that had tinged both cases. Ward was smiling as he reported this, but Ward always smiles. Laura, on the other hand, looked pissed off. Laura is black; I didn't blame her.

Angie came back out of the shower, newly dressed in a pair of my gray shorts and a white Polo sweatshirt. The sweatshirt was mine too, but damn if she didn't look better than me in it. She said, "Where's my coffee?"

"Same place as the bell. Let me know when you find the both of them."

She frowned, brushing out her hair, head tilted to one side.

The photograph of Socia's corpse flashed on the screen. She stopped brushing for a moment. I said, "How do you feel?"

She nodded toward the TV. "Fine, as long as I don't think about it. Come on, let's get out of here."

"And go where?"

"Well, I don't know about you, babe, but I want to spend some of that bonus money. And," she said, straightening up, tossing her long hair behind her, "we have to visit Bubba."

"Have you considered that he may be angry with us?"

She shrugged. "You got to die some time, right?"

I picked up a Nintendo Gameboy for Bubba, bought a bunch of Kill-the-Commie-Terrorist games to go with it. Angie bought him a Freddy Krueger doll and five issues of *Jugs* magazine.

There was a police guard at his door, but after making a few phone calls, he allowed us to go in. Bubba was reading a worn copy of *The Anarchist's Cookbook* when we entered, learning all sorts of new and nifty ways to build a hydrogen bomb in his backyard. He looked up at us, and for the single longest second of my life, I couldn't tell if he was angry or not.

He said, " 'Bout time someone I liked showed up."

I learned how to breathe again.

He was paler than I'd ever seen him and the whole left side of his chest and arm was in a cast, but take away the cast and I've seen people with a bad cold who looked less healthy. Angie bent over and kissed his forehead, then suddenly pulled his head to her chest and held it there for a moment, her eyes closed. "I was worried about you, you maniac."

"What don't kill me only makes me bloody."

Bubba. Deep as always.

He said, "A Freddie Krueger doll! Hot shit!" He looked at me. "What'd you bring me, homeboy?"

We left after a half hour or so. The doctors had initially thought he'd be in ICU for at least a week, but now they were saying he could be released in another two days. He'd face an indictment, of course, but he assured us, "What's a witness? Really. I never met one. They those people who always seem to get amnesia just before I'm supposed to go to trial?"

We walked down Charles Street into the Back Bay, Angie's credit card burning a hole in her pocket. Bonwit Teller never stood a chance. She hit the place like a cyclone and by the time we left, we were carrying half the first floor in paper bags.

I did a half hour's shopping at Eddie Bauer, another twenty minutes at the Banana Republic in Copley Place, my stomach beginning to churn in the atmosphere of four-story marble waterfalls and solid gold window frames and Neiman-Marcus displays of eighty-five-dollar argyle socks. If Donald Trump puked, Copley Place is probably what would hit the toilet.

We took the back entrance out of there, the best place to find a cab in the city in midafternoon. We were trying to figure out where we were going to eat lunch, when I saw Roland standing at the bottom of the escalator, his huge frame spread lazily across the exit way, one arm in a cast, one eye closed shut, the other looking steadily at us.

I reached under my untucked shirt, got a firm grip on the nine millimeter, cold against my stomach but warm in my hand.

Roland stepped back. "I want to talk."

I kept my hand on my gun.

Angie said, "So talk."

"Take a walk with me." He turned and walked out through the revolving door.

I'm not quite sure why we followed him, but we did.

The sun was strong, the air warm but not too humid as we walked up Dartmouth, away from the staid hotels and the quaint shops, the yuppies sipping cappuccino amidst the illusion of civilization. We crossed Columbus Avenue and went down through the South End, the restored brownstones eventually giving way to the sorrier-looking ones, those that hadn't been touched by the frontier mentality of the fern-and-Perrier crowd yet. We kept going, none of us saying a word, farther down into Roxbury. As soon as we crossed over the border, Roland said, "Just want to speak to you a minute."

I looked around me, saw nothing that gave me comfort, but somehow, I trusted him. Having checked inside the hollows of the sling that supported his arm and seeing no gun there, I had one concrete reason to feel this way. But that wasn't all of it. What I knew of Roland, he wasn't like his father. He didn't lull you into death with a few words and a hypnotist's inflection. He just came straight at you and sent you to your coffin.

Another thing I was realizing, for sure—the kid was huge. I'd never been this close to him when he'd been on his feet, and it was damn near awe-inspiring. He was closing in on six foot four or so and every inch of skin that covered his body was bunched tight with coiled muscle. I'm six feet even and I felt like a dwarf.

He stopped in a wornout field, a construction site waiting to happen, the next place big business would go to encroach and keep encroaching, pushing Roxbury west or east until it became another South End, another place to have a good drink and hear underground music. And its people would roll east or west too, while politicians cut ribbons and shook the hands of entrepreneurs and talked of progress, pointed to declining crime statistics in the area with pride, while ignoring the rising crime statistics in the areas where the displaced had settled. Roxbury would become a nice word again, Dedham or Randolph a bad one. And another neighborhood would dissolve.

Roland said, "You two killed Marion."

We didn't say anything.

"You think it would . . . please me? That it? Keep me from your door?"

I said, "No. Didn't have much to do with you at the time, Roland. He pissed us off. Simple as that."

He looked at me, then off beyond the lot. We weren't too far from the decrepit tenements where he'd chased us the night before. All around us were worn buildings and sparse fields of city growth. Not much more than a stone's throw from Beacon Hill.

He seemed to read my thoughts. He said, "That's right. We're sitting on your doorstep."

I looked back, saw the skyline glittering above us in the midafternoon sun, close enough to kiss. I wondered what it must be like, living here, this close, knowing you'd never get to taste it. Not for free. A couple of miles and a world away.

I said, "Oh well."

Roland said, "You can't keep doing this to us forever. Can't hold us back."

I said, "Roland, 'we' didn't create you. Don't try and put that off on the white man too. Your father and you made you what you are."

"And what am I?" he said.

I shrugged. "A sixteen-year-old killing machine."

"Damn right," he said. "Damn right." He spit on the ground to the left of my foot. He said, "But I wasn't always."

I thought of the skinny boy in the photographs, tried to imagine what benevolent, possibly hopeful thoughts had run through his brain before someone had burned it out of him, overloaded the circuits until the good had to go just to make way for all the bad. I looked at the sixteen-year-old man in front of me, the massive, bulked-up stone with the bad eye and the arm in the cast. I couldn't, for the life of me, connect the two.

I said, "Yeah, well, we were all little boys once, Roland." I looked at Angie. "Little girls too."

Roland said, "The white man—"

Angie dropped her shopping bag and said, "Roland, we're not going to listen to this 'white man' shit. We know all about the white man. We know he has the power and we know the black man doesn't. We know the way the world works and we know that way sucks. We know all that. We're not too pleased with ourselves either, but there you are. And maybe if you had some suggestions on how to change things for the better, we'd have something to talk about. But you kill people, Roland, and you sell crack. Don't expect violins."

He smiled at her. It wasn't the warmest smile I'd ever seen—Roland has about as much warmth in him as a polar cap—but it wasn't completely cold either. He said, "Maybe. Maybe." He scratched at the skin just above his cast with his free hand. "You kept . . . that thing out of the papers, so maybe you think I owe you." He looked at us. "I don't. Don't owe nobody nothing, because I don't ask for nothing." He rubbed the skin beside his bad eye. "But, then, I don't see much point in killing you no more either."

I had to remind myself he was sixteen years old.

I said, "Roland, let me ask you something."

He frowned, seemed bored suddenly. "Go ahead."

"All this hate, all this anger in you—any of it go away when you found out your father was dead?"

He turned a cube of cinder block over with his foot and shrugged. "No. Maybe if I'd been able to pull the trigger myself, maybe then."

I shook my head. "Doesn't work that way."

He kicked at another hunk of cinder block. "No," he said, "I suppose it don't." He looked off beyond the weeds and the tenements on the other side of the lot, past the torn brick blocks with coils of soldered metal sticking out of them like flags.

His empire.

He said, "You two go on home. We forget about each other."

I said, "Deal," but I had a feeling I'd never forget Roland, even after I read his obituary.

He nodded, more to himself than us, and started to walk off. He'd crested a small slope of industrial waste, when he stopped, his back to us. Somewhere, not far away, a siren rang hollowly. He said, "My mother, she was all right. Decent."

I took Angie's hand in mine. "She was," I said. "But she was never needed."

His shoulders moved slightly, possibly a shrug, possibly something else. "Can't say that she was," he said and started walking again. He crossed the lot as we watched him, shrinking slowly as he neared the tenements. A lone prince on his way to the throne, wondering why it didn't feel as sweet as it should.

We watched him disappear through a dark doorway as a breeze—cool for this time of summer—came off the ocean and swept north past the tenement, past us with chilled fingers that mussed our hair and widened our eyes, moving on into the heart of the city. Angie's warm hand tightened around mine as we turned and sidestepped the rubble, following the breeze back to our part of town.

DARKNESS, TAKE MY HAND

This novel is dedicated to Mal Ellenburg and Sterling Watson for a thousand good arguments about the nature of the craft and the nature of the beast.

acknowledgments

For answering what I'm sure were a lot of stupid questions about the medical and correctional professions, I thank Doctor Jolie Yuknek, Department of Pediatrics, Boston City Hospital, and Sergeant Thomas Lehane, Massachusetts Department of Corrections.

For reading, responding to, and/or editing the manuscript (as well as answering even more stupid questions), thanks to Ann Rittenberg, Claire Wachtel, Chris, Gerry, Susan, and Sheila.

We should be thankful we cannot see the horrors and degradations lying around our childhood, in cupboards and bookshelves, everywhere.

—GRAHAM GREENE
The Power and the Glory

When I was a kid, my father took me up on the roof of a freshly burned building.

He'd been giving me a tour of the firehouse when the call came in, and I got to ride beside him in the front seat of the fire engine, thrill to the feel of it turning corners as its back half buckled and the sirens rang and the smoke poured blue and black and thick ahead of us.

An hour after they'd doused the flames, once my hair had been ruffled by his fellow firemen a dozen times, and I'd been fed my limit of street vendor hot dogs as I sat on the curb and watched them work, my father came and took my hand and led me up the fire escape.

Oily wisps of smoke curled into our hair and caressed the brick as we climbed, and through broken windows I could see charred, gutted floors. Gaps in the ceilings rained dirty water.

I was terrified of that building, and my father had to pick me up when he stepped out on the roof.

"Patrick," he whispered as we walked across the tar paper, "it's okay. Don't you see?"

I looked out and saw the city rising steel blue and yellow beyond the stretch of neighborhood. I could smell the heat and damage below me.

"Don't you see?" my father repeated. "It's safe here. We stopped the fire in the low floors. It can't reach us up here. If you stop it at its base, it can't rise."

He smoothed my hair and kissed my cheek.

And I trembled.

Prologue

Christmas Eve
6:15 p.m.

Three days ago, on the first official night of winter, a guy I grew up with, Eddie Brewer, was one of four people shot in a convenience store. Robbery was not a motive. The shooter, James Fahey, had recently broken up with his girlfriend, Laura Stiles, who was a cashier on the four-to-twelve shift. At eleven fifteen, as Eddie Brewer filled a styrofoam cup with ice and Sprite, James Fahey walked through the door and shot Laura Stiles once in the face and twice in the heart.

Then he shot Eddie Brewer once in the head and walked down the frozen food aisle and found an elderly Vietnamese couple huddling in the dairy section. Two bullets each for them, and James Fahey decided his work was complete.

He walked out to his car, sat behind the wheel, and taped the restraining order Laura Stiles and her family had successfully filed against him to the rearview mirror. Then he tied one of Laura's bras around his head, took a pull from a bottle of Jack Daniel's, and fired a bullet into his mouth.

James Fahey and Laura Stiles were pronounced dead at the scene. The elderly Vietnamese man died en route to Carney Hospital, his wife a few hours later. Eddie Brewer, however, lies in a coma, and while doctors say his prognosis isn't good, they also admit his continued existence is all but miraculous.

The press have been giving that description a lot of play lately, because Eddie Brewer, never anything close to a saint when we were growing up, is a priest. He'd been out jogging the night he was shot, dressed in thermals and sweats, so Fahey didn't know his vocation, though I doubt it would have mattered much. But the press, sensing both a nostalgia for religion so close to the holidays, and a fresh spin on an old story, played his priesthood for all it was worth.

TV commentators and print editorialists have likened Eddie Brewer's random shooting to a sign of the apocalypse, and around-the-clock vigils have been held at his parish in Lower Mills and outside the Carney. Eddie Brewer, an obscure cleric and a completely unassuming man, is heading for martyrdom, whether he lives or not.

None of this has anything to do with the nightmare that descended on my life and that of several others in this city two months ago, a nightmare that left me with wounds the doctors say have healed as well as can be expected, even though my right hand has yet to regain most of its feeling, and the scars on my face sometimes burn under the beard I've grown. No, a priest getting shot and the serial killer who entered my life and the latest "ethnic cleansing" being wrought in a former Soviet republic or the man who shot up an abortion clinic not far from here or another serial killer who's killed ten in Utah and has yet to be caught—none of it is connected.

But sometimes it *feels* like it is, as if somewhere there's a thread to all these events, all these random, arbitrary violences, and that if we can just figure out where that thread begins, we can pull on it, unravel everything, make sense of it.

Since Thanksgiving, I've grown the beard, the first one of my life, and while I keep it trimmed, it continues to surprise me in the mirror every morning, as if I spend my nights dreaming of a face that is smooth and unruptured by scars, flesh that is clean the way only a baby's is, skin untouched by anything but sweet air and a mother's tender caresses.

The office—Kenzie/Gennaro Investigations—is closed,

gathering dust I assume, maybe the first stray cobweb in a corner behind my desk, maybe one behind Angie's too. Angie's been gone since the end of November, and I try not to think about her. Or Grace Cole. Or Grace's daughter, Mae. Or anything at all.

Mass has just ended across the street, and with the unseasonably warm weather—still in the low forties, though the sun's been down for ninety minutes—most of the parishioners mill about outside, and their voices are sharp in the night air as they wish each other good cheer and happy holidays. They remark on the strangeness of the weather, how erratic it's been all year, how summer was cold and autumn warm and then just as suddenly bitter and icy, how no one should be surprised if Christmas morning were to bring a Santa Ana and a mercury reading in the seventies.

Someone mentions Eddie Brewer, and they speak about it for a moment, but a brief one, and I sense they don't want it to spoil their festive mood. But, oh, they say, what a sick, crazy world. Crazy is the word, they say, crazy, crazy, crazy.

I spend most of my time sitting out here lately. From the porch, I can see people, and even though it's often cool out here, their voices keep me here as my bad hand stiffens with cold and my teeth begin to chatter.

In the mornings, I carry my coffee out, sit in the brisk air and look across the avenue to the schoolyard and watch the small boys in their blue ties and matching blue pants and the small girls with their plaid skirts and glinting barrettes run around the yard. Their sudden shrieks and darting movements, their seemingly bottomless supply of frenetic energy, can be wearying or invigorating depending on my mood. When it's a bad day, those shrieks ride my spinal column like chips of broken glass. On good days, though, I get a flush of something that may be a memory of what it was like to feel whole, when the simple act of breathing didn't ache.

The issue, he wrote, is pain. How much I feel, how much I parcel out.

He came during the warmest, most erratic autumn on record, when the weather seemed to have flipped completely off its usual course, when everything seemed up-side down, as if you'd look at a hole in the ground and see stars and constellations floating at the bottom, turn your head to the sky and see dirt and trees hanging sus-pended. As if he had his fingers on the globe, and he slapped it, and the world—or at least my portion of it—spun.

Sometimes Bubba or Richie or Devin and Oscar drop by, sit out here with me and we talk about the NFL play-offs or the college bowls or the latest movies in town. We don't talk about this past autumn or Grace and Mae. We don't talk about Angie. And we never talk about him. He's done his damage, and there's nothing left to say.

The issue, he wrote, is pain.

Those words—written on a piece of white, 8×11 copy paper—haunt me. Those words, so simple, sometimes seem as if they were written in stone.

1

Angie and I were up in our belfry office trying to fix the air conditioner when Eric Gault called.

Usually in the middle of a New England October, a broken air conditioner wouldn't be a problem. A broken heater would. But it wasn't turning out to be a normal autumn. At two in the afternoon, the temperature hung in the mid-seventies and the window screens still carried the damp, baked odor of summer.

"Maybe we should call someone," Angie said.

I thumped the window unit on the side with my palm, turned it on again. Nothing.

"I bet it's the belt," I said.

"That's what you say when the car breaks down, too."

"Hmm." I glared at the air conditioner for about twenty seconds and it remained silent.

"Call it foul names," Angie said. "Maybe that'll help."

I turned my glare on her, got about as much reaction as I got from the air conditioner. Maybe I needed to work on my glare.

The phone rang and I picked it up, hoping the caller knew something about mechanics, but I got Eric Gault instead.

Eric taught criminology at Bryce University. We met when he was still teaching at U/Mass and I took a couple of his classes.

"You know anything about fixing air conditioners?"

"You try turning it on and off and then back on?" he said.

6

"Yes."

"And nothing happened?"

"Nope."

"Hit it a couple of times."

"I did."

"Call a repairman then."

"You're a lot of help."

"Is your office still in a belfry, Patrick?"

"Yes. Why?"

"Well, I have a prospective client for you."

"And?"

"I'd like her to hire you."

"Fine. Bring her by."

"The belfry?"

"Sure."

"I said I'd like her to hire you."

I looked around the tiny office. "That's cold, Eric."

"Can you stop by Lewis Wharf, say about nine in the morning?"

"I think so. What's your friend's name?"

"Diandra Warren."

"What's her problem?"

"I'd prefer it if she told you face to face."

"Okay."

"I'll meet you there tomorrow."

"See you then."

I started to hang up.

"Patrick."

"Yeah?"

"Do you have a little sister named Moira?"

"No. I have an older sister named Erin."

"Oh."

"Why?"

"Nothing. We'll talk tomorrow."

"See you then."

I hung up, looked at the air conditioner, then at Angie, back at the air conditioner, and then I dialed a repairman.

Diandra Warren lived in a fifth-story loft on Lewis Wharf. She had a panoramic view of the harbor, enormous bay windows that bathed the east end of the loft with soft morning sunlight, and she looked like the kind of woman who'd never wanted for a single thing her whole life.

Hair the color of a peach hung in a graceful, sweeping curve over her forehead and tapered into a page boy on the sides. Her dark silk shirt and light blue jeans looked as if they'd never been worn, and the bones in her face seemed chiseled under skin so unblemished and golden it reminded me of water in a chalice.

She opened the door and said, "Mr. Kenzie, Ms. Gennaro," in a soft, confident whisper, a whisper that knew a listener would lean in to hear it if necessary. "Please, come in."

The loft was precisely furnished. The couch and armchairs in the living area were a cream color that complemented the blond Scandinavian wood of the kitchen furniture and the muted reds and browns of the Persian and Native American rugs placed strategically over the hardwood floor. The sense of color gave the place an air of warmth, but the almost Spartan functionalism suggested an owner who wasn't given to the unplanned gesture or the sentimentality of clutter.

By the bay windows, the exposed brick wall was taken up by a brass bed, walnut dresser, three birch file cabinets, and a Governor Winthrop desk. In the whole place, I couldn't see a closet or any hanging clothes. Maybe she just wished a fresh wardrobe out of the air every morning, and it was waiting for her, fully pressed, by the time she came out of the shower.

She led us into the living area, and we sat in the armchairs as she moved onto the couch with a slight hesitation. Between us was a smoked-glass coffee table with a manila envelope in the center and a heavy ashtray and antique lighter to its left.

Diandra Warren smiled at us.

We smiled back. Have to be quick to improvise in this business.

Her eyes widened slightly and the smile stayed where it was. Maybe she was waiting for us to list our qualifications, show her our guns and tell her how many dastardly foes we'd vanquished since sunup.

Angie's smile faded, but I kept mine in place for a few seconds longer. Picture of the happy-go-lucky detective, putting his prospective client at ease. Patrick "Sparky" Kenzie. At your service.

Diandra Warren said, "I'm not sure how to start."

Angie said, "Eric said you may be in some trouble we could help you with."

She nodded, and her hazel irises seemed to fragment for a moment, as if something had come loose behind them. She pursed her lips, looked at her slim hands, and as she began to raise her head, the front door opened and Eric entered. His salt-and-pepper hair was tied back in a ponytail and balding on top, but he looked ten years younger than the forty-six or -seven I knew he was. He wore khakis and a denim shirt under a charcoal sport coat with the lower button clasped. The sport coat looked a bit strange on him, as if the tailor hadn't counted on a gun sticking to Eric's hip.

"Hey, Eric." I held out my hand.

He shook it. "Glad you could make it, Patrick."

"Hi, Eric." Angie extended her hand.

As he leaned over to shake it, he realized he'd exposed the gun. He closed his eyes for a moment and blushed.

Angie said, "I would feel a lot better if you placed that gun on the coffee table until we leave, Eric."

"I feel like a fool," he said, trying to crack a smile.

"Please," Diandra said, "just put it on the table, Eric."

He unsnapped the holster as if it might bite and put a Ruger .38 on top of the manila envelope.

I met his eyes, confused. Eric Gault and a gun went together like caviar and hot dogs.

He sat beside Diandra. "We've been a little on edge lately."

"Why?"

Diandra sighed. "I'm a psychiatrist, Mr. Kenzie, Ms. Gennaro. I teach at Bryce twice a week and provide counseling for staff and students in addition to maintaining my practice off campus. You expect a lot of things in my line

of work—dangerous clients, patients who have full psychotic episodes in a tiny office with you alone, paranoid
dissociative schizophrenics who find out your address. You
live with those fears. I guess you expect them to be realized one day. But this . . .'' She looked at the envelope on
the table between us. ''This is . . .''

I said, ''Try telling us how 'this' started.''

She sat back on the couch and closed her eyes for a
moment. Eric placed a hand lightly on her shoulder, and
she shook her head, eyes still closed, and he removed it,
placed it on his knee and looked at it as if he wasn't sure
how it had gotten there.

''A student came to see me one morning when I was at
Bryce. At least she said she was a student.''

''Any reason to think otherwise?'' Angie said.

''Not at the time. She had a student ID.'' Diandra
opened her eyes. ''But once I did some checking I found
there was no record of her.''

''What was this person's name?'' I said.

''Moira Kenzie.''

I looked at Angie and she raised an eyebrow.

''You see, Mr. Kenzie, when Eric said your name I
jumped on it, hoping you're related to this girl.''

I thought about it. Kenzie isn't a terribly common name.
Even back in Ireland, there's only a few of us around Dublin and a few more scattered up near Ulster. Given the
cruelty and violence that festered in the hearts of my father
and his brothers, it wasn't necessarily a bad thing that the
bloodline looked to be close to its end.

''You said this Moira Kenzie was a girl?''

''Yes?''

''So she was young?''

''Nineteen, maybe twenty.''

I shook my head. ''Then, no, I don't know her, Doctor
Warren. The only Moira Kenzie I know is a cousin of my
late father. She's in her mid-sixties and she hasn't left Van-
couver in twenty years.''

Diandra nodded, a curt, bitter one, and her pupils
seemed to dim. ''Well, then . . .''

"Doctor Warren," I said, "what happened when you met this Moira Kenzie?"

She pursed her lips and looked at Eric, then up at a heavy ceiling fan above her. She exhaled slowly through her mouth and I knew she'd decided to trust us.

"Moira said she was the girlfriend of a man named Hurlihy."

"Kevin Hurlihy?" Angie said.

Diandra Warren's golden skin had paled to eggshell in the last minute. She nodded.

Angie looked at me and again raised her eyebrows.

Eric said, "You know him?"

"Unfortunately," I said, "we've met Kevin."

Kevin Hurlihy grew up with us. He's pretty silly-looking—a gangly, tall guy with hips like doorknobs and unruly, brittle hair that looks like he styles it by sticking his head in a toilet bowl and flushing. When he was twelve years old, a cancerous growth was successfully removed from his larynx. The scar tissue from the surgery, however, left him with a cracked, high-pitched mess of a voice that sounds like the perpetual angry whine of a teenage girl. He wears Coke-bottle glasses that make his eyes bulge like a frog's, and he has the fashion sense of an accordionist in a polka band. He's Jack Rouse's right-hand man and Jack Rouse runs the Irish Mafia in this city, and if Kevin looks and sounds comical, he isn't even close.

"What happened?" Angie said.

Diandra looked up at the ceiling and the skin over her throat trembled. "Moira told me Kevin scared her. She told me he had her followed constantly, forced her to watch him have sex with other women, forced her to have sex with associates, how he beats men who even look at her casually, and how . . ." She swallowed, and Eric placed a tentative hand on top of her own. "Then she told me how she'd had an affair with a man and Kevin found out and how he . . . killed the man and buried him in Somerville. She begged me to help her. She . . ."

"Who contacted you?" I said.

She wiped her left eye, then lit a long white cigarette with the antique lighter. As afraid as she was, her hand only betrayed the slightest tremor. "Kevin," she said, the word popping out of her mouth like it was sour. "He called me at four in the morning. When the phone rings at four in the morning, do you know how you feel?"

Disoriented, confused, alone, and terrified. Just the way a guy like Kevin Hurlihy wants you to feel.

"He said all these foul things. He said, and I quote, 'How's it feel to be living your last week on earth, you useless cunt?' "

Sounded like Kevin. Class all the way.

She inhaled with a hiss.

I said, "When did you receive this call?"

"Three weeks ago."

"Three weeks?" Angie said.

"Yes. I tried to ignore it. I called the police, but they said there was nothing they could do since I had no proof it was Kevin who called." She ran a hand through her hair, curled into herself a bit more on the sofa, looked at us.

"When you talked to the police," I said, "did you mention anything about this body buried in Somerville?"

"No."

"Good," Angie said.

"Why have you waited so long before seeking some help?"

She reached over and slid Eric's gun off the manila envelope. She handed the envelope to Angie, who opened it and pulled out a black-and-white photograph. She looked at it, then handed it to me.

The young man in the photo looked to be about twenty—handsome, with long, sandy brown hair and two days' beard stubble. He wore jeans with rips in the knees, a T-shirt under an unbuttoned flannel shirt, and a black leather jacket. The college grunge uniform. He had a notebook under his arm and was walking past a brick wall. He seemed unaware his picture was being taken.

"My son, Jason," Diandra said. "He's a sophomore at Bryce. That building is the corner of the Bryce Library. The photograph arrived yesterday by regular mail."

"Any note?"

She shook her head.

Eric said, "Her name and address are typed on the front of that envelope, nothing else."

"Two days ago," Diandra said, "when Jason was home for the weekend, I overheard him telling a friend on the phone that he couldn't shake the feeling someone was stalking him. Stalking. That's the word he used." She pointed at the photo with her cigarette and the tremor in her hand was more noticeable. "The next day, that arrived."

I looked at the photo again. Classic Mafia warning—you may think you know something about us, but we know everything about you.

"I haven't seen Moira Kenzie since that first day. She isn't enrolled at Bryce, the phone number she gave me is for a Chinese restaurant, and she's not listed in any local phone directories. But yet she came to me. And now I have this in my life. And I don't know why. Christ." She slapped both palms down into her thighs and closed her eyes. When she opened them, all the courage she'd presumably been sucking out of the thin air for the last three weeks was gone. She looked terrified and suddenly aware of how weak the walls we erect around our lives truly are.

I looked at Eric, his hand on Diandra's, and tried to gauge their relationship. I'd never known him to date a woman and always assumed he was gay. Whether true or not, I'd known him for ten years and he'd never mentioned a son.

"Who's Jason's father?" I said.

"What? Why?"

"When a child's involved in a threat," Angie said, "we have to consider custody issues."

Diandra and Eric shook their heads simultaneously.

"Diandra's been divorced almost twenty years," Eric said. "Her ex-husband is friendly but distant with Jason."

"I need his name," I said.

"Stanley Timpson," Diandra said.

"Suffolk County District Attorney Stan Timpson?"

She nodded.

"Doctor Warren," Angie said, "since your ex-husband

is the most powerful law enforcement officer in the Commonwealth, we'd have to assume that—"

"No." Diandra shook her head. "Most people don't even know we were married. He has a second wife, three other children, and his contact with Jason and me is minimal. Believe me, this has nothing to do with Stan."

I looked at Eric.

"I'd have to agree," he said. "Jason has taken Diandra's name, not Stan's, and he has almost no contact with his father outside of a birthday phone call or Christmas card."

"Will you help me?" Diandra said.

Angie and I looked at each other. Hanging out in the same zip code as people like Kevin Hurlihy and his boss, Jack Rouse, isn't something either Angie or I consider healthy. Now we were being asked to cruise right up to their dinner tables and ask them to stop bothering our client. What fun. If we took Diandra Warren's case, it would go down as one of the more patently suicidal decisions we'd ever made.

Angie read my mind. "What," she said, "you want to live forever?"

2

As we left Lewis Wharf and walked up Commercial, the schizophrenic New England autumn had turned an ugly morning into a glorious afternoon. When I woke up, a breeze so chilly and mean it seemed the exhalation of a Puritan god was hissing through the cracks under my windows. The sky was hard and pale as baseball leather, and people walking to their cars on the avenue were hunched into thick jackets and oversized sweaters, breath steaming around their faces.

By the time I left my apartment, the temperature had risen into the high forties, and the muted sun, trying to push through the sheet of hard sky, looked like an orange trapped just beneath the surface of a frozen pond.

Walking up Lewis Wharf toward Diandra Warren's apartment, I'd removed my jacket as the sun finally broke through, and now as we drove back to the neighborhood, the mercury hovered in the high sixties.

We drove past Copp's Hill, and the warm breeze sweeping off the harbor rustled the trees overlooking the hill and several handfuls of burnished red leaves crested the slate headstones and fluttered down onto the grass. On our right, the stretch of wharfs and docks glinted under the sun, and to our left the brown, red, and off-white brick of the North End hinted of tile floors and old open doorways and the smells of thick sauces and garlic and freshly baked bread.

"Can't hate the city on a day like this," Angie said.

"Impossible."

She grasped the back of her thick hair with one hand

15

and twisted it into a makeshift ponytail, tilting her head toward the open window to catch the sun on her face and neck. Watching her with her eyes closed and a small grin on her face, I was almost prepared to believe that she was completely healthy.

But she wasn't. After she left her husband, Phil, left him in a bloody heap retching off her front porch, payment for having tried to batter her body one time too many, Angie passed the winter in the mist of an increasingly short attention span and a dating ritual which left a succession of males scratching their heads as she abandoned them without notice and moved on to the next.

Since I've never been a paragon of moral virtue, I couldn't say much to her without sounding like a hypocrite, and by early spring she seemed to have bottomed out. She quit bringing warm bodies home and started to participate fully in case work again, even fixed up her apartment a bit, which for Angie meant she cleaned the oven and bought a broom. But she wasn't whole, not like she used to be.

She was quieter, less cocky. She'd call or drop by my apartment at the oddest hours to talk about the day we just shared. She also claimed she hadn't seen Phil in months, but for some reason I couldn't fully explain, I didn't believe her.

This was all compounded by the fact that for only the second time in all the years we've known each other, I couldn't always be there for her at a moment's notice. Since July, when I met Grace Cole, I'd been spending whole days and nights, sometimes full weekends, with her whenever we could get time together. Occasionally I'm also enlisted into babysitting duty for Grace's daughter, Mae, and so I'm often beyond the reach of my partner except in the case of an absolute emergency. It wasn't something either of us ever really prepared for, since as Angie once put it: "There's a better chance of seeing a black guy in a Woody Allen movie than seeing Patrick in a serious relationship."

She caught me watching her at a light, opened her eyes

fully and looked at me with a tiny smile playing on her lips. "Worrying about me again, Kenzie?"

My partner the psychic.

"Just checking you out, Gennaro. Purely sexist, nothing more."

"I know you, Patrick." She leaned back from the window. "You're still playing big brother."

"And?"

"And," she said, running the backs of her fingers along my cheek, "it's time for you to stop."

I lifted a strand of hair out of her eye, just before the light turned green. "No," I said.

We stopped inside her house long enough for her to change into a pair of cut-off denim shorts and for me to take two bottles of Rolling Rock from her fridge. Then we sat out on her back porch listening to her neighbor's over-starched shirts crack and snap in the breeze and enjoyed the day.

She leaned back on her elbows, stretched her legs out in front of her. "So, we have a case suddenly."

"We do," I said, glancing at her smooth olive legs and faded denim cut-offs. There might not be much good in this world, but show me anyone who has a bad thing to say about denim cut-offs and I'll show you a lunatic.

"Any ideas how to play it?" she said. Then, "Stop looking at my legs, you pervert. You're practically a married man now."

I shrugged, leaned back myself, looked up at the bright marble sky. "Not sure. Know what bothers me?"

"Besides Muzac, infomercials, and New Jersey accents?"

"About this case."

"Pray tell."

"Why the name Moira Kenzie? I mean, if it's a fake, which we can probably assume, why my last name?"

"There's something known as coincidence. Maybe you've heard of it. It's when the—"

"Okay. Something else."

"Yes?"

"Kevin Hurlihy seem like the type of guy who'd have a girlfriend to you?"

"Well, no. But it's been years, really, since we've known him."

"Still . . ."

"Who knows?" she said. "I've seen a lot of weird, ugly guys with beautiful women and vice versa."

"Kevin's not just weird, though. He's a sadist."

"So are a lot of professional boxers. You always see them with women."

I shrugged. "I guess. Okay. So how do we deal with Kevin?"

"And Jack Rouse," she said.

"Dangerous guys," I said.

"Very," she said.

"And who deals with dangerous people on a daily basis?"

"Certainly not us," she said.

"No," I said, "we're wusses."

"And proud of it," she said. "Which leaves . . ." She turned her head, squinted into the sun to look at me. "You don't mean—" she said.

"I do."

"Oh, Patrick."

"We must visit Bubba," I said.

"Really?"

I sighed, not real happy about it myself. "Really."

"Damn," Angie said.

3

"**Left,**" **Bubba said.** Then, "About eight inches to your right. Good. Almost there."

He was walking backward a few feet ahead of us, his hands held up near his chest, his fingers wiggling like he was backing in a truck. "Okay," he said. "Left foot about nine inches to your left. That's it."

Visiting Bubba in the old warehouse where he lives is a lot like playing Twister on the edge of a cliff. Bubba's got the first forty feet of the second floor wired with enough explosives to vaporize the eastern seaboard, so you have to follow his directions to the letter if you want to breathe without artificial assistance for the rest of your life. Both Angie and I have been through the process countless times before, but we've never trusted our memories enough to cross those forty feet without Bubba's help. Call us overly cautious.

"Patrick," he said, looking at me gravely as my right foot hovered a quarter inch off the ground, "I said six inches to the right. Not five."

I took a deep breath and moved my foot another inch.

He smiled and nodded.

I set my foot down. I didn't blow up. I was glad.

Behind me, Angie said, "Bubba, why don't you just invest in a security system?"

Bubba frowned. "This is my security system."

"This is a minefield, Bubba."

"You say tomato," Bubba said. "Four inches left, Patrick."

Angie exhaled loudly behind me.

"You're clear, Patrick," he said as I stepped onto a patch of floor about ten feet away from him. He narrowed his eyes at Angie. "Don't be such a sissy, Ange."

Angie was standing with one knee raised looking a lot like a stork. A very put-out stork, actually. She said, "When I get there, I'm shooting you, Bubba Rogowski."

"Oooh," Bubba said. "She used my full name. Just like my mom used to."

"You never knew your mother," I reminded him.

"Psychically, Patrick," he said and touched his protruding frontal lobe. "Psychically."

Booby traps aside, sometimes I worry about him.

Angie stepped onto the patch of floor I'd just vacated.

"You're clear," Bubba said and she punched his shoulder.

"Anything else we should worry about?" I said. "Spears falling from the ceiling, razor blades in the chairs?"

"Not unless I activate them." He walked back toward an old fridge which sat beside two worn brown sofas, an orange office chair, and a stereo system so old it had an eight-track deck. In front of the office chair was a wooden crate, and its several cousins were stacked on the other side of a mattress thrown down just beyond the couches. A couple of the crates were open and I could see the ugly butts of oiled black firearms sticking up through yellow straw. Bubba's daily bread.

He opened the fridge, pulled a bottle of vodka from the freezer. He produced three shot glasses from the trench coat I've never seen him without. Dead of summer or heart of winter, it doesn't matter. Bubba and his trench coat do not part. Like Harpo Marx with a really bad attitude and homicidal tendencies. He poured the vodka and handed us each a glass. "I hear it steadies the nerves." He tossed his back.

It steadied mine. By the way Angie closed her eyes for a moment, I think it steadied hers. Bubba showed no reaction, but then Bubba doesn't have nerves or, as far as I know, most other things humans need to function.

He plopped his two hundred and thirty-plus pounds down into one of the sofas. "So, why you need a meet with Jack Rouse?"

We told him.

"Doesn't sound like him. That picture shit, I mean, maybe it's effective, but it's far too subtle for Jack."

"What about Kevin Hurlihy?" Angie said.

"If it's too subtle for Jack," he said, "then it's completely beyond Kevin." He drank from the bottle. "Come to think of it, most things are beyond Kev. Addition and subtraction, the alphabet, shit like that. Hell, you guys must remember that from the old days."

"We'd wondered if he'd changed."

Bubba laughed. "Nope. Gotten worse."

"So he's dangerous," I said.

"Oh, yeah," Bubba said. "Like a junkyard dog. Knows how to rape and fight and scare hell out of people and that's about it, but he does those things well." He handed me the bottle and I poured another shot.

I said, "So two people who knowingly took a case that pitted them against him and his boss . . ."

"Would be morons, yeah." He took the bottle back.

I glared at Angie and she stuck her tongue out at me.

Bubba said, "Want me to kill him for you?" and stretched out on the couch.

I blinked. "Ahm . . ."

Bubba yawned. "It's not a problem."

Angie touched his knee. "Not at the moment."

"Really," he said, sitting up, "no sweat. I built this new thing, and what you do is clamp it around the guy's skull, right here, and—"

"We'll let you know," I said.

"Cool." He lay back on the couch, looked at us for a moment. "I didn't figure a freak like Kevin for having a girlfriend, though. He seems like a guy either pays for it or takes it by force."

"That bothered me too," I said.

"Anyway," Bubba said, "you don't want to meet Jack Rouse and Kevin alone."

"We don't?"

He shook his head. "You go up to them, and say, 'Back off our client,' they'll kill you. They'd have to. They ain't real stable."

A guy who used a minefield for home protection was telling us Jack and Kevin weren't stable. This was good news. Now that I knew just how dangerous they really were, I considered walking back into that minefield, doing a jig, getting it over with quick.

"We'll go through Fat Freddy," Bubba said.

"Are you serious?" Angie said.

Fat Freddy Constantine was the godfather of the Boston Mafia, the man who'd wrested control from the once pre-eminent Providence outfit and consolidated his power. Jack Rouse, Kevin Hurlihy, anyone who so much as sold a nickel bag in this city answered to Fat Freddy.

"It's the only way," Bubba said. "You go through Fat Freddy, you're showing him respect, and if I set up the meet, they know you're friends, they won't whack you."

"Bonus," I said.

"When you want the meet?"

"Soon as possible," Angie said.

He shrugged and picked up a cordless phone off the floor. He dialed and took another swig from the bottle as he waited. "Lou," he said, "tell the man I called." He hung up.

" 'The man?' " I said.

He held out his hands. "They all watch Scorsese movies and cop shows, think it's the way they're supposed to talk. I humor them." He reached across his whale's-hump chest and poured another shot into Angie's glass. "You officially divorced yet, Gennaro?"

She smiled and downed the shot. "Not officially."

"When?" He raised his eyebrows.

She propped her feet up on an open crate of AK-47s and leaned back in her chair. "The wheels of justice turn slowly, Bubba, and divorce is complicated."

Bubba grimaced. "Smuggling surface-to-air missiles from Libya is complicated. But divorce?"

Angie ran both hands through the hair along her temples, looked up at the peeling heating pipes stretched across Bubba's ceiling. "A relationship in your hands, Bubba, lasts about as long as a six-pack. So what do you know about divorce? Really?"

He sighed. "I know people seem to go out of their way to fuck up things usually should be snapped off clean." He swiveled his legs off the couch, dropped the soles of his combat boots to the floor. "How about you, homeboy?"

"Moi?" I said.

"Si," he said. "How was your divorce experience?"

"Piece of cake," I said. "Like ordering Chinese—one phone call, and everything's taken care of."

He looked at Angie. "See?"

She waved a dismissive hand in my general direction. "You'd take his word for it? Mr. Introspection?"

"I doth protest," I said.

"You doth full of shit," Angie said.

Bubba rolled his eyes. "Would you guys just bang each other and get it over with?"

There was one of those awkward pauses that comes up every time someone suggests there's a lot more than friendship between me and my partner. Bubba smiled, getting a charge out of it, and then, thankfully, his phone rang.

"Yeah." He nodded at us. "Mr. Constantine, how you doing?" He rolled his eyes as Mr. Constantine elaborated on just how he was. "Glad to hear it," Bubba said. "Listen, Mr. C., I got a couple friends need to speak with you. Take a couple minutes."

I mouthed, "Mr. *C.*?" and he shot me the bird.

"Yes, sir, they're good folks. Civilians, but they may have stumbled onto something could maybe interest you. Has to do with Jack and Kevin." Fat Freddy began talking again and Bubba made the universal masturbatory gesture with his fist. "Yes, sir," he said eventually. "Patrick Kenzie and Angela Gennaro." He listened, then blinked and looked at Angie. He put his hand over the mouthpiece and said, "You related to the Patriso Family?"

She lit a cigarette. " 'Fraid so."

"Yes, sir," Bubba said into the phone. "The very same Angela Gennaro." He raised his left eyebrow at her. "Ten tonight. Thanks, Mr. Constantine." He paused, looked at the wooden crate Angie was using as a footstool. "What? Oh, yeah, Lou knows where. Six cases. Tomorrow night. You bet. As a whistle, Mr. Constantine. Yes, sir. Take care." He hung up and sighed loudly, shoved the antenna back into the phone with the heel of his hand. "Fucking wops," he said. "Everything's 'Yes, sir. No, sir. How's the wife?' Least the Harp mobs, they're too mean to give a fuck how the wife is."

Coming from Bubba, this was high praise for my ethnicity. I said, "Where do we meet him?"

He was looking at Angie with something akin to awe on his rubbery face. "At his coffee shop on Prince Street. Ten tonight. How come you never told me you were connected?"

She flicked her cigarette ash on his floor. It wasn't disrespectful; it was Bubba's ashtray. "I'm not connected."

"According to Freddy, you are."

"Well," she said, "he's mistaken. An accident of blood, that's all."

He looked at me. "You know she was related to the Patriso mob?"

"Yup."

"And?"

"And she never seemed like she cared, so I didn't either."

"Bubba," she said, "it's not something I'm proud of."

He whistled. "All these years, all the scrapes you two been in, and you never called on them for backup?"

Angie looked at him through the long bangs that had fallen in her face. "Never even considered it."

"Why?" He was genuinely confused.

"'Cause you're all the Mafia we need, handsome."

He blushed, something only Angie can get him to do, something that's always worth the effort. His huge face swelled like an overripe grape and for a moment he looked almost harmless. Almost.

"Stop," he said, "you're embarrassing me."

*   *   *

Back at the office, I brewed some coffee to counteract the vodka buzz and Angie played back the messages on our answering machine.

The first was from a recent client, Bobo Gedmenson, owner of Bobo's Yo-Yo chain of under-twenty-one dance clubs and a few strip joints out in Saugus and Peabody with names like Dripping Vanilla and The Honey Dip. Now that we'd located Bobo's ex-partner and returned most of the money he'd embezzled from Bobo, Bobo was suddenly questioning our rates and crying poormouth.

"People," I said, shaking my head.

"Suck," Angie agreed as Bobo beeped off.

I made a mental reminder to toss the collection job to Bubba, and then the second message played:

"Hallo. Just thought I'd wish you jolly good luck on your new case and all that rubbish. I gather it's a splendid one. Yes? Well, I'll be in touch. Cheerio."

I looked at Angie. "Who the hell was that?"

"I thought you knew. I don't know anyone British."

"Me either." I shrugged. "Wrong number?"

" 'Good luck on your new case'? Sounds like he knew what he was talking about."

"Accent sound fake to you?"

She nodded. "Like someone who's watched a lot of *Python.*"

"Who do we know who does accents?"

"Beats me."

The next voice was Grace Cole's. In the background I could hear the assaultive human noise and babble of the emergency room where she worked.

"I actually got ten minutes for a coffee break so I tried to catch you. I'm here till at least early tomorrow morning, but call me at my place tomorrow night. Miss you."

She beeped off and Angie said, "So, when's the wedding?"

"Tomorrow. Didn't you know?"

She smiled. "You're whipped, Patrick. You do know that, don't you?"

"According to who?"

"According to me and all your friends." Her smile

faded a bit. "I've never seen you look at a woman the way you look at Grace."

"And if I am?"

She looked out her window at the avenue. "Then I say more power to you," she said softly. She tried to get the smile back but it cracked weakly and disappeared. "I wish you both all the best."

4

By ten that night, Angie and I were sitting in a small coffee shop on Prince Street, learning more than we ever wanted to know about prostates from Fat Freddy Constantine.

Freddy Constantine's coffee shop on Prince Street was a narrow shop on a narrow street. Prince Street cuts across the North End from Commercial to Moon Street, and like most of the streets in that neighborhood, it's barely wide enough to squeeze a bicycle through. The temperature had dropped into the mid-fifties by the time we arrived, but up and down Prince Street, men sat in front of shops and restaurants wearing only T-shirts or tank tops under open short-sleeves, leaning back in lawn chairs and smoking cigars or playing cards and laughing suddenly and violently as people do in neighborhoods they're sure they own.

Freddie's coffee shop was nothing but a dark room with two small tables out front and four inside on a white-and-black-tile floor. A ceiling fan rotated sluggishly and flipped the pages of a newspaper back and forth on the counter as Dean Martin warbled from somewhere behind a heavy black curtain drawn across the back doorway.

We were met at the front door by two young guys with dark hair and bodies by Bally and matching pink-champagne V-necks and gold chains.

I said, "Is there like a catalog all you guys shop from?"

One of them found this so witty that he patted me down extra hard, the heels of his hands chopping between my rib cage and hips like they expected to meet in the middle.

We'd left our guns in the car, so they took our wallets.
We didn't like it, they didn't care, and soon they led us to
a table across from Don Frederico Constantine himself.

Fat Freddy looked like a walrus without the mustache.
He was immense and smoke gray and he wore several
layers of dark clothing, so that his square chopping-block
head on top of all that darkness looked like something that
had erupted from the folds of the collar and spilled toward
the shoulders. His almond eyes were warm and liquid, paternal, and he smiled a lot. Smiled at strangers on the
street, at reporters as he came down courtroom steps, presumably at his victims before his men kneecapped them.

He said, "Please, sit down."

Except for Freddy and ourselves, there was only one
other person in the coffee shop. He sat about twenty feet
back at a table beside a support beam, one hand on the
table, legs crossed at the ankles. He wore light khakis and
a white shirt and gray scarf under an amber canvas jacket
with a leather collar. He didn't quite look at us, but I
couldn't swear he was looking away either. His name was
Pine, no first name that I ever heard, and he was a legend
in his circles, the man who'd survived four different
bosses, three family wars, and whose enemies had a habit
of disappearing so completely people soon forgot they'd
ever lived. Sitting at the table, he seemed a perfectly normal, almost bland guy: handsome, possibly, but not in any
way that stuck in the memory; he was probably five eleven
or six feet with dirty blond hair and green eyes and an
average build.

Just being in the same room with him made my skull
tingle.

Angie and I sat down and Fat Freddy said, "Prostates."

"Excuse me?" Angie said.

"Prostates," Freddy repeated. He poured coffee from a
pewter pot into a cup, handed it to Angie. "Not something
your gender has to worry about half as much as ours." He
nodded at me as he handed me my cup, then nudged the
cream and sugar in our direction. "I'll tell you," he said,
"I've reached the height of my profession, my daughter
just got accepted to Harvard, and financially, I want for

little." He shifted in his chair, grimaced enough so that his huge jowls rolled in toward the center of his face and completely obscured his lips for a moment. "But, I swear, I'd trade it all in tomorrow for a healthy prostate." He sighed. "You?"

"What?" I said.

"Have a healthy prostate?"

"Last time I checked, Mr. Constantine."

He leaned forward. "Count your blessings, my young friend. Count them twice. A man without a healthy prostate is . . ." He spread his hands on the table. "Well, he's a man without secrets, a man without dignity. Those doctors, Jesus, they flop you down on your stomach and they go in there with their evil little tools and they poke and they prod, they tear and they—"

"Sounds terrible," Angie said.

It slowed him down, thank God.

He nodded. "Terrible isn't quite the word." He looked at her suddenly as if he'd just noticed her. "And you, my dear, are far too exquisite to be subjected to such talk." He kissed her hand and I tried not to roll my eyes. "I know your grandfather quite well, Angela. Quite well."

Angie smiled. "He's proud of the association, Mr. Constantine."

"I'll be sure to tell him I had the pleasure of meeting his lovely granddaughter." He looked at me and his twinkling eyes faded a bit. "And you, Mr. Kenzie, you're keeping a careful eye on this woman, making sure she keeps out of harm's way?"

"This woman does a pretty good job of that herself, Mr. Constantine," Angie said.

Fat Freddy's eyes stayed on me, growing darker by the second, like he wasn't too keen on what he saw. He said, "Our friends will join us in just a minute."

As Freddy leaned back to pour himself another cup of coffee, I heard one of the bodyguards out front say, "Go right on in, Mr. Rouse," and Angie's eyes widened slightly as Jack Rouse and Kevin Hurlihy came through the door.

Jack Rouse controlled Southie, Charlestown, and everything between Savin Hill and the Neponset River in Dorchester. He was thin, hard, and his eyes matched the gunmetal of his close-cropped hair. He didn't look particularly threatening, but he didn't have to—he had Kevin for that.

I've known Kevin since we were six, and nothing that lives in his brain or his bloodstream has ever been stained by a humane impulse. He walked through the door, avoided looking at Pine or even acknowledging him, and I knew Pine was who Kevin aspired to be. But Pine was all stillness and economy, while Kevin was a walking exposed nerve, his pupils lit with a battery charge, the kind of guy who might shoot everyone in the place simply because the idea occurred to him. Pine was scary because killing was a job to him, no different than a thousand others. Kevin was scary because killing was the only job he wanted, and he'd do it for free.

The first thing he did after shaking Freddy's hand was sit down beside me and put his cigarette out in my coffee cup. Then he ran a hand through his coarse, thick hair and stared at me.

Freddy said, "Jack, Kevin, you know Mr. Kenzie and Ms. Gennaro, don't you?"

"Old friends, sure," Jack said as he took the seat beside Angie. "Neighborhood kids like Kevin." Rouse shrugged off an old blue Members' Only jacket and hung it behind him on his chair. "Ain't that the God's truth, Kev?"

Kevin was too busy staring at me to comment.

Fat Freddy said, "I like everything to be above board. Rogowski says you two are okay, and maybe you got a problem I can help you with—so be it. But you two come from Jack's neighborhood, so I ask Jack if he'd like to sit in. You see what I'm saying?"

We nodded.

Kevin lit another cigarette, blew the smoke into my hair.

Freddy turned his palms up on the table. "We're all agreed, then. So, tell me what you need, Mr. Kenzie."

"We've been hired by a client," I said, "who—"

"How's your coffee, Jack?" Freddy said. "Enough cream?"

"It's fine, Mr. Constantine. Very good."

"Who," I repeated, "is under the impression she annoyed one of Jack's men."

"Men?" Freddy said and raised his eyebrows, looked at Jack, then back at me. "We're small businessmen, Mr. Kenzie. We have employees, but their loyalties stop with their paychecks." He looked at Jack again. "Men?" he said and they both chuckled.

Angie sighed.

Kevin blew some more smoke into my hair.

I was tired, and the last vestiges of Bubba's vodka were chewing at the base of my brain, so I really wasn't in the mood to play cute with a bunch of cut-rate psychopaths who'd seen *The Godfather* too many times and thought they were respectable. But I reminded myself that Freddy, at least, was a very powerful psychopath who could be dining on my spleen tomorrow night if he wanted to.

"Mr. Constantine, one of Mr. Rouse's . . . associates, then, has expressed anger at our client, made certain threats—"

"Threats?" Freddy said. "Threats?"

"Threats?" Jack said, smiled at Freddy.

"Threats," Angie said. "Seems our client had the misfortune of speaking with your associate's girlfriend, who claimed to know of her boyfriend's criminal activities, including the—how can I put it?" She met Freddy's eyes. "The waste management of some formerly animate tissue?"

It took him a minute to get it, but then his small eyes narrowed and he threw back his massive head and laughed, booming it up into the ceiling, sending it halfway down Prince Street. Jack looked confused. Kevin looked pissed off, but that's the only way Kevin's ever looked.

"Pine," Freddy said. "You hear that?"

Pine made no indication he'd heard anything. He made no indication he was breathing. He sat there, immobile, simultaneously looking and not looking in our direction.

" 'Waste management of formerly animate tissue,' " Freddy repeated, gasping. He looked at Jack, realized he hadn't gotten the joke yet. "Fuck, Jack, go out and pick up a brain, huh?"

Jack blinked and Kevin leaned forward on the table, and Pine's head turned slightly to look at him, and Freddy acted like he hadn't noticed any of it.

He wiped the corners of his mouth with a linen napkin, shook his head slowly at Angie. "Wait'll I tell the guys at the club that one. I swear. You might have taken your father's name, Angela, but you're a Patriso. No question."

Jack said, "Patriso?"

"Yeah," Freddy said. "This is Mr. Patriso's grand-daughter. You didn't know?"

Jack hadn't known. It seemed to annoy him. He said, "Give me a cigarette, Kev."

Kevin leaned across the table, lit the cigarette for him, his elbow about a quarter inch from my eye.

"Mr. Constantine," Angie said, "our client doesn't wish to make the list of what your associate considers disposable."

Freddy held up a meaty hand. "We're talking about what here exactly?"

"Our client believes she may have angered Mr. Hurlihy."

"What?" Jack said.

"Explain," Freddy said. "Quickly."

Without using Diandra's name, we did.

"So, what," Freddy said, "some cooze Kevin's bumping tells this psychiatrist some bullshit about—I got this?— a body or something, and Kevin gets a little hot and calls her and makes some noise." He shook his head. "Kevin, you want to tell me about this?"

Kevin looked at Jack.

"Kevin," Freddy said.

Kevin's head turned.

"You got a girlfriend?"

Kevin's voice sounded like ground glass running through a car engine. "No, Mr. Constantine."

Freddy looked at Jack and they both laughed.

Kevin looked like he'd been caught buying pornography by a nun.

Freddy turned toward us. "You kidding me with this?" He laughed harder. "With all due respect to Kevin, he ain't exactly a ladies' man, if you understand me."

Angie said, "Mr. Constantine, please see our position— this isn't something we made up."

He leaned in, patted her hand. "Angela, I'm not saying you did. But you've been duped. Some broad claims she was threatened by Kevin because of his *girlfriend*? Come now."

"This," Jack said, "is what I left a card game for? This shit?" He snorted and started to stand up.

"Sit down, Jack," Freddy said.

Jack froze half in, half out of his chair.

Freddy looked at Kevin. "Sit, Jack."

Jack sat.

Freddy smiled at us. "Have we cleared up your problem?"

I reached into the inside pocket of my jacket for the photo of Jason Warren, and Kevin's hand dove into his jacket and Jack leaned back in his chair and Pine shifted slightly in his seat. Freddy's eyes never left my hand. Very slowly, I withdrew the photo and placed it on the table.

"Our client received this in the mail the other day."

One of the mustaches above Freddy's eyes arched. "So?"

"So," Angie said, "we'd thought it might be a message from Kevin letting our client know that he knew her weaknesses. Now, we assume it isn't, but we're confused."

Jack nodded at Kevin and Kevin's hand came out of his jacket.

If Freddy noticed, he gave no indication. He looked down at the photo of Jason Warren and sipped his coffee. "This kid, he your client's son?"

"He's not mine," I said.

Freddy raised his huge head slowly, looked at me. "Someone know you, asshole?" Those once warm eyes of his seemed about as comforting as ice picks. "Don't you ever talk to me like that. Understood?"

My mouth suddenly felt like I'd swallowed a wool sweater.

Kevin chuckled softly under his breath.

Freddy reached into the folds of his jacket, his eyes never leaving my face as he produced a leather-bound notepad. He opened it, leafed through a few pages, found the one he was looking for.

"Patrick Kenzie," he read. "Age, thirty-three. Mother and father deceased. One sibling, Erin Margolis, aged thirty-six, lives in Seattle, Washington. Last year you grossed forty-eight thousand dollars as part of your partnership with Miss Gennaro here. Divorced seven years. Ex-wife currently resides in parts unknown." He smiled at me. "But we're working on it, believe me." He turned a page, pursed his fat lips. "Last year, you shot a pimp in cold blood under an expressway overpass." He winked, reached out and patted my hand. "Yes, Kenzie, we know about that. You kill someone again, here's simple advice: Don't leave a witness." He looked back at the notebook. "Where were we? Oh, right. Favorite color is blue. Favorite beer is St. Pauli Girl, favorite food is Mexican." He turned another page, glanced up at us. "How'm I doing so far?"

"Boy," Angie said, "are we impressed."

He turned toward her. "Angela Gennaro. Currently estranged from husband, Phillip Dimassi. Father deceased. Mother, Antonia, lives with second husband in Flagstaff, Arizona. Also involved in killing of pimp last year. Currently residing on Howes Street in a first-floor apartment with a weak deadbolt on the back door." He closed the notebook, looked at us benignly. "Me and my friends can come up with information like this, why the fuck would we need to mail someone a photograph?"

My right hand was pressed against my thigh, the fingers digging into the flesh, telling me to stay calm. I cleared my throat. "Seems unlikely."

"Fucking right, it is," Jack Rouse said.

"We don't send photographs, Mr. Kenzie," Freddy said. "We send our messages a bit more directly."

Jack and Freddy stared at us with predatory humor in their eyes, and Kevin Hurlihy had a shit-eating grin on his face the size of a canyon.

Angie said, "I have a weak deadbolt on my back door?"

Freddy shrugged. "So I hear."

Jack Rouse's fingers rose to the tweed scally cap on his head and he tipped it in her direction.

She smiled, looked at me, then at Freddy. You'd have to have known her for a while to realize exactly how irate she was. She's one of those people whose anger you can gauge by her reduction in movement. By the statue's position she'd taken at the table, I was pretty sure she'd cruised past the extremely pissed-off point about five minutes ago.

"Freddy," she said and he blinked. "You answer to the Imbruglia Family in New York. Correct?"

Freddy stared at her.

Pine uncrossed his legs.

"And the Imbruglia Family," she said, leaning into the table slightly, "they answer to the Moliach Family, who in turn are still considered glorified caporegimes to the Patriso Family. Correct?"

Freddy's eyes were still and flat, and Jack's left hand was frozen halfway between the edge of the table and his coffee cup, and beside me I could hear Kevin taking long deep breaths through his nose.

"And you—do I have this right?—sent men to find security weaknesses in the apartment of Mr. Patriso's only granddaughter? Freddy," she said and reached across the table and touched his hand, "do you think Mr. Patriso would consider these actions respectful or disrespectful?"

Freddy said, "Angela—"

She patted his hand and stood. "Thanks for your time."

I stood. "Nice seeing you guys."

Kevin's chair made a loud scraping noise on the tile as he stepped in my path, looked at me with those depth-charge eyes of his.

Freddy said, "Sit the fuck down."

"You heard him, Kev," I said. "Sit the fuck down."

Kevin smiled, ran his palm across his mouth.

Out of the corner of my eye, I saw Pine cross his legs at the ankles again.

"Kevin," Jack Rouse said.

In Kevin's face I could see years of howling class rage and the bright sheen of true psychosis. I could see the little, pissed-off kid whose brain had been stunted and blighted sometime during the first or second grade and had never grown beyond that point. I could see murder.

"Angela," Freddy said, "Mr. Kenzie. Please sit down."

"Kevin," Jack Rouse said again.

Kevin placed the hand that had wiped the smile off his face on my shoulder. Whatever passed between us in the second or two it lay there wasn't pleasant or comfortable or clean. Then he nodded once, as if answering a question I'd asked, and stepped back by his chair.

"Angela," Freddy said, "could we—?"

"Have a nice day, Freddy." She came around behind me and we walked out onto Prince Street.

We reached the car on Commercial, a block from Diandra Warren's apartment, and Angie said, "I got some things to do, so I'm going to cab it home from here."

"You sure?"

She looked at me like a woman who'd just backed down a room full of Mafioso and wasn't in the mood to take any shit. "What're you going to do?"

"Talk to Diandra, I guess. See if I can find out any more about this Moira Kenzie."

"You need me?"

"Nope."

She looked back up Prince Street. "I believe him."

"Kevin?"

She nodded.

"Me too," I said. "He has no reason to lie, really."

She turned her head, looked over at Lewis Wharf, at the single yellow light glowing in Diandra Warren's apartment. "So where's that leave her? If Kevin didn't send that photograph, who did?"

"Haven't a clue."

"Some detectives," she said.

"We'll figure it out," I said. "It's what we're good at."

I looked up Prince and saw two men walking down

toward us. One was short and thin and hard and wore a scally cap. The other was tall and thin and probably giggled when he killed people. They reached the end of the street and stopped at a gold Diamante directly across from us. As Kevin opened the passenger door for Jack, he stared at us.

"That guy," a voice said, "doesn't like you two much."

I turned my head, saw Pine sitting on the hood of my car. He flicked his wrist and my wallet hit me in the chest.

"No," I said.

Kevin came around the driver's side of the car, still looking at us, then climbed in and they pulled out onto Commercial, drove up around Waterfront Park, and disappeared at the curve of Atlantic Ave.

"Miss Gennaro," Pine said, leaning forward and handing her her wallet.

Angie took it.

"That was a very nice performance in there. Bravo."

"Thank you," Angie said.

"I wouldn't try it twice, though."

"No?"

"That would be stupid."

She nodded. "Yes."

"That guy," Pine said, looking off to where the Diamante had disappeared and then back at me, "is going to cause you some grief."

"Not much I can do about it," I said.

He came off the car hood fluidly, as if he were incapable of an awkward gesture or the embarrassment of a stumble.

"It was me," he said, "and he looked at me like that, he wouldn't have made his car alive." He shrugged. "That's me, though."

Angie said, "We're used to Kevin. We've known him since kindergarten."

Pine nodded. "Probably should have killed him back then." He passed between us and I felt ice melting in the center of my chest. "Good night." He crossed Commercial and went up Prince, and a crisp breeze swept the street.

Angie shivered in her coat. "I don't like this case, Patrick."

"Me either," I said. "Don't like it at all."

5

Except for a single white track light in the kitchen where we sat, Diandra Warren's loft was dark, the furniture rising out of the empty spaces in hulking shadows. Lights from neighboring buildings glazed her windows but barely penetrated the interior, and across the harbor Charlestown's lights checkered the black sky in hard squares of yellow and white.

It was a relatively warm night, but it seemed cold from Diandra's loft.

Diandra placed a second bottle of Brooklyn Lager on the butcher-block table in front of me, then sat down and idly fingered her wine glass.

"You're saying you believe these Mafioso?" Eric said.

I nodded. I'd just spent fifteen minutes telling them about my meeting at Fat Freddy's place, omitting only Angie's relationship with Vincent Patriso.

I said, "They don't gain much by lying."

"They're criminals." Eric's eyes widened at me. "Lying is second nature to them."

I sipped my beer. "This is true. But criminals usually lie out of fear or to maintain an edge."

"Okay . . ."

"And these guys, believe me, have no reason to fear me. I'm nothing to them. If they were threatening you, Doctor Warren, and I came around on your behalf, their response would have been, 'Fine, we're threatening her. Now mind your own business or we'll kill you. End of discussion.'"

"But they didn't say that." She nodded to herself.

"No. Add to this that Kevin just isn't the type to have a steady girlfriend, and it seems unlikelier by the second."

"But—" Eric started.

I held up a hand, looked at Diandra. "I should have asked this at our first meeting, but it never occurred to me that this could be a hoax. This guy who called claiming to be Kevin—was there anything odd about his voice?"

"Odd? How?"

I shook my head. "Think."

"It was a deep voice, husky, I guess."

"That's it?"

She took a sip of wine, then nodded. "Yes."

"Then it wasn't Kevin."

"How do you—?"

"Kevin's voice is ruined, Doctor Warren. Has been since he was a kid. It sounds like it's perpetually cracking, like the voice of a teenager going through puberty."

"That wasn't the voice I heard on the phone."

"No."

Eric rubbed his face. "So, if Kevin didn't make the call, who did?"

"And why?" Diandra said.

I looked at both of them and held out my hands. "Frankly, I have no idea. Either of you have any enemies?"

Diandra shook her head.

Eric said, "How do you define enemies?"

"Enemies," I said. "As in people who call up to threaten you at four A.M., or send you pictures of your child without a note of explanation or generally wish you dead. Enemies."

He thought about it for a moment, then shook his head.

"You're sure?"

He grimaced. "I have professional competitors, I guess, and detractors, people who disagree with me—"

"In what sense?"

He smiled, somewhat ruefully. "Patrick, you took my courses. You know that I don't agree with a lot of the experts in the field and that people disagree with my disagreements. But I doubt such people wish me physical harm. Besides, wouldn't my enemies come after me, not Diandra and her son?''

Diandra flinched, lowered her eyes, and sipped her wine.

I shrugged. ''Possibly. You never know, though.'' I looked at Diandra. ''You said that in the past you've feared patients. Any of them recently released from wards or prisons who might hold a grudge?''

''I'd have been notified.'' She met my eyes and hers were vibrant with confusion and fear, a deep, encompassing fear.

''Any current patients who might have the motive and resourcefulness to do this?''

She spent a good minute thinking about it, but eventually shook her head. ''No.''

''I'll need to speak to your ex-husband.''

''Stan? Why? I don't see the point.''

''I need to rule out any possible connection to him. I'm sorry if it upsets you, but I'd be a fool if I didn't.''

''I'm not obtuse, Mr. Kenzie, but I promise you Stan has no connection to my life and hasn't for almost two decades.''

''I have to know everything I can about the people in your life, Doctor Warren, particularly anyone with whom you have a relationship that is not picture perfect.''

''Patrick,'' Eric said, ''come on. What about privacy?''

I sighed. ''Fuck privacy.''

''Excuse me?''

''You heard me, Eric,'' I said. ''Fuck privacy. Doctor Warren's, and yours too, I'm afraid. You brought me into this, Eric, and you know how I work.''

He blinked.

''I don't like the way this case feels.'' I looked out at the darkness of Diandra's loft, at the icy sheen on her windows. ''I don't like it and I'm trying to catch up on some details so I can do my job and keep Doctor Warren and her son out of danger. To accomplish that, I need to know everything about your lives. Both of you. And if you refuse me that access''—I looked at Diandra—''I'll walk away.''

Diandra watched me calmly.

Eric said, "You'd leave a woman in distress? Just like that?"

I kept my eyes on Diandra. "Just like that."

Diandra said, "Are you always this blunt?"

For a quarter second, an image flashed through my brain of a woman cascading down onto hard cement, her body filled with holes, my face and clothes splattered with her blood. Jenna Angeline—dead before she hit the ground on a soft summer morning as I stood an inch away.

I said, "I had someone die on me once because I was a step too slow. I won't have that happen again."

A small tremble rippled the skin at the base of her throat. She reached up and rubbed it. "So you definitely think I'm in serious danger."

I shook my head. "I don't know. But you were threatened. You did receive that photo. Someone's going to a lot of trouble to screw with your life. I want to find out who that is and make them stop. That's why you hired me. Can you call Timpson for me, set up an appointment for tomorrow?"

She shrugged. "I suppose."

"Good. I also need a description of Moira Kenzie, anything you can remember about her, no matter how small."

As Diandra closed her eyes for a full minute to conjure up a complete image of Moira Kenzie, I flipped open a notepad, uncapped a pen, and waited.

"She was wearing jeans, a black river-driver's shirt under a red flannel shirt." She opened her eyes. "She was very pretty with long, dirty-blond hair, a bit wispy, and she chain-smoked. She seemed authentically terrified."

"Height?"

"Five five or so."

"Weight?"

"I'm guessing about one ten."

"What kind of cigarettes did she smoke?"

She closed her eyes again. "Long with white filters. The pack was gold. 'Deluxe' something or other."

"Benson and Hedges Deluxe Ultra Lights?"

Her eyes snapped open. "Yes."

I shrugged. "My partner switches to them every time she tries to quit by cutting back. Eyes?"

"Green."

"Any guesses on ethnic background?"

She sipped her wine. "Northern European maybe, a few generations back and maybe mixed. She could have been Irish, British, even Slavic. She had very pale skin."

"Anything else? Where did she say she was from?"

"Belmont," she said with a note of mild surprise.

"Does that seem incongruous for any reason?"

"Well . . . if someone's from Belmont, usually they go to the finer prep schools, et cetera."

"True."

"And one of the things they lose, if they ever had it, is a Boston accent. Maybe they have a light one. . . ."

"But not a 'If you come to my pahty don't fahget the beah' type of accent."

"Exactly."

"But Moira did?"

She nodded. "It didn't register at the time, but now, yes, it does seem a bit odd. It wasn't a Belmont accent, it was Revere or East Boston or . . ." She looked at me.

"Or Dorchester," I said.

"Yes."

"A neighborhood accent." I closed my notebook.

"Yes. What will you do from here, Mr. Kenzie?"

"I'm going to watch Jason. The threat's to him. He's the one who feels 'stalked,' it was his picture you received."

"Yes."

"I want you to limit your activities."

"I can't—"

"Keep your office hours and appointments," I said, "but take some time off from Bryce until I have some answers."

She nodded.

"Eric?" I said.

He looked at me.

"That gun you're carrying, you know how to use it?"

"I practice once a week. I'm a good shot."

"It's a little different shooting at flesh, Eric."

"I know that."

"I need you to stick as close as you can to Doctor Warren for a few days. You can do that?"

"Certainly."

"If anything happens, don't waste time trying to get a head shot or put one in some attacker's heart."

"What should I do, then?"

"Empty the gun into the body, Eric. Six shots should put down anything smaller than a rhino."

He looked deflated, as if his time spent at the gun club had just been revealed for the futile exercise it usually was. And maybe he really was a good shot, but I doubted anyone who attacked Diandra would be wearing a bull's-eye in the center of his forehead.

"Eric," I said, "would you walk me out?"

He nodded and we left the loft, walked down a short hall to the elevator.

"Our friendship can't get in the way of how I do my job. You understand that, don't you?"

He looked at his shoes, nodded.

"What's your relationship with her?"

He met my eyes and his were hard. "Why?"

"No privacy, Eric. Remember that. I have to know what your stake is here."

He shrugged. "We're friends."

"Sleep-over friends?"

He shook his head and smiled bitterly. "Sometimes, Patrick, I think you need a little polish."

I shrugged. "I'm not paid for my table manners, Eric."

"Diandra and I met when I was at Brown working on my doctorate and she was just entering the graduate program."

I cleared my throat. "Again—are you two intimate?"

"No," he said. "We're just very good friends. Like you and Angie."

"You understand why I made the assumption."

He nodded.

"Is she intimate with anyone?"

He shook his head. "She's . . ." He looked up at the ceiling, then back at his feet.

"She's what?"

"She's not sexually active, Patrick. By philosophical choice. She's been celibate for at least ten years."

"Why?"

His face darkened. "I told you—choice. Some people aren't ruled by their libidos, Patrick, hard as that concept may be for someone such as yourself to understand."

"Okay, Eric," I said softly. "Is there anything you're not telling me?"

"Like what?"

"Skeletons in your closet," I said. "A reason why this person would be threatening Jason to get to you?"

"What're you implying?"

"I'm not implying anything, Eric. I asked a direct question. *Yes* or *no* is all that's required."

"No." His voice was ice.

"Sorry I have to ask these questions."

"Are you?" he said and turned and walked back to the apartment.

6

It was close to midnight when I left Diandra's, and the city streets were quiet as I drove south along the waterfront. The temperature was still in the mid-fifties and I rolled down the windows on my latest hunk of shit and let the soft breeze cleanse the musty confines.

After my last company car suffered a coronary on a bleak, forgotten street in Roxbury, I found this '86 nut brown Crown Victoria at a police auction my friend Devin, a cop, had told me about. The engine was a work of art; you could drive a Crown Vic off a thirty-story building and the engine would keep chugging long after the rest of the car had shattered into small pieces. I spent money on everything under the hood and I had it outfitted with top-of-the line tires, but I left the interior the way I'd found it—roof and seats yellowed by the previous owner's cheap cigars, back seats torn and spilling foam rubber, broken radio. Both rear doors were sharply dented, as if they'd been squeezed by forceps, and the paint on the trunk was torn off in a jagged circle that revealed the primer underneath.

It was a hideous eyesore, but I was reasonably certain no respectable car thief would want to be caught dead in it.

At the traffic light by the Harbor Towers, the engine hummed happily as it guzzled a few gallons of gas a minute, and two attractive young women crossed in front of the car. They looked like office workers: Both wore tight but drab skirts and blouses under wrinkled raincoats. Their dark panty hose disappeared at the ankles into identical white tennis shoes. They walked with just a hint of uncertainty, as if the pavement were sponge, and the quick laugh of the redhead was a bit too loud.

The brunette's eyes met mine and I smiled the innocuous smile of one human soul acknowledging another on a soft, quiet night in an often bustling city.

She smiled back and then her friend hiccupped loudly and they both fell into each other and laughed uproariously as they reached the curb.

I pulled away, slid onto the central artery, with the dark green expressway girded above me, found myself thinking I was a pretty odd guy if a smile from a tipsy woman could still lift my spirits as easily as it had.

But it was an odd world, too often populated with Kevin Hurlihys and Fat Freddy Constantines and people like a woman I'd read about in the paper this morning who'd left her three children to fend for themselves in a rat-infested apartment while she went on a four-day bender with her latest boyfriend. When child welfare officials entered her apartment, they had to pull one of the kids, screaming, from the mattress his bedsores had fastened him to. It sometimes seemed in a world like this—on a night when I was filled with a growing sense of dread about a client who was being threatened for unknown reasons by unknown forces whose unknown motives couldn't possibly be good enough—that a smile from a woman shouldn't have any effect. But it did.

And if her smile picked up my spirits, it was nothing compared to what Grace's did when I pulled up to my three-decker and saw her sitting on the front porch. She was wearing a forest green canvas field jacket that was four or five sizes too big for her over a white T-shirt and blue hospital scrub pants. Usually the bangs of her short auburn hair fanned the edges of her face, but she'd obviously been running her hands through it during the last thirty hours of her shift, and her face was drawn from too little sleep and too many cups of coffee under the harsh light of the emergency room.

And she was still one of the most beautiful women I'd ever seen.

As I climbed the steps, she stood and watched me with a half-smile playing on her lips and mischief in her pale eyes. When I was three steps from the top, she spread her arms wide and tilted forward like a diver on a high board.

"Catch me." She closed her eyes and fell forward.

The crush of her body against mine was so sweet it bordered on pain. She kissed me and I braced my legs as her thighs slid over my hips and her ankles crossed against the backs of my legs. I could smell her skin and feel the heat of her flesh and the tidal pull of each one of our organs and muscles and arteries hanging as if suspended beneath our separate skins. Grace's mouth came away from mine and her lips grazed my ear.

"I missed you," she whispered.

"I noticed." I kissed her throat. "How'd you escape?"

She groaned. "It finally slowed down."

"You been waiting long?"

She shook her head and her teeth nipped my collarbone before her legs unwrapped themselves from my waist and she stood in front of me, our foreheads touching.

"Where's Mae?" I said.

"Home with Annabeth. Sound asleep."

Annabeth was Grace's younger sister and live-in nanny.

"You see her?"

"Just long enough to read her a bedtime story and kiss her good night. Then she was out like a rock."

"What about you?" I said, running my hand up and down her spine. "You need sleep?"

She groaned again and nodded and her forehead hit mine.

"Ouch."

She laughed softly. "Sorry."

"You're exhausted."

She looked into my eyes. "Absolutely. More than sleep, though, I need you." She kissed me. "Deep, deep inside me. You think you can oblige me, Detective?"

"I'm a hell of an obliger, Doctor."

"I've heard that. You going to take me upstairs or are

we going to put on a show for the neighbors?"

"Well . . ."

Her palm found my abdomen. "Tell me where it hurts."

"A little lower," I said.

As soon as I closed the apartment door behind me, Grace pinned me against the wall and buried her tongue in my mouth. Her left hand grasped the back of my head tightly, but her right ran over my body like a small, hungry animal. I'm usually on the perpetually hormonal side, but if I hadn't quit smoking several years ago, Grace would've put me in intensive care.

"The lady is in command tonight, I take it."

"The lady," she said and nipped my shoulder, not very lightly, "is so horny she might have to be hosed down."

"Again," I said, "the gentleman is happy to oblige."

She stepped back and stared at me as she pulled off her jacket and tossed it somewhere into my living room. Grace wasn't a big neat freak. Then she kissed my mouth roughly and spun on her heel and started walking down my hallway.

"Where you going?" My voice was a tad hoarse.

"To your shower."

She peeled off her T-shirt as she reached the door to the bathroom. A small shaft of streetlight cut through the bedroom into the hall and slanted across the hard muscles in her back. She hung the T-shirt on the doorknob and turned to look at me, her arms crossed over her bare breasts. "You're not moving," she said.

"I'm enjoying the view," I said.

She uncrossed her arms and ran both hands through her hair, arching her back, her ribcage pressing against her skin. She met my eyes again as she kicked off her tennis shoes, then peeled off her socks. She ran her hands over her abdomen and pulled the drawstring on her scrub pants. They fell to her ankles and she stepped out of them.

"Coming out of your stupor yet?" she said.

"Oh, yeah."

She leaned against the doorjamb, hooked her thumbs in the elastic band of her black panties. She raised an eyebrow as I walked toward her, her smile a wicked thing.

"Oh, would you like to help me remove these, Detective?"

I helped. I helped a lot. I'm swell at helping.

It occurred to me as Grace and I made love in my shower that whenever I think of her, I think of water. We met during the wettest week of a cold and drizzly summer, and her green eyes were so pale they reminded me of winter rain, and the first time we made love, it was in the sea with the night rain bathing our bodies.

After the shower, we lay in bed, still damp, her auburn hair dark against my chest, the sounds of our lovemaking still echoing in my ears.

She had a scar the size of a thumbtack on her collarbone, the price she had paid for playing in her uncle's barn near exposed nails when she was a kid. I leaned over and kissed it.

"Mmm," she said. "Do that again."

I ran my tongue over the scar.

She hooked her leg over mine, ran the edge of her foot against my ankle. "Can a scar be erogenous?"

"I think anything can be erogenous."

Her warm palm found my abdomen, ran over the hard rubber scar tissue in the shape of a jellyfish. "What about this one?"

"Nothing erogenous about that, Grace."

"You keep evading me about it. It's obviously a burn of some sort."

"What're you—a doctor?"

She chuckled. "Allegedly." She ran her palm up between my thighs. "Tell me where it hurts, Detective."

I smiled, but I doubt it was much of one.

She rose up on her elbow and looked at me for a long time. "You don't have to tell me," she said softly.

I raised my left hand, used the backs of my fingers to brush a strand of hair off her forehead, then allowed the fingers to drop slowly down the edge of her face, along the soft warmth of her throat, and then the small, firm curve of her right breast. I grazed the nipple with my palm as I turned the hand, moved it back up to her face and pulled her down on top of me. I held her so tightly for a moment that I could hear our hearts drumming through our chests like hail falling into a bucket of water.

"My father," I said, "burned me with an iron to teach me a lesson."

"Teach you what?" she said.

"Not to play with fire."

"What?"

I shrugged. "Maybe just that he could. He was the father, I was the son. He wanted to burn me, he could burn me."

She raised her head and her eyes filled. Her fingers dug into my hair and her eyes widened and reddened as they searched mine. When she kissed me, it was hard, bruising, as if she were trying to suck my pain out.

When she pulled back, her face was wet.

"He's dead, right?"

"My father?"

She nodded.

"Oh, yeah. He's dead, Grace."

"Good," she said.

When we made love again a few minutes later, it was one of the most exquisite and disconcerting experiences of my life. Our palms flattened against each other and our forearms followed suit and at every point along my body, my flesh and bone pressed against hers. Then her thighs rose up my hips and she took me inside of her as her legs slid down the backs of mine and her heels clamped just below my knees and I felt utterly enveloped, as if I'd melted through her flesh, and our blood had joined.

She cried out and I could feel it as if it came from my own vocal cords.

"Grace," I whispered as I disappeared inside her. "Grace."

Close to sleep, her lips fluttered against my ear.

" 'Night," she said sleepily.

" 'Night."

Her tongue slid in my ear, warm and electric.

"I love you," she mumbled.

When I opened my eyes to look at her, she was asleep.

I woke to the sound of her showering at six in the morning. My sheets smelled of her perfume and her flesh and a vague hint of hospital antiseptic and our sweat and lovemaking, imprinted into the fabric, it seemed, as if it had been there a thousand nights.

I met her at the bathroom door and she leaned into me as she combed back her hair.

My hand slid under her towel and the beads of water on her lower thighs glided off the edge of my hand.

"Don't even think about it." She kissed me. "I have to go see my daughter and get back to the hospital and after last night, I'm lucky I can walk. Now, go clean up."

I showered alone as she found clean clothes in a drawer we'd agreed she could commandeer, found myself waiting for that usual sense of discomfort I feel when a woman has spent more than, oh, an hour in my bed. But I didn't.

"I love you," she'd mumbled as she drifted off to sleep.

How odd.

When I came back to the bedroom, she was stripping the sheets from the bed, and she'd changed into a pair of black jeans and a dark blue oxford shirt.

I came up behind her as she bent over the pillows.

"Touch me, Patrick," she said, "and you die."

I put my hands back by my sides.

She smiled as she turned with sheets in hand and said, "Laundry. Is that something you're familiar with?"

"Vaguely."

She dropped the pile in a corner. "Can I expect that you'll remake the bed with fresh sheets or are we sleeping on a bare mattress next time I come over?"

"I will do my best, madam."

She slid her arms around my neck and kissed me. She hugged me fiercely and I hugged back just as hard.

"Someone called when you were in the shower." She leaned back in my arms.

"Who? It's not even seven in the morning."

"That's what I thought. He didn't leave his name."

"What'd he say?"

"He knew my name."

"What?" I unclasped my hands from her waist.

"He was Irish. I figured it was an uncle or something."
I shook my head. "My uncles and I don't talk."

"Why not?"

"Because they're my father's brothers and they aren't
any different than he was."

"Oh."

"Grace"—I took her hand, sat her beside me on the
bed—"what did this Irish guy say?"

"He said, 'You must be the lovely Grace. Grand to meet
you.'" She looked at the pile of bedclothes for a moment.
"When I told him you were in the shower, he said, 'Well,
just tell him I called and I'll be dropping in on him sometime,' and he hung up before I could get a name."

"That's it?"

She nodded. "Why?"

I shrugged. "I don't know. Not many people call me
before seven, and when they do, they usually leave a
name."

"Patrick, how many of your friends know we're dating?"

"Angie, Devin, Richie and Sherilynn, Oscar, and
Bubba."

"Bubba?"

"You met him. Big guy, always wears a trench coat—"

"The scary one," she said. "The one who looks like
he might just walk into a Seven-Eleven one day and kill
everyone inside because the Slurpee machine isn't working."

"That's the guy. You met him at—"

"That party last month. I remember." She shuddered.

"He's harmless."

"Maybe to you," she said. "Christ."

I tilted her chin toward me. "Not just me, Grace. Anyone I care about. Bubba's insanely loyal that way."

Her hands ran the wet hair back off my temples. "He's still a psychopath. People like Bubba fill emergency rooms with fresh victims."

"Okay."

"So I don't ever want him near my daughter. Understand?"

There's a look a parent gets when she's feeling protective of her child and it's an animal's look, and the danger that steams off it is palpable. It's not something that can be reasoned with, and even though it stems from the depths of love, it knows no pity.

Grace had that look now.

"Deal," I said.

She kissed my forehead. "Still doesn't solve the identity of the Irish guy who called."

"Nope. He say anything else?"

" 'Soon,' " she said as she came off the bed. "Where'd I leave my jacket?"

"Living room," I said. "What do you mean—'Soon'?"

She paused on her way to the doorway, looked back at me. "When he said he'd be dropping by your place. He waited a few seconds and then he said, 'Soon.' "

She walked out of the bedroom and I heard a weak floorboard creak in the living room as she walked through.

Soon.

7

Shortly after Grace left, Diandra called. Stan Timpson would give me five minutes on the phone at eleven.

"Five whole minutes," I said.

"For Stan, that's generous. I gave him your number. He'll call you at eleven on the dot. Stanley's prompt."

She gave me Jason's class schedule for the week and his dorm room number. I copied it all down as fear made her voice sound tiny and brittle, and just before we hung up she said, "I'm so nervous. I hate it."

"Don't worry, Doctor Warren. This will all work out."

"Will it?"

I called Angie and the phone was picked up on the second ring. Before I heard a voice, there was a rustling noise, as if the phone were being passed from one hand to another and I heard her whisper, "I got it. Okay?"

Her voice was hoarse and hesitant with sleep. "Hello?"

"Morning."

"Uh-huh," she said. "It's that." There was another rustling noise from her end, a disentangling of sheets, and a bed spring groaned. "What's up, Patrick?"

I gave her the rundown on my conversation with Diandra and Eric.

"So it definitely wasn't Kevin who called her." Her voice was still sluggish. "This makes no sense."

"Nope. You got a pen?"

"Somewhere. Let me find it."

More of that rustling sound and I knew she'd dropped

the phone on the bed as she rummaged around for a pen. Angie's kitchen is spotless because she's never used it, and her bathroom sparkles because she hates filth, but her bedroom always looks like she just unpacked from a trip in the middle of a windstorm. Socks and underwear spill from open drawers, and clean jeans and shirts and leggings are strewn across the floor or hang from doorknobs or the posts of her headboard. She's never, as long as I've known her, worn the first wardrobe she's considered in the morning. Amid all this carnage, books and magazines, spines bent or cracked, peek up from the floor.

Mountain bikes have been lost in Angie's bedroom, and now she was looking for a pen.

After several drawers were banged open and change and lighters and earrings were moved around on the tops of nightstands, someone said, "What're you looking for?"

"A pen."

"Here."

She came back on the line. "Got a pen."

"Paper?" I said.

"Oh, shit."

That took another minute.

"Go ahead," she said.

I gave her Jason Warren's class schedule and dorm room number. She'd tail him while I waited for Stan Timpson's call.

"Got it," she said. "Damn, I got to get moving."

I looked at my watch. "His first class isn't till ten-thirty. You got time."

"Nope. Got an appointment at nine-thirty."

"With who?"

Her breathing was slightly labored, and I assumed she was tugging on jeans. "My attorney. See you at Bryce whenever you get there."

She hung up and I stared out at the avenue below. It seemed cut from a canyon, the day was so clear, striped hard as a frozen river between rows of three-deckers and brick. Windshields were seared white and opaque by the sun.

An attorney? Sometimes in the heady flush of my past

three months with Grace, I'd remember with something like surprise that my partner was also out there living a life. Separate from my own. Her life with its attorneys and entanglements and minidramas and men who handed her pens in her bedroom at eight-thirty in the morning.

So, who was this attorney? And who was the guy who handed her the pen? And why should I care?

And what the hell did ''soon'' mean?

I had ninety minutes or so to kill before Timpson called, and after I exercised, I still had over an hour. I went looking for something in my fridge that wasn't beer or soda, and came up empty, so I walked up the avenue to the corner store for my coffee.

I took it back out onto the avenue and leaned against a light pole for a few minutes, enjoyed the day, and sipped my coffee as traffic rolled by and pedestrians rushed past on their way to the subway stop at the end of Crescent.

Behind me I could smell the stench of stale beer and soaked-in-wood whiskey wafting from The Black Emerald Tavern. The Emerald opened at eight for those getting off the graveyard shift, and now, close to ten, it sounded no different than it did on a Friday night, a gaggle of slurred, lazy voices punctuated by the occasional bellow or the sharp crack of a pool cue making impact with a rack of balls.

''Hey, stranger.''

I turned and looked down into the face of a petite woman with a hazy, liquid grin. She had her hand over her eyes to block the sun and it took me a minute to place her because the hair and clothes were different and even her voice had deepened since the last time I'd heard it, though it was still light and ephemeral, as if it might lift off into the breeze before the words had time to dig in.

''Hi, Kara. When'd you get back?''

She shrugged. ''A while ago. How you doing, Patrick?''

''Fine.''

Kara pivoted back and forth on her heel and rolled her eyes off to the side, her grin playing softly up the left side of her face, and she was instantly familiar again.

She'd been a sunny kid, but a loner. You'd see her in the playground scribbling or drawing in a notepad while the other kids played kickball. As she grew older and took her place on the corner overlooking the Blake Yard, her group filling the place my group had abandoned ten years earlier, you'd notice her sitting off to herself against a fence or porch post, drinking a wine cooler and looking out at the streets as if they seemed suddenly foreign to her. She wasn't ostracized or labeled weird because she was beautiful, more beautiful by half than the next most beautiful girl, and pure beauty is valued in this neighborhood like no other commodity because it seems more accidental than even a cash windfall.

Everyone knew, from the time she could walk, that she'd never stay in the neighborhood. It could never hold the beautiful ones and the leaving was entrenched in her eyes like flaws in the irises. When you spoke to her, some part of her—whether it was her head, her arms, her twitching legs—was incapable of remaining still, as if it were already moving past you and the boundaries of the neighborhood into that place she saw beyond.

As rare as she would have seemed to her circle of friends, a version of Kara came along every five years or so. In my days on the corner, it was Angie. And as far as I know, she's the only one who thwarted the strangely defeated neighborhood logic and stuck around.

Before Angie there was Eileen Mack, who hopped an Amtrak in her graduation gown and was next seen a few years later on *Starsky and Hutch*. In twenty-six minutes, she met Starsky, slept with him, gained Hutch's approval (though it was touch-and-go there for a while), and accepted Starsky's stumbling marriage proposal. By the next commercial break, she was dead, and Starsky went on a rampage and found her killer and blew him away with a fierce, righteous look on his face, and the episode ended with him standing over her grave in the rain and we were left knowing he'd never get over her.

By the next episode, he had a new girlfriend and Eileen was never mentioned or seen again by Starsky or Hutch or anyone in the neighborhood.

Kara'd gone to New York after a year at U/Mass and that's the last I'd heard of her, too. Angie and I had actually seen her board the bus as we came out of Tom English's one afternoon. It was the middle of summer, and Kara stood across the avenue at the bus stop. Her natural hair color was a wispy, wheaty blonde, and it blew in her eyes as she adjusted the strap on her bright sundress. She waved and we waved back and she lifted her suitcase as the bus pulled in and scooped her up and took her away.

Now her hair was short and spiky and ink black and her skin was pale as bleach. She wore a sleeveless black turtleneck tucked into painted-on charcoal jeans, and a nervous, half-gasping sound, almost a hiccup, punctuated the ends of her sentences.

"Nice day, huh?"

"I'll take it. Last October, we had snow by this time."

"New York, too." She chuckled, then nodded to herself and looked down at her scuffed boots. "Hmm. Yeah."

I sipped some more coffee. "So how you doing, Kara?"

She put her hand over her eyes again, looked at the slow-motion morning traffic. Hard sunlight glanced off the windshields and shafted through the spikes of her hair. "I'm good, Patrick. Really good. How about you?"

"No complaints." I glanced at the avenue myself and when I turned back she was looking into my face intently, as if trying to decide whether it attracted or repelled her.

She swayed slightly from side to side, an almost imperceptible movement, and I could hear two guys shouting something about five dollars and a baseball game through the open doorway of The Black Emerald.

She said, "You still a detective?"

"Uh-huh."

"Good living?"

"Sometimes," I said.

"My mom mentioned you in a letter last year, said you were in all the papers. A big deal."

I was surprised Kara's mother could climb out of the inside of a scotch glass long enough to read a paper, never mind write her daughter a letter about the experience.

"It was a slow news week," I said.

She looked back at the bar, ran a finger above her ear as if tucking back hair that wasn't there. "What do you charge?"

"Depends on the case. You need a detective, Kara?"

Her lips looked thin and oddly abandoned for a moment, as if she'd closed her eyes during a kiss and opened them to find her lover gone. "No." She laughed, then hiccupped. "I'm moving to L.A. soon. I landed a part on *Days of Our Lives*."

"Really? Hey, congrat—"

"Just a walk-on," she said, shaking her head. "I'm the nurse who's always fiddling with papers behind the nurse who stands at the admitting desk."

"Still," I said, "it's a start."

A man stuck his head out of the bar, looked to his right, then to his left, saw us through bleary eyes. Micky Doog, part-time construction worker, full-time coke dealer, a former local heartthrob from Kara's age group, still trying to hold the line of his youth against the advance of a receding hairline and softening muscles. He blinked when he saw me, then stuck his head back inside.

Kara's shoulders tensed, as if she'd felt him there, then she leaned in toward me and I could smell the sharp odor of rum floating from her mouth at ten in the morning.

"Crazy world, huh?" Her pupils glinted like razors.

"Um . . . yeah," I said. "You need help, Kara?"

She laughed again, followed it with a hiccup.

"No, no. No, I just wanted to say hey, Patrick. You were one of the big brothers to our crew." She tilted her head back toward the bar so I could see where some of her "crew" had ended up this morning. "I just wanted to, you know, say hi."

I nodded and watched tiny tremors ripple the skin along her arms. She kept glancing at my face as if it might reveal something to her, then looked away when it didn't, only to come back to it a second later. She reminded me of a kid with no money standing in a group of kids with plenty at an ice cream truck, as if she were watching cones and chocolate eclairs pass over her head into other hands, and half of her knew she'd never get one, and the other half held out hope that the ice cream man might hand her one out of error or pity. Bleeding inside from the embarrassment of wanting.

I pulled out my wallet and extracted a business card.

She frowned at it, then looked at me. Her half-smile was sarcastic and a bit ugly.

"I'm fine, Patrick."

"You're half in the bag at ten in the morning, Kara."

She shrugged. "It's noon somewhere."

"Not here, though."

Micky Doog stuck his head out the door again. He looked directly at me and his eyes weren't as bleary, emboldened by some blow or whatever else he was selling these days.

"Hey, Kara, you coming back inside?"

She made a little movement with her shoulders, my card dampening in her palm. "Be right in, Mick."

Micky seemed ready to say more, but then he patted the door in a drum beat, nodded once and disappeared inside.

Kara glanced at the avenue, stared at the cars for a long time.

"You leave a place," she said, "you expect it to look smaller when you come back." She shook her head and sighed.

"It doesn't?"

She shook her head. "Looks just the fucking same."

She took a few steps backward, tapping my card against her hip, and her eyes widened as she looked at me and rolled her shoulders elaborately. "Take care, Patrick."

"You too, Kara."

She held up my card. "Hey, now that I got this, right?"

She tucked it into the back pocket of her jeans and turned toward the open doorway of The Black Emerald. She stopped then, turned and smiled at me. It was a wide, gorgeous smile, but her face seemed unaccustomed to it; her cheeks quivered around its edges.

"Be careful, Patrick. Okay?"

"Careful of what?"

"Of everything, Patrick. Everything."

I gave her what I'm sure was a quizzical look and she nodded at me as if we shared a secret, and then she ducked into the bar and was gone.

8

My father, even before he entered the arena himself, had been active in local politics. He was a sign holder and a door knocker, and the bumpers of the various Chevys we'd owned throughout my childhood and adolescence had always borne stickers attesting to my father's partisan loyalty. Politics had nothing to do with social change to my father, and he didn't give a shit what most politicians promised in public; it was the private bonds that drew him. Politics was the last great tree house, and if you got in with the best kids on the block, you could roll the ladder up on the fools below.

He'd supported Stan Timpson when Timpson, fresh out of law school and new to the DA's office, had run for alderman. Timpson was from the neighborhood, after all, a comer, and if things went right, soon he'd be the guy to call when you needed your street plowed or your noisy neighbors rousted or your cousin put on the union dole.

I vaguely remembered Timpson from my childhood, but couldn't completely separate where my own recollection of Timpson differed from the one I'd seen on TV. So when his voice filtered through my phone receiver, it seemed strangely disembodied, as if it were prerecorded.

"Pat Kenzie?" he said heartily.

"Patrick, Mr. Timpson."

"How are you, Patrick?"

"Just fine, sir. How about yourself?"

"Great, great. Couldn't be better." He laughed warmly

as if we'd shared a joke I somehow missed. "Diandra tells me you have some questions for me."

"I do, yes."

"Well, fire away, son."

Timpson was only ten or twelve years older than I was. I wasn't sure how that made me *son*.

"Diandra told you about the photo of Jason she received?"

"She sure did, Patrick. And I got to tell you, it seems a bit strange."

"Yes, well—"

"Personally I think someone's playing a trick on her."

"Pretty elaborate trick."

"She told me you dismissed the Mafia connection?"

"At the moment, yes."

"Well, I don't know what to tell you, Pat."

"Is there anything your office is working on, sir, which could have caused someone to threaten your ex-wife and son?"

"That's the movies talking, Pat."

"Patrick."

"I mean, maybe in Bogotá they go after their district attorneys on personal vendettas. Not in Boston. Come on, son—that's the best you can do?" Another hearty laugh.

"Sir, your son's life may be in danger and—"

"Protect him, Pat."

"I'm trying to, sir. But I can't do that if—"

"You know what I think this is? I'll tell you the truth, it's one of Diandra's crazies. Forgot to take his Prozac and decided to make her nervous. You look over her patient list, son. That's my suggestion."

"Sir, if you'd just—"

"Pat, listen to me. I haven't been married to Diandra in almost two decades. When she called last night, that's the first time I'd heard her voice in six years. No one knows we were ever married. No one knows about Jason. The last campaign, believe me, we were waiting for the issue to be raised—how I left my first wife and baby boy and have maintained very little contact. Guess what, though, Pat? It never came up. A dirty political race in a dirty political town, and it never came up. No one knows about Jason or Diandra in relation to me.''

"What about—?''

"It's been a pleasure talking to you, Pat. Tell your father Stan Timpson said hi. I miss that old guy. Where's he hiding these days?''

"Cedar Grove Cemetery.''

"Got himself a groundskeeper job, did he? Well, got to run. Take care, Pat.''

"This kid,'' Angie said, "is an even bigger slut than you used to be, Patrick.''

"Hey,'' I said.

Our fourth day of following Jason Warren and it was beginning to feel like tailing a young Valentino. Diandra had stressed that we not let Jason know we were tailing him, citing a male's reluctance to let anyone else control or alter his destiny and Jason's own ''formidable'' sense of privacy, as she called it.

I'd be private too, I guess, if I averaged three women in three days.

"A hat trick,'' I said.

"What?'' Angie said.

"The kid scored a hat trick on Wednesday. That officially puts him in the hound hall of fame.''

"Men,'' she said, "are pigs.''

"This is true.''

"Wipe that smirk off your face.''

If Jason were being stalked, the most likely suspect was a jilted lover, some young woman who didn't much appreciate being a notch on a belt, the number two of three. But we'd been watching him almost nonstop for over eighty hours and we'd seen no one following him but us. He wasn't hard to find either. Jason spent his days in class, usually arranged a nooner in his dorm room (an arrangement he seemed to have worked out with his roommate, a stoner from Oregon who held bong parties every night at seven when Jason was out of the room), studied on the lawn until sunset, ate in the cafeteria with a tableful of women and no men, then hit the bars around Bryce at night.

The women he slept with—at least the three we'd seen—all seemed to know of one another without jealousy. All were somewhat of a type, too. They wore fashionable clothing, usually black, with even more fashionable rips in them somewhere. They wore tacky costume jewelry which—given the cars they drove and the soft imported leather of their boots, jackets, and knapsacks—they presumably knew was tacky. So un-hip as to be hip, I guess— their ironic postmodern wink at a hopelessly out of touch world. Or something. None of them had boyfriends.

They were all enrolled in the School of Arts and Sciences. Gabrielle majored in literature. Lauren majored in art history, but spent most of her time playing lead guitar in an all-female ska/punk/speed metal band which seemed to have spent far too much time taking Courtney Love and Kim Deal seriously. And Jade—small and lean and self-consciously foul-mouthed—was a painter.

None of them appeared to bathe much. This would have been a problem for me, but it didn't seem to bother Jason. He didn't bathe much, either. I've never been particularly conservative when it comes to my taste in women, but I do have one rule about bathing and one rule about clitoral rings and I'm pretty unyielding about both of them. Makes me a killjoy with the grunge set, I guess.

Jason made up for the slack, though. Jason, from what we'd seen, was the male campus pump. Wednesday, he climbed out of Jade's bed and they both went to a bar called Harper's Ferry, where they met Gabrielle. Jade stayed in the bar, but Jason and Gabrielle retired to Gabrielle's BMW. There they had oral-genital contact, which I had the misfortune to observe. When they returned, Gabrielle and Jade went into the ladies' room where, according to Angie, they gleefully compared notes.

"Thick as a python allegedly," Angie said.

"It's not the size of the wand—"

"Keep telling yourself that, Patrick—maybe one day you'll believe it."

The two women and their boy-toy then moved on to TT

the Bear's Place in Central Square, where Lauren and her band played like tone-deaf Hole wannabes. After the show, Jason took a ride home with Lauren. They went into her room, lit incense, and fucked like sea otters to old Patty Smith CDs until shortly before dawn.

On the second night, in a bar on North Harvard, I bumped into him as I was coming out of the bathroom. I had my eyes on the crowd, trying to spot Angie, and I didn't even notice Jason until my chest hit his shoulder.

"Looking for someone?"

"What?" I said.

His eyes were full of mischief, but without malice, and shone a bright green in the light shafting from the stage.

"I said, 'Are you looking for someone?' " He lit a cigarette, drew it from his mouth with the same fingers that held his scotch glass.

"My girlfriend," I said. "Sorry I bumped you."

"No problem," he said, shouting a bit over the band's tepid guitar riffs. "You looked a little lost is all. Good luck."

"What's that?"

"Good luck," he shouted into my ear. "Finding your girl or whatever."

"Thanks."

I cut into the crowd as he turned back to Jade, said something in her ear that made her laugh.

"At first it was fun," Angie said on our fourth day.

"Which?"

"The voyeurism."

"Don't knock voyeurism. American culture wouldn't exist without it."

"I'm not," she said. "But it's getting kind of, well, sodden watching this kid fuck everything that isn't nailed down. You know?"

I nodded.

"They seem lonely."

"Who?" I said.

"All of them. Jason, Gabrielle, Jade, Lauren."

"Lonely. Hmm. Well, they seem to be doing a good job hiding it from the rest of the world."

"So did you for a long time, Patrick. So did you."

"Ouch," I said.

The end of the fourth day, we split the duties. For a kid who packed so many women and so many bars into his day, Jason was very structured. You could predict, almost to the minute, where he'd be at any given moment. That night, I went home, and Angie watched his dorm room.

She called while I was cooking dinner to tell me that Jason seemed to have settled in for the night with Gabrielle in his own room. Angie was going to grab a cat-nap and walk him to class in the morning.

After dinner, I sat on my porch and looked out the avenue as night deepened and chilled. It wasn't a minor lessening in warmth, either. It was a total plummet. The moon burned like a slice of dry ice and the air smelled the way it does after an evening high-school football game. A stiff breeze swept the avenue, bit its way through the trees, nibbled at the dry edges of leaves.

I came off the porch when Devin telephoned.

"What's up?" I said.

"What do you mean?"

"You don't call to chat, Dev. It's not your style."

"Maybe this is the new me."

"Nope."

He grumbled. "Fine. We have to talk."

"¿Porque?"

"Because someone just smoked a girl on Meeting House Hill and she has no ID and I'd like to know who she is."

"Which has what, exactly, to do with me?"

"Maybe nothing. But she did have your card in her hand when she died."

"My card?"

"Yours," he said. "Meeting House Hill. See you in ten minutes."

He hung up and I sat with the phone in my ear, listening

until the dial tone returned. I sat there longer still, hearing the tone, waiting for it to tell me that the dead girl on Meeting House Hill wasn't Kara Rider, waiting for it to tell me something. Anything.

9

By the time I reached Meeting House Hill, the temperature had dropped into the low thirties. It was a barren cold, one without wind or spirit, the kind that sinks into your bone marrow and fills your blood with shards of ice.

Meeting House Hill is the dividing line where my neighborhood ends and Field's Corner begins. The hill starts below the pavement, sloping the streets into a steep upgrade that turns a car's third gear into reverse on icy nights. Where several streets converge at an apex, the tip of Meeting House Hill rises through the grid of cement and tar to form a pauper's field in the middle of a neighborhood so blighted you could fire a missile through its center and no one would notice unless you hit a bar or a food stamp office.

The bell of St. Peter's tolled once as Devin met me at my car and we trudged up the hill. The sound of the bell was hollow, ringing blithely on a cold night in an area some god had clearly forgotten. The ground was beginning to harden and patches of dead grass crunched under our feet.

I could see only a few figures silhouetted under the streetlight atop the hill, and I turned to Devin. "You bring the entire force out tonight, Dev?"

He looked at me, his head shrunk low in his jacket. "You'd prefer we made a media event out of it? Have a bunch of reporters and townies and rookies trampling evidence?" He glanced at the rows of three-deckers overlooking the hill. "Great thing about homicides in shitty neighborhoods, nobody gives a fuck, so nobody gets in the way.''

"Nobody gives a fuck, Devin, then nobody's going to tell you anything.''

"That's the downside, sure.''

His partner, Oscar Lee, was the first cop I recognized. Oscar is the largest guy I've ever met. He'd make Refrigerator Perry look anorexic and Michael Jordan look like a midget, and even Bubba looks puny beside Oscar. He wore a leather watch cap over a black head the size of a circus balloon and smoked a cigar that smelled like beachfront after an oil slick.

He turned as we approached. "The hell's Kenzie doing here, Devin?''

Oscar. My friend in need, my friend indeed.

Devin said, "The card. Remember?''

"So you might be able to ID this girl, Kenzie.''

"If I could see her, Oscar. Maybe.''

Oscar shrugged. "She's probably looked better.''

He stepped aside so that I had a clear view of the body lying under the streetlight.

She was naked except for a pair of light blue satin underpants. Her body was swollen from the cold or rigor or something else. Her bangs were swept back off her forehead and her mouth and eyes were open. Her lips were blue from the cold and she seemed to look at something just over my shoulder. Her thin arms and legs were spread wide, and dark blood—chilled to slush—puddled out from the base of her throat, the heels of her upturned palms, and the soles of her feet. Small, flat circles of metal glinted from the center of each palm and each upturned ankle.

It was Kara Rider.

She'd been crucified.

"Three-penny nails,'' Devin said later as we sat in The Black Emerald Tavern. "Very basic. Only two thirds of the homes in this city have them. Preferred by carpenters everywhere.''

"Carpenters,'' Oscar said.

"That's it,'' Devin said. "The perp's a carpenter. Pissed

off about that Christ thing. Taking it upon himself to avenge the hero of his trade.''

"You writing this down?'' Oscar asked me.

We'd come to the bar looking for Micky Doog, the last person I'd seen Kara with, but he hadn't been seen since the early afternoon. Devin got his address from Gerry Glynn, the owner, and sent a few patrolmen by, but Micky's mother hadn't seen him since yesterday.

"There was a few of them in here this morning,'' Gerry told us. "Kara, Micky, John Buccierri, Michelle Rourke, part of that crew used to run around together a few years back.''

"They leave together?''

Gerry nodded. "I was just coming in as they were going out. They were pretty hammered and it wasn't even one in the afternoon. She's a good kid, though, that Kara.''

"Was,'' Oscar said. "Was a good kid.''

It was close to two in the morning and we were drunk.

Gerry's dog, Patton, a massive German shepherd with a coat of black and dusky amber, lay on the bar top ten feet away, watching us as if deciding whether he'd be taking our car keys or not. Eventually he yawned, and a great bacon strip of a tongue lolled from his mouth as he looked away from us with what seemed a studied disinterest.

After the medical examiner had shown up, I'd stood in the cold for another two hours while Kara's body was carted into an ambulance and shipped off to the morgue and then while the forensics team swept the area for the evidence and Devin and Oscar canvassed the homes fronting the park for anyone who might have heard anything. It wasn't so much that no one heard anything, just that women screamed in this neighborhood every night and it was sort of like a car alarm—once you heard it enough times, you stopped noticing.

From the cloth fibers Oscar noticed stuck to Kara's teeth, and the lack of blood Devin found in the nail holes that bored through the frozen dirt under her hands and feet, they assumed the following: She'd been killed at another location after the killer had shoved a handkerchief or piece of shirt in her mouth, then made an incision in the base of her throat with either a stiletto or a very sharp ice pick to demobilize her larynx. He'd then been free to watch her die from either severe shock trauma, a heart attack, or slow suffocation due to drowning in her own blood. For whatever reason, the killer had then transported the body to Meeting House Hill and crucified Kara to the frozen dirt.

"He's a sweetheart, this guy," Devin said.

"Probably just needs a good hug," Oscar said. "Straighten him right out."

"No such thing as a bad boy," Devin said.

"You're damn skippy," Oscar said.

I hadn't said much since I'd seen her body. Unlike Oscar and Devin, I'm no pro when it comes to violent death. I've seen my share, but not on a level even remotely comparable with either of these guys.

I said, "I can't handle this."

"Yes," Devin said, "you can."

"Drink more," Oscar said. He nodded in the direction of Gerry Glynn. Gerry'd owned the Black Emerald since the days when he was a cop, and even though he usually shuts down at one, he never closes his doors to people on the Job. He had our drinks in front of us before Oscar finished his nod, and he was back at the other end of the bar before we even realized he'd been by. The definition of a good bartender.

"Crucified," I said for the twentieth time that night as Devin placed a fresh beer in my hand.

"I think we're all agreed on that point, Patrick."

"Devin," I said, trying to focus on him, pissed off that he wouldn't remain still, "the girl was barely twenty-two years old. I've known her since she was two."

Devin's eyes remained still and blank. I looked at Oscar. He chewed a half-smoked, unlit cigar and looked back at me like I was a piece of furniture he hadn't decided where to place.

"Fuck," I said.

"Patrick," Devin said. "Patrick. You listening?"

I turned in his direction. For a brief moment, his head stopped moving. "What?"

"She was twenty-two. Yes. A baby. And if she'd been

fifteen or forty, it wouldn't be any better. Death is death and murder's murder. Don't make it worse by getting sentimental about her age, Patrick. She was murdered. Atrociously. No argument. But . . .'' He leaned haphazardly on the bar, closed one eye. "Partner? What was my *but*?"

"But," Oscar said, "don't matter if she was male or female, rich or poor, young or old—"

"Black or white," Devin said.

"—black or white," Oscar said, scowling at Devin, "she was still murdered, Kenzie. Murdered bad."

I looked at him. "You ever seen anything that bad?"

He chuckled. "Seen a whole lot worse, Kenzie."

I turned to Devin. "You?"

"Hell, yes." He sipped his drink. "Violent world, Patrick. People enjoy killing. It—"

"Empowers them," Oscar said.

"Exactly," Devin said. "Some part of it makes you feel pretty goddammed good. All that power." He shrugged. "But why're we telling you? You'd know all about that."

"Excuse me?"

Oscar put a hand the size of a catcher's mitt on my shoulder. "Kenzie, everyone knows you did Marion Socia last year. We got you pegged for a couple punks in the projects off the Melnea Cass too."

"What," I said, "and you haven't had me arraigned?"

"Patrick, Patrick, Patrick," Devin said, slurring just a bit, "it was up to us, you'd get a medal for Socia. Fuck him. Fuck him twice, far as I'm concerned. But," he said, closing one eye again, "you can't tell me some part of you didn't feel real good watching the light go out of his eyes when you popped one through his head."

I said, "No comment."

"Kenzie," Oscar said, "you know he's right. He's drunk, but he's right. You drew on that pile of shit Socia, looked in his eyes, and put his ass down." He made a pistol with his index finger and thumb, shoved it against my temple. "Bang. Bang. Bang." He removed the finger. "No more Marion Socia. Kind of feels like being God for a day, don't it?"

How I felt when I killed Marion Socia under an ex-

pressway as trucks hammered the metal extensions overhead was one of the more conflicted set of emotions I'd
ever had in my life, and I sure as hell didn't feel like
reminiscing about it in a bar with two homicide detectives
when I was half in the bag. Maybe I'm paranoid.

Devin smiled. "Killing someone feels very good, Patrick. Don't kid yourself."

Gerry Glynn came down the bar. "Another round,
boys?"

Devin nodded. "Hey, Ger."

Gerry stopped halfway down the bar.

"You ever kill anyone on the Job?"

Gerry looked a bit embarrassed, as if he'd heard the
question too many times. "Never even pulled my gun."

"No," Oscar said.

Gerry shrugged, his kind eyes completely at odds with
the job he'd done for twenty years. He scratched Patton's
abdomen absently. "Those were different days, then. You
remember, Dev."

Devin nodded. "Different days."

Gerry pulled the tap to fill my beer mug. "Different
world, really."

"Different world," Devin said.

He brought our fresh drinks down to us. "Wish I could
help you out, guys."

I looked at Devin. "Someone notify Kara's mother?"

He nodded. "She was passed out in her kitchen, but
they woke her up and told her. Someone's sitting with her
now."

"Kenzie," Oscar said, "we're going to get this Micky
Doog. It was someone else, a gang, whatever, we'll get
'em all. In a few hours, we know everyone's awake, we're
going to recanvass every house and someone probably will
have seen something. And we'll pick the punk motherfucker up and sweat him and mess with his head till he
breaks. Won't bring her back, but maybe we speak for her
a bit."

I said, "Yeah, but . . . ."

Devin leaned toward me. "The prick who did this is going down, Patrick. Believe it."

I wanted to. I really did.

Just before we left, while Devin and Oscar were in the bathroom, I looked up from the blurred bar top and found both Gerry and Patton staring at me. In the four years Gerry'd had him, I'd never known Patton to so much as bark, but one look in the dog's still, flat eyes and you'd never consider messing with it. That dog's eyes had probably forty different casts for Gerry—ranging from love to sympathy—but it had only one for everyone else—bare warning.

Gerry scratched behind Patton's ears. "Crucifixion."

I nodded.

"How many times you think that's happened in this city, Patrick?"

I shrugged, not trusting my tongue to enunciate properly anymore.

"Probably not many," Gerry said, then looked down as Patton licked his hand and Devin came back into the room.

That night, I dreamed of Kara Rider.

I was walking through a cabbage field filled with Black Angus cows and human heads whose faces I didn't recognize. In the distance, the city burned, and I could see my father's silhouette standing atop an engine ladder, hosing the flames with gasoline.

The fire was rolling steadily out from the city, kissing the edges of the cabbage field. Around me, the human heads were beginning to speak, an incoherent babble at first, but soon I could distinguish a stray voice or two.

"Smells like smoke," one said.

"You always say that," one of the cows said and spit cud onto a cabbage leaf as a stillborn calf fell from between its legs and puddled by its hoofs.

I could hear Kara screaming from somewhere in the field as the air grew black and oily and the smoke bit my eyes, and Kara kept screaming my name, but I couldn't tell the human heads from the cabbage heads and the cows were moaning and tipping in the breeze and the smoke was all around me, and pretty soon Kara's screams stopped and I felt grateful as the flames began to lick at my legs. So I sat down in the middle of the field to get my wind back and watch the world burn around me as the cows chewed the grass and swayed back and forth and refused to run.

When I woke up in bed, I was gasping for air and the smell of burning flesh clung to my nostrils. I watched the sheet shake over my racing heart and swore I'd never go drinking with Oscar and Devin again.

10

I'd crawled into bed at four that morning, been awakened by my Salvador Dali dream sometime around seven, and didn't fall back asleep until about eight.

Which meant nothing to Lyle Dimmick and his buddy, Waylon Jennings. At exactly nine, Waylon started screaming about the woman who'd done him wrong, and the harsh grate of a country fiddle climbed over my windowsills and rattled china in my brain.

Lyle Dimmick was a permanently sunburned housepainter who'd come here from Odessa, Texas, because of a woman. He'd found her, lost her, got her back, and lost her again when she ran back to Odessa with some guy she met in a neighborhood pub, an Irish pipefitter who decided he'd always been a cowpoke at heart.

Ed Donnegan owned almost every three-decker on my block, save for my own, and every ten years, he got around to painting them, and every time he did, he hired a single painter for as long as it took to paint them all, rain, snow or shine.

Lyle wore a ten-gallon hat and a red handkerchief around his neck and black wrap-around Gargoyle sunglasses that took up half of his small, pinched face. Those sunglasses, he said, seemed like something a city boy would wear, and they were his only concession to living in a god-awful world of Yankees who had no appreciation for God's three great gifts to mankind—Jack Daniel's, the horse, and, of course, Waylon.

I stuck my head in between the shade and the screen

and saw that his back was to me as he painted the house next door. The music was so loud he'd never hear me, so I pulled down the window instead, then stumbled up and pulled down all the others in the bedroom, and reduced Waylon to just another tinny voice ringing in my head. Then I crawled back into bed and closed my eyes and prayed for quiet.

Which meant nothing to Angie.

She woke me shortly after ten by bouncing around the apartment making coffee, opening windows to another fresh autumn day, and rattling through my refrigerator, as Waylon or Merle or Hank Jr. poured back through my screens.

When that didn't rouse me from bed, she opened the bedroom door and said, "Get up."

"Go away." I pulled the covers over my head.

"Get up, ya baby. I'm bored. Now."

I threw a pillow at her and she ducked and it arced over her head and shattered something in the kitchen.

She said, "You weren't fond of those dishes, I hope."

I stood and wrapped the sheet around my waist to cover my glow-in-the-dark Marvin the Martian boxer shorts and stumbled out into the kitchen.

Angie stood in the middle of the room, coffee cup held in both hands, a few broken plates on the floor and sink.

"Coffee?" she said.

I found a broom, began sweeping up the mess. Angie put her cup on the table, bent by me with a dustpan.

I said, "You're still a bit unclear on this sleep concept, aren't you?"

"Overrated." She scooped up some glass and dumped it in the wastebasket.

"How would you know? You've never tried it."

"Patrick," she said, dumping another load of glass, "it's not my fault you stayed out until the wee hours drinking with your little friends."

My little friends.

"How do you know I was out drinking with anybody?"

She dumped the last bit of glass, straightened. "Because your skin is a shade of green I've never seen before, and there was an incredibly drunken message on my answering machine this morning.''

"Ah." I vaguely recollected a pay phone and a beep from some point last night. "What did this message say?''

She took her coffee cup off the table, leaned against the washing machine. "Something like 'Where are you, it's three in the morning, something's really fucked up, we gotta talk.' The rest I couldn't understand, but by then you'd started speaking Swahili anyway.''

I put the dustpan, broom, and wastebasket in the pantry, poured myself a cup of coffee. "So," I said, "where were you at three in the morning?''

"You're my father now?" She frowned and pinched my waist just above the sheet. "You're getting love handles.''

I reached for the cream. "I don't have love handles.''

"And you know why? Because you still drink beer like you're in a frat.''

I looked at her steadily, poured extra cream into my coffee. "You going to answer my original question?''

"About my whereabouts last night?''

"Yes.''

She sipped her coffee, looked over the mug rim at me. "Nope. I did wake up with a warm, fuzzy feeling, though, and a big smile on my face. Big smile.''

"Big as the one you're wearing now?''

"Bigger.''

"Hmm,'' I said.

She hoisted herself up onto the washing machine. "So, you called me, shit-faced, at three A.M. to do more than check up on my sex life. What's up?'' She lit a cigarette.

I said, "You remember Kara Rider?''

"Yeah.''

"Someone murdered her last night.''

"No.'' Her eyes were huge.

"Yes.'' With all the extra cream, my coffee tasted like baby's formula. "Crucified her on Meeting House Hill.''

She closed her eyes for a moment, opened them. She looked at her cigarette like it might tell her something. "Any idea who did it?'' she said.

"No one was parading around Meeting House Hill with

a bloody hammer singing, 'Boy, oh boy, do I like to cru-
cify women,' if that's what you mean.'' I tossed my coffee
in the sink.

Quietly, she said, "You done snapping for the day?"

I poured fresh coffee into the cup. "Don't know yet.
It's still early." I turned around and she slipped off the
washing machine and stood in front of me.

I saw Kara's thin body lying in the cold night, swollen
and exposed, her eyes blank.

I said, "I ran into her the other morning outside the
Emerald. I had a feeling, I dunno, that she was in trouble
or something, but I let it go. I blew it off."

"And what?" she said. "You're somehow to blame?"

I shrugged.

"No, Patrick," she said. She ran a warm palm up the
side of my neck, forced me to look in her eyes. "Understand?"

Nobody should die like Kara did.

"Understand?" she said again.

"Yeah," I said. "Yeah, I guess."

"No guessing," she said. She removed her hand and
pulled a white envelope from her purse and handed it to
me. "This was taped to the front door downstairs." She
pointed to a small cardboard box on my kitchen table.
"And that was leaning against the door."

I have a third-floor apartment with a bolt lock on both
the front and back doors and usually two guns stored inside
somewhere, and none of this probably deters break-ins as
much as the two front doors to the three-decker itself.
There's an outside one and an interior one, and they're
both reinforced with steel and made of heavy black
German oak. The portal glass in the first one is wired with
alarm tape, and my landlord has fitted both doors with a
total of six locks that require three different keys. I have
a set. Angie has a set. My landlord's wife, who lives in
the first-floor apartment because she can't stand his company, has one. And Stanis, my crazy landlord—terrified
that a Bolshevik hit squad is going to come for him—has
two sets.

All in all, my building is so secure I was surprised some-

one could even tape an envelope to the front door or lean
a box against it without setting off nine or ten alarms and
waking five city blocks.

The envelope was plain, white, letter-size with "patrick
kenzie" typed in the center. No address, no stamp, no
return address. I opened it and pulled a piece of typing
paper from inside, unfolded it. There were no address
headings, no date, no salutation, no signature. In the middle of the page, centered, someone had typed one word:

HI!

The rest of the page was virgin.

I handed it to Angie. She looked at it, turned it over,
turned it back to the front. " 'Hi,' " she read aloud.

"Hi," I said.

"No," she said, "more like 'Hi!' Give it that girlish
giggle."

I tried it.

"Not bad."

HI!

"Could it be Grace?" She poured another cup of coffee.

I shook my head. "She says hi an entirely different way,
believe me."

"So, who?"

I honestly didn't know. It was such an innocuous note,
but weird too. "Whoever wrote it is a master of brevity."

"Or has an extremely limited vocabulary."

I tossed the note on the table, pulled back the tape on
the box and opened it as Angie looked over my shoulder.

"What the hell?" she said.

The box was filled with bumper stickers. I pulled out a
handful, and there was still another two handfuls waiting.

Angie reached in, grabbed a fistful.

"This is . . . odd," I said.

Angie's brow was furrowed and she had a curious half
smile on her face. "You could say that, yeah."

We took them into the living room and laid them out
on the floor in a collage of blacks and yellows and reds
and blues and shiny iridescents. Looking down at all

ninety-six of them was like standing over a world of pet-
ulance and hollow sentiment and the hopelessly inept
search for the perfect sound-bite:

HUGS NOT DRUGS; I'M PRO-CHOICE AND I
VOTE; LOVE YOUR MOTHER; IT'S A CHILD NOT A
CHOICE; I JUST FUCKING LOVE TRAFFIC; IF YOU
DON'T LIKE MY DRIVING DIAL 1-800-EAT-SHIT;
ARMS ARE FOR HUGGING; IF I'M A ROAD HOG,
YOUR WIFE'S A PIG; VOTE FOR TED KENNEDY
AND PUT A BLONDE IN THE WATER; YOU CAN
HAVE MY GUN WHEN YOU PRY IT FROM MY
COLD DEAD FINGERS; I'LL FORGIVE JANE FONDA
WHEN THE JEWS FORGIVE HITLER; IF YOU'RE
AGAINST ABORTION, DON'T HAVE ONE; PEACE—
AN IDEA WHOSE TIME HAS COME; DIE YUPPIE
SCUM; MY KARMA BEATS YOUR DOGMA; MY
BOSS IS A JEWISH CARPENTER; POLITICIANS LIKE
THEIR PEASANTS UNARMED; FORGET 'NAM?
NEVER; THINK GLOBALLY, ACT LOCALLY; HONK
IF YOU'RE RICH AND HANDSOME; HATE IS NOT
A FAMILY VALUE; I'M SPENDING MY CHILD'S IN-
HERITENCE; WE ARE OUT & WE ARE EVERY-
WHERE; SHIT HAPPENS; JUST SAY NO; MY WIFE
RAN OFF WITH MY BEST FRIEND AND I'M SURE
GOING TO MISS HIM; DIVERS DO IT DEEP; I'D
RATHER BE FISHING; DON'T LIKE THE POLICE?
NEXT TIME YOU'RE IN TROUBLE, CALL A LIB-
ERAL; FUCK YOU; FUCK ME; MY CHILD IS AN
HONOR STUDENT AT ST. CATHERINE'S ELEMEN-
TARY; MY CHILD BEAT UP YOUR HONOR STU-
DENT; HAVE A NICE DAY, ASSHOLE; FREE TIBET;
FREE MANDELA; FREE HAITI; FEED SOMALIA;
CHRISTIANS AREN'T PERFECT, JUST FOR-
GIVEN . . .

   . . . And fifty-seven more.

Standing there, looking at all of them, trying to comprehend the enormous gulf of difference in the myriad of
messages, my head began to throb. It was like looking at
a schizophrenic's cat scan while all the poor bastard's per-
sonalities got into a shouting match.

"Screwy," Angie said.

"There's a word, sure."

"Can you see anything any of these have in common?"

"Besides that they're all bumper stickers?"

"I think that goes without saying, Patrick."

I shook my head. "Then, no, I'm at a loss."

"Me too."

"I'll think about it in the shower," I said.

"Good idea," she said. "You smell like a wet bar rag."

With my eyes closed in the shower, I saw Kara standing on the sidewalk as the stale beer stench flowed from the bar behind her, looking out at the traffic on Dorchester Avenue, saying it all looked just the fucking same.

"Be careful," she'd said.

I stepped back out of the shower and dried off, saw her pale exposed body crucified, nailed to a dirt hill.

Angie was right. It wasn't my fault. You can't save people. Particularly when a person isn't even asking to be saved. We bounce and collide and smash our way through our lives, and for the most part, we're on our own. I owed Kara nothing.

But nobody should die like that, a voice whispered.

In the kitchen, I called Richie Colgan, an old friend and columnist for *The Trib*. As usual, he was busy, his voice distant and rushed, the words all running together: "GoodtohearfromyouPat. What'sup?"

"Busy?"

"Ohyeah."

"Could you check something for me?"

"Shoot, shoot."

"Crucifixions as a method of murder. How many in this city?"

"In?"

" 'In?' "

"How far back?"

"Say twenty-five years."

"Library."

"Huh?"

"Library. Heardofit?"

"Yeah."

"Ilooklikeone?"

"Usually when I get info from a library, I don't buy the librarian a case of Michelob afterward."

"Heineken."

"Of course."

"I'monit. Talktoyousoon." He hung up.

When I came back into the living room, the "HI!" note was lying on the coffee table, the bumper stickers were stacked in two neat piles underneath it, and Angie was watching TV. I'd changed into jeans and a cotton shirt and entered the living room toweling my hair dry.

"Whatcha watching?"

"CNN," she said, looking at the newspaper on her lap.

"Anything exciting going on in our world today?"

She shrugged. "An earthquake in India killed over nine thousand people, and a guy in California shot up the office where he works. Killed seven with a machine gun."

"Post office?" I said.

"Accounting firm."

"That's what happens when CPAs get ahold of automatic weapons," I said.

"Apparently."

"Any other happy news I should hear?"

"At some point, they broke in to tell us Liz Taylor's getting divorced again."

"Oh joy," I said.

"So," she said, "what's our plan?"

"Go sit on Jason again, maybe drop by Eric Gault's office, see if he can tell us anything."

"And we continue to work under the assumption that neither Jack Rouse or Kevin sent the photo."

"Yup."

"Which leaves how many suspects?" She stood.

"How many people live in this city?"

"I dunno. City proper, six hundred thousand, give or take; greater metro area, four million or so."

"Then somewhere between six hundred thousand and four million suspects it is," I said, "less two, give or take."

"Thanks for narrowing it down, Skid. You're swell."

11

The second and third floors of McIrwin Hall housed the offices of Bryce's Sociology, Psychology and Criminology faculty, including Eric Gault's. The first floor contained classrooms, and one of those classrooms contained Jason Warren at the moment. According to Bryce's course catalog, the class he took here, "Hell as a Sociological Construct," explored the "social and political motives behind the masculine creation of a Land of Punishment from the Sumerians and Akkadians up to, and including, the Christian Right in America." We'd run checks on all of Jason's teachers and found that Ingrid Uver-Kett had recently been expelled from a local NOW chapter for espousing views that made Andrea Dworkin's look mainstream. Her class ran three and a half hours without a break and met twice a week. Ms. Uver-Kett drove down from Portland, Maine, on Mondays and Thursdays to teach it, and spent the rest of her time, as far as we could see, writing hate mail to Rush Limbaugh.

Angie and I decided Ms. Uver-Kett seemed to spend far too much time being a threat to herself to possibly threaten Jason and eliminated her as a suspect.

McIrwin Hall was a white Georgian set off in a grove of birch and violently red maples with a cobblestone walk leading up to it. We'd watched Jason disappear in a crowd of students pouring through the front doors. We heard tramping and catcalls and then a sudden, almost total silence.

We had breakfast and came back to see Eric. By then,

only a forlorn and forgotten pen at the foot of the stairs gave any indication that a single soul had been through the doors this morning.

The foyer smelled of ammonia and pine solvent and two hundred years of intellectual perspiration, of knowledge sought and knowledge gained and grand ideas conceived under the mote-rich glow of the fractured sunlight streaming through a stained glass window.

There was a reception desk to our right, but no receptionist. At Bryce, I guess, you were already supposed to know your every destination.

Angie took off her denim shirt, yanked at the hem of her untucked T-shirt to clear it of static cling. "The atmosphere alone makes me want to get a degree here."

"Probably shouldn't have flunked high school geometry."

The next thing I said was, "Ooof."

We climbed a curved mahogany staircase, the walls laden with paintings of past Bryce presidents. Dour looking men all, faces weighted and strained from carrying so much genius in their brains. Eric's office was at the end of the hall and we knocked once and heard a muffled, "Come in," from the other side of the pebbled glass.

Eric's long salt-and-pepper ponytail fell over the right shoulder of his blue and maroon cardigan. Underneath the cardigan was a denim Oxford and a hand-painted navy blue tie with a plaintive baby seal staring out at us.

I cocked an eyebrow at the tie as I took a seat.

"Sue me," Eric said, "for being a slave to fashion." He leaned back in his chair and waved a hand at his open window. "Some weather, isn't it?"

"Some weather," I agreed.

He sighed and rubbed his eyes. "So, how's Jason doing?"

"He lives a very busy existence," Angie said.

"He used to be an insular kid, believe it or not," Eric said. "Very sweet, never a moment's trouble to Diandra, but introverted since day one."

"Not anymore," I said.

Eric nodded. "Ever since he came here, he's broken out.

It's common, of course, for kids who didn't fit in with the jock or beautiful-people cliques in high school to find themselves in college, stretch a bit.''

"Jason does a lot of stretching," I said.

"He seems lonely," Angie said.

Eric nodded. "I could see that. The father leaving when he was so young explains some things, but still, always there's been this . . . distance. I wish I could explain it. You see him with his . . ."—he smiled—". . . harem, I guess, when he doesn't know you're watching, and it's like he's a completely different person from the shy kid I've always known.''

"What does Diandra think about it?" I said.

"She doesn't notice it. He's very close to her, so when he talks to anyone with any degree of depth, he talks to her. But he doesn't bring women home, he doesn't even hint at his lifestyle here. She knows he's holding a piece of himself back, but she tells herself he's just very good at keeping his own counsel, and she respects that.''

"But you don't think so," Angie said.

He shrugged and looked out the window a moment. "When I was his age, I was living in the same dorm on this campus and I'd been a pretty introverted kid myself, and here, like Jason, I came out of my shell. I mean, it's college. It's study, drink, smoke weed, have sex with strangers, take naps in the afternoon. It's what you do if you come to a place like this at eighteen.''

"You had sex with strangers?" I said. "I'm shocked."

"And I feel so bad about it now. I do. But, okay, I was no saint either, but with Jason, this radical change and his charge into almost de Sadian excess is a bit drastic.''

" 'De Sadian'?" I said. "You intellectuals, I swear, talk so damn cool.''

"So why the change? What's he trying to prove?" Angie said.

"I don't know, exactly." Eric cocked his head in such a way that, not for the first time, he reminded me of a cobra. "Jason's a good kid. Personally I can't imagine him being mixed up in anything that would harm either himself or his mother, but then I've known the boy all his life and he's the last person I would've ever predicted would succumb to a Don Juan complex. You've dismissed the Mafia connection?''

''Pretty much,'' I said.

He pursed his lips, exhaled slowly. ''You got me then. I know what I just told you about Jason and that's about it. I'd like to say who he is or isn't with total certainty, but I've been at this long enough to realize that no one truly knows anyone else.'' He waved his hand at bookshelves crammed with criminology and psychology texts. ''If my years of study have taught me anything, that's the sum total.''

''Deep,'' I said.

He loosened his tie. ''You asked my opinion of Jason and I gave it you, prefaced by my belief that all humans have secret selves and secret lives.''

''What're yours, Eric?''

He winked. ''Wouldn't you like to know?''

As we walked into the sunlight, Angie slipped an arm through mine and we sat on the lawn under a tree and faced the doors through which Jason would exit in a few minutes. It's an old trick of ours to play lovers when we're tailing someone; people who'd possibly see either one of us as incongruous in a given place rarely give us a second glance as a couple. Lovers, for some reason, can often pass easily through doors the solitary person finds barred.

She looked up at the fan of leaves and limbs in the tree above. Humid air stirred yellow leaves against brittle pikes of grass and Angie leaned her head into my shoulder and left it there for a long time.

''You okay?'' I said.

Her hand tightened against my bicep.

''Ange?''

''I signed the papers yesterday.''

''The papers?''

''The divorce papers,'' she said softly. ''They've been sitting in my apartment for over two months. I signed them and dropped them at my attorney's office. Just like that.'' She moved her head slightly, resettled it in the space between my shoulder and neck. "As I signed my name, I had the distinct feeling it was going to make everything much cleaner somehow." Her voice had grown thick. "Was that how it was for you?"

I considered how I'd felt sitting in an attorney's climate-controlled office, bundling and bagging up my short, barren, ill-conceived marriage by signing on a dotted line and folding pages neatly three times before sliding them into an envelope. No matter how therapeutic, there's something pitiless about wrapping up the past and tying a ribbon to it.

My marriage to Renee had lasted less than two years, and it had been over in most respects in under two months. Angie had been married to Phil over twelve years. I had no conception what it was like walking away from twelve years, no matter how bad many of them had been.

"Did it make everything cleaner and clearer?" she said.

"No," I said, pulling her tight. "Not at all."

12

For another week, Angie and I tailed Jason around campus and town, up to classroom and bedroom doors, put him to bed at night, and rose with him in the morning. It wasn't exactly a thrill a minute, either. Sure, Jason led a pretty lively existence, but once you got the gist of it— wake, eat, class, sex, study, eat, drink, sex, sleep—it got old pretty quick. I'm sure if I'd been hired to tail de Sade himself in his prime, I'd have tired of that too by the third or fourth time he drank from a baby's skull or arranged an all-night fivesome.

Angie had been right—there was something lonely and sad about Jason and his partners. They bobbed through their existence like plastic ducks on hot water, tipping over occasionally, waiting as long as it took for someone to right them, and then back to more of the same bobbing. There were no fights, but no real passion, either. There was only a sense of them—the whole group—as flippantly self-aware, marginally ironic, as detached from the lives they led as a retina would be from an eye which no longer controlled it.

And there was no one stalking him. We were positive. Ten days and we'd seen no one. And we'd been looking.

Then, on the eleventh, Jason broke his routine.

I'd had no information on Kara Rider's murder because Devin and Oscar wouldn't return my calls, and from newspaper accounts I could tell the case had reached an impasse.

Following Jason kept my mind off it initially, but by now I was so bored I had no choice but to brood, and the brooding got me nowhere. Kara was dead. I couldn't have stopped it. Her murderer was unknown and free. Richie Colgan hadn't gotten back to me yet, though he'd left a message saying he was working on it. If I'd had the time, I could have looked into it, but instead I had to watch Jason and his band of studiously feckless groupies bleed the brilliance out of a magnificent Indian Summer by spending most of their time in cramped smoky rooms dressed in black or nothing at all.

"He's moving," Angie said and we left the alley we'd been in and followed Jason through Brookline Village. He browsed at a bookstore, bought a box of 3.5 diskettes at Egghead Software, then strolled into The Coolidge Corner Theater.

"Something new," Angie said.

For ten days, Jason had never varied substantially from his routine. Now he was going into a movie theater. Alone.

I looked up at the marquee, knowing I might have to follow him in and hoping it wasn't a Bergman film. Or worse, Fassbinder.

The Coolidge Corner leans toward esoteric art films and revivals, which is wonderful in this age of cookie-cutter Hollywood product. However, the price for this is that you do get those weeks when The Coolidge runs nothing but kitchen-sink dramas from Finland or Croatia or some other frigid, doom-laden country where all the pale, emaciated inhabitants seem to do is sit around talking about Kierkegaard or Nietzsche or how miserable they are instead of talking about moving someplace with more light and a more optimistic class of people.

Today, though, they were showing a restored print of Coppola's *Apocalypse Now*. As much as I like the movie, Angie hates it. She says it makes her feel like she's watching it from underneath a swamp after taking too many Quaaludes.

She stayed outside, and I went in. One of the benefits of having a partner at a time like this is that following someone into a movie theater, particularly if it's only half filled, is risky. If the target decides to leave halfway through the film, it's hard to follow without being conspicuous. But a partner can pick him right up outside.

The theater was almost empty. Jason took a seat near the front in the center, and I sat ten rows back to the left. A couple sat a few rows up on my right, and another lone person—a young woman with squinting eyes and a red bandana tied around her head—took notes. A film student.

About the time that Robert Duvall was holding a barbecue on the beach, a man came in and sat in the row behind Jason, about five seats to his left. As Wagner boomed on the soundtrack and gunships shredded the early morning village with gunfire and explosives, the light from the screen bathed the face of the man and I could see his profile—smooth cheeks interrupted by a trim goatee, close-cropped dark hair, a stud glinting from his earlobe.

During the Do-Long Bridge sequence, as Martin Sheen and Sam Bottoms crawled through a beseiged trench looking for the battalion leader, the man moved four seats to his left.

"Hey, soldier," Sheen yelled over the mortar fire at a young, scared black kid as flares lit up the sky. "Who's in command here?"

"Ain't you?" the kid screamed and the guy with the goatee leaned forward and Jason's head tilted back.

Whatever he said to Jason was brief, and by the time Martin Sheen left the trench and returned to the boat, the guy was stepping out into the aisle and walking back toward me. He was roughly my height and build, maybe thirty, and very good looking. He wore a dark sport coat over a loose green tank-top, battered jeans, and cowboy boots. When he caught me staring, he blinked and looked down at his feet as they carried him out of the theater.

On screen, Albert Hall asked Sheen, "You find the C.O.?"

"There's no fucking C.O.," Sheen said and climbed into the boat as Jason left his seat and walked up the aisle.

I waited a full three minutes, then left my seat as the PT boat floated inexorably toward Kurtz's compound and Brando's lunatic improvisations. I stuck my head in the bathroom to be sure it was empty, then left the theater.

Out on Harvard, I blinked into the sudden glare, then looked both ways for Angie, Jason, or the guy with the goatee. Nothing. I walked up to Beacon, but they weren't there either. Angie and I long ago agreed that the one separated from the chase was the one who went home without the car. So I hummed "O Sole Mio" until I flagged down a cab and rode it back to the neighborhood.

Jason and the guy with the goatee had met for lunch at the Sunset Grill on Brighton Avenue. Angie photographed them from across the street, and in one shot, the hands of both men had disappeared under the table. My initial assumption was drug deal.

They split the tab and, back out on Brighton Ave., their hands grazed against each other, and they both smiled shyly. The smile on Jason's face wasn't one I'd seen in the previous ten days. His usual smile was something of a cocky smirk, a lazy grin, rife with confidence. But this smile was unaffected, with a hint of a gush to it, as if he'd had no time to consider it before it broke across his cheeks.

Angie caught the smile and hand-grazing on film. And my assumption changed.

The guy with the goatee walked up Brighton toward Union Square, while Jason walked back to Bryce.

Angie and I spread her photos on her kitchen table that night and tried to decide what to tell Diandra Warren.

This was one of those points when my responsibility to my client was a bit unclear. I had no reason to think Jason's apparent bisexuality had anything to do with the threatening calls Diandra had received. And I had no reason, on the other hand, not to tell her about the encounter. Still, I didn't know if Jason was out of the closet or not, and I wasn't comfortable outing him, particularly when, in that one photograph, I was looking at a kid who, in all the time I'd observed him, looked purely happy for the one and only time.

"Okay," Angie said, "I think I have a solution."

She handed me a photograph of Jason and the guy with the goatee in which both were eating, neither really looking at the other, but instead concentrating on their food.

"He met him," Angie said, "had lunch, that's all. We show this to Diandra, along with ones of Jason and his women, ask if she knows this guy, but unless she offers, we don't bring up the possibility of a romance."

"Sounds like a plan."

"No," Diandra said. "I've never seen this man before. Who is he?"

I shook my head. "I don't know. Eric?"

Eric looked at the photo for a long time, eventually shook his head. "No." He handed it back to me. "No," he said again.

Angie said, "Doctor Warren, in over a week, this is all we've come up with. Jason's social circle is pretty limited and until this day, exclusively female."

She nodded, then tapped the head of Jason's friend with her finger. "Are they lovers?"

I looked at Angie. She looked at me.

"Come now, Mr. Kenzie, you don't think I know about Jason's sexuality? He's my son."

"So he's open about it?" I said.

"Hardly. He's never spoken to me about it, but I've known, I think, since he was a child. And I've let him know that I have absolutely no problem with homosexuality or bisexuality or any possible permutation thereof without mentioning the possibility of his own. But I still think he's either embarrassed or confused by his sexuality." She tapped the photo again. "Is this man a threat?"

"We don't have any reason to think so."

She lit a cigarette, leaned back in her couch and watched me. "So where does that leave us?"

"You've received no more threats or photos in the mail?"

"No."

"Then I don't see that we're doing much more than wasting your money, Doctor Warren."

She looked at Eric and he shrugged.

She turned back toward us. "Jason and I are going up to a house we have in New Hampshire for the weekend.

When we come back, would you resume watching Jason
for just a few more days, put a mother's mind at rest?''
"Sure."

Friday morning Angie called to say Diandra had picked
up Jason and left for New Hampshire. I'd watched him all
through Thursday evening and nothing had happened. No
threats, no suspicious characters lurking outside his dorm,
no liaison with the guy with the goatee.

We'd worked our asses off trying to identify the guy
with the goatee, but it was as if he'd come from mist and
to mist he'd returned. He wasn't a student or teacher at
Bryce. He didn't work at any of the establishments in a
mile radius of campus. We'd even had a cop friend of
Angie's run his face through a computer for a felon match,
and come up empty. Since he'd met Jason in the open and
their meeting had been more than cordial, there was no
reason to consider him a threat, so we decided to keep our
eyes open until he popped back up again. Maybe he was
from out of state. Maybe he was a mirage.

"So we got the weekend off," Angie said. "What're
you going to do?"

"Spend as much of it as possible with Grace."

"You're whipped."

"I am. How about yourself?"

"I'll never tell."

"Be good."

"No," she said.

"Be safe."

"Okay."

I cleaned my house and it was short work because I'm
rarely there long enough to mess it up. When I came across
the ''HI!'' note and bumper stickers again, I felt a warm
prickle begin to knot under the skin at the base of my
brain, but I shrugged it off, tossed everything in a cabinet
of my entertainment center.

I called Richie Colgan again, got his voice mail, left a
message, and then there was nothing left to do but shower
and shave and go meet Grace at her place. Oh happy day.

As I went down the stairs, I could hear two people

breathing heavily in the foyer. I turned the last corner and there were Stanis and Liva, squaring off for round one million or so.

Stanis was wearing about a half gallon of oatmeal for a hat and his wife's blowsy housecoat was covered with ketchup and scrambled eggs so fresh they steamed. They stared at each other, the veins in his neck protruding, her left eyelid twitching madly as she kneaded an orange in her right hand.

I knew better than to ask.

I tiptoed past and opened the first door, closed it behind me as I entered the small hallway and stepped on a white envelope on the floor. The black rubber strip underneath the front door clamps so tightly over the threshold you'd have an easier time squeezing a hippo through a clarinet than you would sliding a piece of paper under the front door.

I looked at the envelope. No scuff marks or wrinkles.

The words "patrick kenzie" were typed in the center.

I opened the door into the foyer again and Stanis and Liva were still frozen as I'd left them, food on their bodies steaming, Liva's hand wrapped around the orange.

"Stanis," I said, "did you open the door to anyone this morning? In the last half hour or so?"

He shook his head and some oatmeal fell to the floor, but he never took his eyes off his wife. "Open door to who? Stranger? You think I crazy?" He pointed at Liva. "She crazy."

"I show you crazy," she said and hit him in the head with the orange.

He screamed, "Aaargh," or something similar and I backed out quickly and shut the door.

I stood in the hallway, envelope in my hands, and I felt a greasy swelling of dread in my stomach, though I couldn't articulate why completely.

Why? a voice whispered.

This envelope. The "HI!" note. The bumper stickers.

None of which are threatening, the voice whispered. At least not overtly. Just words and paper.

I opened the door, stepped out onto the porch. In the

schoolyard across from me, recess was in full swing and the nuns were chasing children around by the hopscotch area, and I saw a boy pull the hair of a girl who reminded me of Mae, the way she stood with her head cocked slightly to one side as if listening for the air to tell her a secret. When the boy pulled her hair, she screamed and slapped at the back of her head as if she were being attacked by bats, and the boy ran off into a crowd of other boys and the girl stopped shrieking and looked around, confused and alone, and I wanted to cross the avenue and find the little prick and pull his hair, make him feel confused and alone, even if I'd probably done the same thing myself a hundred times when I was his age.

I guess my impulse had something to do with growing older, with looking back and seeing very few innocent violences committed against the young, in knowing that every tiny pain scars and chips away at what is pure and infinitely breakable in a child.

Or maybe I was just in a bad mood.

I looked down at the envelope in my hand and something told me I wasn't going to be too keen on what I read if I opened it. But I did. And after I read it, I looked back at my front door and its imposing, heavy wood and portal glass fringed by alarm tape and three brass bolt locks gleaming in the late morning sunlight, and it seemed to mock me.

The note read:

> *patrick,*
> *don'tforgettolockup.*

13

"**Careful, Mae,**" **Grace** said.

We were crossing the Mass. Ave. Bridge from the Cambridge side. Below us the Charles was the color of caramel in the dying light and the Harvard crew team made chugging noises as they slid along, their oars slicing as clean as cutlasses through the water.

Mae stood up on the six-inch shoulder that separated the sidewalk from traffic, the fingers of her right hand resting loosely in mine as she tried to keep her balance.

"Smoots?" she said again, her lips smacking around the word as if it were chocolate. "How come smoots, Patrick?"

"That's how they measured the bridge," I said. "They turned Oliver Smoot over and over again, across the bridge."

"Didn't they like him?" She looked down at the next yellow smoot marker, her face darkening.

"Yeah, they liked him. Everyone was just playing."

"A game?" She looked up into my face and smiled.

I nodded. "That's how they got the Smoot measurements."

"Smoots," she said and giggled. "Smoots, smoots."

A truck rumbled past, shaking the bridge under our feet.

"Time to come down, honey," Grace said.

"I—"

"Now."

She hopped off beside me. "Smoots," she said to me with a crazy grin, as if it were our private joke now.

In 1958, some MIT seniors laid Oliver Smoot end to end across the Mass. Ave. Bridge and declared the bridge to be 364 smoots long, plus an ear. Somehow, the measurement became a treasure to be shared by Boston and Cambridge, and whenever the bridge is touched up, the Smoot markings are freshly painted.

We walked off the bridge and headed east along the river path. It was early evening and the air was the color of scotch and the trees had a burnished glow, the smoky dark gold of the sky contrasting starkly with the explosion of cherry reds, lime greens, and bright yellows in the canopies of leaves stretched above us.

"So run this by me again," Grace said, wrapping her arm in mine. "Your client met a woman who claimed she was the girlfriend of a mob guy."

"But she wasn't, and he has nothing to do with any of this as far as we can tell, and the woman vanished, and we can't find any record of her having existed in the first place. The kid, Jason, doesn't seem to have any skeletons in his closet outside of maybe bisexuality, which doesn't bother the mother. We've tracked the kid for a week and a half and come up with nothing but some guy in a goatee who might be having an affair with the kid, but who vanished into the air."

"And this girl you knew? The one who was killed?"

I shrugged. "Nothing. All her known acquaintances have been cleared, even the scumbags she hung out with, and Devin isn't taking my calls. It's sort of fuck—"

"Patrick," Grace said.

I looked down, saw Mae.

"Whoops," I said. "It's sort of messed up."

"Much better."

"Scottie," Mae said. "Scottie."

Just ahead, a middle-aged couple sat on the lawn by the jogging path, a black Scottish terrier lying beside the man's knee as he petted it absently.

"Can I?" Mae asked Grace.

"Ask the man first."

Mae walked off the path onto the grass with a slight hesitancy as if approaching a strange, uncharted frontier.

The man and woman smiled at her, then looked at us and we waved.

"Is your dog friendly?"

The man nodded. "Too friendly."

Mae held out a hand about nine inches from the head of the Scottie, who still hadn't noticed her. "He won't bite?"

"He never bites," the woman said. "What's your name?"

"Mae."

The dog looked up and Mae jerked her arm back, but the dog merely rose slowly on its hind legs and sniffed.

"Mae," the woman said, "this is Indy."

Indy sniffed Mae's leg and she looked back over her shoulder at us, uncertain.

"He wants to be petted," I said.

In increments, she lowered her body and touched his head. He turned his snout into her palm, and she lowered herself even more. The closer she got to him, the more I wanted to ask the couple if they were sure their dog didn't bite. It was an odd feeling. On the danger scale, Scottish terriers fall somewhere in between guppies and sunflowers, but that wasn't much comfort as I watched Mae's tiny body inch closer and closer to something with teeth.

When Indy jumped on Mae, I almost dove at them, but Grace put a hand on my arm, and Mae shrieked and she and the dog rolled around on the grass like old pals.

Grace sighed. "That was a clean dress she was wearing."

We sat down on a bench and watched for a while as Mae and Indy chased each other and stumbled into each other and tackled each other and got up and did it again.

"You have a beautiful daughter," the woman said.

"Thank you," Grace said.

Mae came dashing past the bench, hands up at her head, shrieking as Indy nipped at her heels. They went about another twenty yards and then went down in a tiny explosion of grass and dirt.

"How long have you been married?" the woman asked.

Before I could answer, Grace dug her fingers into my thigh.

"Five years," she said.

"You seem like newlyweds," the woman said.

"So do you."

The man laughed and his wife poked him with an elbow.

"We feel like newlyweds," Grace said. "Don't we, honey?"

"We put Mae to bed around eight, and she dropped off quickly, her fuel supply exhausted by our long walk around the river and her game of tag with Indy. When we came back into the living room, Grace immediately began picking things up off the floor—coloring books, toys, tabloid magazines, and horror paperbacks. The tabloids and books weren't Grace's, they were Annabeth's. Grace's father died when she was in college, and he left both girls a modest fortune. Grace depleted hers pretty quickly by paying what wasn't covered by her scholarship during her final two years at Yale, then supporting herself, her then-husband Bryan, and Mae before Bryan left her and Tufts Medical accepted her on fellowship, and she burned through most of what remained on living expenses.

Annabeth, four years younger, did a year of community college and then blew through the bulk of her inheritence during a year in Europe. She kept photographs of the trip taped to her headboard and vanity, and every one of them was taken in a bar. How to Drink Your Way Through Europe on Forty Grand.

She was great with Mae, though—made sure she was in bed on time, made sure she ate right and brushed her teeth and never crossed the street without holding her hand. She took her to children's school shows and to the Children's Museum and to playgrounds and did all the things that Grace didn't have time for while working ninety-hour weeks.

We finished cleaning up after Mae and Annabeth and then curled up on the couch and tried to find something worth watching on TV and failed. Springsteen was right—fifty-seven channels and nothing on.

So we shut it off and sat facing each other, legs crossed at the knees, and she told me about her past three days in ER, how they kept coming, the bodies stacking up on gurneys like cordwood in a winter cabin, and the noise level reaching the pitch of a heavy metal concert, and an old woman who'd been knocked over in a purse-snatching and banged her head against the sidewalk holding Grace's wrists as silent tears leaked from both eyes and she died just like that. Of fourteen-year-old gang members with baby's faces and blood sluicing off their chests like wet paint as doctors tried to plug the leaks and a baby brought in with a left arm twisted completely backwards at the shoulder joint and broken in three places around the elbow, his parents claiming he'd fallen. Of a crack addict screaming and fighting the orderlies because she needed her next fix and didn't give a shit if the doctors wanted to remove the knife from her eye first.

"And you think my job is violent?" I said.

She placed her forehead against mine. "One more year and I'm in cardiology. One more year." She leaned back, took my hands in hers, rested them on her lap. "That girl who got killed in the park," she said, "isn't connected to this other case, is she?"

"What gave you that idea?"

"Nothing. I was just wondering."

"No. Just happens we took the Warren case around the same time Kara was murdered. Why'd you think that?"

She ran her hands up my arms. "Because you're tense, Patrick. Tenser than I've ever seen you."

"How so?"

"Oh, you're acting real well, but I can feel it in your body, see it in the way you stand, like you're expecting to get hit by a truck." She kissed me. "Something's got you wigged out."

I thought of the last eleven days. I'd sat at a dinner table with three psychotics, four if you counted Pine. Then I saw a woman crucified to a hill. Then someone sent me a package of bumper stickers and a "HI!" Then I found the "don'tforgettolockup" note. People were shooting up abortion clinics and subway cars and blowing up embassies. Homes were sliding off the sides of hills in California and falling through the earth in India. Maybe I had reason to be wigged out.

I slid my arms around her waist and pulled her up on top of me, leaned back on the couch and slid my hands up under her sweater, ran my palms along the edges of her breasts. She bit down on her lower lip and her eyes widened slightly.

"You said something to me the other morning," I said.

"I said a lot of things to you the other morning," she said. "I said, 'Oh God' a few times if I remember right."

"That wasn't it."

"Oh," she said, clapping her hands against my chest. "The 'I love you' phrase. Is that what you mean, Detective?"

"Yes, ma'am."

She unbuttoned my shirt down to my navel and ran her hands over my chest. "Well, what of it? I. Love. You."

"Why?"

"Why?" she said.

I nodded.

"That's the silliest question you've ever asked. Don't you feel worthy of love, Patrick?"

"Maybe not," I said as she touched the scar on my abdomen.

She met my eyes and hers were kind and warm, like benedictions. She leaned forward and my hands came out of her sweater as she slid down my body until her head was at my lap. She tore open the rest of my shirt and laid her face on the scar. She traced it with her tongue, then kissed it.

"I love this scar," she said, resting her chin on it and looking up into my face. "I love it because it's a mark of evil. That's what your father was, Patrick. Evil. And he tried to pour it into you. But he failed. Because you're kind and gentle, and you're so good with Mae and she loves you so much." She drummed the scar with her fingernails. "So, you see, your father lost because you are good, and if he didn't love you, that's his fucking problem, not yours. He was an asshole, and you are worthy of love." She rose on all fours above me. "All of mine and all of Mae's."

I couldn't speak for a minute. I looked into Grace's face and I saw the flaws, I saw what she'd look like when she was old, how in fifteen or twenty years many men would never be able to see what an aesthetic wonder her face and body had been, and it was just as well. Because it didn't mean shit in the long haul. I have said "I love you" to my ex-wife, Renee, and heard her say it, and we both knew it was a lie, a desperate want perhaps, but far removed from a reality. I loved my partner and I loved my sister and I'd loved my mother, though I never really knew her.

But I don't think I ever felt anything like this.

When I tried to speak, my voice was shaky and hoarse and the words were strangled in my throat. My eyes felt wet and my heart felt as if it were bleeding.

When I was a boy, I loved my father, and he just kept hurting me. He wouldn't stop. No matter how much I wept, no matter how much I pleaded, no matter how hard I tried to figure out what he wanted, what I could do to be worthy of his love instead of victim of his rage.

"I love you," I'd tell him and he'd laugh. And laugh. And then he'd beat me some more.

"I love you," I said once as he rammed my head into a door, and he spun me around and spit in my face.

"I hate you," I told him, very calmly, not long before he died.

He laughed at that one too. "Score one for the old man."

"I love you," I told Grace now.

And she laughed. But it was a beautiful laugh. One of surprise and relief and release, one that was followed by two tears that dropped off her cheekbones and landed in my eyes and mingled with mine.

"Oh my God," she groaned, lowering herself to my body, her lips grazing my own. "I love you too, Patrick."

14

Grace and I weren't quite at the point yet where one stayed over at the other's house long enough for Mae to find us in bed together. That moment was coming soon, but it wasn't one either of us was going to approach lightly. Mae knew I was her mother's "special friend," but she didn't have to know what special friends do together until we were sure this special friend would be around for a long time. I had too many friends growing up who had no fathers but an amazing supply of uncles parading through their mothers' beds—and I'd seen how it had fucked them up.

So I left shortly after midnight. As I was fitting my key into the downstairs lock, I heard my phone ringing distantly. By the time I made it up the stairs, Richie Colgan was talking to my answering machine:

". . . name of Jamal Cooper in September of seventy-three was—"

"I'm here, Rich."

"Patrick, you're alive. And your answering machine's working again."

"It was never broken."

"Well, it must not like taking messages from the black man, then."

"You haven't been getting through?"

"I've called you half a dozen times in the last week, got nothing but ring-ring-ring."

"Try my office?"

"Same thing."

I picked up my answering machine, looked underneath. I wasn't looking for anything particular, it just seemed like what one did. I checked the jacks and portals in back; nope, everything was hooked up properly. And I had received other messages all week.

"I don't know what to tell you, Rich. It seems to be working fine. Maybe you misdialed."

"Whatever. I got the info you need. By the way, how's Grace?"

Richie and his wife, Sherilynn, had played matchmaker between Grace and me last summer. It had been Sherilynn's theory for the past decade that all I needed to straighten out my life was a strong woman who'd kick my ass on a regular basis and take none of my shit. Nine times she'd been wrong, but the tenth, so far, seemed to be working out.

"Tell Sheri I'm smitten."

He laughed. "She's gonna love that. Love it! Ha-ha, I knew your ass was done the first time you looked at Grace. Cooked and smoked and marinated and hung up in strips."

"Mmmm," I said.

"Good," he said to himself and clucked. "Awright, you want your info?"

"Pen and paper are at the ready."

"Case of Heinies better be at the ready, too, Slim."

"Goes without saying."

"In twenty-five years," Richie said, "there's been one crucifixion in this city. Kid name of Jamal Cooper. Black male, twenty-one, found crucified to the floorboards in the basement of a flophouse in old Scollay Square in September of seventy-three."

"Quick bio of Cooper?"

"He was a junkie. Heroin. Rap sheet the length of a football field. Mostly small-time shit—petty burglary, solicitation, but a couple of home invasions, too, bought him two years at the old Dedham House of Corrections. Still, Cooper wasn't nothing but a nickel-and-dimer. If he hadn't been crucified, nobody would have noticed he died. Even then, cops didn't seem to be busting their asses on the case at first."

"Who was the investigating officer?"

"Two guys. An Inspector Brett Hardiman and, lemme see, yeah, a Detective Sergeant Gerald Glynn."

That stopped me. "They make an arrest?"

"Well, here's where it gets interesting. I had to dig a bit, but there was a local stir in the papers for a day when they brought a guy named Alec Hardiman in for questioning."

"Wait a minute, didn't you just—?"

"Yup. Alec Hardiman was the son of the chief investigating officer, Brett Hardiman."

"What happened?"

"The younger Hardiman was cleared."

"Coverup?"

"It doesn't look that way. There really wasn't much evidence against him. He'd known Jamal Cooper casually, I guess, and that was that. *But . . .*"

"What?"

Several phones rang at once on Richie's end and he said, "Hold on."

"No, Rich. No, I—"

He put me on hold, the bastard. I waited.

When he came back on the line, his voice had changed back to its City Desk rush. "Patrick, Igottago."

"No."

"Yes. Look, this Alec Hardiman was convicted for another murder in seventy-five. He's doing life in Walpole. That's all I got. Gottarun."

He hung up and I looked down at the names on my notepad: Jamal Cooper. Brett Hardiman. Alec Hardiman. Gerald Glynn.

I thought about calling Angie but it was late and she'd been beat from watching Jason do nothing all week.

I stared at the phone for a bit, then took my jacket and left the apartment.

I didn't need the jacket. Past one in the morning, and the humidity lathered my skin until the pores felt sticky and fetid and sickly soft.

October. Right.

Gerry Glynn was washing glasses at the bar sink when

I entered The Black Emerald. The place was empty, the
three TV screens on, but the volume muted, the Pogues'
version of "Dirty Old Town" coming out of the jukebox
at whisper volume, stools up on the bar, floor swept, amber
ashtrays clean as boiled bones.

Gerry was looking into the sink. "Sorry," he said without looking up. "Closed."

On top of the pool table near the back, Patton raised his
head and looked at me. I couldn't see his face very distinctly through the cigarette smoke that still hovered there
like a cloud, but I knew what he'd say if he could speak:
"Didn't you hear the man? We're *closed.*"

"Hi, Gerry."

"Patrick," he said, confused but with enthusiasm.
"What brings you by?"

He wiped his palms and offered me his hand.

I shook it and he pumped mine hard, looking me dead
in the eyes, a habit of the older generation that reminded
me of my father.

"I needed to ask you a question or two, Ger, if you got
the time."

He cocked his head and his usually kind eyes lost their
softness. Then they cleared and he hoisted his bulk onto
the cooler behind him and spread his hands, palms up.
"Sure. You need a beer or something?"

"Don't want to put you out, Ger." I settled into the bar
stool across from him.

He opened the door of the cooler next to him. His thick
arm dug down inside and ice rattled. "No problem. Can't
promise what I'll come up with."

I smiled. "Long as it isn't a Busch."

He laughed. "Nope. It's a . . ." His arm came out
washed in ice water, dimples of cold jellied white against
the flesh under his forearm. ". . . Lite."

I smiled as he handed it to me. "Like sex in a sailboat,"
I said.

He laughed loudly and sputtered the punchline. "It's
fucking too close to water. I love that one." He reached
behind himself and, without looking, pulled a bottle of
Stolichnaya from the shelf. He poured some into a tall shot

glass, put the bottle back, then raised the glass.

"Cheers."

"Cheers," I said and drank some Lite. Tasted like water, but it was still better than Busch. Of course, a cup of diesel is usually better than Busch.

"So what's your question?" Gerry said. He patted his ample gut. "Jealous of my physique?"

I smiled. "A bit." I drank some more Lite. "Gerry, what can you tell me about someone named Alec Hardiman?"

He held his shot glass up to the fluorescent light and the clear liquid disappeared in a shimmer of white. He stared at it and rotated the glass in his fingers.

"Now," he said quietly, eyes still on the glass, "where would you come up with that name, Patrick?"

"It was mentioned to me."

"You've been looking for matches to the MO of Kara Rider's killer." He brought the glass down and looked across at me. He didn't seem angry or irritated and his voice was flat and monotonous, but there was a stillness to his squat body that hadn't been there a minute before.

"Per your suggestion, Ger."

On the jukebox behind me, the Pogues had at some point given way to The Waterboys' "Don't Bang the Drum." The TV screens above Gerry's head were tuned to three different channels. One broadcast Australian Rules Football, one what looked like an old *Kojak* episode, and the third showed Old Glory wavering in the breeze as it signed off for the night.

Gerry hadn't moved, hadn't so much as blinked, since he'd brought the shot glass back down by his side, and I could just make out the sound of his breathing, shallow and thin, as he exhaled through his nostrils. He didn't study me so much as stare through me, as if what he was seeing was on the other side of my head.

He reached back for the bottle of Stoli, poured himself another shot. "So, Alec comes back to haunt us all again." He chuckled. "Ah, well, I should have known."

Patton jumped down from the pool table and padded into the main bar area, gave me a look like I was sitting in his seat, then hopped up on the bar top in front of me and lay down, his paws over his eyes.

"He wants you to pet him," Gerry said.

"No, he doesn't." I watched Patton's rib cage rise and fall.

"He likes you, Patrick. Go ahead."

I felt like Mae for a moment as I reached out a tentative hand toward that gorgeous coat of black and amber. I felt coiled muscle hard as a pool ball under the coat, and then Patton raised his head and mewed and flicked his tongue over my free hand, nuzzled it gratefully with a chilly nose.

"Just a big softy, huh?" I said.

"Unfortunately," Gerry said. "Don't let the secret get around, though."

"Gerry," I said, as Patton's rich coat undulated and curled around my hand, "this Alec Hardiman could have killed—?"

"Kara Rider?" He shook his head. "No, no. That would be pretty hard to do even for Alec. Alec Hardiman's been in prison since nineteen seventy-five, and he won't be getting out during my lifetime. Probably not during yours, either."

I finished my Lite and Gerry, ever the bartender, had his hand in the ice before I set it down on the bar. This time he came up with a Harpoon IPA, spun it in his meaty palm and popped the cap off in the opener mounted on the cooler wall. I took it from him and some foam spilled down the side onto my hand and Patton licked it up.

Gerry leaned his head back against the edge of the shelf above it. "Did you know a kid name of Cal Morrison?"

"Not real well," I said, swallowing against a shudder that threatened to rise every time I heard Cal Morrison's name. "He was a few years older than me."

Gerry nodded. "But you know what happened to him."

"He was stabbed to death in the Blake Yard."

Gerry stared at me for a moment, and then he sighed. "How old were you at the time?"

"Nine or ten."

He reached for another shot glass, poured a finger of Stoli in it and set it on the bar in front of me. "Drink."

I was reminded of Bubba's vodka and its ragged chewing on my spinal column. Unlike my father and his brothers, I must have missed some crucial Kenzie gene, because I never could drink hard liquor for shit.

I gave Gerry a weak smile. "Dosvidanya."

He raised his and we drank and I blinked away tears.

"Cal Morrison," he said, "wasn't stabbed to death, Patrick." He sighed again and it was a low, melancholy sound. "Cal Morrison was crucified."

15

"**Cal Morrison wasn't** crucified," I said.

"No?" Gerry said. "You saw the body, did you?"

"No."

He sipped from the shot glass. "I did. I caught the squeal. Me and Brett Hardiman."

"Alec Hardiman's father."

He nodded. "My partner." He leaned forward and poured some vodka into my shot glass. "Brett died in eighty."

I looked at my shot glass, nudged it six inches away from me as Gerry refilled his own.

Gerry caught me at it, smiled. "You're not like your father, Patrick."

"Thanks for the compliment."

He chuckled softly. "You look like him, though. A dead ringer. You must know that."

I shrugged.

He turned his wrists upward, looked down at them for a moment. "Blood's a strange thing."

"How's that?"

"It's passed into a woman's womb, creates a life. Could be near identical to the parent who created it, could be so different the father starts suspecting the mailman delivered more than the mail. You got your father's blood, I got my father's, Alec Hardiman had his father's in him."

"And his father was . . . ?"

"A good man." He nodded more to himself than to me and took a sip from his glass. "A fine, fine man actually.

113

Moral. Decent. So, so, so smart. If no one told you, you'd have never guessed he was a cop. You'd have taken him for a minister or a banker. He dressed impeccably, spoke impeccably, did everything . . . impeccably. He had a simple white colonial house in Melrose and a sweet, kind wife and a beautiful, blond son, and you'd swear you could eat lunch off the seat of his car.''

I sipped my beer as the second TV gave way to Old Glory followed by a blue screen and noticed that it was now The Chieftains' ''Coast of Malabar'' on the jukebox.

''So he's this perfect guy with this perfect life. Perfect wife, perfect car, perfect house, perfect son.'' He peered at his thumbnail. Then he looked at me and his soft eyes were slightly unhinged, as if they'd stared too long at the sun and were just regaining a sense of the shapes and colors before them. ''Then Alec, I dunno, something went in him. It just . . . went. No psychiatrist could ever explain it. One day he was this normal, regular kid, and the next . . .'' He held up his hands. ''The next, I don't know.''

''And he killed Cal Morrison?''

''We don't know that,'' he said and his voice was thick.

He couldn't look at me for some reason. His face had grown ruddy and the veins in his neck stuck out like cables and he looked at the floor and kicked his heel into the wall of the cooler. ''We don't know that,'' he said again.

''Gerry,'' I said, ''let me in here. Last I knew, Cal Morrison was stabbed in the Blakey by some drifter.''

''Black guy,'' he said, the soft grin again playing on his lips. ''That was the rumor at the time, wasn't it?''

I nodded.

''Can't find someone to blame, blame a jig. Right?''

I shrugged. ''That was the story back then.''

''Well, he wasn't stabbed. That was just what we told the media. He was crucified. And it wasn't a black guy did it. We found red hair and blond hair and brown hair in Cal Morrison's clothing, but no black. And Alec Hardiman and a friend of his, Charles Rugglestone, had been seen in the neighborhood earlier that night, and we were already on edge about the other killings, so until we busted someone, we didn't mind the black guy story circulating for a while." He shrugged. "Not like too many black guys were going to stumble into this neighborhood back then, so it seemed a safe cover for a while."

"Gerry," I said, "what other killings?"

The bar door opened, the heavy wood banging against the brick exterior and we both looked at a man with spiky hair and a nose ring and a torn T-shirt hanging untucked over fashionably eviscerated jeans.

"Closed," Gerry said.

"Just a wee spot to warm me stumuch on a lonely night," the guy said in a horrendously fake brogue.

Gerry came off the cooler and walked around the bar. "You even know where you are, son?"

Underneath my hand, Patton's muscles tightened and he raised his head, stared at the kid.

The kid took a step forward. "Just a wee spot of whiskey." He giggled into his hand, blinked into the light and his face was swollen with booze and God knows what else.

"Kenmore Square is that way," Gerry said and pointed back out the door.

"Don't want Kenmore Square," the guy said. He swayed slightly from side to side as he fumbled in his waistband for his cigarettes.

"Son," Gerry said, "it's time for you to be moving on."

Gerry put his arm on the guy's shoulder and for a moment the guy looked ready to shrug it off, but then he looked at me and then Patton and then down at Gerry. Gerry's demeanor was kind and warm, and he was four inches shorter, but even this guy, drunk as he was, sensed how quickly that kindness could disappear if he pushed it.

"Just wanted a drink," he mumbled.

"I know," Gerry said. "But I can't give you one. You got cab fare? Where you live?"

"I just wanted a drink," the guy repeated. He looked up at me and tears leaked down his cheeks and the damp cigarette hung flacid between his lips. "I just . . ."

"Where you live?" Gerry asked again.

"Huh? Lower Mills." The guy sniffled.

"You can walk around Lower Mills dressed like that

without getting your ass kicked?'' Gerry smiled. ''Place must have changed a lot in ten years.''

''Lower Mills,'' the guy sobbed.

''Son,'' Gerry said, ''ssshh. It's okay. It's all right. You go out this door, you take a right, there's a cab half a block up. Cabbie's name is Achal and he's there till three on the dot. You tell him to take you to Lower Mills.''

''I don't got no money.''

Gerry patted the kid's hip and when he pulled his hand away there was a ten-dollar bill in the kid's waistband. ''Looks like you got a sawbuck you forgot about.''

The kid looked down at his waistband. ''Mine?''

''It ain't mine. Now go get in that cab. Okay?''

''Okay.'' The kid sniffled as Gerry led him back out the door, and then suddenly he spun and hugged as much of Gerry as he could get his arms around.

Gerry chuckled. ''Okay. Okay.''

''I love you, man,'' the kid said. ''I love you!''

A cab pulled to the curb outside and Gerry nodded at the driver as he disentangled himself. ''Go on now. Go on.''

Patton lowered his head and rolled into a fetal position on the bar, closed his eyes. I scratched his nose and he nipped my hand gently, seemed to smile sleepily at me.

''I love you!'' the kid bellowed as he stumbled out.

''I'm moved,'' Gerry said. He shut the door to the bar and we heard the taxi's axles clack as it pulled a U-turn on the avenue to head down to Lower Mills. ''Deeply moved.'' Gerry locked the door and raised his eyebrows at me, ran a hand through the rusty stubble on his head.

''Still Officer Friendly,'' I said.

He shrugged, then frowned. ''Did I do that at your school—the Officer Friendly lecture?''

I nodded. ''Second grade at St. Bart's.''

He took his bottle and shot glass over to a table by the jukebox and I joined him, left my shot glass on the bar, seven feet away from me, where it belonged. Patton remained on the bar, eyes closed, dreaming of large cats.

He leaned back in his chair and arched his back, stretched his arms behind his head and yawned loudly.

"You know something? I remember that now."

"Oh, please," I said. "That was over twenty years ago."

"Mmm." He brought the chair legs back to the floor, poured himself another drink. By my count he'd had six shots and there was absolutely no noticeable effect. "That class was something, though," he said, tilting the glass toward me in toast. "There was you and Angela and that shitbird she married, what was his name."

"Phil Dimassi."

"Phil, yeah." He shook his head. "Then there was that head case Kevin Hurlihy and that other nut job, Rogowski."

"Bubba's okay."

"I know you guys are friends, Patrick, but give me a break. He's a suspect in maybe seven unsolved homicides."

"Real nice guys, I'm sure, the victims."

He shrugged. "Killing is killing. You take a life without cause, you should be punished. All there is to it."

I sipped my beer, glanced at the jukebox.

"You don't agree?" he said.

I held out my hands, leaned back in my chair. "I used to. Sometimes, though, I mean come on, Gerry—Kara Rider's life was worth more than the life of the guy who killed her."

"Beautiful," he said and gave me a dark smile. "Utilitarian logic at its best, and the cornerstone of most facist ideologies, if you don't mind me mentioning." He downed another shot, watching me with clear, steady eyes. "If you presuppose that a victim's life is worth more than a murderer's, and then you yourself go and kill that murderer, doesn't that then make your own life less worthy than the murderer you killed?"

"What," I said, "you're a Jesuit now, Gerry? Going to wrap me up in syllogisms?"

"Answer the question, Patrick. Don't be glib."

Even when I'd been a kid, there'd always been something oddly ethereal about Gerry. He didn't exist on the same plane as the rest of us. You sensed that some part of him swam in the spiritual murk that the priests told us existed just above the realm of our everyday consciousness. The place from which dreams and art and faith and divine inspiration were sprung.

I went behind the bar for another beer, and he watched me with those calm, kind eyes. I dug around the cooler, found another Harpoon, and came back to the table.

"We could sit here and debate it all night, Gerry, and maybe in an ideal world, it wouldn't be true, but in this one, yeah, some lives are worth a lot more than others." I shrugged at his cocked eyebrow. "Might make me a facist but I'd say Mother Teresa's life is worth more than Michael Millken's. I'd say Martin Luther King's was worth a lot more than Hitler's."

"Interesting." His voice was almost a whisper. "So if you are able to judge the worth of another human life, you are yourself, by inference, superior to that life."

"Not necessarily."

"Are you better than Hitler?"

"Absolutely."

"Stalin?"

"Yes."

"Pol Pot?"

"Yes."

"Me?"

"You?"

He nodded.

"You're not a killer, Gerry."

He shrugged. "Is that how you judge? You're better than someone who kills or orders others to kill?"

"If those killings are done to victims who pose no real physical threat to the killer or the person who orders the killing, then yes, I am better than them."

"So you're superior to Alexander, Caesar, several U.S. presidents, a few popes."

I laughed. He'd set me up and I'd felt it coming, but I hadn't seen where it would come from.

"Like I said, Gerry, I think you're half Jesuit."

He smiled and rubbed his bristled scalp. "I'll admit, they taught me well." His eyes narrowed and he leaned into the table. "I just hate this idea that some people have more of a right to take a life than others. It's an inherently corrupt concept. You kill, you should be punished."

"Like Alec Hardiman?"

He blinked. "You're part pit bull, aren't you, Patrick?"

"What my clients pay me for, Ger." I reached across and refilled his shot glass for him. "Tell me about Alec Hardiman and Cal Morrison and Jamal Cooper."

"Maybe Alec killed Cal Morrison and Cooper, too, I don't know for sure. Whoever killed those boys was making some kind of statement, that's for sure. Crucified Morrison below the Edward Everett statue, shoved an ice pick through his larynx so he couldn't scream, cut off pieces of him that were never found."

"What pieces?"

Gerry's fingers drummed the tabletop for a moment, his lips pursed as he decided how much to tell me. "His testicles, a kneecap, both big toes. It fit with some other victims we knew about."

"Other victims besides Cooper?"

"Not long before Cal Morrison was killed," Gerry said, "a few winos and hookers from the Zone downtown to as far away as the Springfield bus depot were murdered. Six in all, starting with Jamal Cooper. The murder weapons varied, the victim profiles varied, the methods of execution varied, but Brett and I believed it was all the work of the same two killers."

"Two?" I said.

He nodded. "Working in tandem. Conceivably it could have been one guy, but he would have had to be astonishingly strong, ambidexterous, quick as lightning."

"If the murder weapons and MO and victim selection were so varied, why'd you think it was the same killers?"

"There was a level of cruelty to the kills like I'd never seen before. Never seen since, either. Not only did these guys enjoy their work, Patrick, but they—or he—were also thinking of the people who found the bodies, how they'd react. They cut a wino into a hundred sixty-four pieces. Think about it. One hundred and sixty-four pieces of flesh and bone, some no bigger than a fingertip, left on the bureau top and along the headboard, spaced out on the floor, hanging from hooks along the shower rod in this little flophouse room down in the Zone. Place ain't even there no more, but I can't drive by the space it used to occupy without thinking about that room. A sixteen-year-old runaway in Worcester, he snapped her neck and then twisted her head around a hundred eighty degrees, wrapped it in duct tape so it would stay that way for the first person through the door. It was beyond anything I've ever come up against, and no one can tell me that those six victims, all still officially unsolved cases, weren't killed by the same one or more people."

"And Cal Morrison?"

He nodded. "Number seven. And Charles Rugglestone, possibly, would be number eight."

"Wait," I said, "the Rugglestone who was friends with this Alec Hardiman?"

"You bet." He raised his glass, put it back down, stared at it. "Charles Rugglestone was murdered in a warehouse not far from here. He was stabbed with an ice pick thirty-two times, bludgeoned with a hammer so hard that the holes in his skull looked like small animals had been living in his brain and decided to eat their way out. He was also burned, piece by piece, from his ankles to his neck, most of it while he was still breathing. We found Alec Hardiman passed out in the dispatch office with Rugglestone's blood all over him and the ice pick a few feet away, his prints all over it."

"So he did it."

Gerry shrugged. "Every year, because his father asked me to, I visit Alec at Walpole. And, maybe, I dunno, because I like him. I still see the little kid in him. Whatever. But as much as I like him, he's a cipher. Is he capable of murder? Yeah. I don't doubt that for a second. But I can also tell you that no single man, no matter how strong—and Alec wasn't all that strong—could have done what was done to Rugglestone." He pursed his lips and downed the shot. "But as soon as Alec went to trial, the killings I'd been investigating dried up. His father, of course, retired not long after the arrest, but I kept looking into the

Morrison murder and the six that came before it, and I cleared Alec of involvement in at least two of those.''

"But he was convicted.''

"For Rugglestone's murder only. Nobody wanted to admit that they'd suspected a serial killer was out there and didn't notify the general public. No one wanted more egg on their faces after the son of a decorated cop was arrested for a brutal murder. So Alec went to trial for Rugglestone's murder and he was sentenced to life in prison and he's up at Walpole rotting away. His father went to Florida, probably died trying to figure out where it all went so wrong. And none of this would matter, I suppose, except that someone crucified Kara Rider on a hill and someone else gave you my name and the name Alec Hardiman.''

"So,'' I said, "if there actually was more than one killer, and Alec Hardiman was one of them . . .''

"Then the other one's still out there, yeah.'' Dark pockets had formed under his eyes and hollowed them out. "And if he's still out there after almost twenty-something years, and he's been holding his breath all this time for some sort of comeback, I'd say he's probably pretty pissed off.''

16

It was snowing on a bright summer day when Kara Rider stopped me to ask how the Jason Warren case was going.

She'd changed her hair back to its original blond and she was sitting in a lawn chair outside The Black Emerald wearing only a pink bikini bottom and the snow fell to either side of her and piled up by the chair, but only sun fell on her skin. Her small breasts were hard, and beaded with perspiration, and I had to keep reminding myself that I'd known her since she was a little kid, and I shouldn't be noticing them in a sexual context.

Grace and Mae were half a block up, Grace placing a black rose in Mae's hair. Across the avenue a pack of white dogs, small and gnarled like fists, watched them and drooled, thick streams pouring from the sides of their mouths.

"I got to go," I said to Kara, but when I looked back, Grace and Mae were gone.

"Sit," Kara said. "Just for a sec."

So I sat and the snow fell down the back of my collar and chilled my spine. My teeth chattered as I said, "I thought you were dead."

"No," she said. "I just went away for a while."

"Where'd you go?"

"Brookline. Shit."

"What?"

"This place looks just the fucking same."

122

Grace stuck her head out of The Black Emerald. "You ready, Patrick?"

"Got to go," I said and patted Kara's shoulder.

She took my hand and laid it against her bare breast.

I looked at Grace, but she didn't seem to mind. Angie stood beside her and they both smiled.

Kara stroked her nipple with my palm. "Don't forget about me."

Snow was pouring on her body now, burying it.

"I won't. I gotta go."

"Bye."

The legs of her lawn chair collapsed under the weight of the snow, and when I looked back I could just make out her form under drifts of soft white.

Mae came out of the bar and took my hand and fed it to her dog.

I watched my blood foam in the dog's mouth, and it didn't hurt—it was almost sweet.

"See," Mae said, "he likes you, Patrick."

The last week of October, we bailed out of the Jason Warren case by mutual agreement with Diandra and Eric. I know guys who would've milked it, played up to the fears of a worried mother, but I don't milk cases. Not because I'm particularly moral, but because it's bad business when half your living comes from repeat clients. We had files on all of Jason's teachers since he'd come to Bryce (eleven) and all his known acquaintances (Jade, Gabrielle, Lauren, and his roommate) except the guy with the goatee, and nothing about any of them suggested they were a threat to Jason. We had write-ups of our daily observation work, as well as synopses of our meeting with Fat Freddy, Jack Rouse, and Kevin Hurlihy, and my own telephone discussion with Stan Timpson.

Diandra had received no more threats, phone calls, or pictures in the mail. She'd spoken with Jason in New Hampshire, mentioned that a friend of hers had seen him with a guy in the Sunset Grill the previous week, and Jason had described him as "just a friend" and offered no more information.

We spent another week tailing him, and it was more of the same—explosions of sexual activity, solitude, studying.

Diandra agreed that we were all getting nowhere, that there was nothing outside of her having received that photograph to suggest Jason was in any danger whatsoever, and we finally came to the conclusion that maybe our original perception—that Diandra had inadvertently angered Kevin Hurlihy—had been correct after all. Once we'd met with Fat Freddy, every hint of threat had disappeared; maybe Freddy, Kevin, Jack and the whole mob had decided to back off, but hadn't wished to lose face to a couple of PIs.

Whatever the situation, it was over now, and Diandra paid us for our time and thanked us, and we left our cards and home numbers in case anything sprang back up and went back to our lives during our business's dullest season.

A few days later, at his behest, we met Devin in The Black Emerald at two o'clock in the afternoon. There was a "Closed" sign in the doorway, but we knocked and Devin opened the door, locked it behind us after we came in.

Gerry Glynn was behind the bar, sitting on the cooler, not looking very happy, and Oscar sat by a plate of food at the bar, and Devin took his seat beside him and bit into the bloodiest cheeseburger this side of an open flame.

I took the seat beside Devin, and Angie took the one beside Oscar and stole one of his fries.

I looked at Devin's cheeseburger. "They just lean the cow against a radiator?"

He growled and stuffed some more in his mouth.

"Devin, you know what red meat does to your heart, never mind your bowels?"

He wiped his mouth with a cocktail napkin. "You turn into one of those holistic, health PC douchebags while I wasn't looking, Kenzie?"

"Nope. But I saw one picketing out front."

He reached for his hip. "Here. Take my gun and shoot the prick. See if you can pop a mime while you're at it. I'll see it gets written up right."

A throat cleared behind me and I looked into the bar mirror. A man sat in a shadowed booth just over my right shoulder.

He wore a dark suit and dark tie, a crisp white shirt and a matching scarf. His dark hair was the color of polished mahogany. He sat stiffly in the booth, as if his spine had been replaced with pipe.

Devin jerked a thumb over his shoulder. "Patrick Kenzie, Angela Gennaro, meet FBI Special Agent Barton Bolton."

I turned on my barstool and Angie turned on hers and we both said, "Hi."

Special Agent Barton Bolton said nothing. He looked each of us up and down like a concentration camp commandant trying to decide if we were best fit for work or extermination, then shifted his gaze to a point somewhere over Oscar's shoulder.

"We have a problem," Oscar said.

"Could be a small problem," Devin said, "could be a big one."

"And it is?" Angie said.

"Let's all sit together." Oscar pushed his plate away.

Devin did the same and we all joined Special Agent Barton Bolton in the booth.

"What about Gerry?" I said, watching him clear the plates off the bar.

"Mr. Glynn's already been questioned," Bolton said.

"Ah."

"Patrick," Devin said, "your card was found in Kara Rider's hand."

"I told you how it got there."

"And when we were working on the presumption that Micky Doog or one of his puke friends had killed her because she wouldn't blow him or whatever, it wasn't a problem."

"Your presumption has changed?" Angie said.

" 'Fraid so." Devin lit a cigarette.

"You quit," I said.

"Unsuccessfully." He shrugged.

Agent Bolton removed a photograph from his briefcase,

handed it to me. It was of a young man, mid-thirties, built like a Grecian statue. He wore only shorts and was smiling at the camera and his upper torso was all hard cuts and coiled muscle, biceps the size of baseballs.

"Do you know this man?"

I said, "No," and handed the photo to Angie.

She looked at it a moment. "No."

"You're sure?"

Angie said, "I'd remember that body. Trust me."

"Who is he?"

"Peter Stimovich," Oscar said. "Actually his full name is The Late Peter Stimovich. He was killed last night."

"Did he have my business card too?"

"Not as far as we know."

"Then why am I here?"

Devin looked across the bar at Gerry. "What did you and Gerry talk about when you came in here a few days ago?"

"Ask Gerry."

"We did."

"Wait," I said, "how do you know I came in here a few days ago?"

"You've been under surveillance," Bolton said.

"Excuse me?"

Devin shrugged. "This is bigger than you, Patrick. A lot bigger."

"How long?" I said.

"How long what?"

"Have I been watched?" I looked at Bolton.

"Since Alec Hardiman refused our request to speak with him," Devin said.

"So?"

"When he refused our request," Oscar said, "he did it by saying you're the only one he'll talk to."

"Me?"

"You, Patrick. Only you."

17

"**Why's Alec Hardiman** want to talk to me?"

"Good question," Bolton said. He waved at the smoke coming from Devin's cigarette. "Mr. Kenzie, everything said from this point on is absolutely confidential. Understood?"

Angie and I gave Bolton our best shrugs.

"Just so we're clear—if you repeat anything we speak of today, you'll be charged with Federal obstruction charges carrying a maximum penalty of ten years."

"You enjoy saying that, don't you?" Angie said.

"What's that?"

She deepened her voice. " 'Federal obstruction charges.' "

He sighed. "Mr. Kenzie, when Kara Rider was murdered, she had your card in her hand. Her crucifixion, as you probably know, bore remarkable similarities to the crucifixion of a boy in this neighborhood in 1974. Sergeant Amronklin, you might not know, was a patrolman back then who worked with former Detective Sergeant Glynn and Inspector Hardiman."

I looked at Devin. "Did you think Kara's murder might have been connected to Cal's the night we saw her body?"

"I considered the possibility."

"But you didn't say anything to me."

"Nope." He stubbed out his cigarette. "You're a private citizen, Patrick. It's not my job to let you in. Besides, I thought it was a hell of a long shot. Just something I kept in the back of my mind."

The phone on the bar rang and Gerry picked it up, his eyes on us. "Black Emerald." He nodded as if he'd expected the caller's question. "Sorry, no. We're all closed up here. Plumbing problem." He closed his eyes for a moment, nodded hurriedly. "You're so desperate for a drink, try another bar. You better get going." He looked about to hang up. "What'd I tell you? Closed. I'm sorry, too."

He hung up, gave us a shrug.

"This other victim," I said.

"Stimovich."

"Right. Was he crucified?"

"No," Bolton said.

"How'd he die?"

Bolton looked at Devin and Devin looked at Oscar and Oscar said, "Who gives a shit? Tell them. We need all the help we can get before we have more bodies on our hands."

Bolton said, "Mr. Stimovich was tied to a wall, his skin removed in strips, and then he was disemboweled while he was still alive."

"Jesus," Angie said and blessed herself so quickly I'm not even sure she was aware she did it.

Gerry's phone rang again.

Bolton frowned. "Can you yank that out of the hook for a little while, Mr. Glynn?"

Gerry looked pained. "Agent Bolton, with all due respect to the dead, I'll keep my place closed as long as you feel you need it, but I got regulars wondering why my door's closed."

Bolton waived dismissively and Gerry answered the phone.

After a few seconds of listening, he nodded. "Bob, Bob, listen, we have a plumbing situation. I'm sorry, but I got three inches of water on the floor and . . ." He listened. "So do what I'm telling you—go to Leary's or The Fermanagh. Go *somewhere*. Okay?"

He hung up, gave us another shrug.

I said, "How do you know Kara wasn't killed by someone she knew? Micky Doog? Or a gang initiation rite?"

Oscar shook his head. "It doesn't play that way. All her known acquaintances have alibis, including Micky Doog. Plus there's a whole lot of her time unaccounted for while she was back in the city."

"She wasn't hanging around the neighborhood much," Devin said. "Her mother had no idea where she went. But she was back in town only three weeks and it wasn't like she could have made that many acquaintances over in Brookline."

"Brookline?" I said, remembering my dream.

"Brookline. That's the one place we know she went several times. Credit card receipts from Cityside, a couple of restaurants around Bryce University."

"Jesus," I said.

"What?"

"Nothing. Nothing. Look, how do you know these cases are connected if the vics were killed in different ways?"

"Photographs," Bolton said.

A block of dry ice melted in my chest.

"What photographs?" Angie said.

Devin said, "Kara's mother had a stack of mail she hadn't opened in a few days before Kara died. One of them was an envelope, no return address, no note, just a photograph of Kara inside, innocent photo, nothing—"

Angie said, "Gerry, can I use your phone?"

"What's the matter?" Bolton said.

She was already at the bar, dialing.

"And the other guy, Stimovich?" I said.

"No one at his dorm room," Angie said and hung up, dialed another number.

"What's up, Patrick?" Devin said.

"Tell me about Stimovich," I said, trying to keep the panic from my voice. "Devin. Now."

"Stimovich's girlfriend, Alice Boorstin—"

"No one at Diandra's office," Angie said and slammed the phone down, picked it up, began dialing again.

"—received a similar photo of him in the mail two weeks ago. Same thing. No note or return address, just a photo."

"Diandra," Angie said into the phone, "where's Jason?"

"Patrick," Oscar said, "tell us."

"I *have* his class schedule," Angie said. "He only has one class today and it was over five hours ago."

"Our client received a similar photograph weeks ago," I said. "Of her son."

"We'll be in touch. Stay there. Don't worry." Angie hung up the phone. "Fuck, fuck, fuck," she said.

"Let's go." I stood up.

"You're not going anywhere," Bolton said.

"Arrest me," I said and followed Angie out the door.

18

We found Jade, Gabrielle, and Lauren dining together in the student union, but no Jason. The women gave us "Who the fuck are you?" looks, but answered our questions. None of them had seen Jason since this morning.

We stopped by his dorm room, but he hadn't been by since the previous night. His roommate stood in a haze of pot fumes with Henry Rollins's pissed-off wail booming through his speakers and said, "Nah, man, I got like no idea where he'd be. 'Cept with that dude, you know."

"We don't know."

"That dude. You know, that, like, dude he hangs out with sometimes."

"This dude got a goatee?" Angie said.

The roommate nodded. "And like the most hollow eyes. Like he ain't walking among the living. Be a babe if he was a chick, though. Weird, huh?"

"Dude got a name?"

"None I ever heard."

As we walked back to the car, I could hear Grace asking me a few nights ago, "Are these cases connected in any way?"

Well now, yeah, they were. So what did that mean?

Diandra Warren receives a photograph of her son and makes a reasonable logical leap that it's connected to the Mafia hood she inadvertently angered. Except—she didn't inadvertently anger him. She was contacted by an imposter, and they met in Brookline. An imposter with a harsh Boston accent and wispy blond hair. Kara Rider's hair, when I saw it, looked freshly dyed. Kara Rider used to have blonde hair and her credit card receipts put her in Brookline around the same time "Moira Kenzie" had contacted Diandra.

Diandra Warren had no TV in her apartment. If she read a newspaper, she read *The Trib,* not *The News. The News* had plastered Kara's photograph across page one. *The Trib,* far less sensationalistic and actually late on the story, hadn't published a photograph of Kara at all.

As we reached the car, Eric Gault pulled behind it in a tan Audi. He looked at us with mild surprise as he got out.

"What brings you kids by?"

"Looking for Jason."

He opened his trunk, began picking up books from a pile of old newspapers. "I thought you'd given up on the case."

"There've been some new developments," I said and smiled with confidence I didn't feel. I looked at the newspapers in Eric's trunk. "You save them?"

He shook his head. "I toss them in here, take them to a recycling station when I can't close the trunk anymore."

"I'm looking for one about ten days old. May I?"

He stepped back. "Be my guest."

I pulled back the top *News* on the pile, found the one with Kara's photo four down. "Thanks," I said.

"My pleasure." He shut the trunk. "If you're looking for Jason, try Coolidge Corner or the bars on Brighton Avenue. The Kells, Harper's Ferry—they're big Bryce hangouts."

"Thanks."

Angie pointed at the books under his arm. "Overdue at the library?"

He shook his head, looked at the stately white and red-brick dorm buildings. "Overtime. In this recession, even us tenured profs have to stoop to tutoring now and again."

We climbed into our car, said good-bye.

Eric waved, then turned his back to us and walked up to the dorms, whistling softly in the gradually cooling air.

*   *   *

We tried every bar on Brighton Ave., North Harvard, and a few in Union Square. No Jason.

On the drive to Diandra's place, Angie said, "Why'd you grab that newspaper?"

I told her.

"Christ," she said, "this is a nightmare."

"Yeah, it is."

We rode the elevator up to Diandra's as the waterfront rose, then fell away from us into an overturned bowl of black ink harbor. The apprehension that had been sitting tightly in my stomach for the last few hours expanded and eddied until I felt nauseous.

When Diandra let us in, the first thing I said was, "This Moira Kenzie, did she have a nervous habit of tucking her hair behind her right ear, even if there was nothing to tuck?"

She stared at me.

"Did she?"

"Yes, but how did you . . . ?"

"Think. Did she make this weird, sort of laughing, sort of hiccuping sound at the ends of her sentences?"

She closed her eyes for a moment. "Yes. Yes, she did."

I held up *The News*. "Is this her?"

"Yes."

"Son of a bitch," I said loudly.

"Moira Kenzie" was Kara Rider.

I paged Devin from Diandra's.

"Dark hair," I told him. "Twenty. Tall. Good build. Cleft in his chin. Usually dresses in jeans and flannel shirts." I looked at Diandra. "Do you have a fax here?"

"Yes."

"Devin, I'm faxing you a photo. What's the number?"

He gave it to me. "Patrick, we'll have a hundred guys looking for this kid."

"You get two hundred, I'll feel better."

The fax machine was at the east end of the loft, by the desk. I fed it the photo Diandra had received of Jason, waited for the transmission report, walked back to Diandra and Angie in the living area.

I told Diandra we were slightly concerned because we'd received conclusive proof that neither Jack Rouse nor Kevin Hurlihy could have been involved. I told her that because Kara Rider had died shortly after impersonating Moira Kenzie, I wanted to reopen the case. I didn't tell her that everyone who'd received a photo had had loved ones murdered.

"But he's okay?" She sat on the couch, tucked her legs under her and searched our faces.

"As far as we know," Angie said.

She shook her head. "You're worried. That's obvious. And you're holding something back. Please tell me what. Please."

"It's nothing," I said. "I just don't like it that the girl who impersonated Moira Kenzie and got this whole thing rolling has turned up dead."

She didn't believe me and she leaned forward, her elbows on her knees. "Every night, no matter what, between nine and nine-thirty, Jason calls."

I looked at my watch. Five past nine.

"Is he going to call, Mr. Kenzie?"

I looked at Angie. She was peering intently at Diandra.

Diandra closed her eyes for a moment. When she opened them, she said, "Do either of you have children?"

Angie shook her head.

I thought of Mae for a moment.

"No," I said.

"I didn't think so." She walked to a window, her hands on the backs of her hips. As she stood there, lights from an apartment in the building next door went out one by one and pools of darkness spread across her blond floor.

She said, "You never stop worrying. Never. You remember the first time he climbed out of his crib and fell to the floor before you could reach him. And you thought he was dead. Just for a second. And you remember the horror of that thought. When he grows older and rides his bike and climbs trees and walks to school on his own and darts out in front of cars instead of waiting for the light to change, you pretend it's okay. You say, 'That's kids. I did the same thing at his age.' But always in the back of your throat is this scream, barely suppressed. Don't. Stop. Please don't get hurt.'' She turned from the window and stared at us from the shadows. "It never goes away. The worry. The fear. Not for a second. That's the price of bringing life into this world.''

I saw Mae reaching her hand down by the mouth of that dog, how I'd felt ready to jump, to tear the head off that Scottish terrier if need be.

The phone rang. Nine-fifteen. All three of us jerked at once, and Diandra crossed the floor in four strides. Angie looked at me and rolled her eyes upward in relief.

Diandra picked up the phone. "Jason?" she said. "Jason?"

It wasn't Jason. That was immediately apparent when she ran her free hand up along her temple and pressed it hard against the hairline. "What?" she said. She turned her head and looked at me. "Hold on."

She handed me the phone. "Someone named Oscar."

I took the phone from her and turned so that my back was to her and Angie as another set of lights went out in the building beside us and spread the darkness across the floor like liquid while Oscar told me that Jason Warren had been found.

In pieces.

19

In an abandoned trucking depot along the waterfront in South Boston, the killer had shot Jason Warren once in the stomach, stabbed him several times with an ice pick and bludgeoned him with a hammer. He'd also amputated his limbs and placed them on windowsills, left his torso sitting in a chair facing the door, and tied his head to a dead power cable hanging from an elevated conveyor belt.

A crew of forensics cops spent the night and most of the next morning in there and never found Jason's kneecaps.

The first two cops on the scene were rookies. One quit the force within a week. The other, Devin told me, took a leave of absence to seek counseling. Devin also told me that when he and Oscar entered the truck depot, he'd first thought Jason had run afoul of a lion.

When I hung up that night after receiving word from Oscar and turned to Diandra and Angie, Diandra already knew.

She said, "My son is dead, isn't he?"

And I nodded.

She closed her eyes, and held one hand up by her ear as if motioning for a room to be quiet so she could hear something. She swayed slightly, as if to a breeze, and Angie stepped up beside her.

"Don't touch me," she said, eyes still closed.

By the time Eric arrived, Diandra was sitting on her window seat, staring out at the harbor, the coffee Angie'd made sitting cold and untouched beside her. In an hour, she hadn't spoken a single word.

When Eric entered, she stared at him as he removed his raincoat and hat, placed them on a hook, looked at us.

We stepped into the kitchen alcove, and I told him.

"Jesus," he said, and for a moment he looked as if he'd be sick. His face turned the color of paste and he gripped the bar until his knuckles whitened. "Murdered. How?"

I shook my head. "Murdered is enough for now," I said.

He rested both hands on the bar top, lowered his head. "What's Diandra been like since she heard?"

"Quiet."

He nodded. "That's her way. You contact Stan Timpson?"

I shook my head. "I assume the police will."

His eyes filled. "That kid, that poor beautiful kid."

"Tell me," I said.

He stared past my shoulder at the fridge. "Tell you what?"

"Whatever you know about Jason. Whatever it is you've been hiding."

"Hiding?" His voice was small.

"Hiding," I said. "You haven't felt right in this since the beginning."

"On what do you base—"

"Call it a hunch, Eric. What were you doing at Bryce tonight?"

"I told you. Tutoring."

"Bullshit. I saw the books you pulled out of the car. One of them was a Chilton car guide, Eric."

"Look," he said, "I'm going to go to Diandra now. I know how she'll react and I really think you and Ange should leave. She won't want you to have seen her when she cracks."

I nodded. "I'll be in touch."

He adjusted his glasses, walked past me. "I'll see you get full payment for whatever remains on the bill."

"We've already been paid, Eric."

He crossed the loft to her and I looked at Angie, cocked

my head toward the door. She picked her purse up off the floor and her jacket off the couch as Eric placed a hand on Diandra's shoulder.

"Eric," she said. "Oh, Eric. Why? Why?"

She fell off the window seat into his arms as Angie reached me. And as I opened the door, Diandra Warren howled. It was one of the worst sounds I've ever heard—a raging, tortured, ravaged noise that blew from her chest and reverberated across the loft and clamored in my head long after I'd left the building.

In the elevator, I said to Angie, "Eric's wrong."

"Wrong about what?"

"He's wrong," I said. "He's dirty. Or he's hiding something."

"What?"

"I don't know. He's our friend, Ange, but I don't like the feeling I get from him on this."

"I'll look into it," she said.

I nodded. I could still hear Diandra's awful howl in my head and I wanted to curl up and cover myself against it.

Angie leaned against the glass elevator wall and hugged herself tightly and we didn't speak once on the ride home.

One of the things being around children teaches you, I think, is that no matter what the tragedy, you must keep moving. You have no choice. Long before Jason's death, before I'd even heard of him or his mother, I'd agreed to take Mae for a day and a half while Grace worked and Annabeth went to Maine to see an old friend from her year in college.

When Grace heard about Jason, she said, "I'll find someone else. I'll find a way to get the time off."

"No," I said. "Nothing changes. I want to take her."

And I did. And it was one of the best decisions I ever made. I know society tells us it's good to talk about tragedy, to discuss it with friends or qualified strangers, and maybe so. But I often think we talk way too much in this society, that we consider verbalization a panacea that it very often is not, and that we turn a blind eye to the sort of morbid self-absorption that becomes a predictable by-product of it.

I'm prone to brooding as it is, and I spend a lot of time by myself which makes it worse, and maybe some good would have come if I'd discussed Jason's death and my own feelings of guilt about it with someone. But I didn't.

Instead, I spent my time with Mae, and the simple act of keeping up with her and keeping her entertained and feeding her and putting her down for her nap and explaining the antics of the Marx Brothers to her as we watched *Animal Crackers* and *Duck Soup* and then reading Dr. Seuss to her as she settled into the daybed I'd set up in the bedroom—the simple act of caring for another, smaller human being was more therapeutic than a thousand counseling sessions, and I found myself wondering if past generations had been right when they accepted that as common knowledge.

Halfway through *Fox in Sox* her eyelids fluttered and I tucked the sheet up under her chin and put the book aside.

"You love Mommy?" she said.

"I love Mommy. Go to sleep."

"Mommy loves you," she mumbled.

"I know. Go to sleep."

"You love me?"

I kissed her cheek, tucked the blanket under her chin. "I adore you, Mae."

But she was asleep.

Grace called around eleven.

"How is my tiny terror?"

"Perfect and asleep."

"I hate this. She spends whole weeks being a perfect bitch around me, and she spends a day with you and she's Pollyanna."

"Well," I said, "I'm so much more fun to be around."

She chuckled. "Really—she's been good?"

"Fine."

"You doing any better about Jason?"

"Long as I don't think about it."

"Point taken. You okay about the other night?"

"With us?" I said.

"Yeah."

"Something happen the other night?"

She sighed. "Such a dick."

"Hey."

"Yeah?"

"I love you."

"I love you too."

"Nice, ain't it?" I said.

"Nicest thing in the world," she said.

The next morning, while Mae still slept, I walked out onto my porch and saw Kevin Hurlihy standing out front, leaning against the gold Diamante he drove for Jack Rouse.

Ever since my pen pal sent his "don'tforgettolockup" note, I'd been carrying my gun wherever I went. Even downstairs to pick up my mail. Especially downstairs to pick up my mail.

So when I walked out to my porch and saw Psycho Kevin looking up at me from the sidewalk, I assured myself that at least my gun was only a reach away. And luckily, it was my 6.5 mm. Beretta, with a fifteen-shot clip, because with Kevin, I had a feeling I'd have to use every bullet I had.

He stared at me for a long time. Eventually, I sat down on the top step, opened my three bills, and leafed through my latest issue of *Spin,* read some of an article on Machinery Hall.

"You listen to Machinery Hall, Kev?" I said eventually.

Kevin stared and breathed through his nostrils.

"Good band," I said. "You should pick up their CD."

Kevin didn't look like he'd be dropping by Tower Records after our chat.

"Sure, they're a little derivative, but who isn't these days?"

Kevin didn't look like he knew what derivative meant.

For ten minutes, he stood there without saying a word, his eyes never leaving me, and they were dull murky eyes, as lively as swamp water. I guessed this was the morning

Kevin. The night Kevin was the one with the charged-up eyes, the ones that seemed to pulse with homicide. The morning Kevin looked catatonic.

"So, Kev, I'm guessing here, but I'd say you're not a big alternative music fan."

Kevin lit a cigarette.

"I didn't used to be, but then my partner pretty much convinced me that there was more out there than the Stones and Springsteen. A lot of it is corporate bullshit, and a lot is overrated, don't get me wrong. I mean, explain Morrisey. But then you get a Kurt Cobain or a Trent Reznor, and you say, 'These guys are the real deal,' and it's all enough to give you hope. Or maybe I'm wrong. By the way, Kev, how did you feel about Kurt's death? Did you think we lost the voice of our generation or did that happen when Frankie Goes to Hollywood broke up?"

A sharp breeze creased the avenue and his voice sounded like nothing—an ugly soulless nothing—when he spoke.

"Kenzie, a guy skimmed over forty large from Jackie a few years back."

"It speaks," I said.

"This guy is like two hours from taking a flight to Paraguay or some fucking place when I find him at his girlfriend's." He flicked his cigarette into the bushes fronting the three-decker. "I made him lie face down on the floor, Kenzie, and then I jumped up and down on his back until his spine broke in half. Made the same sound a door makes when you kick it in. Exact same sound. There's that one big loud crack and all those little splintering noises at the same time."

The sharp breeze rode up the avenue again, and the crisp leaves in the gutters made a crackling sound.

"Anyway," Kevin said, "the guy's screaming, his girlfriend's screaming, and they keep looking at the door to this shitty fucking apartment, not because they think they got a chance of getting to it, but because they know that door means they're locked in. *With me.* I have the power. I decide what images they take to hell with them."

He lit another cigarette and I felt the breeze bore through the center of my chest.

"So," he said, "I turn this guy over. I make him sit up on his broken spine, and I rape his girlfriend for, I dunno, a few hours. Had to keep throwing whiskey in the guy's face to keep him from passing out. Then I shot his girlfriend like eight, maybe nine, times. I pour myself a drink and I look in the guy's eyes for a while.

"It's all gone. All his hope. All his pride. All his love. I own it. Me. I own it all. And he knows it. And I walk behind him. I put my gun against the back of his head, right at the brain stem. And then, you know what I do?"

I didn't say anything.

"I wait. I wait like five minutes. And guess what? Guess what the guy did, Kenzie. Guess."

I folded my hands across my lap.

"He begs, Kenzie. Fucking guy's paralyzed. He's just let another guy rape and kill his girl and he couldn't do shit. He's got nothing to live for. Nothing. But he begs to stay alive anyway. This fucking crazy world, I swear."

He flicked his cigarette into the steps below me and the coals shattered and were picked up and swirled by the wind.

"I shot him in the brain just as he started to pray."

Usually when I'd looked at Kevin in the past, I'd seen nothing, a great hole of it. But now I realized it wasn't nothing, it was everything. Everything rancid in this world. It was swastikas and killing fields and labor camps and vermin and fire that rained from the sky. Kevin's nothing was simply an infinite capacity for all of that and more.

"Stay away from the Jason Warren thing," he said. "That guy who ripped off Jackie? His girlfriend? They were friends of mine. You," he said, "I don't ever remember liking."

He stood there a full minute, his eyes never leaving mine, and I felt filth and depravity violate my blood and stain, stain, stain every inch of my body.

He walked around to the driver's side of the car, rested his hands on the hood.

"I hear you went out and got yourself a ready-made

family, Kenzie. Some doctor cunt and her little girl cunt. This little girl, she's what, like four years old?''

I thought of Mae sleeping only three stories up.

"How strong you think a four-year-old's spine is, Kenzie?"

"Kevin," I said and my voice felt thick and filled with phlegm, "if you—"

He held up a hand and pantomimed a chatterbox, then looked down as he opened his door.

"Hey, fuckhead," I said, my voice loud and hoarse on the empty avenue, "I'm talking to you."

He looked at me.

"Kevin," I said, "you go anywhere near that woman or her child and I'll put enough bullets in your head to make it look like a fucking bowling ball."

"Words," he said, opening his door. "Lotta words, Kenzie. See you around."

I pulled the gun from against the small of my back and fired a round through his passenger window.

Kevin jumped back as the glass imploded onto his seat, then looked at me.

"A promise, Kevin. Take it to the fucking bank."

For a moment, I thought he'd do something. Right there. Right then. But he didn't. He said, "You just bought a plot at Cedar Grove, Kenzie. You know that."

I nodded.

He looked in at the glass on the seat and fury suddenly exploded across his face and he reached into his waistband and started around the car fast.

I aimed the gun at the center of his forehead.

And he stopped, hand still in his waistband, and then very slowly, he smiled. He walked back to the driver's door, opened it, then rested his arms on the hood and looked at me. "Here's what's going to happen. Enjoy your time with that girlfriend of yours, fuck her twice a night if you can, and make sure you're extra special nice to the kid. Soon—maybe later today, maybe next week—I'll come calling. First, I'll kill you. Then I'll wait a while. Maybe I'll get something to eat, go to the track, have a few beers. Whatever. And after that, I'm going to drop by your woman's place and kill her and her little girl. And then I'm going to go home, Kenzie, and laugh my ass off.''

He got in the car and drove away and I stood on the porch, my blood popping and boiling against the bone.

20

When I got back upstairs, the first thing I did was check in on Mae. She was curled on her side, hugging one of the pillows, her bangs covering her eyes, her cheeks slightly flushed with heat and sleep.

I looked at my watch. Eight-thirty. Whatever sleep her mother lost working so much, this kid made up for.

I shut the door, went into the kitchen, and fielded three phone calls from irate neighbors who wanted to know what the hell I was doing discharging a firearm at eight in the morning. I couldn't tell if it was the discharging of the firearm or the time of morning I chose to do it that pissed them off most, but I didn't bother asking. I apologized and two hung up in my ear, while a third suggested I seek professional help.

After I hung up for the third time, I called Bubba.

"What's up?"

"You free to shadow some people for a couple days?"

"Who?"

"Kevin Hurlihy and Grace."

"Sure. They don't seem like they run in the same circles, though."

"They don't. He may fuck with her to get to me, so I need to know where both of them are at all times. It's a two-man job."

He yawned. "I'll use Nelson."

Nelson Ferrare was a guy from the neighborhood who worked with Bubba on his arms deals whenever he needed an extra trigger man or driver. He was a short guy, no more than 5'4", and I'd never heard him speak above a whisper or utter more than five words in a given day. Nelson was as shit-house crazy as Bubba, with a Napoleon complex to boot, but like Bubba, he could reign in his psychosis as long as he had something to occupy his time.

"Okay. And Bubba? If anything happens to me in the next week, let's say I meet with an accident, will you do something for me?"

"Name it."

"Find a safe place for Mae and Grace . . ."

"Okay."

". . . and then cancel Hurlihy's ticket."

"No problem. That it?"

"That's it."

"Okee-doke. See ya."

"Let's hope so."

I hung up and saw that the tremors that had been rippling through my wrists and hands since I'd shot out Kevin's window had stopped.

I called Devin next.

"Agent Bolton wants to talk to you."

"I'm sure."

"He doesn't like you being associated with two out of four dead."

"Four?"

"We think he killed another one last night. I can't get into it right now. You going to come by or is Bolton going to have to come for you?"

"I'll be by."

"When?"

"Soon. Kevin Hurlihy just paid me a house call and told me to back off the investigation, by the way."

"We've had him under surveillance for days. He ain't our killer."

"I didn't think he was. He lacks the imagination for what this guy is pulling. But he's involved somehow."

"It's curious, I'll admit. Look, get your ass over to FBI Headquarters. Bolton's ready to send out a dragnet, pull in you, Gerry Glynn, Jack Rouse, Fat Freddy, everyone else who was anywhere near any of the victims."

"Thanks for the tip."

I hung up, and an explosion of country music rocked the apartment through my open kitchen screen. Of course, if you're hearing Waylon, it must be nine.

I looked at my watch. Nine on the dot.

I stepped out on my back porch. Lyle was working on the house closest to mine, and he turned the radio down when he saw me.

"Hey, Patrick, how y'all doing, son?"

"Lyle," I said, "I got my girlfriend's daughter sleeping over. Could we maybe keep it down a bit?"

"Sure thing, son. Sure thing."

"Thanks," I said. "We'll be cutting out pretty soon, so you can turn it back up when we go."

He shrugged. "Only doing a third of a day here myself. Got me a bad tooth kept me up half the night."

"Dentist?" I said and winced.

"Yeah," he said morosely. "Hate paying those bastards, but I tried pulling the tooth myself last night with some pliers and the sumbitch only come out like so far and then it wouldn't budge. Plus, them pliers got all slippery cause of all the blood and, well—"

"Good luck at the dentist, Lyle."

"Thanks," he said. "I'll tell you, bastard ain't using no Novocaine on me neither. Ol' Lyle just about faints dead away he sees a needle. I'm some kind of coward, huh?"

Sure, Lyle, I thought. A big fraidy cat. Go pull a few more of your teeth out with pliers, no one will be able to stop talking about what a wuss you are.

I went back into the bedroom and Mae was gone.

The comforter was crumpled by the foot of my bed and Miss Lilly, her doll, lay on the top of the daybed, staring up at me with her dead doll eyes.

Then I heard the toilet flush and I stepped out into the hall as Mae stepped out of the bathroom rubbing her eyes.

My heart jackhammered into my dust-dry mouth, and I wanted to drop to my knees under the weight of the relief that washed over my body.

"I'm hungry, Patrick," she said and walked into the kitchen in her Mickey Mouse pajamas with padded feet.

"Apple Jacks or Sugar Pops?" I managed.

"Sugar Pops."

"Sugar Pops it is."

While Mae was in the bathroom changing out of her pajamas and brushing her teeth, I called Angie.

"Hey," she said.

"How you doing?"

"I'm . . . okay. Still trying to convince myself there was nothing we could've done to keep Jason alive."

A silence hung between us because I was trying to convince myself of the same.

"You find out anything about Eric?" I said.

"A little. Five years ago, when Eric was still teaching part-time at U/Mass–Boston, a city councilor from Jamaica Plain named Paul Hobson filed suit against the school and Eric."

"For what?"

"I don't know. Everything pertaining to the case is sealed. Looks like an out-of-court settlement followed by gag orders all around. Eric left U/Mass, though."

"Anything else?"

"So far, no, but I'm still digging."

I told her about my encounter with Kevin.

"You shot out his car window, Patrick? Jesus."

"I was a tad perturbed."

"Yeah, but shooting out his car window?"

"Angie," I said, "he threatened Mae and Grace. He does anything that uncool next time I see him, maybe I'll just forget the car and shoot him."

"There's going to be a reprisal," she said.

"I'm aware of that." I sighed, felt the weight behind my eyes, the stench of fear in my shirt. "Bolton's ordered me down to the JFK Building."

"Me too?"

"You weren't mentioned."

"Good."

"I'll have to take care of Mae somehow."

"I'll take her," she said.

"Yeah?"

"I'd love it. Bring her by. I'll take her to the playground across the street."

I called Grace and told her I'd gotten hung up. She thought Mae hanging out with Angie was a fine idea as long as Angie didn't mind.

"She's looking forward to it, believe me."

"Great. You okay?"

"Fine. Why?"

"I don't know," she said. "There's a tremor in your voice."

Guys like Kevin will do that, I thought.

"I'm fine. I'll see you soon."

Mae walked into the kitchen as I hung up.

"Hey, pal," I said, "want to go to the playground?"

She smiled and it was her mother's smile, guileless and open and without hesitation. "Playground? They got swings?"

" 'Course they got swings. Wouldn't be much of a playground without swings."

"They got a jungle gym?"

"They got one of those too."

"They got roller coasters?"

"Not yet," I said, "but I'll put in a suggestion to management."

She hoisted herself up on the chair across from me and put her untied sneakers on my chair. "Okay," she said.

"Mae," I said as I tied her sneakers, "I have to go see a friend, though, and I can't take you with me."

The momentary look of confusion and abandonment in her eyes broke my heart in quarters.

"But," I said hurriedly, "you know my friend Angie? She wants to play with you."

"How come?"

"Because she likes you. And she likes playgrounds."

"She got pretty hair."

"Yeah, she does."

"It's black and tangly and I like it."

"I'll tell her you said so, Mae."

*   *   *

"Patrick, why we stopped?" Mae said.

We were standing on the corner of Dorchester Ave. and Howes Street. If you looked directly across the avenue, you saw the Ryan Playground.

If you looked horizontally down Howes Street, you saw Angie's house.

And, at this moment, Angie. Standing out front.

Kissing her ex-husband Phil on the cheek.

I felt something clench in the center of my chest and then just as suddenly unclench and fill with a gust of chilled air which seemed to hollow out my insides like the flick of a spade.

"Angie!" Mae said.

Angie turned, and so did Phil, and I felt like a voyeur. An angry voyeur with violence in my heart.

They crossed the street and walked to the corner together. She looked, as usual, stupendous in a pair of blue jeans, purple T-shirt, black leather jacket slung over her shoulder. Her hair was wet and a single strand had come out from behind her ear and clung to her cheekbone. She tucked it back as she approached and waved her fingers at Mae.

Phil, unfortunately, also looked good. Angie'd told me he'd quit drinking, and you could see the effects. He'd dropped at least twenty pounds since I'd last seen him, and his jawline was smooth and hard, his eyes devoid of the puffiness that had all but swallowed them over the last five years. He moved loosely in a white shirt and pleated charcoal trousers that matched the color of the hair swept off his forehead. He looked fifteen years younger and his pupils carried a spark I hadn't seen since childhood.

"Hey, Patrick," he said.

"Hi, Phil."

He paused at the curb and clutched a hand to his heart. "Is this her?" he said. "Is this the one? Is this the great, the unforgettable, the world-renowned Mae?"

He squatted by her and she smiled broadly.

"I'm Mae," she said softly.

"It is a pleasure, Mae," he said and shook her hand

formally. "I bet you turn frogs into princes in your spare time. You are definitely something to see."

She looked at me, curious and slightly confused, but I could see by the flush of her face and the charge in her pupils that Phil had already worked his magic.

"I'm Mae," she said again.

"And I'm Phillip," he said. "This guy taking care of you all right?"

"He's my pal," Mae said. "He's Patrick."

"No greater pal to have," Phil said.

You didn't have to know Phil when he was younger to recognize his ability with people, no matter what their age. Even when he was drinking too much and abusing his wife, it was still there. Phil, since he climbed out of the crib, had had this gift. It wasn't cheap or vaudevillian or contrived or consciously manipulative. It was a simple but rare ability to make the person he talked to feel like he or she was the only person on the planet worthy of attention, as if his ears were placed on his head specifically so he could listen to what you had to say, as if his eyes existed only to see you, as if his sole reason for being was to have his encounter—whatever its nature—with you.

I'd forgotten that until I saw him with Mae. It was so much easier to remember him as the drunken asshole who'd somehow managed to marry Angie.

But Angie had remained married to him for twelve years. Even while he beat her. And there was a reason for that. No matter how unforgivable a monster Phil had become, he was still—somewhere inside of him—the Phil who made you glad you'd met him.

That was the Phil who rose from his place by Mae as Angie said, "How you doing, pretty girl?"

"I'm great." Mae reached up to touch Angie's hair.

"She likes your hair," I said.

"You like this mess?" Angie dropped to one knee as Mae ran her hand through her hair.

"It's very tangly," Mae said.

"That's what my hairdresser says."

"How you doing, Patrick?" Phil held out his hand.

I considered it. On a bright autumn morning with the

air so fresh it felt like a tonic and the sun dancing lightly on the orange leaves, it seemed silly to not be at peace with my surroundings.

I let my hesitation speak for itself, then reached out and shook the hand. "Not bad, Phil. How about yourself?"

"Good," he said. "Still taking it day by day and all, but, you know how it is, everyone's life has static."

"True." I looked some of my own static dead in the face.

"Yeah, well . . ." He looked over his shoulder at his ex-wife and a child playing with each other's hair. "She's a prize."

"Which one?" I said.

He smiled, a rueful one. "Both of them, I guess. But I was talking about the four-year-old at the moment."

I nodded. "She's something else, yeah."

Angie walked up beside him, Mae's hand in hers. "What time you have to be at work?"

"Noon," he said. He looked at me. "Guy I'm working for now's an *artiste* in the Back Bay, got me ripping up his entire duplex, ripping up nineteenth-century parquet floors so we can inlay it all with black—black—marble. You believe that?" He sighed and ran his hands through his hair.

"I was wondering," Angie said, "if maybe you wouldn't mind pushing Mae on the swings with me?"

"Oh, I dunno," he said, looking at Mae, "my arm's kinda sore."

"Don't be a big baby," Mae said.

"Can't be called a big baby now, can I?" Phil said as he scooped her up with one arm and settled her on his hip and the three of them crossed the avenue toward the play-ground, waving brightly to me before they walked up the steps and headed for the swing sets.

21

"**You're going to** go see Alec Hardiman," Bolton said without looking up as I walked into the conference room.

"I am?"

"You have an appointment this afternoon at one."

I looked at Devin and Oscar. "I do?"

"This office will be monitoring the entire visit."

I sat down in a seat across from Devin, a deep cherry-wood table the size of my apartment between us. Oscar sat to Devin's left and a half dozen Feds in suits and ties filled the rest of the table. Most of them were talking on telephones. Devin and Oscar didn't have telephones. Bolton had two in front of him at the other end of the table, regular and special Batphone, I guessed.

He stood up and came down the table toward me. "What did you and Kevin Hurlihy discuss?"

"Politics," I said, "the current value of the yen, things of that nature."

Bolton put his hand on the back of my chair and leaned in close enough for me to smell the Sucrets in his mouth. "Tell me what you talked about, Mr. Kenzie."

"What do you think we talked about, Special Agent Bolton? He told me to back off the Warren investigation."

"So you fired a round into his car."

"Seemed an appropriate response at the time."

"Why does your name keep coming up on this case?"

"I have no idea."

"Why does Alec Hardiman want to talk only to you?"

"Again, no clue."

He snapped the chair back as he walked around the table, stopped behind Devin and Oscar and put his hands in his pockets. He looked like he hadn't slept in a week.

"I need answers, Mr. Kenzie."

"I don't have any. I faxed Devin copies of my case files on the Warren case. I sent over photos of the guy with the goatee. I told you everything I remember about my meeting with Kara Rider. Beyond that, I'm as in the dark as you guys."

He pulled a hand out of his pocket, rubbed the back of his neck. "What do you, Jack Rouse, Kevin Hurlihy, Jason Warren, Kara Rider, Peter Stimovich, Freddy Constantine, District Attorney Timpson and Alec Hardiman have in common?"

"This a riddle?"

"Answer the question."

"I. Don't. Fucking. Know." I held up my hands. "Clear enough for you?"

"You have to help us out here, Mr. Kenzie."

"And I'm trying, Bolton, but your interviewing technique is about as socially skilled as a loan shark's. You piss me off, I'm not going to be able to be much help, because I won't be able to think past my anger."

Bolton walked to the back wall at the other end of the room. It was the width of the office, at least thirty feet, and about twelve feet tall. He tugged at the sheet covering it and when it came away in his hands I was looking at a corkboard that covered ninety percent of the wall.

Photographs and crime scene diagrams, spectral analysis sheets and evidence lists were stuck by pushpins and thin wires to the cork. I came out of my seat and walked slowly down the length of the table, trying to take it all in.

Behind me, Devin said, "We've interviewed everyone involved in either case that we know of, Patrick. Plus interrogations of everyone who knew Stimovich and the latest victim, Pamela Stokes. Nothing. Nothing at all."

All the victims were represented by photos, two each of them living, several of them dead. Pamela Stokes looked to have been about thirty. One of the photos showed her squinting against the sun, her hand held over her forehead, a bright smile lighting up an otherwise bland face.

"What do we know about her?"

"Saleswoman for Anne Klein," Oscar said. "Last seen leaving The Mercury Bar on Boylston Street two nights ago."

"Alone?" I said.

Devin shook his head. "With a guy wearing a baseball cap, sunglasses, and a goatee."

"He's wearing sunglasses in a bar, and nobody's suspicious?"

"You ever been to the Mercury?" Oscar said. "It's filled with très chic Euro-trash wannabes. They all wear sunglasses indoors."

"So there's our killer." I pointed at the photo of Jason and the guy with the goatee.

"One of them anyway," Oscar said.

"You're sure there's two?"

"We're working on that assumption. Jason Warren, without a doubt, was killed by two men."

"How do we know that?"

"He scratched them," Devin said. "Two different types of blood under his fingernails."

"Did the families of all the victims receive photographs of them before they were killed?"

"Yes," Oscar said. "It's the closest we have to an MO. Three of the four victims were killed in places other than where their bodies were found. Kara Rider was then dumped in Dorchester, Stimovich in Squantum, and what was left of Pamela Stokes was found in Lincoln."

Below the current victims' photos were photos under a heading "Victims. 1974." Cal Morrison's slightly cocky, boyish face stared out at me and even though I hadn't thought of him for years until that night at Gerry's bar, I could immediately smell the Piña Colada shampoo he'd worn in his hair, and I remembered how we'd all razzed him about it.

"All the victims have been cross-referenced for similarities?"

"Yes," Bolton said.

"And?"

"Two," Bolton said. "Both Kara Rider's mother and Jason Warren's father grew up in Dorchester."

"The other?"

"Both Kara Rider and Pam Stokes wore the same perfume."

"What kind?"

"Lab analysis says it was Halston for Women."

"Lab analysis," I said as I looked at photos of Jack Rouse, Stan Timpson, Freddy Constantine, Diandra Warren, Diedre Rider. There were two of each. One from the present, the other at least twenty years old.

"No clues whatsoever as to motive?" I looked at Oscar and he looked away and then over at Devin and Devin passed the ball to Bolton.

"Agent Bolton?" I said. "What do you have?"

"Jason Warren's mother," he said eventually.

"What about her?"

"She's occasionally been consulted as a psychological expert in criminal trials."

"So?"

"So," he said, "she provided a psychological profile of Hardiman during his trial that effectively crushed his insanity defense. Diandra Warren, Mr. Kenzie, put Alec Hardiman away."

Bolton's mobile command post was a black RV with tinted windows. It was waiting for us, idling, when we came out onto New Sudbury Street.

Inside, two agents, Erdham and Fields, sat at a black-and-gray computer station that took up the right wall. On the tabletop was a serpent's nest of cable, two computers, two fax machines, two laser-jet printers. Above the hutch was a bank of six monitors with a matching bank of six across from them on the left wall. Down at the end of the work center I could see digital receivers and recorders, a dual-deck VCR, audio- and videocassettes, diskettes, and CDs.

The left wall supported a small table and three captain's chairs bolted to the wall. As the RV lurched into traffic, I fell into one and rested my hand on a small fridge.

"You take this thing on camping trips?" I said.

Bolton ignored me. "Agent Erdham, you have that writ?"

Erdham handed him a piece of paper and Bolton slipped it into his inside pocket.

He sat beside me. "You'll be going into the meeting with Warden Lief and the chief prison psychologist, Doctor Dolquist. They'll brief you on Hardiman, so there's very little I can bother adding except to say that Hardiman is not to be taken lightly, no matter how pleasant he may seem. He's suspected in three murders behind bars, but no one in the entire population of a maximum-security pen will come forward with evidence. These are multiple murderers and arsonists and serial rapists, and they're all afraid of Alec Hardiman. You understand?"

I nodded.

"The cell in which the meeting will be held is completely wired. We'll have both audio and video access from this control booth. We'll be watching you every step of the way. Hardiman will have both legs manacled and at least one wrist. Even still, tread lightly with him."

"Hardiman gave you consent for the audio and video?"

"The video isn't up to him. Only the audio infringes upon his rights."

"And did he give consent?"

He shook his large head. "No, he did not."

"But you're doing it anyway."

"Yes. I'm not looking to take it into court. I could need to consult it from time to time as the case goes on. You have a problem with that?"

"Can't think of one."

The RV lurched again as it swung past Haymarket and made the turn onto 93, and I sat back and looked out the windows and wondered how I'd ever gotten myself into this.

Doctor Dolquist was a small but powerfully built man who'd only meet my eyes for a moment before glancing away at something else.

Warden Lief was tall, with his black head shaven so smooth it gleamed.

Dolquist and I were left alone for several minutes in Lief's office while Lief met with Bolton to hammer out surveillance details. Dolquist looked at a photograph of Lief and two friends holding a marlin by a stucco hut under a blazing Florida sun while I waited for the silence to become less uncomfortable.

"You married, Mr. Kenzie?" He stared at the photo.

"Divorced. A long time ago."

"Kids?"

"No. You?"

He nodded. "Two. It helps."

"Helps what?"

He waved a hand toward the walls. "Dealing with this place. It helps to return home to children, to the clean smell of them." He looked at me and then away.

"I'm sure it does," I said.

"Your work," he said, "must bring you into contact with a lot of what's negative in humanity."

"Depends on the case," I said.

"How long have you been doing it?"

"Almost ten years."

"You must have started young."

"I did."

"Do you see it as your life's work?" That quick glance again, skipping across my face.

"I'm not sure yet. How about you, Doctor?"

"I believe so," he said with extreme slowness. "I do believe so," he said unhappily.

"Tell me about Hardiman," I said.

"Alec," he said, "is an unexplainable. He had a very proper upbringing, no history of child abuse or childhood trauma, and no early indicators of a diseased mind. As far as we know he didn't torture animals or display morbid obsessions or act out in any notable way. He was very bright in school and quite popular. And then one day . . ."

"What?"

"We don't know. Around the time he was sixteen or so, trouble started. Neighborhood girls who claimed he'd exposed himself to them. Cats strangled and hung from telephone wires near his house. Violent outbursts in the classroom. And then, nothing again. At seventeen, he reverted to an appearance of normalcy. And if it weren't for the falling out with Rugglestone, who knows how long they would have gone on killing.''

"There had to be *something*.''

He shook his head. "I've worked with him for almost two decades, Mr. Kenzie, and I haven't found it. Even now, to all outward appearances, Alec Hardiman seems a polite, reasonable, perfectly harmless man.''

"But he isn't.''

He laughed, a sudden harsh sound in the small room. "He's the most dangerous man I've ever met.'' He lifted a pencil holder off Lief's desk, looked at it absently and set it back down. "Alec has been HIV positive for three years.'' He looked at me and for a moment, his eyes held. "Recently his condition has worsened into full-blown AIDS. He's dying, Mr. Kenzie.''

"You think that's why he called me here? Deathbed confessions, last-minute change in morals?''

He shook his head. "Not at all. Alec has no morals. Since he's been diagnosed, he's been kept out of general population. But I think Alec knew he'd contracted long before we did. In the two months leading up to his diagnosis, he raped at least ten men. At least ten. It's my firm belief that he did this not to satisfy his sexual urges, but to satisfy his homicidal ones.''

Warden Lief stuck his head back in. "Show time.''

He handed me a pair of tight canvas gloves, and he and Dolquist donned pairs of their own.

"Keep your hands away from his mouth,'' Dolquist said softly, his eyes on the floor.

And we left the office, none of us speaking as we took a long walk down an oddly hushed cellblock toward Alec Hardiman.

22

Alec Hardiman was forty-one years old, but looked fifteen years younger. His pale blond hair was plastered wetly across his forehead like a grade-schooler's. His eye-glasses were small and rectangular—granny glasses—and when he spoke his voice seemed as light as air.

"Hi, Patrick," he said as I came into the room. "Glad you could make the trip."

He sat at a small metal table bolted to the floor. His frail hands were cuffed and looped through two holes in the table and his feet were manacled. When he looked up at me, the fluorescent seared the lenses of his glasses white.

I took a seat across from him. "I heard you could help me, Inmate Hardiman."

"You did?" He slouched loosely in his chair and gave off the impression of a man completely at ease with his surroundings. The lesions that covered his face and neck seemed raw and alive, their surfaces carrying a sheen. His pupils seemed to emanate brightly from recessive caverns in their hollow sockets.

"Yes. I heard you wanted to talk."

"Absolutely," he said as Dolquist took the seat beside my own and Lief took up position against the wall, eyes impassive, hand on his nightstick. "I've wanted to talk to you for a long time, Patrick."

"To me? Why?"

"You interest me." He shrugged.

"You've been in prison for most of my life, Inmate Hardiman—"

"Please call me Alec."

"Alec. I don't understand your interest."

He tilted his head so that the glasses, which had been sliding down his nose, righted themselves.

"Water?"

"Excuse me?" I said.

He tilted his head to indicate a plastic pitcher and four plastic glasses on the table to his left.

"Would you like some water?" he said.

"No, thank you."

"Candy?" He smiled softly.

"What?"

"Do you enjoy your work?"

I glanced at Dolquist. Career seemed to be an obsession behind these walls.

"It pays the bills," I said.

"But it's more than that," Hardiman said. "Isn't it?"

I shrugged.

"Do you see yourself doing it at fifty-five?" he asked.

"I'm not sure I see myself doing it at thirty-five, Inmate Hardiman."

"Alec."

"Alec," I said.

He nodded the way a priest will in a confessional. "What other options do you have?"

I sighed. "Alec, we didn't come here to discuss my future."

"That doesn't mean we can't, Patrick. Does it?" He raised both eyebrows and his skeletal face softened with innocence. "I'm interested in you. Humor me, please."

I looked at Lief and he shrugged his wide shoulders.

"Maybe I'll teach," I said.

"Really?" He leaned forward.

"Why not?"

"What about working for a large agency?" he said. "I've heard they pay well."

"Some do."

"Offer a benefits package, health insurance, the like."

"Yes."

"Have you considered it, Patrick?"

I hated the way he said my name, but I wasn't sure why. "I've considered it."

"But you prefer your independence."

"Something like that." I poured myself a glass of water and Hardiman's bright eyes fixed on my lips as I drank. "Alec," I said, "what can you tell us about—"

"You're familiar with the parable of the three talents."

I nodded.

"Those who horde or are afraid to answer to their gifts, 'are neither hot nor cold' and shall be spewed from the mouth of God."

"I'm familiar with the tale, Alec."

"Well?" He sat back and raised his palms against the cuffs. "A man who turns his back on his vocation is neither hot nor cold."

"What if the man isn't sure he's found his vocation?" He shrugged.

"Alec, if we could just discuss—"

"I think you've been blessed with the gift of fury, Patrick. I do. I've seen it in you."

"When?"

"Have you ever been in love?" He leaned forward.

"What's that got to—"

"Have you?"

"Yes," I said.

"Are you now?" He peered into my face.

"Why do you care, Alec?"

He leaned back, looked up at the ceiling. "I've never been in love. I've never been in love and I've never held a woman's hand and walked on a beach with her and talked about, oh, domestic things—who will cook, who will clean that night, if we should call a repairman for the washing machine. I've never experienced such things and sometimes when I'm alone, late at night, it makes me weep." He chewed his lower lip for a moment. "But we all dream of other lives, I suppose. We all want to live a thousand different existences during our time here. But we can't, can we?"

"No," I said. "We can't."

"I asked about your career goals, Patrick, because I believe you're a man of impact. Do you understand?''

"No.''

He smiled sadly. "Most men and women pass their time on this earth without distinction. Lives of quiet desperation and all that. They are born, they exist for a time with all their particular passions and loves and dreams and pains, and then they die. And barely anyone notices. Patrick, there are billions of these people—tens of billions—throughout history who have lived without impact, who may as well not have been born at all.''

"The people you're talking about might disagree.''

"I'm sure they would.'' He smiled broadly and leaned in as if he were about to tell me a secret. "But who would listen?''

"Alec, all I need to know here is why—''

"You are potentially a man of impact, Patrick. You could be remembered long after you die. Think what an achievement that would be, particularly in this disposable culture of ours. Think of it.''

"What if I have no desire to be a 'man of impact'?''

His eyes disappeared in the wash of fluorescence. "Maybe the choice isn't yours. Maybe you'll be turned into one whether you like it or not.'' He shrugged.

"By who?'' I said.

He smiled. "Whom.''

"By *whom,* then?'' I said.

"The Father,'' he said, "the Son, and the Holy Ghost.''

"Of course,'' I said.

"Are you a man of impact, Alec?'' Dolquist said.

We both turned our heads, looked at him.

"Are you?'' Dolquist said.

Alec Hardiman's head turned back slowly to face me, and his glasses slipped halfway down his nose. The eyes behind the lenses were the milky green of Carribbean shallows. "Forgive Doctor Dolquist's interruption, Patrick. He's a little on edge lately about his wife.''

"My wife,'' Dolquist said.

"Doctor Dolquist's wife, Judith,'' Hardiman said, "left him once for another man. Did you know that, Patrick?''

Dolquist picked at some lint on his knee, concentrated on his shoes.

"And then she came back, and he took her back. I'm sure there were tears, pleas for forgiveness, some minor snide remarks on the doctor's part. One can only assume. But that was three years ago, wasn't it, Doctor?"

Dolquist looked at Hardiman and his eyes were clear but his breathing was slightly shallow and his right hand still picked absently at his pant leg.

"I have it on good authority," Hardiman said, "that on the second and fourth Wednesday of every month, Doctor Dolquist's Queen Judith allows penetration of her every orifice by two former inmates of this institution at the Red Roof Inn on Route One in Saugus. I wonder how Doctor Dolquist feels about that."

"Enough, Inmate," Lief said.

Dolquist looked at a point somewhere over Hardiman's head and his voice was smooth, but the back of his neck bore a swath of hard bright red. "Alec, your delusions are for another time. Today—"

"They're not delusions."

"—Mr. Kenzie is here at your behest and—"

"Second and fourth Wednesdays," Hardiman said, "between two and four at the Red Roof Inn. Room two seventeen."

Dolquist's voice faltered for just a moment, a pause or an intake of breath which wasn't quite natural and I heard it and so did Hardiman, and Hardiman smiled slightly at me.

Dolquist said, "The point of this meeting—"

Hardiman waved his thin fingers dismissively and turned his full attention to me. I could see myself mirrored in the icy fluorescent light that ran along the upper half of both lenses, his green pupils floating just below my melting features. He leaned forward again and I resisted the urge to lean back because I could suddenly feel the heat of him, smell the torpid, fleshy stench of a decayed conscience.

"Alec," I said, "what can you tell me about the deaths

of Kara Rider, Peter Stimovich, Jason Warren, and Pamela Stokes?''

He sighed. ''When I was a boy, I was attacked by a nest of yellow jackets. I was walking along a lake, and I have no idea where they came from, but then, like a mirage, they surrounded me and swarmed my body in this great big cloud of black and yellow. Through the cloud I could just make out my parents and some neighbors rushing down the sand toward me, and I wanted to tell them it was all right. It was fine. But then the bees stung. A thousand needles pierced my flesh and drank from my blood, and the pain was so excruciating it was orgasmic.'' He looked at me as a drop of sweat fell from his nose and landed on his chin. ''I was eleven years old and I had my first orgasm, right there in my swimsuit, as a thousand yellow jackets drank my blood.''

Lief frowned and leaned back against the wall.

''The last time it was wasps,'' Dolquist said.

''It was yellow jackets.''

''You said wasps, Alec.''

''I said yellow jackets,'' Alec said mildly and looked back at me. ''Have you ever been stung?''

I shrugged. ''Probably once or twice when I was a little kid. I can't remember.''

There was a silence then which lasted several minutes. Alec Hardiman sat across from me and looked at me as if he were considering how I'd look laid out in sections on a piece of bone-white china, forks and knives and a full service tray at his disposal.

I looked back, aware that he'd refuse to answer any questions I had at the moment.

When he spoke, I didn't see his lips move until afterward, in memory.

''Could you adjust my glasses, Patrick?''

I looked at Lief and he shrugged. I leaned forward and pushed them back up to Alec's eyes and he tilted his nostrils toward the space of bare skin between my gloved palm and shirt cuff, sniffed audibly.

I removed my hand.

''Did you have sex this morning, Patrick?''

I didn't say anything.

"I can smell her sex on your hand," he said.

Lief came off the wall just enough so that I could see the warning in his face.

"I want you to understand something," Hardiman said. "I want you to understand that there are choices. You can make the right one or the wrong one, but the choice will be presented. Not everyone you love can live."

I tried to get some saliva working through the sand stiffening in my throat and against my tongue. "Diandra Warren's son is dead because she put you away. That one I get. What about the other victims?"

He hummed, softly at first, and I couldn't recognize the tune until he lowered his head and the volume rose slightly. "Send in the Clowns."

"The other victims," I repeated. "Why did they have to die, Alec?"

"Isn't it bliss?" he sang.

"You brought me here for a reason," I said.

"Don't you approve . . ."

"Why did they die, Alec?" I said.

"One who keeps tearing around . . ." His voice was thin and high. "One who can't move . . ."

"Inmate Hardiman—"

"So send in the clowns . . ."

I looked at Dolquist, then at Lief.

Hardiman wagged a finger at me. "Don't bother," he sang, "they're here."

And he laughed. He laughed hard, his vocal cords booming, his mouth wide and spittle forming at the corners, and his eyes even wider as they remained on me. The air in the cell seemed to go into that mouth with him, as if he were sucking it down into his lungs until it filled his whole body and we'd be left airless and gasping.

Then his mouth clamped shut and his eyes glazed and he looked as reasonable and gentle as a small-town librarian.

"Why did you bring me here, Alec?"

"You've tamed the cowlick, Patrick."

"What?"

He turned his head, spoke to Lief. "Patrick used to have an awful cowlick near the back of his head. It stuck out like a broken finger."

I resisted the urge to raise my hand to my head, pat down a cowlick I haven't had in years. My stomach felt weak suddenly and very cold.

"Why'd you bring me here? You could have spoken to a thousand police officers, a thousand Feds, but—"

"If I claimed my blood was being poisoned by the government or that alpha waves from other galaxies were infiltrating my faculties or that I'd been forcibly sodomized by my mother—what would you say to that?"

"I wouldn't know what to say."

"No, you wouldn't. Because you know nothing, and none of those things are true, and even if they were, it would be largely irrelevent. What if I told you I was God?"

"Which one?"

"The only one."

"I'd wonder how God got Himself locked up in the joint and why he couldn't just miracle His ass out."

He smiled. "Very good. Very glib, of course, but that's your nature."

"What's yours?"

"My nature?"

I nodded.

He looked at Lief. "Are we having the baked chicken again this week?"

"Friday," Lief said.

Hardiman nodded. "That's good. I like the baked chicken. Patrick, it was a pleasure meeting you. Drop by again."

Lief looked at me and shrugged. "Interview's over."

I said, "Wait."

Hardiman laughed. "Interview's over, Patrick."

Dolquist stood up. After a minute, I did too.

"Doctor Dolquist," Hardiman said, "say hello to Queen Judith for me."

Dolquist turned toward the cell gate.

I turned with him, stared at the bars, and felt them holding me, closing me in, blocking me from ever seeing the outside world again, locking me in here with Hardiman.

Lief walked up to the gate and produced a key, all three of us with our backs to Hardiman now.

And he whispered, "Your father was a yellow jacket."

I turned around and he was staring at me impassively.

"What was that?"

He nodded and closed his eyes, drummed the fingertips of his cuffed hands on the table. When he spoke, his voice seemed to come from the corners of the room and the ceiling, and the bars themselves—anywhere but from his mouth:

"I said, 'Eviscerate them, Patrick. Kill them all.' "

He pursed his lips, and we stood there waiting, but it was useless. A minute passed in complete silence, as he remained that way without so much as a tremor coursing his tight, pallid skin.

As the doors opened and we walked out into the corridor of C Block past the two guards posted as sentries outside the cell, Alec Hardiman sang the words, "Eviscerate them, Patrick. Kill them all," in a voice so light but rich and strong that we could have been hearing an aria.

"Eviscerate them, Patrick."

The words flowed like birdsong down the cellblock corridor.

"Kill them all."

23

Lief led us through a maze of maintenance corridors, the sounds of the prison muffled by the thick walls. The corridors smelled of antiseptic and industrial solvent and the floors had the yellowish shine of the floors in all state institutions.

"He has a fan club, you know."

"Who?"

"Hardiman," Lief said. "Criminology students, law students, lonely middle-aged women, a couple of social workers, some church-group types. Pen pals who he's convinced of his innocence."

"You're shitting me."

Lief smiled and shook his head. "Oh, no. Alec has this favorite thing he does—he invites them to visit, to see his eminence in the flesh or some such. And some of these people, they're poor. They spend a life's savings just to get here. And then guess what ol' Alec does?"

"Laughs at them?"

"He refuses to see them," Dolquist said. "Always."

"Yup," Lief said. He punched numbers into a keypad by the door in front of us and it opened with a soft click. "He sits in his cell and looks out the window as they walk back down the long road to their cars, confused and humiliated and alone, and he jerks off into his hand."

"That's Alec," Dolquist said as we came out into the light by the main gate.

"What was that crack about your father?" Lief said as

169

we left the prison and headed toward Bolton's RV sitting halfway down the gravel walkway.

I shrugged. "I don't know. As far as I know, he didn't know my father."

Dolquist said, "Sounds like he wants you to think he did."

"And that cowlick shit," Lief said. "Either he did know you, Mr. Kenzie, or he made a hell of a guess."

Gravel crunched under our feet as we crossed toward the RV and I said, "I've never met the guy before."

"Well," Lief said, "Alec's good at fucking with people's heads. I heard you were coming, I dug this up." He handed me a piece of paper. "We intercepted this when Alec tried to send it by one of his couriers to a nineteen-year-old boy he'd raped after he knew he was HIV positive."

I opened the note:

> *The death in my blood*
> *I gave it to you.*
> *On the other side of the grave*
> *I'll be waiting for you.*

I handed the note back as if it were on fire.

"Wanted the kid to be afraid even after he was dead. That's Alec," Lief said. "And maybe you never did meet, but he asked for you specifically. Remember that."

I nodded.

Dolquist's voice was hesitant. "Do you need me?"

Lief shook his head. "Write me up a report, have it on my desk in the morning, and I think we're okay, Ron."

Dolquist stopped just outside the van and shook my hand. "Nice meeting you, Mr. Kenzie. I hope everything works out."

"Same here."

He nodded but wouldn't meet my eyes and then he nodded curtly at Lief and turned to walk away.

Lief patted him on the back, a slightly awkward gesture, as if he'd never done it before. "Take care, Ron."

We watched the little muscular man walk down the path

a bit before he stopped and seemed almost to jerk to his left and cut across the lawn toward the parking lot.

"He's a little weird," Lief said, "but he's a good man."

The great shadow of the prison wall cut across the lawn and darkened the grass and Dolquist seemed wary of it. He walked along its edge, in the strip of sunlit grass, and he did so gingerly, as if he were afraid he'd step too much to his left and sink through the dark grass.

"Where do you think he's going?"

"To check on his wife." Lief spit into the gravel.

"You think what Hardiman said was true."

He shrugged. "Don't know. The details were precise, though. If it was your wife, and she'd been unfaithful before, wouldn't you go check?"

Dolquist was a tiny figure now as he reached the edge of the grass and cut around the shadow of the prison into the parking lot before disappearing from view.

"Poor bastard," I said.

Lief spit into the gravel again. "Pray Hardiman don't make someone say that about you someday."

A sudden stiff breeze curled out of the dark shadows under the wall and I shrugged my shoulders against it as I opened the back door of the RV.

Bolton said, "Nice interviewing technique. You study?"

"I did my best," I said.

"You did shit," he said. "You learned absolutely zero about these current killings in there."

"Oh well." I looked around the RV. Erdham and Fields sat at the thin black table. Above them, the bank of six monitors played five recordings of our interview with Hardiman, the sixth covering real time as Alec sat in the same position we'd left him in, his eyes closed, head thrown back, lips pursed.

Beside me Lief watched the second bank of monitors on the opposite wall as a series of prisoner photos rolled across, angry faces being replaced by fresh angry faces at a rate of six every two minutes. I looked over and watched Erdham's fingers whiz over a computer keypad and I realized he was rifling through the prison files of every inmate.

"Where'd you get authorization?" Lief said.

Bolton looked bored. "A federal magistrate at five this morning." He handed Lief a writ. "See for yourself."

I looked up at the bank of monitors above his head as a fresh row of convicts materialized. As Lief bent beside me and went over the writ slowly, his index finger running under the words as he read, I watched the six convicts' faces above me until they were replaced with six more. Two were black, two white, one had so many facial tatoos he could have been green for all I could tell, and one looked like a young Hispanic except his hair was a shock of pure white.

"Freeze that," I said.

Erdham looked over his shoulder at me. "What?"

"Freeze those faces," I said. "Can you do that?"

He took his hands off the keyboard. "It's done." He looked at Bolton. "None of them are a match so far, sir."

"What's a match?" I said.

Bolton said, "We're running every inmate's file against all prison documentation, no matter how minor, to see if there's any sort of relationship with Alec Hardiman. We're nearing the end of the "A"s now."

"First two are completely clean," Erdham said. "Not a single incident of contact with Hardiman."

Lief was staring up at the monitors now too. "Run the sixth," he said.

I came up beside him. "Who is that guy?"

"You seen him before?"

"I don't know," I said. "He seems familiar."

"You'd remember that hair, though."

"Yeah," I said, "I would."

"Evandro Arujo," Erdham said. "No match on cellblock, no match on work detail, no match on recreational time, no match on—"

"Lot that computer won't tell you," Lief said.

"—sentencing. I'm punching up incident reports now."

I looked at the face. It was smooth and feminine, the face of a pretty woman. The white hair contrasted starkly with large almond eyes and amber skin. The thick lips were also feminine, pouty, and his eyelashes were long and dark.

"Major incident, number one—Inmate Arujo claims he was raped in hydrotherapy room, August sixth, eighty-seven. Inmate refuses to identify alleged rapists, requests solitary confinement. Request denied."

I looked at Lief.

"I wasn't here then," he said.

"What was he in for?"

"Grand theft auto. First offense."

"In here?" I said.

Bolton was standing beside us now and I could smell the Sucrets on his breath. "Grand theft isn't maximum."

"Tell that to the judge," Lief said. "And the cop whose car Evandro totaled, who was a drinking buddy of said judge."

"Second major incident—suspicion of mayhem. March eighty-eight. No further information."

"Means he raped someone himself," Lief said.

"Third major incident—arrest and trial for manslaughter. Convicted June eighty-nine."

"Welcome to Evandro World," Lief said.

"Print this," Bolton said.

The laser jet hummed, and the first thing out was the photo we were all staring up at.

Bolton took it, looked at Lief. "Was there contact between this inmate and Hardiman?"

Lief nodded. "Won't find documentation of it, though."

"Why not?"

"Because there's what you know and can prove and what you just know. Evandro was Hardiman's bitch. Walked in here a half-decent kid to do nine months on a car theft, walked out nine and a half years later a fucking freak show."

"How'd he get that hair?" I said.

"Shock," Lief said. "After the gang-bang in hydro, he was found on the floor bleeding from every orifice with his hair shocked white. After he got out of the infirmary, he went back into population because the previous warden didn't like spics, and by the time I got here, he'd been bought and sold a thousand times and ended up with Hardiman.''

''When was he released?'' Bolton said.

''Six months ago.''

''Run all his photos and print them,'' Bolton said.

Erdham's fingers flew back over the keyboard and suddenly the bank of monitors showed five different photos of Evandro Arujo.

The first was a mug shot from the Brockton PD. His face was swollen and his right cheekbone looked broken and his eyes were tender and terrified.

''Crashed the car,'' Lief said. ''Hit his head on the steering wheel.''

The next was taken the day he arrived at Walpole. Eyes still huge and terrified, cuts and swelling gone. He had rich black hair and the same feminine features, but they were even softer, still carrying a hint of baby fat.

The next one was the first I'd seen. His hair was white, and the large eyes were altered somehow, as if someone had scraped off a layer of emotion the way you'd scrape the thinnest film of egg-white from the shell.

''After he murdered Norman Sussex,'' Lief said.

In the fourth, he'd lost a lot of weight and his feminine features seemed grotesque, the face of a haggard witch on a young man's body. The large eyes were bright and loud, somehow, and the full lips sneered.

''The day he was convicted.''

The final photo was taken the day of his release. He'd streaked his hair with what looked like charcoal and gained weight, and he puckered his lips at the photographer.

''How did this guy get out?'' Bolton said. ''He looks completely deranged.''

I stared up at the second photo, the young Evandro, dark-haired, face clear of bruises, eyes wide and afraid.

''He was convicted of involuntary manslaughter,'' Lief said. ''Not murder. Not even man two. I know he cleaved open Sussex without provocation, but I couldn't prove it. And wounds on both Sussex and Arujo at the time were consistent with those of men who'd been in a shank fight.''

He pointed at Arujo's forehead in the most recent photo. There was a thin white line creasing the forehead. "See that? Shank mark. Sussex couldn't tell us what happened, so Arujo claimed self-defense, said the shank belonged to Sussex, and he draws eight years, because the judge didn't believe him, but he couldn't prove otherwise either. We got a serious overcrowding problem in our prisons, in case no one told you, and Inmate Arujo was in every other respect a model prisoner who served his time, earned his parole."

I stared up at the various incarnations of Evandro Arujo. Injured. Young and scared. Blighted and ruined. Gaunt and barren. Petulant and dangerous. And I knew, beyond any doubt, that I'd seen him before. But I couldn't place where.

I rifled through possibilities:

On the street. In a bar. On a bus. In the subway. Driving a cab. At the gym. In a crowd. At a ballgame. In a movie theater. At a concert. In—

"Who's got a pen?"

"What?"

"A pen," I said. "Black. Or a marker."

Fields held up a felt tip and I snatched it, pulled a photo of Evandro out of the laser printer and started scribbling on it.

Lief came up and looked over my shoulder, "Why you drawing a goatee on the man, Kenzie?"

I stared down at the face I'd seen in the movie theater, the face in a dozen photos Angie had taken.

"So he can't hide anymore," I said.

24

Devin faxed us a copy of Evandro Arujo's photo from the set Angie'd given him and Erdham fed it into his computer.

We crawled north on 95, the RV stuck in a midday traffic snarl as Bolton said, "I want an all-points issued on him immediately," to Devin, then turned and barked at Erdham, "Punch up his probie's name."

Erdham glanced at Fields and Fields hit a button and said, "Sheila Lawn. Office in the Saltonstall Building."

Bolton was still talking to Devin. ". . . five eleven, one hundred sixty-three pounds, thirty years old, only distinguishing mark is a thin scar, one inch long, on his upper forehead, just below the hairline, shank wound . . ." He cupped his hand over the phone. "Kenzie, call her."

Fields gave me the phone number and I picked up a handset and dialed as Evandro's photo materialized on Erdham's screen. He immediately began to punch buttons and enhance the texture and color.

"Sheila Lawn's office."

"Ms. Lawn, please."

"This is she."

"Ms. Lawn, my name's Patrick Kenzie. I'm a private detective and I need information on one of your parolees."

"Just like that?"

"Excuse me?"

The RV lumbered into a lane that was moving an inch or two faster per minute and several horns blared.

"You don't think I'm going to reveal anything about a

client to a man claiming to be a private investigator on the phone, do you?''

"Well . . ."

Bolton was watching me as he listened to something Devin said, and he reached out and grabbed the phone from me, spoke into it out of the corner of his mouth while still listening to Devin through his other ear.

"Officer Lawn, this is Special Agent Barton Bolton of the FBI. I'm assigned to the Boston office and my identification number is six-oh-four-one-nine-two. Call and verify who I am and keep Mr. Kenzie on the line. This is a federal matter and we expect your cooperation."

He tossed the phone back to me and said to Devin, "Go ahead, I'm listening."

"Hi," I said.

"Hi," she said. "I feel chastised. By a man with a name like Barton no less. Hold on."

While I was on hold, I looked out the window as the RV switched lanes again and saw what the tie-up had been. A Volvo had rear-ended a Datsun and the owner of one of them was being escorted down the breakdown lane to an ambulance. His face was covered in blood and pricked with small shards of glass and he held his hands in front of him awkwardly, as if he wasn't sure they were attached anymore.

The accident wasn't blocking traffic anymore, if it had ever been, but everyone had slowed to a standstill to get a proper look. Three cars ahead of us, the backseat passenger was recording it all on video camera. Home movies for the wife and kids. Look, son, severe facial lacerations.

"Mr. Kenzie?"

"I'm here."

"I've been chastised twice now. The second time by Agent Bolton's boss for wasting the FBI's precious time on something as trivial as protecting my client's rights. So, which of my choirboys do you need information on?"

"Evandro Arujo."

"Why?"

"We just need it, that's all I can say."

"Okay. Shoot."

"When's the last time you saw him?"

"Two weeks ago Monday. Evandro's punctual. Hell, compared to most, he's a dream."

"How's that?"

"Never misses an appointment, is never late, got a job within two weeks of his release—"

"Where?"

"Hartow Kennel in Swampscott."

"What's the address and phone number at Hartow Kennel?"

She gave it to me and I wrote it down, ripped off the sheet and handed it to Bolton as he hung up the phone.

Lawn said, "His boss, Hank Rivers, loves him, said he'd hire nothing but ex-cons if they were all like Evandro."

"Where's Evandro live, Officer Lawn?"

"Ms. is fine. His address is, lemme see . . . here it is— two-oh-five Custer Street."

"Where's that?"

"Brighton."

Bryce was right next door. I wrote down the address and handed it to Bolton.

"Is he in trouble?" she said.

"Yes," I said. "If you see him, Ms. Lawn, do not approach him. Call the number Agent Bolton just gave you."

"But what if he comes here? He has another appointment in less than two weeks."

"He won't be coming there. And if he does, lock the door and call for help."

"You think he crucified that girl a few weeks ago, don't you?"

The RV was moving briskly now, but inside, it felt like traffic had come to a dead stop.

I said, "What would make you think that?"

"It was something he said once."

"What did he say?"

"You have to understand, like I said, he's one of the easiest parolees I have and he's never been anything but sweet and polite and, hell, he sent me flowers in the hospital when I broke my leg. I'm no virgin when it comes to ex-cons, Mr. Kenzie, but Evandro really seemed like a decent guy who'd taken his fall and didn't want to take another.''

''What did he say about crucifixions?''

Bolton and Fields looked at me and I could see that even the usually disinterested Erdham was watching my reflection on his LED screen.

''We were finishing up here one day and he started fixating on my chest. At first I thought, you know, he's checking out my breasts, but then I realize he's staring at the crucifix I wear. Usually I keep it tucked under my shirt, but it fell out that day and I didn't even notice until I caught Evandro looking at it. And it wasn't just a benign look, it was a bit obsessive, if you know what I'm saying. When I asked him what he was looking at, he said, 'What do you think about crucifixions, Sheila Lawn?' Not Officer Lawn or Ms. Lawn, but *Sheila* Lawn.''

''What did you say?''

''I said, 'In what context?' or something like that.''

''And Evandro?''

''He said, 'In the sexual context, of course.' I think it was the 'of course' that really got to me, because he seemed to think it a perfectly normal context in which to consider a crucifixion.''

''Did you report this conversation?''

''To who? Are you kidding? I have ten men a day, Mr. Kenzie, who say far worse to me, and they're not breaking any laws, though I could consider it sexual harassment if I didn't know that my male colleagues hear the same thing.''

''Ms. Lawn,'' I said, ''you jumped right from my original questions to asking if Evandro crucified someone, yet I never mentioned wanting him for murder—''

''Yet you're hanging out with the FBI and you said I should hide if I saw him.''

''But if Evandro was such a model parolee, why would you make that leap? If he was so nice, how could you think—''

''Of him crucifying that girl?''

''Yes.''

"Because.... You put things out of your mind every day in this job, Mr. Kenzie. It's, well, what you do to keep at it. And I'd completely forgotten that crucifix conversation with Evandro until I saw the article on that girl who was killed. And then it came back fast and I remembered how I'd felt as he looked at me, just for a second, while he said, 'In the sexual context, of course,' and the way I felt was dirty and naked and completely vulnerable. But more than that, I felt terrified—again, for only a second—because I thought he was considering . . ."

There was a long silence as she groped for words.

"Crucifying you?" I asked.

She inhaled sharply. "Absolutely."

"Beyond the hair-coloring and the goatee," Erdham said as we watched Evandro's photograph take on full color and total clarification on the LED screen, "he's definitely had his hairline altered."

"How?"

He held up the last photo taken of Evandro in prison. "See the scar from the shiv on his upper forehead?"

Bolton said, "Shit."

"Now you don't," Erdham said and tapped his screen.

I looked at the photo Angie'd taken of Evandro exiting the Sunset Grill. The hairline was at least a half-inch lower than it had been when he left prison.

"Now I don't think that's necessarily part of a disguise," Erdham said. "It's too minimal. Most people would never notice the change."

"He's vain," I said.

"Exactly."

"What else?" Bolton said.

"See for yourself."

I looked at the two photos. It was hard to get past the shock of white hair turning to dark brown at first, but gradually . . .

"His eyes," Bolton said.

Erdham nodded. "Brown naturally, but green in the photo Mr. Kenzie's partner took."

Fields set down his phone. "Agent Bolton?"

"Yeah?" He turned away from us.

"His cheekbones," I said, noticing my own reflection transposed over Evandro's in the screen.

"You're good at this," Erdham said.

"No go at either his address or his place of work," Fields was saying. "Landlord hasn't seen him in two weeks, and his boss said he called in sick two days ago and hasn't been seen since."

"I want agents at both places yesterday."

"They're already on their way, sir."

"What about the cheekbones?" Bolton said.

"Implants," Erdham said. "That would be my guess. You see?" He punched a button three times and Evandro's photo was magnified until we were staring at nothing but his calm green eyes, the top half of his nose, and his cheekbones. Erdham touched a pen to the left cheekbone. "The tissue here is much softer than it is in that photo. Hell, there's almost no flesh in that one. But here . . . And see how the skin seems almost chapped, just a bit reddened? That's because it isn't used to being stretched out that far, like skin over a blister that's on its way to the surface."

"You're a genius," Bolton said.

"Definitely," Erdham said and his eyes lit up behind his glasses like a little kid's looking at birthday candles. "But he's pretty damn smart, too. He didn't go for big changes which would alarm his probation officer or a landlord. Except for the hair," he said hurriedly, "and anyone would understand that. Instead, he went for subtle cosmetic changes. You could run this current photo through a computer, and unless you knew *exactly* what you were looking for, it might not match up with any of those prison photos."

The RV tipped a bit as we made the turn onto 93 in Braintree, and Bolton and I palmed the roof for a moment.

"If he thought that far ahead," I said, "then he knew we'd end up looking for him or at least for someone who looked like that." I pointed at the computer screen.

"Absolutely," Erdham said.

"So," Bolton said, "he's assuming he'll be caught."

"Seems to be the case," Erdham said. "Why else would

he duplicate some of Hardiman's murders?''

"He knows he'll be caught," I said, "and he doesn't care."

"Might be even worse than that," Erdham said. "Maybe he even wants to be caught, which means all these deaths are some sort of message, and he's going to keep killing until we figure out what it is."

"Sergeant Amronklin told me some interesting things while you were on the phone with Arujo's probie."

The RV turned off 93 at Haymarket and again Bolton and I had to push against the roof to maintain balance.

"Such as."

"He caught up with Kara Rider's roommate in New York. Ms. Rider met a fellow actor in a class three months ago. He said he was from Long Island, only made it into Manhattan once a week for this class." He looked at me. "Guess."

"The guy had a goatee."

He nodded. "Went by the name Evan Hardiman. Like that? Ms. Rider's roommate also said, and I'm quoting here, 'He was the most sensual man who ever walked the earth.' "

"Sensual," I said.

He grimaced. "She's, you know, dramatic."

"What else did she say?"

"She said Kara said he was the best fuck she'd ever had. 'The be-all and end-all' was how she described it."

"She got the end-all right."

"I want a psych profile immediately," Bolton said as we rode up in the elevator. "I want to know everything about Arujo from the moment they snipped his umbilical to now."

"Got it," Fields said.

He wiped his face with his sleeve. "I want the same list we ran on Hardiman, cross-reference everyone who ever came in contact with Arujo while he was in prison and have an agent at every one of their doorsteps by tomorrow morning."

"Got it." Fields scribbled furiously in his pad.

"Agents sitting on his parents' house if they're still alive," Bolton said, taking off his coat and breathing heavily. "Shit, even if they're not. Agents on the homes of every girlfriend or boyfriend he ever had, on any friends he's had, any girls or boys who ever spurned his advances."

"That's a lot of manpower," Erdham said.

Bolton shrugged. "Minuscule compared to what Waco cost this government and we might actually win here. I want recanvasses of all crime scenes, fresh interviews of every BPD slug who touched them before we came on the scene. I want all principals on Kenzie's list"—he ticked off on his fingers—"Hurlihy, Rouse, Constantine, Pine, Timpson, Diandra Warren, Glynn, Gault—reinterviewed and extensive, no, *exhaustive* checks run on their backgrounds to see if they ever crossed paths with Arujo." He reached into his breast pocket for his inhaler as the elevator came to a stop. "Got it? Got it? Get to it."

The doors opened and he charged out, sucking audibly on the inhaler.

Behind me, Field asked Erdham, " 'Exhaustive'—is that spelled with one dick or two?"

"Two," Erdham said. "But they're both pretty small."

Bolton loosened his tie until the knot hung at his sternum and dropped heavily into the chair behind his desk.

"Close the door behind you," he said.

I did. His face was deep pink, his breathing ragged.

"You okay?"

"Never better. Tell me about your father."

I took a seat. "Nothing to tell. I think Hardiman was reaching, trying to rattle me with bullshit."

"I don't," he said and took a small hit off his inhaler. "You three had your back to him when he said it, but I was watching him on film. He looked like he blew a load when he said your father was a yellow jacket, like he'd been saving it for maximum impact." He ran a hand through his hair. "You had a cowlick when you were younger, didn't you?"

"A lot of kids did."

"A lot of kids didn't grow up to have their presence requested by a serial killer."

I held up a hand, nodded. "I had a cowlick, Agent Bolton. Usually only noticeable if I'd been sweating a lot."

"Why?"

"Because I was vain, I guess. I put shit in my hair to keep it down usually."

He nodded. "He knew you."

"I don't know what to tell you, Agent Bolton. I've never seen the guy before."

Another nod. "Tell me about your father. You know I've already got people researching him."

"I assumed as much."

"What was he like?"

"He was an asshole who enjoyed inflicting pain, Bolton. And I don't like talking about him."

"And I'm sorry," he said, "but your personal qualms mean nothing to me right now. I'm trying to bring Arujo down and stop the bloodshed—"

"And get a nifty promotion out of the deal."

He raised an eyebrow and nodded vigorously. "Absolutely. Bank on it. I don't know any of these victims, Mr. Kenzie, and in a general sense, I don't want any human beings to die. Ever. But in a particular sense, I feel nothing for these individuals. And I'm not paid to. I'm paid to bring down guys like this Arujo, and that's what I'm doing. And if by doing so, I advance my career, then isn't it a perfect world?" His tiny eyes dilated. "Tell me about your father."

"He was a lieutenant with the Boston Fire Department most of his life. Later, he switched to local politics, became a city councilor. Not long after that, he got lung cancer and died."

"You two didn't get along."

"No. He was a bully. Everyone who knew him feared him, and most hated him. He had no friends."

"Yet you seem to be his opposite."

"How so?"

"Well, people like you. Sergeants Amronklin and Lee

are very fond of you, Lief took an instant liking to you, and from what I've learned of you since I took this case over, you've formed very strong bonds with people who are such polar opposites as a liberal newspaper columnist and a psychotic weapons supplier. Your father had no friends, yet you are very rich with friends. Your father was a violent man, yet you don't seem to have an uncontrollable propensity for it.''

Tell that to Marion Socia, I thought.

''What I'm trying to figure out here, Mr. Kenzie, is if Alec Hardiman made Jason Warren pay for the sins of his mother, maybe you're being set up to pay for the sins of your father.''

''Which is fine, Agent Bolton. But Diandra had a direct effect on Hardiman's incarceration. So far, though, there's no link between my father and Hardiman.''

''Not one we've uncovered.'' He leaned back. ''Look at this from my perspective. This all started when Kara Rider, an actress, contacted Diandra Warren using the alias Moira *Kenzie*. That wasn't a mistake. That was a message. We can assume, I think, that Arujo put her up to it. She then points fingers at Kevin Hurlihy and by implication, Jack Rouse. You make contact with Gerry Glynn, who worked with Alec Hardiman's father. He points you toward Hardiman himself. Hardiman killed Charles Rugglestone in your neighborhood. We also assume that he killed Cal Morrison. Also in your neighborhood. Back then, you and Kevin Hurlihy were kids, but Jack Rouse ran a grocery store, Stan Timpson and Diandra Warren lived a few blocks away, Kevin Hurlihy's mother, Emma, was a housewife, Gerry Glynn was a cop, and your father, Mr. Kenzie, was a fireman.''

He handed me an 8×11 map of the Edward Everett Square, Savin Hill, and Columbia Point neighborhoods. Someone had penned a circle around what constituted St. Bart's parish—Edward Everett Square itself, the Blake Yard, JFK/UMass Station, a stretch of Dorchester Avenue beginning at the South Boston line and ending at St. William's Church in Savin Hill. Within the circle, someone had also marked in five small black squares and two large blue dots.

"The squares are?" I looked at him.

"Approximate locations of the residences in 1974 of Jack Rouse, Stan and Diandra Timpson, Emma Hurlihy, Gerry Glynn, and Edgar Kenzie. The two blue dots are the murder sites of Cal Morrison and Charles Rugglestone. Both the squares and dots are within a quarter square mile of each other."

I stared at the map. My neighborhood. A tiny, mostly forgotten, hardscrabble place of three-deckers and faded A-frames, cubbyhole taverns and corner stores. Outside of the occasional bar brawl, not the type of place that called much attention to itself. Yet here was the FBI shining a national spotlight down on it.

"What you're looking at there," Bolton said, "is a kill zone."

I called Angie from an empty conference room.

She answered on the fourth ring, out of breath. "Hey, I just came through the door."

"Whatcha doing?"

"Talking to you, ya pinhead, and opening my mail. Bill, bill, bill, take-out menu, bill . . ."

"How was Mae?"

"Fine. I just dropped her off with Grace. How was your day?"

"The guy with the goatee's name is Evandro Arujo. He was Alec Hardiman's partner-in-life in the joint."

"Bullshit."

"Nope. Looks like he's our guy."

"But he doesn't know you."

"This is true."

"So why would he leave your card in Kara's hand?"

"Coincidence?"

"Fine. But Jason getting killed, too?"

"Really, really, big coincidence?"

She sighed and I could hear her rip into an envelope. "This doesn't make total sense yet."

"Agreed," I said.

"Tell me about Hardiman."

I did and then I took her through my day as she ripped open more envelopes and said, "Yeah, yeah," in a distracted tone which would have annoyed me if I hadn't known her well enough to know she could talk on the telephone, listen to the radio, watch TV, and cook pasta while carrying on a half-conversation with someone else in the room and she'd still hear every word I said.

But halfway through my story, the "yeahs" stopped and I got nothing but silence, and it wasn't a rapt silence, it was a thick one.

"Ange?"

Nothing.

"Ange?" I said again.

"Patrick," she said and her voice was so small, it seemed to have no body attached to it.

"What? What's wrong?"

"I just got a photograph in the mail."

I stood up from the chair so quickly I could see the lights of the city jerk and slant and spin around me. "Of who?"

"Of me," she said. Then, "And Phil."

25

"I'm supposed to be afraid of this guy?" Phil held up one of the photos Angie'd taken of Evandro.

"Yes," Bolton said.

Phil flapped the photo in his hand. "Well, I'm not."

"Believe me, Phil," I said, "you should be."

He looked at all of us—Bolton, Devin, Oscar, Angie, and myself, packed into Angie's tiny kitchen—and shook his head. He reached under his jacket and pulled out a pistol, pointed it at the floor and checked the load.

"Jesus, Phil," Angie said. "Put it away."

"You got a permit for that?" Devin said.

Phil kept his eyes down, the roots of his hair dark with sweat.

"Mr. Dimassi," Bolton said, "you won't need that. We'll protect you."

Phil said, "Sure," very softly.

We waited as he glanced back at the photo he'd left on the counter and back to the gun in his hand and fear began to seep out his pores. He looked at Angie once and then back at the floor and I could tell he was trying to process it all. He'd come home from work and been met outside his apartment by Federal agents who took him over here, where he was informed that someone he'd never met was determined to stop the beating of his heart, probably within the week.

Eventually he looked up from the floor and his normally olive skin was the color of skim milk. He caught my eye and flashed his boyish grin, shook his head as if we were somehow in this together.

"Okay," he said. "Maybe I'm a little scared."

The bubble of tension that had hung pregnant in the kitchen popped softly and bled out under the back door.

He laid the gun on the oven top and hoisted himself up on the counter, raised a slightly bemused eyebrow at Bolton.

"So tell me about this guy."

An agent stuck his head into the kitchen. "Agent Bolton, sir? No signs that anyone's been tampering with any locks or access areas to the house. We swept for bugs, and it's clean. Back yard is overgrown and shows no evidence it's been walked in for at least a month."

Bolton nodded and the agent left.

"Agent Bolton," Phil said.

Bolton turned back to him.

"Could you please tell me about this guy who wants to kill me and my wife?"

"Ex, Phil," Angie said softly. "Ex."

"Sorry." He looked at Bolton. "Me and my ex-wife, then?"

Bolton leaned against the fridge as Devin and Oscar settled into chairs and I sat up on the counter on the other side of the oven.

"The man's name is Evandro Arujo," Bolton said. "He's a suspect in four murders in the last month. In every one of these cases, he's sent photographs to his intended victims or their loved ones."

"Photos like that one." Phil indicated the picture of him and Angie which lay on the kitchen table, powdered with fingerprint dust.

"Yes."

It had been taken recently. Fallen leaves littering the foreground were multicolored. Phil was listening to something Angie was saying, his head down, hers turned toward him as they walked the stretch of grass and pavement which cut through the center of Commonwealth Avenue.

"But there's nothing threatening about that picture."

Bolton nodded. "Except that it was taken at all and then

sent to Ms. Gennaro. Have you ever heard of Evandro
Arujo?''

''No.''

''Alec Hardiman?''

''Nope.''

''Peter Stimovich or Pamela Stokes?''

Phil thought about it. ''Both sound vaguely familiar.''

Bolton opened the file in his hand, passed photos of
Stimovich and Stokes to him.

Phil's face darkened. ''Wasn't this guy stabbed to death
last week?''

Bolton said, ''A lot worse than stabbed.''

''The papers said stabbed,'' Phil said. ''Something
about his girlfriend's ex-boyfriend being a suspect.''

Bolton shook his head. ''That's the story we leaked.
Stimovich's girlfriend had no ex-boyfriend of note.''

Phil held up the Pamela Stokes photo. ''She dead, too?''

''Yes.''

Phil rubbed his eyes. ''Fuck,'' he said and it came out
in a ripple as if riding a laugh or a shudder.

''Have you ever met either of them?''

Phil shook his head.

''How about Jason Warren?''

Phil looked over at Angie. ''The kid you were trying to
protect? The one who died?''

She nodded. She hadn't spoken much since we arrived.
She chain-smoked and stared out the window facing the
back yard.

''Kara Rider?'' Bolton said.

''She was killed by this asshole too?''

Bolton nodded.

''Jesus.'' Phil came off the counter gingerly, as if not
sure there'd be a floor waiting to meet him. He crossed
stiffly to Angie, took a cigarette from her pack, lit it, and
looked down at his ex-wife.

She watched him the way you'd watch someone who's
just been informed he has cancer, not sure if you should
give him space to lash out or stay close to catch him if he
crumbles.

He placed a hand on her cheek and she leaned into it

and something deeply intimate—some acknowledgment of what rooted them to each other—passed between them.

"Mr. Dimassi, did you know Kara Rider?"

Phil withdrew his hand from Angie's cheek in a slow caress and walked back to the counter.

"I knew her when she was growing up. We all did."

"Had you seen her recently?"

He shook his head. "Not in three or four years." He stared at his cigarette, then flicked ash into the sink. "Why us, Mr. Bolton?"

"We don't know," Bolton said and there was an edge of desperate irritation in his voice. "We're hunting Arujo now and his face will be plastered over every newspaper in New England by tomorrow morning. He can't hide long. We still don't know why he's targeting the people he's targeting, except in the Warren case where we have a possible motive—but at least now we know who he's targeting and we can watch both you and Ms. Gennaro."

Erdham came into the kitchen. "Perimeters of both this house and Mr. Dimassi's apartment building are secure."

Bolton nodded and rubbed his face with fleshy hands.

"Okay, Mr. Dimassi," he said, "here it is. Twenty years ago a man named Alec Hardiman murdered his friend, Charles Rugglestone in a warehouse about six blocks from here. We believe that Hardiman and Rugglestone were responsible for a string of murders at the time, the most notorious of which was Cal Morrison's crucifixion."

"I remember Cal," Phil said.

"Did you know him well?"

"No. He was a couple years older than us. I never heard about a crucifixion, though. He was stabbed."

Bolton shook his head. "Again, a story leaked to the media to buy time and eliminate nutcases who'd confess to killing Hoffa and both Kennedys before breakfast. Morrison was crucified. Six days later, Hardiman went berserk and did the work of ten psychotic men on his partner, Rugglestone. No one knows why, except that both men had large quantities of PCP and alcohol in their systems at the time. Hardiman went to Walpole for life, and twelve

years later he took Arujo and turned him into a psychopath. Arujo was relatively innocent when he went in, but
now he's anything but.''

"You see him," Devin said, "you run, Phil."

Phil swallowed and gave a small nod.

"Arujo's been out for six months," Bolton said. "We
believe Hardiman has a contact on the outside, a second
killer who either fosters Arujo's need to kill or vice versa.
We're not positive about this, but we're leaning that way.
For some unknown reason, Hardiman, Arujo, and this unknown third man are pointing us in one direction only—
this neighborhood. And they're pointing us toward certain
people—Mr. Kenzie, Diandra Warren, Stan Timpson,
Kevin Hurlihy and Jack Rouse—but we don't know why.''

"And these other people—Stimovich and Stokes—
what's their connection to the neighborhood?''

"We believe they might just be random. Thrill kills, no
motivation outside of the kill itself."

"So why are Angie and me being targeted?''

Bolton shrugged. "Could be a ruse. We don't know.
Could be they're just trying to rattle Ms. Gennaro's cage
because she's involved in tracking them. Whoever Arujo's
partner is, they both intended for Mr. Kenzie and Ms. Gennaro to be in this from the start. Kara Rider's role was
specifically designed for that purpose. And then, maybe,''
Bolton said, and looked at me, "he's trying to force Mr.
Kenzie to make that choice Hardiman spoke of.''

Everyone looked at me.

"Hardiman said I'd be forced to make some kind of
choice. He said, 'Not everyone you love can live.' Maybe
my choice is between saving Phil or saving Angie.''

Phil shook his head. "But anyone who knows us knows
we haven't been close in over a decade, Patrick.''

I nodded.

"But you used to be?'' Bolton said.

"Like brothers," Phil said and I tried to detect bitterness
and self-pity in his voice; I only heard a quiet, sad accep-
tance.

"For how long?'' Bolton said.

"From the crib 'til we were, like, twenty. Right?''

I shrugged. "Around there, yeah."

I looked at Angie but she stared at the floor.

Bolton said, "Hardiman said you'd met before, Mr. Kenzie."

"I never met the man."

"Or you don't recall it."

"I'd remember that face," I said.

"If you saw it as an adult, sure. But as a kid?"

He handed Phil two photos of Hardiman—one from '74, the other from the present.

Phil stared at them and I could see he wanted to recognize Hardiman, to have this make sense, for there to be a reason this man had targeted him for death. Eventually he closed his eyes, exhaled loudly, and shook his head.

"I've never seen this guy before."

"You're sure?"

He handed the photos back. "Positive."

"Well, that's too bad," Bolton said, "because he's part of your life now."

An agent drove Phil home at eight, and Angie, Devin, Oscar, and I headed to my place so I could fill an overnight bag.

Bolton wanted Angie to appear vulnerable, alone, but we convinced him that if Evandro or his partner had been studying us, we should appear as normal as possible. And hanging out with Devin and Oscar was something we did at least once a month, though not usually sober.

As for my moving in with Angie, I insisted upon it, whether Bolton gave a shit or not.

Actually, though, he liked the idea. "I've thought you two were sleeping together since we met, so I'm sure Evandro assumes the same."

"You're a pig," Angie said and he shrugged.

Back at my place, we settled into the kitchen while I pulled clothes from my dryer and stuffed them into a gym bag. Looking out my window, I saw Lyle Dimmick finishing up for the day, wiping paint off his hands and placing the brush in a can of thinner.

"So how's your relationship with the Feds?" I asked Devin.

"Deteriorating by the day," he said. "Why do you think we were shut out of the Alec Hardiman visit this afternoon?"

"So you're demoted to babysitting us?" Angie said.

"Actually," Oscar said, "we asked for this specifically. Can't wait to see how you two do in close quarters."

He looked at Devin and they both laughed.

Devin found a stuffed frog Mae had left behind on my counter and picked it up. "Yours?"

"Mae's."

"Sure." He held it up in front of him and made faces at it. "You two might want to keep this guy," he said, "if only to provide some counterbalance."

"We've lived together before," Angie said and scowled.

"True," Devin said, "for two weeks. But you'd just walked out on your husband, Ange. And neither of you spent too much time around each other back then, if I remember. Patrick practically moved into Fenway Park and you were always out nights clubbing your way through Kenmore Square. Now, you'll be forced together for the length of this investigation. Could be months, even years, before it's over." He spoke to the frog. "What do you think of that?"

I looked out the window as he and Oscar giggled and Angie fumed. Lyle descended the scaffolding, radio and cooler grasped awkwardly in one hand, bottle of Jack sticking out of his back pocket.

Watching him, something bugged me. I'd never known him to work past five and it was eight-thirty now. Beyond that, he'd told me this morning that his tooth hurt. . . .

"Got any chips around here?" Oscar said.

Angie stood, went to the cabinets over the oven. "With Patrick, a good food supply is never a safe bet." She opened the left cabinet, rummaged through some cans.

This morning, Mae and I ate breakfast, but that was after I talked to Lyle. After I talked to Kevin. I'd come back in the kitchen, called Bubba . . .

"What'd I tell you?" Angie said to Oscar and opened the middle cabinet. "No chips here, either."

"You two'll get along just fine," Devin said.

After Bubba, I'd asked Lyle to keep his music down because Mae was still asleep. And he said . . .

"Last try." Angie reached for the right cabinet door.

. . . he didn't mind because he had a dentist's appointment and was only working a half day.

I stood up and looked out the window, down into the yard below the scaffolding, as Angie screamed and jumped back from the cabinet.

The yard was empty. "Lyle" was gone.

I looked at the cabinet and the first thing I noticed were eyes staring back at me. They were blue and they were human and they weren't attached to anything.

Oscar grabbed his walkie-talkie. "Get me Bolton. Now."

Angie stumbled back along the table. "Oh, shit."

"Devin," I said, "that housepainter . . ."

"Lyle Dimmick," he said. "We ran a check on him."

"That wasn't Lyle," I said.

Oscar caught on to our conversation as Bolton came over the walkie-talkie.

"Bolton," Oscar said, "fan your men out. Arujo's in the area dressed like a cowboy housepainter. He just left."

"Heading in which direction?"

"I don't know. Fan out your men."

"We're rolling."

Angie and I took my back stairs three at a time and vaulted the porch railing into my back yard, guns drawn. He could have gone in three directions. If he'd gone west through back yards, he'd still be doing it because there wasn't a cross street on this side for four city blocks. If he'd gone north toward the school, he would have run into the FBI. That left south to the block behind mine, or east to Dorchester Avenue.

I took south, Angie went east.

And neither of us found him.

And neither did Devin or Oscar.

And none of the FBI had any luck either.

By nine, a helicopter flew over the neighborhood and they'd brought in dogs, and agents were doing house-to-house searches. My neighbors weren't too keen on me last year when I nearly brought a gang war to their doorsteps; I could only imagine what ancient Celtic curses they were hurling at my soul tonight.

Evandro Arujo had bypassed the security system by posing as Lyle Dimmick. Any neighbor looking out a window and seeing a ladder propped up by my third-floor windows would just have assumed Ed Donnegan now owned my building too and had hired Lyle to paint it.

The motherfucker had been inside my home.

The eyes, it was assumed, belonged to Peter Stimovich, who'd been found without his own, a detail Bolton had omitted.

"Thanks for telling me," I said.

"Kenzie," he said with his perpetual sigh, "I'm not paid to keep you in the loop. I'm paid to bring you into it only insofar as it suits our needs."

Under the eyes, which a federal ME lifted gelatinously from my cupboard and placed in separate plastic bags, I'd been left another note, a white envelope, and a large stack of flyers. The note said, "sonicetoseeUagain" in the same typeface as the first two.

Bolton took the envelope before I could open it, then looked at the other notes I'd received in the last month. "How come you never came forward with these?"

"I didn't know they were from him."

He handed them to a lab tech. "Kenzie and Gennaro's prints are on file with Agent Erdham. Take the bumper stickers too."

"What do you make of the flyers?" Devin said.

There were over a thousand of them in two neat stacks bound by rubber bands, some yellowed by age, some wrinkled, some only ten days old. They all showed photographs in the left corner of missing children, with vital statistics listed below the photos, and they all bore the same legend: Have You Seen Me?

Well, no, I hadn't. Over the years I'd received hundreds

of these flyers in the mail, I suppose, and I always looked closely just to be sure, before tossing them in the trash, but in all that time I'd never seen a face I recognized. Receiving them once a week or so, it was easy to forget about them, but now, leafing through them with rubber gloves bound over my hands so tightly I could feel the sweat bleeding from the pores of my palms, it was overwhelming.

Thousands of them. Gone. A country unto themselves. A half-dreamt litter of misplaced lives. So many of them, I assumed, were dead. Others, I'm sure, had been found, always worse off than when they'd disappeared. The rest of them were cast adrift and floating like a traveling carnival across our landscape, passing like blips through the hearts of our cities, sleeping on stone and grates and discarded mattresses, hollow-cheeked and sallow-skinned, eyes blank and hair filled with nits.

"It's the same as the bumper stickers," Bolton said.

"How so?" Oscar said.

"He wants Kenzie to share his postmodern malaise. That the world is off its hinges and can't be reattached, that a thousand voices shout inane opinions at one another and not one will change any of the others. That we are constantly at cross purposes and there's no holistic, shared accumulation of knowledge. That children disappear every day and we say, 'How tragic. Pass the salt.'" He looked at me. "Sound right?"

"Maybe."

Angie shook her head. "No. Bullshit."

"Excuse me?"

"Bullshit," she said. "Maybe that's part of it, but it isn't all of his message. Agent Bolton, you've accepted that we probably have two killers, not just one little Evandro Arujo on our hands. Correct?"

He nodded.

"This second one, he's been waiting or, hell, incubating for two decades. That's the prevailing theory, right?"

"That's it."

She nodded. She lit a cigarette and held it up. "I've

tried to quit smoking several times. You know how much effort that takes?''

''You know how much I would have appreciated it at this moment if you'd succeeded?'' Bolton said, ducking from the cloud of smoke which filtered over the kitchen.

''Too bad.'' She shrugged. ''My point is that we all have our addiction of choice. The one thing that gets us to our soul. That *is* us, in a way. What couldn't you live without?''

''Me?'' he said.

''You.''

He smiled and looked away, slightly embarrassed. ''Books.''

''Books?'' Oscar laughed.

He turned on him. ''What's wrong with that?''

''Nothing, nothing. Go on, Agent Bolton. You the man.''

''What kind of books?'' Angie said.

''The great ones,'' Bolton said, a little sheepish. ''Tolstoy, Dostoyevsky, Joyce, Shakespeare, Flaubert.''

''And if they were outlawed?'' Angie said.

''I'd break the law,'' Bolton said.

''You wild man,'' Devin said. ''I am appalled.''

''Hey.'' Bolton glared at him.

''What about you, Oscar?''

''Food,'' Oscar said and patted his belly. ''Not health food, but real tasty heart-attack food. Steaks, ribs, eggs, chicken-fried steak and gravy.''

Devin said, ''What a shock.''

''Damn,'' Oscar said. ''Just went and made myself hungry.''

''Devin?''

''Cigarettes,'' he said. ''Booze probably.''

''Patrick?''

''Sex.''

''You,'' Oscar said, ''are a whore, Kenzie.''

''Fine,'' Angie said. ''These are the things that get us through, make life bearable. Cigarettes, books, food, cigarettes again, booze, and sex. That's us.'' She tapped the

stack of flyers. "What about him? What can't he go without?"

"Killing," I said.

"That'd be my guess," she said.

"So," Oscar said, "if he's been forced to take a vacation for twenty years—"

"No way he'd make it," Devin said. "No fucking
way."

"But he hasn't been calling attention to his kills," Bolton said.

Angie lifted a stack of flyers. "Until now."

"He's been killing kids," I said.

"For twenty years," Angie said.

Erdham came in at ten to report that a man wearing a
cowboy hat and driving a stolen red Jeep Cherokee had
blown a red light at an intersection on Wollaston Beach.
Quincy Police had given chase and lost him on a steep
curve of 3A in Weymouth, which he maneuvered and they
didn't.

"Chasing a fucking Jeep on a curve?" Devin said in
disbelief. "These Mario Andrettis slide out, but a somer-
sault machine like a Cherokee holds the curve?"

"That's the size of it. Last seen heading south over the
bridge by the old naval yard."

"What time was that?" Bolton said.

Erdham checked his notes. "Nine thirty-five on Wollaston. Nine forty-four when they lost him."

"Anything else?" Bolton said.

"Yeah," Erdham said slowly, looking at me.

"What?"

"Mallon?"

Fields stepped into the kitchen holding a stack of small
tape recorders and at least fifty feet of coaxial cable.

"What's that?" Bolton said.

"He bugged the entire apartment," Fields said, refusing
to look at me. "The recorders were fastened by electrical
tape to the underside of the landlord's porch. No tapes
inside. The cables fed into a junction port up on the roof,
mixed in with the cable TV and electrical and phone lines.

He ran the cables down the side of the house with the rest of the wires and you'd never notice unless you were looking for it.''

"You're shitting me," I said.

Fields gave me an apologetic shake of his head. " 'Fraid not. By the amount of dust and mildew I found on these cables, I'd say he's been listening to everything going on inside your apartment for at least a week.'' He shrugged. "Maybe more.''

26

"**Why didn't he** take off the cowboy hat?" I said as we drove back to Angie's.

I'd left my apartment behind gratefully. Currently it was filled with technicians and cops stampeding around, ripping up the floorboards, covering it in a cloud of fingerprint dust. One bug was found in the living room baseboard, another attached to the underside of my bedroom dresser, a third sewed into the kitchen curtain.

I was trying to distract myself from the deep incision made by my total lack of privacy, and that's when I fixated on the cowboy hat.

"What?" Devin said.

"Why was he still wearing the cowboy hat when he blew the light in Wollaston?"

"He forgot to take it off," Oscar said.

"If he was from Texas or Wyoming," I said, "I'd say okay. But he's a Brockton boy. He's going to be aware of a cowboy hat on his head while he drives. He knows there're Feds after him. He's got to know that once we found the eyes we'd figure he was impersonating Lyle."

"Yet he's still wearing the hat," Angie said.

"He's laughing at us," Devin said after a moment. "He's letting us know we're not good enough to get him."

"What a guy," Oscar said. "What a swell fucking guy."

Bolton had his agents stashed in the apartments on either side of Phil and in the Livoskis' house across from

Angie's house and the McKays' behind it. Both families had been paid well for the imposition and put up downtown at the Marriott, but even so, Angie called them both and apologized for the inconvenience.

She hung up and took a shower while I sat in the dining room at her dusty table with the light off and the shades drawn. Oscar and Devin were in a car down the street and they'd left two walkie-talkies behind. They sat on the table in front of me, hard and square, and their twin silhouettes looked like transmitters to another galaxy in the soft dark.

When Angie came out of the shower, she wore a gray Monsignor Ryan Memorial High School T-shirt and red flannel shorts that swam around her thighs. Her hair was wet and she looked tiny as she placed ashtray and cigarettes on the table and handed me a Coke.

She lit a cigarette. Through the flame I had a momentary glimpse of how drawn and afraid her face was.

"It'll be okay," I said.

She shrugged. "Yeah."

"They'll get him before he ever comes near this place."

Another shrug. "Yeah."

"Ange, he won't get to you."

"His batting average has been pretty good so far."

"We're very good at protecting people, Ange. We can protect each other, I think."

She exhaled a missile of smoke over my head. "Tell that to Jason Warren."

I put my hand on hers. "We didn't know what we were dealing with when we pulled out of the Warren case. We do now."

"Patrick, he got into your place pretty easily."

I wasn't prepared to even think about that right now. The violation I'd been living with since Fields held up those tape recorders was total and ugly.

I said, "My place didn't have fifty agents—"

Her hand turned under mine so that our palms met and she tightened her fingers around my wrist. "He's beyond reason," she said. "Evandro. He's . . . nothing like we've ever dealt with. He's not a person, he's a force, and I think if he wants me bad enough, he'll get to me."

She sucked hard on her cigarette; the coal flared and I could see red pockets under her eyes.

"He won't—"

"Sssh," she said and removed her hand from mine. She stubbed out the cigarette and cleared her throat. "I don't want to sound like a wimp here or the pathetic little woman, but I need to hold someone now and I . . ."

I came out of my chair and knelt between her legs and she wrapped her arms around me and pressed the side of her face against mine and dug her fingers into my back.

Her voice was a warm whisper in my ear. "If he should kill me, Patrick—"

"I won't—"

"If he should, you have to promise me something."

I waited, felt the terror rattling up through her chest and squirming out the pores of her skin.

"Promise me," she said, "that you'll stay alive long enough to kill him. Slowly. For days, if you can manage it."

"What if he gets to me first?" I said.

"He can't kill us both. No one's that good. If he gets to you before me"—she leaned back a bit so her eyes could meet mine—"I'll paint this house with his blood. Every last inch of it."

She went to bed a few minutes later and I turned on a small light in the kitchen and read through the files Bolton had given me on Alec Hardiman, Charles Rugglestone, Cal Morrison, and the murders of 1974.

Both Hardiman and Rugglestone looked numbingly normal. Alec Hardiman's only distinguishing characteristic was that, like Evandro, he was extremely handsome, almost to a degree you'd consider feminine. But there are plenty of handsome men in the world, several of whom hold no sway over anyone.

Rugglestone, with his widow's peak and long face, looked more like a West Virginia coal miner than anything else. He didn't look particularly friendly, but he didn't look like a man who crucified children and disembowled winos.

The faces told me nothing.

People, my mother once claimed, cannot be fully understood, only reacted to.

My mother was married to my father for twenty-five years so she probably did a lot of reacting in her time.

Right now, I had to agree with her. I'd spent time with Hardiman, read how he'd turned from an angelic boy into a demon overnight, and nothing could tell me why.

Less was known about Rugglestone. He'd served in Vietnam, been honorably discharged, came from a small farm in East Texas and hadn't had any contact with his family in over six years by the time he was killed. His mother was quoted as calling him "a good boy."

I turned a page of the Rugglestone file, saw diagrams of the empty warehouse where Hardiman had inexplicably turned on him. The warehouse was gone now, a supermarket and dry cleaner's in its place.

The diagram showed me where Rugglestone's body had been found, tied to a chair, stabbed, beaten, and burned. It showed where Hardiman had been found by Detective Gerry Glynn, who was responding to an anonymous call, curled naked into a fetal position in the old dispatch office, his body saturated with Rugglestone's blood, the ice pick four feet away from him.

How had Gerry felt, responding to an anonymous tip, walking in and finding Rugglestone's body and then finding his partner's son curled up with the murder weapon?

And who had called in the anonymous tip?

I flipped another page, saw a yellowed photo of a white van registered to Rugglestone. It looked old and uncared for and it was missing the windshield. The interior of the van, according to the report, had been hosed down within the last twenty-four hours prior to Rugglestone's death, the panels wiped clean, yet the windshield had been demolished only recently. Glass filled the driver and passenger seats, glistened in rocks on the floor. Two cinderblocks rested in the center of the van floor.

Somebody, probably kids, had tossed the cinderblocks through the windshield while the van was parked outside the warehouse. Committing vandalism while Hardiman committed murder only a few feet away.

Maybe the vandals had heard noise from inside, recognized it as something insidious and called in the anonymous tip.

I looked at the van for another minute, and I felt something akin to dread.

I've never liked vans. For some reason which I'm sure Dodge and Ford would love to eradicate, I associate them with sickness—with drivers who molest children, with rapists idling in supermarket parking lots, with childhood rumors of killer clowns, with evil.

I turned the page, came upon Rugglestone's toxicology report. He'd had large quantities of both PCP and methylamphetamine in his system, enough to keep him awake for a week. He'd counterbalanced these with a blood alcohol level of .12, but even that much booze, I was sure, couldn't override the effects of so much artificial adrenaline. His blood would have been electrified.

How did Hardiman, twenty-five pounds lighter, manage to tie him down?

I flipped another page, found the postmortem report of Rugglestone's injuries. Even though I'd heard both Gerry Glynn and Bolton's accounts, the magnitude of damage done to Rugglestone's body was almost impossible to comprehend.

Sixty-seven blows from a hammer found under a chair in the dispatch office with Alec Hardiman. Blows came from a height of seven feet and from as close as six inches. They came from the front, the back, the left, and the right.

I opened the Hardiman file, placed the two side by side. At his trial, Hardiman's defense lawyer had argued that his client had suffered nerve damage to his left hand as a child, that he wasn't ambidexterous, that he couldn't have swung a hammer with such force using his left hand.

The prosecution pointed out the evidence of PCP in Hardiman's system, and judge and jury agreed that the drug could give an already deranged man the strength of ten.

No one believed the defense attorney's argument that the PCP in Hardiman's system was negligible compared

to the amount found in Rugglestone's and that Hardiman
hadn't added to it with speed, but cut into it with a combination of morphine and seconol. Add the alcohol to the
mix, and Hardiman was lucky he could stand that afternoon, never mind perform physical feats of such staggering
magnitude.

He'd burned Rugglestone in sections over the course of
four hours. He started with the feet, and just before the
fire had worked its way up to the lower calves, he doused
it, went back to work with the hammer or the ice pick or
a straight razor, which was used to lacerate Rugglestone's
flesh over one hundred and ten times, also from right and
left angles. Then he burned the lower calves and knees,
doused the flames again, and so on.

Examination of Rugglestone's wounds had revealed the
presence of lemon juice, hydrogen peroxide, and table salt.
Facial and head lacerations had shown evidence of two
facial compounds—Ponds cold cream and white Pan-Cake
makeup.

He'd been wearing makeup?

I checked the Hardiman file. At the time of his arrest,
Hardiman, too, had been found with traces of white Pan-
Cake compound in the roots of the hair closest to his face,
as if he'd wiped it off but hadn't had time to wash his
hair.

I rifled through Cal Morrison's file. Morrison had left
his house at three on an overcast afternoon to head for a
sandlot football game at Columbia Park. His house was
less than a mile away, and while police had checked every
possible route he could've taken, they'd found no witnesses who'd seen Cal past the point when he waved to a
neighbor on Sumner Street.

Seven hours later, he'd been crucified.

Forensics teams had found evidence that Cal had spent
several hours lying on his back on a rug. A cheap rug, the
kind cut in sections unprofessionally, so that tufts of it
stayed in his hair. The rug had also contained sediments
of oil and brake fluid.

Under the nails of his left hand, they found type A blood
and the chemicals used to form white Pan-Cake makeup.

Detectives had momentarily entertained the idea that they could be looking for a female killer.

Hair fibers and plaster casts of footprints quickly discounted the theory.

Makeup. Why were Rugglestone and Hardiman wearing makeup?

27

Around eleven, I called Devin on the walkie-talkie
and told him about the makeup.

"Bothered me too at the time," he said.

"And?"

"And it ended up being just one of those incidental
things. Hardiman and Rugglestone *were* lovers, Patrick."

"They were homosexual, Devin—that doesn't mean
they were cross-dressers or fems. There's nothing in any
of these files about them ever being seen wearing
makeup."

"I don't know what to tell you, Patrick. It never added
up to shit. Hardiman and Rugglestone killed Morrison and
then Hardiman killed Rugglestone, and if they were wearing pineapples on their heads and dressed in purple tu-tus
at the time, it wouldn't change those facts."

"Something's wrong in those files, Devin. I know it."

He sighed. "Where's Angie?"

"Asleep."

"Alone?" He chuckled.

"What?" I said.

"Nothing."

In the backround I could hear Oscar's guttural guffaw.

"Spit it out," I said.

Devin's amused sigh followed the squawk of the walkie-
talkie. "Me and Oscar just made a little side bet."

"Pertaining to?"

"You and your partner and how long you'll be able to

stay cooped up together before one of two things happens.''

''And those things would be?''

''I say you'll kill each other, but Oscar says you'll get buck wild before the weekend.''

''Nice,'' I said. ''Aren't you guys late for your political correctness training session?''

''Police department calls it Human Sensitivity Dialogues,'' Devin said, ''and me and Sergeant Lee decided we're sensitive enough.''

''Of course.''

''You sound like you don't believe us,'' Oscar chimed in.

''Oh, no. You're posterboys for the New Sensitive Male.''

''Yeah?'' Devin said. ''Think it'll help us pick up chicks?''

After I hung up with Devin, I called Grace.

I'd been stalling most of the night. Grace was mature and understanding, but even so I wasn't sure how I'd explain moving in with Angie to her. I'm not a particularly possessive person, yet I'm not sure how well I'd take it if Grace called me and said she was shacking up for a few days with a male friend.

As it happened, the issue didn't come up immediately.

''Hi,'' I said.

Silence.

''Grace?''

''I'm not sure I feel like talking to you, Patrick.''

''Why?''

''You damn well know why.''

''No,'' I said, ''I don't.''

''If you're going to play games with me, I'll hang up.''

''Grace, I have *no* idea what you're talking—''

She hung up.

I stared at the phone for a minute, considered banging it into the wall several times. Then I took a few deep breaths and called her back.

''What?'' she said.

"Don't hang up."

"That depends on how much bullshit you try to sling."

"Grace, I can't respond to something if I don't know what I did wrong."

"Is my life in danger?" she said.

"What're you talking about?"

"Answer the question. Is my life in danger?"

"Not as far as I know."

"Then why are you having me followed?"

Canyons opened in the pit of my stomach and ice melted against my spine.

"I'm not having you followed, Grace."

Evandro? Kevin Hurlihy? The mystery killer? Who?

"Bullshit," she said. "That psychotic in the trenchcoat didn't get this idea all on his own and just go—"

"Bubba?" I said.

"You know very fucking well Bubba."

"Grace, slow down. Tell me exactly what happened."

She exhaled slowly through the receiver. "I'm in the St. Botolph Restaurant with Annabeth and my daughter—my *daughter,* Patrick—and there's a guy sitting at the bar checking me out. And he's not being really subtle about it, okay, but he wasn't threatening either. And then—"

"What did this guy look like?"

"What? He looked sort of like Larry Bird before Madison Avenue got a hold of him—tall, very pale, horrible hair, long jaw, and big Adam's apple."

Kevin. Fucking Kevin. Sitting a few feet away from Grace and Mae and Annabeth.

Considering various ways he could crack their spines.

"I'll kill him," I whispered.

"What?"

"Go on, Grace. Please."

"So he finally works up his nerve and gets up from the bar and comes over to the table to try out whatever pathetic pickup line he'd use, and then, then your certifiable mutant friend comes out of nowhere and drags him out of the restaurant by his hair. In full view of thirty people, he banged the man's face off a hydrant several times."

"Oh, my," I said.

" 'Oh my'?'' she said. "That's all you can say. *Oh my?* Patrick, the hydrant was just on the other side of the window from our table. Mae saw the whole thing. He smashed that man's face in, and she watched. She's been crying all day. And that poor, poor man, he—"

"Is he dead?"

"I don't *know*. Some friends of his pulled up in a car and that . . . fucking *lunatic* and some midget henchman of his just stood back and watched as they dragged the man into a car and drove off."

"That 'poor, poor man' Grace, is a contract killer for the Irish Mafia. His name's Kevin Hurlihy and he told me this morning he'd hurt you to fuck up my life."

"You're joking."

"I wish I were."

A long hard silence hung over the line between us.

"And now," Grace said eventually, "he's in my life? In my daughter's life, Patrick? In my daughter's?"

"Grace, I—"

"What?" she said. "What, what, what, what? Huh? That freak in the trenchcoat, he's supposed to be my guardian angel? He's supposed to make me feel safe?"

"Sort of."

"You brought this into my life. This violence. You . . . Jesus!"

"Grace, listen—"

"I'll call you later," she said and her voice was distant and small.

"I'm at Angie's."

"What?"

"I'm staying here tonight."

"At Angie's," she said.

"It's possible she's the next target of the guy who killed Jason Warren and Kara Rider."

"At Angie's," she said again. "I'll call you later maybe."

She hung up.

No good-bye. No "take care." Just a "maybe."

* * *

It took her twenty-two minutes to call back. I was sitting at the table, staring at photographs of Hardiman and Rugglestone and Cal Morrison until they all blurred in my head and joined as one, the same questions nagging my brain, the answers, I knew, lying in front of me, but floating simultaneously, just beyond the limits of my vision.

"Hi," she said.

"Hi."

"How's Angie?" she said.

"Scared."

"I don't blame her." She sighed into the phone. "How are you, Patrick?"

"Okay, I guess."

"Look, I won't apologize for being pissed earlier."

"I don't expect you to."

"I want you in my life, Patrick . . ."

"Good."

"—but I'm not sure I want your life in my life."

"I don't understand," I said.

The line hummed, empty, and I found myself eyeing Angie's cigarette pack, wanting one very badly.

"Your life," Grace said. "The violence. You seek it out, don't you?"

"No."

"Yes," she said softly. "The other day, I went into the library. I looked up those newspaper articles on you from last year. When that woman got killed."

"And?"

"And I read about you," she said. "And I saw the photos of you kneeling by that woman and the man you shot. You were covered in blood."

"It was hers."

"What?"

"The blood," I said. "It was Jenna's. The woman who got killed. Maybe some from Curtis Moore, the guy I wounded. But not mine."

"I know," she said. "I know. But as I was looking at pictures of you and reading about you, I felt, well, 'Who is this guy?' I don't know the guy in those photos. I don't know the guy who shoots people. I don't know this person. It was so strange.''

"I don't know what to say, Grace.''

"Have you ever killed anyone?'' Her voice was sharp. I didn't answer at first.

Eventually, I said, "No.''

So easy, the first lie I ever told her.

"You're capable of it though, aren't you?''

"We all are.''

"Maybe so, Patrick. Maybe so. But most of us don't choose situations that force the issue. You do.''

"I didn't choose this killer in my life, Grace. I didn't choose Kevin Hurlihy in it either.''

"Yes,'' she said, "you did. Your whole life is a conscious attempt to confront violence, Patrick. You can't beat him.''

"Who?''

"Your father.''

I reached for the pack of cigarettes, slid them across the table until they were in front of me.

"I'm not trying to,'' I said.

"Could've fooled me.''

I removed a cigarette from the pack, tapped it in the center of the fan of photos of Hardiman and Rugglestone's burned corpse, a crucified Cal Morrison.

"Where's this conversation going, Grace?''

"You hang around with people like . . . Bubba. And Devin and Oscar. And you live in a world of such violence and surround yourself with violent people.''

"It'll never touch you.''

"It already has. Shit. And I know you'd die before you'd let anyone harm me physically. I know that.''

"But . . .''

"But at what price? What happens to you? You can't clean sewers for a living and come home smelling like soap, Patrick. It'll eat at you, as long as you do this work. It'll hollow you out.''

"Has it so far?''

For a long dark moment, I heard only silence.

"Not yet," she said. "But it's a miracle. How many miracles do you have left, Patrick?"

"I don't know," I said and my voice was raw.

"I don't either," she said. "But I don't like the odds."

"Grace—"

"I'll talk to you soon," she said and her voice stumbled around the *soon*.

"Okay."

"G'night."

She hung up, and I listened to the dial tone. Then I crushed the cigarette between my fingers and pushed the pack away from me.

"Where are you?" I asked Bubba when I finally reached him on his cell phone.

"Outside one of Jack Rouse's chop shops in Southie."

"Why?"

"Because Jack's in there and so's Kevin and so's most of their crew."

"You fucked up Kevin good today," I said.

"Christmas came early, yeah." He chuckled. "Ol' Kev's sucking his boiled dinner through a straw for a while, buddy."

"You broke his jaw?"

"Nose, too. Got the two-for-one special."

I said, "But, Bubba—in front of Grace?"

"Why not? Lemme tell you something, Patrick, that's one ungrateful woman you're dating."

"You were expecting a tip?" I said.

"I was expecting a smile," he said. "A thank you or just a grateful roll of the eyes would have been acceptable."

"You bludgeoned a man in front of her daughter, Bubba."

"So? He had it coming."

"Grace didn't know that and Mae's too young to understand."

"What can I say, Patrick? Bad day for Kev, good day for me. Oh fucking well."

I sighed. Trying to talk social conventions and concepts

of morality to Bubba is like trying to explain cholesterol
to a Big Mac.

"Is Nelson still watching Grace?" I said.

"Like a hawk."

"Until all this is over, Bubba, he can't take his eyes off
her."

"Don't think he wants to. I think he's falling in love
with the woman."

I almost shuddered. "So what're Kevin and Jack doing?"

"Packing. Looks like they're taking a trip."

"Where?"

"I don't know. We'll find out."

I could hear a slightly deflated edge in his voice.

"Hey, Bubba."

"Yeah?"

"Thanks for looking out for Grace and Mae."

His tone lightened. "Anytime. You'd do the same for
me."

Probably a bit more delicately, but . . .

"Of course," I said. "Should you maybe lay low a
while?"

"Why?"

"Kevin might come back at you."

He laughed. "So fucking what?" He snorted. "Kevin."

"What about Jack? He'll probably have to save face,
whack you for banging up one of his men."

Bubba sighed. "Jack is all bullshit, Patrick. That's
something you never got. He's made his bones, he's dangerous, sure, but only to people who're vulnerable. Not to
someone like me. He knows to take me out he'd have to
use fucking humungous amounts of manpower and be
ready for an all-out war if he misses me. He's like . . .
when I served in Beirut, they gave us rifles with no bullets.
That's Jack. He's a rifle with no bullets. And I'm this
deranged Shiite Muslim motherfucker driving a truck full
of bombs around his embassy. I'm death. And Jack's too
pussy to fuck with death. I mean, this is the guy who got
his first taste of power running EEPA."

"Eepa?" I said.

"E-E-P-A. The Edward Everett Protection Association. The neighborhood vigilante group. 'Member? Back in the seventies?''

"Vaguely.''

"Shit, yeah. They were all good citizens, all geared up to protect their neighborhood from niggers and spics and people who looked at 'em funny. Hell, they rousted me twice. Your old man gave me an ass-whupping, boy, that—''

"My old man?''

"Yeah. Seems funny now, looking back on it. Hell, the whole group only lasted maybe six months, but they made punks like me pay when we got caught, I'll give 'em that.''

"When was this?'' I said as some of it came back to me a bit—the meetings in my father's living room, the sound of loud, self-righteous voices and ice clinking in glasses and hollow threats delivered in reference to the car thieves and B&E operators and graffiti artists of the neighborhood.

"I don't know.'' Bubba yawned. "I was stealing hubcaps back then, so I was probably just out of the crib. We were maybe, like, eleven or twelve. Probably seventy-four or -five. Right around busing, yeah.''

"And my father and Jack Rouse . . .''

"Were the leaders. And then there was, like, lemme see—Paul Burns and Terry Climstich and some small guy always wore a tie, didn't live in the neighborhood long, and like, oh yeah, two women. I'll never forget it—they bust me clipping caps off Paul Burns's car and they're putting the boots to me, no big deal, but I look up and I see two chicks doing it. I mean, Christ.''

"Who were the women?'' I said. "Bubba?''

"Emma Hurlihy and Diedre Rider. You believe that? A couple of chicks kicking my ass. Crazy world. Huh?''

"Gotta go, Bubba. Call you soon. Okay?''

I hung up and dialed Bolton.

28

"What did these people do?" Angie said.

We were standing over her coffee table with Bolton, Devin, Oscar, Erdham, and Fields, all of us staring down at copies of a photo Fields had acquired by waking the editor of *The Dorchester Community Sun,* a local weekly that had been covering the neighborhoods since 1962.

The photo was from a puff piece done on neighborhood watch groups the week of June 12, 1974. Under the headline NEIGHBORS WHO CARE, the article gushed about the daring exploits of the EEPA, as well as the Adams Corner Neighborhood Watch in Neponset, the Savin Hill Community League, the Field's Corner Citizens Against Crime, and the Ashmont Civic Pride Protectors.

My father was quoted in the third column: "I'm a fireman, and one thing firemen know is that you have to stop a fire in the low floors, before it gets out of control."

"Your old man had a feel for the sound bite," Oscar said. "Even back then."

"It was one of his favorite sayings. He'd had years of practice with it."

Fields had blown up the photo of the EEPA members and there they stood on the basketball court of the Ryan Playground, trying to look mean and friendly at the same time.

My father and Jack Rouse were kneeling at the center of the group, on either side of an EEPA sign with shamrocks in the upper corners. They both looked like they were posing for football cards, as if emulating the stance of defensive linemen, fists dug into the ground, opposite hands holding up the sign.

Behind them stood a very young Stan Timpson, the only person wearing a tie, followed from left to right by Diedre Rider, Emma Hurlihy, Paul Burns, and Terry Climstich.

"What's this?" I said and pointed at a tiny bar of black to the right of the photo.

"The photographer's name," Fields said.

"Can we magnify it somehow, get a look at it?"

"I'm ahead of you, Mr. Kenzie."

We turned and looked at him.

"Diandra Warren took that photograph."

She looked like death.

Her skin was the color of white formica and the clothes hanging to her skeletal frame were beseiged by wrinkles.

"Tell me about the Edward Everett Protection Association, Diandra. Please," I said.

"The what?" She stared at me with bleary eyes. As she stood before me, I felt I was looking at someone I'd known in youth but hadn't seen in several decades, only to discover that time had not only worn her down, but had laid waste to her without mercy.

I placed the photograph on the bar in front of her.

"Your husband, my father, Jack Rouse, Emma Hurlihy, Diedre Rider."

"That was fifteen or twenty years ago," she said.

"Twenty," Bolton said.

"Why didn't you recognize my name?" I said. "You knew my father."

She cocked her head, looked at me as if I'd just claimed she was a long-lost sister.

"I never knew your father, Mr. Kenzie."

I pointed at the photo. "There he is, Doctor Warren. Standing a foot away from your husband."

"That's your father?" She stared at the photo.

"Yes. And that's Jack Rouse beside him. And just over his left shoulder, that's Kevin Hurlihy's mother."

"I didn't . . ." She peered at the faces. "I didn't know these people by name, Mr. Kenzie. I took this photo because Stan asked me to. This silly group was something he was involved with, not me. I wouldn't even allow them to have meetings at our house.''

''Why not?'' Devin said.

She sighed and waved a frail hand. ''All that macho posturing under the guise of community service. It was so ridiculous. Stan would try to convince me how good it would look on his résumé, but he was no different than the rest, forming a street gang and calling it socially benevolent.''

Bolton said, ''Our records indicate that you filed for separation from Mr. Timpson in November of nineteen seventy-four. Why?''

She shrugged and yawned into her fist.

''Doctor Warren?''

''Jesus Christ,'' she said sharply. ''Jesus Christ.'' She looked up at us and for a moment life returned to her, and then just as suddenly dissipated. She dropped her head into her hands and limp strands of hair fell over her fingers.

''Stanley,'' she said, ''showed his true colors that summer. He was a Roman basically, convinced of his own moral superiority. He'd come home with blood on his shoe from kicking some unlucky car thief and try to tell me it was about justice. He became ugly . . . sexually, as if I were no longer his wife but his purchased courtesan. He changed from an essentially decent man with some unanswered questions about his manhood into a storm trooper.'' She stabbed her finger into the photo. ''And it was this group that caused it. This ridiculous, silly group of fools.''

''Was there any one particular incident that you can recall, Doctor Warren?''

''In what way?''

''Did he ever tell you war stories?'' Devin said.

''No. Not after we fought about the blood on his shoe that time.''

''And you're sure it was a car thief's blood?''

She nodded.

''Doctor Warren,'' I said and she looked up at me, ''if

you were estranged from Timpson, why did you help the DA's office during the Hardiman trial?''

"Stan had nothing to do with the case. He was prosecuting prostitutes in night court back then. I had helped the DA's office once before when a defendant was claiming insanity, and they liked the result, so they asked me to interview Alec Hardiman. I found him to be sociopathic, given to delusions of grandeur, and paranoid, but legally sane, fully aware of the difference between right and wrong.''

"Was there any connection between EEPA and Alec Hardiman?'' Oscar said.

She shook her head. "None that I ever knew of.''

"Why did EEPA disband?''

She shrugged. "I think they just got bored. I really don't know. I'd moved out of the neighborhood by then. Stan followed a few months later.''

"There's nothing else you can remember from that time?''

She stared at the photograph for a long time.

"I remember,'' she said wearily, "that when I took this picture I was pregnant, and I was feeling nauseous that day. I told myself it was the heat and the baby growing inside me. But it wasn't. It was them.'' She pushed the photo away. "There was a sickness to that group, a corruption. I had the feeling, as I took this picture, that they'd hurt someone very badly some day. And like it.''

In the RV, Fields removed his headphones and looked at Bolton. "The prison shrink, Doctor Dolquist, has been trying to reach Mr. Kenzie. I can patch him through.''

Bolton nodded, turned to me. "Put it on speaker.''

I answered the phone on the first ring.

"Mr. Kenzie? Ron Dolquist.''

"Doctor Dolquist,'' I said, "may I put you on speaker phone?''

"Certainly.''

I did, and his voice picked up a metallic quality, as if it were bouncing off several satellites at once.

"Mr. Kenzie, I've spent a lot of time going over all the

notes I've kept of my sessions with Alec Hardiman over the years, and I think I may have stumbled on something. Warden Lief tells me you believe Evandro Arujo is working on the outside at Hardiman's behest?"

"That's correct."

"Have you considered the possibility that Evandro has a partner?"

There were eight of us packed in the RV, and we all looked at the speaker simultaneously.

"Why would you say that, Doctor?"

"Well, it was something I'd forgotten about, but the first few years he was here, Alec spent a lot of time talking about someone named John."

"John?"

"Yes. At the time, Alec was working hard to have his conviction overturned on the grounds of insanity, and he pulled out all the stops to convince the psychiatric staff that he was delusional, paranoid, schizophrenic, you name it. This John, I believed, was just his attempt to establish multiple personality syndrome. After nineteen seventy-nine, he never mentioned him again."

Bolton leaned over my shoulder. "What changed your mind, Doctor?"

"Agent Bolton? Oh. Well, at the time I did allow for the possibility that John was a manifestation of his own personality—a fantasy Alec, if you will, who could walk through walls, disappear in mist, that sort of thing. But as I went through my notes last night, I kept coming upon references to a trinity, and I recalled that he'd told you, Mr. Kenzie, that you'd be transformed into a 'man of impact' by—"

"The 'Father, Son, and Holy Ghost,'" I said.

"Yes. Often, when Alec spoke of this John, he called him Father John. Alec would be the son. And the ghost—"

"Arujo," I said. "He vanishes into mist."

"Exactly. Alec's grasp of the true meaning of the Blessed Trinity leaves a lot to be desired, but it's like a lot of mythological and religious imagery with him—he takes what he needs and molds it to suit his purposes, tosses out the rest."

"Tell us more about John, Doctor."

"Yes, yes. John, according to Alec, disguises himself as his polar opposite. Only with his victims and his closest intimates—Hardiman, Rugglestone, and now Arujo—does he remove the mask, lets them see the 'pure fury of his true face,' as Alec put it. When you look at John, you see what *you want to see* in a person; you see benevolence and wisdom and gentleness. But John is none of these things. According to Alec, John is a 'scientist' who studies human suffering first hand for clues to the motives behind creation."

"The motives behind creation?" I said.

"I'm going to read to you from notes I took during a session with Alec in September of seventy-eight, shortly before he stopped mentioning John entirely. These are Alec Hardiman's words:

" 'If God is benevolent, then why do we have such a capacity to feel pain? Our nerves are supposed to alert us to dangers; that's the biological reason for pain. Yet we can feel pain far past the level necessary to alert us to danger. We can feel acute levels of pain beyond description. And not only do we have *this* capacity, as all animals do, but we further have the mental capacity to suffer it again and again emotionally and psychically. No other animal shares that capacity. Does God hate us that much? Or does He love us that much? And if neither, if it's just an arbitrary flaw in our DNA, then isn't the point of all this pain He's given us to inure us? Make us as indifferent to the suffering of others as He is? And so shouldn't we emulate Him, do as John does—revel in and prolong and improve upon pain and our methods of inflicting it? John understands that this is the essence of purity.' "

Dolquist cleared his throat. "End quote."

Bolton said, "Doctor?"

"Yes?"

"Right off the top of your head, describe John."

"He's physically powerful, and if you met him, you'd be able to see that, but it wouldn't be overt. He's not a bodybuilder, you understand, just a strong man. He appears to others to be quite sane and rational, maybe even wise. I would expect that he's beloved in his community, a doer of good deeds on a small level.''

"Is he married?'' Bolton said.

"I doubt it. Even he'd have to know that no matter how good his facade, his spouse and his children would sense his disease. He may have been married once, but not anymore.''

"What else?''

"I don't think he's been able to stop killing for the past two decades. It would be impossible for him. I believe he chose only to keep his kills quiet.''

We all looked at Angie and she tipped an imaginary hat.

"What else, Doctor?''

"The primary thrill for him is the kills. But secondary to that, and only barely, is the joy he gets living behind his mask. John stares out at you from behind that mask and laughs at you from behind the cover it provides. It's very sexual to him, and that's why he has to finally take it off after all these years.''

"I'm not following you,'' I said.

"Think of it as a prolonged erection, if you will. John has been waiting to climax for over twenty years now. As much as he enjoys that erection, his need to ejaculate is even more pressing.''

"He wants to be caught.''

"He wants to *expose* himself. It's not the same thing. He wants to take off the mask and spit in your face as you're looking into his *real* eyes, but that's not to say he'll accept handcuffs willingly.''

"Anything else, Doctor?''

"Yes. I think he knows Mr. Kenzie. I don't mean *knows of* him. I mean, he's known him for a long time. They've met. Face to face.''

"Why do you say that?'' I said.

"A man like this establishes odd relationships, but no matter how odd, they're extremely important to him. It would be paramount to him that he know one of his pursuers. For whatever reason, he chose you, Mr. Kenzie. And he let you know by having Hardiman send for you. You

and John know each other, Mr. Kenzie. I'd stake my reputation on it.''

"Thank you, Doctor," Bolton said. "I'm assuming the
reason you read from your notes is because you have no
intention of releasing them to us."

"Not without a court order," Dolquist said, "and even
then you'd be in for a battle. If I find anything else in there
which I think can stop these murders, I'll call immediately.
Mr. Kenzie?"

"Yes?"

"If I could have a word with you alone?"

Bolton shrugged and I shut off the speaker, cradled the
phone to my ear. "Yes, Doctor?"

"Alec was wrong."

"About?"

"About my wife. He was wrong."

"That's good to hear," I said.

"I just wanted that . . . to be clear. He was wrong," Dolquist repeated. "Good-bye, Mr. Kenzie."

"Good-bye, Doctor."

"Stan Timpson is in Cancun," Erdham said.

"What?" Bolton said.

"It's correct, sir. Took the wife and kids down there
three days ago for a little R and R."

"A little R and R," Bolton said. "He's the district attorney of Suffolk County during a serial-killer crisis. And
he goes to Mexico?" He shook his head. "Go get him."

"Sir? I'm not a field agent."

Bolton pointed his finger at him. "Send someone, then.
Send two agents, and bring him back."

"Under arrest, sir?"

"For questioning. Where's he staying?"

"His secretary said he was staying at the Marriott."

"There's a *but* here. I can feel it."

Erdham nodded. "He never checked in there."

"Four agents," Bolton said. "I want *four* agents on the
next plane to Cancun. And bring his secretary in, too."

"Yes, sir." Erdham picked up a phone as the RV turned
on to the expressway.

"They've all gone for cover, haven't they?" I said.

Bolton sighed. "It appears so. Jack Rouse and Kevin Hurlihy can't be found. Diedre Rider hasn't been seen since her daughter's funeral."

"What about Burns and Climstich?" Angie said.

"Both deceased. Paul Burns was a baker who stuck his head in one of his own ovens back in seventy-seven. Climstich died of a coronary in eighty-three. Neither left descendants." He dropped the photo into his lap and stared at it. "You look just like your father, Mr. Kenzie."

"I know," I said.

"You said he was a bully. Was that all?"

"How do you mean?"

"I need to know what the man was capable of."

"He was capable of anything, Agent Bolton."

Bolton nodded, leafed through his file. "Emma Hurlihy was committed to the Della Vorstin Home in seventy-five. Before that, there was no record of metal illness in her family, nor did she evidence any disturbing behavior until late seventy-four. Diedre Rider's first arrest for drunk and disorderly occurred in February of seventy-five. After that, she was getting picked up by police on regular basis. Jack Rouse went from being a slightly corrupt corner-store owner to the head of the Irish Mafia in five years. Reports I obtained from the Organized Crime Bureau as well as BPD's Major Crime Unit say that Rouse's rise to power was allegedly the bloodiest in the history of the Irish Mafia here. He attained power by killing anyone who got in his way. How did this happen? How did an extremely low-level bookie get the stones to become a made man overnight?"

He looked at us and we shook our heads.

He turned another page in the file. "District Attorney Stanley Timpson, now here's an interesting guy. Graduated near the bottom of his class at Harvard. Reached only the middle of his law school class at Suffolk. Failed his bar twice before he finally passed. The only reason he got in the DA's office at all was because of Diandra Warren's father's connections, and his early performance evaluations were low. Then, starting in seventy-five, he turns into a tiger. He earns a reputation, in night court mind you, for refusing to cut deals. He graduates to superior court, more of the same. People begin to fear him, and the DA's office starts throwing him felony work, and his star continues rising. By eighty-four he is considered the most feared prosecutor in New England. Again, how did this happen?''

The RV swung off the expressway in my neighborhood and headed for St. Bart's Church, where Bolton was holding his morning debriefing.

"Your father, Mr. Kenzie, runs for city council in seventy-eight. The only thing he seems to do while in office is aquire a reputation for ruthlessness and power-craving which would have made Lyndon Johnson blush. He is, by all accounts, a negligible public servant, but a ferocious politician. Again, we have an obscure person—a fire fighter, for Christ's sake—who rises far beyond any normal expectations one would hold for him.''

"What about Climstich?'' Angie said. "Burns killed himself, but did Climstich show signs of a transformation?''

"Mr. Climstich became something of a hermit. His wife left him in the fall of seventy-five. Divorce affidavits attest that Mrs. Climstich cited irreconcilable differences after twenty-eight years of marriage. She stated that her husband had become withdrawn, morbid, and addicted to pornography. She further stated that said pornography was particularly vile in nature and that Mr. Climstich seemed obsessed with bestiality.''

"Where are you going with all this, Agent Bolton?'' Angie asked.

"I'm saying something very strange happened to these people. They either became successful—rose beyond any reasonable expectation of their stations in life, or''—he ran his index finger over Emma Hurlihy and Paul Burns—"their lives fell apart and they imploded.'' He looked at Angie as if she held the answer. "Something altered these people, Ms. Gennaro. Something transformed them.''

The RV pulled up behind the church and Angie looked down at the photograph and said it again:

"What did these people do?"

"I don't know," Bolton said and shot a wry smile my way. "But as Alec Hardiman would say, it definitely had impact."

29

Angie and I walked to a donut shop on Boston Street with Devin and Oscar following at a discreet distance.

We were both well beyond tired and the air danced with transparent bubbles which popped before my eyes.

We barely spoke as we sipped our coffee by the window and stared out at the gray morning. All the pieces seemed to be falling together in our puzzle, but somehow, the puzzle itself still refused to take on a recognizable image.

EEPA, I had to assume, had had some sort of encounter with either Hardiman, Rugglestone, or potentially, the third mystery killer. But what kind of encounter? Did they see something that Hardiman or the mystery killer believed compromised them? If so, what could that have been? And why not just knock off the original members of the EEPA back in the mid-seventies? Why wait twenty years to go after their descendants, or the loved ones of their descendants?

"You look beat, Patrick."

I gave her a weary smile. "You too."

She sipped her coffee. "After this debriefing, let's go home to bed."

"That didn't sound right."

She chuckled. "No, it didn't. You know what I mean."

I nodded. "Still trying to get me in the sack after all these years."

"You wish, slick."

"Back in seventy-four," I said, "what possible reasons could a man have for wearing makeup?"

"You're stuck on this point, aren't you?"

"Yeah."

"I don't know, Patrick. Maybe they were very vain men. Maybe they were covering up crow's feet."

"With white Pan-Cake?"

"Maybe they were mimes. Or clowns. Or goth freaks."

"Or KISS fans," I said.

"That, too." She hummed a bar of "Beth."

"Shit."

"What?"

"The connection's there," I said. "I can feel it."

"You mean to the makeup?"

"Yes," I said. "And the connection between Hardiman and EEPA. I'm certain. It's staring us in the face and we're too tired to see it."

She shrugged. "Let's go see what Bolton has to say at his debriefing. Maybe that'll make sense of everything."

"Sure."

"Don't be a pessimist," she said.

Half Bolton's men were working this neighborhood for information, others were staking out Angie's place, Phil's apartment, and mine, too, so Bolton had gotten permission from Father Drummond to gather in the church.

As it usually did in the mornings, the church bore the burnt aroma of incense and candle wax from the seven o'clock mass, a stronger scent of pine solvent and oil soap in the pews, and the sad smell of wilting chrysanthemums. Mottled dust spun in the pewter shafts of light that slanted through the east windows over the altar and disappeared in the middle rows of pews. A church, on a cold fall morning, with its smoky browns and reds, its whiskey-hued air and multicolored stained glass just warming to a frigid sun, always feels as the founders of Catholicism probably intended—like a place cleansed and purified of earthly imperfection, a place meant to hear only whispers and the rustling hush of fabric against a bending knee.

Bolton sat on the altar in the gilded red priest's celebrant chair. He'd moved it forward a bit to prop his feet on the chancel rail while agents and several cops sat in the front four pews, most holding pens, paper, or tape recorders at the ready.

"Glad you could make it," Bolton said.

"Don't do that," Angie said, glancing at his shoes.

"What?"

"Sit on the altar in the priest's chair with your feet on the rail."

"Why not?"

"Some people would find it offensive."

"Not me." He shrugged. "I'm not Catholic."

"I am," she said.

He watched her to see if she was joking, but she stared back so calmly and firmly that he knew she wasn't.

He sighed and got out of the chair, placed it back where it belonged. As we headed back for the pews, he crossed the altar and climbed into the raised pulpit.

"Better?" he called.

She shrugged, as Devin and Oscar took their places in the pew ahead of us. "It'll do."

"So glad I'm no longer offending your delicate sensibilities, Ms. Gennaro."

She rolled her eyes at me as we took seats in the fifth pew and I once again felt an odd flush of admiration for my partner's faith in a religion I had long ago abandoned. She doesn't advertise it or announce it at every turn, and she has nothing but scorn for the patriarchal hierarchy that runs the church, but she nevertheless holds firm to a belief in the religion and ritual with a quiet intensity that can't be shaken.

Bolton was quickly taking a liking to the pulpit. His thick hands caressed the Latin words and Roman art carved ornately in its sides and his nostrils flared slightly as he looked down on his audience.

"The previous night's developments include the following: One, a search of Evandro Arujo's apartment yielded photographs discovered under a floorboard below a steel radiator. Sightings of men fitting Arujo's description have tripled since seven o'clock this morning, when the daily papers carried two photographs of him—one with goatee, one without. Most sightings seem baseless. However, five alleged sightings have occurred in the lower South Shore and two more recent sightings in Cape Cod, around Bourne. I have deployed agents who searched the upper South Shore last night to head for the lower edges and the Cape and Islands. Roadblocks have been installed along both sides of Routes 6, 28, and 3, as well as I-495. Two sightings put Arujo in a black Nissan Sentra, but again, the validity of any of these sightings is always suspect in the wake of sudden public hysteria.''

"The Jeep?" an agent said.

"As yet, nothing. Maybe he's still in it, maybe he ditched it. A red Cherokee was stolen from the parking lot of the Bayside Expo Center yesterday morning, and we're working under the assumption that this is the car Evandro was spotted in yesterday. License plate number is 299-ZSR. Wollaston police got a partial plate number yesterday off the Jeep they chased, which matches."

"You mentioned photographs," Angie said.

Bolton nodded. "Several photographs of Kara Rider, Jason Warren, Stimovich, and Stokes. These photos are similar to the ones sent to the victims' loved ones. Arujo is, beyond any doubt now, the prime suspect in these killings. Other photos found are of unknown people who we must assume are intended victims. The good thing, ladies and gentlemen, is that we may be able to predict where he'll strike next."

Bolton coughed into his hand. "Forensic evidence," he said, "has now unequivocally determined that there are two killers involved in the four deaths of this investigation. Bruises on Jason Warren's wrists confirm he was held by one person while another sliced his face and chest with a straight razor. Kara Rider's head was gripped tightly by two hands while two other hands shoved an ice pick into her larynx. Wounds to Peter Stimovich and Pamela Stokes confirm the presence of two killers."

"Any idea where they were killed?" Oscar said.

"Not at this time, no. Jason Warren was killed in the South Boston warehouse. The rest were killed somewhere else. For whatever reason, the killers felt a need to kill Warren quickly." He shrugged. "We have no idea why.

The other three had only minimal amounts of hydroclorophyl in their systems, which suggests they were only
unconscious while the killers transported them to the site
where they were killed.''

Devin said, "Stimovich was tortured for at least an hour,
Stokes for twice that. They made a lot of noise.''

Bolton nodded. "We're looking for an isolated murder
site.''

"Which leaves how many sites?'' Angie said.

"Countless. Tenements, abandoned buildings, environ-
mentally protected wetlands, a half dozen small islands off
the coast, closed prisons, hospitals, warehouses, you name
it. If one of these killers has been lying dormant for two
decades, we can assume he's planned everything in detail.
He could have easily outfitted his home with a soundproof
basement or suite of rooms.''

"Has there been any further proof to suggest the killer
who's been lying dormant may have been killing children?''

"No definitive proof,'' Bolton said. "But of the one
thousand one hundred and sixty-two flyers you received,
covering over ten years, two hundred eighty-seven children
are confirmed dead. Two hundred eleven of those cases
officially unsolved.''

"How many in New England?'' an agent said.

"Fifty-six,'' Bolton said quietly. "Forty-nine unsolved.''

"Percentage-wise,'' Oscar said, "that's an awfully high
number.''

"Yes,'' Bolton said wearily, "it is.''

"How many died in ways similar to the current victims?''

"In Massachusetts,'' Bolton said, "none, although there
were several stabbing victims, several with hand perfora-
tions, so we're still studying those. We have two cases of
violence so extreme it could bear match-up with the current victims.''

"Where?''

"One in Lubbock, Texas, in eighty-six. One outside of
Miami, in unincorporated Dade County, in ninety-one.''

"Amputation?"

"Affirmative."

"Body parts missing?"

"Again, affirmative."

"How old were the kids?"

"Lubbock was fourteen and male. The one in unincorporated Dade was sixteen and female." He cleared his throat and patted his chest pockets for his inhaler, but didn't find it. "Further, as you were all apprised last night, Mr. Kenzie provided us with a possible connection between the murders of seventy-four and those of the present day. Gentlemen, it looks like our killers have an ax to grind with children of EEPA members, but we haven't, as yet, connected the group to Alec Hardiman or Evandro Arujo. We don't know why, but we must assume the connection is primary."

"What about Stimovich and Stokes?" an agent asked. "Where's their connection?"

"We believe there is none. We believe they are two of the 'guiltless' victims the killer spoke of in his letter."

"What letter?" Angie said.

Bolton looked down at us. "The one found in your apartment, Mr. Kenzie. Under Stimovich's eyes."

"The one you wouldn't let me read."

He nodded, glanced down at his notes, adjusted his glasses. "During a search of Jason Warren's dormitory room, a diary belonging to Mr. Warren was discovered in a locked desk drawer. Copies will be provided to agents upon request, but for the moment, I read from an entry dated October 17, the date Mr. Kenzie and Ms. Gennaro observed Warren with Arujo." He cleared his throat, obviously uncomfortable assuming a voice that wasn't his own. " 'E. was in town again. For a little over an hour. He has no idea of his power, has no idea how attractive his fear of self is. He wants to make love to me, but he can't completely face his own bisexuality yet. I understand, I told him. It took me forever. Freedom is painful. He touched me for the first time, and then he left. Back to New York. And his wife. But I'll see him again. I know it. I'm drawing him in.' "

Bolton was actually blushing when he finished.

"Evandro's the lure," I said.

"Apparently," Bolton said. "Arujo leads them in and his mystery partner snares them. All accounts of Arujo—from fellow prisoners to other entries in this diary to Kara Rider's roommate to people in the bar the night he picked up Pamela Stokes—mention the same thing over and over: The man possesses a powerful sexuality. If he's smart enough—and I know he is—to erect hurdles around it for prospective victims to jump, then they ultimately agree to his terms of secrecy and meetings in out-of-the-way places. Hence, the alleged wife he told Jason Warren about. God only knows what he told the others, but I think he sucked them in by pretending to be sucked in by them."

"A male Helen of Troy," Devin said.

"Harry of Troy," Oscar said and a few agents chuckled.

"Further investigation of crime scene evidence has yielded the following: One—both killers weigh between one hundred sixty and one hundred eighty pounds. Two—since Evandro Arujo's shoe size is a match for the size nine and a half we found at the Rider murder scene, his partner is the one with the size eight. Three—the second killer has brown hair and is quite strong. Stimovich was an extremely powerful man and someone subdued him before administering toxins; Arujo is not particularly powerful, so we must assume that the partner is.

"Fourth—reinterviewing of all who had tangential contact with these victims has yielded the following: All but Professor Eric Gault and Gerald Glynn have airtight alibis for all four murders. Both Gault and Glynn are currently being interrogated at JFK and Gault has failed a polygraph. Both men are strong, and both are small enough to wear a size eight shoe, though both claim to wear size nines. Any questions?"

"Are they suspects?" I said.

"Why do you ask?"

"Because Gault recommended me to Diandra Warren and Gerry Glynn provided me with crucial information."

Bolton nodded. "Which only confirms our suspicion of the mystery killer's pathology."

"Which is?" Angie said.

"Doctor Elias Rottenheim from the Behavioral Sciences division has posited this theory concerning the mystery, dormant killer. Also refer to transcripts of this morning's conversation with Doctor Dolquist. I'm quoting here from Doctor Rottenheim: 'Subject conforms to all criteria prevalent among those suffering the dual affliction of narcissistic personality disorder combined with a shared psychotic disorder in which subject is the inducer or primary case.'"

"English would be nice," Devin said.

"The gist of Doctor Rottenheim's report is that a sufferer of narcissistic personality disorder, in this case our dormant killer, is under the impression that his acts exist at a level of grandiosity. He deserves love and admiration simply for *existing*. He evidences all the hallmarks of the sociopath, is obsessed with his own sense of entitlement and believes himself to be special or even godlike. The killer who suffers the shared psychotic disorder is able to convince others that his disorder is perfectly logical and natural. Hence the word *shared*. He's the primary case, the inducer of *others'* delusions."

"He's convinced Evandro Arujo or Alec Hardiman," Angie said, "or both, that killing is good."

"It seems so."

"So how does that profile apply to either Gault or Glynn?" I asked.

"Gault pointed you to Diandra Warren. Glynn pointed you to Alec Hardiman. From a benign perspective, such actions would suggest that neither man could be involved since he's trying to help. However, remember what Dolquist said—this guy has a relationship with you, Mr. Kenzie. He's daring you to catch him."

"So Gault or Glynn could be Arujo's mystery partner?"

"I think anything's possible, Mr. Kenzie."

The November sun was fighting a losing battle with the encroachment of thickening layers of slate in the sky. In direct sunlight, you felt warm enough to remove your jacket. Outside of it, you were ready to look for a parka.

"In the letter," Bolton said as we crossed the school-yard, "the writer said some of the victims would be 'worthy' and others would meet the reproach of the guiltless."

"What's that mean?" I said.

"It's a line from Shakespeare. In *Othello,* Iago states, 'All guiltless meet reproach.' Several scholars argue that this is the very moment in which Iago passes from a criminal with motive into a creature beset by what Coleridge called 'motiveless malignancy.'"

"You're losing me," Angie said.

"Iago had a reason to wreak vengeance on Othello, slim as it was. But he had no reason to destroy Desdemona or gut the Venetian army of talent and officers the week before a Turkish onslaught. Yet, the argument goes, he became so impressed with his own capacity for evil that it became, in and of itself, enough motive to destroy anyone. He starts the play by pledging to destroy the guilty—Othello and Cassio—but by the fourth act, he's set on destroying *anyone*—'all guiltless meet reproach'—simply because he can. Simply because he enjoys it."

"And this killer—"

"May be a similar creature. He kills Kara Rider and Jason Warren because they are the children of his enemies."

"But killing Stimovich and Stokes?" Angie said.

"No motive at all," he said. "He does it for fun."

A light, misting rain speckled our hair and jackets.

Bolton reached into his briefcase and handed Angie a piece of paper.

"What's this?"

Bolton squinted into the mist. "A copy of the killer's letter."

Angie held the letter away from her, as if its contents might be contagious.

"You wanted in the loop," Bolton said. "Right?"

"Yes."

He pointed at the letter. "Now you're in the loop." He shrugged and walked back toward the schoolyard.

30

patrick,

the issue is pain. understand this.

initially, there wasn't any grand plan. I killed someone almost by accident, really, and I felt all those things you're supposed to feel—guilt, revulsion, fear, shame, self-hatred. I took a bath to clean Myself of her blood. sitting in the tub, I vomited, but I didn't move. I sat there as the water stank with her blood and My shame, the stink of My mortal sin.

then I drained the tub and showered and . . . went on. what do humans do, after all, once they've done something immoral or inconceivable? they go on. there's no other choice if you've slipped past the grasp of the law.

so I went about My life and then those feelings of shame and guilt went away. I thought they'd linger forever. but they didn't.

and I remember thinking, it can't be this simple. but it was. and pretty soon, more out of curiosity than anything, I killed someone else. and it felt, well, nice. calming. the way a cold glass of beer must feel to an alcoholic coming off a dry spell. the way the first night of sexual intercourse must feel to lovers who've been kept apart.

taking another life is a lot like sex actually. sometimes its a transcendent, orgasmic act. other times, it's just a so-so, okay, no big deal, but what're you going to do? sort of sensation. but it's never less than interesting. it's something you remember.

I'm not sure why I'm writing you, patrick. who I am as I write this isn't who I am during My day job, nor who I am when I kill. I wear a lot of faces, and some you'll never see, and some you'd never want to. I've seen a few of your faces—a pretty one, a violent one, a reflective one, some others—and I wonder which you'll wear if we ever meet with carrion between us. I do wonder.

all guiltless, I've heard, will meet reproach. maybe so. and so be it. I'm not sure the worthy victims are worth all the trouble actually.

I dreamed once that I was stranded on a planet of the whitest sand. and the sky was white. that's all there was—Me, spilling drifts of white sand as wide as oceans, and a burning white sky. I was alone. and small. after days of wandering, I could smell My own rot, and I knew I'd die in these drifts of white under a hot sky, and I prayed for shade. and eventually it came. and it had a voice and a name. "Come," Darkness said, "come with me." but I was weak, I was rotting, I couldn't rise to My knees. "Darkness," I said, "take My hand. Take Me away from this place." and Darkness did.

so you see what I'm teaching you, patrick?

best,
The Father

"Oh," Angie said, tossing the letter on her dining room table, "this is good. This guy sounds sane." She scowled at the letter. "Jesus."

"I know."

"People like this," she said, "exist."

I nodded. In and of itself that was horrifying. There's enough evil in the average person who gets up every day, goes to work, thinks of himself as good as much as possible. But maybe he cheats on his wife, maybe he fucks over a co-worker, maybe, in his heart of hearts, he thinks there's a race or two of people who are inferior to him.

Most of the time, our powers of rationalization being what they are, he never has to face it. He can go to his death thinking he's good.

Most of us can. Most of us do.

But the man who wrote this letter had embraced evil. He enjoyed the pain of others. He didn't rationalize his hate, he reveled in it.

And reading his letter was, above all else, tiring. In a uniquely sordid way.

"I'm beat," Angie said.

"Me too."

She looked at the letter again and touched her palms to her shoulders, closed her eyes.

"I want to say it's inhuman," she said. "But it isn't."

I looked at the letter. "It's human all right."

I'd made myself a bed on her couch and was trying to get comfortable when she called to me from the bedroom.

"What?" I said.

"C'mere a second."

I walked to the bedroom, leaned against the doorway. She was sitting up in the bed, the down comforter spread over and around her like a rose pink sea.

"You okay on the couch?"

"Fine," I said.

"Okay."

"Okay," I said and headed back for the couch.

"Because—"

I turned back. "Huh?"

"It's big, you know. Plenty of room."

"The couch?"

She frowned. "The bed."

"Oh." I narrowed my eyes at her. "What's up?"

"Don't make me say it."

"Say what?"

Her lips turned up in an attempt at a grin and it came out looking horrible. "I'm afraid, Patrick. Okay?"

I have no idea what it cost her to say that.

"Me too," I said and came into the bedroom.

Sometime during our nap, Angie's body shifted and I opened my eyes to find her leg curled over mine, wrapped tightly between my thighs. Her head was tucked into my shoulder, her left hand draped across my chest. Her breath fluttered against my neck, rhythmic with sleep.

I thought of Grace, but for some reason I couldn't picture her fully in my head. I could see her hair and her eyes, but when I tried to form an image of her face, whole, it wouldn't come.

Angie groaned and her leg tightened against mine.

"Don't," she mumbled very softly. "Don't," she repeated, still asleep.

This is the way the world ends, I thought, and faded back to dreams.

Late in the day, Phil called and I answered on the first ring.

"You awake?" he said.

"I'm awake."

"Thought I'd drop by."

"Angie's asleep."

"That's cool. I just . . . sitting alone, waiting for this guy to try something, it's driving me nuts."

"Come on by, Phil."

While we slept, the temperature had dropped fifteen degrees and the sky turned to granite. Wind roared down from Canada and poured across the neighborhood, rattled windows and bucked the bodies of cars parked along the avenue.

The hail unleashed itself shortly afterward. When I went into Angie's bathroom for a shower, it spit against the windows like sand carried by sweeps of water off the ocean. By the time I was drying off, it spewed against windows and walls as if the wind were ejecting nails and lug nuts.

Phil brewed coffee while I changed into fresh clothes in the bedroom, then come back into the kitchen.

"She still asleep?" he said.

I nodded.

"Goes out like Spinks fighting Tyson, don't she? One minute she's all bright-eyed energy, the next she's crashed like she ain't slept in a month." He poured some coffee into a mug. "Always been that way, that girl."

I got myself a Coke, sat at the table. "She'll be okay, Phil. No one's going to get to her. Or you either."

"Mmm." He brought his coffee to the table. "You sleeping with her yet?"

I leaned back in my chair, cocked my head, and raised an eyebrow at him. "You're way out of line, Phil."

He shrugged. "She loves you, Patrick."

"Not that way. You never understood that."

He smiled. "I understood a lot, Patrick." He cupped the mug in both hands. "I know she loved me. I'm not arguing that. But she's always been half in love with you, too."

I shook my head. "All those years you beat her, Phil, guess what? She never, not once, fooled around on you."

"I know that."

"Really?" I leaned forward a bit, lowered my voice. "Didn't keep you from calling her a whore on a regular basis. Didn't stop you from pummeling the shit out of her when you felt in the mood. Did it?"

"Patrick," he said softly, "I know what I was. What I . . . am." He frowned and stared into his coffee cup. "I'm a wife beater. And a drunk. And that's that. There you go." He smiled bitterly at the cup. "I beat that woman." He looked over his shoulder toward her bedroom. "I beat her and I earned her hate, and she'll never trust me again.

Ever. We'll never be . . . friends. Not on any level near what we used to be.''

"Probably not.''

"Yeah. So, however I became what I became, I did become that thing. And I've lost her and I deserved to because she's better off without me in her life in the long run.''

"I don't think she's planning to ever boot you out of her life, Phil.''

He gave me that bitter smile. "That's classic Ange, though. Let's face it, Patrick. Angie, for all her fuck-you, I-don't-need-anyone attitude, can't say good-bye. To anything. That's her weakness. Why do you think she still lives in her mother's house? With most of the furniture that was here when she was a kid?''

I looked around, saw her mother's ancient black pots in the pantry, her doilies on the couch in the den, realized Phil and I were sitting in chairs her parents had purchased from the Marshall Field's in Uphams Corner that had burned down sometime in the late sixties. Something can sit in front of you your whole life, waiting to be noticed for what it is, and often you're sitting too close to really see it.

"You got a point,'' I admitted.

"Why do you think she never left Dorchester? A girl as smart and beautiful as her, the only time she's been out of state was on our honeymoon. Why do you think it took her twelve years to leave me? Anyone else would have been gone in six. But Angie can't walk away. It's her flaw. Probably has something to do with her sister being the opposite.''

I'm not sure what kind of look I gave him, but he held up a hand in apology.

"Touchy subject,'' he said. "I forgot.''

"What's your point here, Phil?''

He shrugged. "Angie can't say good-bye, so she'll work hard to keep me in her life.''

"And?''

"And I won't let her. I'm an albatross around her neck. Right now, I need us to—I dunno—heal a bit more. Get some closure. So she knows completely that I was the bad guy. It was all, all, all me. Not her.''

"And when that's done?"

"I'm gone. A guy like me, I can get work anywhere. Rich people are always remodeling their homes. So soon, I'm hitting the road. I think you two deserve your shot.''

"Phil—"

"Please, Pat. Please,'' he said. "This is me. We been friends since forever. I know you. And I know Angela. You might have something real nice with Grace now and I think that's terrific. I do. But know yourself.'' He bumped his elbow into mine and looked hard in my eyes. "Okay? For once in your life, buddy, face yourself. You've been in love with Angie since kindergarten. And she's been in love with you.''

"She married you, Phil.'' I bumped his elbow back.

"Because she was pissed at you—''

"That's not the only reason.''

"I know. She loved me, too. For a while, maybe, she even loved me more. I don't doubt it. But we can love more than one thing simultaneously. We're human, so we're messy.''

I smiled, realized it was the first time I'd smiled naturally in Phil's presence in a decade. "We are that.''

We looked at each other and I could feel the old blood rippling within us—the blood of sacred bonds and shared boyhoods. Neither Phil nor I ever felt accepted in our homes. His father was an alcoholic and an unregenerate womanizer, a guy who slept with every woman in the neighborhood and made sure his wife knew it. By the time Phil was seven or eight, his household was a DMZ of flying plates and accusations. Anytime Carmine and Laura Dimassi were in the same room, it was about as safe as Beirut, and in one of the great perverse misinterpretations of their Catholic faith, they refused to divorce or live apart. They liked the daily skirmishes and nightly makeup sessions of passionate lovemaking that had them thumping against the wall separating their bedroom from their son's.

I was out of my house as much as possible for different reasons, so Phil and I took refuge together, and the first home we both felt comfortable in was an abandoned pigeon coop we found on the roof of an industrial garage on Sudan Street. We cleaned all the white shit out and reinforced it with boards from old pallets and slid some abandoned furniture in there, and pretty soon we picked up other strays like ourselves—Bubba, Kevin Hurlihy for a while, Nelson Ferrare, Angie. The Little Rascals with class rage and larcenous hearts and complete lack of respect for authority.

As he sat across from me at his ex-wife's table, I could see the old Phil again, the only brother I ever had. He grinned, as if remembering it all himself, and I could hear the sounds of our childhood laughter as we roamed the streets and ran like wolves over rooftops and tried to stay three steps ahead of our parents. Jesus, we'd laughed a lot for kids who should have been permanently angry.

Outside Angie's house, the clatter of hail sounded like a thousand sticks beating against the roof.

"What happened to you, Phil?"

His grin disappeared. "Hey, you—"

I held up a hand. "No. I'm not judging. I'm wondering. Like you told Bolton, we were like brothers. We *were* brothers, for Christ's sake. And then you went south on me. When'd all the hate take over, Phil?"

He shrugged. "I never forgave you for some things, Pat."

"Like what?"

"Well . . . You and Angie, you know . . ."

"Sleeping together?"

"Her losing her virginity to you. You were my best friends and we were all so Catholic and repressed and sexually skewed. And you two, that summer, you distanced from me."

"No."

"Oh, yes." He chuckled. "Oh, yes. Left me with Bubba and Frankie Shakes and a bunch of other pituitary cases with mush for brains. And then—what was it, in August?"

I knew what "it" was. I nodded. "August fourth."

"Down at Carson Beach, you two, well, did the deed. And then, genius that you were, you treated her like shit.

And she came running to me. And I was second choice. Again.''

"Again?"

"Again." He leaned back in his chair and spread his arms in an almost apologetic gesture. "Hey," he said, "I always had charm and I always had my looks, but you had instinct."

"You kidding me?"

"No," he said. "Come on, Pat. I was always thinking things through too much, and you were doing them. You were the first guy to realize Angie wasn't just one of the guys anymore, the first to stop hanging out on the corner, the first to—"

"I was restless. I was—"

"You were instinct," he said. "You always could size up any situation before the rest of us and act on it."

"Bullshit."

"Bullshit?" He chuckled. "Come on, Pat. It's your gift. 'Member those spooky fucking clowns in Savin Hill?"

I smiled and shivered at the same time. "Oh, yeah."

He nodded, and I could tell that two decades later he still felt the fear that had gripped us for weeks after our encounter with the clowns.

"If you hadn't thrown that baseball through their windshield," he said, "who knows if we'd even be here today."

"Phil," I said, "we were kids with overactive imaginations and—"

He shook his head violently. "Sure, sure. We were kids and we were on edge because Cal Morrison had been killed that week and we'd been hearing rumors about those clowns since forever and blah, blah, blah. All that's true, but we were *there,* Patrick. Me and you. And you know what would have happened to us if we'd gotten into that van with them. I can still see it. Shit. The grime and grease all over the fenders, that smell coming from the open window—"

The white van with the broken windshield in the Hardiman file.

"Phil," I said. "Phil. Jesus Christ."

"What?"

"The clowns," I said. "You just said it yourself. It was the week Cal was killed. And then, shit, I hummed the baseball through their windshield—"

"Damn straight you did."

"And told my father." I'd raised my hand to my mouth, half covering it because it was wide open in shock.

"Wait a second," he said and I could see that the same knowledge prickling like fire ants against my spinal column had invaded Phil. His eyes lit up like flares.

"I marked the van," I said. "I fucking marked it, Phil, without even knowing it. And EEPA found it."

He stared at me and I could see that he knew it too.

"Patrick, you're saying—"

"Alec Hardiman and Charles Rugglestone were the clowns."

In the days and weeks after Cal Morrison was killed, if you were a kid in my neighborhood, you were afraid.

You were afraid of black guys, because Cal had supposedly been killed by one. You were afraid of mangy, grizzled men who stared too long at you on the subway. You were frightened by cars that paused at intersections for too long after the light had turned green or seemed to slow as they approached you. You were terrified by the homeless and the dank alleys and dark parks in which they slept.

You were afraid of almost everything.

But nothing frightened the kids in my neighborhood as much as clowns.

It seemed so silly, in retrospect. Killer clowns rampaged in pulp fiction and bad drive-in movies. They lived in the realm of vampires and prehistoric monsters stomping Tokyo. Fictions conjured up to scare the only targets gullible enough to be afraid of them—children.

As I reached adulthood, I was no longer afraid of my closet when I woke in the middle of the night. The creaks of the old house I grew up in held no terror either; they were simply creaks—the plaintive whine of aging wood and the relaxed sighs of settling foundations. I grew to fear almost nothing except the barrel of a pistol pointed in my direction or the sudden potential for violence in the eyes of bitter drunks and men realizing their entire lives had passed unnoticed by all but themselves.

But as a child, my fear was embodied by the clowns.

I'm not sure how the rumor started—maybe around a fire at summer camp, maybe after one of our group had seen one of those bad drive-in movies—but by the time I was six or so, every kid knew about the clowns, though no one could actually claim to have seen them.

But the rumors were rampant.

They drove a van and carried bags of candy and bright balloons, and bouquets of flowers exploded out from their oversized sleeves.

They had a machine in the back of that van that knocked kids out in under a second, and once you were unconscious, you never woke back up.

While you were out, but before you died, they took turns on your body.

Then they cut your throat.

And because they were clowns and their mouths were painted that way, they were always smiling.

Phil and I were almost at the age when we would have stopped fearing them, the age when you knew there was no Santa Claus and you probably weren't the long-lost son of a benevolent billionaire who'd return some day to claim you.

We were on our way back from a Little League game in Savin Hill, and we'd lingered until near dark, playing war games in the woods behind the Motley School, climbing the decrepit fire escape to the roof of the school itself. By the time we climbed down, the day had grown long and chilly, the shadows lengthening against walls and spreading out hard against bare pavement as if they'd been carved there.

We began the walk down Savin Hill Avenue as the sun disappeared entirely and the sky took on the cast of polished metal, tossed the ball back and forth to keep the gathering cold at bay and ignored the rumbles in our stomachs because they meant we'd have to go home sooner or later, and home, ours, at least, sucked.

The van slid up behind us as we started down the slope of the avenue by the subway station, and I remember very distinctly noticing that the entire avenue was empty. It lay before us in that sudden emptiness that comes to a neighborhood around dinner time. Though it wasn't yet dark, we could see orange and yellow squares of light in several homes fronting the avenue, and a lone plastic hockey puck curled against the hubcap of a car.

Everyone was in for dinner. Even the bars were quiet.

Phil rifled the ball with his shotgun arm and it rose a bit more than I first expected; I had to jump and twist myself to snag it. When I came down I'd twisted myself to the side and that's when I saw the white face and blue hair and wide red lips staring out the passenger window at me.

"Nice catch," the clown said.

There was only one way kids in my neighborhood responded to clowns.

"Fuck you," I said.

"Nice mouth," the clown said, and I didn't like the way he smiled when he said it, his gloved hand resting on the outside of the door panel.

"Real nice," the driver said. "Real, real nice. Your mother know you talk that way?"

I was no more than two feet from that door, frozen on the pavement, and I couldn't move my feet. I couldn't take my eyes off the clown's red mouth.

Phil, I noticed, was a good ten feet down the hill, frozen too, it seemed.

"You guys need a ride?" the passenger clown said.

I shook my head, my mouth dry.

"He's not so mouthy all of a sudden, this kid."

"No." The driver craned his head around his partner's neck so that I could see his bright red hair and the bursts of yellow around his eyes. "You two look cold."

"I can see goose pimples," the passenger said.

I moved two steps to my right, and my feet felt like they were sinking into wet sponge.

The passenger clown glanced quickly down the avenue and back toward me.

The driver looked in the rearview and his hand disappeared from the wheel.

"Patrick?" Phil said. "Let's go."

"Patrick," the passenger clown said slowly, as if he

were licking the word. "That's a nice name. What's your last name, Patrick?"

Even now, I have no idea why I answered. Total fear, perhaps, a desire to buy time, but even then, I should have known to give a false name, but I didn't. I had some desperate feeling, I guess, that if they knew my last name, they'd see me as a person, not a victim, and I'd receive mercy.

"Kenzie," I said.

And the clown gave me a seductive smile, and I heard the door latch unlock like a round ratcheting into a shotgun.

That's when I threw the baseball.

I don't recall planning it. I merely took two steps to my right—thick, slow steps as if I were in a dream—and I think initially I was aiming for the clown himself as he started to open his door.

Instead, the ball sailed out of my hand and someone said, "Shit!" and there was a loud popping noise as the ball buried itself in the center of the windshield and the glass fractured and webbed.

Phil screamed, "Help! Help!"

The passenger door swung open and I could see fury in the clown's face.

I stumbled as I leaped forward and gravity pushed me down Savin Hill Avenue.

"Help!" Phil screamed and then he ran and I was right behind him, my arms still pinwheeling as I tried to keep my balance and the pavement kept jerking toward my face.

A beefy man with a mustache as thick as a brush head stepped out of Bulldog's bar at the corner of Sydney, and we could hear tires squealing behind us. The beefy man looked angry; he had a sawed-off bat in his hand, and at first I thought he was going to use it on us.

His apron, I remember, bore swaths of meaty red and brown.

"Fuck's going on?" the man said, and his eyes narrowed at something over my shoulder, and I knew the van was coming for all of us. It was going to jump the curb and mangle us.

I turned my head in order to see my own death, and instead I saw a flash of grimy orange tail lights as the van spun the corner onto Grampian Way and disappeared.

The bar owner knew my father and ten minutes later my old man came into Bulldog's as Phil and I sat at the bar with our ginger ales and pretended they were whiskeys.

My father wasn't always mean. He had his good days. And for whatever reason, that day was one of his best. He wasn't angry we'd stayed out past dinner time, though I'd been beaten for the same offense only a week before. Usually indifferent to my friends, he ruffled Phil's hair and bought us several more ginger ales and two heaping corned beef sandwiches, and we sat in the bar with him until night had risen up the doorway on our left and the bar had filled.

When I told him in a faltering voice what had happened, his face grew as tender and kind as I'd ever seen it, and he peered at me with soft worry and wiped my wet bangs off my forehead with a thick, gentle finger and dabbed the corned beef off the corner of my mouth with a napkin.

"You two had some day," he said. He whistled and smiled at Phil and Phil smiled back broadly.

My father's smile, so rare, was a thing of wonder.

"I didn't mean to bust the window," I said. "I didn't mean to, Dad."

"It's okay."

"You're not mad?"

He shook his head.

"I—"

"You did great, Patrick. You did great," he whispered. He took my head to his broad chest and kissed my cheek, smoothed my cow lick with his palm. "You make me proud."

It was the only time I ever heard those words from my father.

"Clowns," Bolton said.

"Clowns," I said.

"Clowns, yeah," Phil said.

"Okay," Bolton said slowly. "Clowns," he repeated and nodded to himself.

"No shit," I said.

"Uh-huh." He nodded again and then turned his huge head, looked directly at me. "You are, I'm assuming, fucking kidding me." He wiped his mouth with the back of his hand.

"No."

"We're perfectly and completely friggin' serious," Phil said.

"Jesus." Bolton leaned against the sink, looked over at Angie. "Tell me you're not part of this, Ms. Gennaro. You, at least, seem like a person of some rationality."

She tightened the belt on her robe. "I don't know what to believe." She shrugged her shoulders in the direction of Phil and me. "They seem pretty certain."

"Listen for a second—"

He crossed to me in three large steps. "No. No. We've blown the surveillance because of you, Mr. Kenzie. You call me over here and say you've cracked the case. You've—"

"I didn't—"

"—figured it all out and you need to see me right away. So I come over here and *he's* here"—he pointed at Phil—"and now *they're* here"—he jerked his head at Devin and Oscar—"and any hopes we had of suckering Evandro into this place are shot because it looks like a fucking law enforcement convention in here." He paused for breath. "And I could have lived with all that as long as we were, oh, I don't know, getting somewhere. But, no, you give me clowns."

"Mr. Bolton," Phil said, "we're serious here."

"Oh. Good. Let me see if I have this right—twenty years ago, two circus performers with bushy hair and rubber pants pull up beside you in a van while you're walking to a Little League game and—"

"From," I said.

"What?"

"We were walking back *from* the game," Phil said.

"Mea culpa," Bolton said and gave us a bow and flourish. "Mea maxima fucking culpa, tu morani."

"I've never been insulted in Latin before," Devin said to Oscar. "You?"

"Mandarin," Oscar said. "Never Latin."

"Fine," Bolton said. "You were accosted by two circus performers coming back *from* a game and because—do I have this right, Mr. Kenzie?—because Alec Hardiman sang 'Send in the Clowns' during the prison interview you think he was one of those clowns and that means, of course, that he's been killing people to get back at you for escaping that day?"

"It's not that simple."

"Oh, well, thank heaven. Look, Mr. Kenzie, twenty-five years ago I asked out Carol Yaeger of Chevy Chase, Maryland, and she laughed in my face. But that doesn't—"

"Hard to believe," Devin said.

"—mean I thought it perfectly logical to wait a couple of decades and kill everyone she ever knew."

"Bolton," I said, "I'd love to keep watching you dig yourself a hole here, but time is short. You bring the Hardiman, Rugglestone, and Morrison files like I asked?"

He patted his briefcase. "Right here."

"Open 'em."

"Mr. Kenzie—"

"Please."

He opened the briefcase, pulled out the files, and set them on the kitchen table. "And?"

"Check the ME's report on Rugglestone. Specifically look at the section on unexplained toxins."

He found it, adjusted his glasses. "Yes?"

"What was found in Rugglestone's facial lacerations?"

He read: " 'Lemon extract; hydrogen peroxide; talc, mineral oil, stearic acid, peg-thirty-two, triethanolamine, lanolin . . . all consistent with ingredients of white Pan-Cake makeup.' " He looked up. "So?"

"Read Hardiman's file. Same section."

He flipped a few pages and did.

"So? They were both wearing makeup."

"*White* Pan-Cake," I said. "The kind mimes use," I said. "And clowns."

"I see what—"

"Cal Morrison was found with the same properties under his fingernails."

He opened the Morrison file, leafed through it until he found it.

"Still," he said.

"Find the photograph of the van found outside the murder site—it was registered to Rugglestone."

He leafed through the file. "Here it is."

"It's missing the windshield," I said.

"Yes."

"But the van had been hosed clean, probably that day. Sometime between the hosing and the time the police found it, someone chucked some cinderblocks through the windshield, probably while Rugglestone was being murdered."

"So?"

"So, I'd marked the windshield. I threw the baseball and put a spiderweb in the center. That was the only thing to suggest Hardiman and Rugglestone were the clowns. Remove the mark, remove the motive."

"What's your point?"

I didn't truly believe it until I said it.

"I think EEPA killed Charles Rugglestone."

"He's right," Devin said eventually.

The hail had turned to rain shortly after eight, and the rain froze almost as soon as it hit. Streaks of water bled down Angie's windows and rippled into veins of crackling ice before our eyes.

Bolton had sent an agent back to the RV to make copies of the Rugglestone, Hardiman, and Morrison files, and we'd spent the last hour reading them in Angie's dining room.

Bolton said, "I'm not so sure."

"Please," Angie said. "It's all here if you look at it right. Everyone goes on the assumption that Alec Hardiman, loaded up on PCP, does the work of ten men when he kills Rugglestone. And if I was convinced Hardiman had killed several other people, I probably would have been swayed, too. But he had nerve damage in his left hand, seconol in his system, and was found passed out. Now, you look at Rugglestone's wounds with the idea that maybe ten people—or, say, seven—*were* involved, and it makes perfect sense."

Devin said, "Patrick's father knew about the damage to the windshield. He and his EEPA friends hunt it down, find Hardiman and Rugglestone . . ."

"EEPA killed Rugglestone," Oscar said with a note of shock in his voice.

Bolton looked at the file, then at me, then back at the file. He peered at it, and his lips moved as he read over the section detailing Rugglestone's wounds. When he looked at me, the flesh on his face drooped and his mouth opened. "You're right," he said softly. "You're right."

"Don't let it go to your head," Devin said. "You prick."

"A child's tale," Bolton said in a low whisper.

"What?"

We sat together in the dining room. The rest of them were in the kitchen while Oscar cooked his famous steak tips.

Bolton held up his hands in the darkness. "It's like something out of the Brothers Grimm. The two clowns, the cavernous van, the threat to innocence."

I shrugged. "At the time, it was just scary."

"Your father," he said.

I watched fingers of ice congeal on the window.

"You know what I'm getting at," he said.

I nodded. "He would have been the one who burned Rugglestone."

"In sections," Bolton said. "While the man screamed."

The ice cracked and fragmented as streams of rain tunneled through it. Immediately, fresh translucent veins replaced it.

"Yes," I said, remembering my father's kiss that evening. "My father burned Rugglestone alive. In sections."

"He was capable of that?"

"I told you, Agent Bolton, he was capable of anything."

"But *that*?" Bolton said.

I remembered my father's lips on my cheek, the rush of blood I'd felt in his chest as he pulled me to him, the love in his voice when he told me I'd made him proud.

Then I thought of the time he'd burned me with the iron, the smell of burning flesh that had risen from my abdomen and choked me as my father stared at me with a fury that bordered on ecstasy.

"Not only was he capable of it," I said, "he probably enjoyed it."

We were eating steak tips in the dining room when Erdham came in.

"Yes?" Bolton said.

Erdham handed him a photograph. "I thought you should see this."

Bolton wiped his mouth and fingers with a napkin, held the photo up to the light.

"This is one of the ones found at Arujo's place. Right?"

"Yes, sir."

"Have you identified the people in the photograph?"

Erdham shook his head. "No, sir."

"So why am I looking at it, Agent Erdham?"

Erdham looked at me and frowned. "It's not so much the people, sir. Look where it was taken."

Bolton squinted at the photo. "Yes?"

"Sir, if you—"

"Wait a minute." Bolton dropped his napkin onto his plate.

"Yes, sir," Erdham said and his body rippled.

Bolton looked at me. "This is your place."

I put down my fork. "What're you talking about?"

"This photo was taken on the front porch of your three-decker."

"Of me or Patrick?" Angie said.

Bolton shook his head. "Of a woman and a little girl."

"Grace," I said.

32

I **was the** first one out of Angie's house. I had a cellular phone to my ear as I stepped onto the porch and several government cars screeched up Howes.

"Grace?"

"Yeah?"

"You okay?" I slipped on some black ice and righted myself by grabbing the railing as Angie and Bolton came onto the porch next.

"What? You woke me up. I have to work at six. What time is it?"

"Ten. Sorry."

"Can we talk in the morning?"

"No. No. I need you to stay on the line and check all your doors and windows."

The cars slid to stops in front of the house.

"What? What's all that noise?"

"Grace, check your doors and windows. Make sure they're all locked."

I made my way to the slick sidewalk. The trees above were heavy and shimmering with daggers of ice. The street and sidewalk were a black glaze.

"Patrick, I—"

"Do it now, Grace."

I hopped in the back of the lead car, a dark blue Lincoln, and Angie sat beside me. Bolton sat up front and gave the driver Grace's address.

"Go." I slapped the driver's headrest. "Go. Go."

"Patrick," Grace said, "what's going on?"

"You check the doors?"

"I'm checking them now. Front door is locked. Cellar door is locked. Hang on, I'm heading to the back."

"Car coming up on our right," Angie said.

Our driver punched the gas as we shot through the intersection heading south and the car racing toward us from the east locked up his brakes on the ice and blared his horn and skidded across the intersection as the caravan of cars behind us jerked right and cruised around his back end.

"Back door's locked," Grace said. "I'm checking windows now."

"Good."

"You're scaring the shit out of me."

"I know. I'm sorry. The windows."

"Front bedroom and living room, all locked. I'm going into Mae's room. Locked, locked . . ."

"Mommy?"

"It's okay, honey. Stay in bed. I'll be right back."

The Lincoln spun onto the 93 on-ramp doing at least sixty. The back wheels skipped over a bubble of ice or frozen slush and banged against the divider.

"I'm in Annabeth's room," Grace whispered. "Locked. Locked. Open."

"Open?"

"Yeah. She left it open just a crack."

"Shit."

"Patrick, tell me what's going on."

"Close it, Grace. Close it."

"I did. What do you think—"

"Where's your gun?"

"My gun? I don't own one. I hate guns."

"A knife then."

"What?"

"Get a knife, Grace. Jesus. Get a—"

Angie ripped the phone out of my hand and shushed me with a finger to her lips.

"Grace, it's Ange. Listen. You may be in danger. We're not sure. Just stay on the line with me and don't move unless you're sure there's an intruder in there with you."

The exit signs flew past—Andrew Square, Massachusetts Avenue—and the Lincoln swerved onto Frontage Road, passed the industrial waste and Big Dig refuse in a blur as we hurtled toward East Berklee.

"Bolton," I said, "she's not bait."

"I know."

"I want her buried so deep in protective custody the President couldn't find her if he wanted to."

"I understand."

"Get Mae," Angie said, "and stay in one room with the door locked. We'll be there in three minutes. If someone tries to get through the door, go out the window and run toward Huntington or Mass. Ave., screaming your head off."

We blew the first red light on East Berklee and a car swerved out of our way, jumped the curb, and smashed into the light pole in front of Pine Street Inn.

"There's a lawsuit," Bolton said.

"No, no," Angie said anxiously. "Don't leave the house unless you hear something inside. If he's waiting outside, that would be just what he wants. We're almost there, Grace. Which room are you in?"

The rear left tire ate the curb as we fishtailed onto Columbus Avenue.

"Mae's bedroom? Good. We're eight blocks away."

The pavement of Columbus Avenue was buried under a quarter inch of ice so black and hard it looked like we were passing over a swath of pure licorice.

I punched the door with the side of my fist as the wheels spun and then caught and then spun again.

"Calm down," Bolton said.

Angie patted my knee.

As the Lincoln turned right on West Newton, black-and-white images exploded in my head like flashbulbs.

Kara, crucified in the cold.

Jason Warren's head swinging from a power cord.

Peter Stimovich staring out from a face with no eyes.

Mae tackling the dog in the grass.

Grace's damp body rolling on top of mine in the heart of a warm night.

Cal Morrison locked in the back of that grimy white van.

The bloody red leer of the clown as he said my name.

"Grace," I whispered.

"It's okay," Angie said into the phone, "we're almost there now."

We turned onto St. Botolph and the driver put on the brakes, caught more ice under his wheels, and we slid past Grace's brownstone before the car jerked to a stop two houses up.

The rear cars were pulling to erratic stops behind us as I got out and ran toward her house. I slipped on the sidewalk and dropped to my knee as a man came charging out between two cars on my right. I turned, pointed my gun at his chest, saw him raising his arm in the dark rain.

My finger was depressing the trigger when he screamed, "Patrick, hold it!"

Nelson.

He lowered his arm, his face wet and frightened, and Oscar hit him from behind like a train, Nelson's small body disappearing completely under Oscar's bulk as the two of them hit the ice.

"Oscar," I said, "he's okay. He's okay. He's working for me."

I ran up the steps to Grace's door.

Angie and Devin came up behind me as Grace opened the door and said, "Patrick, what the hell is going on?" She looked over my shoulder as Bolton barked orders at his men and her eyes widened.

Lights went on up and down the street.

"It's okay now," I said.

Devin's gun was drawn and he stepped up beside Grace. "Where's the child?"

"What? In her bedroom."

He went into the house in a target shooter's stance.

"Hey, wait." She rushed in after him.

Angie and I went in behind her as agents tramped through the surrounding yards with flashlights.

Grace was pointing at Devin's gun. "Put that away, Sergeant. Put it—"

Mae began to cry loudly. "Mommy."

Devin was sticking his head in and out of doorways, his gun held tightly next to his knee.

I felt nauseous as I stood in the warm light of the living room, my hands shaking with adrenaline. I heard Mae weeping from the bedroom and I followed the sound.

A thought—*I almost shot Nelson*—passed through my brain with a shiver, and then was gone.

Grace held Mae to her shoulder, and Mae opened her eyes and saw me and burst into a fresh peal of tears.

Grace looked over at me. "Jesus Christ, Patrick, was this necessary?"

Flashlight beams bounced off her windows from the outside.

"Yes," I said.

"Patrick," she said and her eyes were angry as they stared at my hand. "Get rid of that."

I looked down, noticed the gun in my hand, realized it had brought forth Mae's last burst of tears. I slid it back into the holster, then stared at them, mother and daughter as they hugged on that bed, and I felt soiled and foul.

"The first priority here," Bolton told Grace in the living room as Mae changed in her bedroom, "is to get you and your daughter to safety. A car's waiting outside and I'd like you two to get into it and come with us."

"Where?" Grace said.

"Patrick," a small voice said.

I turned and saw Mae standing in her bedroom doorway, freshly dressed in jeans and a sweatshirt, shoelaces untied.

"Yeah?" I said softly.

"Where's your gun?"

I tried to smile. "Tucked away. Sorry I scared you."

"Is it fat?"

"What?" I bent by her, tied her shoes.

"Is it . . ." She fidgeted, groping for the word, embarrassed that she didn't know it.

"Heavy?" I said.

She nodded. "Yeah. Heavy."

"It's heavy, Mae. Too heavy for you to carry."

"How about you?"

"Pretty heavy for me, too," I said.

"So why do you have it?" She cocked her head to the left, looked up into my face.

"It's sort of equipment for my job," I said. "Like your mom uses her stethoscope."

I kissed her forehead.

She kissed my cheek and hugged my neck with arms so soft they didn't seem as if they could come from the same world that produced Alec Hardimans and Evandro Arujos and knives and guns. She went back into the bedroom.

In the living room, Grace was shaking her head. "No."

"What?" Bolton said.

"No," Grace said. "I won't go. You can take Mae and I'll call her father. He'll—I'm sure of it, yes—he'll take time off and go with Mae so she won't be alone. I'll visit until this is over, but I won't go myself."

"Doctor Cole, that's unacceptable."

"I'm a first-year surgical resident, Agent Bolton. Do you understand that?"

"Yes, I do, but your life's in danger."

She shook her head. "You can protect me. You can watch me. And you can hide my daughter." She looked at Mae's bedroom door and tears welled in her eyes. "But I can't give up my work. Not now. I'll never get a decent job if I walk away in the middle of a residency."

"Doctor Cole," Bolton said, "I can't allow this."

She shook her head. "You'll have to, Agent Bolton. Protect my daughter. I'll take care of myself."

"This man we're dealing with—"

"Is dangerous, I know. You've told me. And I'm afraid, Agent Bolton, but I'm not going to give up what I've spent my life working toward. Not now. Not for anyone."

"He'll get to you," I said and I could still feel Mae's arms on my neck.

Everyone in the room looked up at me.

Grace said, "Not if I—"

"Not if you *what*? I can't protect you all, Grace."

"I'm not asking you—"

"He said I had a choice."

"Who?"

"Hardiman," I said and I was surprised at how loud my voice was. "I had to choose between people I loved. He meant you and Mae and Phil and Angie. I can't protect all of you, Grace."

"Then don't, Patrick." Her voice was cold. "Don't. You brought this to my doorstep. My daughter's doorstep. Your stupid fucking pursuit of a violent life led this person to me. Your life is my life now and my daughter's and neither of us asked for it." She punched her knee with the side of her fist and then looked at the floor, inhaled sharply. "I'll be fine. Take Mae someplace safe. I'll call her father now."

Bolton looked at Devin and Devin shrugged.

"I can't make you go into protective custody—"

"No," I said. "No, no, no. Grace, you don't know this guy. He'll get to you. He will."

I crossed the floor until I was standing over her.

"So?" she said.

"So?" I said. "So?"

I was aware that everyone was looking at me. I was aware that I didn't feel completely like myself. I felt crazed and vindictive. I felt violent and ugly and unhinged.

"So," Grace said again.

"So he'll cut your fucking head off," I said.

"Patrick," Angie said.

I bent over Grace. "You understand that? He'll cut your head off. But last. He'll do that last. First, Grace, he'll rape you for a while and then he'll slice off pieces of your body and then he'll hammer nails through your fucking palms and then—"

"Stop it," she said quietly.

But I couldn't. It seemed important that she know this.

"—he'll disembowel you, Grace. He loves that. Disemboweling people so he can see their insides steam. And then maybe he'll pluck out your eyes while he lets his partner rip into you and—"

The scream came from behind me.

Grace had her hands over her ears by this point, but she pulled them off when she heard the scream.

I turned and Mae was standing behind me, her face bright red, her arms jerking spasmodically by her sides as if she'd been electrified.

"No, no, no!" She screamed it through tears of horror and pushed past me and jumped on her mother and clung to her with ferocity.

Grace looked past her daughter as she held her to her breast, looked at me with a naked and total hatred.

"Leave my house," she said.

"Grace."

"Now," she said.

"Doctor Cole," Bolton said, "I'd like you to—"

"I'll go with you," she said.

"What?"

Her eyes were still fixed on me. "I'll go into protective custody with you, Agent Bolton. I won't leave my daughter. I'll go," she said softly.

I said, "Look, Grace—"

She placed her hands over her daughter's ears.

"I thought I told you to get the fuck out of my home."

The phone rang and she reached for it, her eyes never leaving me. "Hello." She frowned. "I thought I told you this afternoon not to call back. If you want to talk to Patrick—"

"Who is it?" I said.

She tossed the receiver on the floor by my feet. "You gave my number to that psycho friend of yours, Patrick?"

"Bubba?" I picked up the phone as she brushed past me, carried Mae into the bedroom.

"Hello, Patrick."

"Who's this?" I said.

"How'd you like all those pictures I took of your friends?"

I looked at Bolton, mouthed "Evandro."

He ran from the house, Devin a step behind him.

"They didn't do much for me, Evandro."

"Oh," he said. "I'm sorry to hear that. I've been working on my technique, trying to play with light and space, respect the spatial tableau, that sort of thing. I think I'm developing artistically. Don't you?"

Outside the window, an agent scaled the telephone pole in Grace's side yard.

"I don't know, Evandro. I doubt you got Annie Leibovitz looking over her shoulder or anything."

Evandro chuckled. "But I've got you looking over yours, don't I, Patrick?"

Devin came back in holding a piece of paper with the words "Keep him on for *two* minutes" written on it.

"Yes, you do. Where are you, Evandro?"

"Watching you."

"Really?" I resisted the urge to turn and look out the windows fronting the street.

"Watching you and your girlfriend and all those nice policemen tramping around the house."

"Well, since you're in the neighborhood, drop on by."

Another soft chuckle. "I'd rather wait. You look very handsome at the moment, Patrick—the phone clenched tightly against your ear, brow furrowed with concern, hair disheveled from the rain. Very handsome."

Grace came back into the living room, dropped a suitcase on the floor by the door.

"Thanks for the compliment, Evandro."

Grace blinked when she heard the name, looked over at Angie.

"My pleasure," Evandro said.

"What am I wearing?"

"What's that?" he said.

"What am I wearing?"

"Patrick, when I took the pictures of your girlfriend and her—"

"What am I wearing, Evandro?"

"—little girl, I—"

"You don't know, because you're not watching this house. Are you?"

"I see a lot more than you can imagine."

"You're full of shit, Evandro." I laughed. "Trying to come off as—"

"Don't you dare laugh at me."

"—some all-seeing, all-knowing master criminal—"

"Change the tone of your voice. Immediately, Patrick."

"—when from where I'm standing you look like a punk."

Devin looked at his watch, held up three fingers. Thirty seconds to go.

"I'm going to cut the child in half and mail her to you."

I turned my head, saw Mae standing over her suitcase in the bedroom, rubbing her eyes.

"You're not going to get anywhere near her, jerkoff. You had your chance and you choked."

"I will annihilate everyone you know." His voice was ragged with rage.

Bolton came through the front door, nodded.

"Pray I don't see you first, Evandro."

"You won't, Patrick. No one ever does. Good-bye."

And another voice, huskier than Evandro's, came over the line: "We'll be seeing you, laddies."

The connection broke, and I looked at Bolton.

"Both of them," he said.

"Yup."

"You recognize that second voice?"

"Not with the phony accent."

"They're on the North Shore."

"The *North* Shore?" Angie said.

Bolton nodded. "Nahant."

"They're holed up on an island?" Devin said.

"We can lock them down," Bolton said. "I've already alerted the Coast Guard and sent police cars from Nahant, Lynn, and Swampscott to block the bridge leading off the island."

"So we're safe?" Grace said.

"No," I said.

She ignored me, looked at Bolton.

"I can't take the chance," Bolton said. "You can't either, Doctor Cole. I can't risk your safety and your daughter's until we've got them."

She looked at Mae as Mae came out of the bedroom with her Pocahontas suitcase. "Okay. You're right."

Bolton turned to me. "I have two men on Mr. Dimassi's place, but I'm stretched thin. Half my men are still on the South Shore. I need the ones I have."

I looked at Angie and she nodded.

"Those are state-of-the-art alarms on both front and back doors of your house, Ms. Gennaro."

"We can protect ourselves for a few hours," I said.

He clapped a hand on my shoulder. "We've got them, Mr. Kenzie." He looked at Grace and Mae. "Ready?"

She nodded, held out her hand to Mae. Mae took it and looked up at me, her face a mask of confusion and a sadness older than herself.

"Grace."

"No." Grace shook her head as I reached my hand toward her shoulder. She turned her back to me and left the house.

The car that took them away was a black Chrysler New Yorker with bulletproof windows and a driver with cold, brightly alert eyes.

I said, "Where are you taking them?"

"Far away," Bolton said. "Far away."

A helicopter touched down in the center of Massachusetts Avenue, and Bolton and Erdham and Fields jogged gingerly to it on the ice.

As the helicopter lifted up and blew trash against storefronts along the avenue, Devin and Oscar pulled up beside us.

"I put your dwarf buddy in the hospital," Oscar said, holding out his hands in apology. "Cracked six of his ribs. I'm sorry."

I shrugged. I'd make it up to Nelson someday.

"I've sent a unit to Angie's house," Devin said. "I know the guy. His name's Tim Dunn. You can trust him. Head back there."

We stood together in the rain and watched them pull into the police and FBI car caravan and head down Massachusetts Avenue, and the patter of the rain against the ice was one of the loneliest sounds I've ever heard.

33

Our cab driver maneuvered the icy streets with a deft touch, keeping the needle around the 20 mph mark and rarely touching the brake unless he had no other choice.

The city was encased in ice. Great glassy sheets covered building facades, and gutters bent under the weight of cascading white daggers. Trees shimmered platinum, and cars along the avenues had turned to sculptures.

"We gonna have many blackouts tonight, man," the cab driver said.

"You think so," Angie said absently.

"Oh, you bet, pretty lady. That ice, she gonna pull all those power lines to the ground. You wait and see. Nobody should be out on this bad night. No."

"Why're you?" I said.

"Got to feed the little ones, sure. Little ones don't have to know how tough this world is for their papa. No. Just got to know they get fed."

I saw Mae's face, scrunched in confusion and abject terror. The words I'd spewed at her mother echoed in my ears.

The little ones don't have to know.

How could I have forgotten that?

Timothy Dunn clicked his flashlight beam at us twice as we walked up Angie's front walkway.

He crossed the street to us with careful steps. He was a slim kid with a wide, open face under his dark blue cap.

It was the face of a farm boy or a boy whose mother raised him for the priesthood.

His cap was encased in plastic to keep it dry and his heavy black raincoat was slick with drizzle. He tipped the cap as he met us at the front steps.

"Mr. Kenzie, Ms. Gennaro, I'm Officer Timothy Dunn. How we doing tonight?"

"Been better," Angie said.

"Yes, ma'am, I heard."

"Miss," Angie said.

"Excuse me?"

"Please call me Miss or Angie. Ma'am makes me feel like I'm old enough to be your mother." She peered at him through the rain. "I'm not, am I?"

He smiled sheepishly. "I sure doubt it, Miss."

"How old are you?"

"Twenty-four."

"Whew."

"And you?" he said.

She chuckled. "Never ask a woman her weight or her age, Officer Dunn."

He nodded. "Just seems like, in either case, the Lord's been awful kind to you, Miss."

I rolled my eyes.

She leaned back, took a second look at him.

"You will go far, Officer Dunn."

"Thank you, Miss. People keep telling me that."

"Believe them," she said.

He looked down at his feet for a moment, shuffled them slightly, and tugged on his right earlobe in such a way that I was sure it was a nervous habit of his.

He cleared his throat. "Sergeant Amronklin said the FBI boys would be sending reinforcements by as soon as they get them all rounded up on the South Shore. He said by two or three in the morning, the latest. I understand front and back doors are protected by alarms and the back of the house is secure."

Angie nodded.

"I'd still like to take a look back there."

"Be my guest."

He tipped his hat again and walked back around as we stood on the porch and listened to his footsteps crunch through the frozen grass.

"Where'd Devin get this kid?" Angie said. "Mayberry?"

"Probably a nephew," I said.

"Of Devin's?" She shook her head. "No way."

"Trust me. Devin's got eight sisters and half of them are nuns. Literally. The other half are married to men who know they take a back seat to the Lord."

"How'd Devin come out of that gene pool?"

"It's a mystery, I admit."

"This one's so innocent and forthright," she said.

"He's too young for you."

"Every boy needs a woman to corrupt him," she said.

"And you're just the girl to do it."

"Bet your ass. Did you see the way those thighs of his moved in those tight pants?"

I sighed.

The flashlight beam preceded Timothy Dunn's crunching feet as he came back around the house.

"All clear," he said as we came back out on the steps.

"Thank you, Officer."

He met her eyes and his pupils dilated, then fluttered to his right.

"Tim," he said. "Please call me Tim, Miss."

"Then call me Angie. He's Patrick."

He nodded and his eyes glanced guiltily over my face.

"So," he said.

"So," Angie said.

"So, I'll be in the car. If I need to approach the house I'll call first. Sergeant Amronklin gave me the number."

"What if the line's busy?" I said.

He'd thought of that. "Three flashes from my flashlight directed at that window." He pointed at the living room. "I've seen a diagram of the house and that should carry into any room except the kitchen and bathroom. Correct?"

"Yes."

"And finally, if you're asleep or don't see it, I'll ring the bell. Two short rings. Okay?"

"Sounds good," I said.

"You'll be fine," he said.

Angie nodded. "Thank you, Tim."

He nodded, but couldn't meet her eyes. He walked back across the street and down to his car and climbed in.

I grimaced at Angie. "Tim," I said.

"Oh, shut up."

"They'll get over it," Angie said.

We sat in the dining room talking about Grace and Mae. From there, I could see the dot of red light pulsing from the alarm console by the front door. Instead of reassuring me, it seemed only to underscore our vulnerability.

"No, they won't."

"If they love you, they'll see you were just cracking under stress. Cracking badly, I admit, but cracking."

I shook my head. "Grace was right. I brought it into her home. And then I became it. I terrified her child, Angie."

"Kids are resilient," she said.

"If you were Grace, and I pulled that performance on you, gave your child nightmares for a month probably, what would you do?"

"I'm not Grace."

"But if you were."

She shook her head, looked down at the beer in her hand.

"Come on," I said.

She was still looking at the beer when she spoke. "I'd probably want you out of my life. Forever."

We moved to the bedroom, sat in chairs on either side of the bed, both of us exhausted but still too wired to sleep.

The rain had stopped and the lights in the bedroom were off as the ice cast silver light against the windows and bathed the room in pearl.

"It'll eat us eventually," Angie said. "The violence."

"I always thought we were stronger than it."

"You were wrong. It infests you after a while."

"You talking about me or you?"

"Both of us. Remember when I shot Bobby Royce a few years ago?"

I remembered. "You saved my life."

"By taking his." She took a deep drag on her cigarette. "I told myself for years that I didn't feel what I felt when I pulled the trigger, that I couldn't have."

"What'd you feel?" I said.

She leaned forward in the chair, her feet on the edge of the bed, and hugged her knees.

"I felt like God," she said. "I felt great, Patrick."

Later, she lay in bed with the ashtray on her abdomen, staring up at the ceiling while I remained in the chair.

"This is my last case," she said. "Least for a while."

"Okay."

She turned her head on the pillow. "You don't mind?"

"No."

She blew smoke rings at the ceiling.

"I'm so tired of being scared, Patrick. I'm so tired of all that fear turning into anger. I'm exhausted by how much all of it makes me hate."

"I know," I said.

"I'm tired of dealing with psychotics and deadbeats and scumbags and liars on a continual basis. I'm starting to think that's all there is in the world."

I nodded. I was tired of it, too.

"We're still young." She looked over at me. "You know?"

"Yeah."

"We're still young enough to change if we want. We're young enough to get clean again."

I leaned forward. "How long have you felt this way?"

"Ever since we killed Marion Socia. Maybe ever since I killed Bobby Royce, I don't know. But a long time. I've felt so dirty for so long, Patrick. And I didn't used to."

My voice was a whisper. "Can we get clean, though, Ange? Or is it already too late?"

She shrugged. "It's worth a try. Don't you think?"

"Sure." I reached across and took her hand. "If you think so, it's worth it."

She smiled. "You're the best friend I've ever had."

"Back at you," I said.

"I sat up in Angie's bed with a start.

"What?" I said, but no one was talking to me.

The apartment was still. Out of the corner of my eye, I saw something move. I turned and looked at the far window. As I stared at the frozen panes, dark leaf silhouettes pressed flat against the glass, then snapped back into the darkness as the poplar tree outside bowed in the wind.

I noticed that the red digital numbers of her alarm clock were black.

I found my watch on the dresser, leaned down to catch the icy light from the window: 1:45.

I turned on the bed and lifted the window shade behind me, looked at houses around me. Every light was out, even porch lights. The neighborhood looked like a mountain hamlet, glazed in ice, deprived of electricity.

When the phone rang, it was a shattering sound.

I grabbed it. "Hello."

"Mr. Kenzie?"

"Yes."

"Tim Dunn."

"The lights are out."

"Yes," he said. "In pockets all over the city. The ice is turning heavy and yanking down lines, blowing transformers across the state. I've apprised Boston Edison of our situation, but it's still going to take a while."

"Okay. Thanks, Officer Dunn."

"Don't mention it."

"Officer Dunn?"

"Yes?"

"Which of Devin's sisters is your mother?"

"How'd you know?"

"I'm a detective, remember?"

He chuckled. "Theresa."

"Ah," I said. "One of the older sisters. Devin's afraid of the older ones."

He laughed softly. "I know. It's kind of funny."

"Thanks for looking out for us, Officer Dunn."

"Any time," he said. " 'Night, Mr. Kenzie."

I hung up, stared out at the hushed mixture of deep black and bright silver and pearl.

"Patrick?"

Her head rose up off the pillow and her left hand pulled a mass of tangled hair off her face. She pushed herself up on an elbow and I was very aware of her breasts moving under her Monsignor Ryan Memorial High School T-shirt.

"What's going on?"

"Nothing," I said.

"Bad dream?" She sat up, one leg under her, the other slipping out, smooth and bare, from under the sheet.

"I thought I heard something." I nodded in the direction of the window. "Turned out to be a tree branch."

She yawned. "I keep meaning to trim that."

"Lights are out, too. All over town."

She peeked under the shade. "Wow."

"Dunn said transformers are blowing all over the state."

"No, no," she said abruptly and threw back the sheet, got out of bed. "No way. Too dark."

She rummaged through her closet until she found a shoebox. She placed it on the floor and pulled out a handful of white candles.

"You want a hand?" I said.

She shook her head and walked around the room, placing the candles in holders and stands I couldn't see in the dark. She had them tucked everywhere—on the two nightstands, the dresser, the vanity chest. It was almost unsettling to watch her light the wicks, her thumb never once releasing the ignitor on her lighter as she pivoted from one candle to the next until the shadows of flame flickered and expanded against the walls in the light they'd created.

In under two minutes she turned the room into one that resembled a chapel far more than a bedroom.

"There," she said as she slid back under the covers.

For at least a minute, neither of us said anything. I watched the flames flicker and grow, the warm yellow light play off our flesh, begin to glow in the strands of her hair.

She turned on the bed so that she was facing me, her

legs crossed at the knees, tucked against her, the sheet bunched at her waist. She kneaded it between her hands, and tilted her head and shook it so that her hair untangled some more and fell down her back.

"I keep seeing corpses in my dreams," she said.

"I just see Evandro," I admitted.

"What's he doing?" She leaned forward a bit.

"Coming for us," I said. "Steadily."

"In my dreams, he's already arrived."

"So those corpses . . ."

"They're ours." Her hands clenched together in her lap and she looked at them as if she expected them to tear apart from each other on their own.

"I'm not ready to die, Patrick."

I sat up against the headboard. "Neither am I."

She leaned forward. With her hands clenched on her lap and her upper body leaning in toward me, her thick hair framing her face so that I could barely see it, she seemed conspiratorial, vested in secrets she might never share.

"If anyone can get to us—"

"That's not going to happen."

She leaned her forehead against mine. "Yes, it is."

The house creaked, settling another hundredth of an inch closer to the earth.

"We're ready if he comes for us."

She laughed and it was a wet, strangled sound.

"We're basket cases, Patrick. You know it, I know it, and he probably knows it. We haven't eaten or slept decently in days. He's screwed us emotionally and psychologically and just about every other way you can think of." Her damp hands pressed against my cheeks. "If he chooses, he can bury us."

I could feel tremors, like sudden jolts of electricity, explode under her palms. The heat and blood and tidal tuggings of her body pulsed through her T-shirt and I knew she was probably right.

If he wanted to, he'd bury us.

And that knowledge was so goddamned ugly, so polluted with the basest sort of self-awareness—that we were nothing, any of us, but a pile of organs and veins and muscle and valves hanging suspended in currents of blood within frail, uselessly vain exteriors. And that with a flick of a switch, Evandro could come along and shut us down, turn us off as easily as turning off a light, and our particular pile of organs and valves would cease to function, and the lights would go out and the darkness would be total.

"Remember what we talked about," I said. "If we die, we're taking him with us."

"So *what*?" she said. "So fucking what, Patrick? I don't want to take Evandro with me. I simply do not want to die. I want him to leave me alone."

"Hey," I said softly. "It's okay. Come on."

She smiled sadly at me. "I'm sorry. It's just that it's the dead of night and I'm more afraid than I've ever been in my life and I'm not up to the tough-guy platitudes right now. They feel terribly hollow lately."

Her eyes were moist and so were her palms as she pulled them down my cheeks, began to lean back on her haunches.

I caught her hands gently at the wrists, and she leaned forward again. Her right hand moved into my hair, pushing it back off my forehead as she lowered her body onto mine and her thighs slid in between mine and her left foot grazed my right as she pushed the sheet down to the foot of the bed.

A strand of her hair tickled my left eye and we both froze with our faces almost touching. I could smell fear on her breath, fear in our hair, on our skin.

Her dark eyes peered into my face with a mixture of curiosity, determination, and the ghosts of old ancient hurts we never talked about. Her fingers dug deeply into my hair and her pelvic bone drove down against my own.

"We shouldn't be doing this," she said.

"No," I said.

"What about Grace?" she whispered.

I let the question hang there because I didn't have an answer.

"What about Phil?" I said.

"Phil's over," she said.

"There are good reasons we haven't done this in seventeen years," I said.

"I know. I'm trying to remember them."

I raised my hand, pushed it through the hair along her left temple and she nipped at my wrist with her teeth and arched her back, drove her pelvic bone even deeper.

"Renee," she said and gripped the hair by my temples with a sudden anger.

"Renee's gone." I gripped her hair just as roughly.

"You're so sure?"

"You ever hear me talk about her?" I slid my left leg along the edge of her right, hooked my ankle over hers.

"Conspicuously," she said. Her left hand slid down my chest, squeezed my hip at the place where bare skin met boxer shorts. "You conspicuously don't talk about a woman you married." The heel of her hand nudged an edge of underwear over my hip.

"Ange—"

"Don't say my name."

"What?"

"Not when we're talking about you and my sister."

There it was. A full decade since we'd so much as broached the subject, and it was back out again with all its sordid implications.

She leaned back until she was sitting on my thighs and my hands had fallen to her hips.

"I've paid enough for her," I said.

She shook her head. "No."

"Yes."

She shrugged. "I'm beyond the point of caring about it, though. At the moment anyway."

"Ange—"

She put a finger to my lips, then she leaned back again and peeled her T-shirt off her body. She tossed it to the side of the bed and grasped my hands and pulled them up over her rib cage and placed them on her breasts.

She lowered her head and her hair fell over my hands. "I've missed you for seventeen years," she murmured.

"Me too," I said hoarsely.

"Good," she whispered.

Her hair fell in my face again as her lips hovered over
mine and her knees locked against my thighs and pushed
my underwear down my legs. Her slim tongue flicked
against my upper lip. "Good," she said again.

I raised my head and kissed her. My right hand caught
in the tangles of her hair, and as my mouth dropped back
from hers, she followed it, closing her lips over it and
burying her tongue inside. My hands dropped down her
back, the fingers pressing either side of her spinal cord
before they hooked under the elastic band of her underpants.

She raised an arm and gripped the headboard, her body
rising up mine as my tongue found her throat and my
hands turned her underpants into a silk coil that rolled
tightly over her hips and the rise of her ass. Her breast
sank into my mouth and she gasped slightly, pulled the
headboard against the mattress. The heel of her hand ran
roughly down my abdomen and into my groin and she
kicked at the coil of underwear around her ankles as she
lowered herself back down my body.

And the phone rang.

"Fuck 'em," I said. "Whoever it is."

Her nose bumped lightly off mine and she groaned and
then we both laughed, our teeth an inch apart.

"Help me get these off," she said. "I'm all tied up
down here."

The phone rang again, loud and shrill.

Our legs and underwear had become completely inter-
twined and my hand slid down her legs and reached for
them and met Angie's hand down there too and the sudden
touch of it was one of the most erotic sensations I've ever
encountered.

The phone rang again and she arched sideways on the
bed as our ankles came free and I could see sweat glisten-
ing on her olive skin in the candlelight.

Angie groaned, but it was a groan of pure annoyance
and exasperation, and our bodies slid against each other as
she reached over me for the phone.

"It could be Officer Dunn," she said. "Shit."

"Tim," I said. "Call him Tim."

"Fuck you," she said with a throaty laugh and slapped my chest.

She brought the receiver back over my body with her and fell away from me onto the bed, her olive skin further darkened by the white sheet below it.

"Hello," she said and blew at wet strands of hair clinging to her forehead.

I could hear the sound of something scratching. Softly, but persistently. I looked at the window to my right, saw the dark leaves scrape the pane.

Scratch, scratch.

Angie's right leg pulled away from mine, and my flesh suddenly felt cold.

"Phil, please," she said. "It's almost two in the morning."

She pressed her head and shoulders into the pillow, crooked the phone between ear and shoulder, raised her lower back and ass off the bed, and pulled the underpants back up to her hips.

"And I am glad you're okay," she said. "But, Phil, can't we talk in the morning?"

The leaves scratched the window again, and I found my boxers, pulled them on.

Angie's palm caressed my hip absently and she turned and gave me a "Can you believe this?" roll of her eyes. She suddenly squeezed the flesh over my hip, where she'd claimed I had love handles, and she bit her lower lip in an attempt to keep from smiling. She failed.

"Phil, you've been drinking. Haven't you?"

Scratch. Scratch.

I looked at the window, but the leaves were gone, bowing back in the dark breeze.

"I know that, Phillip," she said sadly. "I know. And I'm trying." Her hand fell away from my hip and she turned toward the phone and stood up from the bed. "I don't. I don't hate you."

She stood with one knee on the bed, looking out the window, the phone cord pressed against the backs of her thighs, and worked her way back into her T-shirt.

I got out of the bed, too, tossed my jeans and shirt back

on. The house was cold without the press of body heat, and I didn't feel like crawling back under the covers while she chatted with Phil.

"I'm not judging," she said. "But if Arujo picks tonight to come after you, wouldn't you rather have sharp wits?"

The white beam of light crested her shoulder and the glow of candlelight and blinked three times against the upper wall in front of her. She had her head down and didn't notice, so I left the bedroom and walked down the hallway, hugging my arms against the cold and watched through the living room window as Tim Dunn crossed the street toward the house.

I reached to deactivate the alarm, saw that it had lost its power in the blackout.

I opened the door before he could ring the bell.

"What's up?" I said.

He had his head down against the moisture sweeping off the trees and I realized he was looking at my bare feet.

A walkie-talkie squawked from the living room.

"Cold?" Dunn said and tugged his earlobe.

"Yeah. Come on in," I said. "Shut the door behind you."

I turned in the hallway and Devin's voice burst over the walkie-talkie: "Patrick, get the fuck out of the house. Arujo set us up. Arujo set us up. He's not in Nahant."

I turned back as Dunn raised his head and Evandro Arujo's face stared out at me from under the cap brim.

"Arujo's not in Nahant, Patrick. He's right here. In the rest of your life."

34

Before I could speak, Evandro pressed a stiletto against the skin under my right eye. He dug the point into the socket bone and closed the door behind him.

There was already blood on the knife.

He noticed me looking at it and smiled sadly.

"Officer Dunn," he whispered, "won't be turning twenty-five, I'm afraid. Bummer, huh."

He pushed me backward by digging the point in harder against the bone and I took a few steps down the hallway.

"Patrick," he said, his other hand on Dunn's service revolver, "if you make a sound, I'll pluck out your eye and shoot your partner before she's halfway out of the bedroom. Understood?"

I nodded.

In the faint light from the candles in the bedroom I could see he wore Dunn's uniform shirt; it was dark with blood.

"Why'd you have to kill him?" I whispered.

"He used gel in his hair," Evandro said. He held a hand to his lips as we reached the bathroom, midway down the center hall, and motioned for me to stop.

I did.

He'd shaved the goatee and the hair peeking out from under the cap brim was dyed a honey blond. His colored contacts were a faded gray, and I assumed the inch of sideburns by each ear were fake, since he didn't have them when I saw him last.

"Turn around," he whispered. "Slowly."

From the bedroom I could hear Angie sigh. "Phil, re-ally, I'm very tired."

She hadn't heard the walkie-talkie. Fuck.

I turned around as Evandro placed the flat edge of the stiletto to my face and allowed it to slide with the skin as my head turned away. I felt the point skip across the back of my neck and then bite into the hollow space under my right ear, in the gap between my skull and jaw.

"You fuck with me," he whispered in my ear, "and this point comes out through your nose. Take small steps."

"Phillip," Angie said. "Please . . ."

The bedroom had two doorways. One fronted the hall, the other, six feet beyond, led into the kitchen. We were four feet from the first doorway when Evandro pressed the stiletto point into my skin to stop me. "Ssh," he whis-pered. "Ssh."

"No," Angie said and her voice sounded weary. "No, Phil, I don't hate you. You're a good man."

"I was twelve feet away out there," Evandro whispered. "You and your partner and poor Officer Dunn chatting about securing the house against me, and I'm crouched in the neighbor's hedge. I could smell you from there, Pat-rick."

I felt a small popping sensation as the stiletto point broke the skin at the edge of my jaw like a pin.

I couldn't see my options. If I tried for an elbow to Evandro's chest, which would be the first thing he'd ex-pect, there was still more than a fifty percent chance he'd be able to shove the knife through my brain anyway. All other possibilities—fist to the groin, foot brought down hard on his instep, sudden pivot to my left or right—car-ried the same likelihood of success. One of his hands held the knife, the other the gun, and both weapons dug into my body.

"If you'd just call back in the morning," Angie said, "we'll talk then."

"Or not," Evandro whispered. He nudged me forward.

At the edge of the doorway, he suddenly jerked the gun from my side. The point of the knife left my ear and dug into the back of my head where my spinal column and the base of my skull met. He spun in front of the doorway with my body blocking his.

Instead of standing by the bed where I'd left her, Angie was gone. The phone lay off the hook in the center of the bed, and I could hear Evandro's breath quicken as he craned his head over my shoulder to get a better look.

The sheet on the bed still bore the imprints of our bodies. Her cigarette fed ash into the ashtray and a pirouette of smoke into the air. The candle flames glowed like the yellow eyes of jungle cats.

Evandro looked toward the closet, saw that it was filled with enough clothes to hide a body.

He nudged me again and I again considered elbowing him.

He pointed Dunn's service revolver over my shoulder at the closet, pulled back the hammer.

"She in there?" he whispered, shifting his body to my left as he drew a bead on the closet and dug the knife harder against my skull.

"I don't know," I said.

I heard her voice before I even knew she was there.

It came from two inches behind me and it was preceded by the hard metal crack of a pistol hammer pulling back.

"Don't. Fucking. Move."

Evandro twisted the point of the knife into the base of my skull so hard that I stood up on my toes and felt a stream of blood flow down the back of my neck.

The movement turned my head to the left and I could see the barrel of Angie's .38 sticking out of Evandro's right ear, see how white her knuckles were around the butt.

Angie knocked the gun out of Evandro's hand with a quick swipe. When it hit the floor by the footboard, I expected it to fire, but it lay there, hammer cocked, pointing at the vanity chest.

"Angela Gennaro," Evandro said. "Nice to meet you. Very slick pretending you were still on the phone."

"I still *am* on the phone, asshole. It look hung up to you?"

Evandro's eyelids fluttered. "No, it doesn't."

"What does that tell you?"

"It tells me someone forgot to hang it up." He sniffed the air. "Smells like sex in here. The commingling of flesh. I hate that smell. You enjoyed yourselves, I hope."

"The police are on their way, Evandro, so put the knife down."

"I'd love to, Angela, but I have to kill you first."

"You won't get both of us."

"You're not thinking clearly, Angela. Must be the sex making you foggy. It'll do that. It's the stench of cave-dwellers really, the stink of sex is. After I fucked Kara and Jason—and believe me, it wasn't my choice, it was theirs—I wanted to cut their throats then and there. But I was convinced to wait. I was—"

"He's trying to lull you with talk, Ange."

She shoved the gun harder against his ear. "I seem lulled to you, Evandro?"

"Remember what you've learned over these last few weeks. I don't work alone, or did you forget that?"

"I'd say you're alone now, Evandro. So put the fucking knife down."

He dug it deeper and a white flash erupted in my brain.

"You're out of your depth," Evandro said. "You think we can't beat you both, but instead you can't beat both of us."

"Shoot him," I said.

"What?" Evandro said wildly.

"Shoot him!"

To our right, from the kitchen, someone said, "Hello."

Angie turned her head, and I could smell the bullet when it hit her. It smelled like sulfur and cordite and blood.

Her own gun went off between Evandro and me and the muzzle flash was like fire in my eyes.

I jerked forward and felt the stiletto pop back out of my flesh and clatter to the floor behind us as Evandro's nails tore across my face.

I drove my elbow back into his head and heard bone break and a scream and suddenly Angie's gun roared twice and glass shattered in the kitchen.

Evandro and I wrestled our way blindly into the bedroom and then shapes began to take form again through the blaring white in my eyes. My foot hit Dunn's service revolver and it discharged loudly and skittered out into the kitchen.

Evandro's hands clawed at my face and I dug my hands into the flesh under his rib cage. I spun, tightening my fingers on his lowest ribs, and hurled him over Angie's vanity chest and into the mirror.

The flash of white disappeared as I watched his slim body crest her makeup and crash through the glass. The mirror cracked in large, jagged pieces the shape of dorsal fins and the candle flames sputtered, then flared as they fell to the floor. I dove over the bed as he came down and the entire vanity came with him.

I grabbed my gun from Angie's nightstand as I went over it, came up on the other side of the bed and fired without hesitation at the place where I'd seen him last.

But he wasn't there anymore.

I turned my head, saw Angie sitting up on the floor, one eye squinting as she aimed down her barrel and steadied her arm, a fallen candle burning on the floor beside her. Footsteps paused on the kitchen floor, and Angie pulled the trigger.

And then she pulled it again.

Someone in the kitchen screamed.

And I heard another scream from outside, but it was the scream of metal, the howl of an engine, and suddenly the kitchen exploded in bursts of angry fluorescent, and the hum of electrical appliances followed.

I stamped out the candle by Angie's arm and stepped out into the hall behind her, pointed my gun at Evandro. His back was to us, his arms held down by his sides. He swayed from side to side in the middle of the kitchen floor, as if to music only he could hear.

Angie's first shot had found the center of his back and a large hole was torn through Dunn's black leather patrolman's jacket. As we watched, it filled with red, and Evandro stopped swaying and dropped to one knee.

Her second shot had blown off a flap of his head just over his right ear.

He raised his gun hand to it absently, and Dunn's service revolver fell and skittered across the linoleum.

"You okay?" I said.

"Stupid question," she groaned. "Jesus. Get in the kitchen."

"Where's the guy who shot you?"

"He went out through the kitchen door. Get in there."

"Fuck that. You're hurt."

She grimaced. "I'm okay. Patrick, he can still pick up that gun again. Will you get in there?"

I came up behind Evandro and picked up Dunn's service revolver, came around to face him. Evandro stared at me as he gingerly fingered the place where a piece of his head used to be, his face bathed gray in the sputtering fluorescence overhead.

He wept silently and the tears mixed with blood flowing down his face and his skin was so pale I was reminded of the clowns from long ago.

"It doesn't hurt," he said.

"It will."

He stared up at me with those confused, lonely eyes.

"It was a blue Mustang," he said, and it seemed important to him that I understand that.

"What was?"

"The car I stole. It was blue and it had white leather bucket seats."

"Evandro," I said, "who's your partner?"

"The hubcaps," he said, "gleamed."

"Who's your partner?"

"Do you feel *anything* for me?" he asked, his eyes wide and his hands held out like a supplicant's.

"No," I said and my voice was flat and dead.

"We're getting to you, then," he said. "We're winning."

"Who's we?" I said.

He blinked at the blood and tears. "I've been to hell."

"I know."

"No. No. I have been to *hell*," he screamed and fresh tears poured out of his eyes as his face contorted.

"And then you created some for other people. Quick, Evandro, who's your partner?"

"I don't remember."

"Bullshit, Evandro. Tell me."

I was losing him. He was dying in front of me as he placed his palm on his head and tried to staunch the flow of blood, and I knew he could go any second or within a few hours, but he was going.

"I don't remember," he repeated.

"Evandro, he left you behind. You're dying. He's not. Come on. I—"

"I don't remember who I was before I went in that place. I have no idea. I can't even remember—" His chest heaved suddenly and his cheeks puffed up like a blowfish and I heard something rumble in his chest.

"Who's—"

"—can't remember what I looked like as a child."

"Evandro?"

He vomited blood onto the floor and looked at it for a moment. When he looked back at me, he was terrified.

My face probably didn't provide much hope because as I looked down at what had just left his body, I knew he couldn't live long without it.

"Oh, shit," he said and he held out his hands and looked at them.

"Evandro—"

But he died that way—staring at his hands as they dropped back to his sides, one knee bent to the floor, his face confused and afraid and utterly alone.

"Is he dead?"

I came back into the hall after stepping into her bedroom long enough to stamp out a single candle trying to burn through her floor. "Oh, yeah. How're you?"

Her skin glistened with fat beads of sweat. "I'm sorta fucked up here, Patrick."

I didn't like the sound of her voice. It was much higher than usual and there was a keening to it.

"Where you hit?"

She lifted her arm and I could see a dark red hole just above her hip and below her rib cage that seemed to breathe.

"How's it look?" She lay her head against the door-jamb.

"Not bad," I lied. "Let me get a towel."

"I only saw his body," she said. "The shape of it."

"What?" I pulled a towel from the rack in the bath-room, came back into the hall. "Who?"

"The prick who shot me. When I shot back, I saw his body. He's short but built. You know?"

I pressed the towel into her side. "Okay. Short but built. Got it."

She closed her eyes. "Screavly," she said.

"What? Open your eyes, Ange. Come on."

She opened them, smiled wearily. " 'S gun," she said, " 's heavy."

I took the gun from her hand. "Not anymore. Ange, I need you to stay awake while—"

There was a loud crash at the front door and I spun in the hall, took aim at Phil and two EMTs as they burst inside the house.

I lowered my gun as Phil slid to his knees in the hall beside Angie.

"Oh, Jesus," he said. "Honey?" He wiped wet hair off her brow.

One of the EMTs said, "Give me some room. Come on."

I stepped back.

"Honey?" Phil screamed.

Her eyes fluttered open. "Hi," she said.

"Step back, sir," the EMT said. "Step back now."

Phil fell back on his haunches and slid a few feet away.

"Miss," the EMT said, "can you feel that pressure?"

Outside, patrol cars screeched to a halt and bathed the windows in lights the color of raging flame.

"So scared," Angie said.

The second EMT dropped the wheels to a stretcher in the hallway and flipped up a metal rod by its head.

A sudden rattle erupted in the hallway and I looked down and saw Angie's heels hammering the floorboards.

"She's going into shock," the EMT said. He grabbed her shoulders. "Get her legs," he shouted. "Get her legs, man."

I grabbed her legs and Phil said, "Oh, Jesus. Do something, do something, do something."

Her legs kicked into my armpit and I pressed them between my arm and chest, held on as her eyes rolled back white in the sockets and her head slipped off the side of the doorjamb and banged into the floor.

"Now," the first EMT said and the second one handed him a syringe and he plunged it into Angie's chest.

"What're you doing?" Phil said. "Jesus Christ, what're you doing to her?"

She jerked in my arms one last time and then she seemed to almost float back down to the floor.

"We're going to lift her," the EMT told me. "Gently, but fast. On three. One . . ."

Four cops appeared in the doorway, hands on their weapons.

"Two," the EMT said. "Get the fuck out of the doorway! We got an injured woman coming through."

The second EMT pulled an oxygen mask out of his bag, held it at the ready.

The cops backed off onto the porch.

"Three."

We lifted her, and her body felt far too light in my arms, as if it had never moved or jumped or danced.

We settled her onto the stretcher and the second EMT clamped the oxygen mask down over her face and yelled, "Coming through," and they pulled her down the hall and onto the porch.

Phil and I followed and the moment I stepped out onto the icy porch I heard the sounds of at least twenty weapons being cocked and aimed in my direction.

"Put the guns down and drop to your fucking knees!"

I knew better than to argue with nervous cops.

I placed my gun and Dunn's on the porch and knelt over them and held my hands up.

Phil was too worried about Angie to think that they could be talking to him too.

He took two steps after her stretcher and a cop clubbed his collarbone with a shotgun butt.

"He's the husband," I said. "He's the husband."

"Shut the fuck up, asshole! Keep your fucking hands in the air. Do it! Do it! Do it!"

I did. I remained kneeling as the cops moved cautiously closer and the bitter air found my bare feet and thin shirt and the paramedics lifted Angie into the back of the ambulance and took her away.

35

By the time the cops sorted everything out, Angie was in her second hour of surgery.

Phil was allowed to leave around four, after he'd called City Hospital, but I had to stick around and walk four detectives and a nervous young ADA through everything.

Timothy Dunn's body had been found stuffed naked into a trash barrel by the swing sets in the Ryan Playground. The assumption was that Evandro had lured him there by doing something suspicious enough to catch Dunn's eye, but not so obvious as to be taken as a direct threat or sign of danger.

A white sheet was found hanging from the basketball hoop that would have been directly in Dunn's field of vision from his unmarked cruiser. A man hanging a sheet to a hoop at 2:00 A.M. on an icy night could conceivably have been odd enough to draw a young cop's curiosity, but not a call for backup.

The sheet froze to the pole and hung there, a diamond of white against a pewter sky.

Dunn had been approaching the playground steps when Evandro came up behind him and buried the stiletto in his right ear.

The man who shot Angie had come in through the back door. His footprints—size eight—were found all over the back yard, but disappeared on Dorchester Avenue. The alarms Erdham had installed were rendered useless by the blackout, and all the man had to do was pick a second-rate bolt lock on the back door and walk on in.

Both Angie's shots had missed him. One was found in the wall by the door. The other had ricocheted off the oven and shattered the window over the sink.

Which left only Evandro to explain.

Cops, when one of their own has been killed, are scary people to be around. The anger that commonly seethes just under their surfaces comes fully to the fore and you pity the poor bastard they arrest next.

Tonight was even worse than usual because Timothy Dunn had been related to a decorated brother cop. A promising cop himself, he'd also been young and innocent, stripped of his blues and stuffed in a barrel.

As Detective Cord—a white-haired man with a kind voice and merciless eyes—interviewed me in the kitchen, Officer Rogin—a balled-up bull of a cop—circled Evandro's body, opening and closing his fists.

Rogin struck me as the kind of guy who becomes a cop for the same reason a lot of guys become jail guards— because they're sadists who need socially acceptable outlets.

Evandro's corpse was as I'd left it, defying the laws of physics and gravity as I'd come to know them by remaining on one knee, hands by his sides, looking down.

He was heading for rigor that way, and it pissed Rogin off. He looked at Evandro for a long time and breathed through his nostrils and balled his fists, as if by standing there long enough, exuding enough menace, he'd resurrect Evandro long enough to shoot him again.

It didn't happen.

So Rogin took a step back and kicked the corpse in the face with a steel-toed shoe.

Evandro's corpse flipped onto its back and the shoulders bounced off the floor. One leg collapsed under him, his head lolled to the left, and his eyes stared at the oven.

"Rogin, the fuck you doing?"

"Nice going, Hughie."

"You're going on report," Detective Cord said.

Rogin looked at him and it was clear they had a history. Rogin shrugged elaborately and spit on Evandro's nose.

"Showed him," a cop said. "Fucker won't have the nerve to die on you twice, Rogin."

And then the house was cored by a deep quiet. Rogin blinked uncertainly at something in the hallway.

Devin entered the kitchen with his eyes on Evandro's corpse, his face pink with cold. Oscar and Bolton came in behind him, and stayed a few steps back.

Devin kept his eyes on the corpse for a full minute, during which no one spoke. I'm not sure anyone breathed.

"Feel better?" He looked up at Rogin.

"Sergeant?"

"Do you feel better now?"

Rogin wiped a hand on his hip. "I'm not sure what you mean, sir."

"Pretty simple question," Devin said. "You just kicked a corpse. Do you feel better?"

"Ahm . . ." Rogin looked at the floor. "Yeah. I do."

Devin nodded. "Good," he said softly. "Good. I'm glad you have a sense of accomplishment, Officer Rogin. That's important. What else have you accomplished to-night?"

Rogin cleared his throat. "I established a crime-scene perimeter—"

"Good. That's always good."

"And I, ahm—"

"Clubbed a guy on the porch," Devin said. "Correct?"

"I thought he was armed, sir."

"Understandable," Devin said. "Tell me, did you en-gage in a search for the second shooter?"

"No, sir. That was—"

"Did you, perhaps, provide a blanket for the naked body of Officer Dunn?"

"No."

"No. No." Devin nudged Evandro's corpse with his toe, stared down at it with pure apathy. "Did you take any steps to ascertain the location of the second shooter or interview neighbors or conduct a house-to-house search?"

"No. But again, I—"

"So, outside of kicking a corpse and clubbing a de-fenseless man and stretching out some yellow crime-scene tape, you haven't accomplished much, have you, Officer?''

Rogin studied something on the stove. "No."

"What was that?" Devin said.

"I said no, sir."

Devin nodded and stepped over the corpse until he was standing beside Rogin.

Rogin was a tall man and Devin wasn't, so Rogin had to lean down when Devin beckoned him to do so. He bent his head and Devin turned his lips toward his ear.

"Leave my crime scene, Officer Rogin," Devin said.

Rogin looked at him.

Devin whispered, but the whole kitchen could hear:

"While your arms are still attached to your shoulders."

"We fucked up," Bolton said. "Actually *I* fucked up."

"No," I said.

"This is my fault."

"This is Evandro's fault," I said. "And his partner's."

He leaned his head back against the wall in Angie's hallway. "I was over-eager. They offered bait, and I bit. I never should have left you alone."

"You couldn't have predicted a blackout, Bolton."

"No?" He raised both hands, then dropped them in disgust.

"Bolton," I said, "Grace is safe. Mae is safe. Phil is safe. They're the civilians in all this. Not me and Angie."

I started to walk down the hall toward the living room.

"Kenzie."

I looked back at him.

"If you and your partner aren't civilians and you're not cops, what are you?"

I shrugged. "Two idiots who aren't half as tough as we thought we were."

Later, in the living room, a mottled gray light told us morning was advancing.

"You tell Theresa?" I asked Devin.

He stared out the window. "Not yet. I'm heading over there in a few minutes."

"I'm sorry, Devin." It wasn't much, but it was all I could think to say.

Oscar coughed into his fist, looked at the floor.

Devin ran his finger over the window ledge, stared at the dust he came back with. "My son turned fifteen yesterday," he said.

Devin's ex-wife, Helen, and their two children lived in Chicago with her second husband, an orthodontist. Helen had custody, and Devin had lost visitation rights after an ugly Christmas incident four years ago.

"Yeah? How's Lloyd doing these days?"

He shrugged. "He sent me a picture a few months back. He's big, got hair so long I couldn't see his eyes." He studied his hard, scarred hands. "He plays drums in some local band. Helen says his grades are suffering."

He looked back out at the street, and the mottled gray seemed to dampen and stretch his skin. When he spoke again, his voice was tremulous.

"I figure there's a lot worse things to be than a musician, though. You know, Patrick?"

I nodded.

Phil had taken my Crown Victoria to the hospital, so Devin drove me over to the garage where I store my Porsche as the morning lightened around us.

Outside the garage, he sat back in his seat and closed his eyes as the heat sputtering from his cracked exhaust pipe enveloped the car.

"Arujo and his partner rigged a phone to a computer modem in an abandoned house in Nahant," he said. "Rigged it so they could call from a pay phone down the street and the call would be traced back to the computer phone. Pretty smart."

I waited as he rubbed his face with his hands and closed his eyes tighter, as if warding off a fresh wave of hurt.

"I'm a cop," he said. "It's everything I am. I have to do my job. Professionally."

"I know."

"Find this guy, Patrick."

"I will."

"By any means necessary."

"Bolton—"

He held up a hand. "Bolton wants this to end, too. Don't call attention to yourself. Don't be seen. From me and Bolton's end, we offer you privacy. You won't be watched." He opened his eyes, turned on the seat, looked at me for a long time. "Don't let this guy write books from prison or give interviews to Geraldo."

I nodded.

"They'll want to study his brain." He picked at a loose piece of vinyl peeling from his cracked dashboard. "They can't do that if there's no brain left to study."

I patted his arm once and got out of the car.

Angie was still in surgery when I called the hospital. I asked them to page Phil, and when he got on the phone he sounded washed out.

"What's going on?" I said.

"She's still in there. They won't tell me anything."

"Stay calm, Phil. She's strong."

"You coming here?"

"Soon," I said. "I have to see someone first."

"Hey, Patrick," he said carefully, "you stay calm, too."

I found Eric at his apartment in the Back Bay.

He answered the door in a tattered bathrobe and gray sweatpants, and his face was drawn, three days' worth of gray stubble along his jawline. His hair wasn't tied back into a ponytail and it made him look ancient as it flowed around his ears and over his shoulders.

"Talk to me, Eric."

He glanced at the gun in my waistband. "Leave me alone, Patrick. I'm tired."

Behind him I could see discarded newspapers on the floor, a pile of plates and cups in the sink.

"Fuck you, Eric. We have to talk."

"I've already talked."

"With the FBI, I know. You failed your polygraph, Eric."

He blinked. "What?"

"You heard me."

He scratched his leg, yawned, and looked at a point over my shoulder. "Polygraphs aren't admissable in court."

"This isn't about court," I said. "This is about Jason Warren. This is about Angie."

"Angie?"

"She's got a bullet in her, Eric."

"She . . . ?" He held a hand out in front of him as if not sure what to do with it. "Jesus, Patrick, is she going to be okay?"

"I don't know yet, Eric."

"You must be losing your mind."

"I'm completely fucking deranged right now, Eric. Take that into consideration."

He winced, and a tide of something bitter and hopeless washed through his eyes.

He turned his back to me, leaving the door open, and walked back into his apartment. I followed him through the wreckage of a living room strewn with books and empty pizza boxes, bottles of wine and empty beer cans.

In the kitchen he poured himself a cup of coffee and the coffee maker was stained by days of splattered coffee he'd neglected to wipe off. It was also unplugged. God knew how old the coffee was.

"Were you and Jason lovers?" I said.

He sipped his cold coffee.

"Eric? Why'd you leave U/Mass?"

"You know what happens to male professors who sleep with male students?" he said.

"Professors sleep with students all the time," I said.

He smiled and shook his head. "Male professors sleep with female students all the time." He sighed. "And in the current political atmosphere on most campuses, even that's becoming dangerous. *In loco parentis*. Not a terribly threatening phrase unless it's applied to twenty-one-year-old men and women in the one country where the last thing we would want of our children is that they actually grow up."

I found a clean spot of counter, leaned against it.

Eric looked up from his coffee cup. "But, yes, Patrick, a prevailing attitude exists that it's okay for male professors to sleep with female students as long as those students aren't currently taking those professors' classes."

"So where's the problem?"

"The problem is gay professors and gay students. That sort of relationship, I promise you, is still frowned on."

"Eric," I said, "give me a break. This is Boston academia we're talking about here. The most strongly fortified bastion of liberalism in America."

He laughed softly. "You think so, don't you?" He shook his head again, a strange smile playing on thin lips. "If you had a daughter, Patrick, and let's say she's twenty, she's smart, she's at Harvard or Bryce or B.U., and you found out she was fucking a professor, how would you feel?"

I met his hollow gaze. "I'm not saying I'd like it, Eric, but I wouldn't be surprised. And I'd figure she's an adult, it's her choice."

He nodded. "Same scenario, but it's your son and he's fucking his male professor?"

That stopped me. It stirred some deeply repressed part of myself that was more Puritan than Catholic, and the image I had in my head—of a young man in a tiny cramped bed with Eric—revolted me for just a moment before I got control of it, started to distance myself from the image, grasp on to the intellectual handholds of my own social liberalism.

"I'd—"

"See?" He was smiling brightly, but his eyes were still hollow and unhinged. "The thought repulsed you, didn't it?"

"Eric, I—"

"Didn't it?"

"Yes," I said quietly. And wondered what that made me.

He held up a hand. "It's okay, Patrick. I've known you for ten years, and you're one of the least homophobic straight men I know. But you're still homophobic."

"Not when it comes to—"

"You and your gay friends," he said, "you're fine. I grant you that. But when it comes to the possibility of your *son* and his gay friends . . ."

I shrugged. "Maybe."

"Jason and I had an affair," he said and poured his coffee into the sink.

"When?" I said.

"Last year. It ended. It only lasted a month in the first place. I was a family friend, and I felt like I was betraying Diandra. Jason, for his part, I think wanted to be with someone closer to his own age, and he still had a pretty powerful attraction to women as well. But the breakup was very amicable."

"Did you tell the FBI this?"

"No."

"Eric, for Christ's sake, why not?"

"It'll destroy my career," he said. "Remember your reaction to my hypothetical. No matter how liberal you think academia is, the trustees of most colleges are straight white males. Or their country-club wives. And as soon as they think a fag professor is turning their children or their friends' children into fag students, they'll ruin him. Bank on it."

"Eric, it's going to come out. The FBI, Eric. The FBI. They're going through your life right now with magnifying glasses. They'll turn over the right rock sooner or later."

"I can't admit this, Patrick. I can't."

"What about Evandro Arujo? Did you know him?"

He shook his head. "No. Jason was scared, Diandra was scared, so I called you in."

I believed him. "Eric, please consider talking to the Feds."

"Will you be telling them what I told you?"

I shook my head. "I don't work that way. I'll tell them, for what it's worth, that I don't think you're a suspect, but I don't think it'll change their minds without proof."

He nodded and walked out of the kitchen to the door. "Thanks for coming by, Patrick."

I paused in the doorway. "Tell them, Eric."

He put a hand on my shoulder and smiled at me, trying

to look brave. "The night Jason was killed, I was with a
student. A lover. The student's father is a high-powered
attorney from North Carolina and a ranking member of the
Christian Coalition. What do you think he'll do when he
finds out?"

I looked down at his dusty carpet.

"Teaching's all I know, Patrick. It *is* me. Without it, I
disappear."

I looked at him and he seemed to be disappearing as he
said it, floating away to mist right in front of me.

"I stopped at The Black Emerald on my way over to
the hospital, but it was closed. I looked up at Gerry's apartment above it. The shades were drawn. I looked for
Gerry's Grand Torino, usually parked out in front of the
bar. It wasn't here.

If the killer had met me face to face since all this began,
as Dolquist theorized, then it narrowed the field of suspects. Eric and Gerry were both considered suspects by the
FBI. And Gerry was definitely physically strong.

But what possible motive could he have?

I'd known Gerry my entire life. Could he kill?

We're all capable of murder, the voice in my head whispered. Every one of us.

"Mr. Kenzie."

I turned, saw Agent Fields standing by the trunk of a
dark Plymouth. He tossed recording equipment into the
trunk. "Mr. Glynn's in the clear."

"How?"

"We had this place staked out last night. Glynn went
up to his apartment at one, watched TV until three, and
went to bed. We sat here all night, and he never left. He's
not our man, Mr. Kenzie. Sorry."

I nodded, part of me relieved, part of me feeling guilty
for suspecting Gerry in the first place.

Of course there was another part of me that was disappointed. Maybe I'd wanted it to be Glynn.

Just so it would finally be over.

*   *   *

"The bullet did a lot of damage," Dr. Barnett told me. "It tore up her liver, knicked both kidneys, settled in her lower intestines. We almost lost her twice, Mr. Kenzie."

"How is she now?"

"She's not out of the woods," he said. "Is she a strong person? Got a big heart?"

"Yes," I said.

"Then she's got a better chance than some. That's really all I can tell you right now."

They brought her into ICU at eight-thirty after ninety minutes in post-op.

She looked like she'd lost fifty pounds and her body seemed adrift in the bed.

Phil and I stood over her as a nurse hooked up her IVs and switched on a life-support monitor.

"What's that for?" Phil said. "She's okay now. Right?"

"She hemorrhaged twice, Mr. Dimassi. We're monitoring to make sure she doesn't do it again."

Phil took Angie's hand and it looked so small in his.

"Ange?" he said.

"She'll be asleep for most of the day," the nurse said. "There's very little you can do for her now, Mr. Dimassi."

"I'm not leaving her," Phil said.

The nurse looked at me and I gave her back nothing but a flat stare.

At ten, I came out of ICU and found Bubba sitting in the waiting room.

"How is she?"

"They think," I said, "she's going to be okay."

He nodded.

"We'll know more when she wakes up, I guess."

"When's that?"

"Late this afternoon," I said. "Maybe the evening."

"Anything I can do?"

I leaned over the fountain, gulped water like a man come in from a desert.

"I need to speak to Fat Freddy," I said.

"Sure. Why?"

"I need to find Jack Rouse and Kevin Hurlihy and ask them some questions."

"I don't think Freddy'll have a problem with that."

"If they don't answer my questions," I said, "I'll need permission to shoot them until they do."

Bubba leaned over the fountain, looked at me. "You're serious?"

"You tell Freddy, Bubba, that if I don't get his permission, I'll do it anyway."

"Now you're talking," he said.

Phil and I worked in shifts.

If one of us had to use the bathroom or get a drink, the other held Angie's hand. All day, her hand was enclosed in one of ours.

At noon, Phil went looking for the cafeteria, and I lifted her hand to my lips and closed my eyes.

The day I met her, she was missing both front teeth and her hair was cut so short and so badly that I thought she was another boy. We were in the gym at the Little House Recreation Center on East Cottage, and it was a free-for-all for six-year-olds. This was back before there was much official after-school care in my neighborhood, but parents could drop their kids at the Little House for three hours for five dollars a week, and the staff pretty much gave us free rein as long as we didn't break anything.

That day, the floor of the gym was littered with maroon dodgeballs and orange Nerfs and hard plastic footballs and floor hockey sticks and pucks and basketballs and maybe twenty-five uncoordinated six-year-olds running around and screaming like maniacs.

The pucks were in short supply, and after I picked up a hockey stick I honed in on the short kid with the bad haircut as she pushed one awkwardly around the edge of the gym. I snuck up behind her, lifted her stick off the floor with my own, and stole the puck.

And she tackled me, punched me in the head, and stole it back.

With her hand to my face in the ICU unit, I could remember that day as vividly as any in my life.

I leaned in and placed my cheek against hers, pressed her hand tightly to my chest, closed my eyes.

When Phil came back, I bummed a cigarette off him and went out to the parking lot to smoke it.

I hadn't smoked in seven years, but the tobacco smelled like perfume as I lit it and the smoke that filled my lungs felt clean and pure in the frigid air.

"That Porsche," someone on my right said, "is one nice ride. Sixty-six?"

"Sixty-three," I said and turned to look at him.

Pine wore a camel hair topcoat and burgundy twill trousers and a black cashmere sweater. His black gloves looked like a second skin over his hands.

"How'd you afford it?" he said.

"I pretty much bought a body only," I said. "Acquired parts over several years."

"You one of those guys who loves his car more than his wife or friends?"

I held up the keys. "It's chrome and metal and rubber, Pine, and it couldn't mean less to me right now. You want it, take it."

He shook his head. "Far too ostentatious for my tastes. Drive an Acura myself."

I took my second drag on the cigarette and immediately felt light-headed. The air danced in front of my eyes.

"Shooting Vincent Patriso's only granddaughter," he said, "was an extremely uncool thing for someone to do."

"Yes."

"Mr. Constantine has been informed that two people he ordered to cooperate with your investigation did not."

"That's correct."

"And now Ms. Gennaro lies in ICU."

"Yes."

"Mr. Constantine wants you to know that he had nothing to do with this."

"I know."

"Mr. Constantine also wants you to know that you have carte blanche when it comes to whatever you have to do to identify and apprehend the man who shot Ms. Gennaro."

"Carte blanche?"

"Carte blanche, Mr. Kenzie. If Mr. Hurlihy and Mr. Rouse were never seen again, Mr. Constantine assures you that neither he nor his associates would have any desire to look for them. Understood?"

I nodded.

He handed me a card. Scribbled on one side was an address—411 South Street, 4th floor. Scribbled on the other side was a phone number I recognized as Bubba's cell phone.

"Meet Mr. Rogowski there as soon as you can."

"Thanks."

He shrugged, looked at my cigarette. "Shouldn't smoke those things, Mr. Kenzie."

He walked off into the parking lot and I stubbed out the cigarette and went back inside.

"Angie opened her eyes at two forty-five.

"Honey?" Phil said.

She blinked and tried to speak but her mouth was too dry.

As instructed earlier by the nurse, we gave her some chips of ice but no water, and she nodded gratefully.

"Don't call me honey," she croaked. "How many times do I have to tell you, Phillip?"

Phil laughed and kissed her forehead and I kissed her cheek and she slapped feebly at both of us.

We sat back.

"How do you feel?" I said.

"Real stupid question," she said.

Dr. Barnett dropped his stethoscope and penlight back into his pockets and told Angie, "You're going to be in ICU until tomorrow, just so we can keep a close eye on you, but it looks like you're coming along well."

"Hurts like hell," she said.

He smiled. "I'd expect so. That bullet took a particularly nasty course, Ms. Gennaro. And later we'll discuss some of the damage. I can promise you that there's a whole lot of foods you'll never be able to eat again. Just about any liquid besides water is going to be out of the question for a while too.''

"Damn," she said.

"And there'll be other restrictions to talk about, but—"

"What about . . . ?" She looked at Phil and me and then away.

"Yes?" Barnett said.

"Well," she said, "the bullet sort of rattled around down in my lower regions and . . ."

"It affected none of your reproductive organs, Ms. Gennaro."

"Oh," she said and caught me smiling, glared at me. "Don't say a damn word, Patrick."

The pain returned in force around five and they shot her up with enough Demerol to mellow out a Bengal tiger.

I touched my palm to her cheek as she blinked at the drug's effect.

"The guy who shot me?" she said thickly.

"Yeah?"

"You identify him yet?"

"No."

"But you will, won't you?"

"Absolutely."

"Well, then . . ."

"Yeah?"

"Go get him, Patrick," she said. "Shut his ass down."

36

Four eleven South Street was the only vacant building on a street of artist's lofts and carpet makers, costumers, rag merchants, and by-appointment-only galleries. Boston's two-block equivalent of SoHo.

Four eleven was four stories tall and had been a parking garage before the city actually needed one. It changed hands in the late forties and the new owner turned it into an entertainment complex for sailors. The first floor had been a bar and billiards parlor, the second a casino, and the third a whorehouse.

The place had been vacant most of my life, so I never knew what the fourth floor was used for until my Porsche rose up past the dark floors in an ancient car elevator and the doors opened onto a dank, musty bowling alley.

Light fixtures hung haphazardly from a section of caved-in ceiling and several alleys were nothing but corridors of rubble. Shattered bowling pins lay in heaps of white dust in the gutters and the hand dryers had long ago been ripped from the floors and presumably sold for parts. Several of the runway shelves still held bowling balls, though, and I could see target arrows through the dust and grime on a couple of alleys.

Bubba sat in a captain's chair by the center alley as we left the car and exited the elevator. The chair still bore screws at the base from wherever he'd torn it up, and the leather was ripped in several places and spilling foam stuffing onto the floor by his feet.

"Who owns this place?" I said.

"Freddy." He sipped from a bottle of Finlandia. His face was ruddy and his eyes slightly watery, and I knew that he was easily into his second bottle, never a good sign.

"Freddy keeps an abandoned building on his books for fun?"

He shook his head. "The second and third floor only look like shit from the elevator. They're actually pretty nice. Freddy and his boys use them for functions sometimes, shit like that." He looked at Phil and there was nothing friendly in his glance. "Fuck you doing here, pussy?"

Phil took a step back, but still did better than most people facing Bubba in full psychotic tilt.

"I'm in this now, Bubba. All the way."

Bubba smiled and the darkness that covered the entire rear of the alleys seemed to rise up behind him. "Well, now," he said. "How nice for you. Pissed off someone put Angie in the hospital and it wasn't you this time? Someone stepping into your area of expertise, faggot?"

Phil shifted toward me a step. "This has nothing to do with the bad blood between us, Bubba."

Bubba raised his eyebrows at me. "He grow some balls or's he just stupid?"

I'd seen Bubba like this only a few times before, and it was always a case of being far too close to the demon for my liking. By my amended estimate, he had to be three bottles of vodka in, and there was no telling if he'd allow his blacker instincts to be reined in.

Bubba cared about exactly two people in the world— me and Angie. And Phil had spent too much time hurting Angie over the years for Bubba to feel anything for him but pure hate. Being the object of another's hate is relative. If the person who hates you is an advertising exec whose Infiniti you cut off in traffic, you're probably not going to worry much. If Bubba hates you, though, putting a couple of continents between the two of you is not a bad idea.

"Bubba," I said.

He turned his head slowly to look up at me and his gaze was muddy.

"Phil is on our side for this one. That's all you need to

know right now. He wants to be in on whatever we do."

He showed no reaction, just turned his head back toward Phil, fixed that muddy gaze on him.

Phil held the look for as long as he could, long after sweat had slid down by his ears, but eventually he looked at the floor.

"All right, douche," Bubba said. "We'll let you sit in for a few hands, you want to find redemption for what you did to your wife or whatever bullshit you told yourself." He stood and towered over Phil until Phil looked up. "Just so there's no misunderstanding—Patrick forgives. Angie forgives. I don't. Someday I'm going to hurt you."

Phil nodded. "I know that, Bubba."

Bubba used his index finger to prop Phil's chin up. "And if anything that happens in this room leaks, I'll know it didn't come from Patrick. Which means I'll kill you, Phil. Got it?"

Phil tried to nod, but Bubba's finger kept his head from moving.

"Yes," Phil said through gritted teeth.

Bubba looked up at a dark wall on the other side of the elevator. "Lights," he called.

Someone behind the wall flicked a switch and a sickly green-and-white neon flickered in the few remaining light fixtures over the back half of the alleys. There was more sputtering and several gauzy yellow bars of light shafted over the bowling pits themselves.

Bubba raised his arms and turned around grandly, like Moses parting the Red Sea, and we looked down the alleys as a rat scurried for safety along one of the gutters.

"Holy shit," Phil said under his breath.

"You say something?" Bubba said.

"No. Nothing," Phil managed.

At the end of the alley directly in front of me, Kevin Hurlihy was kneeling in the pit. His hands were tied behind his back and his legs were tied at the ankles and a noose around his neck was tied to a nail in the wall over the pit. His face was swollen and shiny with bloody welts. The nose Bubba had broken was flabby and blue, and his broken jaw was wired shut.

Jack Rouse, looking even worse for wear, was tied in an identical fashion in the next alley over. Jack was a lot older than Kevin and his face was almost green and slick with sweat.

Bubba took in our shocked faces and smiled. He leaned in toward Phil and said, "Take a good look at them. Then think what I'm going to do to you someday, pussy."

As Bubba sauntered down the alley toward them, I said, "What, you already interrogated them?"

He shook his head and swigged some vodka. "Hell, no. I had no idea what questions to ask."

"So why they all beat to shit, Bubba?"

He reached Kevin and bent down by him, looked back at me with his deranged grin. "Because I was bored."

He winked and slapped Kevin's jaw and Kevin screamed through his wired teeth.

"Jesus, Patrick," Phil whispered. "Jesus."

"Relax, Phil," I said, though my own blood churned.

Bubba stepped over beside Jack and slapped him in the side of the head so hard you could hear the sound ring across the fourth floor, but Jack didn't scream, just closed his eyes for a moment.

"Okay." Bubba turned around and his trench coat lifted and swirled around him for a moment. He staggered back to us and his combat boots sounded like the hoofs of Clydesdales. "Ask your questions, Patrick."

"How long they been there?" I said.

He shrugged. "Few hours." He picked up a dusty bowling ball from the rack, wiped it with his sleeve.

"Maybe we should get them some water or something."

He spun on me. "What? You fucking kidding me? Patrick"—he placed his arm around me, used the bowling ball to gesture in their direction—"that's the asshole who threatened to kill you and Grace. Remember? Those are the fucks who could have stopped this a month ago, before Angie got shot, before Kara Rider got crucified. They're the enemy," he hissed and the alcohol on his breath rode over me like a wave.

"True," I said as Kevin shook involuntarily. "But—"

"No buts!" Bubba said. "No buts! You said today you

were ready to shoot them if necessary. Right? Right?''

"Yes."

"Well, then? What? There they are, Patrick. Be a man of your word. Don't fucking embarrass me. Don't.''

He removed his arm and pulled the bowling ball close to his chest, caressed it.

I'd said I'd shoot them to get information, and at the time I'd felt it. But it was real easy to say and real easy to feel standing in a hospital waiting room, far distanced from the actual human flesh and bone and blood I was threatening.

Now, here were two bloodied human beings rendered completely helpless and at my mercy. And they weren't vague concepts, they were breathing. And shaking.

At *my* mercy.

I left Bubba and Phil and walked down the alley toward Kevin. He watched me come and seemed to gather strength from it. Maybe he thought that I was the weak link here.

When Grace had told me he'd approached her table, I'd said I'd kill him. And at that moment, if he'd walked into the room, I would have. That was rage.

This was torture.

As I neared him, he sucked air and shook his head as if to clear it and then fastened his numb eyes on my own.

Kevin tortures, a voice in my head whispered. He kills. He enjoys it. He'd give you no mercy. So you owe him none.

"Kevin," I said and lowered myself until I was on one knee in front of him, "this is bad. You know this is bad. You don't tell me what I need to know, Bubba will do the Spanish Inquisition on your head.''

"Fuck you.'' His cracked voice broke through gritted teeth. "Fuck you, Kenzie. Okay?''

"No, Kev. No. You don't help me out here, you're going to be fucked up ten different ways. Fat Freddy gave me carte blanche with you. And Jack.''

The left half of his face sagged a bit.

"It's true, Kev.''

"Bullshit.''

"You think we'd be here if it wasn't? You let Vincent Patriso's granddaughter get shot."

"I didn't—"

I shook my head. "That's how he sees it. Doesn't matter what you say now."

His eyes were red and bulging as he shook his head and stared up at me.

"Kevin," I said softly, "tell me what happened between EEPA and Hardiman and Rugglestone. Who's the third guy?"

"Ask Jack."

"I will," I said. "But I'm asking you first."

He nodded and the noose bit into his neck and his throat gurgled. I pulled the rope back out of the center of his Adam's apple and he sighed, his eyes on the floor.

He shook his head adamantly and I knew he wouldn't talk.

"Fore!" Bubba yelled.

Kevin's eyes widened and his neck jerked back in the noose and I stepped out of the way as the bowling ball rocketed down the alley and seemed to pick up speed by the second as it hurtled across the splinters in the ancient floor and made contact with Kevin Hurlihy's groin.

He howled and jerked forward against the noose and I yanked at his shoulders to keep his neck from snapping and tears streamed down his cheeks.

"Only a spare," Bubba said.

"Hey, Bubba," I said, "hold up."

But Bubba was already into his windup. He crossed one leg in front of the other at the foul line and the ball left his hand and arced out by the target arrows, hit the alley with a hint of a backward spin and then streaked across the wood and shattered Kevin's left knee.

"Jesus!" Kevin screamed and flipped to his right.

"Your turn, Jack." Bubba picked up a ball and stepped into the next lane.

"I'll die, Bubba." Jack's voice was soft and resigned and it stopped Bubba for a moment.

"Not if you talk, Jack," I said.

He looked at me as if just noticing me. "You know

what the difference between you and your old man is, Patrick?''

I shook my head.

"Your old man would be throwing those bowling balls himself. You, you'll use what torture can get you, but you won't do it yourself. You're vomit.''

I looked at him and suddenly felt the same crazed rage I'd felt in Grace's house. This piece-of-shit Irish Mafia killer was getting self-righteous with me? While Grace and Mae were holed up in some FBI bunker in Nebraska or someplace with Grace's career in ruins? While Kara Rider lay in the ground and Jason Warren lay in pieces and Angie lay in a hospital bed and Tim Dunn was stripped of his clothes and shoved in a barrel?

I'd spent weeks standing by while people like Evandro and his partner and Hardiman and Jack Rouse and Kevin Hurlihy wreaked violence on innocents for fun. Because they enjoyed the pain of others. Because they could.

And suddenly I wasn't just angry at Jack or Kevin or Hardiman, I was furious at every person who practiced violence willingly. People who blew up abortion clinics and bombed airliners and butchered families and gassed subway tunnels and executed hostages and killed women who looked like women who'd spurned them in the past.

In the name of *their* pain. Or *their* principles. Or *their* profit.

Well, I was sick of *their* violence and *their* hate and my own codes of decency, which may have cost people their lives in the last month. Sick to fucking death of it all.

Jack was staring up at me defiantly and I could feel blood roaring in my ears and still hear Kevin hissing in pain through clenched teeth beside me. I met Bubba's eyes and saw a gleam in them and it invigorated me.

I felt omnipotent.

I kept my eyes on Jack and pulled out my gun and rammed the butt into Kevin's gritted teeth.

The shriek he sent out into the atmosphere was one of complete disbelief and sudden, utter fear.

I grabbed his hair in my hand, my eyes still on Jack, and the hair felt slick and oily between my fingers as I rammed the barrel into his temple and cocked the hammer.

"You have any feelings for this guy, Jack, talk."

Jack looked at Kevin and I could see it pained him. I was once again surprised by the bonds that could exist between two people who knew so little about love.

Jack's mouth opened and he looked so, so old.

"You got five seconds, Jack. One. Two. Three . . ."

Kevin moaned and his broken teeth rattled against the wire in his mouth.

"Four."

"Your father," Jack said quietly, "burned Rugglestone from head to toe over the course of four hours."

"I know that. Who else was there?"

His mouth opened wide again and he looked at Kevin.

"Who else, Jack? Or I start counting again. From four."

"All of us. Timpson. Kev's mother. Diedre Rider. Burns. Climstich. Me."

"What happened?"

"We found Hardiman and Rugglestone hiding out in that warehouse. We'd been looking for the van all night and that morning, we found it right in our neighborhood." Jack licked his upper lip with a tongue so pale it was almost white. "Your father came up with the idea of tying Hardiman to a chair and making him watch while we did Rugglestone. At first, we were just going to take a few shots each, then work on Hardiman, then call in the police."

"Why didn't you?"

"I don't know. Something happened to us in there. Your father found a box hidden under the floorboards. The box was inside a cooler. There were body parts in it." He looked at me wildly. "Body parts. Of kids. Adults, too, but, Jesus, there was a child's foot in there, Kenzie. Still in a small red sneaker with blue polka-dots. Christ. We saw that and we lost it. That's when your father got the gasoline. That's when we started using the ice picks and razor blades."

I waved my hand at him because I didn't feel like hearing any more about the good citizens of EEPA and their systematic torture-killing of Charles Rugglestone.

"Who's doing Hardiman's killing for him now?"

Jack looked confused. "What's-his-name. Arujo. The guy your partner killed last night. Right?"

"Arujo had a partner. You know who it is, Jack?"

"No," he said. "I don't. Kenzie, we made a mistake. We let Hardiman live, but—"

"Why?"

"Why what?"

"Why'd you let him live?"

"Because it was our only way out once G busted us. That was the deal he made with us."

"G? What the hell are you talking about?"

He sighed. "We got caught, Patrick. Standing around Rugglestone watching his body go up in flames with blood all over our clothes."

"Who caught you?"

"G. I told you."

"Who's G, Jack?"

He frowned. "Gerry Glynn, Kenzie."

I felt light-headed suddenly, as if I'd just tried to smoke another cigarette.

"And he didn't arrest you?" I asked Jack.

Jack nodded slightly. "He said it was understandable. He said most people would do the same."

"*Gerry* said this?"

"Who the fuck am I talking about? Yeah. Gerry. He made sure each one of us knew what we owed him, and then he sent us on our way and arrested Alec Hardiman."

"What do you mean, you owed him?"

"We owed him. Favors, shit like that, for the rest of our lives. Your father pulled strings and got him the zoning and the liquor license for his bar. I got him some creative financing. Other people did other things. We were forbidden to talk with each other, so I have no idea who gave him what outside of me and your old man."

"You were forbidden to talk with each other? By Gerry?"

"Of course by Gerry." He stared at me and the veins in his neck were bright blue and hard. "You don't know who you're dealing with when it comes to Gerry, do you?

Jesus.'' He laughed loudly. ''Holy shit! You bought all
that Officer Friendly bullshit, didn't you? Kenzie,'' he said
and strained against the noose, ''Gerry Glynn is a fucking
monster. He makes me look like a parish priest.'' He
laughed again and it was a shrill, awful sound. ''You think
that gypsy cab he keeps out front always takes people
where they want to go?''

I remembered that night in the bar, the drunk kid who
Gerry sent into that cab with ten bucks. Had he made it
home? And who was the cab driver? Evandro?

Bubba and Phil had come down the alley by this point
and I looked at them as I removed the gun from Kevin's
head.

''You guys know this?''

Phil shook his head.

Bubba said, ''I knew Gerry was a little shady, ran some
blow and some hookers out of the bar, but that's it.''

''He duped your whole fucking generation,'' Jack said.
''The whole pack of ya. Jesus.''

''Be specific,'' I said. ''Very specific, Jack.''

He smiled at us and his old eyes danced. ''Gerry Glynn
is one of the meanest motherfuckers who ever came out
of the neighborhood. His son died. You know that?''

I said, ''He had a son?''

'' 'Course he had a fucking son. Brendan. Died in
'sixty-five. Had some bizarre hemorrhage at his brain stem.
No one could ever explain it. Kid was four years old, he
grabs his head, drops dead in Gerry's front yard while he's
playing with Gerry's wife. Gerry snapped. He killed his
wife.''

''Bullshit,'' Bubba said. ''Guy was a cop.''

''So? Gerry got it in his head that it was her fault. That
she'd been fucking around on him and God had punished
her by killing their kid. He punched her to death, framed
some spook for it. The spook got shivved to death in Dedham a week after his arraignment. Case closed.''

''How's Gerry reach out and touch a guy locked up?''

''Gerry was a bull at Dedham. Back in the old days,
when they still allowed cops to work two jobs in the same
system. Some witness, a con, supposedly heard Gerry set

it up. Gerry whacked the guy in Scollay Square a week after he was released.''

Jamal Cooper. Victim Number One. Jesus.

''Gerry's one of the scariest guys on the planet, you dumb fuck, Kenzie.''

''And it never occurred to you that he could be Hardiman's partner?'' I asked.

Everyone looked at me.

''Hardiman's . . . ?'' Jack's mouth opened wide again and the muscles in his jaws rotated against thin skin. ''No, no. I mean, Gerry's dangerous, but he's not . . .''

''He's not what, Jack?''

''He's, well, not serial-killer-psycho crazy.''

I shook my head. ''How fucking dumb could you be?''

Jack looked at me. ''Shit, Kenzie, Gerry's from the neighborhood. We don't breed crazies like that in the neighborhood.''

I shook my head. ''You're from the neighborhood, Jack. So was my father. Look what you two pulled off in that warehouse.''

I started to walk back down the alley and he called after me: ''What about you, Kenzie? What about what you pulled off here today?''

I looked back, saw Kevin trying to stay conscious against the pain, blood painted on his mouth and chin.

''I didn't kill anyone, Jack.''

''But if I hadn't talked, you would have, Kenzie. You would have.''

I turned, kept walking.

''You want to think of yourself as good, Kenzie? Huh? Think about what I just said. Remember what you would have done.''

The shots came out of the darkness in front of me.

I saw the muzzle flash and actually felt the first bullet streak past my shoulder.

I dropped to the floor as a second bullet burst through the darkness and out into the light.

Behind me, I heard two deep metal-into-flesh sounds. Sucking sounds.

As Pine walked out of the darkness, he unscrewed a

silencer from his pistol, his gloved hand shrouded in smoke.

I turned my head and looked back down the lanes.

Phil was on his knees, hands over his head.

Bubba tilted his head back as he poured vodka down his throat.

Kevin Hurlihy and Jack Rouse stared blankly back at me, identical bullet holes in the centers of their foreheads.

"Welcome to my world," Pine said and offered me his gloved hand.

37

I **didn't like** the way Pine stood over the elevator shaft with his eyes on Phil as we descended. Phil had his head down and his hand on the roof of the Porsche as if he needed its support to remain standing. Pine's gaze never wavered.

As we neared the first floor Pine said something to Bubba, and Bubba stuffed his hands in his trench coat pockets and shrugged.

The elevator doors opened and we climbed in the car and pulled out the back of the building and turned up the alley that led to South Street.

"Jesus," Phil said.

I drove slowly up the alley, my eyes on the headlights cutting through the hard dark in front of us.

"Pull the car over," Phil said desperately.

"No, Phil."

"Please. I'm going to be sick."

"I know," I said. "But you're going to have to hold it down until we're out of sight of the building."

"Why, for God's sake?"

I pulled out onto South Street. "Because if Pine or Bubba sees you puke, they'll be convinced they can't trust you. Now hold on."

I drove up the block, turned right and picked up speed on Summer Street. A half block past South Station, I pulled in behind the Post Office, checked each loading bay until I was sure they hadn't started filling the trucks yet, and then pulled in behind a Dumpster.

Phil was out of the car before we came to a complete stop and I turned up the radio so I wouldn't have to hear the sounds of his body revolting against what he'd just witnessed.

I reached down and turned the volume higher and the windows reverberated as Sponge's "Plowed" poured through my speakers, the vicious guitar riffs carving through my skull.

Two men were dead and I may as well have pulled the trigger myself. They weren't innocent. They weren't clean. But they were human, nonetheless.

Phil came back to the car and I handed him Kleenex from the glove compartment and turned down the volume. He pressed the tissue to his mouth as I swung back onto Summer and headed toward Southie.

"Why'd he kill them? They told us what we wanted to know."

"They disobeyed his boss. Don't get caught up in the whys, Phil."

"But Christ, he just shot them. He just pulled his gun and they were tied up and I'm standing there, looking at them, and then—shit—no sound, nothing, just those holes."

"Phil, listen to me."

I pulled to the side of the road on a dark stretch by the Araban Coffee Building, smelled the roasted aroma trying to overide the oily stench of the docks off to my left.

He put his hands over his eyes. "Oh, my God."

"Phil! Fucking look at me!"

He lowered his hands. "What?"

"It never happened."

"What?"

"It never happened. You got it?" I was shouting, and Phil recoiled from me in the dark of the car, but I didn't care. "You want to die, too? Do you? That's what we're talking about here, Phil."

"Jesus. Me? Why?"

"Because you're a witness."

"I know, but—"

"*But* is not an option. This is very simple, Phil. You're

alive because Bubba would never kill anyone I care about. You're alive because he's convinced Pine that I'll keep you in line. I'm alive because they know I won't talk. And both of us, by the way, would go to jail for double homicide if we did, because we were *there*. But it'd never come to that, Phil, because if Pine has any reason to worry, he'll kill you and he'll kill me and he'll probably kill Bubba, too."

"But—"

"Stop with the fucking buts, Phil. I swear to God. You convince yourself that this never happened. It was all a bad dream. Kevin and Jack are on vacation somewhere. Because if you don't get clear on that concept, you'll talk."

"I won't."

"You will. You'll tell your wife or your girlfriend or someone in a bar, and then we're all dead. And the person you told is dead, too. Do you understand?"

"Yes."

"You'll be watched."

"What?"

I nodded. "Face it and find a way to live with it. For quite a while, you'll be watched."

He swallowed hard and his eyes bulged, and I thought he might get sick again.

Instead he jerked his head around and stared out the window and curled into himself on the seat.

"How do you do this?" he whispered. "Day in and day out?"

I sat back in my seat and closed my eyes and listened to the German engine rumble.

"How do you live with yourself, Patrick?"

I slid the shift into first and didn't speak again as we drove through Southie and down into the neighborhood.

I left the Porsche in front of my house and headed for the Crown Victoria, parked a few cars back, because a '63 Porsche is just about the last thing you want to be driving in my neighborhood if you want to remain anonymous.

Phil stood by the passenger door, and I shook my head.

"What?" he said.

"You're staying behind, Phil. I'm alone on this one."

He shook his head. "No. I was married to her, Patrick, and this prick shot her."

"Want him to shoot you, too, Phil?"

He shrugged. "You think I'm not up to this?"

I nodded. "I think you're not up to this, Phil."

"Why? Because of the bowling alley? Kevin—he was someone we grew up with. A friend once. So okay, I didn't handle him getting shot real well. But Gerry?" He held his gun up on the car top, worked the slide, and jacked a round into the chamber. "Gerry's dogshit. Gerry dies."

I stared at him, waited for him to see how silly he looked working the slide like a character in a movie, spitting out his bravado.

He stared back, and the muzzle of his gun slowly turned until it was facing me over the roof.

"You going to shoot me, Phil? Huh?"

His hand was firm. The gun never wavered.

"Answer me, Phil. You going to shoot me?"

"You don't open this door, Patrick, I'll blow the window out, climb in anyway."

I looked steadily at the gun in his hand.

"I love her, too, Patrick." He lowered the gun.

I got in the car. He rapped on the window with the gun and I took a deep breath, knowing he'd follow me on foot if it came down to it or shoot out the window of my Porsche and hot-wire it.

I reached across the seat and unlocked the door.

The rain started around midnight, not even a drizzle at first, just a few spits that mingled with the dirt on my windows and bled down to my wipers.

We parked in front of a senior citizens home on Dorchester Avenue, a half block up from The Black Emerald. Then the clouds broke and the rain clattered the roof and swept down the avenue in great dark sheets. It was a freezing rain, identical to yesterday's, and the only effect it had on the ice still clinging to sidewalks and buildings was to make it seem simultaneously cleaner and more lethal.

Initially, we were grateful for it, because our windows steamed up, and unless someone was standing right beside the car, he wouldn't be able to see the two of us inside.

But this worked against us, too, because pretty soon we couldn't see the bar very well or the door to Gerry's apartment. The defrost in the car was broken, and so was the heater, and damp cold bit into my bones. I cracked my window, and Phil cracked his, and I used my elbow to wipe at the condensation on the inside until Gerry's doorway and the doorway to the Emerald reappeared, diluted and rubbery.

"How're you so sure it's Gerry who's been working with Hardiman?" Phil said.

"I'm not," I said. "But it feels right."

"So why aren't we calling the cops?"

"To tell them what? Two guys with fresh bullet holes in their heads told us Gerry was a bad guy?"

"What about the FBI then?"

"Same problem. We don't have any proof. If it is Gerry, and we tip him too early, maybe he slips away again, goes into hibernation or whatever, only kills runaways nobody's looking for."

"So why are we here?"

"Because if he makes a move, any kind of move, I want to see it, Phil."

Phil wiped at his side of the windshield, peered out at the bar. "Maybe we should just go in there, ask him some questions."

I looked at him. "Are you nuts?"

"Why not?"

"Because if it is him, he'll kill us, Phil."

"There's two of us, Patrick. We're both armed."

I could see he was trying to talk himself into it, to suck up the courage necessary to go through that door. But he was still a long way from doing it.

"It's the tension," I said. "The waiting."

"What about it?"

"Sometimes it seems a lot worse than any confrontation could be, like if you could just do something, you'd stop feeling like you need to climb out of your skin."

He nodded. "That's the feeling, yeah."

"Problem is, Phil, if Gerry's the guy we think he is, the confrontation will be a lot worse than the wait. He'll kill us, guns or no guns."

He swallowed once, then nodded.

For a full minute I stared hard at the door to the Emerald. In the time we'd been here, I'd seen no one enter or exit, and that was more than a little odd just after midnight at a bar in this neighborhood. A solid sheet of water the size of a building swept along the avenue, its edges curling, and the wind howled distantly.

"How many people?" Phil said.

"What?"

Phil tilted his head in the direction of the Emerald. "If he is the guy, how many people you think he's killed? Over his entire lifetime? I mean, taking into consideration that maybe he killed all those runaways over the years, and maybe a shitload of people no one even knows about and—"

"Phil."

"Yeah?"

"I'm nervous enough. There are some things I don't want to think about just now."

"Oh." He rubbed the stubble under his chin. "Right."

I stared at the bar, counted off another full minute. Still no one went in or out.

My cell phone rang and both Phil and I jerked so hard our heads hit the roof.

"Jesus," Phil said. "Jesus Christ."

I flipped it open. "Hello."

"Patrick, it's Devin. Where are you?"

"In my car. What's up?"

"I just talked to Erdham with the FBI. He pulled a partial print from under the floorboard in your house where one of the bugs was placed."

"And?" The oxygen circulating through my body slowed to a crawl.

"It's Glynn, Patrick. Gerry Glynn."

I looked through my steamed windows and could just

make out the shape of the bar, and I felt unequivocal terror like I'd never felt in my life.

"Patrick? You there?"

"Yeah. Look, Devin, I'm outside Gerry's place now."

"You're what?"

"You heard me. I came to the same conclusion an hour ago."

"Jesus, Patrick. Get out of there. Now. Don't fuck around. Go. Go."

I wanted to. Christ, I wanted to.

But if he was in there now, packing a bag with ice picks and straight razors, preparing to head out to pick up another victim . . .

"I can't, Dev. If he's here and he moves, I'm following him wherever he goes."

"No, no, no. No, Patrick. You hear me? Get the fuck out of there."

"Can't do it, Dev."

"Fuck!" I heard him bang something hard. "All right. I'm on my way over there now with an army. You got it? You sit tight, and we'll be there in fifteen minutes. He moves, you call this number."

He gave it to me and I scribbled it on the pad velcroed to my dash.

"Hurry," I said.

"I'm hurrying." He hung up.

I looked at Phil. "It's confirmed. Gerry's our guy."

Phil looked at the phone in my hand and his face was a mixture of nausea and desperation.

"Help's on the way?" he said.

"Help's on the way."

The windows had fogged over completely and I wiped at mine again, saw something dark and heavy move out of the corner of my eye, near the back door.

Then the door opened and Gerry Glynn hopped inside and put his wet arms around me.

38

"**How you guys** doing?" Gerry said.

Phil's hand had slipped into his jacket, and I looked at him so he knew I didn't want him pulling a gun in the car.

"Good, Gerry," I said.

I met his eyes in the mirror and they were kind and slightly amused.

His thick hands patted my sternum. "I surprise you?"

"Oh, yeah," I said.

He chuckled. "Sorry. Just I saw you guys sitting in here and I thought to myself, 'Now why are Patrick and Phil sitting in a car on Dot Ave. at twelve-thirty in the morning during a rainstorm?' "

"Just having a chat, Ger," Phil said and his attempt at sounding casual came out sounding forced.

"Oh," Gerry said. "Well. Hell of a night for it."

I looked at the wet red hairs spreading limply down his forearms.

"You looking to get lucky with me?" I said.

He narrowed his eyes at me in the mirror, then looked down at his arms.

"Oh, Jeez." He removed his arms. "Whoops. Forgot how wet I was."

"You're not working the bar tonight?" Phil said.

"Huh? No. No." He propped his forearms on the back of our seat between the two headrests, leaned his head in. "Bar's closed at the moment. I figured, weather like this, you know, who's going to come out?"

"Too bad," Phil said and coughed out a ragged half chuckle. "Could have used a drink tonight."

I looked at the driver's wheel to conceal my fury. Phil, I thought, how could you have just said that?

"Bar's always open to friends," Gerry said happily and slapped our shoulders. "Yes, sir. No problem there."

I said, "I don't know, Ger. It's getting a little late for me and—"

"On the house," Gerry said. "On me, my friends. 'A little late,'" he said, and nudged Phil. "What's with this guy?"

"Well—"

"Come on. Come on. One drink."

He hopped out of the car and opened my door before I thought to reach for it.

Phil was giving me a What-do-we-do? look and the rain was spitting through the open door into my face and neck.

Gerry leaned into the car. "Come on, guys. Trying to drown me out here?"

Gerry kept his hands in the pouch of his hooded warm-up sweater as we jogged to the bar door, and when he removed the right to open the door with his key, the left remained in the pouch. In the dark, with the wind and rain in my face, I couldn't tell if he had a weapon in there or not, so I wasn't about to pull my own and attempt a citizen's arrest on the street with a jittery partner for back-up.

Gerry opened the door and swept his hand out ahead of him so we'd pass first.

A muted halo of yellow illuminated the bar itself, but the rest of the place was dark. The pool room, just beyond the bar, was pitch black.

"Where's my favorite dog?" I said.

"Patton? Up in the apartment, dreaming doggie dreams." He snapped the bolt-lock, and Phil and I looked back at him.

He smiled. "Can't have any regulars stumbling in, getting pissed at me for closing up earlier."

"Can't have that," Phil said and laughed like an idiot.

Gerry gave him a quizzical look, then glanced at me.

I shrugged. "Neither of us has slept in a good while, Gerry."

His face immediately jellied into an expression of the deepest sympathy.

"I almost forgot. Jesus. Angie was hurt last night, wasn't she?"

"Yeah," Phil said and now his voice was too hard.

Gerry went behind the bar. "Oh, guys, I'm sorry. She's okay, though?"

"She's okay," I said.

"Sit, sit," Gerry said and rummaged in the cooler. His back to us, he said, "Angie, she's, well, special. You know?"

He turned back to us as we sat and placed two bottles of Bud in front of us. I removed my jacket, tried to appear normal, shook my hands free of rain.

"Yes," I said. "She is."

He frowned at his hands as he popped the tops off the bottles. "She's . . . well, every now and then you get someone in this town who's just unique. Full of spirit and life. Angie's like that. I'd rather die myself than see harm come to a girl like that."

Phil was gripping his beer bottle so hard I was afraid it would shatter in his hand.

"Thanks, Gerry," I said. "She's going to be fine, though."

"Well, that calls for a drink." He poured himself a shot of Jameson's, raised the glass. "To Angie's recovery."

We touched bottles to glass and drank.

"You're okay though, Patrick?" he asked. "I heard you were in the middle of the firefight, too."

"Fine, Gerry."

"Thank the good Lord for that, Patrick. Yes, sir."

Behind us, music suddenly exploded in our ears and Phil jerked around in his seat. "Fuck!"

Gerry smiled and touched a switch under the bar, and the volume descended rapidly until the wall of noise became a song I recognized.

"Let It Bleed." Absolutely fucking perfect.

"Jukebox kicks on automatically two minutes after I

come through the door," Gerry said. "Sorry to spook you."

"No problem," I said.

"You okay, Phil?"

"Huh?" Phil's eyes were the size of hubcaps. "Fine. Fine. Why?"

Gerry shrugged. "You just seem a little jumpy."

"No." Phil shook his head violently. "Not me. Nope." He gave us both a broad, sickly smile. "I'm aces, Gerry."

"O-kay," Gerry said and smiled himself, gave me another curious look.

This man kills people, a voice whispered. For fun. Dozens of people.

"So anything new?" Gerry asked me.

Kills, the voice whispered.

"Huh?" I said.

"Anything new?" Gerry repeated. "I mean outside of getting in a shootout last night and all."

He dissects people, the voice hissed, while they're still alive. And screaming.

"No," I managed. "Outside of that, everything's been pretty status quo, Ger."

He chuckled. "A wonder you've made it this far, Patrick, the life you lead."

They beg. And he laughs. They pray. And he laughs. This man, Patrick. This man with the open face and the kind eyes.

"Luck of the Irish," I said.

"Don't I know it." He raised his glass of Jameson's and winked, downed it. "Phil," he said as he poured another, "what're you doing these days?"

"What?" Phil said. "How do you mean?"

Phil clung to his seat like a rocket to its booster, as if the countdown had already begun and any second he'd shoot up through the roof.

"For work," Gerry said. "You still work for Galvin Brothers?"

Phil blinked. "No, no. I'm, ah, a private contractor now, Gerry."

"Steady work?"

This man opened Jason Warren's body up and amputated his limbs, severed his head.

"What?" Phil sucked some beer from the bottle. "Oh, yeah, pretty steady."

"You guys are a little slow tonight," Gerry said.

"Ha-ha," Phil said weakly.

This man hammered Kara Rider's hands into frozen dirt.

His fingers snapped in front of my face.

"You still with us, Patrick?"

I smiled. "Take another beer, Gerry."

"Sure thing." He kept his eyes on me, steady and curious, as he reached behind him into the cooler.

Behind us "Let It Bleed" had given way to "Midnight Rambler" and the harmonica sounded like a persistent chuckle from the grave.

He handed me the beer, and his hand touched mine around the icy bottle as he did so and I resisted the urge to recoil.

"FBI interrogated me," he said. "You hear about that?"

I nodded.

"The questions they asked, my God. Sure, they're just doing their jobs, I understand, but the miserable cunts, I swear."

He flashed his smile at Phil, but it didn't fit those words, and suddenly I was aware of a smell that had been in here with us since we entered. It was a sweaty, musky smell, commingled with the stewy stench of matted hair and flesh.

It wasn't coming from Gerry or Phil or me, because it wasn't the smell of a human. It was the smell of an animal.

I glanced at the clock over Gerry's shoulder. Fifteen minutes exactly since I'd talked to Devin.

Where was he?

I could still feel his hand where it had glanced off mine around the beer bottle. The skin burned.

That hand plucked out Peter Stimovich's eyes.

Phil was leaning to his right, peering at something

around the corner of the bar and Gerry looked at both of us and his smile evaporated.

I knew the silence was heavy and uncomfortable and suspicious, but I couldn't think how to break it.

That smell rose into my nostrils again, and it was sickly warm, somehow, and I knew it came from my right, from the pitch black of the pool room.

"Midnight Rambler" ended and the silence that replaced it for a moment filled the bar.

I could just barely hear a low, almost imperceptible chugging sound coming from the pool room. The sound of breathing. Patton was back in the dark somewhere, watching us.

Talk, Patrick. Talk or die.

"So, Ger," I said and my throat felt dry, as if the words would strangle in my throat, "what's new with you?"

"Not much," he said, and I knew he'd given up on small talk. He watched Phil openly now.

"You mean outside of being interrogated by the FBI and all?" I grinned, tried to bring the forced lightness back to the room.

"Outside of that, yeah," Gerry said, his eyes on Phil.

"The Long Black Veil" took "Midnight Rambler's" place. Just one more song about death. Wonderful.

Phil stared at something around the corner of the bar, on the floor, out of my eyesight.

"Phil," Gerry said. "Something interest you?"

Phil looked up sharply and then his eyes half-hooded over, as if he were completely nonplussed.

"No, Ger." He smiled and held out his hands. "Just looking at that dog bowl on the floor, and, you know, the food in there's wet, like Patton was just chewing it. You sure he's upstairs?"

It was supposed to sound casual. I'm sure that's how he intended it. But it came out sounding anything but.

The kindness in Gerry's eyes disappeared into a vortex of pure black cold, and he glanced at me as if I were a bug under a microscope.

And I knew all pretense had ended.

I reached for my gun as tires screeched to a stop outside and Gerry reached under the bar.

Phil was still frozen when Gerry said, "Iago!"

It wasn't just the name of a Shakespeare character, it was an attack code.

I had my gun clear of my waistband when Patton burst out of the darkness and I saw the hard glint of the straight razor in Gerry's hand.

Phil said, "Oh, no. No." And ducked.

And Patton vaulted over his shoulder toward me.

Gerry's arm shot out and I leaned back as the razor cleaved through the flesh by my cheekbone and Patton hit me like a wrecking ball and knocked me off my stool.

"No, Gerry! No!" Phil screamed, his hand stuck in his belt as he dug for his gun.

The dog's teeth bounced off my forehead and its head reared back and its jaws opened and plunged toward my right eye.

Someone screamed.

I grasped Patton's neck with my free hand and the noise he made was a savage combination of screaming and barking. I squeezed his throat but it constricted and my hand slid up his sweaty fur and his head plunged toward my face again.

I shoved the gun into his midsection as he kicked at my arm with his back feet and when I pulled the trigger— twice—Patton's head snapped back as if he heard his name being called, and then he jerked and shuddered and a low hissing sound escaped his mouth. His flesh went soft in my hands as he tipped to his right and toppled into the row of bar stools.

I sat up and fired six rounds into the mirrors and bottles behind the bar, but Gerry wasn't there.

Phil was on the floor by his stool, grasping his throat.

The front door shattered off its hinges as I crawled to him and I heard Devin yell, "Don't shoot! Don't shoot! He's a good guy!" Then, "Kenzie, put your gun down!"

I laid it on the floor beside Phil as I reached him.

Most of the blood came from the right side of his throat,

where Gerry had made his initial incision before cutting a smile toward the other side.

"An ambulance!" I screamed. "We need an ambulance!"

Phil looked up at me, confused, as the bright blood flowed between his fingers and over his hand.

Devin handed me a bar towel and I pressed it to Phil's throat, placed my hands tightly on either side.

"Shit," he said.

"Don't speak, Phil."

"Shit," he said again.

Twin pearls of defeat were imprinted in his eyes as if he'd been expecting this since he was born, as if you come out of a womb with a winner's luck or a loser's and he'd always known he'd find himself on the floor of a bar some night, the stench of stale beer soaked in rubber tile all around him, his throat cut.

He tried to smile and tears spilled from the corners of his eyes, slid across his temples, and were lost in his dark hair.

"Phil," I said, "you're going to be okay."

"I know," he said.

And died.

39

Gerry had run down to the cellar and crossed into the building next door, let himself out the back door as he'd done the night he'd shot Angie. He hopped into his Grand Torino in the alley behind the bar and drove toward Crescent Avenue.

A cruiser almost collided with him as he shot out the alley onto Crescent, and by the time he squealed onto Dorchester Avenue, four police cars were in pursuit.

Two more cruisers and an FBI Lincoln came down the Avenue and formed a blockade by the corner with Harborview Street as Gerry's car slid along the ice toward them.

Gerry spun the wheel at the Ryan Playground and drove straight up entrance stairs so slick with ice they might as well have been a ramp.

He fishtailed in the center of the playground as the cops and the Feds were getting out of their cars and aiming their weapons and then he popped the trunk and pulled his hostages out.

One was a twenty-one-year-old woman named Danielle Rawson, who'd been missing from her parents' house in Reading since this morning. The other hostage was her two-year-old son, Campbell.

When Gerry pulled Danielle out of the trunk, there was a twelve-gauge attached to her head by electrical tape.

He strapped Campbell to his back using the backpack Danielle had been wearing when he kidnapped them.

Both of them had been drugged and only Danielle came

to as Gerry wrapped his finger around the shotgun trigger and doused himself and Danielle in gasoline, then poured a circle of it around the three of them in the ice.

Then Gerry asked for me.

I was still in the bar.

I was kneeling over Phil's body, weeping into his chest.

I hadn't cried since I was sixteen years old, and my tears flooded out in waves as I knelt by my oldest friend's body and felt sheared, in strips, of anything I'd ever known by which to define myself or my world.

"Phil," I said and buried my head in his chest.

"He's asking for you," Devin said.

I looked up at him and felt removed from everything and everyone.

I noticed a fresh swath of blood on Phil's shirt, where my head had been, and remembered that Gerry had cut me.

"Who?" I said.

"Glynn," Oscar said. "He's trapped in the playground. With hostages."

"You got sharpshooters?"

"Yes," Devin said.

I shrugged. "So shoot him."

"Can't do it." Devin handed me a towel for my cheek.

Then Oscar told me about the baby strapped to Glynn's back and the shotgun taped to the mother's head and the gasoline.

It didn't seem real to me, though.

"He killed Phil," I said.

Devin grasped my arm roughly and pulled me to my feet.

"Yes, Patrick, he did. And now he might kill two more people. Care to help us prevent that?"

"Yeah," I said, and my voice didn't sound like my own. It sounded dead. "Sure."

*   *   *

They followed me out to my car as I shrugged on the bulletproof vest they gave me and put a fresh clip in my Beretta. Bolton joined us on the avenue.

"He's surrounded," he said. "Boxed in."

I felt as numb as I've ever felt, as if I'd been cored clean of emotions as swiftly as you'd core an apple.

"Be quick," Oscar said. "You got five minutes or he maims a hostage."

I nodded, pulled my shirt and jacket on over the vest as we reached my car.

"You know Bubba's warehouse," I said.

"Yeah."

"The fence that runs around it also runs around the playground."

"I'm aware of this," Devin said.

I opened the car, popped the glove compartment, began pulling out its contents and spilling them on the seats.

"What're you doing, Patrick?"

"The fence," I said, "has a hole in it. You can't see it in the dark because it's just a cut. You push at it and it flaps forward."

"Okay."

I saw the edge of a small steel cylinder sticking up from the pile of matchbooks and warranty information and various papers and screws on my seat.

"The hole is at the east corner of the fence where the posts meet at the beginning of Bubba's land."

Devin looked at the cylinder as I shut the door and headed up the avenue toward the playground.

"What's that in your hand?"

"It's a one-shot." I loosened my watchband, slid the cylinder between the leather strap and my wrist.

"A one-shot."

"Christmas present from Bubba," I said. "Years ago." I flashed it at him. "One bullet. I depress this button, it's like a trigger. The bullet leaves the cylinder."

He and Oscar looked at it. "That's a fucking suppressor with a couple of hinges and screws, a blasting cap, and a bullet. It'll blow up in your hand, Patrick."

"Possibly."

The playground loomed in front of us, the fifteen-foot-high fence glazed in ice, the trees black and heavy with it.

"Why do you even need that?" Oscar said.

"Because he'll make me give up my gun." I turned and looked at them. "The hole in the fence, guys."

"I'll send a man in," Bolton said.

"No." I shook my head. I nodded at Devin and Oscar. "One of them. They're the only ones I trust. One of you go through it and crawl up on him from behind."

"And do what? Patrick, he's got—"

"—a baby strapped to his back. Trust me. You're going to have to break his fall."

"I'll do it," Devin said.

Oscar snorted. "With your knees? Shit. You won't get ten yards across that ice."

Devin looked at him. "Yeah? How you going to drag your whale's ass across a playground without getting seen."

"I'm a brother, partner. I'm one with the night."

"Which is it?" I said.

Devin sighed, jerked his thumb at Oscar.

"Whale's ass," Oscar said grumpily. "Huh."

"See you in there," I said and walked over the sidewalk to the playground.

I came up the steps by pulling myself, hand over hand, up the railing.

The streets and avenues had been burned free of ice by salt and tires during the day, but the playground was a skating rink. At least two inches of blue-black ice covered the center where the pavement sloped and the water had pooled.

The trees and basketball hoops and jungle gyms and swings were pure glass.

Gerry stood in the center of the playground, in what was intended as a fountain spring or frog pond before the city ran out of money and it became merely a cement basin with benches surrounding it. A place to go with the kids and watch your tax dollars at work.

Gerry's car sat sideways; he leaned against the hood as

I approached. I couldn't see the baby on his back from my angle, but Danielle Rawson bore the hollow gaze of someone who'd already accepted her own death as she knelt on the ice by Gerry's legs. Twelve hours in a trunk had matted her hair to the left side of her head as if a hand were pressed there, and her face was streaked with dirty fingers of ruined mascara, the corners of her eyelids burned red by gasoline.

She reminded me of pictures of women I've seen in Auschwitz or Dachau or Bosnia. She seemed to know her life had passed beyond the reach of human protection.

"Hi, Patrick," Gerry said. "That's far enough."

I stopped six feet from the car, four feet from Danielle Rawson, found myself toeing the ring of gasoline.

"Hi, Gerry," I said.

"You're awful calm." He raised an eyebrow, and it was sodden with gasoline. His rusty hair was pasted to his head.

"Tired," I said.

"Your eyes are red."

"If you say so."

"Phillip Dimassi is dead, I take it."

"Yup."

"You wept for him."

"Yes, I did."

I looked at Danielle Rawson, tried to find the energy necessary to care what happened to her.

"Patrick?"

He leaned back against the car and the shotgun taped to Danielle Rawson's head pulled her back with him.

"Yeah, Gerry?"

"Are you in shock?"

"I dunno." I turned my head, looked around at the prisms of ice and the dark drizzle and the blue and white lights from the police cruisers and the cops and federal agents stretched across car hoods, splayed haphazardly on telephone poles, kneeling on the roofs surrounding the playground. All of them, to the man, with guns extended.

Guns, guns, guns. Three hundred and sixty degrees of pure violence.

"I think you're in shock." Gerry nodded to himself.

"Well, shit, Gerry," I said and found myself scratching my head as it was pelted with rain, "I haven't slept in two days and you've killed or wounded just about everybody I care about. So, I dunno, how'm I supposed to feel?"

"Curious," he said.

"Curious?"

"Curious," he repeated and wrenched the shotgun so that Danielle Rawson's neck twisted in his grip and her head banged off his knee.

I looked at her and she wasn't terrified or angry. She was defeated. Just like me. I tried to find a bond based on that, to force emotion to rise in me, but it wouldn't come.

I looked back at Gerry.

"Curious about what, Gerry?" I rested my hand against my hip, felt the butt of my gun. He hadn't asked me for my gun, I realized. How odd.

"About me," he said. "I've killed a lot of people, Patrick."

"Kudos," I said.

He twisted the shotgun and Danielle Rawson's knees lifted off the ice.

"You're amused?" he said and his finger curled tight around the shotgun trigger.

"No, Gerry," I said, "I'm apathetic."

Just over the trunk of the car I noticed a piece of the fence push forward in the darkness and a gaping space open in its place. Then the fence fell back and the space disappeared.

"Apathetic?" Gerry said. "Tell you what, Pat—let's see how apathetic you are." He reached behind his head and came back with the baby, his fist gripping its clothes at the back, and held it aloft. "Weighs less than some rocks I've thrown," he said.

The baby was still drugged. Maybe dead, I didn't know. His eyelids were clenched shut, as if from pain, and his small head was feathered with blond whiskers. He seemed softer than a pillow.

Danielle Rawson looked up and then she banged her

head into Gerry's knees, her screams muffled by the tape over her mouth.

"You going to chuck the baby, Gerry?"

"Sure," he said. "Why not?"

I shrugged. "Why not. He ain't mine."

Danielle's eyes bulged and their pupils damned me.

"You're burned out, Pat."

I nodded. "I got nothing left, Gerry."

"Take your gun out, Pat."

I did. I went to toss it into the frozen snow.

"No, no," Gerry said. "Hold on to it."

"Hold on to it?"

"Absolutely. In fact, jack a round into the chamber and point at me. Come on. It'll be fun."

I did as he asked, raised my arm and centered it on Gerry's forehead.

"Much better," he said. "I'm kind of sorry you're all burned out on me, Patrick."

"No, you're not. That was one of the alleged points of this. Wasn't it?"

He smiled. "How do you mean?"

"You wanted to practice your bullshit theory of dehumanization. Right?"

He shrugged. "Some people would say it's not bullshit."

"Some people would buy sunblock in the Arctic, Gerry."

He laughed. "Worked on Evandro pretty well."

"Is that why it took you twenty years to come back?"

"I never went away, Patrick. But, in terms of my experiment with the human condition in general, and a certain belief I have in the charm of threes, yeah, Alec and I had to wait until you had all grown a bit and until Alec had found a worthy candidate in Evandro. And then there were all my years of planning and all Alec's efforts with Evandro until we could be sure he was one of us. I'd say it was all a great success, wouldn't you?"

"Sure, Gerry. Whatever."

He cocked his arm so that the baby's head was pointed

directly at the ice and stared at the ground as if looking for the perfect impact point.

"What're you going to do, Patrick?"

"Don't know there's much I can do, Ger."

He smiled. "You shoot me now, the mother definitely dies and the baby probably does."

"Agreed."

"You don't shoot me now, I might just hurl this baby's head against the ice."

Danielle bucked against the gun.

"I do that," Gerry said, "you lose them both. So here we have choice. Your choice, Patrick."

The ice under Gerry's car was darkened by Oscar's shadow as he inched along the other side of it.

"Gerry," I said, "you won. Right?"

"How do you see it?"

"Correct me if I'm wrong. I was supposed to pay for what my father did to Charles Rugglestone. Right?"

"Partially," he said and looked up at the baby's head, tilted it so he could see the clenched eyes.

"Okay. You got me. Shoot me, if you want. It's cool."

"I never wanted to kill you, Patrick," he said, his eyes still on the baby. He pursed his lips and made cooing sounds. "Last night at your partner's place? Evandro was supposed to kill her and leave you alive with the guilt, with the pain."

"Why?"

Oscar's shadow was preceding him across the ice. It leaked out in front of the car and spread raggedly across the stone animals and hobby horses directly behind Gerry. The shadow was thrown by the streetlight in the rear of the playground and I found myself wondering which genius hadn't thought of shutting it off before Oscar went through the fence.

All Gerry had to do was turn his head, and this whole mess would reach boiling point.

Gerry turned his hand, pivoted the baby back and forth.

"Used to hold my own son like this," he said.

"Over ice?" I said.

He grinned. "Mmmm. No, Patrick. Just hold him in my

arms and smell him and kiss the top of his head occasionally.''

''And he died.''

''Yes.'' Gerry peered up at the child's face, scrunched
his own in imitation.

''So—what, Gerry—because of that everything makes
some sort of sense?''

It was in my voice, I'm not sure why or how, but there
it was—the barest hint of emotion.

Gerry heard it. ''Toss your gun to your right.''

I looked at it like I didn't care, like I hadn't even known
it was there.

''Now.'' Gerry opened his palm and the baby dropped
into space.

Danielle shrieked against the tape and banged her head
into the shotgun.

''Okay,'' I said. ''Okay.''

The baby's head was plummeting toward the ice when
Gerry closed his hand over the ankles.

I tossed my gun into the slushy sand pit under the jungle
gym.

''Now your backup,'' Gerry said and swung the baby
like a pendulum in his hands.

''Fuck you,'' I said and watched his perilous grip on
the small ankles.

''Patrick,'' he said and raised his eyebrows, ''it sounds
like you're coming out of your stupor. The backup.''

I pulled the gun Phil had been grasping when Gerry
slashed his throat, tossed it beside my own.

Oscar must have noticed his shadow, because it began
to recede back behind the car and his legs appeared between the front and rear tires again.

''When my son died,'' Gerry said and pulled Campbell
Rawson in against his cheek, nuzzled his soft face, ''there
was no warning. He was out in the yard, four years old,
making noise, and then . . . he wasn't. A valve in his brain
slipped.'' He shrugged. ''Just slipped. And his head filled
with blood. And he died.''

''Tough way to go.''

He gave me his soft, kind smile. ''Patronize me again,

Patrick, and I smash the child's skull." He tilted his head and kissed Campbell's cheek. "So, my son's dead. And I find out there's no way what happened to him could have been predicted or prevented. God decided Brendan Glynn dies today. And so it was."

"And your wife?"

He smoothed Campbell's hair against his head and the baby's eyes remained shut.

"My wife," he said. "Hmm. I killed her, yeah. Not God. Me. I don't know what sort of plan God had for the woman, but I definitely fucked them up. I had plans for Brendan's life, He fucked them up. He probably had plans for Kara Rider's life, but He's had to change them, hasn't He?"

"And Hardiman," I said, "how did he come into this?"

"Did he tell you about his childhood encounter with bees?"

"Yes."

"Mmm. It wasn't bees. Alec likes to embellish. I was there and it was mosquitos. He disappeared in a cloud of them, and when he came out, I could see the mark of conscience had been removed from him." He smiled, and I could see the cloud of bugs and the dark lake in his eyes. "So, after that, Alec and I established a mentor-student relationship which later blossomed into so much more."

"And he—what?—went to jail willingly to protect you?"

Gerry shrugged. "Jail meant nothing to someone like Alec. His freedom is total, Patrick. It's in his mind. Bars can't hold it. He's more free in jail than most people are on the outside."

"So why punish Diandra Warren for sending him there?"

He frowned. "She reduced Alec. On the stand. She presumed to *explain* him to a jury of dunces. It was fucking insulting."

"So, all this"—my arm swept the playground—"is about you and Alec getting back at who exactly?"

"Whom," he corrected me and his smile returned.

"God?" I said.

"That's a bit reductive, but if that's the sort of glib shit you have to feed the media after I'm dead, be my guest, Patrick."

"You're going to die, Gerry? When?"

"As soon as you make your move, Patrick. You'll kill me." He tilted his head in the direction of the police. "Or they will."

"What about the hostages, Gerry?"

"One of them dies. Minimum. You can't save them both, Patrick. There's no way. Accept that."

"I have."

Danielle Rawson searched my face to see if I was joking and I met her eyes long enough for her to see I wasn't.

"One of them dies," Gerry said. "We're agreed on that?"

"Yup."

I pivoted my left foot to the right and then back and then to the right again. To Gerry, hopefully, it seemed an absent-minded gesture. To Oscar, again hopefully, it was more than that. I couldn't risk looking at the car again. I'd just have to assume he was there.

"A month ago," Gerry said, "you would've done anything to save both of them. You'd be racking your brain. But not now."

"Nope. You've taught me well, Gerry."

"How many lives did you shatter to get to me?" he asked.

I thought of Jack and Kevin. Then of Grace and Mae. Phil, of course.

"Enough," I said.

He laughed. "Good. Good. It's fun, isn't it? I mean, okay, you've never killed anyone intentionally. Have you? But I'll tell you, I didn't exactly plan for it to be my life's work. After I killed my wife, in pure fury, not premeditated at all, really . . . after I killed her, I felt awful. I threw up. I had the cold sweats for two weeks. And then one night, I'm driving out on an old stretch of road near Mansfield, no other car for miles. And I pass this guy riding his bike, and I got this impulse—strongest impulse I'd ever had in my life. I'm passing him on the right, I can see the reflec-

tors on his bike, see his face all serious and full of concentration and this voice says to me, 'Flick the wheel,
Gerry. Flick the wheel.' So I did. I just turned my hand a
quarter inch to the left and he went vaulting off into a tree.
And I went back to him, he was still barely alive, and I
watched him die. And I felt fine. And it just kept getting
better. The nigger kid who knew I'd gotten someone else
to take the fall for my wife, all the ones after him, Cal
Morrison. It just kept feeling better and better. I have no
regrets. Sorry, but I don't. So when you kill me—''

"I'm not going to kill you, Gerry."

"What?" His head reared back.

"You heard me. Let someone else send you to your
blaze of glory. You're a speck, man. You're nothing.
You're not worth the bullet or the mark on my soul for
taking you out."

"You trying to piss me off again, Patrick?" He removed
Campbell Rawson from his shoulder and held him aloft.

I tilted my wrist so the cylinder dropped into my palm,
shrugged. "You're a joke, Gerry. I'm just calling it like I
see it."

"That so?"

"Absolutely." I met his hard eyes with my own. "And
you'll be replaced, just like everything else, in maybe a
week, tops. Some other dumb, sick shit will come along
and kill some people and he'll be all over the papers, and
all over *Hard Copy* and you'll be yesterday's news. Your
fifteen minutes are up, Gerry. And they've passed without
impact."

He flipped Campbell Rawson upside down in his hand,
grasped his ankles again, and his finger depressed the shotgun trigger an eighth of an inch and Danielle closed one
eye against the blast she was sure was coming, but kept
the other eye on her baby.

"They'll remember this," Gerry said. "Believe me."

He swung his arm back in a softball pitcher's windup
and Campbell slid back into the darkness behind him, the
small white body disappearing as if it had gone back to
the womb.

But when Gerry swung his arm forward to release the

baby into the air, Campbell was no longer in his hand.

He looked down, confused, and I jumped forward, hit the ice on my knees and slid the index finger of my left hand in between the shotgun trigger and the guard.

Gerry clamped back on the trigger. When he met my finger, he looked at me and then clamped down so hard that my finger broke.

The straight razor appeared in his left hand and I shoved the one-shot into his right palm.

He shrieked even before I pulled the trigger. It was a high-pitched sound, the yip-and-bark of a kennel's worth of hyenas, and the razor felt like the tip of a lover's tongue as it sank into my neck, then snagged against my jawbone.

I depressed the trigger on the one-shot and nothing happened.

Gerry shrieked louder, and the razor came out of my flesh, then swung back in immediately, and I clenched my eyes shut and depressed the trigger frantically three times.

And Gerry's hand exploded.

And so did mine.

The razor hit the ice by my knee as I dropped the one-shot and fire roared up the electrical tape and gasoline on Gerry's arm and caught the wisps of Danielle's hair.

Gerry threw his head back and opened his mouth wide and bellowed in ecstasy.

I grabbed the razor, could barely feel it because the nerves in my hand seemed to have stopped working.

I slashed into the electric tape at the end of the shotgun barrel, and Danielle dropped away toward the ice and rolled her head into the frozen sand.

My broken finger came back out of the shotgun and Gerry swung the barrels toward my head.

The twin shotgun bores arced through the darkness like eyes without mercy or soul, and I raised my head to meet them, and Gerry's wail filled my ears as the fire licked at his neck.

Good-bye, I thought. Everyone. It's been nice.

Oscar's first two shots entered the back of Gerry's head and exited through the center of his forehead and a third punched into his back.

The shotgun jerked upward in Gerry's flaming arm and then the shots came from the front, several at once, and Gerry spun like a marionette and pitched toward the ground. The shotgun boomed twice and punched holes through the ice in front of him as he fell.

He landed on his knees and, for a moment, I wasn't sure if he was dead or not. His rusty hair was afire and his head lolled to the left as one eye disappeared in flames but the other shimmered at me through waves of heat, and an amused derision shone in the pupil.

Patrick, the eye said through the gathering smoke, you still know nothing.

Oscar rose up on the other side of Gerry's corpse, Campbell Rawson clutched tight to his massive chest as it rose and fell with great heaving breaths. The sight of it— something so soft and gentle in the arms of something so thick and mountainous—made me laugh.

Oscar came out of the darkness toward me, stepped around Gerry's burning body, and I felt the waves of heat rise toward me as the circle of gasoline around Gerry caught fire.

Burn, I thought. Burn. God help me, but burn.

Just after Oscar stepped over the outer edge of the circle, it erupted in yellow flame, and I found myself laughing harder as he looked at it, not remotely impressed.

I felt cool lips smack against my ear, and by the time I looked her way, Danielle was already past me, rushing to take her child from Oscar.

His huge shadow loomed over me as he approached, and I looked up at him and he held the look for a long moment.

"How you doing, Patrick?" he said and smiled broadly.

And, behind him, Gerry burned on the ice.

And everything was so goddamned funny for some reason, even though I knew it wasn't. I knew it wasn't. I did. But I was still laughing when they put me in the ambulance.

Epilogue

A month after Gerry Glynn's death, his killing ground was discovered in what had been the cafeteria of the long-closed Dedham House of Correction. Along with several of his victims' body parts stored in a half dozen coolers, police also found a list Gerry'd compiled of all the people he'd killed since 1965. Gerry was twenty-seven when he murdered his wife, fifty-eight when he died. In those thirty-one years, he killed—either by himself or with the aid of Charles Rugglestone, Alec Hardiman, or Evandro Arujo—thirty-four people. According to the list.

A police psychologist speculated that the number could actually be higher. Someone of Gerry's ego, he argued, could easily have differentiated between "worthy" victims and "lesser" ones.

Of the thirty-four, sixteen were runaways, one in Lubbock, Texas, and another in unincorporated Dade County, Florida, just as Bolton had suspected.

Three and a half weeks after his death, Cox Publishers published the true-crime book, *The Boston Manglers*, by a staff reporter with the *News*. The book sold fast for two days, and then the discovery was made in Dedham, and people lost interest because even a book produced in twenty-four days wasn't able to keep up with the times.

An internal police investigation into Gerry Glynn's death concluded that officers and federal agents had used "necessary, extreme force" when sharpshooters fired fourteen bullets into his body after Oscar's first three had effectively killed him.

*   *   *

Stanley Timpson was arrested on charges of conspiracy to commit murder in the Rugglestone case and obstruction of a federal investigation upon arriving at Logan Airport from Mexico.

The state, upon reviewing the Rugglestone case, decided that since the only witnesses to Rugglestone's murder were a catatonic mental patient, an unhinged alcoholic, and an AIDS victim who wouldn't live to see a trial and because there was no longer any physical evidence left, that they'd leave prosecution of Timpson to federal authorities.

Last I heard, Timpson was planning to enter a plea on the obstruction charge in exchange for dismissal of the conspiracy.

Alec Hardiman's attorney petitioned the State Supreme Court for immediate reversal of his client's conviction and immediate commutation of his prison term due to allegations surfacing against Timpson and EEPA in relation to the Rugglestone murder. The attorney then filed a second suit in civil court against the State of Massachusetts, the current governor and chief of police as well as the men who'd held those positions in 1974. For wrongful imprisonment, the attorney argued, Alec Hardiman was entitled to sixty million dollars—or three million dollars for every year he spent behind bars. His client, the attorney argued, was further victimized by the state when he contracted AIDS due to inferior policing fellow inmates, and should be released immediately while he still had some life left.

A reversal of Hardiman's decision is currently pending.

Jack Rouse and Kevin Hurlihy were rumored to be hiding out in the Cayman Islands.

Another rumor, rarely reported in the papers, suggested they'd been murdered on the orders of Fat Freddy Constantine. Lieutenant John Kevosky of the Major Crime Unit said, "Negative. Both Kevin and Jack have a history of disappearing when the heat gets turned up. Besides,

Freddy had no reason to kill them. They made him money. They're hiding out in the Carribean.''
   Or not.

Diandra Warren quit her consulting position at Bryce and put her private practice on hiatus.
   Eric Gault continues to teach at Bryce, his secret safe for now.

Evandro Arujo's parents sold a diary their son had written as a teenager to a TV tabloid for $20,000. Producers later sued for return of the money on the basis that the diary revealed the musings of what was, back then, a perfectly healthy mind.
   The parents of Peter Stimovich and Pamela Stokes joined together in a class action suit against the state, the governor (again), and Walpole Penitentiary for releasing Evandro Arujo.

Campbell Rawson was, quite miraculously, according to doctors, unaffected by the overdose of hydroclorophyl administered by Gerry Glynn. He should have had permanent brain damage, but instead he woke with a headache and nothing more.
   His mother, Danielle, sent me a Christmas card with a rambling thank-you note inside and an assurance that any time I passed through Reading I was welcome to a hot meal and friendship at the Rawson household.

Grace and Mae returned from a safe house in Upstate New York two days after Gerry's death. Grace resecured her position at Beth Israel and called me the day I was released from the hospital.
   It was one of those uncomfortable conversations in which polite reserve replaces intimacy and as it stumbled toward a close, I asked her if she'd like to meet for a drink sometime.
   ''I don't think that would be a good idea, Patrick.''
   ''Ever?'' I asked.
   A long, unpopped bubble of a pause followed and was

an answer in and of itself, and then she said:

"I'll always care for you."

"But."

"But my daughter comes first, and I can't risk exposing her to your life again."

A pit opened and yawned and extended from my throat to my stomach.

"Can I talk to her? Say 'bye?"

"I don't think that would be a healthy thing. For either of you." Her voice cracked and her quick inhalation was a wet hiss. "Sometimes it's better to let things fade."

I closed my eyes and placed my head against the phone for a moment.

"Grace, I—"

"I have to go, Patrick. Take care of yourself. I mean that. Don't let that job destroy you. Okay?"

"Okay."

"Promise?"

"I promise, Grace. I—"

" 'Bye, Patrick."

" 'Bye."

Angie left the day after Phil's funeral.

"He died," she said, "because he loved us too much and we didn't love him enough."

"How do you figure?" I stared into an open grave cut through hard, frozen earth.

"It wasn't his fight, but he fought it anyway. For us. And we didn't love him enough to keep him out of it."

"I don't know if it's that simple."

"It is," she assured me and dropped flowers in the grave onto his coffin.

Mail has piled up in my apartment—bills, solicitations from supermarket tabloids and local TV and radio talk shows. Talk, talk, talk, I find myself thinking, talk all you want and it won't change the fact that Glynn existed. And so many others like him still do.

The only thing I've pulled from the pile is a postcard from Angie.

It arrived two weeks ago from Rome. Birds flap their wings over the Vatican.

Patrick,

Gorgeous here. What do you think the guys in this building are deciding about my life and my body these days? Men keep pinching our butts over here and I'm going to clock one soon, start an international incident, I just know it. Going to Tuscany tomorrow. Then, who knows? Renee says Hi. Says don't worry about the beard, she always thought you'd look hot with one. My sister—I swear. Take care.

Miss you,
Ange

Miss you.

On the advice of friends, I consulted a psychiatrist during the first week in December.

After an hour, he told me I was suffering from clinical depression.

"I know that," I said.

He leaned forward. "And how are we going to help you with that?"

I glanced at the door behind him, a closet, I assumed.

"You got Grace or Mae Cole back there?" I said.

He actually turned his head to check. "No, but—"

"How about Angie?"

"Patrick—"

"Can you resurrect Phil or make the last few months not have happened?"

"No."

"Then you can't help me, Doctor."

I wrote him a check.

"But, Patrick, you're deeply depressed and you need—"

"I need my friends, Doctor. I'm sorry, but you're a stranger. Your advice may be great, but it's still a stranger's advice, and I don't take advice from strangers. Something my mother taught me."

"Still, you need—"

"I *need* Angie, Doctor. That simple. I know I'm depressed, but I can't change it right now, and I don't want to."

"Why not?"

"Because it's natural. Like autumn. You go through what I went through, and you'd be nuts not to be depressed. Right?"

He nodded.

"Thank you for your time, Doctor."

Christmas Eve
7:30 p.m.

So here I sit.

On my porch, three days after someone shot a priest in a convenience store, waiting for my life to begin again.

My crazy landlord, Stanis, actually invited me in for Christmas dinner tomorrow, but I declined, said I'd made other plans.

I might go to Richie and Sherilynn's. Or Devin's. He and Oscar invited me to join their bachelor's Christmas. Microwaved turkey dinners and generous portions of Jack Daniel's. Sure sounds tempting, but . . .

I've been alone on Christmas before. Several times. But never like this. I never felt it before, this dire loneliness, the hollowing despair of it.

"You can love more than one person at the same time," Phil said once. "Humans are messy."

I definitely was.

Alone on the porch, I loved Angie and Grace and Mae and Phil and Kara Rider and Jason and Diandra Warren, Danielle and Campbell Rawson. I loved them all and missed them all.

And felt all the more lonely.

Phil was dead. I knew that, but I couldn't accept it enough not to want—desperately—that he wasn't.

I could see us climbing out windows in our respective homes as children and meeting on the avenue, running up it together as we laughed at the ease of our escapes and headed through the bitter night to rap on Angie's window and pull her into our desperado pack.

And then the three of us took off, lost to the night.

I have no idea what we used to do on half our midnight jaunts, what we used to talk about as we made our way through the dark cement jungle of our neighborhood.

I only know that it was enough.

Miss you, she'd written.

Miss you, too.

Miss you more than the severed nerves in my hand.

"Hi," she said.

I'd been dozing in the chair on the porch and I opened my eyes to the first snowflakes of this winter. I batted my eyes at them, shook my head against the cruel, sweet sound of her voice, so vivid I'd been ready to believe for a moment, like a fool, that it wasn't a dream.

"Aren't you cold?" she said.

I was awake now. And those last words didn't come from a dream.

I turned in my chair and she stepped onto the porch gingerly, as if worried she'd disturbed the gentle settling of the virgin flakes on the wood.

"Hi," I said.

"Hi."

I stood and she stopped six inches from me.

"I couldn't stay away," she said.

"I'm glad."

The snow fell in her hair and glistened white for just a moment before it melted and disappeared.

She took a faltering step and I took one to compensate and then I was holding her as the fat white flakes fell on our bodies.

Winter, real winter, was here.

"I missed you," she said and crushed her body against mine.

"Missed you, too," I said.

She kissed my cheek, ran her hands into my hair, and

looked at me for a long moment as flakes collected on her eyelashes.

She lowered her head. "And I miss him. Badly."

"Me too."

When she raised her head her face was slick, and I couldn't tell if it was all just melted snow or not.

"Any plans for Christmas?" she said.

"You tell me."

She wiped her left eye. "I'd kind of like to hang with you, Patrick. That okay?"

"That's the best thing I've heard all year, Ange."

In the kitchen, we made hot chocolate, stared over the rims of our mugs at each other as the radio in the living room updated us on the weather.

The snow, the announcer told us, was part of the first major storm system to hit Massachusetts this winter. By the time we woke in the morning, he promised, twelve to sixteen inches would have fallen.

"Real snow," Angie said. "Who would've thought?"

"It's about time."

The weather report over, the announcer was updating the condition of Reverend Edward Brewer.

"How long you think he can hold on?" Angie said.

I shrugged. "I don't know."

We sipped from our mugs as the announcer reported the mayor's call for more stringent handgun laws, the governor's call for tougher enforcement of restraining orders. So another Eddie Brewer wouldn't walk into the wrong convenience store at the wrong time. So another Laura Stiles could break up with her abusive boyfriend without fear of death. So the James Faheys of the world would stop instilling us with terror.

So our city would one day be as safe as Eden before the fall, our lives insulated from the hurtful and the random.

"Let's go in the living room," Angie said, "and turn the radio off."

She reached out and I took her hand in the dark kitchen as the snow painted my window in soft specks of white, followed her down the hall toward the living room.

Eddie Brewer's condition hadn't changed. He was still in a coma.

The city, the announcer said, waited. The city, the announcer assured us, was holding its breath.

DENNIS LEHANE is the *New York Times* bestselling author of *Mystic River, Shutter Island,* and *Coronado,* as well as *A Drink Before the War,* which won the Shamus Award for Best First Novel; *Darkness, Take My Hand; Sacred; Gone, Baby, Gone;* and *Prayers for Rain.* A native of Dorchester, Massachusetts, he lives in the Boston area. Visit his website at *www.dennislehanebooks.com.*